Redemption

Graeme Gibson

Published by Kilbryde Press 2017

First published 2017

Cover design by Flipside Creative

www.flipsidecreative.co.uk

Author's Note

Redemption is the third book in the Dark Secrets Trilogy. In writing it, as with the two previous books, I have tried to be historically accurate. Unfortunately, this is sometimes difficult to achieve, particularly so when dealing with locations within towns and cities. The topographies of cities like Belfast and Glasgow have changed dramatically since the 1970s and if I have misquoted street names and locations then I ask your forgiveness.

The political situation at the time was one of turmoil and I have done my best to be even handed when dealing with the parties involved in the conflict in Northern Ireland. There is not, and never has been (as far as I am aware) a clandestine British organisation known as Ultra (though it is not beyond the bounds of plausibility that such an organisation exists or has existed). Contrary to what some would have us believe, political skulduggery is not restricted to the CIA and KGB and MI5 and MI6 certainly are not strangers to it (the Britsh didn't build an Empire by being nice). Nor was there a splinter group of the IRA known as the Mhílíste Náisiúnaíoch Ulster, the Ulster Nationalist Militia. Indeed, those with any knowledge of Nationalist politics in Ireland will be well aware that no such group would ever include the word "Ulster" in its title.

But the story is not about organisations. It is about one man trying to come to terms with his part in the shadowy world of political intrigue and assassination and the effect it has on him and on those closest to him. Organisations are not affected by love, hate or loyalty, only individuals.

Acknowledgements

This is where I give thanks to the various people who have helped me along the way and encouraged me to finish this book. One of the big questions facing me as I wrote this final part of the trilogy was whether to kill off my hero or to keep him alive for further adventures. His survival, in great part, is down to my good friend Duncan McCallum who insisted that Jamie Raeburn has become a real person to him and an early death would be a waste of a great character. Many others voiced the same opinion so my thanks (and Jamie's) go to all of you.

As with all my other books, the help and encouragement given me by Indie Authors World (Kim and Sinclair McLeod) cannot go unmentioned. They are an inspiration to all aspiring authors.

Writing about places and events set in the past, even the recent past, requires quite a bit of research. It is important that these, as far as possible, be authentic. In this respect the internet is a boon and I am grateful to all who have made contributions to various websites giving information on old Glasgow... and also to those who have responded to cries for help.

I also want to thank Gus Macdonald of The Parkhead Welding Company for general advice and information on welding techniques back in the 1970s. That was invaluable.

Once again, as with The Janus Complex and Archangel, the cover design for Redemption was created by my talented daughter-in-law, Louise. I can't thank her enough.

And finally, for all her help and encouragement, I have to thank my wife. She has had to put up with a lot!

In Memory of John Andrew

(1936 – 2016)
A good friend and an exceptional human being. Sadly missed.

Prologue

Friday 2nd March 1973, England.

So Michael Messenger was dead. It was official. It had come from the lips of "God" himself, dropped into the conversation as though it were of no real consequence.

Jamie Raeburn tried hard to concentrate on the Old Man's words. They weren't having a conversation, not really. It was more of a monologue delivered by the Brigadier to a captive audience of one. Him. He might have argued, just for the hell of it, but he wasn't up to it, not yet at least - not to conversation, and certainly not to argument.

Lying in his makeshift hospital bed, he let the news sink in. If it was true – and that was always in doubt when listening to Sir Charles Redmond - then his alter ego was departed from this world.

'*Good riddance*,' part of his brain responded, while the other part, the rational part, tried to work out the consequences.

Was it good news, he pondered? There would be a downside... There was *always* a downside, but, for the moment, he couldn't see it.

Look on the bright side, he told himself, you're still alive. And he was, though it had been a close run thing. Saint Peter's outer guards at the "The Pearly Gates" had drawn him from the queue and turned him back, back to this purgatory. Perhaps he should enjoy this tiny respite, he counselled himself, and, behind the swathes of cotton bandages, his face broke into a tentative smile.

'So what happens now?' he asked in a weak voice, peering at the man opposite through the narrow slit in the dressings swathed around his head. His breathing was weak and rasping. The noise of it rattled around in his head.

Sir Charles laughed quietly. 'Well, what happens now is that we bury you, old boy,' he announced. 'But it'll be a while before the big day. There are still a few things to arrange.'

That, Jamie decided, sounded ominous. When the Head of Ultra arranged "a few things", it usually ended badly for some poor bugger. He hoped it was not to be him on this occasion. 'Like a body?' he mumbled. 'Or have you got something else in mind?'

Sir Charles seemed to read his thoughts and gave him a knowing look. 'Oh, don't worry about that old chap, of course there will be a body... we already have one and it isn't yours,' he added, laughing and allowing his face to break into a grin.

'Is it someone you've had your eye on for a while or was the poor bugger just in the wrong place at the wrong time?' Jamie didn't want to sound cynical but it was difficult in the circumstances.

There was silence in the room for a moment as someone padded down the corridor outside. It would be a nurse, Jamie assumed. No one else, other than the small medical team attending him, had access to this floor of the big Georgian house.

Sir Charles glanced towards the door and cocked an ear theatrically. The nurse probably couldn't hear anything through the thick walls, but Brigadier Redmond wasn't one for taking chances. The devastating events at Kiltyclogher, the sleepy little hamlet in County Leitrim, Eire, less than a week earlier, were, in spy speak, sensitive. Knowledge of what happened there was restricted to very few people and Charles Redmond intended it should stay that way. As the sound of the footsteps faded, he turned his attention back to Jamie.

'Wrong time, wrong place,' he confirmed, returning to Jamie's earlier question. 'There's a surfeit of available bodies in Northern Ireland, Raeburn, you know that. Let's just say that someone who was about to disappear into a drab, anonymous little hole in County Armagh is now going to be interred over here, in England's green and pleasant land... and with full Military Honours, I might add.'

Jamie grimaced beneath the bandages. 'Poor bastard,' he mumbled, his words still muffled.

'Oh *please*,' Sir Charles retorted disparagingly. 'Poor is hardly fair. He would have been very lonely where he was going. When he takes your place, at least some visitors will drop by... and his grave will be neat and tidy. He can bask in your glory; what's poor about that?' He laughed again, clearly amused by a new thought. He decided to share it. 'Mark you, he'll probably haunt the graveyard until the end of time,' he said, 'His coffin will be draped with the Union Jack, not the Green, White and Gold of his beloved Ireland. That's bound to turn any self-respecting Nationalist into a wailing spectre.' His chortle continued for a moment longer before he fell silent.

Jamie felt sick. Everyone, even he, was disposable in the old boy's world. A silence hung heavily between them for a while. Outside, a car engine revved loudly before it pulled away over the gravel drive. The crunch of its tyres on the tiny stones faded gradually with the distance. Voices carried up from the lower floors - indistinct conversation and female laughter. Further away, a dog barked and, somewhere in the house, a radio provided background music. It was playing classical music... Brahms, Beethoven or Bach, perhaps?

In truth, Jamie hadn't a clue, it wasn't his cup of tea, but in his current situation it was strangely soothing. All of these things; the voices, the laughter, the music, the barking dog, presented a picture of normality. But what was normal in his world, he mused grimly?

He lay still. His pain, controlled for the moment, would intensify again quickly as the morphine wore off. That was as sure as night follows day. The doctor spoke of weaning him off it. "I don't want you addicted", he said.

Jamie didn't want to be addicted to it either but, given the choice, addiction was marginally preferable to the pain he suffered without it. The pain was hellish. His body felt as though a psychopath was attacking it with a steam hammer and his head was on fire as another deranged psycho shoved red-hot needles into his skull; hundreds, thousands at a time.

The morphine took it all away. When the drug kicked in, he floated on a cloud of soft, fluffy cotton wool. When it wore off, as it was doing now, concentration became difficult. Fortunately, the Brigadier's visits were usually short. That, on the other hand, would soon change. It was inevitable. And then the questions would start.

'And what is to happen to me?' he asked, struggling to maintain focus.

Sir Charles rose from his chair and wandered over to the window. He was now out of Jamie's line of vision. When he eventually spoke, his voice seemed to come from far away. 'When you're up to it, you'll be debriefed. After that...well, maybe it's the end of the road.'

'End of the road?' Jamie croaked, uncertainty creeping in. That didn't sound good. Not good at all.

'Retired, decommissioned, de-activated, put out to grass...call it what you like.'

'As simple as that?' Jamie said, breathing a silent sigh of relief

Sir Charles laughed and turned from the window, returned to his chair and eased himself down onto it. He could guess what was going through Jamie's mind. 'Not entirely,' he said, knowing the effect his words would have. 'There's a complication.'

'What sort of complication?' Jamie asked anxiously. He was finding it more and more difficult to stay with it now.

Sir Charles relented. 'I think you've had enough for now,' he said solicitously. 'We'll talk again later.'

'And my wife... When can I see her?'

'Soon, old boy; she'll be here soon. Just relax. I'll return later. Sleep now.' As Sir Charles made for the door, he turned back. He saw Jamie's eyelids close, and smiled inwardly. Now for the hard part, he mused.

***

It was early evening when Sir Charles returned. The sun was sinking slowly to the horizon, bathing the room in a deep, blood red glow. Jamie felt stronger but he was in some pain. His morphine had been reduced and movement of any sort was difficult with pain racking his body and his head. He was bandaged heavily, like an Egyptian Mummy, which wasn't surprising. He had drifted between life and death. His memory was returning now, slowly, and the memories weren't pleasant.

He had been awake for a while, contemplating his future, before the Brigadier let himself into the room. His future, he mused grimly... if he had one. He still wasn't convinced that "the end of the road" meant retirement. If anything it sounded too good to be true and, in Jamie's experience, anything that sounded too good to be true, usually was.

Liam Fitzpatrick figured prominently in his thoughts. The Irishman could prove to be his downfall. Did Sir Charles know they had a past, he wondered. That was, as Jerry Pearce, host of the popular TV game show said each week, the $64,000 question. He decided to keep his acquaintanceship with Liam to himself. There was no point in muddying the already murky waters.

His thoughts kept returning to the events that night at Kiltyclogher. The IRA bastards had been waiting for him. He had known it from the outset. It was the old sixth sense thing. What hadn't been clear at the time, and still wasn't, was *how* they knew. The look of shock on Liam's face when he pulled off Jamie's mask would remain with him until the day he died.

Jamie's life had been hanging by a thread at that moment and the fact he was still alive today raised another baffling question. Why hadn't Liam Fitzpatrick simply put a bullet between his eyes there and then? Friendship? No, it wasn't that; they weren't friends. Sure, they had met, but only briefly, and that had been years before.

So why am I still alive when I should be down below stoking coal for Old Nick?

Sir Charles gave a polite little cough to gain his attention and settled down into his usual chair. With the setting sun behind him and his face hidden in dark shadow, he could have been the Devil himself. 'How are you feeling now?' the old boy asked.

Was that real or was it professional concern, Jamie wondered?

'Just dandy,' he replied sarcastically. 'How do you think I'm feeling?' He closed his eyes for added effect. When he opened them, Sir Charles was watching him carefully. He was evaluating him, the way he always did.

'What am I to do with you?' the Brigadier said softly.

Jamie suspected that was a rhetorical question but answered anyway. 'I thought you had decided I was past my best...ready for retirement, you said.'

Sir Charles laughed. 'Yes, I did, didn't I,' he replied. 'But I also mentioned that there was a complication.'

'Which you said we'd talk about later,' Jamie reminded him. 'Now is later,' he continued quietly, his voice deadened by the gauze. 'I'm all ears.'

Sir Charles regarded him thoughtfully for a moment. The sun had sunk lower and the room was darkening.

The gates of hell are opening, Jamie mused darkly.

'What happened to you at Kiltyclogher has been puzzling me,' the old man started.

'You and me both,' Jamie laughed, instantly regretting his foolhardiness as a spasm of pain lanced through him. His breathing became rapid for a few seconds then settled again.

Throughout this episode, the Brigadier watched him dispassionately. 'I keep asking myself why the Irishman didn't just kill you,' he continued, at length. He paused for a moment as if awaiting a response but Jamie remained silent on this occasion. 'I mean, it's clear you were expected. They were waiting for a British agent...'

'An assassin,' Jamie pointed out. 'They knew I was an Archangel.'

'Quite,' Sir Charles concurred. 'Though whether or not they know what an Archangel actually does is still a matter of conjecture. That, however, is irrelevant. What really perplexes me is why you are still with us,' he continued. 'Do you know?'

Jamie tried not to sound bored when he replied. He wished the man would use simple English instead of talking as though he were lecturing Ph.D. students. 'No,' he replied, keeping it short. He was conscious of the old man's eyes boring into him and he sensed his disbelief. One thing was encouraging though; if Sir Charles knew about his and Liam's past, he would have raised the subject by now. So maybe he was off the hook after all.

Sir Charles shook his head slowly. 'It doesn't make sense, does it?'

'I suppose not,' Jamie agreed.

'So what am I missing?'

It was a pointed question and Jamie was grateful for the bandages that enshrouded his head. They hid his guilt. He could lie with the best of them but Sir Charles Redmond wasn't easily fooled. He had the uncanny ability to detect falsehood and he did not need a polygraph machine.

'Like what?' Jamie mumbled.

The Brigadier was staring at him, his gaze steely, unwavering. He remained like that for a long time before letting out a sigh. 'You know, Raeburn, I am never quite sure about you,' he said quietly.

Jamie said nothing. What was there to say?

'The fact he *didn't* kill you is the complication I spoke of earlier,' Sir Charles continued.

Jamie swivelled his eyes towards him. That was not what he had expected to hear.

'So my being alive is a complication,' he said, his words accompanied by a nervous laugh. 'How, exactly, is that?' he continued. He was being drawn into something, the final outcome of which was still in doubt...in *his* mind at least.

There was another pregnant pause. Was that a psychological turning of the screw, Jamie wondered, or was the old man just having difficulty framing the answer? Either way, it didn't bode well.

The Brigadier gave a small cough and began searching in his pocket for his pipe and tobacco pouch. This was what he always did when he needed a moment to think, without it being too obvious. The ploy didn't work well with people who knew him. Suddenly appearing to realise where he was he stopped his fumbling and placed his hands on his lap, grinning guiltily.

'Sorry old chap, I should have known better,' he said. His professional face had now replaced the grin.

Back to inscrutability, Jamie thought grimly. Things were not looking any better for him.

Sir Charles gave another small cough, announcing his reply. 'Actually, the complication is not that you are alive, Raeburn' he started, paused again, then: 'The problem, or complication, is that the man who shot you belongs to me.' His voice had dropped, giving it all the dramatic effect it needed.

Not that it needed any, Jamie mused. 'Shit,' he murmured involuntarily. 'He's an Archangel too?'

Sir Charles smiled coldly. 'No, he's not an Archangel; he's not one of *you*. What I said was, he belongs to me. Granted the difference is subtle. He's an informer and his code name is "Corkscrew",' he added. After a moment's silence, he continued. 'Now do you see my problem?' he asked.

'Not really.'

Sir Charles shook his head slowly. 'Corkscrew...his name is Liam Fitzpatrick, has been working for me inside the Provisional IRA, and more particularly inside the UNM, the Mhílíste Náisiúnaíoch Ulster, for about 18 months. He is a veritable goldmine of information and, as you would expect, I keep his existence a closely guarded secret. I am selective about what I do or don't do with the information he gives me and not even our friends in MI5 know I have him.'

They might be your friends, Jamie thought silently, *but they are certainly not mine.*

Sir Charles stopped his delivery and began fumbling again. Jamie knew the signs. This time he really *did* need a smoke. 'Don't let me stop you,' he said.

The Brigadier smiled appreciatively before pulling out the offending items from his pocket, his trusty briar, the battered leather pouch containing his "special" tobacco, and a box of Bryant & May matches. He ranged them carefully on the bed and began the ritual of filling his pipe, tamping down the shag with the top of the little penknife he kept in the pouch, and striking a match. The rasp of the match head on the abrasive strip on the side of the box was strangely comforting to Jamie, as was the flare given off as the potassium chlorate and phosphorus as the match head ignited, followed then by the aroma of the heavy, smouldering tobacco.

Sir Charles saw his reaction to the striking match and smiled grimly. He lifted the still burning match for Jamie to see. 'A little pin head of potassium chlorate and a little phosphorus to produce that tiny explosion, eh?' he said. 'No wonder the terrorists pack it into beer kegs and cars...and even trucks. Without the phosphorus, it makes a great weed killer. With it, it's a cheap and effective explosive.'

Both men lapsed into silence. Jamie ruminated on what he now knew and the Brigadier sucked contentedly on the stem of his briar. The comfortable silence did not last for long.

'They knew you were coming,' Sir Charles said at last. 'And *that* is as much a puzzle as it is worrying. I can count the people who knew of your mission on the fingers of one hand,' he continued. 'And until that night at Kiltyclogher I trusted each one of them.'

'And this informer of yours, Corkscrew, he didn't know?' Jamie probed, avoiding the use of Liam's name.

'No, he did not. News of your mission came as something of a shock to the poor blighter. Gave him nightmares, I imagine. Envisaged his cover being blown...not a pleasant thought,' he laughed coldly. 'You know what they do to touts.'

Jamie gave a shudder. Yes, he knew what they did to touts. They did the same to spies too, if memory served him well.

'I still don't see your problem,' Jamie reiterated. 'Even if they had managed to take me alive, I didn't know anything worthwhile.'

Sir Charles gave a grim smile. 'You knew enough. Names are unimportant. You knew the reason you were there and that, together with your just being there would have been enough. They would have started searching for the source of the leak...and they are thorough, if nothing else. How long do you think it would have taken them to work it out?'

Jamie sighed. 'So why didn't he kill me?'

Sir Charles' smile turned colder. 'As I said before, that question has been taxing me for quite some time. No doubt he had his reasons...which he still refuses to reveal, I might say...but it was something of an aberration on his part, don't you think?'

There was a further moment's silence, broken ultimately by Jamie. 'Okay, I see all that, but they think he executed me so his stock is probably even higher than before. What, exactly, is the complication?' he continued, restating his earlier question.

'I'm disappointed in you, Raeburn,' the Brigadier replied slowly as though addressing a dim child. 'You're not thinking clearly,' he continued. 'Though, in the circumstances, that is understandable.' Another pause, then he continued. 'You are supposed to be dead...executed by Corkscrew. If the IRA or UNM learn that you are alive, where does that leave Corkscrew?'

Jamie lapsed into silence once again. The strain was beginning to tell. His head was throbbing and pain was beginning to course through his body. He wanted all of this to be over. He couldn't see how that could happen, but he could see where the Brigadier was heading. 'So I have to disappear,' he said at length.

'That may well be the only answer,' Sir Charles agreed.

'And my family?'

'That all depends, old boy. It may be they will have to disappear with you.'

Jamie considered that response with some trepidation. Given Ultra's track record, the definition of "disappear" was a variable. He coughed and gave a soft groan. The pain was building again, becoming unbearable.

Sir Charles regarded him dispassionately. He was considering his options.

'I might have a solution for your dilemma,' Jamie said at last. The Brigadier smiled humourlessly at that; just like the wolf in the story of Little Red Riding Hood, Jamie mused.

'Yes, I rather hoped you might,' the man whispered.

Part I

Chapter One

The early afternoon sun was high in the sky. It baked the earth below like bread in the boulangerie's ovens, forming a hard crust on the dry soil. It had been like this for weeks now, day after day of endless sunshine with temperatures soaring up into the thirties Celsius. Only brave souls were out in the searing heat. Even the animals sought shade where they could find it. Cows clustered in the meagre shade of isolated trees, their tails swishing furiously in the fruitless battle with the flies that swarmed around them. Cats and dogs too - with more sense than their human masters – hid indoors or found shade beneath crumbling walls or in shrivelling shrubberies.

Those who could, like the cats and dogs, remained indoors with windows fully open behind closed shutters. There at least in the darkened rooms with their tiled floors people could find a semblance of coolness.

Jamie Raeburn was one of the few braving the heat, the words of Noel Coward's song *Mad dogs and Englishmen* repeating over and over again in his head, like a grainy record stuck in a groove. He smiled inwardly. Was he insane, he wondered?

He breathed a sigh and leaned on his garden fork. It was hard going, he had to admit, but he had expected nothing else. The soil had not seen a spade or fork for close on two years before the family's arrival. That meant two years of scorching, hot summers and bitingly cold winters that had transformed the ground into something akin to concrete.

Sweat gathered on his brow and stung his eyes. It glistened on his body and trickled in tiny rivulets down his naked chest and back, before gathering in the cotton waistband of his cut off denims. His breathing returned to normal and he cast an eye around his domain. The fruit trees were his pride and joy. Their branches, dense with foliage and heavy with fruit, cast deep and tempting shadows on the scorched grass. He broke into a grin as he remembered his first thoughts on seeing the place - the broken fences, the ramshackle lean-to chicken coop and the waist high wild grass and weeds. What he had managed to achieve in the months since, filled him with pride. Still grinning, he casually wiped the sweat from his brow with the back of his hand.

He was at peace here. The place had grown on him - and on his family too. The early weeks had been hard. Harder for his wife and children than for him, he reflected. For him it had been the sheer physical and mental effort required to get his body, and his mind, back into shape. For Kate and his kids the barriers had been more psychological, watching him push himself through the pain while they dealt with their own uncertainties.

Coming here had been a crazy impulse, he thought, but it had paid off. His body had repaired itself. He was fitter and stronger now than ever before... physically at least. His mind was another matter. It was still fragile. He laughed quietly to himself at that assessment. Fragile was an understatement.

The physical punishment to his body was as nothing compared to the psychological mutilation he had suffered. Kate saw his body heal but his mind was closed to all but him. He hid the darkest thoughts behind a quick and easy smile and a friendly word. The garden had saved him, he mused. It had given him a sense of purpose.

His once pale skin was now a deep, dark bronze but evidence of his past life, the stark white scars, still marked his body. They always would. He accepted that. They were reminders.

His hair was longer than before. It was longer than he liked it but that was a price worth paying. It concealed the ugly scar above his left ear, left there by Liam Fitzpatrick's well-placed gunshot. He had been millimetres from death, he mused stoically from time to time. A couple of millimetres deeper and he would not be here now worrying about the length of his hair.

He now sported a full beard, brown tinged with red. It reminded him of his mother's auburn hair. It was the final piece in his transformation. Kate had objected fiercely at first but over the weeks, she had grown to accept it. More than accept it. She liked when it tickled her skin, or so she said.

The overall effect was astonishing. Old friends back home would scarcely recognise him. When he looked into a mirror, he scarcely recognised himself. He imagined he looked like a Hippy. Stick some roses in his hair and he could be in California.

But did all that matter? There was little chance of old friends bumping into him here. Not now. This wasn't Glasgow; not even Scotland. The old Jamie Raeburn was dead. Jean-Luc Rochefort was very much alive. He had a new name, a new life, and a new future.

He looked out over the fields behind his house. The landscape stretched away into the distance, an irregular pattern of fields. All of them of different sizes and colours. Dust covered roads, some no more than tracks, criss-crossed the terrain connecting the surrounding villages with the nearby town of Epernay and with each other.

On the far side of the gentle valley of the River Surmelin, an elderly tractor driven by an equally elderly farm worker, laboured up the incline. A cloud of dust followed in its wake as its wheels and the heavy plough behind it tore and ripped the parched soil. It was stage one in the cycle, a cycle repeated three or four times each year, as the ground was prepared for the next crop. Soon, the second stage of metamorphosis would take place when the new seeds germinated. The earth would turn green as the early shoots pressed through the soil and then the colour would change again. The green would become gold, or yellow, or brown, depending on the crop, as it ripened, ready for harvest. The colours of the landscape changed constantly. Jamie loved it.

The move here had been sudden. It had been forced on him... forced on all of them. He and Kate had spoken of doing something like this in the past.

Disappearing. But back then, it had been a means of escape. Now it was a form of exile. Pleasant exile but exile none the less.

Thinking back, there had been no alternative. He could see the way the Brigadier's mind was working. Michael Messenger was dead... his usefulness exhausted. Jamie Raeburn was now a liability... and if he was a liability, so too was his family. That had been the deciding factor that led to their move. Yes, there were still risks and dangers out there, he had known that from the beginning, but the risks would have been greater had they stayed. And then some.

That was one of his darker thoughts, one he kept firmly to himself. Sharing it with Kate was not a good idea. Why upset her, he reasoned. Better to let her believe they were free of the nightmare.

He heard her pottering about in the house behind him. She laughed and his children squealed happily. That made him smile again. His children were amazing. They had coped with everything over these last months... including his mood swings in the early days. Children, he decided, cope with most things when they have their parents around them. Adults, however, are a different matter. For Kate, the change had been challenging. Life in rural France was not what she was used to. Adjusting had been difficult for her. It still was, he mused.

Language was the major problem. It still was, though Kate would never admit it. The kids had mastered it easily, as children do. They spoke like natives now. Kate still struggled and she found it hard. No one in the village spoke English. She felt isolated. Being separated from her family back in England was bad enough, being unable to speak to them was awful. She missed her mother, her father with his quirky ways, and her brother and his family. She didn't complain, but she missed them. Jamie knew that. He missed his own mother and father. He had tried to talk about it with her but her response was always the same... she said she was happy, happy they were safe, happy they were together. That, she insisted, was all that mattered.

Jamie smiled thoughtfully and wiped more sweat from his brow.

Are we safe, he wondered? Has the nightmare really ended?

It didn't feel like it sometimes. Sure, some of the spectres from his past to rest, his erstwhile fellow travellers on the road to Hades, had been laid to rest. He was the boatman who carried them across the Styx and then turned back. Alone. They were still in his mind. They always would be, he imagined, lying there passively, like cadavers, in an air-conditioned mortuary with tiny "Do Not Disturb" labels attached to their big toes. Could he ever redeem himself, he wondered? That was a private thought. A dark one. He smiled grimly and pushed it to the back of his mind. They were the past. He could forget them... for the moment at least.

Until Judgement Day, when they all rise up to indict me before Saint Peter...but not today. Today it's only the living that concern me.

He gave an involuntary little shudder as the sound of a vehicle, faint at first, came to him from the Epernay road. It was coming towards the village at speed, its engine roaring throatily as the driver pushed it to its limit on the long straight. He turned towards the sound and found it just where he expected it to be. It started as a black speck and grew rapidly in size, like an ugly, bloating beetle. A cloud of dust hung in the air in its wake, lending it a sense of menace.

Jamie felt tense and uncomfortable. Why, he couldn't say, but it was happening more and more these days. The feeling didn't relate to this particular car, it came with any car. He couldn't rationalise it, but suspected the reason was that one day, sooner or later, another car would come down the Epernay road and he would be forced to leave this place.

Kate shared his fear. He knew that, but it was never discussed. It was taboo. Superstition it undoubtedly was, but each believed that talking about it would bring it about. And so, they never spoke of it. But that did not remove it from their thoughts. Thinking about it was something neither of them could avoid.

The car, a big black Citroën DS21, sped into the village, its brakes squealing in protest as the driver slowed for the right hand bend and then, with a roar, it accelerated past the house. The sound of it faded quickly after that as the driver negotiated the series of bends that wound, tortuously, through the village and on to the South.

He smiled again as the tension eased. That too was irrational. The car's passage through the village was a daily event; he could virtually set his watch by it. The answer was simple. It wasn't the car that caused his problems; it was the thoughts that came with it.

He sensed Kate's presence and turned, smiling sheepishly. She was looking at him quizzically, as though reading his thoughts. She could read him like a book. It was a knack she had exhibited almost from the day they first met, years before.

She returned his smile but said nothing. She held out her hand. Jamie pushed the fork into the sun-baked ground and came to her, wiping the dirt from his hands onto his already soiled trousers.

Kate laughed as she wrapped her arms around his neck. 'Day dreaming again Monsieur Rochefort?' she giggled, avoiding the subject she knew was on his mind. 'Any excuse to avoid digging the garden,' she continued, pulling him closer. She felt his hands on her and turned her head to him, kissing him hungrily and pressing her heavily swollen belly against him. It never changed. Even after five years of marriage and three, soon to be four, children, she still wanted him... and he felt the same. Maybe it was everything they had been through... all of the trials and tribulations they had faced together.

The patter of tiny feet put an end to any thoughts she had of luring him into the relative cool of their bedroom. She could wait for that but she sensed that the baby kicking inside her was impatient to join them. It was due any day now. She had worried about that at first. Giving birth in a foreign land, unable to speak the language, had filled her with dread. That fear was gone. She could speak a few words and phrases of French now and her confidence was growing. She could communicate now; could understand and be understood. More importantly, she felt accepted... and she had made new friends. Friends who promised help when the time came. Maybe she should be warning them to be ready, she thought with a smile.

Jamie pulled away from her and shrugged, smiling down at the children, his message clear. 'So it's back to the digging then,' he laughed. 'Come on, you lot,' he grinned, tousling the hair of his two younger children. 'You can help me for a while and then I'll fill the pool for you; deal?'

They bounded away, eager to help, while Lauren, the eldest, gave him a 'no way' look. She was growing up so fast, Jamie mused, and looking more like her mother every day.

Another few years and I will have to keep a shotgun handy, he laughed inwardly.

'I'll help Mum,' the girl announced, taking Kate's hand. 'We'll make you a cake.'

Jamie laughed and nodded. 'Offer accepted,' he replied.

'We'll make you a fruit tart then,' Kate decided, laughing. 'Just don't spend too long out here in your kingdom, my lord,' she continued. 'If you do, Lauren and I might just bake it and eat it before you come in.'

Jamie laughed and bowed, then turned to his younger offspring. 'Right, you two,' he said with a grin. 'You heard that; we have to finish quickly or there will be no tart for us.'

The children squealed with delight and began digging furiously with their tiny spades. That would keep them busy for a while, he hoped. This was what he had craved so much. A normal family life. Somehow, he doubted it would last. His sixth sense was picking up dark clouds on the horizon.

***

That night it was oppressively warm. Even with the windows opened wide behind firmly closed wooden shutters, it was hot in the house. Jamie and Kate came outside for respite and sat, close together, at the tiny table on the stone terrace at the back of the house. A bottle of red wine, already opened, sat beside two glasses sat on the table beside a spluttering lantern. The stars twinkled and sparkled in the sky and The Milky Way stretched across the heavens like diamonds spilled out onto a black velvet cloth - millions of tiny, sparkling diamonds.

The heavens always filled Jamie with awe and, occasionally, fear. It was, to him, like being in the presence of some supernatural power. Some might say God - and being in the presence of God, given Jamie's history, wasn't necessarily a good thing.

He thought of home. He was a city boy. His life, until now, had been lived in the industrial heartland of Scotland, with its factories, shipyards and steel works pumping soot and grime into the air and blackening the sky. Even the sun, when it did manage to make an appearance, seemed to shine through a perpetual haze of polution.

It was so different here, he mused. Here, the sun shone, almost daily, from a clear blue sky and at night, the glow of the moon covered the countryside in a pale, white radiance. There was nothing to match it back home. Maybe, in the Highlands and Islands, away from the cities and their pollution, it might be as clear as this, he mused. But it wouldn't be as warm.

'Do you miss home?' he murmured quietly to Kate, breaking the silence... and the taboo. He could see the flickering candlelight from the lantern dancing in his wife's eyes as she turned towards him.

'This is my home,' she replied gently. 'Wherever we are, as long as we're together, is my home,' she continued, fending him off in her usual way. 'Anyway, what's to miss?' she laughed. 'It's beautiful here and we have made new friends... though I suppose I miss our old friends sometimes.'

'But our new friends aren't family,' Jamie riposted softly.

'You're my family. The kids are my family,' she retorted instantly. She heard him sigh and knew he was preparing his next line. She decided to beat him to it. 'Your turn,' she said. 'Do you miss it?' she posed.

'What? Miss Glasgow?' he laughed. 'Like you said, what's to miss... the rain, the grime, the endless grey sky?'

'No, not Glasgow,' Kate said, her voice now tinged with sadness. 'Though I think that you do sometimes. No, I was thinking more of your old life, sweetheart... our old life,' she added quickly, correcting herself. 'Digging a garden, cutting grass and growing fruit and vegetables isn't really you,' she laughed. 'I sometimes get the feeling that all the peace and inactivity around here is getting to you.'

Jamie smiled. Was it showing so clearly?

He turned his attention back to the sky for a moment as he gathered his thoughts. After a moment, he spoke again. 'I suppose there are things I miss,' he admitted, somewhat reluctantly. 'The danger was addictive. It was a bit like taking drugs, I suppose. I felt alive. It was that feeling you get on a giant roller coaster - fear and elation in equal measure.' He turned guiltily to her then. 'That's selfish,' he continued. 'I'm sorry. I knew what it was doing to you.'

Kate Raeburn nodded slowly and pulled a face. 'When you went away each time I wondered if I would ever see you again. I knew it was much more dangerous than you made out.'

Jamie sighed softly. What else had she worked out, he mused?

'It all changed with Terence Magill,' he whispered after a moment. He saw Kate's brow furrow in response to that and realised he had broken a cardinal rules: Never, ever, mention a name. He carried on quickly, hoping she would forget it. 'That's when I realised there wasn't much difference between me and the guys getting "the good news" - no difference at all, in fact,' he added, his voice fading.

'The good news? Kate queried with a laugh, her brow knitting. 'That's a strange way of putting it.'

He laughed back but his laugh had a cold, callous ring to it. 'It's black humour, sweetheart,' he replied grimly. 'It's what the SAS who trained me guys call a hit.' His mood was darkening dangerously now. It was time to pull back.

Kate refused to let go. She raised her left eyebrow inquisitively and reached for his hand, squeezing it gently. She knew the signs. She thought he had beaten the depression that had engulfed him but now doubt was setting in. Something was troubling him. She could see it clearly. Something deep, and something dark.

'Why are you bringing this up now, Jamie?' she asked softly, failing miserably to hide her anxiety. 'It's over... you're not that man any more...' Her voice trailed off as she searched his face for acknowledgement but found none. His face was just a vague, dark blur in the darkness. She sensed the worst and an involuntary shudder ran down her spine. 'It is over... isn't it?' she continued, her voice now no louder than a whisper. She saw his head move slowly from side to side. Not denial, she mused, but uncertainty.

'I don't know,' he replied, his voice matching hers. 'For the last few weeks things have been crowding in on me... flashbacks, bits of conversation - things that, on their own, don't make sense. I feel I'm being watched, talked about, stalked even... I think they're getting ready to draw me back in.' He paused a moment. 'Am I being paranoid?' he asked at last, accompanying it with a small laugh to make light of it.

'Maybe, maybe not,' Kate replied softly. She squeezed his fingers again, tighter this time. She too was growing anxious. 'What aren't you telling me, my love?' she continued gently.

Jamie leaned towards the table and poured two glasses of wine, passing one over to her. He took a mouthful and stared up into the heavens. The Milky Way stretched away to infinity, the tiny stars so clear he felt he could count them all, though it would take him a lifetime... maybe even three lifetimes. There was silence for a while, only the occasional sounds of the night disturbing it; owls, dogs barking in the distance, bats squeaking out their sonar as they flew acrobatically in the dark searching for food.

'I never really did tell you about that last job, did I?' he murmured eventually. His voice was so low Kate had to strain to hear him. When she did, the words sent a shiver down her spine.

She pulled him closer and laid her head gently against his shoulder. 'Is that what's worrying you?' she asked. Her voice was gentle. 'The sudden realisation that you're not immortal?'

Jamie laughed harshly. 'No, it's not that,' he said, still laughing. 'I've never doubted that. Mortality is just about time frame and we're not in charge of the clock.'

'If it's not about that then what, or who, is it about?' Kate continued. Her anxiety was mounting.

Jamie sighed heavily and downed another mouthful of wine. He refilled his glass and stared at it pensively for a moment. 'A man risked his life to save me that night,' he said at last. 'I don't know why. I've gone over it again and again, more so recently, but there's no logical reason for it. I keep seeing his face... his eyes boring into me. He'll be back to call in the debt.'

'You can't know that, Jamie. How could he find us here anyway? No one knows we're here.' Jamie looked away. Was there guilt there, Kate wondered? What was he hiding?

Jamie's voice broke into her thoughts again. 'It wasn't just his look,' he said. 'He said something. He was telling me he would be back to call in the debt.'

"Don't forget Dermott, ye owe me; ye owe me big time". Liam Fitzpatrick's words, just before he fired that final shot, reverberated around Jamie's head.

Kate's brow furrowed, the worry lines clear on her face. She didn't want to know what had happened. It was too harrowing even to contemplate, but clearly, Jamie wanted to unburden himself of something. 'I don't understand, Jamie,' she said, almost inaudibly. 'You were wounded. Soldiers, the SAS was sent to bring you back. That's their job. They risk their lives all the time...like you,' she added sadly. 'Is this man you speak of one of them?' Even as she asked the question, she knew that wasn't the answer. She also knew that the real answer was at the root of what was troubling him.

Jamie sighed and reached for her with one hand and raised the other to his left temple, lifting his hair to reveal the scar that lay beneath. 'The man who risked his life is the man who gave me this,' he said quietly. He felt her tense as the shock hit her. He took a deep breath and ploughed on. 'His name is Liam Fitzpatrick. I met him back in '67 when I was over in Belfast.' He hesitated a moment, having second thoughts, then sighed heavily and continued. 'Liam was there that night...at Kiltyclogher, with the IRA unit. He could have killed me,' he said, looking at Kate with sad eyes. 'He probably should have...for his own good,' he added with a wry laugh. 'But he faked it. Convinced his mates that I was dead and left me there for the SAS boys to find. If he'd been rumbled, we would both be dead now.' He shook his head, still wrestling with the problem. 'What I don't understand is why he did it. It just doesn't make sense.'

Kate sat still, frozen with shock. The reality of what had happened hit home. She had always known he had been near to death that night; she just didn't know how near. She felt herself shake and a knot formed in her stomach.

'Why did he do that?' Jamie continued, breaking into the apprehension that was building in her. 'I don't know if I would.'

Kate laughed despite the horror of it. 'Yes you would,' she said with absolute certainty. 'Remember Conor?' she added.

Jamie forced a smile but there was no warmth in it.

How could I forget Conor?

She was right, of course. Conor Whelan had been a stranger to him that fateful night back in 1966. If he could not abandon a stranger, how could he abandon someone he knew? Kate knew him better than he knew himself.

They sat in silence for a while, sipping wine and gazing up at the firmament. Off in the distance the same dog barked and laughter drifted to them on the warm night air. A gentle breeze swept across the garden, cooling them briefly.

Kate was perturbed. She knew the potency of Jamie's sixth sense and guessed that something else was troubling him, something he hadn't been able to share. Not yet.

'So, back to my original question,' she whispered eventually, squeezing his fingers tenderly once again. 'Why are you bringing this up now? What is really worrying you?'

He smiled grimly. He hoped that the darkness hid the worst of his haunted expression from her. But the darkness wasn't just around him, he mused, it was inside him, and that made it difficult to disguise. He leaned closer to her. She needed to see, he decided, and she needed to know. He sighed again, a deeper sigh this time. 'I think Liam Fitzpatrick is going to come looking for me...looking for that debt to be repaid,' he said. 'And when he does...' He let his voice trail off, leaving the conclusion unsaid.

'I've done some really bad things, Kate,' he murmured. 'Maybe this will be fate giving me an opportunity to redeem myself. My final redemption,' he added, with another cold laugh.

Kate shivered despite the balmy heat. He pulled her close, wrapping his arms tightly around her. 'I'm sorry,' he whispered.

A silent tear ran down Kate's face. Redemption, she mused, usually comes at a price. There seemed to be a sense of inevitability to it now. Jamie's instincts were rarely wrong; she knew that from bitter experience. So, it could only be a matter of time, she fretted, and that frightened her. All her old fears, the fears she thought were behind them, now came rushing back with a vengeance.

Chapter Two

Same day, West Belfast, Northern Ireland.

The old man hobbled unsteadily from Falls Road into Divis Street towards Albert Street and St. Peter's, his head down and his shoulders hunched. The church, the pro-Cathedral, was close now. So far so good, he mused grimly. He was beginning to think he was too old for this sort of thing.

His appearance, carefully crafted, attracted no attention from the people who passed him by. Life was too precarious here to worry about people like him. Those who did look turned away guiltily, the heart ripped from them in recent years. And there were many old men like him in Belfast these days, especially in Roman Catholic enclaves like West Belfast. His clothes were worn and stained, the old coat he sported belted around his waist with a piece of frayed cord, and his shoes had seen better days, their heels worn and the leather badly scuffed. Grey stubble covered his chin and his hair, hanging limply to his shoulders beneath a battered, sweat-stained cap, was greasy and lank.

An Army patrol made its way towards him, the young soldiers hugging the walls of the buildings for cover, their eyes darting from window to window and to the roofs opposite. These boys did pay attention, scrutinising him carefully before passing on by. In a city where any man could pose a threat, he appeared to pose none.

There was a smell of burning in the air. It was dismal here, he thought darkly. Gaps appeared in the housing stock where some of the dwellings had been burned to the ground. Other houses stood gaunt, their roofs gaping and their glassless windows blackened by fire. It reminded him of towns in Germany at the end of the war when the Allied armies had pushed through and he felt a grudging sympathy for the Catholic population. They were not all mindless thugs, he reminded himself, just as the Protestants weren't all choirboys.

Once in Albert Street he followed it for about 100 yards before turning left into St Peter's Close. Ahead of him now the twin spires of St Peter's, the Roman Catholic pro-cathedral, rose majestically into the slate grey sky. It was, without doubt, an imposing sight. Was it Divine intervention that had helped it avoid the ravages of the war that was tearing the city apart and leaving so many other places devastated, he wondered? If so, he hoped the man upstairs didn't take his eye off the ball.

How times change, he thought grimly. One of the original Catholic Churches in Belfast - St. Mary's Chapel Lane – had been built with the aid of "Protestant and Dissenter" money. A Catholic Church built with Protestant money, he mused on. Where did it all go wrong?

He was early for his rendezvous. He had intended to be. He eased himself down onto a dwarf wall bordering the square and settled to wait. There were few passers-by here. He fished a battered packet of cigarettes from his coat pocket and lit up. He would have preferred his pipe but that didn't fit the image he was portraying.

It was about twenty minutes before Liam Fitzpatrick appeared. The man made his way into the square, walking at a steady pace, and headed directly for the Chapel entrance. He looked neither right nor left, his mind clearly elsewhere. He had met the old man sitting on the dwarf wall once before but there was no likelihood he would recognise him now. They were different beings.

Sir Charles Redmond smiled coldly. Fitzpatrick was right on time. He, on the other hand, intended being late for their appointment. He drew heavily on his cigarette and coughed. As a theatrical prop, it was ideal, but smoking cigarettes was not something he enjoyed. The square remained deserted, with no one entering it behind Fitzpatrick.

Not yet, anyway; don't be hasty.

Another five minutes and then he could be sure. That was why he had picked this place for the rendezvous. If anyone was following Corkscrew, they would stick out like a sore thumb. He puffed on the cigarette, refusing to inhale its noxious fumes, and waited. Still no one entered the square. The tension in him was ebbing now. Not that it would ever leave him, not while he was here, but he was reasonably confident that his man had not been followed. That, of course, depended on whether or not Corkscrew was his man, he reminded himself, but that was a risk he had to take.

Still in character, he hauled himself stiffly up from the wall and hobbled towards the Chapel entrance. He, like Liam Fitzpatrick, looked neither right nor left and anyone watching would see only an old man, a vagrant perhaps, entering the church for solace. Once inside, he stopped and searched for the Irishman. Stretching ahead of him was the main aisle, with pews ranged right and left towards a series of columns and arches that bounded the outer aisles. The altar faced him, the Bishop's Chair set against the far wall beneath ornate decoration and high, arched windows stretching up to the domed roof. The floor was intricately tiled, mosaic like, he noted. It was, quite simply, stunning and modern buildings could never match its opulence. On any other day he might have enjoyed sitting here in quiet contemplation, but not today.

He found Corkscrew about half way down the line of wooden pews, a few yards in from the central aisle. The man's head was bent forward as though he were engaged in silent prayer but that, Sir Charles thought, was unlikely. Although nominally a Roman Catholic, and brought up in "The Faith", Liam Fitzpatrick believed in no God. His religion was Socialism and he had joined the IRA to fight for social justice and a Socialist Republic, not, like some of his fellow terrorists, out of blind, religious hatred and sectarianism.

Sir Charles shuffled down the aisle and entered the line of pews behind his man. He slid along on the wooden seat on his bottom, stopping just before reaching Corkscrew. He was now just behind and to Corkscrew's left. All the pews around them were vacant, the nearest visitors to the church congregated nearer the altar. He saw Corkscrew's head rise and anticipated the man turning around to face him, and that was something he didn't want.

'Don't turn round,' he hissed. There was no chance of their conversation being overheard but Sir Charles kept his voice low, almost to a whisper. Liam Fitzpatrick's head dropped once again as he complied with the instruction.

'What is so urgent you dragged me here?' Sir Charles continued. 'This is against every rule in the book.'

'Scared, are ye?' Liam murmured sarcastically.

The old man laughed quietly. 'Not particularly, merely annoyed. I've been doing this sort of thing most of my adult life...I can smell danger. How about you?'

When Liam spoke, the sarcasm was gone. 'Aye, I'm scared...and I'd like to enjoy a long adult life. That's why you're here. You can give me that; no one else can.'

Another soft laugh came from Sir Charles. 'Isn't that in the power of your God? Wasn't that what you were praying for when I arrived?' he asked. It was his turn for the sarcasm.

Liam Fitzpatrick snorted derisively. 'What God? If there's a God he seems to have lost sight of this country,' he retorted. 'No, I'll settle for you.'

'Then get to the point. Say your piece.'

There was a moment of silence. From the nave, the sound of murmuring voices could just be heard. Sir Charles waited patiently. Some gut instinct told him that what he was about to learn was significant.

'Things are goin' to hell, so they are,' Liam started. 'Youse Brits have made a real arse o' things; curfews, internment an' Bloody Sunday...youse need to wise up, so ye do! An' now there's this "power sharin'" shite,' he laughed coldly. 'A wee chat around the table an' that'll sort everything, is that what youse think?'

'I've heard all this before,' Sir Charles hissed. 'You didn't need to meet me to let me have these pearls of wisdom. So why am I here?'

Liam stared down at his feet as though in supplication, biting back anger and fear in equal proportions. 'Not everybody's goin' to be sittin' round the feckin' table,' he whispered at last. 'There are some who don't want to talk...an' they're plannin' a wee alternative, so they are...a wee fireworks party. The Army Council don't agree with it, the UNM don't agree with it, an' from what I hear, some of the feckin' Loyalists aren't too keen on it either.' A series of big "spectaculars" is bein' planned...to remind the people who really calls the shots here.'

Sir Charles was interested now. This was worth the visit at least. There had been nothing in recent briefings by MI5 along these lines although, reading between the lines, some in that branch of the Security Services weren't entirely behind the proposal either. 'Who's planning it and what is it?' he asked, his eyes scanning the church nervously.

'The UNM is involved...The Army too,' Liam responded quietly. Sir Charles knew only too well that Liam's reference to "The Army" had nothing to do with the British Army and everything to do with the IRA. 'As to what they're plannin', I don't know yet...but it's not just one, it's three or four an' they'll all be co-ordinated for maximum effect.'

Sir Charles was more than worried now. There was nothing coming in from any intelligence sources that pointed to this so if it was true a major crisis was looming. He was so taken up with thoughts of it that he almost missed Liam's next bit.

'I'm bein' sent over to England with three other UNM men. I don't know who yet, but we're to be part of it. All the operations are bein' planned separately...if youse lot penetrate one, youse won't get the others. I can give ye the information on the job I'm part of but that's all...ye'll have to work the rest out fer yerselves...unless youse have some other poor fuck like me in yer pocket,' he added darkly.

He paused, waiting for Sir Charles' response to that but none came. 'I've had enough,' he murmured. 'I don't want anythin' to do with it...somethin' tells me it's all goin' to end badly, so I'm playin' my get out of jail free card.'

Sir Charles sat quietly, absorbing the information before replying. 'And you don't know the targets?' he asked, avoiding Liam's demand.

'I told ye, they're keepin' those close to their chests. Security's tight. All I know is it'll make Joe Public sit up an' take notice...so whatever they are, they're big,' the Irishman reiterated.

'Yes, so you say...but you've given me nothing to judge that on. I need more. What about timescale?'

'I don't know that either...but I'm goin' over to the Mainland in January so it won't be before that. I think we're waitin' for a special delivery.'

Sir Charles' interest piqued. 'What "special delivery"...and where is it coming from, do you know?'

Liam shook his head despairingly.

'You don't know much, do you?' Sir Charles continued. It was more a statement than a question and it brought no response. 'Okay, I need more. When you get it you pass it on...and I want it all. Then I'll get you out.' He let that hang in the air for a moment before continuing. 'And then, of course, there's the other thing you still have to get me,' he said, his voice cold.

Liam groaned softly before replying. 'I've told ye before, I don't know who planted that feckin' bomb. It was before my time. If I start askin' too many questions then someone else will start askin' questions about me. I'm not a feckin' ganch, I'm not goin' down that road. There's already rumours about a tout high up in The Army Council; I don't want caught up in the fallout from that.' He turned round to face Sir Charles now. 'An' I'll not be contactin' McClure again,' he continued adamantly.

Sir Charles bit back his anger. 'You're playing a dangerous game, laddie,' he said menacingly.

'Aye, but I've been playin' this dangerous game fer a while now...an' I don't trust the feckin' RUC any more,' he stated simply.

'McClure has been your contact for almost two years and you're still in the clear...what's brought this on?'

Liam Fitzpatrick stared back at him grimly. 'No harm to McClure, he's a dacent enough man, so he is. It's not him that worries me,' he replied. 'But the deeper I get into this shit the more chance there is of a fuck-up. Somebody says the wrong thing at the wrong time, a careless word or an innocent slip of the tongue, an' before ah've had time to pack a bag an' slip away there's a knock at the door an'...well, ye know the rest.'

Sir Charles returned his look, studying the informer closely. He expected to see fear, that was only natural, but what he saw was beyond that. Corkscrew was genuinely afraid.

'Okay,' he conceded. 'You want out, I accept that, and I'll fix it, but before I do I want everything you can get on these attacks; targets, dates and who's involved. That's my price. But that still leaves us with a problem, does it not? If you insist in cutting yourself off from McClure, how do you intend passing that intelligence to me?'

Liam smiled for the first time since the conversation started, though the effect was hardly encouraging to Sir Charles.

'Ah've been thinkin' about that, so ah have,' Liam responded. 'There is someone ah think ah can trust... Dermott Lynch. You get him to help me an' ah'll pass everythin' to him.'

Sir Charles knotted his brow. The conversation was taking an unexpected and confusing turn. 'Dermott Lynch?' he parried, his mind now in overdrive.

The name meant nothing to him but the Irishman obviously thought it did. So who was Dermott Lynch? He had to play it carefully, no slips.

'Why should Dermott get involved?' he asked, keeping it formal.

Liam's laugh was almost soundless. 'Ah saved his feckin' neck,' Liam retorted. 'He'd be rottin' in a wood in County Leitrim if it wasn't for me, so he would,' he continued, sounding almost matter of fact. 'Ask him.'

Sir Charles maintained his bland expression but he was stunned. The one thing that had puzzled him most about Raeburn's miraculous escape from Kiltyclogher was now laid bare. Jamie Raeburn, Michael Messenger and now Dermott Lynch... an unholy trilogy, almost like father, son and Holy Ghost... and Raeburn, it turns out, was all three.

He stared at the back of Fitzpatrick's head as he spoke. 'Dermott's been out of it since Kiltyclogher,' he said quietly. 'I retired him... for his sake and for yours. He almost bled to death... and hypothermia nearly took him too.' He noticed Corkscrew was no longer staring at the floor. He was looking straight ahead now, his eyes screwed tightly shut. He obviously hadn't thought of that, Sir Charles mused.

'I don't know where he is now, or how to contact him. Sorry,' the Brigadier continued, his voice steady.

Liam laughed cynically, his eyes still firmly shut. 'Ye don't expect me to believe that shite, do ye? You know exactly where he is, so ye do,' he retorted disdainfully. He paused for a second or two, opened his eyes and turned his head slightly to face Sir Charles. 'If he is retired, like ye say, then ye'd better un-retire him. Ah'll do this through Dermott, or not at all.'

'You're cutting off your nose to spite your face. Cut yourself off from me it'll be open season on you, you do realise that?'

'An you'll have a major feckin' incident that'll bite ye on the arse,' Liam retaliated.

Sir Charles sensed he was wasting his time. The man wasn't going to budge. He smiled and gave a resigned sigh. 'Alright,' he agreed. 'I'll talk to Dermott but I can't promise you anything. It will be up to him... He might not agree.'

Liam looked grimly ahead as he replied. 'Then ye'd better use yer best powers o' persuasion and convince him to change his mind, so ye had,' Liam responded irreverently.

Two men and two women accompanied by two elderly nuns in long black habits and white coifs, the starched cotton headwear that covers their necks and cheeks, made their way up the central aisle towards the exit. Their animated chattering stopped when they spied the two men and six pairs of curious eyes settled on them. Sir Charles returned their looks and forced a smile. Their curiosity was understandable, he reflected. What could a down and out, a vagrant, have in common with a seemingly respectable working man? Liam, unnerved by the attention, turned his head away from Sir Charles and stared belligerently back at them until the party, embarrassed, looked away and passed them by.

Sir Charles waited until the group had exited into the Atrium before slipping a small, crumpled scrap of paper across to the Irishman. On it was scribbled a sequence of numbers, nothing more. 'Call me on that number on Saturday morning between eight and mid-day,' he said softly. 'If you can't make it, the fall-back will be on Monday evening between seven and eleven. If you don't call by then, you'll be too late. The number will be unobtainable... and you'll be on your own. Understood?'

Liam faced the altar ahead of him, his back again to Sir Charles, and nodded his acknowledgement, his head moving up and down almost imperceptibly.

The meeting was over.

'Good,' Sir Charles murmured quietly. 'I'll leave first,' he continued. 'Wait ten minutes before you follow. You can spend the time talking to your God and seeking his forgiveness... or his intervention with Dermott,' he added, chuckling coldly, before sliding along the pew on his backside towards the aisle. He didn't look back.

Liam Fitzpatrick stared forward towards the altar and the magnificent stained glass windows beyond. He wasn't talking to his God or to any other god, come to that; he had given up on God many years before.

Sir Charles, still in character, hobbled out of the church and into the grey, Belfast afternoon. The small group of pilgrims, still accompanied by the nuns, was taking photographs. They paid him no heed. He meant nothing to them.

He smiled to himself. That was as it should be. Slowly, he limped his way back through the square to Albert Street and turned towards the city centre.

The crack of rifles came from the bottom of The Falls. The Army and the Provos were at it again. Corkscrew was right in one thing at least. Things were getting worse.

His pick-up would take place in Chichester Street near Belfast City Hall in ten minutes. It was far enough away from St. Peter's but, even so, it would be well stage-managed by Chief Inspector McClure. The Special Branch man, like Sir Charles, never took unnecessary risks.

Sir Charles remained vigilant. His senses were still attuned to the danger around him but he could not help his thoughts turning to the challenge ahead.

And it will be a challenge, he told himself.

But as well as presenting him with a challenge it also raised an awkward problem. A problem he had hoped he would never have to face. The fallout from it would be unavoidable...and personal. 'Such is life,' he murmured to no one but himself, a grim smile settling on his craggy face.

He followed his pre-determined route, conscious of everyone and everything around him, but still pondering Liam Fitzpatrick's proposition.

'Dermott Kelly, Dermott Kelly, Dermott Kelly,' he murmured quietly to himself, repeating the name over and over again, like a mantra. Everything was clear now. The puzzle solved. He had always had his suspicions but his questions on the matter had been rebuffed by Raeburn time and time again. He had not given an inch. Denial had followed denial. He did not know why the Irishman hadn't executed him, he didn't know the man, he could offer no explanation, had no idea why his life had been spared.

Raeburn had even gone so far as to suggest it was simply luck, a poor shot by the IRA man in the heat of the moment, grazing his skull rather than penetrating it. He had been close to death so the suggestion was, in some ways, plausible, but the "poor shot" bit Sir Charles had never accepted. Even in the heat of the moment it would be impossible to miss at such close range. A blind man could have done it.

Now everything had fallen into place but only out of necessity on Corkscrew's part, Sir Charles reminded himself.

He cursed quietly under his breath. Raeburn had fooled him, no mean feat...but in reality, he had fooled himself. He had given up; it was as simple as that. Pragmatism had won the day. As far as the rest of the world was concerned, Captain Michael Messenger was dead and Raeburn was gone, out of it. It had been irrelevant by then.

But that was six months ago. It may have been irrelevant then, but it was not irrelevant now. Whist he was mildly annoyed, with himself as much as with both men, he could, he realised, use what he had learned to advantage.

He had regretted the loss of "Michael". It had irked him. The impending loss of Corkscrew also irked him but, with luck and some subtle machinations, he might be able to use it to bring his best Archangel back.

That thought, the raising of his errant Archangel from the dead like some latter day Lazarus, invigorated him. If he could do it, it would be a miracle of sorts. But there would be no Divine intervention, simply tact and gentle persuasion. A feeling of euphoria settled on him. It might just work and if it did he could kill two birds with one stone, so to speak.

He was in Chichester Street now, about fifty yards short of City Hall, when a Royal Ulster Constabulary Land Rover, heavily armoured with mesh grills covering its windows, pulled to a halt beside him. Two officers, their torsos protected by flak jackets, clambered from the vehicle and circled him. Nothing was said. He simply looked at them, waiting, his face projecting an image of apprehension. Suddenly, he was gripped by the arms and frog marched to the rear of the idling vehicle. The doors were flung open from the inside where another man waited and he was thrown unceremoniously inside. The doors slammed shut behind him. He heard the front doors of the Land Rover close and the vehicle pulled away, swinging out into the afternoon traffic.

Sir Charles cursed softly and twisted his body on the floor where he had fallen to look up at the man sitting on the bench seat above him.

'Sorry about that, Brigadier,' Chief Inspector Ewan McClure of RUC Special Branch said with a lopsided grin. 'The lads like to make it look authentic.' He held out a hand and helped Sir Charles to the bench opposite. 'Worthwhile, was it?' the policeman asked, raising an eyebrow questioningly as the Brigadier settled down on the bench seat facing him.

Sir Charles shook his head. 'That remains to be seen, Chief Inspector,' he replied. 'If what he says is true, there's a major attack in the offing. Trouble is, he doesn't know the details.'

'So you'll be wanting me to stay on top of him then,' the RUC man continued.

'Yes, and no, Ewan,' Sir Charles came back. 'You are not to have any more contact with Corkscrew,' he continued, taking the RUC man by surprise. 'He's getting jumpy,' he said, by way of explanation. 'It's no reflection on you, he assures me, and I believe him. Apparently there's talk of a tout somewhere in the upper echelons and he's scared he'll get caught up in the paranoia.'

Ewan McClure snorted derisively. 'It's that bloody woman he's seeing,' he countered. 'I don't know about any other informer. Having an affair with that lass is crazy in the extreme,' he added. 'That's probably what's really behind it.'

'Yes, probably,' Sir Charles agreed, allowing himself a wry smile.

'So where does that leave me?'

The Brigadier smiled grimly. 'I said Yes, and no, Ewan. The fact you are no longer his contact does not mean I want you to stop watching him. Quite the opposite, in fact; I want you to stick to him like a limpet. We need to watch his back...and I want to know everything about everyone he meets, talks to...even dreams about.'

The Special Branch man gave a frosty laugh. 'And his new contact? What about him...or her?' he continued. 'Do you want them watched too?'

Sir Charles chuckled. 'That might prove a little too complicated, Ewan. One, you'd be following a ghost and, two, I doubt he'll come anywhere near your bailiwick. But who knows? If he does, I'll let you know.' He smiled at his RUC contact, the conversation over. 'Now, tell your boys to get me to Castlereigh toute de suite, I have to speak to someone there and need to be somewhere else by tomorrow.'

Chapter Three

South of Epernay, Marne, France, Thursday 30th August 1973

'We're almost there, Chief,' the driver called out, just loud enough to be heard over the steady purr of the engine.

Sir Charles Redmond, opened his eyes and stretched out his legs in the back of the car. With his eyes opened, the bright sunlight seared into his retina and forced him to screw them shut again. It was like staring right into a brilliant searchlight. He opened them again, carefully this time, and let them adjust to the glare. The sleep had done him little good and he was beginning to question the sense of what he was doing here. But it was necessary so he put a brave face on it. 'How long to go?' he asked.

'About five minutes, I reckon,' his driver replied. 'We passed through Epernay a few minutes back. The village is five or six kilometres up ahead. Do you want to go straight to the house?'

Sir Charles smiled. 'No, I don't think so George. It's late. We'll take rooms at one of the hotels in the village and I'll pay my respects to Monsieur Rochefort in the morning.' He paused for a moment. 'And you can drive back into Epernay and get me some champagne for my wife. I won't need you,' he added.

George gave him a quick look in the rear view mirror, trying to catch his eye to convey his concern over that, but Sir Charles' attention was already elsewhere. He hoped the old boy was calling this one right. From what little he knew of Monsieur Rochefort from Sir Charles' occasional remark on the man, the meeting between them probably wouldn't be amicable. But it was his Chief's call. He just followed orders. Even when they made no sense to him.

Sir Charles turned his head to the window. He was here on a wing and a prayer, and he knew it. A lot depended on Raeburn's fitness, physical and mental. Had the lad recovered sufficiently from his injuries, he wondered anxiously. That was the big question.

And if he hasn't?

Then I'll cross that bridge when I come to it, he decided. He didn't feel particularly good about what he was doing here but that came with the job. If there had been an alternative he would have taken it, he told himself, but he was simply appeasing his conscience with that. Even if there had been an alternative, he would still be here.

Outside the car, a dense wall of trees flashed past. The road stretched ahead of them, straight as a die, flanked on both sides by impenetrable forest set behind high fences. He had never visited this part of the Region before but he knew places like it where the deep, dark forest had saved his life. The same forests had provided shelter for the men and women of the FFI, the Resistance. It seemed a lifetime ago and yet, here he was, on another mission.

Abruptly, the trees disappeared behind them and fields now stretched away towards the horizon. He felt the car begin a gentle descent and pulled his eyes away from the fields to the road ahead. It ran downhill, more steeply, to what appeared to be a bridge over a small river and then climbed gently towards a cluster of houses that sat on the high ground beyond. Their destination, he surmised. His eyes were immediately drawn to the imposing chateau that towered over the village, dominating it. It was an outlandish structure, fairy-tale like, with turrets and chimneys rising haphazardly into the sky and the sun reflecting off myriad windows. It was a statement of power and control looming as it did over the surrounding peaceful countryside. Was it not ever thus, he mused?

Again, his thoughts drifted to the past. Not the recent past but back to his younger days when things had been black and white. At least he thought they were black and white. But wasn't that the problem with memories? You remember what you want to remember and erase the rest, he mused. They were good times, people said, when in truth they were probably darker than today.

Too much philosophising!

He shook his head to chase them away but the memories kept piling in. His wife's parents lived not too far from here. About 50 kilometres or thereabouts, he guessed, in the village of Saint Gibrien, near Chalons-sur-Marne. They were retired now, living out their days in peace and tranquillity. He wondered if they thought of the past as "the good times". They were dangerous times, exciting times, scary times...but good?

He shook his head and smiled. They had been good in one way. It was then he had met his wife, Estelle, and had fallen head over heels in love. The young British spy and the beautiful young French Resistance fighter; him leading raids against the railway marshalling yards at Chalons, blowing up telephone exchanges and derailing trains, and Estelle acting as courier, carrying information between the different Resistance units in the area. He had been a man of principle in those days; where had it all gone wrong.

'That's us, Sir,' he heard George say as the car glided to a halt and his thoughts reverted to the present. He would visit Saint Gibrien and his in-laws before he returned home. Spring a surprise. Estelle didn't know he was here so he could avoid the visit, without domestic repercussions, had he wanted to but his conscience would not allow it. Conscience? He laughed inwardly. Maybe all was not yet lost.

They were parked in what appeared to be the village square, facing an imposing stone building. At least, it had been imposing at some time in its past. A giant arched gateway led through its thick stone walls to a shaded courtyard beyond. Wooden shutters, paint flaking from the wood, covered its windows and the stonework was badly in need of some tender loving care. Gaps had appeared in the mortar between the enormous stone blocks and weeds grew from dilapidated gutters, pointing majestically skywards. But it was the ivy, clinging tenaciously to great swathes of wall, its green leaves turning to a deep red with the approach of autumn that turned the ancient building into a thing of beauty.

Behind them was another imposing building, this of more recent origin but still a great age. A tall, square bell tower with an enormous round clock that faced out over the square rose grandly above the building. The French Tricolour hanging limply in the still air from a flagpole set above the door identified this building as the Mairie, the Town Hall. The flag gave it away.

To their left was a white painted two-storey structure boasting the name Hotel de la Place on a board fixed above its wide, ground floor window. That would do, Sir Charles decided. Two doors served the building. One, on the left, led to what appeared to be the bar with restaurant beyond and the other to the hotel's reception area. The windows on the upper floor were bedecked with flower boxes, all of them filled with geraniums. A profusion of colour. It was, the he had to admit, a very pretty village. But it was quiet; and that gave him cause for some concern.

He eased himself out of the Rover and stood on the cobbles. The car stood out like a thoroughbred among nags, he noted, even though there were few of the latter. He saw a small Citroen van, a garishly painted Citroen 2CV and a sleek, though old, black Citroen DS5. The only other vehicle was a Renault truck that had seen better days. Set against those, his black Rover 3500 looked exactly what it was, an official vehicle. He should have thought things out a little better, he mused. If Raeburn saw the car or heard any of the locals gossiping about it, his suspicions would be aroused. That, Sir Charles decided, would never do. He wanted surprise on his side when he finally knocked on the young man's door.

'Change of plan, George,' he said, coming to a decision. 'You can leave me here and head back into Epernay. Find yourself a hotel. I won't need you until tomorrow afternoon.'

George was taken by surprise. It showed all over his finely chiselled face. 'Don't worry. I don't imagine anyone here is going to set about me,' Sir Charles laughed. 'I don't want my quarry spooked,' he continued. 'So don't hang about. Chop-chop.'

George still looked sceptical but set to the task, removing the Brigadier's overnight bag from the boot and placing it beside the old man's feet on the cobbles. Sir Charles handed him a fistful of francs. 'There should be more than enough there for a decent hotel,' he said. 'And try to stay out of trouble,' he said jokingly. Of all the men who worked for him, George Fox was the least likely to get into trouble...of any sort.

As the big car pulled away and retraced its route to Epernay, Sir Charles picked up his bag and entered the hotel, looking around furtively. His change of plan might have come too late to avoid discovery, he realised. If so, he would just have to deal with the consequences. 'Que sera, sera,' he murmured, as he entered the comfortable gloom of the reception hall. It was time to settle in, have a meal and a drink, and plan his tactics.

Chapter Four

Next day, Friday 31 August 1973

Sir Charles breakfasted alone in the restaurant to the rear of the hotel. It was early. If there were other guests staying in the hotel, either they were very early risers, or they were enjoying a lie in. As it was, he was the only guest in the cavernous dining room, which suited him to a T.

He was more relaxed now. There had been no surprise late night visit to the hotel by an irate Jamie Raeburn seeking him out so he felt reasonably confident the lad didn't know he was here.

Just before eight, he left the hotel and set out on a walk to reconnoitre the village. Old habits born out of long training and even longer experience, died hard. He had been desk bound for years now with only occasional forays out into the field, but he didn't forget the rules. They had kept him alive in the past and, who knows, he might have to rely on them again to keep him alive in the future. Or the present, come to that, he mused.

The walk would clear his head. After his meal the night before, he had spent just over an hour in the small hotel bar with the proprietor, sharing a bottle of Armagnac. Drinking on an operation was an indulgence he would normally have foregone but last night, from an operational point of view, he convinced himself later, it had been worthwhile. The Frenchman, naturally reticent it appeared, became less so as the level of the Armagnac sank lower down the bottle. By the end of the evening, when the mistress of the house appeared with a face that portended a night in the doghouse for the poor man, he was positively garrulous.

He was a caricature of the English notion of the typical Frenchman. Everything about him screamed of his French roots, from his large proboscis, bushy eyebrows and even bushier moustache to his swollen stomach hanging loosely over his waistline and the obligatory Gauloise Bleu cigarette hanging limply from his lips.

Their conversation, Sir Charles was pleased to find, had been enlightening. As the proprietor of the biggest hotel in the village and the man who ran the bar and tabac, he knew everything there was to know about the village and its inhabitants, the Montmortais. The discussion had, after Sir Charles judged sufficient Armagnac to have been consumed, turned to the tourist trade and the influx of foreigners to the village. As far as the Frenchman was concerned, "foreigners" included anyone born out with the Champagne Region. He didn't like foreigners, he said; Germans, Belgians, Parisians, and the English of course, but Sir Charles detected impish jocularity in that and played along. He joined the man's laughter and probed gently on. There was one "foreigner", however, the Frenchman conceded, albeit grudgingly, that he did like quite a lot. This foreigner had a French name but he was not French, the man had whispered conspiratorially. Monsieur Rochefort, he asserted with a wink, was English and was probably a spy, though why he should be spying here was a mystery. The joke was growing legs. Sir Charles had laughed politely but inside he was roaring with laughter. If only the Frenchman knew...and Raeburn would be delighted to learn he was thought of by the locals as English. That would not go down well, Sir Charles mused with amusement, hoping he would get the opportunity to pass on that particular tit-bit.

The Frenchman's comment that his new neighbour was English had given the Brigadier the opening he needed to probe further, and he took it. Small talk, he knew, could produce a mine of information, and on this occasion, it did just that. By the time he took his leave of the Frenchman and his stony faced wife, Sir Charles knew all he needed to know about Monsieur Rochefort. All that he didn't already know, that is, and that was quite a lot.

With that information tucked away, he headed away from the hotel towards the west, putting distance between himself and the Rochefort house, which, he had learned, lay at the eastern edge of the village. He still wanted his forthcoming visit to his former Archangel to come as a surprise.

He thought about Jamie Raeburn as he strolled out of the village. The countryside around him was peaceful and it gave him an opportunity to think things through without distraction. Raeburn had been an important asset to Ultra and losing him had damaged the organisation. Yes, the man was a loose cannon, prone to taking matters into his own hands rather than following instructions to the letter, but he had been an effective operative. Probably the most effective Archangel he had ever had on the books, he ruminated. The others were good, but Michael, as he had been known, was exceptional. He had an instinctive awareness of danger. He could have achieved great things, risen through the ranks to the top...maybe not right to the top, his politics would prevent that, but he could have gone far. The shambles at Kiltyclogher had put an end to that, he mused... Or had it?

His rendezvous with Corkscrew in Belfast earlier in the week had presented him with an opportunity to reopen a vault he had thought, until now, was firmly closed and bolted. Corkscrew could be his locksmith and Raeburn the treasure hidden away in that vault. If he played his cards right, he reminded himself.

Persuading the young man would not be easy. The operation at Kiltyclogher had taken him to the edge. He had been out of the game for six months now and his wife, according to Sir Charles' new best friend, the hotel proprietor, was just about to give birth. That would make things doubly difficult. Raeburn's motivation was, and always had been, the safety and integrity of his family. He smiled grimly with that thought. Jamie Raeburn was not a natural killer, but he would do it without compunction to protect his family. His recent past proved that beyond any shadow of doubt. Sir Charles' problem now, as he saw it, was that he might be perceived as a threat. That, after all, was the main reason why Raeburn had elected to come here with his family in the first place.

The lad had said nothing like that at the time but Sir Charles knew it had prompted his decision. He believed his life was in danger and that that danger could extend to his wife and children. That was something he could have dispelled at the time but it had suited him to let Jamie believe it. That might count against him now.

He had been walking for some time before he finally came to a halt. He was on a narrow country road leading to another small village, trees lining both sides of the road. Small, white houses appeared in the distance ahead of him and wood pigeons cooed from their perches in the trees. It was tranquil, a scene of complete calm, and he ruminated on the benefits of living his life in a place like this. Raeburn's life for the last five years had been filled with danger, intrigue and fear. None of those existed here, he imagined. That posed the question; was that a factor that made his job easier, or more difficult?

He tended towards the latter, but Raeburn was a complex character and a man who would always "do the right thing". Could he be persuaded that returning to help Corkscrew was "the right thing"? Only time would tell. If not, he would have to think of some other lever to apply...but apply with care, he reminded himself.

He checked his watch. It was now approaching nine o'clock and the village would be like Sleepy Hollow again, he imagined. The children would be at school, the men would be in the fields or in Epernay, and the women would be attending to their domestic chores behind closed doors. It was getting warm and by afternoon, it would be scorching. He hoped he had finished his task by then.

At ten o'clock on the button he rapped at the door of the Rochefort's house at the end of a quiet cul-de-sac, or impasse as the French called it. The smell of flowers filled his nostrils and he breathed it in deeply. The more time he spent here the more difficult he imagined his task was going to be. It was idyllic. Even his own thoughts had turned to retirement and his wife would, he knew, love to return to her home country.

He listened for the sound of footsteps behind the door but there was only silence. He knocked again, rapping his knuckles hard on the solid wood, louder this time. Still there was only silence. He began to worry that he had miscalculated and the house was, in fact, empty, and then he heard the lock turn and the door swung open. A sigh of relief escaped his lips just before Kate Raeburn's face appeared in the doorway.

He had hoped it would be Jamie. Now the element of surprise would be lost, to some degree at least. Strangely, he felt tongue-tied. This was his first meeting with Kate Raeburn and she exceeded all expectations. The photographs he had seen of her in the past did not do her justice, he mused. She was looking at him intently with her big green almond shaped eyes and he could almost see the tiny cogs turning in her brain as she tried to work out who he was.

'It's Kate, isn't it?' he said, as disarmingly as possible, and saw her eyes widen in horror as realisation dawned on her. That was not the sort of surprise he wanted to deliver.

'Jamie!' she screamed, her voice verging on hysteria.

Sir Charles braced himself. It was not going well. Footsteps raced towards the door and he took a step backwards. An angry Jamie Raeburn was something better handled from a distance, he mused, but there was no hiding place here. He could have handled this better, he thought, chastising himself.

Jamie appeared in the doorway, easing his wife protectively aside and ready to confront whatever had caused her fright. His eyes were ablaze and the sight of the Brigadier standing there did little to calm him. 'It's alright, Kate, it's alright,' he said soothingly, his arm protectively around his wife's shoulder.

Sir Charles closed his eyes. He had been warned that Kate Raeburn was pregnant; had known that before Raeburn moved here. Christ, even the hotel owner had mentioned it the night before... and he had ignored it. Frightening Kate Raeburn was one thing, frightening a heavily pregnant Kate Raeburn was another thing entirely. He had messed up. He should have been more careful and now he would have a mountain to climb convincing Raeburn to return to the fold. 'I'm sorry,' he said lamely. 'I didn't mean to startle you,' he continued, directing his words to Kate.

'What do you want? Why are you here?' Jamie fired at him, still enraged.

'We need to talk,' the old man replied. He was now at a disadvantage despite his efforts to spring a surprise. Well, he had sprung a surprise alright, he mused, just not the one he had intended.

'To talk?' Jamie repeated derisively. 'You've come all this way for a chat?' he continued, his anger clearly unabated. The fire was still raging, Sir Charles noted. 'A Scottish guy called Alexander Graham Bell invented a thing called a telephone years ago,' he continued sarcastically. 'If it was just a talk you wanted, you could have used that instead of scaring the life out of my wife. Christ...'

'I'm sorry,' the old man repeated. 'I didn't think. It was stupid of me, I accept that, but it really is imperative that I talk to you.' Judging by the look in Jamie's eyes, he wasn't about to relent and his not insignificant bulk was still filling the doorway. Despite Kate Raeburn's presence, it seemed he would have to play his final card.

'It concerns an old friend of yours,' he said, pausing before adding: 'Liam Fitzpatrick.' He saw Kate Raeburn's eyes widen at the mention of Liam's name and she glanced, surprised, at her husband.

She knows all about him, he surmised.

Dropping Liam's name into the mix had also had an effect on Jamie too, it appeared, as he stepped aside, giving his wife a resigned look.

'It's okay,' he said to her, gently. 'I'll deal with it.' He turned back to the Brigadier. 'You'd better come in,' he said, but there was still a barrier between them. He refused to lower his guard.

Sir Charles stepped into the cool of a stone-flagged hallway illuminated by light streaming in from an open doorway on the left and another at the far end that appeared to lead out to a garden beyond. He waited as Kate Raeburn entered the room on the left and closed the door behind her, glancing back at him anxiously as she did so. Only then did he follow Jamie down the long hallway and outside onto a spacious stone terrace.

A table and chairs sat haphazardly on the terrace and children's toys filled much of the remaining space. Jamie gestured to one of the chairs and sat down heavily on another. Sir Charles drew the chair out from the table and lowered himself onto it before turning his attention to his host.

The lad looked good, he noted. Hardly recognisable from the man he had last seen six months before. The garden beyond the terrace showed signs of work, a lot of work, and it showed on Jamie's physique. That was a definite plus, he mused. Physically, he looked better than Sir Charles could ever remember. He wondered what Clara would think of him now... but that was by the way. 'You're looking well,' he remarked.

Jamie stared silently back at him. Clearly, his animosity had not ebbed away completely yet, Sir Charles mused. He would have to tread carefully. 'It can't be long now until the baby arrives,' he commented, smiling benevolently. 'Your wife looks good on it,' he added. 'I hope she's keeping well?'

'She was until you came knocking on the door,' Jamie retorted, bitterly, and then seemed to think better of it. 'She's fine, thanks,' he added, a little less confrontational now. 'But you're not here to ask after my wife's health Brigadier, so get to the point.' He gestured out at the garden with a sweeping motion of his arm. 'As you can see, I'm busy; I've got a lot to do out there and it won't get done if I'm sitting here on my arse talking to you about bugger all. You've got five minutes.'

Sir Charles fought back a pained retaliation and smiled manfully. At least I have managed to get this far, he consoled himself. That was something at least.

'I need your help,' he started. He thought it would be better to approach the problem openly.

'I'm retired,' Jamie fired back, without missing a beat. 'I'm toxic, remember?'

Sir Charles nodded slowly. 'I know... and I really do regret having to involve you,' he said, trying to sound sincere. He suspected the effort was wasted.

'You haven't involved me,' Jamie reacted quickly, confirming his suspicion.

The Brigadier carried on. 'This situation has been forced upon me; otherwise I would still be in London and you would be out there breaking your back,' he continued, giving a quiet laugh.

'Where does Liam Fitzpatrick fit into this?' Jamie asked, his voice still flat.

Sir Charles fixed him with a stare. He smiled inwardly as he recalled the futility of that. Fixing Raeburn with a stare to make any argument more convincing was a bit like a rabbit staring at a King Cobra in an effort to convince the snake it wasn't hungry.

'Actually, it's Liam who wants your help, not me,' he said. He hoped it came across as truthful. There was an element of truth in it, after all. He would get round to what he wanted from Jamie in the fullness of time, he decided; when he was a little more malleable.

Jamie was holding the Brigadier's look unblinkingly. Just like that King Cobra, he mused vacantly. It was a waiting game now; he knew that from experience. The next word had to come from Jamie so he waited, gazing back into the unmoving dark brown eyes of his former Archangel. Clara Whitelaw, his deputy, had often spoken of Raeburn's eyes in the early days, he recalled. She said they sparkled and, at the same time, they were opaque. You could see your own reflection in them but you could not see behind them, she said. Looking into them now, that assessment was, he had to conceded, highly accurate. At this moment, he had no idea which way the young man facing him would jump. He could read most people; Jamie Raeburn was one of the few he could not.

'And what about my so called toxicity?'

'Circumstances change. You were toxic but less so now.'

Jamie laughed frostily. 'It doesn't sound like a change of circumstances to me, Brigadier, more like expediency.' He paused and gave a soft sigh. 'Okay, what sort of help does he want?' he said, his voice showing the merest flicker of interest at last.

Sir Charles emulated his sigh but his was one of relief, not resignation. Then he reminded himself it was a little too early for that. He might be winning this battle but the war was a long way from over. He still had work to do, a lot of work, but at least he had Raeburn's interest.

'He has been working for me but now he's scared and he wants out. You know how that feels, don't you?' Jamie smiled but it was hardly encouraging, Sir Charles noted.

'He thinks they're closing in on him,' he continued. 'There are rumours of a tout fairly high up in the organisation... Operations are being blown, people being arrested out of the blue, heavy security being placed around targets, that sort of thing.'

The news of Liam Fitzpatrick being a tout came as a surprise but in this game surprises like it weren't dramatic. He smiled wryly. 'He accepted the risk when he took your thirty pieces of silver,' Jamie retorted. 'If you're worried about him... and I guess you wouldn't be here if you're not, then why don't you just pull him out? Give him a new identity, a suitcase full of money, and pack him off somewhere out of the road... Like you were supposed to have done with me.'

Sir Charles pulled his tobacco pouch from his pocket along with his pipe and held them up for Jamie's approval. Jamie nodded and the old man proceeded to fill his briar, meticulously pushing the shag into the bowl and tamping it down with a finger.

Jamie smiled at the scene. Some things never change, he mused.

He had cut back on his own smoking habit. French cigarettes were proving a little too strong for him, but today he might make an exception. His old jacket hung over the terrace balustrade and there was, he knew, a packet of Gauloise tucked away in a pocket together with his trusty Zippo. He leaned over and pulled the garment to him, retrieving the cigarettes and lighter. He tapped a cigarette loose and slipped it between his lips, flicked the lighter and held the flame out to Sir Charles.

The old man dipped his head and sucked in the flame, the aroma of the burning tobacco immediately filling the still morning air. Jamie brought the Zippo back to his cigarette and lit up, blowing a plume of smoke skywards.

'It isn't that easy,' Sir Charles mumbled at last, the words coming out in a cloud of bluish white smoke. 'There's a complication.' Jamie's raucous laugh in response threw him. Sir Charles didn't think it a laughing matter. 'What's so funny?' he demanded, trying to keep the irritation out of his voice.

'Nothing's funny about it,' Jamie replied, smiling coldly now. 'It's just that I seem to remember hearing those same words about six months ago. I was the complication then, if I remember correctly.'

'You were never the complication, Raeburn,' Sir Charles retorted defensively. 'The situation we found you in was the complication. Nothing more than that... and we resolved that little problem.'

'Did we?' Jamie retorted cynically. He dragged heavily on the cigarette between his lips, feeling his head spin a little. It was his first cigarette for weeks, he reflected, and he wasn't enjoying it. Maybe I should have foregone the pleasure.

"Little problem", he mused, going back over Sir Charles' words. The man could be, when he wanted to be, a master of understatement. 'Okay, I suppose you'd better tell me what the complication is this time,' he continued. He had already made up his mind. Kate was due any day now and there was no way on earth he was leaving her. But listening to what the Brigadier had to say might make his refusal a little more palatable to the old boy.

Sir Charles puffed on his pipe. He had already exceeded his allotted five minutes so the signs were encouraging at last. 'There is talk of major attacks being planned. Corkscrew...you'll remember his code name...he has been told he's part of it...being sent to England as part of one of three or four ASUs. The targets haven't been divulged as yet and he says that "special" weapons training is involved. Some new weapon is to be available to them. It is all being kept very quiet, probably because of their tout fear. He doesn't want to be part of it... He's convinced the targets are military installations and he thinks it will all end badly.'

'That's perceptive of him,' Jamie interrupted acerbically.

'There's more to it than that, of course,' Sir Charles continued.

Of course, there always is.

'Corkscrew has been meeting one of my men over there... he's RUC Special Branch...'

'Does the Chief Constable know?' Jamie asked, unable to resist the barb.

Sir Charles ignored him and carried on. 'Unfortunately, Corkscrew has no faith in the RUC, especially Special Branch.

Now there's a surprise, Jamie mused, but he held his tongue this time.

'He's afraid the fact that he's an informer will leak out...which would, of course, be unfortunate,' the old boy continued. Another understatement. 'He says he will continue to pass me intelligence on these attacks up until it is time for him to take part... but he refuses to go on using his RUC contact. He says he will only do it through you.'

'Me?' Jamie laughed. It was a natural reaction to the suggestion. 'Are you serious? I'm not going back over there. You can forget it Brigadier. Find some other mug to do your dirty work.' His anger was simmering once more.

Sir Charles regarded him pensively. Time for the gentle persuasion phase, perhaps, he was thinking. He mulled over his approach to it. Was it time for the "Dermott Lynch" card or should he keep that up his sleeve for later? Use it, if need be, as part of a stick and carrot approach if all else failed?

'The man is desperate, Raeburn. Seems you are the only person he feels he can trust. Why is that, I wonder? Can you shed any light on it?' the old man continued. 'Could it be because he saved your life? Is that it, perhaps? He sees that as creating some sort of obligation on your part... what do you think?' He kept his voice soft throughout, as though sharing his thoughts rather than probing into Jamie's psyche. He watched carefully for Jamie's reaction, pleased with what he saw.

Come on Raeburn, do the right thing.

'That's unfair Brigadier,' Kate Raeburn said quietly from the doorway, taking both men by surprise. She was carrying a tray with a pot of coffee and the usual accoutrements and, as far as Sir Charles was concerned, her timing could not have been worse. 'He left Jamie for dead,' she continued. 'It was pure chance that he survived... so please, don't try to use it to create some sort of obligation on my husband's part.' She approached the table and placed the tray on the table. Without asking, she began to pour.

Sir Charles regarded her with admiration. She was a formidable young woman... and they made the perfect couple.

Kate filled a cup and passed it to him, her eyes never wavering from his. 'Are you married Brigadier?' she asked quietly. He nodded, his brow knotting a little as he wondered where this was leading. 'Children?' she continued.

'No,' he replied. 'We weren't able to have children,' he replied, the sadness he felt at that reflected in his voice.

Kate did not let up. 'We do have children,' she continued, moving towards Jamie and placing her hand on his shoulder. 'And, as you can see, we'll soon be having another.' Her free hand stroked her swollen belly beneath the cotton material of her dress. Her eyes continued to bore into him, the message clear.

Sir Charles felt uncomfortable now. He knew where she was leading him...and leading her husband too, come to that.

'Aren't we...' she continued, pausing for just a heartbeat. 'Me and his children, that is... aren't we enough of an obligation for him?' she continued.

Sir Charles struggled. Normally in command of most situations, she was running rings round him. She was not aggressive, wasn't pleading or playing on his softer side... perhaps she knew he didn't have a softer side, he smiled inside... but she didn't have to, did she? She had deftly manoeuvred him into a situation he couldn't escape from. The Queen is the most dangerous piece on a chessboard, he reflected, and Kate Raeburn was the "Queen" in this particular game.

He turned to look at Jamie. The doubt that had appeared earlier on the young man's face was gone. His wife's intervention had carried the day. Check mate, Sir Charles mused, reverting to his chess analogy.

It was time for a tactical retreat. 'You're right,' he responded at last, letting out a sigh. 'I should never have come,' he continued, favouring Kate with a wan smile. She didn't return it... she wasn't gloating over her victory. His admiration for her clicked up another notch.

He sipped his coffee. She watched him for a moment then bent and pecked her husband on the cheek. He caught the message that passed between them and smiled again. 'Don't give in,' she was telling him. Clearly, he was going to have to rely on his fall back plan... but that all depended on Corkscrew and how he handled it. He himself would have no control over the outcome.

Kate nodded to him, tacitly acknowledging the matter was now closed, and withdrew back into the cool of the house.

'You are a very lucky young man,' Sir Charles stated when they were once again alone. Jamie simply smiled. 'I had to try,' he continued. 'You know that.' He received a nod in response this time.

'Does Clara know you're here?' Jamie asked, his voice low.

Sir Charles simply raised an eyebrow, finished his coffee and replaced the cup on the table. 'I think it's time for me to go,' he said. He stood, thrusting out his hand. Jamie took it. Each tightened his grip, as if testing the strength of the other. Not the physical strength, they both knew Jamie won that contest, the mental strength. At the end, as they released their grips, Sir Charles' question had been answered. His Archangel's recovery was complete.

Jamie escorted him to the door, waiting as the Brigadier called out goodbye to Kate, and guided him over the threshold. 'Good luck,' he said, his brown eyes twinkling.

Sir Charles smiled. 'Good luck to you too, Jamie Raeburn. A bientôt.' He gave a wave and sauntered away, turning back for a reaction.

Jamie returned the gesture. Unlike Kate, he knew the game wasn't quite over, and the Brigadier's parting shot had just confirmed it. "A bientôt" he repeated to himself. 'See you soon.'

Chapter Five

Belfast, Saturday 1 September 1973

Liam Fitzpatrick whistled tunelessly as he parked his van in Belfast City Centre. He felt chipper despite being stopped twice on the way into the city and having his van turned over and searched for anything that should not be in it; like explosives, a gun, or anything else that could be used to cause mayhem on the streets of the capitol.

He had smiled patiently as the peelers and their soldier escorts had poured all over it with their sniffer dogs and their little mirrors stuck on the end of long poles. He was getting used to it. They seemed to be stopping him more often these days, he thought, but his irritation was tempered by the fact that it was doing his street cred a power of good.

The buggers could search all they liked, they wouldn't find anything. The van contained only his tools as well as odd bits of copper and lead pipe, an assortment of old taps, a chipped sink he was intending to dump, and his welding gear. The soldiers, boys most of them, watched him warily most of the time. Just starting a tour, you could always tell. They would eventually become blasé, but it took a while. These boys hadn't quite reached that stage.

He locked the doors, though why he bothered he never knew. No one in his or her right mind would steal this heap of rusting shite and as for what was in the back, well. His tools might be worth a few quid, he mused, but stealing them was hardly worth the risk. Word would go round quickly that somebody had been stupid enough to rob "a volunteer" of his tools and if the idiot were caught, they wouldn't be able to walk again. Not without sticks anyway, he smiled grimly. It wouldn't be little "love bites" - bullets through the meaty part of the calf and thigh - that these buggers would get. No, for them it would be the full job; a bullet behind the knee that shattered the joint and removed the kneecap. Like he said, stealing his tools really wasn't worth the risk.

Two telephone boxes sat across the road, both in use. He could wait. There was no particular rush; he had until mid-day to make the call, but hanging about was a pain in the arse. Waiting about like a spare dick at a whore's wedding made him a target for the Peelers. And worse; there was always the risk that a Prod with a gun might have a dislike for Catholic plumbers and take a shot at him. I really should take my name off the side of the van, he told himself often when this sort of thought came to him.

But then again, why the fuck should I, was always his response.

The Happy Leprechaun was only a block away and he was always welcome there. He could kill some time over a pint of Guinness and still be back by twelve. He set off, still whistling. Now it was "The Fields of Athenry" he was attempting, maybe not a sensible choice in this neck of the woods, but what the hell, it was Saturday morning and the streets were reasonably quiet.

Given that he was tone deaf and his rendition of the tune was far from note perfect, he would get away with it. He grinned. Soon he would be able to whistle what he liked, when he liked and where he liked...but until then, he reminded himself, he should really watch what he was doing.

Forty minutes later, he left the pub and made his way back to the telephone boxes. It was now twenty to twelve. He was now a little later than he had intended. One pint of Guinness had become two when a freak thunderstorm had started just after his arrival and he had decided his telephone call could wait. It was still raining now as he made his way back towards his van and the telephone boxes, but the air smelled fresher. The thunderstorm had lifted the heavy, turgid heat that had settled over the City in the last few days. He breathed deeply, enjoying the damp freshness of the air even though it was still heavily laced with odours of cordite, smoke, petrol fumes and other human waste.

One telephone box was still in use. A young man lounged inside talking animatedly, totally engrossed in his conversation. He was either talking to a girl, trying to seduce her at long range, or he was discussing football, Liam mused. And if it was the football, it would be about Glasgow Celtic or Glasgow Rangers, depending on which side of the great divide the caller came from. Only those subjects, sex and football, could keep a Belfast man animated the way this one was, Liam smiled.

He pulled open the door of the free phone booth and stepped inside, wrinkling his nose with distaste. Why did these places always smell like public toilets that hadn't been cleaned for months? And you could smoke fish in here, he mused. Why was it everyone who used these cabins smoke like a chimney, he wondered. Simple answer, the smoke smothered the other smells at the time but it left behind a gut wrenching combination of stale smoke and pish that made him want to vomit. He sniffed distastefully. Come to think of it, there was a faint whiff of that in the atmosphere too. He swallowed hard and reminded himself to breathe through his mouth.

His pockets jingled as he fished out a handful of change and laid it on the tiny shelf above the telephone unit. The tiny light set into the roof glinted on the coins as he spread them out. He had no idea how much he would need but he imagined he had enough. He sorted it out in small piles; five pence, ten pence and three fifty pence pieces, the high denomination coins. The half pence, one and two pence coins he returned to his pocket. Now he was ready.

He picked up the handset and fed a couple of ten pence pieces into the machine. As he put his right index finger into the dial a police Landover, its windows covered by wire mesh, cruised past and the peeler in the passenger seat ran his eyes over Liam and the boy in the adjacent box. Liam paused, waiting until the vehicle had passed from view before dialling. It was stupid and illogical, he knew, but in this country, everything was stupid and illogical.

There was a series of clicks and a moment of silence and then the familiar ring tone echoed back to him down the line.

***

Sir Charles answered the phone on the first ring. It was a dedicated line so it could only be one person calling. He had wrestled with what to tell the Irishman and even more with the problem of how to resolve the impasse with Raeburn. He had an idea, but it was risky. Having said that, it was his *only* idea.

'Good morning Corkscrew,' he said quietly down the line. 'Just made it, I see.'

'I was held up by security check,' Liam retorted with the half-truth. 'So, have ye spoken to yer man then?' he continued, not prepared to beat about the bush. He noted the pregnant pause that followed. Never a good sign, he mused. 'Well, have ye or haven't ye?' he persisted.

'Yes, I've spoken to him,' Sir Charles confirmed but went no further.

'And?'

The question was followed by another long pause.

'Christ man,' Liam exploded, unable to contain his frustration. 'What the feck are ye playin' at? Ye told me to call ye today an' I've done that. Tell me what he said.'

Sir Charles decided to take the bull by the horns. 'I think I'll let him tell you that himself,' he said. Have you got paper and pencil handy?'

'Aye,' Liam replied angrily, bringing a grubby piece of oil-stained paper from his jacket pocket and licking the tip of his pencil. 'Ready,' he said.

'0033 63998877...got it?'

'0033 63998877' Liam repeated back to him.

'That's it,' Sir Charles confirmed. 'I couldn't convince him. Maybe you'll have better luck. This line will be active again on Monday evening. Call me then,' he said before terminating the call.

Liam stood looking at the piece of paper, his mood like thunder. Well, there was no time like the present, he decided.

Chapter Six

Same day, France.

Jamie came awake instantly when the phone began its shrill ringing. The room was in darkness, behind closed shutters, and it took his eyes a moment to adjust. His immediate thought was to stop the incessant noise. Kate needed rest. The birth of their second son, baby Jack, in the early hours of the previous day had taken a lot out of her; mentally *and* physically.

Who the hell was calling, he wondered? The phone rarely rang. It had been installed for only one purpose, contact with Sir Charles Redmond or his underlings at Ultra...and even then the old bugger had turned up at his door, he mused angrily. Pushing himself up from his chair, he reached out for the offending instrument.

'Oui, j'écoute,' he shouted angrily into the mouthpiece, still pondering who could be at the other end of the line. Neighbours here didn't phone, they just knocked on your door, and no one else, including family, knew the number. He didn't expect it to be Sir Charles, not so soon after his visit, so who was it?

His question was quickly answered. Even after five years, the voice that came back to him was unmistakable. But it isn't five years, is it, he reminded himself; more like five months. He failed to stifle his gasp of astonishment.

'Hello Dermott,' Liam Fitzpatrick's deep Irish brogue roared down the line. 'Surprised are ye?'

'Liam!' Jamie exclaimed, suppressing the urge to shout. 'How the fuck did you get this number?' Even as he asked the question, the answer was obvious.

Liam laughed, amused, and Jamie winced. 'A little bird gave me it,' the Irishman said, still chuckling.

Jamie stared at the phone dumbly, his anger mounting. His number was restricted - emergency use only, the old man had said - and now he gets a call from Liam Fitzpatrick. That compromised his and his family's safety. 'Bastard!' he murmured, directing his anger not at the Irishman but at Sir Charles Redmond. That was why the old sod had sauntered away from the house without argument, he raged. He had expected some sort of follow up, but not this.

'Ah, ye are surprised,' Liam continued, serious now. 'I take it no one warned ye?'

'No, no one warned me,' Jamie confirmed testily. 'Getting you to turn the screw, is he?'

'The General, ye mean?' Liam laughed. 'He told me he would call you with a proposition. I was to call him back today for your answer but when I asked him, he said I should ask you yourself... get it from the horse's mouth, so to speak.'

Jamie laughed coldly. 'Aye, he spoke to me. I told him I wasn't interested. I'm not goin' back over to Ireland.'

'That's not unreasonable,' Liam replied, seemingly unfazed by Jamie's rejection. 'But I think maybe he didn't explain it properly, me auld son. I need someone I can trust to help me out of the feckin' mess I find myself in. Did he tell ye that?'

'He said you want out, aye... but I don't see how I can help you.'

'Use your imagination, Dermott. It isn't enough for me just to disappear. The IRA doesn't forget touts... memories like elephants when it comes to informers, they have,' he said, laughing humourlessly. 'I need them to believe I'm dead. I need to disappear, just like you did, and I need you to help me with that. It has to be convincin'.'

Jamie laughed softly. 'Convincing,' he said, his sarcasm clear. 'It was convincin' because you nearly did kill me, for fuck sake.'

The Irishman laughed. 'Aye, but you're still here, aren't you. Think about it, you wouldn't be enjoyin' life in sunny France today if I hadn't risked my arse for you, would you now?'

Jamie was silent for a moment, trying to calm himself and gather his thoughts. His heart was pounding, beating in his chest like a big bass drum in an Orange Parade. Sir Charles had trapped him. The way Liam put it, how could he refuse and live with himself? But it wasn't just about him. It was about Kate and his children more than him.

'Well?' Liam pressed. 'Can I rely on you?'

Jamie remained silent for a moment. If he was honest with himself, he had expected something like this one day. When the spectre of it presented itself he always shooed it away. He would cross that bridge when he got to it, he kept telling himself. Well, he was at the bridge now and the prospect of crossing it scared him more than he was prepared to admit. 'I need more information,' he responded at last. 'And you need to understand some things,' he responded at last.

'That's reasonable,' Liam replied. 'An' you know me Dermott, I'm a reasonable man. What do you want to know?'

'Where does Ultra stand in this?' he asked.

'Ultra? What the feck is Ultra?' Liam replied quickly. 'I don't know any Ultra. I pass on intelligence to the General... he's with MI5, that's all I know.'

Jamie laughed coldly. 'He's not a General, he's a Brigadier,' he corrected. 'And you think he's with MI5?'

'Brigadier, General... what the fuck does it matter, he's the feckin' boss. An' he is MI5... they don't let any other bugger into their little games. My contact is a Special Branch man... dour bastard, but he's careful, I'll give him that.'

'Aye, he's the boss. And yes, you're right, he's with MI5,' Jamie lied. It made sense. Liam, an Irish Republican informer, would never be allowed into the secret, for obvious reasons.

The pips sounded, indicating the call was ending, and Jamie heard the Irishman fumble with coins, forcing them into the slot of the phone to allow the conversation to continue. He waited until Liam had finished feeding the machine before continuing. 'Second question,' he said then. 'Why don't you just let the Brigadier arrange your disappearance? He's got the experience and the where withal.'

'Oh, I know that, Dermott, I know that... but his price is too high... way too high.'

'I'm not following you; what price?'

'I can't tell you that. Not until I'm sure I can trust you. Not until I know you're on my side in this,' Liam replied.

What was the cryptic message in that, Jamie pondered. 'I thought we were both on the same side,' he replied as the thought circled his head.

'Oh aye, so did I Dermott, so did I. But there's sides within sides. I can't explain it over the phone.'

'You have to Liam.'

'All in good time, Dermott, all in good time me auld son. I'll tell you when, and if, we meet.'

Jamie grimaced. Liam's habit of repeating everything was getting to him. He gritted his teeth and then continued. 'You're in Ireland; I'm in France... Where are you proposin' we meet? He asked. 'An' I told you, I'm not settin' foot in Ireland again. It's way too risky, even for a dead man like me... an' if you're seen with me it could be injurious to your health too.'

A deep laugh accompanied Liam's response. 'Forget Ireland, me auld son. I've got something else in mind.'

'You'll come here?' His voice mirrored his disbelief.

'Jesus, no, Dermott. France is too far for me to travel an' far too expensive. I need an excuse for travellin' so I was thinkin' Glasgow... your home turf.'

Jamie suppressed a snort of derision. What was the man thinking? Glasgow was almost as bad as Ireland as far as he was concerned. He was supposed to be dead, for God's sake. 'You are joking, aren't you?' he retorted, laughing coldly.

'Why? Have you got a problem with Glasgow?'

'Not with Glasgow... only with going back there.'

'I don't get it Dermott. That's your home. What's the problem?'

'You're forgettin' I disappeared in mysterious circumstances. All my friends probably think I'm dead... that was the story put about. An' there is a lot of your people there too. Do I need to spell it out?'

The Irishman gave a short laugh. 'You worry too much, Dermott. From what I know it was a Brit officer that I "killed" an' you were never a Brit officer... not to your friends anyway.'

Jamie decided not to go into the complications of his disappearance and the possibility that someone could link him to the now deceased Michael Messenger.

'I've got good reasons for suggestin' Glasgow,' Liam went on. 'It's safer for me an' I can visit without awkward questions bein' asked. I've been goin' over regular to watch the Bhoys.'

Jamie laughed aloud despite the seriousness of the situation. 'The world is goin' to hell in a handcart an' you're still goin' to watch Celtic? You're off your fuckin' trolley. Anyway, I still don't like it an' apart from that, I've got commitments over here. I can't just up sticks and come to Glasgow.'

'Commitments? Jeezus, Dermott, this is feckin' important,' Liam retorted angrily.

'So is my family.' There was no immediate answer to that, Jamie noted. Clearly, it was news to the Irishman.

'You're married?' Liam said at last. 'I didn't know that. I'm sorry.'

There's a lot of things you don't know, Liam, Jamie reflected bitterly.

'You could bring your wife with you,' the Irishman suggested after a moment.

'Aye, in a perfect world I could, Liam, but I don't think she'd be happy to leave the kids behind.'

'You've got kids too? Christ Almighty! Why didn't the auld bastard tell me all this? Fuck!'

'Four kids, Liam. The fourth arrived yesterday morning.'

Liam cursed under his breath again and then fell silent. He stayed like that for a while as he digested the news. Now, at least, he understood Dermott's reluctance to get involved but it made things difficult. Maybe even impossible, he thought dejectedly. Suddenly, he made up his mind. 'Listen Dermott,' he said, resigned to failure. 'Let's just forget it. I didn't know about your wife an' kids. I'll get someone else.'

Based on what the Irishman had told him up to now that didn't sound likely, Jamie mused. He felt bad. Liam was right. The guy had risked his life. He owed him that. 'I didn't say I wouldn't help you, Liam,' he said, almost without thinking. 'How long do you think you've got before it blows up in your face?'

Liam sighed heavily at the other end of the line. 'I can't let you,' he said.

'I'm not asking you to let me. If I do it... and I haven't decided yet but when I do it'll be my decision. So, back to my question: How long do you think you've got?'

'Long enough.'

'Come on Liam... don't mess about. How long?'

There was an icy laugh from the other end of the line before Liam answered. 'I don't know, Dermott, an' that's the honest truth. A day? A month? A year? I don't feckin' know.' He was growing hysterical but fought it.

The pips tone sounded again. Time was running out. 'I'm runnin' out of money,' he said urgently. 'I'll be in Glasgow in two weeks. I'll call you again before then. If you decide to come I'll meet you there... an' I'll tell you everything.'

Before Jamie could respond, the line died... and so did Kate's hope that he wouldn't get involved.

Chapter Seven

Jamie sat in the quiet, the phone still in his hand, and thought about what had just taken place. His talk with Kate a couple of weeks earlier came back to him, vividly. *"Liam Fitzpatrick is going to come to me for help, sooner or later".*

Prophetic or what, he mused grimly? Sometimes, I can give the Brahan Seer a run for his money.

So what now, he wondered? He had all but committed himself to help the man and he knew what that was going to do to his wife. Her statement to the Brigadier thrown back in her face; sometimes he could be a complete prick.

He could still get out of it; he hadn't made any promises. But he knew that wasn't going to happen. His conscience would not let him. Breaking the news to his wife was going to be unpleasant. 'Worse than unpleasant,' he mouthed silently.

And it was something he couldn't avoid. She had to know...but maybe not just yet. He would tell her when the time was right; when he had made up his mind and when he knew exactly what the hell was going on.

He rose wearily from his chair, replaced the handset, and started the journey to his and Kate's bedroom on the upper floor of the house. There was no need to tiptoe silently past the other children's rooms today. It had just gone one o'clock in the afternoon and the kids were spending the day with one of the neighbours. They had offered to give Kate a break after the birth of the baby...and now this, he ruminated. Shit!

Kate was exhausted. The delivery had taken a lot out of her and following Sir Charles' visit, her head was all over the place. When he left her earlier she had been asleep, the baby in his cot beside the bed. He hoped the call had not wakened her.

That hope was dashed as soon as he eased open the bedroom door.

'Who was that?' she whispered, concern behind it.

'It was nothing,' he mouthed quietly. The lie came automatically.

'That's not what I asked,' Kate continued, sensing his fib and refusing to let him off the hook. 'You were on the phone a long time for it to be nothing,' she chided. 'Stop trying to wrap me up in cotton wool, Jamie. Tell me who it was...you will eventually anyway.'

Jamie sighed heavily as he slipped into the bed beside her and pulled her gently to him. So much for telling her when the time is right, he mused. He would have preferred more time to break it to her gently but there was little chance of that now. She could be persistent...like a dog with a bone. 'How much did you hear?' he asked, nuzzling into her neck.

'Not much. You laughed at one point and I woke up. After that, I only managed to pick up a few words...mostly your bad language. Should I be worried?'

Jamie looked away guiltily, giving her the answer. She thought for a moment, going over the snatches of conversation she had overheard. 'I heard you mention Glasgow...and you said I'd just had the baby.' She hesitated, waiting for his reaction, but he wasn't ready yet it seemed. 'Who was it Jamie...and what's going on?'

He pulled away from her and stared up at the ceiling. In the darkness of the room he could make out very little, just the darker, spinning blades of the ceiling fan as they wafted cooler air down onto the bed. There was no point in avoiding the issue now. Kate wouldn't let him in any event. The stoic in him was saying that the sooner it was out in the open, the sooner they could deal with it. How they would work their way through it he had no idea, but they would. They always did.

He turned back towards her. She was growing agitated and her anger and frustration were mounting. He could see it in the flush on her cheeks. He took a deep breath and started. 'It was Liam Fitzpatrick,' he said. He saw her eyes widen as her anger and frustration were replaced by fear.

'Why? How?' she mumbled. 'How did he get our number?'

'How do you think?' he answered gently. He didn't want to upset her more than she already was. 'The Brigadier gave him it,' he continued, wrapping his arms around her again. He felt her trembling against him.

'What did he want?' she asked, fighting back tears.

'He picked up where Sir Charles left off,' he replied.

They were silent for a while. Lying in each other's' arms seemed to mitigate the disaster that was building up around them. In his cot, the baby whimpered quietly then was quiet again.

Kate came out of their reverie first, nuzzling her lips to his neck. 'You said you would help him,' she said.

Jamie thought at first it was a question but quickly grasped that she had accepted the situation. She had known all along that he would go.

'Not exactly,' he replied, but her look told him she didn't believe it.

'Not exactly,' she repeated softly. 'So what did you say? Maybe?'

He shook his head. 'No, not maybe. I told him I couldn't go just now...I told him about you, told him about the kids, young Jack,' he continued.

'Go where?'

'Glasgow...that's why you heard me speaking about it.'

'I don't understand. Why Glasgow?' she queried.

Jamie laughed quietly. 'I don't understand either...but he says he has his reasons...and it's safer there.'

'When does he want you to go?'

Jamie gave her a long look. The question seemed to accept he would go. She could have said, "when are you going?" It came to the same thing. In Kate's mind it was already only a question of when. 'We didn't fix a date...but I told him about Jack. Liam suggested we forget it,' he admitted.

Kate smiled sadly. Forgetting it was something Jamie Raeburn couldn't do.

'He's going to be over in Glasgow in a couple of weeks, maybe three. He said he would phone again before he leaves Belfast.' He hesitated, searching her eyes for the response to that. 'I didn't promise him anything,' he added. As if that makes a difference!

She pulled him closer and buried her head in his chest. She couldn't think of anything to say. Her thoughts were a jumble of mixed emotions; pride and fear fighting each other for superiority with resentment coming up close. 'And you won't go over to Ireland,' she whispered. That too came out strangely, a mix of instruction blended with plea.

'No, I won't go over to Ireland,' he said. And he meant it; that was a line he would refuse to cross.

A comfortable silence enveloped them now. It was out in the open. They could deal with it. silence was more comfortable now.

'What are you going to do now?' she asked.

'Phone Redmond, I suppose.'

Kate pulled away from him, giving him an anxious look. 'Do you have to involve him?' she asked fearfully. 'I don't trust him.'

Jamie laughed coldly. 'He's already involved, love. As always, he's the one moving all the pawns around the board. I just want to remind him I'm not one of his pawns any longer.' He turned on his side and reached for her. 'Come here,' he whispered. 'I need you.'

A muffled cry from the cot beside the bed announced the fact that someone else needed her too; a little someone who needed her just as much. Jamie smiled, kissed his wife on the forehead and watched as she picked up their son. How can I leave them, he mused fretfully?

***

Jamie rose early next morning. The sun was already edging its way through the gaps in the exterior shutters, slashes of white light splashed across the tiled floor and walls. It was going to be another hot day but Autumn was on the way and Winter wouldn't be far behind. Their first Winter here in France; at least, that was the plan. He suspected that Liam Fitzpatrick's call the day before might, in the words of the great John Lennon, put a "Spaniard in the Works".

Sunday morning. He enjoyed Sundays here. It really was a day of rest. The kids had returned home early accompanied by the neighbours and their children. Together, they had made a night of it. He had made a glutton of himself, eating and drinking a little too much while Kate, breast-feeding, settled for mineral waters. She had been disapproving at first but eventually accepted it with her normal stoicism. That was something they both shared.

He checked the time, smiling for the first time. Seven o'clock in France, he noted, so it would be six o'clock in England. That made it the perfect time for a rude awakening. It was time to get a little of his own back.

He hadn't slept well. Despite the excessive amount of alcohol he had consumed and Kate's salacious efforts to exhaust him with everything short of actually making love, he had spent most of the night staring at the ceiling going over what had happened. And as the night progressed so his anger had grown. Sir Charles Redmond had a lot to answer for.

He sat where he had sat the day before listening to Liam Fitzpatrick's plea for help and cursed the Brigadier for giving out his number. He calmed himself and lifted the handset. The number he dialled was embedded in his memory, probably always would be, he mused. The usual clicks were followed by the ring tone from the other end in a matter of seconds. It took longer for Sir Charles to answer and with every passing second, Jamie's grin grew. Eventually, the ring tone ceased, signalling Sir Charles' finally picking up. He didn't allow the older man time to speak.

'Good morning, Brigadier; wake you, did I?' he said sarcastically.

'Raeburn!' the old man retorted. 'Do you know what time it is?'

'I imagine it's six o'clock over there...but I haven't really slept, been awake all night.'

Sir Charles leapt to the obvious conclusion from that. It just happened to be the wrong one. 'The baby has arrived?' he cooed. 'How delightful...sleepless nights now is it, eh?'

'Aye, the baby has arrived, but he's not the reason for my sleepless night, Brigadier. You are.'

'Me? Good lord, how can I possibly be responsible for that? Oh, I see; was it my surprise appearance that brought it on? I am sorry old chap,' he gushed.

'Save the apology. It wasn't your surprise appearance; it was your devious attempt to get me involved. That was a surprise too...though it probably shouldn't have been.' His voice was cold now. 'I had an unexpected call yesterday.'

'Ah,' Sir Charles replied instantly. 'Corkscrew called you.'

Jamie laughed mirthlessly. 'Aye, Corkscrew, called me...though it strikes me he's not the one that's twisted.'

Sir Charles laughed. 'Sharp, Raeburn...very droll.'

'You gave him my number Brigadier. I don't like that.'

'It was necessary.'

'Bollocks! I had already given you my answer. I told you I didn't want to get involved in your little game.'

'Yes, you did,' Sir Charles agreed. 'But you know I rarely take things at face value...and I thought it was only good manners for you to tell him yourself that you had no intention of helping him.'

'Fuck off, Brigadier. We both know it had nothing to do with that. You just wanted him to turn the screw you left unturned.'

'And did he?'

The silence from the other end of the line gave Sir Charles the answer he had hoped for.

'So you agreed to help him,' he continued.

'No, I said I would think about it.'

'Uh huh, of course you did. And how long are you going to think about it before you agree?'

Jamie sighed. The conversation was following a course he was familiar with. So much for him letting the Brigadier know he was no longer one of his pawns. 'As you seem to know everything Brigadier, you work it out,' he said, in a vain attempt to regain ground.

Sir Charles laughed. He was enjoying the verbal tussle. 'I don't have to Raeburn. You'll call me...you're going to be his conduit, remember?'

'You said that; he didn't.'

'Immaterial, old chap. Information is the price he has to pay for his new identity and his nest egg. You're going to be the postman.'

Jamie knew he had lost. He grimaced and shook his head slowly, anger simmering inside him. But he still had one point to make. 'Okay,' he conceded. 'I'll be his postman, but I just want you to be aware of something. You gave Liam Fitzpatrick my contact number. That was out of order. If anything happens to my family as a resultmy family is at risk because of that, I'll come for you.'

Sir Charles laughed again but he did not sound amused now.

'You find that funny?' Jamie came back quickly.

The laughter stopped. 'Forgive me,' the older man returned quickly. 'I know your capabilities and I'm certainly not making light of it. I just think you're being melodramatic?'

'Melodramatic!' Jamie spat. 'You've got a fucking nerve.'

'Oh, come now, Raeburn. Think about it. France is a big country...vast. Finding you would be virtually impossible, even for abler people than Corkscrew...'

'People like you, you mean,' Jamie interrupted angrily.

'Yes, if you like, but even for me, without your name it would be difficult.' Sir Charles paused, relishing the next bit. 'But Corkscrew doesn't know your real name, does he? Nor the name you're using now,' he added. He paused again.

He did that a lot, Jamie mused.

When Sir Charles spoke again, his voice was like ice. 'You haven't been entirely honest with me, have you?' he said.

'I'm not with you,' Jamie replied, cautiously. He had a bad feeling.

'Oh, come now, Raeburn, of course you're with me. You told me you had no idea why you weren't killed that night. We went over it again and again. Even when I told you Corkscrew was one of mine you stuck to that.'

'That's right.'

'No, that's not right!' Sir Charles spat back. 'You and Corkscrew know one another, Raeburn. That's why he didn't kill you.'

'Rubbish. Whatever you're on Brigadier, I'll have some.'

'No, not rubbish. I know now, and it makes sense. Why else should he have spared you? Why would he risk everything for a stranger, I kept asking myself.'

'And you've deluded yourself with an answer,' Jamie retorted.

'No, not deluded...Dermott,' Sir Charles replied, pausing for a heartbeat before adding the name. Jamie's silence spoke volumes. 'What, no smart retort this time, Dermott?' He allowed a moment's silence before finishing. 'Game, set and match, I think,' he said, allowing himself a cold chuckle. He let the silence play out for a bit after that.

'How did you find out?' Jamie asked at last.

'Your friend Liam gave it away,' Sir Charles replied, laughing coldly still. 'I told you he asked for you as his contact, remember?'

Jamie nodded.

'What I didn't tell you was that he asked for Dermott Lynch as his controller; Dermott Lynch, the only man in the organisation he can trust, he says. That threw me at first, but when he elaborated and told me Dermott was the man I sent to Kiltyclogher, it all began to fall into place. There was still a loose end. What made him think your name was Dermott, I wondered. You didn't exactly have time to introduce yourselves to one another that night,' he laughed. 'And Dermott isn't, and never has been, one of your cover names.' He broke off for a moment, letting Jamie digest that. 'But Corkscrew was so positive. There was no element of doubt in his use of the name. So, logically, the two of you had met at some time in the past. It was then I remembered your short sojourn in Belfast back in 1967. That was the last little piece of the jigsaw. Have I missed anything?'

'No,' Jamie replied shortly. It was difficult not to sound sullen.

'No, I thought not,' the older man laughed again. 'There's no need to worry by the way,' he added. 'He still thinks your name is Dermott Lynch.'

There was another of the annoying little pauses hated so much by Jamie before he continued. 'That, you see, is why I have no worries about him tracing you in France...and no worries about you "coming for me". Now then, shall we finalise matters?' He didn't wait for a reply. 'When you arrange your meeting with Corkscrew you will call me with the details. All of them. He should have some intelligence for me by then as well, I hope. I need it.'

'And that's it?' Jamie asked.

'For now...but there may be other little tasks required later.'

'Like what?' Sir Charles laughed again and Jamie could feel his hackles rise.

'Use your imagination, Michael. You're still an Archangel.'

'I'm no longer Michael and I told you before; I'm finished with all that,' Jamie retorted defiantly.

'We'll see,' Sir Charles replied.

He sounded confident, Jamie thought. He could almost imagine his smug smile. But the Brigadier couldn't make him pull a trigger, could he? He smiled inwardly.

Yes, Brigadier, we'll see.

'You'll need money, I suppose,' Sir Charles said then, breaking into his thoughts. 'Did you close the Messenger bank account when you left Glasgow?'

'No, I didn't get round to that,' Jamie told him. 'There's still a couple of hundred pounds in it,' he added.

'Good, that will save us some time then. I'll deposit funds into the account tomorrow. You'll be able to withdraw money from it when you get here. Will you need money now to arrange your travel? I can transfer cash into your French account, if you like,' he added quickly.

'No,' Jamie replied, equally quickly. 'I can manage. I'll keep receipts. You can refund the money later.' The Brigadier already knew where he lived and that was more than enough information as far as he was concerned.

'Suit yourself,' the Brigadier replied. 'Okay, if we're finished I'll let you get on with whatever it is you do to pass your time these days. Remember, when you fix the exact time and place of your meeting with Corkscrew, I want to know...I may need to put things in place.' The obligatory pause followed. 'Thank you for agreeing to do this,' he added quietly.

'I'm not doing it for you, Brigadier,' Jamie retorted

'No, I know you're not,' Sir Charles replied magnanimously. 'But even so, thank you anyway. We'll talk again soon.'

Before Jamie could respond the older man had disconnected the call. He sat still, staring at the phone. That was another bad habit, people hanging up on him; first Liam Fitzpatrick, and now Sir Charles. He laughed quietly to himself. He would need to teach them both some manners...it seemed they needed him after all.

Chapter Eight

Sir Charles hung up and considered his next move. He felt mildly euphoric. The gamble involved in providing "Corkscrew" with the means of contacting Raeburn had paid off. His erstwhile Archangel was now back in the fold. He had been reasonably confident of that outcome but with Raeburn, he could never be sure. There were unpredictable people and then there was Jamie Raeburn. That young man was truly in a class of his own when it came to capriciousness.

But now Sir Charles had another problem. It was not so much a problem as an irritation, he mused, but none the less, dealing with it would be unpleasant to say the least. It was something he could put it off for an hour or two. It was still early and it was the weekend. He could deal with Clara later.

He smiled wryly. Raeburn's call was timed to cause him maximum annoyance. He should, on reflection, have expected that. But annoyed he was not. He might have been but for one important factor. Raeburn had thrown in the towel and that opened up a completely new avenue.

Contented, he stretched back out on his bed beside his wife and drifted into a light sleep.

***

Clara Whitelaw, Assistant Director of Ultra, gazed across the kitchen table of her Kensington home into the strained face of her husband. She had not slept well. She doubted that he had either if the look on his face was anything to go by. It was an anniversary they would both rather forget, though both for entirely different reasons. Today will be difficult, she mused; no question.

She had brought work home from the office on Friday and could spend a good part of the day dealing with it. It would take her mind off things. It had not been intentional, bringing work home, but she was glad now that she had. The day would be unbearable otherwise and would probably end in an argument. Casting a quick glance at her husband, she thought it might even start with one.

She did not know what Mark had planned for the day, if anything, but she doubted that it would include her. Not today, she mused a little sadly. The memory of what had happened a year before was still too raw for him though he was trying to put it behind him. She could probably do more to help with that, she realised, but she still felt the loss.

None of this was Mark's fault; he had been the innocent party, after all, but she still blamed him. It was irrational, of course it was, but she could not help herself. God, it was going to be awful.

The ringing of the telephone out in the hall caused them both to jump. It was like a scene from some sort of comic farce, she mused; both of them with furrowed brows, wondering who would be calling, today of all days, and both reluctant to answer the damned thing.

It was Clara who broke the deadlock. With an exaggerated sigh she pushed her coffee cup into the middle of the table and stood up, looking daggers at her husband. If she carried on like this all day it wouldn't simply be an argument that took place, it would be all out war. Get a grip, she chided herself.

She pulled the kitchen door closed behind her and strode angrily down the hallway to the phone, her bare feet slapping loudly on the parquet flooring. Her anger was still simmering when she grabbed the handset and she almost shouted into the mouthpiece.

'Good morning Clara,' Sir Charles said lightly, shrugging off her obvious irritation. Her frosty greeting was not at all what he had expected. 'Is everything alright? I'm not disturbing anything important, am I?' he pressed.

'No, sorry...I had a bad night,' she replied, her temper moderating.

'How is Mark?' her mentor continued. It was a ritual they went through; him asking about Mark, and her avoiding the issue.

'Mark is Mark,' she said flatly. 'Actually, he's feeling down too, I think,' she added, taking him by surprise.

'Argument?'

'No, no argument,' she laughed mirthlessly. 'Just the usual stony silence.' She paused for a moment. 'I'm as much to blame as he is, I suppose,' she continued, accepting less than her fair share of the blame. She was much more to blame, and she knew it, but she was still grieving and that made it difficult.

'So, to what do I owe the pleasure?' she asked. She knew it wouldn't be a social call to find out how she was. He saw her just about every day. He knew how she was...he had been privy to her angst twelve months earlier. He knew exactly how she felt. And contrary to Charles' belief that what had taken place six months earlier would make things easier for her and her husband, it had actually made matters worse.

Sir Charles decided to steer clear of Clara's personal problems for the moment though he was aware that what he had to tell her was likely to make them worse. 'I need to have rather an important chat with you,' he continued quietly. 'How are you fixed today?'

'Today?' she repeated testily. 'It's Sunday Charles; can't it wait until tomorrow when we are back in the office?'

'It isn't something I want to discuss in the office. It's rather delicate. How about you and Mark drive down here this afternoon. Estelle would love to see you both.'

God, no, Clara moaned inwardly; not today, any day but today.

'It's important...and it is something I would rather you heard from me than from anyone else,' he added.

That sounded serious, she thought. 'I suppose we could,' she replied reluctantly. 'I'll ask Mark if he has anything planned and I'll call you back, shall I?'

'Ask him now Clara, I'll hold on,' he continued insistently.

There was no way out of it, she thought grimly. Ah well, que sera, sera. 'Okay, hold on,' she said, reluctantly placing the handset on the tiny telephone table beside. She retraced her steps to the kitchen, pushing the door open. Mark was hovering over The Sunday Times, pretending not to be listening in to her conversation. He looked up at her as she entered, one eyebrow rising imperceptibly.

'Charles and Estelle want to know if we can make it down to Hazelgrove this afternoon?' she said, letting her displeasure be seen. Mark pretended not to notice. He was good at pretending, she thought unhappily...but then, he was a spy, just like her.

He gave her a smile. 'That would be great,' he replied, making sure his voice was just loud enough to carry to the phone for Sir Charles to hear at the other end of the line. Clara's resentful grimace didn't upset him. He was used to these now though he hoped she would soon grow out of them.

She stormed back to the phone. 'I suppose you heard that,' she said, forcing a little laugh. 'What time should we come?'

'Why don't you come for lunch,' Sir Charles said.

It came across as a suggestion but most of Charles' orders come across as suggestions, Clara mused. 'Okay, we'll be there about twelve. Is it just us or are others invited?' she asked.

'No, just you,' he replied, dashing her hopes of avoiding interrogation on the state of her personal life.

'Okay, see you then,' she said, hanging up the phone disconsolately.

'What was that all about?' Mark probed as she returned to her chair.

'I have absolutely no idea,' she replied sincerely. After all the lies and deceit, it felt good to be able to tell the truth for once.

Chapter Nine

The drive down to Hazelgrove in her husband's Triumph 2000 passed in more or less uncomfortable silence. Attempts at conversation were stilted and awkward and Clara prayed that the day ahead would be less difficult than the morning had been. If they could only talk about the problem they might be able to put the whole sorry mess behind them and get through it, but it wasn't easy to talk about. It stirred up too many bitter and sad memories and too many emotions. Clara suspected fear played a part in it. Neither of them wanted to say or do anything that made matters worse but their continued silence on the subject did just that.

Charles and Estelle were waiting for them on the steps of the big house when they drove up the sweeping driveway. Estelle waved and Clara could see from the warm smile on her Godmother's face that she was genuinely pleased to see them. That lifted Clara's spirit but the shadow of Jamie still lurked in the darkness of her memory. If only she had managed to clear the air before...She paused in mid-thought and choked back a sob, unable to deal with its conclusion. It was always the same. She was still grieving.

She glanced at her husband, trying hard to conceal the sadness she knew would be there in her eyes. He gave her a smile, forced maybe, but at least he was trying. If only she could tell him how guilty she really felt, perhaps things would be better. She feared, however, that it would only make matters worse, opening up the old sore.

Mark Whitelaw pulled the Triumph to a halt in front of the broad stone steps and Charles and Estelle descended to greet them. Estelle looked her usual contented self; Charles looked distracted, Clara thought. It brought her back to the real reason she and Mark were here today. What did Charles have on his mind that required to be dealt with today...here...and not in the office? It was worrying her and she could do without the added worry today.

She stepped from the car and was immediately swept into Estelle's arms. The two men shook hands, nothing unusual in that, but Charles' mind was clearly on something else. Mark noticed it too and Estelle was doing her best to divert attention from it. Whatever was bothering her Godfather, Estelle knew about it. Her mind went into overdrive. A health issue, she wondered, it was the only explanation. God no, she had already lost one important man from her life. She didn't know if she could bear the loss of another.

Her concern wasn't diminished when Charles gave her a hug and kissed her on the cheek. The words "I'm so glad you could come, Clara" accompanied by an anxious smile were hardly encouraging.

The little group climbed the steps up to the main door, chatting about nothing, she thought. Estelle had gravitated to Mark while Charles took her hand and assisted her up the stairway. It was the way it had been when she was little, visiting this grand house. Charles always looked after her. He took his duties as her Godfather quite literally and if she were to lose him from her life now it would be devastating. She looked at him questioningly, furrowing her brow. He couldn't fail to see her anxiety but he wasn't ready to divulge his secret, it appeared.

Lunch was already prepared and they went straight in. Suddenly, Clara didn't feel hungry but she knew she couldn't let everyone down. She would have to force herself. Conversation over the meal touched on every conceivable subject except, Clara noted, the subject that had brought her here. Mark was beginning to relax a little. He was always so tense these days, and seeing him with a smile on his face and genuinely happy made a pleasant change. Estelle's charm was working.

The meal seemed to last forever as far as Clara was concerned. She ate sparingly and toyed with her food. She did, on the other hand, take two very large glasses of red wine. It was a particularly good Graves but its quality had nothing to do with her drinking it. That was driven by something much more primitive; the suspicion that bad news was in the offing and a healthy quantity of alcohol in her system might help her deal with it.

It was mid-afternoon when they wandered out onto the terrace at the rear of the house. South facing, it caught the best of the sun for most of the day and they settled down at the old wrought iron table that had graced the terrace for as long as Clara could remember. More drink followed and she watched as Estelle poured a large measure of whisky and soda for Mark. She was chatting away freely with him about anything and nothing and Clara sensed it was all part of a plan set up by her Godparents. When Charles suggested she join him in the rose garden, she knew she was right. Here it comes, she mused. She smiled her acceptance of Charles' suggestion and sauntered off with him, leaving her husband and her Godmother engrossed in conversation.

When they were out of earshot, she turned anxiously to Sir Charles and took hold of his hand. 'What's going on Charles? Are you alright?'

He smiled wanly as he looked back towards the terrace. The others were still deep in talk, an occasional laugh drifting across the lawn towards them. 'I'm alright, Clara. It's not my health I asked you here to talk about...I've never felt better in fact. It's something else.'

'Thank God!' she exclaimed, letting all of her pent up emotion out in one great sigh. 'I thought for a minute...'

'I have a confession to make,' he said quietly, and watched her brow furrow again.

'A confession?' she laughed, a little nervously. 'It sounds very dramatic...and serious if it can't wait until tomorrow.'

He looked down at the ground, his face grave.

'You're really worrying me now, Charles. Please, tell me what's wrong.' She pulled him round to face her, one hand on his arm and the other beneath his chin, tilting his face up towards hers.

He forced a smile. 'Let's sit down,' he said, guiding her towards a bench set behind a hedge of roses.

Clara returned his smile and allowed herself to be led to the seat. She had come here often as a child. She loved this hedge, even remembered the name of the rose from which it was formed, "Commandant Beaurepaire", a Bourbon rose with large double crimson flowers, striped pink flowers and marbled white...and all of these grew here in the hedge. She sat down and drew in the scent of the luxurious blooms, preparing herself.

'How are you and Mark getting along now?' Sir Charles asked, avoiding her eyes.

He hadn't brought her all this way to question her on the state of her marriage, Clara reflected gloomily, so that was simply a diversion while he prepared the ground for whatever it was that was on his mind. It was something he often did.

'We're working on it,' she replied. 'It isn't easy...I can't shake the guilt...and I keep thinking...' She hesitated, thought better of what she was about to say, and veered away in another direction. 'To be honest, I don't know how we would have got through the day if you hadn't called and invited us down.'

'What makes today so bad?' he asked.

Clara's smile turned sad. 'You don't remember, do you?'

Sir Charles knitted his brow. Clearly, he had forgotten something, but what, he wondered.

'It was a year ago today,' Clara continued, sensing his confusion. '1st September last year. Mark had come home on leave. You had met him at lunchtime and brought him back to the office and announced that you were thinking of offering him a post with Ultra and...' She broke off, stifling a sob.

The memory exploded into Sir Charles' brain like a fragmentation grenade, destroying everything in its radius. He sat there, struggling for words, his stupidity engulfing him. That was the day it had all come out, he remembered it now. How could he have been so stupid, so inconsiderate?

Clara was speaking again. 'I thought I had lost your respect that day,' she said. 'You were horrified. I remember it so clearly...remember the whole day so clearly. After that, I wanted to make it all up to you, stay away from Jamie like you said, but inside me, I needed to talk to him again. I needed to know why...' She paused again, wiping a solitary tear away. 'Now I'll never have the opportunity...and I think, maybe, that is why Mark and I struggle so much with it.'

She stopped, suddenly remembering this wasn't why she was here, and searched her Godfather's face for confirmation. He sat still, his expression blank and his face grey. 'It isn't Mark's fault,' she continued, needing to finish. 'It's mine. I really was in love with Jamie and I didn't get the chance to say goodbye.'

Sir Charles coughed nervously and squeezed her hand. 'I'm sorry, my dear, but I think my confession is about to make matters worse,' he said, clearly distressed.

Clara had never seen him like this. What was this confession?

'I lied to you about Jamie,' he started, hesitantly.

Strange, she thought, he had never used Jamie's Christian name before. Usually, he referred to him as "Raeburn" or sometimes "Michael" when he forgot himself, but never Jamie.

'There's no easy way to say this really,' he continued. 'Jamie isn't dead.'

Clara sat stock still, frozen by his statement. She had heard the words but struggled to comprehend them. It wasn't possible.

'I'm sorry, Clara,' he said. He was ready to enlarge on it when she cut him off.

'But I don't understand...I was at his funeral...you were there too. You said the eulogy...'

'Yes, I was there with you, but it wasn't Raeburn in the coffin. He was here at Hazelgrove, being patched up. He was pretty badly shot up...it was touch and go for a while.'

'I don't believe you,' Clara mumbled, tears building behind her eyes. 'Why are you saying this now? You told me he was dead.'

Sir Charles decided to let that pass. The questioning would start soon...and then the recrimination. He hoped Mark Whitelaw was strong enough to deal with the fallout and the jealousy that would inevitably raise its ugly head once again.

'The whole thing was a deception?' Clara said through her sobs.

The first of her questions, one of the easier ones to answer, Sir Charles mused. 'Yes, it was a deception; a necessary deception,' he replied. 'I couldn't tell you,' he added. 'You know that.'

'No, I don't know that!' she retorted bitterly. 'You have let me believe he is dead for six months. You must have seen what it was doing to me...and yet you kept it to yourself.'

'I had to Clara.'

'For operational reasons, naturally,' she murmured sarcastically.

Sir Charles stared up into the clear blue sky. What he had seen as an irritation was clearly presenting itself as something much worse. He had underestimated her feelings for the boy. He had expected her to rail against it but, at the same time, had expected her to rationalise things.

Raeburn had been betrayed. The traitor behind that betrayal was still out there and still believed that an Archangel had been killed that night. He had to ensure that didn't change. He would have to spell it out for her, he realised. 'It wasn't for operational reasons, Clara. My reasons were purely practical...and pragmatic,' he added. 'He was betrayed...and I didn't know by whom. I still don't,' he said.

'Are you suggesting it could have been me?' she blurted angrily through her sobs.

'No, of course not. That's absurd,' he countered. 'What I am suggesting is that the person who betrayed him probably got word that he was dead. I had to ensure that that person continued in that belief. If I had told you that Raeburn was still alive it would have affected your behaviour...and may have aroused suspicion.'

'I thought I was the psychologist, Charles,' she retorted sardonically.

'It isn't psychology, my dear; it's just common sense based on observation. I couldn't take the chance, Clara. Lives were at stake.'

'Lives?' she queried. 'So it wasn't just Jamie you were protecting?' she queried, picking up on it.

Her brain was still working analytically at least, Sir Charles noted gratefully. 'Yes, there was another man in danger at the time. It wasn't just Raeburn.'

'So who was it...or is that something else you have to keep from me?'

Sir Charles sighed. 'No, I don't need to keep it from you...in fact the situation demands that I do tell you,' he said at length. 'The other man in danger is the man who shot Raeburn that night. He works for us...for me.'

Clara stared back at him blankly. Her mind was still working through his earlier statement about the betrayal. 'You think that the traitor is one of us or, at least, someone close to us,' she ruminated aloud, her voice low.

He looked at her, saw her tear stained cheeks and sighed again. Sometimes he wondered if they were too close. He didn't like this, not one bit, but he had to go on.

'I don't know Clara, and that's the truth, but I have to consider the possibility. I just don't know how it could have happened. It's like searching for something in a fog; sometimes I think I'm closing in on it and then it disappears again. Very few people knew of that mission. That narrows the field...but I still can't pinpoint the source.'

Clara gave him a mordant look but said nothing. She was not one of the "very few" he had trusted then either, she reflected. But there was something else lurking behind his eyes, ready to come out. She gave a short snort...whatever it was it couldn't be much worse than what he had already told her, she mused. She waited, trying to focus on the one positive out of all of this. Jamie was alive.

They sat in silence for a while. The rose perfumed air was almost soporific and Clara closed her eyes. The birds sang and somewhere a cricket chirped. She could be dreaming, she mused. None of this was really taking place; it was just a bad dream brought on by thoughts of Jamie on this, the first anniversary of their split.

She felt another tear trickle down her cheek and screwed her eyes tightly shut. No, it was no dream. It was real and she was caught up in it now. Otherwise, Charles would have kept it all to himself, she reasoned.

There has to be a reason, so what is it?

'Why are you telling me this now, Charles?' she probed, her voice barely louder than a whisper. She turned her eyes on him, waiting. 'Why not just keep it all to yourself?'

He smiled, a little regretfully, she thought, and took hold of her hand again.

'Because I need your help,' he said simply. 'He trusts you.'

'Who trusts me?' she fired back. She didn't really want to hear the answer; she already knew it.

Sir Charles began his explanation, avoiding the direct answer to her question. 'My informer has brought me some important intelligence,' he started. 'Three, maybe more, big attacks, "Spectaculars" they call them, are being planned over here. My man doesn't know the targets but he thinks they are all military installations. Seems they might be shying away from civilian targets for the moment. Rumour has it, that is alienating a sizeable chunk of their support, especially in the South, and the Americans have voiced their disgust. The FBI has been coming down hard on their supporters over there and funds are drying up. Money talks, even in the midst of a revolution,' he laughed coldly. 'I doubt it will last, though,' he added prophetically.

He gave her a long look before continuing. 'My man, code name "Corkscrew", is in one of the Active Service Units coming over. He's been told that they are to get "special training" on some new weapon. He doesn't know what this weapon is or who is supplying it. It is all very hush-hush; the bastards are learning,' he added, almost as an afterthought.

'What has this got to do with me...and with Jamie?' she asked.

Sir Charles sighed again. 'Corkscrew is getting jittery. He wants out; usual package, new identity, passport and money to start a new life.'

Clara laughed coldly. 'That's hardly surprising,' she retorted. 'But it doesn't answer my question. Where do I fit it?' she pressed, clearly dubious. 'Presumably your man already has a handler in place. I've never met Corkscrew, didn't even know he existed until now. Changing his handler now is just going to make him even more jittery, I would think.'

'Yes, you're right, and normally I wouldn't be considering it, but he has set the ground rules.'

'I don't follow you.'

'Corkscrew has agreed to stay in place until he can identify the targets and the men coming over but with one proviso. He refuses to deal with his existing controller.'

'But he doesn't know me. How can he possibly trust me?'

'He can't...and probably won't, but you're not the one he has asked for.'

'Oh God, no Charles,' Clara blurted. 'Please, tell me it isn't who I think it is.'

Just when I thought things couldn't get worse; I should have known better, she reflected bitterly.

'Corkscrew and Jamie Raeburn go back a long way, it seems,' Sir Charles replied, confirming her fear. 'Long before Kiltyclogher...'

'I can't do this,' she interrupted, tears welling up again.

'Please Clara, hear me out,' Sir Charles responded, as gently as possible. 'Jamie Raeburn is essential to the success of this operation,' he went on, avoiding further protest. 'He is the key. Putting it bluntly, Corkscrew doesn't trust the RUC and, therefore, his current controller. I won't go into why, he has his reasons, but it creates a problem for us. Raeburn was his choice, not mine,' he continued. 'I suspect he has personal reasons for that too, but that aside, he is adamant he will only deal with Raeburn; no one else.'

'Then what use am I...' she started, but he cut her off.

'Raeburn is the only person Corkscrew trusts; and you, I think, are possibly the only officer in Ultra that Raeburn trusts.'

Clara laughed bitterly. 'Trust!' she snorted. 'I can't believe you have the gall to talk about trust. It seems to me that's in short supply at the moment,' she continued caustically. 'If you want to send Jamie back over there, I won't help you,' she said defiantly, voicing the decision she had reached moments earlier.

'You said he was in danger after Kiltyclogher,' she went on. 'If that's true then he's as much at risk now...as much as Corkscrew, I imagine.'

'There's no plan for him to return to Ireland,' Sir Charles replied patiently. 'The attacks that are being planned are here on the mainland and his role will be to act as Corkscrew's liaison...he can do that from here. We set up a communication system for them...that's all we need to do.'

'You know that won't work, Charles,' she responded. 'And if that was all that's involved you wouldn't need me.' She shook her head slowly. 'I'm superfluous to all that.'

Sir Charles turned away from her and gazed off into the distance. He had hoped to break the real reason for her involvement gently over time but that option was looking increasingly unlikely. 'I can't do this without you,' he said at last, turning back to her.

Here it comes, Clara mused; the truth...or at least part of it. 'Can't do what?' she demanded, knowing she was not going to like the answer.

'There is something else I need him to do. He won't do it for me...but he might do it for you. As I said before, it's all about trust...and he trusts you.'

'No, no, and no!' she repeated defiantly. 'I won't do it, Charles. You're asking me to betray him. I can't do that,' she added, tears welling up behind her eyes again.

Sir Charles smiled. It was the smile he always gave when he was about to spring something, Clara mused unhappily.

'I'm not asking you to betray him or his trust, Clara,' he said. 'I just need you to guide him in the right direction when the time comes. That's all. Nothing more, I promise.'

He said it with such sincerity it was almost believable, Clara thought. Almost, she repeated inwardly.

She shook her head as she spoke. 'You're playing with words, Charles. It still sounds to me as if you want me to betray him no matter how you dress it up.'

Sir Charles sighed heavily. 'That's not what I want Clara. What I want is for Raeburn to betray Corkscrew's trust...and he won't do that for me.'

Clara shook her head sadly. Her day had started badly and it was going downhill now at breakneck speed. Her shoulders sagged and she began to sob quietly. 'Why are you doing this to me?' she challenged. 'You've watched me struggling to come to terms with his death...and now you land this on me. You tell me he's alive and then you tell me you need me to manipulate him. How can you? You know how I felt about him,' she finished accusingly.

'I'm not enjoying this any more than you are, my dear, believe me. I'm doing it because I have to.'

'And what if Jamie refuses to get involved in your scheme?' she asked. 'If he was as badly injured as you said earlier, how do you even know he's up to it?'

Sir Charles gave her a lopsided smile accompanied by another sigh. 'Do you really think we would be having this conversation if I had any doubt on that score?' he said softly. 'He's already involved, Clara...and yes, before you ask, he is up to it; both physically and mentally.'

'You've seen him?' she asked, and watched him nod in confirmation.

Another period of thoughtful silence followed as Clara considered all the information. Sir Charles waited.

'So what is it exactly you want him to do?' Clara said at last, nibbling at the bait. 'It doesn't take my involvement to get Jamie to pass on the intelligence...he's already on board for that. What is it you really want him to do?' she repeated, smiling grimly through her tear-filled eyes.

'I need him to be what he was...an Archangel.'

'With all that that entails?' she said sadly in response.

'Yes, with all that entails.'

Clara grimaced. He didn't need to spell it out to her. She sighed sadly. 'I don't think he'll do it,' she said quietly. 'He's not a natural killer, Charles, you know that. He was disillusioned a year ago. I imagine he's even more disenchanted now...especially after the Kiltyclogher mission.'

Sir Charles gave a hollow laugh. 'Yes, he made that abundantly clear when I met him. Hence your involvement,' he continued. 'Like I say, he trusts you.'

They lapsed into silence again. Minutes passed. Long, tortuous minutes for Sir Charles; pensive, sadness filled minutes for Clara.

'I used to love coming here,' she murmured eventually. 'When I was a little girl...you were like a favourite uncle and Estelle was like an exotic aunt. I learned so much from you...sometimes I wonder if you were grooming me for this from an early age. But back then, I was happy. I wish I could go back to those days.'

Sir Charles was looking at her; sadly, she thought. Did he have similar thoughts?

'Tell me about him,' she said, a little louder.

'Who?' he queried, still watching her.

'Who do you think, Charles?' she smiled sombrely. 'Do you think I'm even remotely interested in Corkscrew?'

He shook his head and let out another sigh. 'He's well. You probably wouldn't recognise him,' he laughed. 'Quiet the Bohemian...long hair, beard, shabby clothes. He seems to be at peace with himself,' he said. 'He looks a lot stronger, and fitter, than when I last saw him.'

'Where is he?'

'He's in France...moved the whole family over there. He's very protective of them.'

'He always was.'

'They have a new addition,' he said quietly, waiting for her reaction to that.

Clara looked up, eyes widening.

'A boy,' he said, anticipating her question. 'Born a few days ago...just after I visited.'

Silence enveloped them again. Sir Charles thought it prudent to let her absorb that information. It was a couple of minutes before Clara spoke again.

'His wife must have been pregnant when he was at Kiltyclogher then?' she said.

'Yes,' he said simply. He knew what she was thinking.

'Did he ask about me?'

'No,' he replied. Why lie, he thought?

Because it's what I do.

He let her reflect on that. He didn't feel any guilt. It was better she believed he hadn't mentioned her. It might make her decision that little bit easier.

'I suppose you'd better tell me the rest then,' she said.

Sir Charles' response was a gracious smile. 'Why don't we leave that until tomorrow? We've covered enough for now and I suspect Mark and Estelle are wondering what we're up to,' he said.

Clara returned his smile though not quite so graciously. Mark perhaps, she was thinking. Estelle? I doubt it.

Chapter Ten

Next day, Curzon Street, London

Clara Whitelaw sat slumped at her desk. She felt miserable. Her head was throbbing because of too much gin unwisely consumed the night before after her, and her return from Hazelgeove. That, at the time, presented as the lesser of two evils; drink herself under the table or face incessant, probing questions from an intrigued, and worried, Mark. Now, it seemed, the table she had attempted to drink herself under was rattling about in her head, reverberating off her skull each time she moved. And Mark was still curious. Maybe the gin had not been such a good choice after all, she mused.

She felt a little sick. Was it because of the gin or because of what she had agreed to do, she wondered haplessly. But what, exactly, had she agreed to do? She would find out soon enough, she mused, that thought bringing a rueful smile to her face. Apparently, Charles thought it was okay to discuss the minutiae of his plan in the office, but not okay to break the news of Jamie's faked death here.

She sank another cup of black coffee and stared aimlessly out of the window at the cloudless blue sky. The coffee was not working and the bright light hurt her eyes. Penance, perhaps, she mused wretchedly.

She rummaged in her desk drawer and found some aspirin. They might work. She popped two and tried to think. After her "chat" with Charles, she had been subdued...but then, she had been subdued beforehand too, though in a different way The big question facing her now was whether or not Mark had noticed the difference between the two. He had said nothing on the way home but he had been building up to it. She could see it. She hadn't given him the opportunity to launch his interrogation. She had sunk half a bottle of gin while he was still working out his plan of attack, thereby winning a temporary reprieve. She had only put off the evil moment, she knew that, and if she wanted to save her marriage then she would have to face his questions. And that was her big question; did she want to save her marriage? Come to that, she wondered, did he?

Her office door opened and Sir Charles filled the frame. His look said it all.

'Yes, alright,' she responded, drawing him a pained look. 'I just couldn't face Mark's questions.'

'That all?'

'Yes, that's all,' she fired back, irritated now.

He raised one eyebrow dubiously and nodded his head in the direction of his office before turning away. Clara pushed her weary body up from the desk and followed. Her head was still thumping.

The Brigadier waited just inside his door until she had passed him, leaned out to his secretary and told her there were to be no interruption, and closed the door. A pot of coffee and cups sat on his desk and Clara had to smile. He had obviously anticipated her condition and taken appropriate steps. Without waiting to be asked, she plumped herself down in her usual chair. Sir Charles circled his desk and followed suit. 'Coffee?' he said, smiling knowingly.

Clara nodded gratefully and watched as he poured. She would probably need the whole pot before she felt the benefit, she laughed inwardly.

Sir Charles pushed the cup across the desk towards her, poured one for himself and sat back, rummaging in his jacket pocket.

'Please don't,' Clara said. The eyebrow was raised again. 'Not the pipe,' she moaned. 'I don't think I could stand it.'

He grinned apologetically and stopped his fumbling.

'Right,' he said at last, lifting his cup and sipping his coffee. 'Are you ready for this?'

Clara nodded.

'As I said yesterday, Corkscrew has laid down certain ground rules for his continued co-operation, principal amongst which is Raeburn as his contact. I told you they go back a long way, though I don't think they were particularly close. You'll remember Raeburn's file?'

Clara nodded again and swallowed more coffee. She was beginning to feel better...marginally.

'There was a job he did for the IRA in Belfast, late 1967. That's when they met. Presumably, Corkscrew thinks that gives him some sort of hold over our boy.' He paused and lifted his cup.

'Was he ever our boy?' Clara mused silently, as she waited for him to continue.

'Raeburn went over there under cover. Pretty rudimentary cover, from what I gather, but sufficient for the task. He was given a driving licence and some papers in the name of one Dermott Lynch...and that is the name Corkscrew still knows him by.'

Clara sat up a little straighter. She was learning things about a man she thought she had known. There were obviously two different strands to knowing someone intimately she smiled wryly to herself. 'How do you know all this?'

'It started with Corkscrew's demand...he asked for "Dermott" and I was flummoxed. I worked my way round it; asked him why Dermott should want to get involved and he enlightened me. He owes me, he said, or words to that effect...he would be dead if it weren't for me. It all fell into place then...not all the detail I have now, but enough to know that Demott Lynch and Jamie Raeburn, not to mention Michael Messenger, are one in the same person. I got most of the rest from Raeburn himself when I visited him last week.'

'So, they know one another...but they're not bosom buddies, is that what you're saying?'

'No, you're right, they're not...but my gut instinct is telling me there's some other link between them...and it's this other link that Corkscrew is relying on. Don't ask me what it is; I haven't got a clue...but it's there.'

'I still don't see where this is leading Charles. Corkscrew will pass on the intelligence through Jamie, it's in his best interests...it's his ticket out. We have other Archangels committed to the job. Why do you need Jamie? Tell me what I'm missing here.'

Sir Charles poured two more cups of coffee. It was lukewarm by now but still palatable and pouring it gave him time to think. As before, he slid Clara's cup across the table towards her and then leaned back in his chair, regarding her pensively. He knew what her reaction would be to the next part. They had discussed it before, on numerous occasions, and she had made her thoughts clear. It was an obsession, she said...always the psychologist!

'Corkscrew isn't giving me everything I want from him,' he said at last.

Clara cocked an eyebrow questioningly. 'Which is?' she probed.

'The Coventry bomber,' he continued. He heard her sigh.

'Christ, Charles, when are you going to let that go?' she exploded. 'There are more important things going on around us at the moment.' She slurped another mouthful of coffee and slammed her cup down onto the desk. 'You're obsessed with this,' she murmured angrily. 'There are other agencies out there looking for the bomber but you seem to be treating it as a personal crusade!' she exclaimed.

'It is. I made a promise to the Prime Minister.'

'Yes, I know you did, and I'm sure he raises your failure to deliver on it each time you meet,' she retorted sarcastically.

The Brigadier stared out of the window. 'Corkscrew knows who it is,' he said.

'How do you know that? Has he told you he knows or is that just supposition on your part?' She was still simmering.

'It's more than supposition. He's a UNM member, he's bound to know,' he replied.

'I'm your deputy at Ultra and I didn't know Jamie Raeburn was still alive until yesterday and the Dermott Lynch bit only came up about two minutes ago. The UNM is not mainstream IRA Charles. It's made up of IRA members, sure, but they are a different breed...it's like a private members' club'

'He knows,' Sir Charles insisted.

'Gut instinct again?' she laughed quietly. Sir Charles ignored the jibe. 'Okay...let's assume he does know...what is more important at the moment, the identity of the Coventry bomber or the locations of three or four impending attacks? Why not get that intelligence first and then pull him out? When we have him here we can sweat it out of him.'

The Brigadier smiled grimly. 'Yes, I had thought of that but, unfortunately, so too has Corkscrew.'

Clara's left eyebrow lifted again.

'He suspects I would try that. He's not stupid. He has made it clear that after he has passed on the intelligence on the attacks he'll have no further contact with anyone...other than Raeburn. Raeburn's job is as the middleman. He is to arrange the new passport, not us. When we have the information from Corkscrew, Raeburn will pass on the passport, documents and the cash and Corkscrew disappears.'

Clara thought about that. 'And you want Jamie to give him up to us before he disappears?'

'Either that, or get the information about the bomber from him,' he said simply.

'And then kill them both?'

'That's what Archangels do.'

Clara smiled sadly. She saw it all clearly now. Charles regarded her as his best hope of manipulating Jamie. She had her doubts. Seducing him had been one thing, it was manipulation of a sort, she supposed, but this was something else entirely. And she couldn't use their relationship any longer...sex was off the menu. She had a funny feeling that if she wasn't extremely careful, Jamie Raeburn would end up manipulating her. That was her gut instinct.

'So, are you with me on this?'

Clara heard Charles' words and turned her face towards him. 'I suppose so,' she agreed. 'I just don't know how I'm going to get close enough to him to manage it.'

The Brigadier smiled. 'Oh, I'm sure we'll find a way,' he said smugly.

Clara's mind was already on her next problem. Mark. What was she going to tell him?

Chapter Eleven

Same day, South of Epernay, France.

While Sir Charles Redmond and Clara Whitelaw were debating Clara's future involvement with Jamie in the old man's grand plan, he was wrestling with the enormity of what now faced him. Once again, against his better judgement, he was involved in the Brigadier's shadowy dealings and he didn't like it. Weighing everything up, it appeared he was to play piggy in the middle in Liam Fitzpatrick's and Brigadier Redmond's little game. Well, fuck them, he thought darkly.

He pondered his situation, thinking aloud. 'What do I know?' he murmured quietly. He laughed quietly and shook his head. 'Not a lot,' he answered himself honestly. He made a mental list. It was short.

One, and bizarre as it seemed, Liam Fitzpatrick was a tout. He thought he was touting for MI5 and Special Branch but he was working for Brigadier Redmond. That was a different thing entirely.

Two; the guy was shitting himself and he wanted out. Who could blame him for that, he reflected sombrely. Anyone with an ounce of sense wanted out of the shit storm that passed for normality in the Six Counties these days.

Three, Liam did not trust Sir Charles. That made him smile. It was conjecture, Liam hadn't actually said that, but he didn't trust the old sod one hundred percent so why should Liam Fitzpatrick?

Four, the IRA was planning what they euphemistically called a Spectacular. They liked "Spectaculars". Spectaculars got them the attention they craved while at the same time putting the shit up the general population which in turn, in theory at least, put pressure on the Government. This particular spectacular was to take place somewhere on the Mainland and Liam was the Brigadier's tool for stopping it. But there was something else... something he wasn't being told. It niggled at the back of his mind. Liam's cryptic message certainly pointed to it but what was it? He let out an audible sigh. No wonder the poor bastard wanted out.

And there was the final point. Liam expected, at some stage in the process, to be shafted. There was no surprise there either, he mused. In this game, everyone was shafted at some point.

I'm living proof. So what the fuck am I getting myself into?

The house was suddenly quiet. His older children were at school and nursery and new baby Jack was asleep. Kate had been pottering about in the kitchen, singing quietly to herself. The tinkle of cutlery and clink of pots and pans conveyed a sense of normality. It was a false sense. Nothing was normal any more. 'If this all goes wrong, what happens to Kate and the kids?' he fretted silently.

Kate's soft singing had stopped and the quiet that followed unnerved him. He looked up to see his wife framed in the doorway, gazing intently over at him. There was a worried frown on her face. She was wearing that look more and more these days. 'What?' he asked, laughing nervously.

She pushed herself away from the door and came towards him. Gently, she eased herself onto his lap and held his face in her hands. He could feel the cool dampness of her fingers against his skin. 'I don't like seeing you like this,' she whispered, leaning forward and brushing her lips against his. 'It's as if you're stepping back into a nightmare.'

'Which is kind of what I am doing,' he replied. 'I'm not in control of any of this,' he added unhappily. 'Maybe if I knew what the hell they both want from me I could come to terms with it. I don't know.'

'And when will you know?'

'When I meet Liam Fitzpatrick in Glasgow, I suppose,' he replied quietly, averting his eyes away from her gaze.

'So you're going then,' Kate replied sadly.

He turned back to her and held her look for a heartbeat before replying. 'I have to, Kate. I don't want to...but I have to. You know that. I won't get involved in anything risky, I promise.'

She nodded. Yes, she knew it, but she had been hoping he would change his mind.

'Don't make promises like that, Jamie,' she said with a sad smile. 'We both know that where you're concerned, fate tends to dictate what you get involved in and what you don't.' She kissed him again, longer this time. When they broke apart, she said. 'And what about us...me and the children; what are we to do?'

He stroked her hair and gazed at her. The worry behind her eyes was all too obvious. He stroked her hair and gazed at her. The worry behind her eyes was all too obvious. 'A few days, no longer,' he replied as gently as possible. 'Are you okay with that?'

'Not really, but I can live with a few days,' she agreed reluctantly. She paused for a moment, weighing things up in her mind. She knew he would object but it was important to her. 'If this thing, whatever it is, means you going back over again I don't want to stay here on my own,' she said firmly, her voice indicating that argument on the subject was futile. 'If anything happened to you I'd be lost,' she added, her voice reduced to a whisper. She had not wanted to voice that thought but it was there in her mind, constantly upsetting her.

Jamie smiled and nodded. He understood. 'Nothing is going to happen to me sweetheart,' he said reassuringly, but he knew all the reassurance in the world would not be enough. He pulled her to him and kissed her hard, his mind made up. 'Maybe we should think about going home,' he whispered as they eased apart.

Kate's face brightened. 'Glasgow?' she asked.

'Eventually...but at first it might be better if we stay in Calverton till I get things sorted out. Phone your brother. Get him to look for a temporary place for us.'

'You mean it?'

'Yes, I mean it. When I get back from Glasgow this time we'll sort things out here and head for home.' He stroked her cheek and kissed her again. It was for the best, he decided, but he would have to make sure she stayed out of the firing line in case anything went wrong. He had bad vibes about it.

Part II

Chapter Twelve

Friday 22 September 1973, Bangor Road - North Belfast.

Liam Fitzpatrick parked his van close to the verge and switched off the engine. It was peaceful here between Belfast and the seaside resort. The only sound assailing his eardrums right now was the irregular tick, tick, tick of the van's cooling motor and the squawking of circling seagulls. Nothing else. He smiled grimly. What else should he expect? This place was segregated from the chaos of West Belfast; the Falls and Crumlin Road. The people here were insulated from the hate and the fear, cocooned in their warm, middle class bastions, with their golf clubs and country walks. It was like apartheid in South Africa, he thought, only here it was rich segregated from poor, not white from black. He smiled grimly. They would shit themselves if they discovered they had a cuckoo in the middle of their comfortable little feathered nests, that was for sure. Maybe a cuckoo in the nest was a poor metaphor; this infiltrator was more of a viper, he mused.

He checked his watch. He was a few minutes early for his appointment but he could not sit here for too long. There were not many houses on this stretch of the road but that did not preclude some nosy neighbour spotting him and phoning the Peelers. Those bastards would be here in jig-time. There were the passing patrols to consider as well. That was not really too much of a problem. On the face of it he had a valid reason for being here; an emergency call out to fix a blocked drain. It would stand up to scrutiny, the torn faced housekeeper would confirm it, but being questioned by the police and army was something he would rather avoid. He was on a list; he knew that. He looked around uneasily, imagining unseen eyes watching his every move. He gave an involuntary little shudder.

No wonder this bloody place is so quiet, there are eyes everywhere, watching everything.

'Better get on,' he mumbled to himself.

He pushed the car door open, leaning his shoulder heavily against it for extra leverage. The bloody thing was reluctant to move but finally succumbed with a harsh, grinding squeal of protest from its rusting hinges.

He wanted to make this repair job quick but, at the same time, it all had to look natural. So not too quick, he cautioned himself. He walked to the back of the van and flung open the doors. These doors were easier to open. Probably because they were hanging off their hinges, he reflected with a grin. If he wasn't about to disappear off the face of the earth he would be forced to buy a new one. That, he decided, was another pleasure he could happily forego. He smiled a genuine smile for the first time since setting out on this "job" and immediately chastised himself. Smiling happily was something a man in his position rarely did and he was doing a lot of it these days. Some people might start to ask why.

His tool bag sat waiting for him just inside the door. It sat precariously on top of a pile of old junk, the same junk that had been lying there for several weeks now.

Clutter was good. It provided excellent cover for things he needed to hide. Hoisting the bag up he slammed the doors closed with a resounding bang. That should attract attention. Let the neighbours see what he was here to do. He was a plumber going about his daily grind, nothing more, and nothing less. At least, that was what he wanted anyone watching to think. He smiled again and started to whistle. There was a song in the charts just now... Part of The Union – by The Strawbs. It was a big hit, though not, admittedly, in The Falls but fuck it, he liked the tune.

He stopped whistling and laughed aloud; part of the bloody Union,' he murmured beneath his breath. Aye, that'll be right.

He pushed open the big wrought iron gate and sauntered casually up the long gravel path to the front door of the old Victorian house. He was the very picture of a man happy at his work.

A large, ornate brass knocker in the form of a horse's head adorned the middle of the solid wooden door. The brass gleamed in the afternoon sun. He remembered it from his earlier visit months before. It seemed out of place to him then and it seemed out of place to him now. It painted a picture of middle class conservatism that didn't sit well with him. He took hold of it, reluctantly almost, and rapped three times; three solid, distinct knocks. There was silence, no movement. He knocked again and turned around to survey the garden and the adjoining house. He imagined eyes on him.

The faint sound of footsteps came to him at last from beyond the door. A woman's footfall, just like before. He turned back just as the door opened. It was the same woman. She looked at him enquiringly before her eyes took in the heavy leather tool bag with the large shifting spanner jutting from it. 'You're the plumber,' she said.

Liam wasn't quite sure if it was a statement or a question. He bit back a sarcastic response. 'That's me,' he said instead, giving her a smile. 'You've got a problem with your upstairs toilet,' he added, stepping over the threshold.

The woman gave him a frosty smile and stepped back to let him enter. He had been here before and she remembered him. She was in her forties, though makeup covered many sins, he mused. Her eyes were as distrustful as a woman being handed a bunch of flowers by a husband who smelled of perfume that wasn't hers, he thought. Her dress sense was as severe as her face which went a long way to explaining why there was no gold ring on the third finger of her left hand. He doubted if she ever got flowers.

In fairness, the rest of her wasn't too bad. Her body made up for the severity of her dress and when she smiled, even frostily, her face changed. In a good light she might even be described as beautiful... but then, he reflected, icebergs, in a good light, could be described as beautiful. That didn't mean you would enjoy hugging one.

He followed her along the long hall, trying to keep his eyes off her swaying behind. She was much more attractive from the back. A radio was playing somewhere, a mournful dirge that sat well with the décor and the cold demeanour of the woman in front of him. Classical music wasn't his scene, he decided. He wondered for a moment if she knew what her esteemed employer was into for recreation and if he ever brought any of his boyfriends home. Probably not, he mused, though he doubted anyone, Fionn Doherty included, could prise the secret from her even if she did.

She stopped at the foot of the stairs and pointed upwards. 'The bathroom is up there,' she said, forgetting he had been before. 'It is the door facing you at the far end of the landing. The other rooms are bedrooms. Do not go into any of those,' she instructed. Liam grinned back at her.

As if I would. He nodded an acknowledgement and started up the stairs, his heavy tool bag catching the edge of each tread with a resounding thump. The woman watched him, despairingly, for a moment and then made her way back to the kitchen. The door closed behind her and the music was immediately silenced.

'Thank God for that,' he murmured gratefully under his breath. When he reached the top of the stair he found himself in semi-darkness. The doors that opened onto the landing were all firmly shut and the only illumination came from tiny quarter lights above each. He remembered this from before. There was a light switch on the far wall, a brass plate with a metallic pin in the middle. It looked like a tiny baton with a knob on the end, like a tiny penis. Suitably phallic, he thought, grinning again.

He flicked the switch and the lights came on. He didn't like old switches and these ones were older than old. They were probably put in when the house was built years earlier. He didn't trust them... was always afraid he would get an electric shock when he touched them. The newer switches these days were Bakelite; much safer, he thought. As he made his way along the landing he wondered, vacantly, if the wiring had ever been upgraded. If not, the place was a bloody death trap.

He made up his mind there and then to pick up the package and get out of the place as quickly as possible. He would wait just long enough to make it look good for any nosy neighbours and then he would scarper.

The dull glow from a weak ceiling light did its failing best to brighten the landing. It had a fight on its hands. The walls were painted in a colour that could only be described as dull, light brown. It was probably once cream or magnolia, he mused, but years of neglect and cigarette smoke had done the damage. The skirting boards were brown too, covered with brown tainted varnish. The doors were no different. It all added to the gloom. A lick of white gloss wouldn't go amiss.

The thought of living in a place like this depressed him. But then, nobody really lived here, did they? It wasn't a home. The owner, Sir Rodney Calder, Member of Parliament and elderly bon vivant, spent most of his time in London these days, sitting on his fat arse in Westminster... When he wasn't dipping his wick in some obliging rent boy's bum, he thought coarsely, and Frosty Knickers downstairs was only the housekeeper. She didn't live in as far as he could remember and neither did the handy man/gardener.

The old poof would shit himself if he discovered what his house was being used for today. The old sod would probably have an apoplectic fit and keel over on the spot. That would be no loss to anyone, particularly his constituents in Belfast, though a battalion of rent boys in London would be out of pocket for a while... until some other Dis-Honourable Member took over from old Sir Rodney, of course.

It might be worth letting it slip sometime, he mused, grinning again.

He pushed open the bathroom door and stepped inside. In contrast to the rest of the house, it was light and airy. He remembered his surprise on finding it the last time he was here. It was an oasis in an otherwise barren desert. There was a large corner bath, with room for two, he noted, a walk in shower, toilet pedestal with wooden seat and lid, a wash-hand basin and one of those French contraptions - a bidet. Great for washing your dick and your rear end after a bit of hanky panky, Liam thought, smiling wryly. There were no prizes for guessing what old Sir Rodney enjoyed doing in here.

He made his way to the toilet and lifted the wooden cover. Sure enough, the water was backed up almost to the rim. To any other plumber the fact the water was clear and not heaving with faeces would have seemed strange, but not to Liam. The blockage wasn't caused by shit, it was there because someone had stuffed a bundle of sanitary pads into the U bend. He already knew that. All he had to do was pull the pads back out again and, hey presto, job done. Well, not exactly. He still had to pick up the package.

He set to work, cursing loudly and making as much other noise as possible to keep the ice maiden downstairs from paying him an unwelcome visit. First, he removed the top of the cistern and placed it carefully into the bath. The package, a polythene envelope containing a BASF C60 cassette tape, lay at the bottom of the tank. He rolled up his sleeve and plunged his hand down into the water, squeezing it past the flushing mechanism. Reaching down with his fingers, he managed to clutch the package and pull. It came away easily. Quickly now, he removed it from the tank and dried it off with a rag before placing it carefully at the foot of his tool bag under a gamut of small tools and plumbing odds and sods.

When he returned to his van he would take it from the bag and add it to the collection of tapes he kept there; Van Morrison, Gene Pitney and about fifteen others on old tapes with handwritten labels. That way he would be hiding the needle in the proverbial haystack, so to speak.

Satisfied, he turned back to the blockage. This sort of thing was normally one of the more unsavoury plumbing tasks, he reflected. Plunging your arm up to the elbow in shit was never fun. He smiled this time though. All he had to do was remove the water sodden incontinence pads; no bum wipes, no stinking water and no excrement. Heaven! He remembered an old plumber's joke and laughed manically. "It might be crap to you, it went, but it's my bread and butter."

But he wouldn't be a plumber for much longer, he reminded himself happily. There were a couple of hoops to jump through first and a few obstacles to work round but he was almost there. Thank God for Dermott

Lynch. Without Dermott, the bloody hoops and obstacles would be impossible to negotiate and he would be at the mercy of the old man in London. When he thought about how close he had come to killing Dermott, he shuddered.

For now, though, he had to finish up here and get back to Duggan with the tape. If he was lucky, the tape might have information on the target. When he learned that, he was out of it. A new life far away beckoned.

The thought spurred him on. Kneeling down, he pushed his hand down into the toilet bowl and felt the icy water creep up his arm. The pads should be packed into the U bend and easily removed, he imagined. If not, then whoever had created the blockage had been too cautious and had pushed the bloody things further into the pipe. If that was the case he would have to use flexible metal tongs he kept with his tools for that very purpose.

His felt around blindly in the bend until his fingers touched the compacted bulk of the sodden pads. Teasing the first of them between his thumb and forefinger, he tried to ease it loose. It resisted and he lost his grip. He tried again, cursing softly, with the same result. On his third attempt, his shirt sleeve now thoroughly soaked, the pad began to move. He manoeuvred it back and forth until he was able to give it a firm pull and then, all at once, there was a gurgling sound and the water began to recede.

'Thank God,' he murmured beneath his breath.

The remainder of the pads now lay in a pile at the foot of the bowl. He suspected one or two had escaped down the waste pipe but he didn't care. If the pipe blocked again maybe he would get another call to come and unblock it. He would be happy to take Sir Rodney's money.

He pulled the pads clear one by one and stuffed them into an old plastic bag before starting to clear up. He was just in time. He heard footsteps climbing the stairs and padding along the landing towards him. He quickly flushed the toilet and turned towards the door as it opened, holding up the dripping plastic bag in triumph.

Frosty Knickers wrinkled her nose and looked distastefully at him and the bag. He wasn't sure which she liked least. Probably him, he mused. 'All done,' he said, nodding in the direction of the now clear toilet bowl.

'Good,' she said, still unsmiling. 'How much?'

'Seven Pounds fifty, missus,' he said. 'I'll just finish up here and come down. Ye'll be wantin' a receipt, I suppose?' She nodded. He was convinced that if she smiled her face would crack.

'Right,' he continued, dismissing her. 'I'll be down in five minutes.' He turned away from her and carried on tidying up. She took the hint and left him to it, striding off along the landing and down the stairs.

When he reached the foot of the stairs a few minutes later she was waiting, money in hand. Liam dropped the plastic bag with the pads at his feet and pulled his receipt book from his dungarees' pocket. He searched for a pen. The only one he could find was red biro but what the hell, it was a receipt he was writing, not the feckin' Magna Carta. He scribbled the date and the amount, signed it with a flourish and handed it over.

The woman took it from him as if it was contaminated and handed over the cash; seven one pound notes and five ten pence pieces. No tip, he noticed. He slipped the money into his pocket, touched his forelock mockingly, and headed for the door. He left her the plastic bag.

Chapter Thirteen

That evening.

Pearce Duggan was a big man. Some might describe him as intimidating, but to most came across as an amiable joker, a gentle giant. He sometimes joked that he was the original "Jolly Green Giant". Appearances, however, can be deceptive. Sure, he smiled a lot, joked a lot and played with children, but behind it all lurked an intelligent, incisive brain aligned with a cunning personality. Everything you saw of Pearce Duggan was only what he wanted you to see. Some people had seen the darker side of Pearce and some of them, the more fortunate ones, were still alive. Many of them were not. He was smiling tonight, Liam Fitzpatrick noted, though that wasn't always a good sign.

The small room at the back of the bar had been reserved for their use. A sign pinned to the door said the local Gaelic Football Club Social Committee was using it. The landlord knew differently but he was a sympathetic to *The Cause* and on nights like tonight he had a very short memory. Within seconds of the meeting ending, he would have forgotten they had even been there.

As well as Liam and Duggan there were three other men in the room. The air was thick with cigarette smoke and the atmosphere was charged. Liam and the three other men were sweating nervously. Duggan was still smiling. He was alone in that.

Liam let his eyes wander round the tiny gathering, letting them rest briefly on each man in turn. He knew them all; Fionn Doherty, Eamonn Macari and Pearce Finnegan. And they knew him. There was no love lost between Liam, Doherty and Macari. Finnegan was new. Liam hadn't formed an opinion on him yet. For the moment, he was alright. He was the youngest of the trio and still full of that righteous indignation and sense of injustice that was common in some of the younger volunteers. It wouldn't be long before disillusionment set in, Liam knew from experience.

If he lived that long, that is.

Doherty and Macari were a different proposition. They were anything but alright in Liam's eyes. The word psychopath could have been thought up just for them and the thought of having to spend time with them on this operation turned Liam's stomach. He detested Doherty especially. He was the worse of the two, completely devoid of humanity. Liam had his own personal reasons for loathing the man. And a score to settle. But that would have to wait.

When he turned his attention back to Duggan he found the man examining him. Duggan's face was expressionless but Liam had the feeling the man was reading his mind. He stared back defiantly, holding Duggan's stare until he saw a hint of a smile appear on the man's lips. Mentally, he breathed a sigh of relief.

'Well lads,' Duggan started, positioning himself on a bar stool next to the bar and bringing the gathering to order. 'You'll be pleased to know the mission's on,' he continued. He had their attention now. The tension in the room had eased. No one was going to need the last rites tonight. Doherty and Macari were excited now. The prospect of killing Brits was something they thrived on. Finnegan, Liam could see, was excited too but he put that down to the prospect of being involved in a major attack at last. And Liam? Well, Liam wasn't excited by the prospect of then attack at all. His excitement had an entirely different source.

Duggan held up a cassette tape and waved it theatrically in front of them. It looked similar to the one Liam had delivered to him earlier. 'Liam here brought me the word, fine man that he is,' the big man continued, turning his black eyes back to Liam. The smile was still on Duggan's lips but his eyes were like dark pits. It was like staring into an abyss, Liam mused, and when Duggan was like this it made him feel a tad uncomfortable. He accepted the praise with a modest nod of his head and glanced at the others. Finnegan was looking at him with something akin to awe. Doherty and Macari had heard it all before and both maintained an air of disinterest and boredom. They did not think much of Liam Fitzpatrick; he was too soft in their eyes.

Squeamish, Doherty had called him. Doherty saw himself as a man of action. Unfortunately, that belief in himself wasn't backed up by thought or tactical ability and that was what, in Duggan's opinion, Liam provided. And Duggan's opinion was all that mattered.

'Ye'se will be goin' over to the mainland at the beginnin' o' January. That'll let ye'se scout the place out,' the big man announced.

Liam knitted his brow. 'Where are we goin', Pearce, an how long for?' he asked.

The big man turned to him. Duggan knew that if any of them were going to ask questions it would be Liam. The others were too thick. He stared back at Liam while he considered the question carefully.

'Why don't I keep my big mouth shut?' Liam mused uncomfortably. But then, he reflected, not asking the question might be just as incriminating as asking it. He was the one Duggan expected to query things. He was the thoughtful one, the planner. And the big man would react like this to any operational question, he reminded himself. It didn't help. His nerves were still on edge. He smiled and hoped the big man would think this one innocuous enough. If not, there was no telling where it could lead.

'Ye don't need to know where yet,' Duggan said at length. 'But ye can plan on bein' away for three weeks.' He paused for a moment, eyeing them all individually. 'People think out security is shite... an' they might have a point,' he went on eventually, his words accompanied by a cold laugh. All four men knew Duggan was of the same opinion. He trusted no one.

'Why three weeks?' Liam asked. 'Why not just a quick in an' out job?'

Duggan didn't hesitate this time. 'Plannin', that's why,' he replied. 'Ye'll need to pick the best spot an' ye'll need to know where ye place the explosives. That's crucial to the success o' this.'

'An' why can't we be told all that here?' The question was out before he could stop it.

'Because there's too many feckin' touts here, all ready to spill their guts to the peelers an' the Brits,' he spat out viciously. 'Anyway, we've got places set up fer ye... nice an' quiet, an' not too far from the target when the time comes.' His eyes swept over them as he spoke. 'If ye'se just do as ye're told, ye'll be fine, so ye will.'

Liam shuddered. He decided to drop it at that rather than push his luck. He already had enough to pass on. There was no point in pressing for more.

Pearce Duggan held up the cassette again. 'It's all on here,' he said. 'An' now it's all up here.' He pointed the index finger of his free hand to his temple. Slowly, he unwound the tape, pulling it in long threads from the spool. It twisted in loops as it played out onto the bar. Carefully, he gathered up the loose strands of the tape and placed them in a large glass ashtray. He lifted a cigarette from a packet lying beside the ashtray and lit it with a match, sucking the flame into the white tube and then placing the still burning match into the centre of the bundled tape, smiling contentedly as it flared up and burned away to nothing. The smell of burnt tape and melted plastic from the cassette body pervaded the space, cancelling out the smoke from the cigarette. It was all so theatrical, Liam mused. Duggan was telling them that only he now had all the information. All stored securely in his head.

The man drew heavily on his cigarette and turned back to face them, smiling. 'January 25 next year,' he said, surprising them. 'That's yer feckin' D-day. Youse'll be the final nail in the Brits' coffin,' he continued.

He turned and looked directly at Liam. 'Liam, here, is in charge. Youse'll follow his orders, just like he follows mine. Got it?' His eyes had now turned from Liam to Doherty and Macari. 'I don't want yer enthusiasm runnin' away wi' yese. If ye blow this, ye're dead men.' Both men nodded nervously.

Liam smiled to himself. Doherty and Macari wouldn't like that but they wouldn't go against it. Nobody in their right mind would disobey a direct order from Pearce Duggan. Not that it would stop them giving him a hard time, mind, and they would watch his every step, Liam reflected.

Duggan turned his attention back to Liam then. 'This will be the biggest fright the Brits ever get. This is between us... no one else, understood? If word gets out then I'll know it has come from this room...' He paused, looking directly at each man in turn. 'An' that would make me very unhappy.' He said no more on the subject. He didn't need to.

He turned to Liam. 'Are ye still goin' over to Glasgow to watch the Celtic these days?' he asked.

Liam paused. It sounded like an innocent question but there were no innocent questions where Duggan was concerned. 'Aye, as often as I can,' he replied. 'But it's gettin' too expensive now, so it is.'

Duggan smiled. 'When are ye goin' over next?'

'There's a match at the beginnin' of next month... I thought I might go over fer that,' Liam answered, wondering where this was leading.

'Ye go by bus, don't ye?'

Liam nodded.

'So do ye think ye could squeeze three more onto the charabanc?'

Liam nodded again. 'I suppose. The coach is never full these days. The boys just don't have the money.'

Duggan pulled a wad of notes from his pocket, peeling off a few and handing them to him. 'This one's on me then,' he said. 'Take this three wi' ye. There's someone there ye all have t' meet.'

'Who would that be?' Liam probed.

'A tailor,' Duggan laughed. 'Ye're bein' measured fer new suits. Arrange it.'

Liam nodded. He was like one of those nodding dogs people kept in the back windows of their cars. The name of the tailor would have been good but he was already walking on eggshells.

'Right,' Duggan said with finality. 'Let me know when ye've arranged the trip. Ah'll give ye the name an' address of yer contact the day ye leave.' Those were Liam's orders. He turned to them all now. 'An' remember; ye tell nobody about this...an' ah mean nobody.' Duggan didn't have to spell out the consequences of not heeding that commandment. They all knew it would lead, inevitably, to the breaking of another... the sixth; thou shalt not kill. And that was one Duggan had broken on more than a few occasions.

Chapter Fourteen

Liam left the meeting and drove home. His mood was a mixture of apprehension and euphoria. The briefing, Duggan had called it that, had provided him with the clearest sign to date that his time as a volunteer on the one hand and as an informer on the other, was nearing an end. Not because Duggan suspected him, but because the attack was only a few months away now...and he didn't expect to be around for it. That thought alone brought a smile to his face. That was the source of the euphoria. By 25th January 1974, he expected to be somewhere else; on the other side of the world in fact. But he still had things to do before that...and time was running out. That was the source of his apprehension.

Pearce Duggan had also presented him with a problem he hadn't envisaged, and it was a dangerous problem. Meeting Dermott in Glasgow was always going to be tricky but now, with the three stooges tagging along, it might be virtually impossible. Macari and Finnegan weren't the problem. The problem was Doherty. Would Doherty recognise Dermott? If he did, the game was up. But would he?

Liam ran over the events at Kiltyclogher in his mind. It had been dark, pitch black in fact. And Dermott had been dressed in combat fatigues, his face blacked up with camouflage paint, and he had been wearing a mask. Christ, I hardly recognised him myself, he mused. But Fionn had pulled off Dermott's mask... just before he stole his watch, and he had given him a good look... and he'd been looking down at him as he peed on him, the dirty little bastard.

'Shit, shit, shit,' he murmured softly. But there had been blood everywhere and Dermott's face was a mess, he reminded himself. 'An' I don't even know what he looks like now,' he murmured again, talking it through with himself. It was a risk but it was a risk he had to take...and if it came to it, Dermott could take care of himself. Better not to tell him though, he decided.

He had considered stopping off at a telephone box on the way home but thought better of it. It was late and it was an hour ahead in France, he had remembered, but it wasn't the thought of that that swayed him. It was the thought that from now on his every move would be watched. Pearce Duggan took security to the level of paranoia and some of that rubbed off. A telephone call at this time of night could raise suspicions. Making such a call after a meeting with Pearce Duggan could be suicidal. No, he would wait until the morning when he could hide the call to Dermott in amongst his calls to customers.

A bottle of Bushmills awaited him and after tonight's news, he needed it. An hour later and half a bottle of the fiery golden liquid inside him, he fell into a fitful sleep.

It was just before nine o' clock next morning when Liam arrived at his yard and opened the little wooden shed that served as his office. He had a few calls to make and his girl would be in at around nine fifteen. He would get the call to Dermott out of the way before that.

He filled a battered kettle with water and set it on the single gas ring that served as a cooker. Better to keep his routine in place. He always filled the kettle and lit the ring before Concepta arrived. Any change to that would set her mind buzzing. She was that type of girl. Not the brightest, but she was always trying to please, always trying to figure out what was bothering him or upsetting him. If he deviated from his usual daily routine it would set her off on one of these quests and he could do without that. He had too many secrets he didn't want her finding out about.

With the kettle sitting precariously on the gas ring, he settled down behind the work bench that served as a desk. He spent little time here in the "office" and sometimes felt a little guilty for allowing poor Concepta to work in such a hovel, but it fit his image. And it wouldn't be for long now. He didn't think about what might happen to Concepta then.

He picked up the phone and dialled the number. The long ring tone came back to him. He remembered it from the first time. He hoped Dermott was at home.

A woman answered. Dermott's wife...he had forgotten he was married.

'Hello,' he said, a little self-consciously. 'Is Dermott around by any chance?' he asked.

There was a momentary pause before she replied. 'Oh, yes, of course,' she said, sounding a little taken aback. 'I'll get him.'

There was noise in the background. Muffled voices and the sound of a baby crying and then Dermott came on the line.

'Liam, I was beginning to think you'd given up on using me,' he said.

Liam laughed. 'Ye were hopin', ye mean,' he retorted. 'Listen, I don't have long. I'm goin' to be in Glasgow on the 6th of next month. Can ye get over fer then?'

There was silence from the other end of the line, not unexpectedly, Liam thought.

'Aye, I suppose I can,' Jamie said eventually.

Liam noted the reluctance in Jamie's voice but it hadn't been unexpected. He smiled to himself. 'Good. In that case ye'd better let the boss know then, I suppose.'

'Aye, I suppose.'

'Right, good,' the Irishman repeated.

There was something in his tone that hinted that it wasn't good, Jamie thought, but before he could probe further, Liam was speaking again.

'While ye're on to him, tell him one big job is set for 25 January...that's all I've got just now. I'll have more for him when I meet ye.' Liam paused then, wanting to frame the next bit carefully. 'Listen,' he continued, hesitantly. 'I don't want yer man knowing exactly where an' when we're goin' to meet.'

And there it was, Jamie mused. 'Why?' he fired back. 'He's going to ask, you know that.'

'Aye, I know, but don't tell him. Fudge it,' Liam retorted. 'I'll explain why when I see ye. Trust me Dermott, don't tell him.'

Jamie considered that for a moment. The Irishman sounded worried. 'Okay,' he said. 'I'll keep that to myself...but exactly where and when are we going to meet?'

Liam laughed nervously. 'Oh, yes. Listen, Celtic have a game against Motherwell at Parkhead on Saturday 6th. Go to the game. Ye'll be able to pay at the turnstile, Celtic end naturally. Make ye're way to Section G, second barrier in on yer left side at row L. I'll see ye there. There will be enough of a crowd to get lost in if we need to.'

Before Jamie could respond to that remark the line was dead and Liam was onto his second call of the morning.

***

Jamie replaced the handset and turned to an anxious looking Kate. His expression told her what she didn't want to hear.

'That's it then, you're going?' she asked, rocking the baby gently in her arms.

He nodded unhappily.

'I thought maybe he'd changed his mind,' Kate continued.

'So did I. I hoped he had.'

'When are you to be there?'

'Beginning of October...the 6th. We've got then days...so you'd better phone your brother and tell him to take that place for us. Tell him we want it for six months.'

Kate forced a laugh. 'You're sure?' she asked. He smiled and nodded. 'So what happens now?'

'Now, I phone the Brigadier.'

'Do you have to? I don't trust that man.'

Jamie gave a short laugh. 'You're not alone,' he said. 'For some reason, Liam doesn't want him to know where and when we're meeting,' he added thoughtfully. 'Says he'll explain why when we meet. He sounded scared.'

'And you're not?'

Jamie pulled her and the baby close. 'These days I'm always scared,' he whispered.

Kate shook her head. 'Scared or not, you're getting involved again,' she said. 'You're like Don Quixote, always finding a windmill to tilt at...just remember, sweetheart, some of these windmills fight back.'

He laughed and kissed her softly. 'No more windmills...this is the last one.'

***

Sir Charles answered the phone on the first ring. He felt tense. It had been weeks since his contact with Corkscrew and Raeburn and nothing since. He had people working on possible targets for the attacks but without more information the list was growing and the Security Services couldn't cover all of them. He had been forced too to involve MI5, something he had wanted to avoid until he had more intelligence, but as time passed the need had become unavoidable.

'Redmond,' he shouted gruffly into the phone.

'And a good morning to you too Brigadier,' Jamie retorted. 'Feeling the pressure?'

'Raeburn, at bloody last!' Sir Charles responded, ignoring the comment. What's going on?'

'I'm meeting Corkscrew on 6th October...'

'Where?' Sir Charles interrupted.

Jamie smiled grimly. The old boy was feeling the pressure. 'Don't know yet. He's still working on that,' he lied easily.

'I need to know.'

'Why do you need to know?'

'Don't be obtuse, Raeburn. I need to protect both your backs...obviously.'

Jamie let that hang for a while. It as plausible, but...thinking about Liam's plea, there was probably an ulterior motive. 'When I know, you'll know,' he said.

'Right, right,' Sir Charles replied quickly, apparently mollified. 'Do you have anything else to report?'

'Yes, I do, as it happens. Whatever is going to happen is scheduled for 25th January...next year.'

'25th January,' Sir Charles repeated, thoughtfully. 'No idea what it is?'

'No, none at all, though I would hazard a guess it isn't a Burns' Supper,' Jamie laughed sarcastically.

The Brigadier sighed heavily. 'Nothing else?'

'Like what?'

'Like anything...names, for example.'

'If he had given me names I would have told you. There's nothing else. He did say he'd have more when I meet him.'

'Okay. Call me again before you leave for your rendezvous with him. Place and time, remember. If he contacts you with anything else meantime pass it on immediately.'

'Yes, Sir,' Jamie replied, caustically.

'I have placed funds at your disposal...a sizeable deposit into the Messenger account.'

'Weapon?' Jamie asked casually.

'I'll give you a name when I know where you're going. Don't want you carrying anything with you.'

'Understood.'

'Good. We're finished then. Goodbye,' Sir Charles said curtly, terminating the call.

Jamie smiled grimly. There was still a lot going on he wasn't being told...by both Liam and the Brigadier. And that reminded him exactly where his loyalties lay.

Chapter Fifteen

Monday 1 October 1973

There had been no further call from Liam but Jamie still had the task of letting the Brigadier know the details of the rendezvous. That would be tricky bearing in mind Liam's plea. He would have to play it carefully.

His call, as before, was answered quickly. The old boy was a bit more relaxed this time.

'I've been expecting your call,' he said. 'So, what do you and Corkscrew have planned?' the Brigadier asked, making it sound like a casual question which, of course, it wasn't.

'I'm meeting him in Glasgow... on Saturday.'

'Glasgow! Strange choice; why Glasgow?' Sir Charles demanded.

'Search me... but I told him there was no chance of getting me to go to Ireland, North or South, so that might have influenced his decision.'

Sir Charles snorted. 'I suppose so,' he conceded, then carried on. 'Time and place?'

Jamie laughed. 'I doubt you'll believe it but he wants to me to go to a football match. Safety in numbers, I think.'

'Meaning?'

'Meaning he's scared and he's surrounding himself with a crowd he can disappear into.' There was no immediate response to that, Jamie noted.

After a moment, the Brigadier pressed on. 'Okay, so what is this football match and how are you going to meet?'

'Glasgow Celtic play Motherwell at Parkhead. There will be a big crowd.'

'And you'll be contacted at the game?'

'Yes.'

'How?' the Brigadier pressed, sounding exasperated now.

'Corkscrew's instructions were explicit,' Jamie replied, referring to Liam by his code name. 'I am to go to Section C and take up a position at one of the barriers on the terracing at row G...the third barrier in on the left.'

'And he'll be there?'

'Don't know... he just said I'd be contacted.'

There was silence at the other end of the line. Jamie waited.

'Is there a fall back rendezvous?' Sir Charles asked eventually.

'Nothing was said... I get the feeling he's scared he'll be picked up there?'

'Picked up?' the Brigadier retorted, laughing aloud. 'You make it sound like a tea-dance, not a football match,' he said flippantly before reverting to serious. 'Picked up by whom?' he asked.

'I don't know... prying Irish eyes that aren't smiling... or you, maybe.'

'Me? Good Lord, Raeburn... he's meeting you; why on earth would I want to lift him? Why would I need to? He tells you everything and you tell me. That's the deal.'

As with all the Brigadier's answers, it sounded plausible and Jamie would have accepted it but for one small matter... Liam had asked him not to let the old boy into the details of where they were meeting and there could only be one reason for that – he didn't trust Sir Charles.

'Did he say anything else?' the Brigadier asked after a moment.

'Not a thing.'

'Damn!' the old boy muttered angrily. He didn't sound just as relaxed now, Jamie noted. 'I expected more. I need intelligence from him. Get it.'

'Woah,' Jamie retorted quickly. 'I'm just the messenger, Brigadier, the middle-man. Remember that. I'll pass on what he tells me. If you expect me to pull out his finger nails with pliers or burn him with cigarettes, forget it.'

'Don't be ridiculous, man. I don't mean anything like that.'

'Good,' Jamie responded.

There was a moment's silence. 'Do you need anything else?' Sir Charles asked at length.

'I don't think so.'

'What about a weapon? You did mention that earlier.'

'I've changed my mind. I'll do without on this occasion. If I need one later I'll let you know.'

'As you wish.'

Jamie thought the conversation was at an end and was about to hang up when the Brigadier posed another question. 'How are you going to travel?' he asked.

'I haven't decided,' Jamie reported. 'I've only just taken his call.'

'Best to fly,' Sir Charles suggested. 'Paris to London, London to Glasgow... means you won't be away from your lovely wife and children for too long.'

Jamie smiled to himself. It also means your people can pick up my trail on route, he mused. 'Thanks, I'll bear that in mind,' he said.

'Good, good,' Sir Charles replied, sounding pleased once again. 'I'll hear from you again soon, I hope,' he continued. 'And Raeburn... watch your back.'

The line was dead when Jamie responded. 'Oh I will Brigadier, I will,' he murmured.

Chapter Sixteen

Jamie left home on Thursday 4th October and travelled overland by train and ferry. Flying would have saved him a couple of days but it would also make it easier for the Brigadier's people to pick up his trail and shadow him...if that was the plan. He didn't want that. More to the point, Liam didn't want it.

Kate had accepted his departure with the stoicism he had come to expect of her but he knew too that her patience was growing thin. He was a husband and a father, she had reminded him, and he had to get his priorities sorted out. He couldn't argue with that.

She had driven him to Epernay in the morning, waving him off at the station with a tear in her eye. It had certainly pulled at his heart strings. It also helped him reach a decision. After this, he was finished. Sir Charles Redmond could do what he liked but it wouldn't work. He hadn't said anything to Kate. One, he hadn't had time and two, she wouldn't have believed him. With his track record, who could blame her?

Paris was warm when the big SNCF locomotive pulled to a halt in the Gare de L'Est. He had slept for the best part of the hour and a half long journey, dozing with his head against the window. He gave the appearance of a man without troubles...but that was all it was, an appearance. His sixth sense was screaming out a warning that all was not as it seemed. Something was wrong with this, very wrong, and he would be a fool to ignore the warning. Jamie Raeburn was no fool.

He walked the short journey from the Gare de L'Est to the Gare du Nord, East to North, with his holdall over his shoulder. It was a short walk, about ten minutes. He strode through the Parisians purposefully today, not pausing to admire their city. One day, he promised himself, he would come back here with Kate and they would stroll through the City of Light during the day, cruise the Seine in the evening and make love all night in one of the best hotels. All he had to do was get back after this job.

The rest of the journey was as tedious as it was necessary; Paris to Calais, still by train, and from Calais to Dover on the Car Ferry. He had expected scrutiny at Dover but his French Passport stood up to it. He had taken a taxi to Dover Priory train station, sat in the cafeteria there for forty minutes and then boarded the train for St. Pancras. Another two hour journey with stops because of work on the line but he was in no hurry. The next stage on the route was London to Glasgow Central by the overnight sleeper and that didn't leave Euston until after eleven o'clock. He had plenty of time.

He ate in London at a pub, the Slug and Lettuce near Euston, and drank a pint of warm bitter. The beer and the meal lay heavily in his stomach but it wasn't those that caused his fitful sleep on the journey. It was the thought of what awaited him at his destination. The first stop was at Crewe. The train jolted to a stop and he gazed out onto the platform from his bunk. Zombie like passengers, wrapped up against the cold night, waited to board. Humanity was getting a bit like that, he mused. Dehumanised. Doors had banged, feet padded down the corridor and people mumbled incoherently outside. Finally, with a series of jarring shudders, the train started to move again and the hypnotic drumming of wheels on rail began to take effect. Sleep had finally taken him at around four o'clock in the morning.

When the train rumbled to a halt at Glasgow Central Jamie was drained. He washed his face in the tiny sink, ran his hands over the stubble on his chin, drank down a cup of tea and munched on a dry Rich Tea biscuit. It would have to do.

It was a grey day in Glasgow but after several months immersed in the torrid heat of a French summer, he found himself enjoying it. It was refreshing. It was cold, luxuriously cold, but this was Scotland and some things never change, he noted with a wry grin. A crowd stood beneath the Arrivals and Departures Board set above the curved frontage of the old Victorian Ticket Office, its brown wooden fascia darkened by years of smoke and soot pollution.

So much for it being cold, he mused, as two hardy young guys, not much younger than him, strode purposefully into the station from Gordon Street. They were sporting shorts and T-shirts and had bags slung across their shoulders. He would need to get acclimatised again, he thought with a grin, but shorts and T-shirt might be a step too far. He hoisted his hold-all onto his shoulder and stepped out from the Central Station into Gordon Street.

He had thought a lot about his rendezvous with Liam the next day. Celtic Park, the football ground known to Celtic supporters as Paradise, sits to the east of the city. Why it was called Paradise was a mystery to him. Aesthetically, it couldn't compete with its counterpart out to the west and Paradise it was not. But he was biased. He supposed if he looked hard enough he could find a hotel close to the ground but that might not be a good idea. With that in mind, he headed west. There were plenty of hotels in the West-end.

It was still early morning, just after seven, and pedestrians were sparse. Another half hour and the crowds would swell but for now it was quiet. Conscious of Liam's request to keep the rendezvous a secret he looked around him as he walked. Keeping it from the Brigadier would be easier said than done. People would be looking for him. The old boy would not have relied on him to take a flight. By arriving a day early and travelling overland, he might have gained some respite but if the watchers were out he would have a hard job avoiding them. He stuck out like a stud at a eunuchs' convention.

This is Glasgow, he reminded himself. It is situated in the West of Scotland, the wettest part of the bloody country, where the sun rarely shines and the nearest people get to a suntan is during the Glasgow Fair fortnight, in mid-July, when skin colour turns from white to a fragile pink. It was now early October and the natives had reverted to their natural peely-wally, off white. With his deep bronze tan and his French clothes he looked out of place. He was out of place. He looked like a foreigner. Sure, he could change his clothes, buy some new ones, and get his hair cut but the tan was always going to be a problem. Maybe he could pass himself off as one of the city's growing Indian or Pakistani community, he mused with a smile, but he doubted if many of them went to Celtic games! So, short of covering his face in Calamine Lotion and ending up looking like Coco the Clown on a bad day, he was noticeable.

Shrugging mentally, he set out on his journey following Hope Street north up past its junctions with St Vincent Street, West George Street and West Regent Street to the corner with Bath Street. The big Watt Brothers Department Store stood on the opposite corner and stretched all the way down to Sauchiehall Street beyond. The shutters were down on the doors but he made a mental note to visit later... for that change of clothes!

Turning west now, he climbed up Bath Street to the plateau at its summit. He stopped there and cast his eyes back down the hill. A few people trudged up the hill towards him but there was no one who gave him any cause for concern. Nobody stopped hesitantly or turned away but they couldn't anyway, he mused, grinning. There was nowhere to turn to and no shop windows to peer innocently into. The people kept moving, heads down.

Still nothing, and yet his sixth sense was telling him otherwise.

But what did it matter? The Brigadier needed Liam Fitzpatrick in place to feed him intelligence on the supposed attacks. It didn't make sense to lift him... unless... unless there was something else; something more important. Was that what this was all about?

He waited a moment longer then set off again, strolling casually now along the top of Bath Street before starting the descent towards Elmbank Street at the foot of the hill. Ahead of him the red sandstone edifice that was the Kings Theatre sat imposingly on the corner. He didn't look back again. If he was being followed then whoever was doing it was good and turning to check would simply make them more careful. There were ways to look for them without being obvious.

At the corner of Pitt Street and Bath Street he turned to move diagonally across the junction towards another imposing building, the now unused Elgin Place Congregational Church. It was more like a Greek Temple than a Christian Church, he mused, with its six great Ionic Columns at the top of a wide stone stairway. Glasgow was full of buildings like this, great examples of Victorian architecture, even though the Corporation was doing its best to demolish them.

He stopped at the kerb and looked both ways, back up Bath Street and down towards Elmbank Street; an innocent check for traffic that allowed him to look for anyone shadowing him. There was still no one and he began to relax.

As he continued downhill past Renfield St Stephen's Church he noticed the doors were open. An A Boards stood outside, its message fluttering in the morning breeze. "With God, all things are possible"...Mark 10, verse 27, it said. Are they, he wondered? Even for sinners like me? He doubted it, but it made him think of Frank Daly, Father Daly, up at St Gregory's. Frank had never given up on him. I wonder if he prayed for my soul, he thought grimly.

He walked on auto-pilot for a while, lost in his thoughts. The noise from the new M8 motorway rose up to him as he crossed over it and passsed the Mitchel Library. He had given up worrying about followers. If they were there, so be it. His meeting with Liam wasn't until the next day. Losing them could wait until then. Suddenly, he had more important things on his mind.

He was on familiar ground now. He felt comfortable here and his mood lifted. A pale, watery sun broke through the cloud for a moment and he smiled. This was home, he mused. He and Kate had been happy here. He loved France too, he had to admit, but he still felt as though he was an exile there. He remembered his words to Kate weeks earlier... What is there to miss about Glasgow, he had asked her; the rain, the grime and the endless grey sky? It was a flippant remark. He wasn't so sure now.

He was in Berkeley Street now, two storey terraced houses served by wide stone stairs lined both sides of the road, some of them converted to offices. It had been a posh area once. It still was, he reflected. Maybe not what it once was, granted, but it was still quite plush. He carried on, turning off Berkely Street into Claremont Street and then into Sauchiehall Street at Royal Terrace. Every time he came here he was reminded of the standing of the city a hundred years and more before. You could still almost smell the filthy lucre secreting from the stone. The buildings were magnificent and if you lifted your eyes to your right, you would find the Park Area, and even more magnificent buildings that overlooked Kelvingrove Park. That was where the rich merchants and ship owners had lived, looking down over the park towards the river. There they could keep an eye on their investments, the tall masts of the sailing ships as they unloaded cotton and tobacco from the Americas and loaded with goods to sell on the return journey. What they wouldn't see were the slums where the men who worked the docks lived with their families in abject poverty. They were blind to that... just like today. Would it ever change, he wondered? Probably not. Greed is a powerful motivator, greed and power, he reminded himself, and he was a tool of the people who exercised the power.

Sauchiehall Street is famous the world over. It stretches from the city centre at Buchanan Street at its junction with Parliamentary Road down past Charing Cross and out towards the city's famous Kelvingrove Art Gallery, The Kelvin Hall and Glasgow University. Jamie was now approaching the Lorne Hotel where the road takes a slight dogleg to the right and then runs parallel with Argyle Street a block down on its left.

The architecture began to change here, the imposing Victorian Town Houses being replaced by what at one time would have been equally imposing sandstone tenements occupied, in the main, by the middle classes. These were now tired looking buildings in need to tender loving care but that would be a long time coming, Jamie thought grimly. Most of them were now owned by unscrupulous private landlords and tenanted by the workers who kept the city alive. As long as the tenants kept paying the rents the buildings would be left, slowly deteriorating. It was that greed thing again.

There were more small hotels along this stretch of road towards Kelvingrove but the Lorne was, by far, the biggest. It was, too, he imagined, the most expensive but money wasn't a problem. Sir Charles had seen to that. The Lorne also provided certain advantages that the smaller hotels and guest houses didn't. Here, with any luck, he would just be another face passing through. It had more than one entrance and exit and it had 24 hour access.

He paused on the other side of the road, casually looking back along Sauchiehall Street towards Charing Cross. He was still alone, so far as he could tell. He crossed over, skipping between two Glasgow Corporation busses in their green, white and gold livery, both now packed with workers. The city was coming alive.

He climbed up the broad stairs to the front of the hotel and pushed through the revolving door. It was warmer in here and he could smell the aromas of coffee and fried foods. He was suddenly hungry. It was still early and he wondered if he would be able to get a room at this hour. If not, he would book, leave his bag and attend to other business.

Two receptionists were on duty behind a wide wooden desk. A couple of people, two young women, were examining leaflets on a table beside the desk..."Visit Kelvingrove, Sample the Beauty of the Trossachs, Save your Soul with a visit to the Cathedral". Judging by their clothes they weren't here for the culture, he thought with a smile.

He approached the desk and the older of the two receptionists, a young woman of about his own age, looked up from the register she was examining and beamed at him, showing a row of perfect, white teeth. Her eyes seemed to be taking in everything, he noticed, so maybe he wasn't going to be just another face. He would have to make sure he didn't give her anything else to remember him by, he thought wryly.

'Can I help?' she asked. Her voice seemed to imply she would be happy to.

'I was wondering if you have a room available for two nights?' Jamie replied, speaking in heavily accented English. His passport said he was French so he slipped into character.

The girl's eyes opened wider. 'We don't have any single rooms I'm afraid,' she said. 'Not until later today, but I can let you have a double now. It is a bit more expensive,' she added apologetically.

Jamie shrugged. 'The price is not important,' he answered. 'And it is only for two nights. I will take it.' He pulled out his passport and made to hand it over.

'No, hold onto your passport... we don't need to take it from you over here,' the girl said. 'All we need is a registration form completed.' She took a card from a box and passed it to him, offering him a pen.

Jamie completed it carefully, conscious of her eyes on him throughout. He looked up as he finished, giving her a smile to match the one she had given him on his arrival and saw her cheeks turn pink. 'Will it be possible to have breakfast?' he asked. 'I have been travelling since yesterday morning and have not eaten well,' he added.

The girl assured him that would be in order and told him simply to charge it to his room. She removed a key from the rack behind her and held it tantalisingly just out of his reach. 'Is there anything else I can help you with, sir?' she asked.

Jamie wondered fleetingly what other help was on offer and smiled. 'Not for the moment,' he said. 'But perhaps later?' he added, his voice rising at the end, making it a question rather than a statement. He was teasing her in the same way that she was teasing him but somehow he suspected it would not take much to move on from that. He took the room key from her long, red nail varnished fingers and turned away. He wouldn't be taking her up on her offer.

***

It was late morning before he emerged from his room. A short sleep and a shower had revived him after the journey. The hotel was quieter now, most guests having departed to visits the delights of the city. The same two girls were running reception. He smiled over and received a couple of smiles in return, one warmer than the other.

Outside, he was met by the noise and pollution he expected but a minor miracle had taken place. The sun, a watery orb, had broken through the grey sky. He set off at a brisk pace towards the city centre, retracing his steps from earlier. He had given up checking for tails. They would find him if they wanted to. All he had to do was make sure they didn't find Liam.

He caught a bus, an old "back-ender" with the door at the rear and a single pole rising from the middle of the platform to the roof to provide support. Two bench seats facing the aisle were set next to the door with front facing seats following. He chose the bench. These busses would give him his best opportunity to flush and lose a tail if that became necessary, he reflected. He could jump on and step off virtually anywhere, without warning, and melt into the crowds. But not today, he decided. Today didn't matter.

He had a plan now. First, his intention was to visit the bank and withdraw money from his Michael Messenger account. Thereafter, he would buy a change of clothes – there were plenty of men's outfitters in the city - and then he would visit a barber. A haircut would change his appearance - a little. Shaving off his beard would have more effect but he was still conscious of the scarring beneath. He decided to settle for having his beard trimmed but there was nothing he could do about the colour of his skin. The changes he could effect might be enough, but he doubted it. Anyone looking for him would have a description; tall, long dark curly hair, heavy beard and deeply tanned face. Professionals would see through the changes and anyone sent to find him would be that. Professional.

He stepped down from the bus in Cathedral Street just after the junction with Dundas Street. The Station Café stood on the adjacent corner on the edge of the bridge over the Queen Street Station main line. He would eat there later. The road trembled beneath his feet and a deep rumbling noise signalled the departure of a train on the track below. A quick change of plan found him in the station concourse searching for a free phone box. He found one easily. He had little left in the way of Sterling, but enough, he hoped, to make the call.

Fishing the once familiar coins from his pocket he inserted them into the coin box and dialled. Her voice came on the line immediately. She sounded breathless. 'Hello sweetheart,' he said warmly.

'You made it in one piece then,' she replied. 'I've been waiting to hear from you all morning.'

'Yeah, I made it. The old place hasn't changed much,' he continued. 'Though they're still knocking down old buildings and putting up new ones.'

'I wish I was with you.' A sigh accompanied that.

'I wish you were with me too. I miss you already.'

They were quiet for a moment as though both had run out of things to say but that wasn't the case. They both had too much to say. Sorting priorities was the problem.

'The kids okay?' Jamie asked at last.

'They're fine. They miss you too. They're already asking when you'll be back.'

Jamie laughed quietly. He could imagine the scene. Kate would have her hands full, especially with the baby. He felt guilty.

'Listen love, I don't have much change. I haven't been to the bank yet. I'll call you later... tonight, when the kids are in bed. I just wanted to hear your voice.'

'I wanted to hear yours too. Okay, phone me later... about eight.'

'Will do... love you.'

'Love you too,' she said just before the line disconnected.

That made him think again.

What in the name of Christ am I doing here?

Chapter Seventeen

The day went relatively smoothly after that. He withdrew two hundred and fifty pounds from the bank, a mix of notes, predominantly ten and five pound notes with a few single pound notes. Fears that the withdrawal might be queried, particularly his identity, were unfounded but he carried his old Michael Messenger passport in his pocket just in case. He was glad they didn't ask for it. He looked nothing like the photograph in it now.

His visit to the bank did prompt one new worry, however. A thousand pounds had been lodged in the account, a large sum for a simple operation. That made him think the job was bigger than he had been led to believe and bigger probably also meant longer. That didn't please him but he shrugged the thought away.

With the money tucked safely in his pocket he set about the task of changing his appearance. There was a John Collier shop in Argyle Street. That was his first stop. A double breasted charcoal grey suit with a broad chalk stripe, a black wool and cashmere overcoat and a white button down Oxford shirt with a conservative tie of maroon and blue stripes, not unlike that worn by ex- Guardsmen, were his first purchases. Next, he visited a nearby Timpson's shoe shop where he acquired a pair of black leather brogues and two pairs of black socks.

Carrying his purchases in three large carrier bags he made his way back to the Station Café. It was lunch time and the place was busy. He found a seat at a table occupied by an elderly couple who seemed to spend all of their time bickering, and feasted on two Scotch Pies with beans and chips. The chips he doused liberally with vinegar and sprinkled them with salt. He had forgotten how good these tasted.

With the pies lying heavily in his stomach which was now used to a lighter Continental diet, he made his way back up through the town to Cambridge Street, stopping from time to time to gaze into shop windows and to check for a tail. He was still clear but it was only a matter of time. He left Sauchiehall Street at Cambridge Street and strolled past Renfrew Street. The Waldorf, his old stomping ground, was closing so the time would be just after two thirty he remembered automatically. Glasgow's pubs opened at eleven and closed at half past two. He could never understand why this was the case other than to curb the Glaswegian men's fabled heavy drinking. But the pubs opened again at five, so it didn't curb much.

A feeling of nostalgia filled him. He wouldn't mind paying the old place a visit, he mused, but it might not be such a good idea. He was supposed to be dead after all. Beyond the Waldorf, just after the corner of Cambridge Street and Hill Street, lay Fusco's, an Italian Barber's shop established in the City years before. Jamie had used them occasionally but he preferred Ionta's in the

Gallowgate. He loved the banter there... that, and his favourite barber, Wee Johnny Ionta. Johnny stood about five foot nothing in his built up heels but his character was ten feet tall. But he had decided not to visit wee Johnny today. He was too well known there.

About forty minutes later he emerged from Fusco's with his long hair cut and his beard neatly trimmed. His partial transformation was almost complete and when he changed out of his old French gear into his new, sophisticated clobber, it would be. But would it be enough?

His next action was, as usual, impulsive. It probably wasn't a good idea but it might be the only chance he would get. And Frank Daly deserved an explanation. He made his way on foot down New City Road, or what was left of it, to St Georges Road. Walking faster now, he continued past Jimmy Logan's "New" Metropole Theatre towards Garscube Road and Possil. Beyond the Metropole, tall tenements rose on each side with new high flats dominating the skyline beyond. Soon, the here tenements would follow the same fate as much of the rest of the City, he mused.

The walk gave him time to think and he covered much of the trek without realising it. As he emerged from beneath the aqueduct carrying the Forth and Clyde Canal and started the climb towards Keppochhill Road and Saracen Street, he had resolved things in his mind. When he turned the corner at Saracen and saw St Gregory's off to his right, he stepped back in time. Nothing had changed here. The tenements stretched into the distance along Saracen Street towards Lambhill; tall, grey, dilapidated buildings that housed a tired and disillusioned community.

The Chapel of St Gregory's appeared before him, set on the hill, imposing itself on its less salubrious neighbours. He climbed the slope towards the main door, unsure whether or not it would be open. If not, he would try the Chapel House, the Priests' residence. He still hadn't worked out what he would say to the Priest who had become his friend. What could he tell him? Frank Daly knew a sizeable chunk of his history and had worked out even more, but he didn't know all of it.

How the old priest would take his resurrection was a worry. Frank thought he was dead, killed in an accident, and that Kate and his kids had moved south to stay with her parents. Without doubt, Frank would have attempted to make contact with her, especially after Jamie's conversation with him just before the end. All his attempts would have ended in failure... Jamie knew that, so now there would be questions asked and explanations expected. Suggesting it was a miracle wouldn't wash, even with a priest. People don't come back from the dead these days. Not in my world anyway.

The door was slightly ajar and he heard voices from inside, muffled voices talking in hushed tones. He pushed the door open further and stepped inside. It was cooler in here and he shivered. Three women were talking in the Vestibule near an open door to the Nave. They fell silent for a moment, their eyes turning in unison to check the intruder, before their chattering kicked off again. He nodded a greeting that was wasted on them and pushed past them into the Chapel itself.

Two priests were ahead of him in the Chancel. A coffin lay before the Altar, lid open. Another pilgrim on his or her way to Paradise... or not, Jamie mused. Some mourners stood by the open casket, women weeping and men grey faced and solemn. The sight brought back memories... Not memories, a memory. He gave an involuntary shudder and his old pal Guilt said hello. How long had it been? 'Six years. Six, long bloody years this month,' he murmured to no one but himself. And how many times in those six years have you visited Jack's grave, Guilt asked? He shook his head sadly. But some things in life can be fixed, he mused, and that was one of them.

He slipped into a pew near the back of the Nave, a few rows down from the Vestibule, and gazed down at the little scene. He felt like an interloper. The priests mingled with the mourners. Did they believe all the platitudes they spouted, he wondered, allowing bitterness to seep into him. The thought brought Guilt back to chide him. Frank Daly believed... and Frank had believed in him. With all the man had seen and everything he had learned about people over the years, Frank Daly still believed. He always sees the good in people... even in me, Jamie smiled sadly.

He was about to leave, flee the scene and allow his old friend to continue in the belief that he was dead, when a voice spoke behind him.

'Can I help you, my son?' the voice said, and Jamie recognised it immediately.

He turned slowly, a shy smile spreading across his face. The priest was still looking at him, a puzzled expression on his face. He was wearing the kind of look you give when you meet someone you think you know, but can't quite place.

'If anyone can help me Frank, it's you,' Jamie said quietly, rising from his seat and holding out his hand.

The older man's face went through a metamorphosis. His jaw dropped, his eyes widened and his lips moved, but words seemed to fail him. Jamie stared back at him, smile fixed on his face, waiting.

'Jamie, is it... is it really you?' Frank Daly mumbled at last, gripping the top of the pew for support.

'Aye Frank, it's really me.'

The older man's brow knotted and his eyes filled with tears. 'They... they told me you were dead...I thought...' he said quietly, stumbling over the words and pausing between each phrase as though coming out of a bad dream.

Jamie smiled sadly. 'Part of me died, Father,' he said, forgetting for a moment his old friend's insistence that they forego his title. When they were alone they were Frank and Jamie.

'But how... I don't understand?' the Priest continued.

'It's a long story Frank, one best left untold. How are you?' Jamie asked, changing tack.

The priest's face was taking on more colour now as he adjusted to the shock. 'I'm fine lad and for a dead man you look remarkably well too,' he said, a smile finally breaking out at the corners of his mouth. 'You've been away... America?' he asked.

Jamie shook his head. America was a fair guess given what Frank knew of his friendship with Conor Whelan, the American he had saved from a severe beating one fateful night in Glasgow all those years before. 'No Frank, somewhere closer to home. France.'

'France?' the priest repeated, his brow knotting again with confusion.

Jamie nodded but offered no explanation.

'And what about Kate and the children?'

'All well Frank... We have a new addition,' Jamie replied, unable to hide his pride. 'Born on the 31st August... a boy; we named him Jack.'

The older man smiled and nodded happily. 'Are they with you?'

'No, I had to leave them. I'm only back to meet an old friend and I'll be heading back to France on Sunday or Monday.'

Frank Daly looked into Jamie's eyes, reading the signs. He could read Jamie well, one of the very few people who could. It was more than just a meeting with an old friend. He didn't ask what. If Jamie Raeburn wanted him to know, he would tell him. If he needed help, he would ask.

The Priest allowed a broader smile to grow on his face. 'You said it's a long story... but you know me lad, I enjoy a good yarn. Can you stay for supper tonight, or do you have things to do?'

It was Jamie's turn to smile. 'The only thing I have to do tonight is phone Kate,' he replied easily. 'Other than that, I'm all yours. But what about you? Don't you have duties to perform?' he said, turning towards the coffin standing before the Altar.

'Father Desmond, there on the left, knows the family well. He is conducting the Vigil... and the burial too tomorrow, up at St Kentigern's.'

'I was thinking of going there while I'm here... I haven't been a good friend in that respect,' he commented sadly.

Father Daly smiled benignly. 'It's what's in your head and your heart that counts lad, not the number of visits you make to a desolate place like that. You remember him... you've called your baby son Jack after him, that's what matters. Maybe I could come with you,' he added after a heartbeat.

Jamie nodded thoughtfully. It would be comforting to have the older man there with him but a darker thought was forming in his mind. Being seen in Jamie's company by the wrong people could bring the older man grief and Jamie didn't want that.

'Your mother will be happy to have you home again,' the priest went on, breaking the silence. Jamie's look in response told him what to expect.

'I'm not staying at home. I booked a room at a hotel in town,' he said. He didn't say which hotel. For some reason he found he couldn't look the Priest in the eye.

'So it's more than just a visit that brings you back, lad.'

Jamie smiled but there was little warmth in it, the old Priest noted.

'You're still involved?' he went on. It was half question, half statement.

Jamie shook his head but his words didn't match the gesture. 'Yes, I'm still involved, but not like before. I'm finished with that.'

Frank Daly was watching him, reading the signs again. Being "finished" with it didn't seem like an option, the old man thought sceptically. 'Do you want to talk about it?' he asked.

Jamie didn't answer. His eyes roamed around the church, finally coming to rest on the coffin in front of the Chancel and the little group of solemn mourners.

'Why don't we go over to the Chapel House? I've got a good bottle of malt. You can phone Kate from there and then tell me some of what has been happening to you.'

'Okay,' Jamie agreed. 'But I won't phone Kate from there... I'll nip down to Saracen Street later. There's a phone box at the corner of Killearn Street, isn't there?'

'Yes, it's still there; whether it's working or not is another matter,' Frank Daly replied. He decided not to push the question of why Jamie wouldn't make his call from the Chapel House. He could guess, but some things were better left unsaid. He smiled and placed a hand on Jamie's arm. 'Come on then,' he continued, easing Jamie gently out towards the aisle. 'Let's go over to the house.'

When they reached the aisle the Priest stopped. 'Wait for me here a minute till I let the others know,' he said and strode off down the aisle towards the Altar.

Jamie watched as he drew the other priests aside from the little gathering and spoke with them. Both men, much younger than Frank Daly, turned their heads in his direction and gave him an appraising look. He smiled back self-consciously but their faces remained impassive. Jamie wondered what drove young men like them to join the priesthood. He had never been able to suss it out in the case of Frank Daly either. He watched, still ruminating on that, as his old mentor turned to the mourners, shaking hands and speaking softly.

It was a few minutes before he returned. He took Jamie by the arm again and ushered him out into the vestibule. The three women who had been chatting there earlier were now gone. It was after five o'clock, nearly "tea time" in Glasgow parlance, and their men would be returning from work. Then again, maybe not; it was Friday, he reminded himself, and Friday usually involved a diversion to the pub before staggering home, the pay packet a few bob lighter. Some things would never change.

They made their way over to the Priests' home in relative silence, Father Frank's only comments being about the weather. That was something else that would probably never change here. Glaswegians loved their city but hated the weather and it seemed they couldn't have one without the other.

Mrs Murphy, the housekeeper Jamie remembered from the past, met them in the hall. 'You're back early, Father,' she said, her eyes gravitating accusingly to Jamie.

'Indeed I am Mrs Murphy... My young friend here turned up unexpectedly and we have some catching up to do,' he replied, pushing Jamie further into the hall and closing the door.

Jamie felt the woman's eyes on him and turned to her with a smile. Her brow was knitted, as though trying to place him, and then a smile cracked across her soft, puffy face and her eyes twinkled. He remembered her doing that once before when he was here.

'Och, I remember you now,' she said. 'My, but you look different.'

'It's the tan and the beard woman,' Father Daly laughed. 'He's the same young man underneath... And he'll be staying for dinner. We'll take it in my study, that'll give the others peace.'

Mrs Murphy nodded knowingly. She wasn't stupid. It was not the others who needed peace; it was Father Frank and the young man. She didn't know much about the boy but she did know that the priest had taken the younger man under his wing. Why, was anyone's guess, but there was something about him... a vulnerability he worked hard to conceal. She knew better than to speculate or probe. If she did either, she wouldn't work here very long. The Chapel House was like the confessional.

'I'll make you a pot of tea just now then. You'll be wanting your dinner about seven?'

'Yes, Mrs Murphy, that'll be grand,' the priest replied gratefully and ushered Jamie down the hall.

***

'So, what happened to you?' the Priest asked as he handed Jamie a glass of Laphraoig.

Jamie sniffed the heady aroma of smoky peat and smiled. 'Not your usual tipple, Frank,' he said, avoiding the question, for the moment at least.

'A gift from a grateful parishioner,' Father Frank replied with a wink and then grew serious once again. 'You look different Jamie... and I'm not just referring to the tan and the beard,' he continued.

Jamie smiled wryly. 'Well. It's been eight or nine months since you last saw me,' he said quietly. 'An eventful eight or nine months,' he added, laughing. It sounded harsh.

The priest waited. He knew the rest would come. It was all a matter of trust with Jamie Raeburn. He took his cigarettes from his jacket pocket and watched as Jamie raised his hand to his left temple and lifted his hair. The jagged scar was clearly visible running front to back along Jamie's skull. He drew in a breath, a gasp really.

Jamie's smile was grim. 'That wasn't all,' he said. 'I took a bullet through the groin - I won't show you that one,' he added, snorting a laugh. 'I'm not sure which one did most damage. I almost bled to death.'

'When did all this happen?' Father Daly asked, taking a cigarette from the packet and handing the carton over.

'I phoned you, remember?' Jamie replied, taking the packet and helping himself to one. 'I asked you to help Kate if anything happened to me?' he continued, leaning forward to accept a light from his friend.

Frank Daly nodded as he lit up. He remembered. The call had been the reason for his attempts to contact Kate Raeburn months earlier only to learn that she had moved south to be with her family. And Jamie was dead, he remembered that part too. The pain it had brought him. 'I remember,' he said simply, drawing in a lungful of smoke and coughing harshly.

Jamie let his hair fall back into place and sipped at the whisky, savouring the flavour and running it around his mouth. 'They were waiting for me... a four man IRA Active Service Unit.' He laughed unexpectedly and Frank Daly furrowed his brow. 'Thing is,' he continued. 'I knew they were there... I sensed it... but I went in just the same.'

The Priest shook his head slowly.

'I know,' Jamie laughed again. 'Not the smartest thing to do, but you know me.' He paused and took another sip of the Laphraoig, looking awkwardly over the rim of the glass at the older man.

'How did you get out?'

Jamie dragged on the cigarette and blew out a perfect ring. 'Ah well, that's the interesting part, Frank. Life is full of little surprises, you know that, and it sprung one on me that night. I was down, leg shot to hell, and one of them was bending down over me. I thought I was on my way to meet your boss,' he laughed, pointing heavenward.

There was another pause as Jamie thought about what had happened that night and how much to disclose. 'The man standing over me pulled off my mask and I looked up into his eyes... and then he did what you did a minute ago. He let out a gasp. He knew me. Why he did what he did after that, I still don't know... other than it's the reason I'm here this weekend. He gave me this,' he continued, lifting his fingers to his temple. 'It was a hell of a shot. A couple of millimetres to the left and I wouldn't be here enjoying this whisky,' he finished, swallowing down what remained in the glass and raising the tumbler for a refill.

Father Daly rose from his chair and went for the bottle, returning with it and sitting down again. He filled Jamie's glass and topped up his own.

'What happened after that is a bit of a blur. I don't remember much. They left me there to die, I suppose. I managed to crawl back towards the border... but I didn't make it. I was picked up by the SAS. They brought me back over the border into the North and I was airlifted to a hospital in Belfast.'

They drank in silence for a while as darkness descended in the room. For Frank Daly, a clue to Jamie's return was in what he had said. It was something to do with the man who had shot him, though what that was he doubted he would find out. Not now anyway. He noticed Jamie eyeing his watch, timing his call to his wife, he surmised.

'Would you like me to walk with you down to the telephone box?' he asked. He didn't add that Possilpark was a rough area and there was safety in numbers, especially when one of the number was wearing a dog-collar. He didn't need to. Jamie Raeburn had no need of help when it came to things like that. The offer was merely one of company.

Jamie smiled. 'Thanks Frank, but I can manage on my own. It'll give me a moment to work out how much more I can tell you... and don't take that the wrong way. I trust you. I just don't want you involved in this.'

'And is that why you won't phone from here?'

Jamie smiled again. 'I suppose,' he conceded. 'The forces of darkness have big ears, sharp eyes and long arms,' he laughed. 'I expect to be followed while I'm here... don't think they've latched onto me yet, but who knows. I don't want them tapping your phone.'

'They wouldn't do that, surely,' the Priest responded indignantly. 'This is a church, a chapel house.'

'For a man of your age who has seen evil in just about all of its forms, Frank, you're still a wee bit naïve,' Jamie laughed dryly. 'They don't care about things like that. They probably even bug the Prime Minister and the toilets in Buckingham Palace. I don't think St Gregory's Chapel House would cause them to lose any sleep.'

The Priest smiled, embarrassed. 'I spoke without thinking... You're right of course. They don't care.'

Jamie rose up from his chair and handed over his empty glass. 'I'll go just now. France is an hour ahead of us.'

The Priest nodded. 'Remember, dinner is at seven and we don't want to upset Mrs Murphy. If you're late I'll hear about it for the next week.'

***

Jamie returned about forty minutes later. The priest watched him as he entered the study. He looked despondent. 'Problem,' he asked, showing his concern.

'Not a problem, not really, I just don't like being away from Kate and the kids, especially just now with the baby just arrived. She doesn't complain but...' He paused. 'I'm not being fair, am I?'

'I'm not the one to ask, am I? Does she know what you do?'

'Not all of it... but she's not stupid Frank, she has worked it out. It's hard to hide wounds like the ones I pick up. If she thinks about it, I come back so somebody else probably doesn't. I haven't spelled it out to her but I don't think I need to.'

'You still want out?'

'It's stronger than want, Frank. I have to get out.'

The Priest poured him another glass of Laphraoig and passed it over, watching as he downed half of it.

They settled down just as Mrs Murphy backed into the room with a tray laden with plates, condiments and utensils. That killed their conversation. She pottered about laying the table for a minute and then scuttled back to her kitchen, returning with a large dish of Irish stew and two smaller dishes of potatoes and peas. It smelled good and Jamie smiled appreciatively but raised his eyebrows inquisitively. 'Should you be eating meat on a Friday?' he whispered with Mrs Murphy out of earshot.

The Priest smiled. 'No, I shouldn't, but I missed it last night and Mrs Murphy wasn't best pleased. Anyway, waste is a greater sin, so tuck in.'

Jamie did just that. The whisky was making him hungry.

The whisky was making him hungry.

Conversation over the meal consisted of small talk. On this occasion it ranged from the sublime to the ridiculous; Britain joining the European

Community, the marriage of Princess Anne and Captain Mark Phillips and the new television sitcom, "The Last of The Summer Wine" and, naturally, the weather. The usual things people talk about when they have nothing important to discuss - or when they are trying to avoid the important things they have to discuss. Their conversation didn't extend to the vote in Northern Ireland to remain a part of the Union. That was too close to the important issues they were trying to avoid... for the moment.

With the meal finished and everything cleared away, Mrs Murphy took her leave. They waited until they heard the front door of the Chapel House close before they returned to the serious matters they had left earlier.

The Priest poured two generous measures of the malt whisky and offered Jamie a cigarette. They lit up and relaxed for a moment, enjoying the Laphroaig, before Father Daly posed the question that was still troubling him.

'Why was it necessary to tell people you were dead?' he asked, keeping his voice low.

Jamie sighed. 'The less you know about that the better, Frank,' he replied, but he knew he would divulge more, even as he said it. 'The IRA man who shot me - the one who knew me – is an informer, a tout.' He paused to let that snippet of information sink in before continuing. Frank Daly's face remained impassive and it was hard to tell what he thought of that. 'The thing is,' he carried on at last. 'That man saved my life... only just, I admit,' he added with a cold laugh. 'But the men with him believed he had killed me. He'd just shot a British agent and that agent, me, had to stay dead. It wasn't hard,' he laughed again, colder still. 'I was already more than half way there. But the thinking was that if the person who betrayed me discovered I was still alive that would be bad for the informer.' He let that statement hang in the air for a moment. 'The options open to me were either to disappear and play dead or... well, I'm sure you can guess the alternative.'

The Priest looked at him open mouthed, clearly shocked. He shook his head in disbelief. 'I can't believe that,' he said. 'What about your wife? Your children?'

Jamie raised an eyebrow but said nothing.

'Never!' Father Frank continued.

Jamie turned to him and drank down some of the whisky. 'I've been doing this too long Frank,' he said dejectedly. 'But I know what they're capable of doing to protect a source or an agent. Remember, they wiped my past clean and I'm sure some of the men I've killed were taken out to protect someone else. It's the way it works,' he said finally, downing the remainder of his drink.

The priest refilled his glass and Jamie nodded his thanks. He shouldn't be here, he was thinking, involving this good man in the evil that was his world. Frank Daly, he knew, would dispute that... tell him it was a Priest's lot to confront evil, but that didn't make him feel any better.

'So why are you here in Glasgow and not still in France?' Frank Daly asked as he settled back in his chair.

'I don't really know the answer to that,' Jamie replied quietly. 'The IRA man insisted he would deal only with me in relation to some big attack that's going to take place. Part of the deal is that once he gives over that intelligence we bring him out... New identity, new life, somewhere far away. That's the part they're telling me about and by "they" I mean my lot and the Irishman, but there's a hidden agenda. I just don't know what it is.'

'And you're here to meet this IRA informer?'

Jamie nodded.

'Can I help?'

Jamie shook his head emphatically this time. 'No Frank, there's nothing you can do. You help enough by listening and that alone can get you into trouble if anyone thinks we're close.'

'They would hardly think we're close Jamie, we meet about once a year,' the older man laughed quietly. 'When are you meeting this man?' he asked.

'Tomorrow afternoon.'

'And do you still want to visit Jack's grave?'

'Aye, I do. I'll go tomorrow morning, early.'

'Then let me come with you.'

Jamie swithered at that suggestion. 'I'm not sure that's wise,' he said.

'Why? What could possibly be suspicious about us visiting Jack's grave. If your people know your background as well as you think they do, they'll check back and they'll come to the obvious conclusion,' he argued and waited for a counter from Jamie. There was none. 'I'm coming with you,' he said with finality.

Jamie smiled grimly and conceded defeat. 'Okay,' he said. 'I'll meet you there in the morning.'

'Indeed you will not,' the Priest retorted indignantly. 'You will come here and I will run you up there and bring you back.'

'You've got a car?'

'An old one, a Morris Countryman, but it runs well and my old legs aren't what they used to be,' Father Daly laughed. 'So I'll expect you here at nine o'clock tomorrow morning... And now we'll have another whisky,' he said, bringing the discussion to an end.

Jamie left St Gregory's Chapel House at nine thirty, Father Daly having insisted that he phone for a taxi. That, on reflection, was a good idea as by that time they had finished off three quarters of the bottle of Laphroaig and Jamie had consumed the greater part of that. His head was beginning to spin and that, in his present situation, was not good. His intended visit to the Waldorf would have to wait until another time.

Chapter Eighteen

Saturday 6 October

It was a bright cold morning. Jamie left the hotel early and set off at a brisk pace along Sauchiehall Street towards the City Centre. A hearty breakfast had cured the lingering effects of the Laphroaig from the night before. The walk now would clear the remaining cobwebs from his head. The night with Frank sent out a warning. There would be no more heavy boozing on this trip, he decided.

He was early for his appointment with the Priest but he had good reason. He had detours to make, lots of them, before arriving at St Gregory's. He was glad now that he had accepted the old Priest's offer of company this morning. It would be a lonely vigil without him. And maybe Frank was right; Ultra knew all about Jack Connolly's murder and his involvement in the aftermath of it. They would be aware of Frank Daly's role so what was suspicious about the two of them, the friend and the Priest who had buried Jack, visiting his grave? Nothing, he decided.

Still, it would be better if their visit to St Kentigern's didn't come to the attention of the Brigadier. The old man had a nasty habit of using little things like that to further his own ends. He kept his head down and strode purposefully towards Charing Cross. The trees were starting to shed their leaves and he kicked his way through mounds of brown, gold and yellow foliage that had gathered on the pavements and roadsides. The leaves added a splash of colour to the otherwise drab city streets and the dull sandstone buildings that bore the evidence of the city's industrial past.

He caught a bus at St George's Road, stepping onto the rear platform at the last moment as the bus pulled away from the stop. If anyone was following him that would have left them flat-footed but he sensed he was still on his own. His personal alarm system, his sixth sense, wasn't sending out any warnings just yet but he didn't want to rely too much on that. He had been out of the field for a while. He was rusty.

The bus conductress arrived at his side, ticket machine and cash bag swinging perilously close to his cheek. She was middle aged with her hair tied back in a severe bun, a skirt about two sizes too small for her and too much makeup covering the cracks. He asked for Keppochill Road and smiled up at her as she rang up his ticket and tore it from the roll. She didn't return the smile and moved on. PMT or menopause, he thought cruelly.

Jamie sat back and watched the buildings drift past. A disturbance at the front of the bus caught his attention. The conductress was arguing with another passenger at the front, a large, rotund man with a florid complexion and poor taste in clothes. The language was choice, the kind that turns air blue, but completely unintelligible to anyone who wasn't a native. Hostilities were still in progress when he stepped down from the bus in Keppochhill Road. Now that was a woman with balls, he decided, revising his opinion of her. Even he would have thought twice about getting into an argument with that bruiser. It took a special kind of woman to work as a clippie in this city.

The road was empty. There was no traffic and no people. He turned back towards Saracen Street and walked quickly to the entrance to St Gregory's. A Corporation bus came trundling down Saracen Street towards him from Lambhill, its engine roaring and its exhaust belching out thick black diesel smoke. He looked up as it passed, scanning the windows for faces he knew. It was an automatic reaction. It was something he did without thinking in the past but in those days there was a chance he would recognise someone. Now, he realised, people had moved on... physically, and in their minds.

Father Daly was waiting for him outside the Chapel House. A highly polished old shooting brake, a Morris Countryman, with its wooden spars varnished and shining in the pale morning sunlight, stood idling beside him. A plume of white exhaust smoke came from its rattling tail pipe and rose into the cold air before disappearing into the ether. The Priest gave him a welcoming wave and then slipped in behind the steering wheel.

Jamie pulled the door opened and gave an appreciative nod. The old car was in excellent condition and had clearly been well looked after by its previous owner. The leather seats were cracked a little but that was only to be expected of a car its age. The fact it was still running was a minor miracle, its condition on the other hand was on par with the raising of Lazarus, he mused. He gave a small snort of a laugh at that particular thought; wasn't he Lazarus?

Frank Daly was dressed for the cold. A heavy black coat covered his suit and a woollen scarf played the same role with his dog-collar. He had a pair of galoshes over his outdoor shoes. 'A precaution,' he said, when he caught Jamie looking at them. A pair of leather driving gloves completed the picture. He eyed Jamie up and down. 'I see you've changed...a bit more conservative today, eh? The suit is a nice touch.'

Jamie wasn't sure if there was sarcasm embedded in the comment so he ignored it, turning instead to the car. 'Nice jalopy,' he said with a grin as he settled into the worn passenger seat. 'Nearly as old as me,' he added.

'But in far better condition,' the old priest laughed. 'Not so many dents to its body work.' They both laughed at that. 'I picked it up from an old lady who had looked after it from the day she picked it up from the garage twelve years ago. She had a stroke about six months ago and can't drive now. I take her out for a drive in it every now and then.'

'One of your flock, is she?'

'No, the wife of an old friend sadly passed. She lives out on the south side, Muirend. You wouldn't expect one of my parishioners here to own a car, never mind a car like this,' he said. He sounded serious but Jamie wasn't sure if he was joking or not.

They drove up Saracen Street past the Connolly's old tenement flat. 'Do the Connollys still live there?' Jack asked, feeling guilty for the fact that he hadn't kept in touch.

'Mr and Mrs Connolly are still there. The children are all gone...moved away to the New Towns, Cumbernauld and East Kilbride.'

'And Anne-Marie?'

'Yes, Anne-Marie too,' the Priest replied with a knowing smile. He hadn't been blind to the closeness of Jamie Raeburn and Anne-Marie Connolly. 'She's married now...I conducted the ceremony...she lives out in Bishopbriggs.'

Jamie nodded absently. Memories of the weeks surrounding Jack's murder and funeral came flooding back to him...a vision of Anne-Marie clinging to him in the big black limousine as they followed this same route six years before foremost in his mind.

'Is she happy?' he asked.

Frank Daly gave a soft laugh. 'I think so. Her husband's a nice lad...they've got a little girl. Don't think you need to play the surrogate big brother with that one,' he added with a grin. His face became serious then. 'She took it hard when she heard you were dead...the whole family did. You were like a son and brother to them.'

So news of my supposed demise spread quickly, did it? Jamie mused.

'How did they find out?' he asked.

'I told them...I thought they had a right to know. They thought a lot of you,' Father Daly responded without hesitation.

Jamie nodded. He knew that part but wondered what they would think of him now if they knew what he had been doing since that fateful day six years earlier.

The old Priest read his thoughts. 'No one knows what you've been up to, Jamie,' he said, smiling softly. 'But to be honest, I don't think it would change their opinion of you even if they did.'

'Well let's hope I never have to test your theory,' Jamie replied, wiping an unintended tear from his eye with a fingertip before regaining control.

They passed the rest of the journey in silence, Jamie gazing out at the houses that lined Balmore Road, tenements becoming four in a block and semi-detached council houses, as they passed through Milton on their right and Lambhill on the left. They stopped at the traffic lights at Skirsa Street for a moment, allowing a milk float and two vans to exit the housing scheme and head off down towards Possil and beyond. It was not much further now, Jamie reflected, and a wave of sadness welled up in him.

Father Daly noticed the change in him but said nothing. He selected first gear and pulled away, turning left into Skirska Street and then right onto Tresta Road. They made their way through the housing estate and the entrance St Kentigern's appeared on their right just before the main entrance to the Western Necropolis.

The Priest parked the Morris beside another two cars in the car park and they alighted, Jamie slipping off his coat and leaving it on the seat. They then made their way through the ranks of grave stones towards Jack Connolly's resting place. A tall black headstone appeared on their left and Jamie stopped, his attention caught by the gold gilt motif of a boxer set atop the polished granite. Benny Lynch, died 6th August 1946, undefeated flyweight champion of the world.

One of Scotland's greats, Jamie reflected, as a thought of another entered his mind; the irrepressible Andy Lynch, also known as "Benny", the wee man with the big heart who had shared digs with him, and much else, in Nottingham. He wondered what had become of him, smiled wanly and moved on.

Jack Connolly's grave was marked by a grey granite headstone erected by his family. Withered flowers wilted limply in a glass beside the stone, their petals forming a carpet of faded colour on the green turf. The grass was wet. Jamie's suit might have been a nice touch, as Frank Daly suggested, but it was ill suited to kneeling beside a grave. He was glad he had left his coat in the car. He crouched down on his haunches and rested one hand on the gravestone for balance.

Father Daly moved back a few paces to give him space and Jamie smiled gratefully. He closed his eyes, picturing Jack in his mind's eye. He saw him as he had been; bright eyed and mischievous. What would he be like today, he wondered? He spoke to Jack in his head, formulating questions that would never be answered and repeating apologies that would never be heard. Not in this world anyway.

He was still hunched over when he heard footsteps on the gravel path that ran alongside the graves and Father Daly murmuring a greeting. He opened his eyes and turned. Anne-Marie Connolly stood there, gazing down at him as though she had seen a ghost which, on reflection, she had.

Her expression was one of bemusement mixed with consternation with a little hope thrown in. She held a fresh bunch of flowers in her hands and her eyes alternated between Jamie and the Priest as though awaiting an explanation.

Jamie pushed himself up to his full height and turned towards her, opening his arms. 'Hello Anne-Marie,' he said quietly.

She ran towards him, throwing herself into his arms and burying her head against his chest. 'It is you,' she exclaimed. 'When I saw you kneeling there I wasn't sure...I was scared to hope. Oh God Jamie, you're still alive.'

'Last time I looked in the mirror, aye, I'm still alive,' he laughed warmly. 'It's great to see you. You've grown up...and Father Daly tells me you're married.'

'I gave up waiting for you,' she laughed, happy for a moment. 'And look at you...you're so different. I almost didn't recognise you, but those big brown eyes of yours gave you away.'

She clung to him tightly, the questions tumbling out now. 'What happened to you? Where have you been? How is your family? How long are you staying? Will you have time to visit Ma and Da?'

Jamie tried to field all of her questions gently but some were harder to answer than others..."what happened to you?" being the most difficult.

She was happy his family was well, disappointed that he was not staying long and would not have time to visit her parents, mollified by his promise to visit next time he was home and bemused by the fact he wasn't staying with his own mother and father. He tactfully avoided the one about what had happened to him.

They stayed by the grave for an hour, reminiscing in the main about Jack but talking too about their families. Father Daly hovered around them, like some spiritual referee, intervening when he perceived the talk to be moving towards Jamie's past.

When they finally parted, Anne-Marie was tearful once again but with Jamie's promise to keep in touch, a smile broke through he sniffles. Jamie and Father Daly waved her off in her little blue Morris Mini before climbing into the Priest's shooting brake and following. They were descending back down Balmore Road towards Hawthorn Street before Frank Daly posed the question Jamie had been awaiting.

'And will you keep in touch?' he asked, almost casually.

Jamie gave him a long stare before replying. 'I want to Frank, I really do...'

'Do I detect a "but" coming here?' the old Priest broke in.

'Not so much a "but" as a "hope"...I was about to say that I hope I can keep the promise. I want my old life back...and Anne-Marie and the rest of the Connollys are a part of that.'

Father Daly gave a faint smile but kept his eyes on the road. 'And the "but" in all that is that it isn't up to you, is it? Knowing you as I do, you'll try to do things yourself,' he added. 'You don't like involving the people who care for you in things that might harm them, I understand that, but sometimes it's prudent to ask for help. It isn't a sign of weakness, you know,' he said, flicking his eyes towards Jamie for an instant as the car came to a halt at the traffic lights.

'If I need help I'll ask Frank, that's a promise. But you're right; I don't like involving others. When I do it means I have to watch out for them as well as myself...and that's a weakness.'

They finished the rest of the journey in silence, Father Daly pulling off Saracen Street and into the Chapel grounds before stopping. They sat in an awkward silence for a while with the engine idling before the old Priest spoke again.

'Will you come up for a cup of tea before you head off to do whatever it is you have to do?' he asked.

Jamie shook his head. 'Thanks Frank, but I've got a lot to do. I really appreciate you being there with me this morning. You talk about me asking for help...but with you I don't need to ask,' he said, smiling. 'Why you give help to a heathen like me I don't know,' he carried on, laughing softly. 'But I do appreciate it.'

He held out his hand and Frank Daly gripped it tightly. 'You'll keep in touch with me though,' he said. It wasn't a question.

Jamie gave another short laugh. 'Aye Frank, I'll keep in touch with you.' He shook his friend's hand and then opened the car door, shivering as the chill air outside caught him. He turned back, smiling. 'Thanks, he said. 'For everything.'

With that, he eased himself out of the car and gently closed the door, tapping the window with his fingers before walking off down the drive towards the roadway. As he stepped through the big stone pillars that held the gates he turned around. The car sat where he had left it, exhaust smoke rising into the cold air and almost obscuring Frank Daly's face. Jamie raised his hand in a wave and disappeared behind the high stone wall.

Chapter Nineteen

He walked steadily down the road. His senses were now on full alert. There had been no one following him earlier, he was sure of that, but they would be out looking for him now. The Brigadier had people everywhere, he reminded himself, thinking of the two men involved in his entrapment back in 1968. They were both professionals and if they or others like them were looking for him now they would find him.

What to do now was a problem. Sir Charles would know by now that he hadn't come by plane. The airports, both London and Glasgow would have been watched. The old boy would be wondering what he was playing at and would probably be livid that his plan had been thwarted. That thought brought a smile to his face. But he still hadn't worked out why the old man would want to pick up Liam Fitzpatrickin the first place if what he said was true. But then, the truth of anything was always in doubt when dealing with the Brigadier. It was there some of the time, not all of the time... and certainly not *most* of the time.

It was still early, not yet ten thirty, and he had time to kill. He returned to the Lorne and made a call home. Kate was surprised to hear from him again but her delight was obvious.

'Missing me?' she teased before he had time to say anything.

'You'll never know how much,' he parried. 'I'd much rather be back there with you than over here on my own.'

'That was your decision,' she retorted, a little too quickly. 'So how is sunny Glasgow?' she asked. 'You didn't really tell me last night. And how is Father Daly?'

'Glasgow is Glasgow... grey and damp, and Frank's fine. He told me to pass on his love.'

'Have you been to Jack's grave?' she asked, her voice low and melancholic. Her sadness was palpable.

'Yeah, Frank insisted on coming with me. He drove me up there in his car.'

'He's got a car?' She queried disbelievingly.

Jamie laughed, despite his gloom. 'Those were my words too,' he said. 'I was glad of his company though. It would have been difficult without him.'

'Yes, I imagine it would have been... it's so sad... and being alone would have made it harder.'

'I wouldn't have been alone,' he replied gently. 'Jack's sister was there... Anne-Marie,' he added.

At the other end of the line Kate smiled sadly. She felt a twinge of jealousy. 'The youngest... the one who had a crush on you?' she said, without thinking. She was angry with herself now. 'I'm sorry, I didn't mean that,' she added quickly. 'How is she?'

'All grown up. She's married with a baby daughter. She asked some awkward questions... Frank being there helped.'

There was an awkward silence for a moment and Jamie could hear the children laughing in the background. 'They don't seem to be missing me much,' he remarked, changing the subject less than subtly. He heard Kate snort a little laugh.

'They haven't stopped asking me when you'll be home from the minute you left,' she retorted. 'They're driving me up the wall,' she added, laughing, before her tone grew serious again. 'When are you coming home?' she asked.

'Sunday,' he replied quickly. 'Monday at the very latest.'

'What awkward questions did Anne-Marie ask?'

Jamie groaned inwardly. He didn't really want to go down this line; wished he hadn't raised it. It brought back too many bad memories, for both of them. 'You know the sort of thing,' he answered, keeping it vague. 'Where had we been, what had happened?'

'Was that all?'

'No, like Frank, she was surprised to see me. Maybe shocked is more accurate... a bit like Mary Magdalene when she found the stone rolled away,' he laughed awkwardly. 'Coming back from the dead seems to have that effect on people.'

'How did she know?'

'Frank told the family... He thought it only right. I can't be angry. The Connollys were like a second family to me. Word of my death spread around and word of my miraculous reappearance will spread as quickly. I didn't want that. It might make things difficult.'

'All the more reason for coming back soon. Be careful. I know you.'

He laughed softly. 'I will be... don't worry.'

'I can't not worry Jamie. I love you.'

'I know, I love you too,' he replied as gently as he could, trying to ease the fear out of her.

'So what are you doing next?'

'Meeting Liam Fitzpatrick, you know that.'

She laughed nervously. 'Of course, I'm sorry. I'm just not thinking. Where are you meeting him?' Jamie didn't answer and Kate suddenly realised why. 'You don't think...' she said with a gasp, not finishing the question.

'No, I don't think that,' he said reassuringly. 'I'm just being cautious, that's all.' He didn't know if the telephone in the house in France could be tapped or not. On balance, he thought it unlikely, but Sir Charles Redmond had contacts everywhere and especially in France. There were people there who owed him and he wouldn't be slow in calling in a debt if it suited him, Jamie mused. Better not to think like that. He heard his baby son cry in the background and Lauren talking urgently to Kate. A deep sadness engulfed him.

What am I doing here?'

'I'll have to go, honey' Kate said awkwardly, torn between him and their son. 'Jack needs me.'

'Okay. I'll call you later. Tell the kids I love them.'

'I will... and Jamie, be careful. I love you.'

'Love you too,' he said as he hung up the phone and lay back on the bed, staring vacantly at the ceiling, oblivious to everything else around him.

He ate a light lunch in the Snaffle-bit pub about a hundred yards from the hotel. It consisted of two rolls filled with crispy rashers of bacon topped with melted cheese, an old favourite from his university days, when he would sit in this same pub and enjoy the banter with his fellow students. That brought back happier memories than those he had been recalling earlier. He washed down the food with a pint shandy; a half of McEwan's 80-shilling Export mixed with a half of lemonade. No more hard liquor, he reminded himself.

It was one o'clock when he left the Snaffle Bit and began his journey to Paradise. He was lucky and picked up a cruising taxi near the Lorne where the cabbie had just dropped a fare. This was where it would start to get tricky. He asked the driver to take him to "The Barras", Glasgow's famous market, telling him to drop him in London Road. Then he settled back to consider his next moves.

He had chosen his drop off point carefully. It was a Saturday and The Barras would be busy with shoppers. The place was also on one of the main routes from the city out to Parkhead and the pubs in the area would be spilling drunks out onto the pavement to start their pilgrimage. He could blend in easily. He paid off the cab at the dogleg on London Road, opposite Glasgow Green, and slipped down Ross Street to Suffolk Street, negotiating his way carefully through the crowds surrounding the stalls.

Nothing and nobody moved fast. People wandered slowly from stall to stall rummaging through bric a brac, old furniture, tools, clothing and fakes of every description. The mass of humanity moved like sluggish tidal water with a coat of heavy oil on top, all seeming to move one way and then another like some choreographed dance sequence. Jamie eased his way through, wrinkling his nose at the smells that assailed his nostrils; cheap perfumes and after shave, sweat, mothballs and damp. He made it at last to Kent Street and from there to the Gallowgate, turning from time to time and retracing his steps as though browsing. If he was being tailed, they were good, he surmised. Bloody good.

He joined the flow of fans in Gallowgate and attached himself to a group of men dressed not unlike himself. Conservatively. He tried to blend in, tagging along as though part of the little band. They passed the main entrance to The Barrowland Ballroom and the crowd swelled. Singing began and "carry outs" were opened, cans of beer being distributed like rationing was imminent. Kick off was still about an hour and a half away but already some of the fans were pished. Jamie grinned. It wasn't a display of cockiness or arrogance with these guys, they just liked their "bevvy" like most Glaswegian men.

It would be no different over in Govan. The pubs at Govan Cross and all along Paisley Road West would be spewing out "Bears" on their way to Ibrox and they would be in a similar state. He grinned wryly to himself. Given the choice, he would rather be in Govan. He thought of Jack. If he was looking down on this scene just now, would be pissing himself.

The throng multiplied as he passed Abercrombie Street and he soon found himself in the middle of a swaying, singing, chanting mass that swept everything before it. Cars, busses and taxis ground to a halt. There was something tribal about it. There would be a similar horde swarming along London Road past Bridgeton Cross and the police would be out in force down there to keep the warring factions apart. Discretion was the better part of valour as far as Jamie was concerned and taking the London Road route was a bit like walking through the valley of the shadow of death to reach Paradise. Then again, he mused, laughing quietly to himself, maybe the guy who penned the words of the 23rd Psalm all those years before had divine foresight and knew all about the Brig'ton Billy Boys.

He stayed close to his chosen group, keeping close enough to appear a part of it but at the same time far enough apart to divorce himself from it if the need arose. He gave his unknowing companions a closer look. They were all about his own age and were all well dressed in a uniform sort of way. That set alarm bells jangling. They could be a team, a gang, and if that were the case he would have to keep his wits about him. War could break out without warning.

The searchers finally caught up with him at Whitevale Street in the shadows of the multi-storey flats. He couldn't see them but he knew they were there. The hairs on the back of his neck stood on end and that was a sure sign. There would be more than one team, probably two or three, interchanging at intervals so that he couldn't pick them out. Shaking them would be difficult.

His kept up with the group but he didn't need it now. He'd been made. He worked through his options. He could try to throw them off his scent but he didn't hold out much hope of that. What else could he do other than hope Liam was on the ball? But there was a downside to that. If Liam spotted the tails and aborted there was no fall back. So what then? If they missed this one his journey was a waste of time unless Liam Fitzpatrick had something else up his sleeve. He couldn't rely on that.

It came to him suddenly. He could confront them. It was an alternative of sorts. Isolate them, challenge them and give them an ultimatum... Back off or I abort the rendezvous. He could picture the Brigadier's face when that message filtered through to him. It was worth doing for that alone. But the outcome would depend on what Sir Charles wanted most; the intelligence about the attacks or Liam Fitzpatrick himself.

That still puzzled him. Why would the old boy want to lift Liam now? And why here? He could have done it at any time in Belfast. It didn't make sense. Then again, he mused, maybe it was only Liam's paranoia trickling down to him.

He remained attached to the group until they reached Fielden Street. His tails would have him boxed in and Fielden Street presented an opportunity. He pulled away from his adopted pals and turned right. That would throw them, he thought grimly. Their box would now be in disarray. The tails in front were now way out of position. The ones behind had to follow and Fielden Street was ideal for what he had in mind. There would be no more interchanging by the teams to avoid detection. They were all out of position. He smiled coldly.

Unlike Gallowgate, Fielden Street was virtually deserted. Not only that, there were no hiding places. This part of the East-end was being redeveloped and where there had once been old tenements there was no only vacant lots, demolition sites with weed growing through the mud, rubble and litter. The place was like a bomb site. There was no reason for anyone to be here. He smiled at his shadows' predicament. Follow and risk being blown or pull back and risk losing him.

He sauntered along casually now, following the road down towards Crownpoint Road. He kept his eyes to the front. He didn't turn round. There was no need. They were either behind him or they weren't. He would soon find out.

When he reached the junction with Crownpoint Road he stopped abruptly, pulled his cigarettes from his coat pocket and took his time in selecting one from the pack. He flicked his lighter, lit the cigarette and drew in a lungful of smoke. Only then did he turn to look back up Fielden Street towards Gallowgate... And there they were, two of them, a couple; a youngish man and a woman of indeterminate age. That was a surprise. He hadn't expected a woman.

They had stopped about thirty yards behind him, trying and failing to look inconspicuous. They were arguing or pretending to argue. Jamie wasn't taken in. He grinned, making sure they saw him, and then, without warning, he walked back up Fielden Street towards them. The argument stopped and their faces took on resigned expressions.

'Nice day for it,' Jamie said easily as he approached them. 'What's the matter? She not coming across?' he added, laughing. The young man looked back at him, bemused. 'Haggling over the price, is she?' Jamie went on. 'Or is she a bit too expensive for you? She looks expensive... and bit out of place in this shit hole,' he carried on relentlessly, starting to laugh. The woman stared back at him and he could see the anger simmering behind her eyes. The man still looked bemused.

'You took your time,' Jamie said. His tone was no longer jocular. 'What kept you?'

The woman stepped closer. 'What the hell are you talking about?' she asked angrily. 'And who the hell are you anyway?'

Jamie laughed aloud. Her voice gave her away. Definitely not east-end Glasgow. And her clothes were more House of Fraser than C&A.

'You think we're following you?' the woman went on, trying to sound incredulous. 'We just happen to be going where you're going,' she continued, unabashed.

'Of course you're not,' Jamie replied, laughing again. His raised eyebrows told her he didn't believe a word. 'Because you think you know where I'm headed anyway - Parkhead, Terracing, Section c and third barrier on the left at row G... Right?'

The woman held his look. She said nothing, just kept staring back at him. The man stared off into space. It was clear who was in charge here.

'There is just one small problem with that,' Jamie continued, concentrating on the woman now. 'I lied.'

Her expression didn't change but a flicker of consternation passed across her eyes. Jamie waited, weighing her up. She was in her late twenties, maybe older, with long dirty blonde hair tied back in a pony-tail. She was quite fit, in every way, he decided. She was dressed in denim dungaree trousers with a green cheesecloth shirt beneath the bib front and a heavy jacket with the buttons open. The Doc Marten boots were a nice touch, he mused, smiling inwardly. She was still looking back at him, probably considering him in the same way, he imagined.

But this was getting them nowhere, Jamie mused. He let out a sigh and continued. 'Here's what we're going to do,' he said. 'I'm heading on down to London Road and you're going to stay here. Tell the rest of your people to back off. Call Sir Charles and tell him I clocked you. He can wait for my report. If I see any of you on my tail or if I even suspect you're there I'll abort the meeting and you can tell the old man that too. I'll be on the next train south after that. Think you can manage that?' he finished off, with just a hint of sarcasm.

The woman stared back at him angrily for a moment then her anger subsided. She gave him a cold smile. 'I was told you were an arrogant sod,' she said. 'They were right.' Jamie simply smiled back at her and cocked one eyebrow. 'Okay,' she conceded at last. 'But you're making a mistake and he's not going to like it. You've no idea what you're getting into,' she added.

Jamie kept smiling. Now that, at least, is the truth, he mused.

She turned to her companion and nodded almost imperceptibly. Jamie tensed but the man just turned away and began the walk back up to Gallowgate. The woman lingered for a moment longer, her eyes fixed on his. He noticed them properly for the first time. They were ice blue, the whites as clear as virgin snow, and they sparkled. Spruced up, she would be quite a looker. She smiled, maybe sensing his thoughts, then turned away to follow her colleague. 'Good luck,' she threw back over her shoulder. 'You might need it.'

'Don't worry about me, love,' he called after her. 'I've got nine lives.' His laugh too would have reached her. He didn't bother to add that he had already used up most of them but he doubted if she would be interested.

Jamie stood at the corner of Crownpoint Road for a while watching them retrace their steps. They didn't look back. They stopped momentarily when they met up with the other two men he had seen and he saw the men look in his direction. He gave them a wave. He took his cigarettes and his Zippo from his pocket and lit another fag. It tasted bitter in his mouth. When the four disappeared into the green mass heading east along Gallowgate he threw the remains of the cigarette to the ground and strolled away.

His ultimatum would be relayed, he had no doubt about that. It probably already had been. The question was, would Sir Charles listen, because the decision, at the end of the day, would be his and his alone.

***

The crowd in London Road swirled around him. It was another surging, swaying, boisterous mass of high spirited humanity heading for Paradise. Years before he had asked Jack why it place was called Paradise. It seemed an incongruous name for a place built in the middle of what was probably the biggest shit hole in the city. Jack had an answer though whether it was Gospel or not was debateable. It all stemmed, Jack said, from when the ground was built. The original pitch had been a few hundred yards away from the present stadium, at the corner of Springfield Road and London Road. The club paid buttons for rent there and then the landlord, a dyed in the wool Hun according to Jack, bumped up the rent from £50 to £450 a year. The club decided to move and when it did a journalist at the time said it was like "leaving the graveyard to enter paradise". The name stuck.

As far as Jamie was concerned, it was still a graveyard. He grinned inanely and joined the "mourners" for what he hoped would be a good funeral today when Motherwell buried them. It might help if somebody tied Jimmy "Jinky" Johnstone's boot laces together, right enough.

The stadium loomed ahead of him. The crowd were in high spirits, the team on a roll after their 3-0 drubbing of Turkish side TPS Turku three days earlier in the first round of the European Cup. The crowd began breaking up ahead of him, funnelling away towards the various turnstiles situated around the park. Football fans are creatures of habit, he ruminated, congregating at the same spot on then terracing week after week and probably on the same spot their fathers had gathered at and their grand-fathers too come to that.

He scanned the high wall surrounding the ground and made for the turnstile serving Section G. Mounted police sat sedately between the turnstiles, the horses docile but carrying enough menace to keep the lines clear. Beat cops stood by each turnstile waiting for an opportunity to lift a drunk or arrest somebody for trying to sneak in without paying. Fathers and kids lined up together, ready for the age old ritual of lifting the kid over the gate and sneaking them into the game. It was an accepted part of each Saturday and the police turned a blind eye to it.

The lines began to bunch as the queue approached the gates and some jostling occurred. Jamie felt himself buffeted from behind and angry voices were raised. He felt hands on his shoulders and people around him staggered about for a moment, holding onto one another for support. A cop by the gate looked over and moved towards the turmoil but stopped when placatory sounds came from the source of the problem and the crowd settled down once again.

A kid of about 9 years of age tugged at his sleeve and Jamie looked down at him. He was wearing shorts and a dirty old jacket and had a smudge of dirt on his face. He was grinning up at Jamie. 'Gimme a lift ower the turnstile Mister?' he pleaded, still holding onto Jamie's coat sleeve.

'You on yer own?' Jamie asked, looking around.

'Naw, ma pals are already away through. Ah jist want a lift ower the gate. Gonnae gies wan?'

Jamie laughed. 'Right, come on,' he said, manoeuvring the urchin in front of him.

They shuffled forward slowly and the clicking of the turnstile gates grew louder. Finally, they were at the gate. Jamie put his arms under the boy's oxters and lifted him up, swung him over the barrier and dropped him on the other side. The gate keeper smiled, took his entry money and the turnstile opened.

The boy was waiting patiently on the other side. 'You still here?' Jamie joked. 'I thought you'd be away to meet yer pals.'

'Aye, ah will. But first ah've tae gie ye this,' he said, holding out a folded piece of paper. Jamie looked around suspiciously as he took the paper.

'Who gave you this?' he said quietly, just loud enough to be heard.

'A man... an Irishman,' the boy said innocently. 'He said ye'd gimme a reward.'

Jamie relaxed and laughed. 'You'll go far, wee man,' he said as he rummaged in his coat pocket. He brought out some coins, found two fifty pence pieces and handed them over. 'Get yourself a pie an' a Bovril at half time,' he said, still laughing. The boy grinned, gave him a mock salute and disappeared into the crowd. Jamie checked his watch. The time was now twenty minutes to three.

He made his way up the stairs leading to the top of the terracing and along to the passage at aisle G, the folded scrap of paper still clutched tightly in his hand. He looked around him, searching for tails, but saw no one suspicious. But in this crowd, how could he be sure.

The teams were out warming up, Celtic nearest this end of the ground in their familiar green and white hoops and Motherwell at the far end in their claret and amber strip. The rain had stayed off and to his surprise, Jamie found himself looking forward to the game. It had been a long time since he had been at a match. So long he couldn't remember the last one but it was before Jack's murder, he reflected gloomily. Maybe it was fitting that his return to the game should be here rather than across the city at Ibrox.

He chose a circuitous route to the barrier at row L and found a gap there. A group of older men already ensconced there edged along to give him room, clearly intrigued by the foreign looking gentleman joining them. He could imagine the rumour mill starting. By tonight he would probably be a spy for the team's next European opponents.

Jamie smiled to himself and dug into his coat pocket for his cigarettes. He drew out his Gauloise and his zippo and offered the cigarettes to the men at the barrier who accepted with alacrity, and lit up. Everyone began puffing on the fags, thanking him in carefully modulated English, obviously still regarding him as a foreigner. The Gauloise cigarettes had strengthened their belief and they were too polite to say the fags were shit. He nodded back, saying nothing, keeping up the appearance they had bestowed on him.

Only when he returned the packet of cigarettes to his pocket did he unfold the scrap of paper. It had been folded in four and the wods on it had been hurriedly scribbled in block capitals. The message jumped out at him - CHANGE OF PLAN – MEET TONIGHT - CLELLAND BAR - HOSPITAL STREET GORBALS - EIGHT – ACT SURPRISED TO SEE ME - L. Jamie read it twice and slipped it into his coat pocket. Liam, it appeared, did have a back-up plan. He wondered what caused the change. Had Liam spotted the tails earlier or was there something else? So, there would be no meeting here which, when he thought about it, was probably for the best. His appearance was already drawing attention. He sighed and puffed on the Gauloise Bleu. Now he could enjoy the game... if enjoy was the right word. It was Celtic, after all. He thought of Jack again and smiled. He would do it for him.

Chapter Twenty

Gorbals was changing. It had been a while since Jamie had spent any time this side of the river and he found the changes dramatic - and depressing. Great swathes of the area were flattened and high, multi-storey buildings were sprouting up from the debris. Out with the old, in with the new, he mused. These were the new dream homes, castles in the sky people were calling them, the answer to the city's housing problems. Something told him it would end badly, destroying the character of the place and its community spirit.

The streets, once lined by ranks of grimy, soot stained tenements, now wound through piles of rubble. It reminded him of photographs he had seen of Hiroshima after the Yanks had dropped their bomb, the roads zigzagging aimlessly through a barren wilderness.

Occasionally, a building had been left untouched, a church or a pub, like isolated black teeth jutting out of a diseased gum in an otherwise toothless mouth. They stood defiantly amid the devastation, reminders of what had once been.

He had taken a taxi from the Lorne, directing the bemused cabbie to follow a convoluted route via Bridgeton to enter Gorbals via Hutchesontown and along Ballater Street from its east end. The driver didn't complain. If that was what the foreign gent wanted, it was alright by him; and it added a few quid to the fare.

Jamie's destination was Gorbals Street, near the Citizen's Theatre, about the mid-way point between Ballater Street and Cumberland Street.

As the cab neared his drop off point he noticed the desolation that was evident at Hutchesontown was less pronounced here. Lights were on in buildings on both sides of the road but signs of depopulation, deprivation and decay were all around him. Maybe, he mused, the plan was to let the demolition squads hack away at the periphery until the beating heart of the place just gave up. By the time the cranes with their swinging wrecking balls reached here to finish the job, there would be fuck all left. The place would be empty and all the people would have moved to Castlemilk, Easterhouse, Cumbernauld, or East Kilbride.

He came out of his reverie as the taxi approached Crown Street. Beyond that was Gorbals Cross. At the Cross, the taxi would turn left into Gorbals Street and seconds later he would be out on the pavement... on his own. He was stepping into the unknown. He shrugged mentally; it wouldn't be for the first time.

The taxi came to a surprisingly gentle halt just beside the Citizen's and Palace Theatres. He paid the driver, added a generous tip, and stepped out onto the pavement. The façade of the Citizen's Theatre loomed above him, its six pillars reaching to the heavens, topped by statues of William Shakespeare,

Robert Burns and the four muses - music, dance, tragedy and comedy. It was all tragedy these days, he thought dispiritedly. Next to it, the more genteel frontage of The Palace Theatre stood bathed in light beneath its entrance portico. It looked a bit tired despite the welcoming glow.

He stood for a moment, gazing pensively at the buildings, wondering if they would survive the onslaught of so-called progress. They deserved to live on, he thought; the architecture alone was worth saving. He doubted they would though. Kate said he was a cynic. Maybe he was but that didn't alter the fact that lots of magnificent buildings had already been smashed to rubble in the pursuit of progress... and the occasional bung.

He found it all depressing. It reminded him of his early childhood. Townhead had been just like the old Gorbals until "Progress" came along. Progress for Townhead destroyed a community to make way for a new motorway. The tenement his family had lived in now lay beneath compacted rubble and giant slabs of concrete.

He shook his head dejectedly and struck off up the street towards the junction with of Cumberland Street. The iron girders and supports of the railway bridge loomed ahead of him in the lamp lit gloom. The Monumental Sculptors, Lipton's, appeared on his right at the corner of Bedford Lane with Cleland Street on his left. A steady stream of boisterous youths and young girls passed him, all heading into the City and the bright lights. Who could blame them? The weekend provided them with an opportunity to escape the monotony and drudgery of their otherwise boring lives.

He decided on the scenic route. At the junction with Cumberland Street, instead of turning left and following it, he carried on into Cathcart Road, heading for the magnificent Church built by Alexander "Greek" Thomson in the mid-1800s. Another great building that deserved to survive, he reflected, but would it. Anywhere else, it would have been cherished. Here, it would probably be abandoned to the elements and its fate.

He walked round it, the great stone slabs forming the south wall supporting six pillars, Greek of course, above. Hospital Street was on his left and Caledonia Road stretched away east towards the Southern Necropolis. He took a sharp left and followed Hospital Street down towards the river, crossed back over Cumberland Street and on towards his destination. The railway line materialised above the arches on his left, a branch line to St Enoch's Station, now disused. He smiled grimly, wondering if the ghosts of ancient engine drivers and firemen were gazing down on him.

The Clelland Bar appeared in the gloom. He wouldn't have chosen it for the rendezvous. Not that he had ever been in the pub before. He didn't know it but where it was located gave him an inkling of what to expect. The clientele would be second and third generation Irish. There might even be a few over from the old country itself for today's game, he mused uncomfortably. That was probably why Liam picked it, he thought anxiously. Unlike him, Liam would be comfortable here.

He pushed through the door into the public bar. It was like walking into a wall of sound. There was a babble of noise. Voices and conversations bounced off him, all of them completely unintelligible. Cigarette smoke hung in the air and he detected the sweet, sickly smell of weed. He was pleasantly surprised. Saturday night in an Irish pub in Gorbals yet you would never have known. There were no pictures of Celtic "Greats" on the walls, no green, white and gold tri-colours and no tear-jerk paintings or prints of the mist-covered Mountains of Mourne. None of those. It was just a working class pub filled with people more interested in enjoying themselves than changing the world. He still felt uncomfortable though.

He eased his way through to the bar and ran his eyes along the beer pumps. Guinness, Murphy's and Beamish ales were prominent but Tennents Lager, Glasgow's own, also had its place. His unease grew as he neared the bar. He was attracting unwanted attention. He put it down to the fact he was alone and he looked foreign. There were few loners in this place and fewer foreigners. He ordered a pint of Murphy's Stout and waited as the barman poured it carefully and let it settle. His eyes roamed around the bar, searching discretely for Liam. There was no sign of him but he was early by about ten minutes. He lit a Gauloise and let it dangle from his lip, a bit like Humphrey Bogart in Casablanca. The smoke from the French cigarette added to the fug around him and blended into the miasma.

The drinkers here in the public bar were all male and mostly older men with tired, wrinkled and lined faces. These men were here for the drink, nothing more. Alcohol was their drug of choice. The smells around him were all manly; cigarette smoke, BO, Old Spice, beer and stale breath.

He wondered what the Lounge was like. A thick dividing wall separated the two but nothing could keep out the sounds from beyond. He could hear female voices, high pitched, and little squeals of delight mixed with the voices and laughter of younger men. The message had said Clelland Bar, no more than that, and he began to wonder if he was in the wrong part.

He was still anxious. He was a stranger here and the regular punters were watching him suspiciously. He stuck out and it wasn't just his bronzed skin causing that. He nursed his pint, sipping sparingly, and watched the big clock above the bar. Twenty minutes had passed and Liam was now ten minutes late. What was wrong? Cold feet? He discarded the thought.

There was a table at the back of the pub with a couple of free seats and he headed there, pint in hand. The crowd parted before him like the Nile parting for Moses. He wasn't the only one feeling uncomfortable it seemed. What was it about him, he wondered, that made people react like that? As he sat down two old men sitting at the table eased away to give him more room, watching him uneasily. There it was again. He nodded to them, pleasantly enough he thought, but if he made them feel any better it appeared to be marginal. He sipped at his Murphy's again and stared over at the door, doing his best to ignore the awkward looks.

His sigh of relief almost palpable when Liam and three other hard looking men finally entered. Liam was dressed in a leather bomber jacket over an open necked shirt and jeans. The others wore heavy polo neck jumpers over sports jackets. They looked like a bunch of folk singers but their faces didn't fit the profile. He watched carefully as Liam looked around the bar, his eyes finally finding him. The faint smile on Liam's face echoed his own relief though his was tempered by the presence of the three men with the Irishman.

Liam turned away and made for the bar. Jamie's eyes followed. The Irishman ordered drinks, laughing and joking with his companions, but the camaraderie seemed strained.

Jamie saw him look over towards him again and speak to the others. The three men turned in unison, their eyes appraising him. There was a succession of nods and then Liam, pint in hand, was easing his way through the throng towards him. From the smiles and nods he was attracting it was he was well known in the pub. He added that to the list of questions he had for the man.

Liam arrived, a smile fixed on his face but there was strain behind the smile. The smile worked for the two old boys at the table who visibly relaxed. It seemed they knew Liam too... or maybe of him.

'It is Dermott, isn't it?' Liam asked with feigned uncertainty.

'The very same,' Jamie grinned, rising from his seat and holding out his hand.

Liam gripped it tightly, pulled out the free chair from beneath the table with his foot and lowered himself down onto it.

'Jesus Dermott, me auld son, I thought it was you,' he said loudly, shaking Jamie's hand like a dog worrying a bone. 'You're lookin' well, though I almost took you for an Indian with that tan,' he added with a laugh. 'Where have you been hidin'?'

Jamie returned Liam's grip and looked him over. This wasn't the Liam he had met in Belfast years before nor was it the Liam who saved his life at Kiltyclogher six months earlier. The man had changed, dramatically, but his voice and his eyes were the same. His voice was still a rough, gravely baritone and his eyes still sparkled though they were now set in deep dark shadowy circles. 'I won't ask you how you're doin',' he said quietly. 'You look like shit.'

'Thanks Dermott,' Liam replied, forcing a laugh. 'That's just what I needed to hear. You've changed a bit yourself, me auld son.'

'Aye, I took early retirement and got out; emigrated,' he said. 'Until you came along, that is,' he added under his breath.

The two old boys with them began to fidget nervously. They sensed a private conversation that, for their own good, they didn't want to overhear. They finished their pints hurriedly and prepared to leave.

Liam tried to placate them. 'It's alright, lads,' he said quickly. 'We're pals from way back. It's just been a while...You know how it is, eh?.' He held out a couple of pounds. 'Get yourselves a drink on me.' The older man of the two took the proffered money, touched the skip of his flat cap and shuffled away behind his pal.

No wonder the old sod was smiling, Jamie mused. For a couple of quid he and his pal could get pissed and still have something left for a hair of the dog in the morning.

'So, here you are,' Liam continued. He was trying hard to maintain a semblance of calm, Jamie thought.

'Aye, here I am,' Jamie replied. 'Though you could have picked a better meeting place,' he murmured irritably. 'Inconspicuous we are not.'

'I couldn't, Dermott,' he replied under his voice. 'The boys over there would be suspicious if I buggered off and left them. They're not exactly the trustin' sort.

Jamie flicked his eyes towards the men. They were engrossed in their drinks. That didn't ease his mounting disquiet. 'I don't need this, Liam,' he hissed angrily.

'Relax. We're safe. The boys think we're old muckers. I told them you were dead on... said you'd done us a turn a few years ago.' He grinned and gave Jamie a friendly slap on the arm.

Jamie smiled easily but his nerves were on edge. 'Relax? You've been lookin' over your shoulder since you came in here an' you're tellin' me to relax.'

'It's just the nerves, you know what it's like,' Liam murmured. 'You jump at shadows. But they know me here... We're fine,' he repeated.

That was the problem; Jamie knew exactly what it was like. Liam's reassurance didn't help. 'Aye, right!' he hissed. 'I'll take your word for it. So what's the news?'

'I need your help, Dermott. I told you that... An' you owe me... remember.'

Jamie laughed. It was cold and humourless. 'Aye, I remember, and I'm here. So why don't you tell me what the fuck it is you want me to do and let me get out of here. I feel like a fuckin' alien surrounded by all you Tims.'

Liam forced another laugh for appearance sake and his eyes flicked nervously around the bar again. 'Like I said, I need your help.'

'Aye, I heard you. Stop repeatin' yourself an' get to the point before I die of old age.' Another furtive look around by Liam and Jamie started to get annoyed. 'Listen,' he whispered. 'If you're havin' second thoughts about this, let's just call it off. We can meet again, another time, another place.'

Liam shook his head and forced another smile.

'Come on, Liam,' Jamie went on. 'Spit it out... an' for fuck sake, stop lookin' over your shoulder, you're makin' me nervous.'

Liam took a long drink of his pint and wiped the back of his hand across his lips as his eyes flicked around the room. That was another nervous gesture, Jamie noted uncomfortably. 'I need you to get me out of the shite I'm in.'

'Aye, so I gather. But there's the old man's quid pro quo...'

'Quid what?' Liam interrupted, confused.

Jamie smiled. Latin obviously wasn't the Irishman's strongpoint which was strange, he thought; didn't Catholic priests spout it all the time. 'Quid pro quo... It's the price you have to pay to get his help.'

'Did he tell you what his "price" is?' Liam asked, his voice dropping further.

It was Jamie's turn to look around. This was getting out of hand and too bloody dangerous. He moved closer to Liam. 'There's goin' to be an attack.

You're involved and you're goin' to tell him all about it so he can fuck it up big time,' he said, his voice matching the other man's.

'An' is that all he told you?'

Jamie knotted his brow. The question reinforced Jamie's earlier feeling that he wasn't being told something. He smiled and shook his head. 'Aye, that was all,' he said. 'But I take from your question, there's more?'

'Aye, there's more.' His voice told Jamie there was a lot more.

'And are you goin' to tell me what it is?' Jamie pressed, taking another sip of his pint. He watched Liam struggle with that and began to lose patience. The Irishman was avoiding his eyes. 'Listen, Liam, I'm getting' a wee bit pissed off with all this crap. Get to the fuckin' point.'

They both took a drink and Jamie took another look at the three men who had arrived with Liam. One of them was watching them closely, his eyes narrowed against the smoke. Someone was taking an interest in them at last, Jamie mused uncomfortably.

Liam lifted his eyes to follow Jamie's gaze and saw the man give a cold smile. Liam returned it, raising his glass.

Jamie felt suddenly apprehensive. There man unsettled him and he detected that Liam was afraid of this one. He felt the Irishman's leg shake against his own. The small man by the bar continued to watch them, his eyes now studying Jamie closely.

'You need to watch that one,' Liam whispered out of the side of his mouth and using his glass to shield it. 'He's a shithawk.'

Jamie took a closer look. He had an uncanny feeling he had met the guy... But where, and when? There was an Army booklet he had been given to study during his training, he remembered... It was full of pictures and details of known terrorists. The Army called it the "A to H" book. Maybe the guy was in that, he mused. Liam certainly was.

And yet, he had a strong sense of having met this man before. He thought back to Belfast in 1967, recalling what he could of the three men he had worked with there. He wasn't one of them, Jamie was sure of that. Different build entirely. They had all been big men with broad shoulders whereas this guy was small and weasel like. A rodent. Jamie shrugged inwardly and pushed the thought away before turning back to Liam.

'Right, I'll watch him,' he said, laughing as though he had cracked a joke. Liam laughed with him. 'Listen, we can't talk here. It's too dangerous... And if you're goin' to tell me what's really behind all this we need privacy.' He paused a moment and looked at the three men again, suddenly remembering who they put him in mind of. 'What are you an' "The Bachelors" doin' later?' he asked, grinning. He wondered if they could sing.

Liam was engrossed in his pint. 'I don't know,' he admitted. 'I don't usually have company. The bastards were landed on me.'

'Just who the fuck are they?'

Liam looked guilty. 'The rest of my unit,' he mumbled quietly.

Jamie said nothing but his eyes conveyed his anger. 'You brought them with you? Are you fuckin' crazy? Why for fuck sake?' he hissed, keeping his voice as low as possible and forcing a smile.

'We're here to meet a volunteer. The game gave us cover for comin'.'

'What, a volunteer here in Glasgow?' Jamie continued, surprised again.

Liam nodded.

'To do with the attack that's comin' up?'

Liam nodded again. He took a drink of his pint and Jamie noticed his hand shake. Not a lot, but enough.

Jamie had heard enough. 'Right,' he said firmly. 'I'm out of here,' he said, pushing himself up from his chair. 'I'm stayin' at the Lorne Hotel, far end of Sauchiehall Street. I'll be waitin' for you. Come alone.' He could see panic in the Irishman's eyes.

'How the feck am I gonnae do that?' Liam groaned.

'Your problem,' Jamie retorted harshly. 'You could get them bladdered or find them women and get them laid. Just lose them.' He hesitated a moment. 'Take them dancin', find yourself a bird, an' slip away from them. I take it that disappearin' for a shag is acceptable behaviour an' your buddies over there won't start askin' awkward questions when you turn up knackered an' bleary eyed in the mornin'?'

Liam forced a smile. 'Nah, they won't. Probably just want to know the details of what we got up to.'

'Perverts!' Jamie murmured, laughing again.

Liam was thinking it through and finding problems. 'What if I can't find a woman?' he complained.

'Then pay for one, an' don't be choosy,' Jamie retorted harshly. He softened then. 'Ach, don't worry, an Irish Casanova like you shouldn't have a problem.'

'An Irish Casa-what like me?'

'Nova, Casanova... Ach, forget it. You must have led a sheltered life,' Jamie said, laughing and rolling his eyes. He placed his glass with the dregs of the pint on the table, ready to go.

Liam gave it one more shot. 'Why don't you come with us?' he asked. 'You could help me out.' It sounded like a plea.

'You're jokin', right? Go dancin' with that lot?' he said, directing his eyes at the three men. 'No chance.'

Liam shrugged acceptance. 'So what are you goin' to do?'

'I told you, I'm goin' back to my hotel. I'll phone my wife and I'll settle down with a bottle of malt an' I'll watch whatever rubbish is on the telly till you get there.' He held out his hand, smiling again. Liam took it and they shook, keeping up appearances.

Jamie hesitated again. 'One more thing,' he went on. 'If you turn up late and it's shut, ring for the night porter. Say your name is Rochefort and you're in room 302, third floor. I'll make sure the key is there for you.'

'Rochefort?' Liam repeated, brow knotting curiously.

Jamie gave him a smile, hiding his exasperation. 'I'm French... Remember?' Liam did not remember. It hadn't occurred to him that Jamie would be using any name other than Lynch.

Jamie turned away and headed for the door, directing a friendly nod to the three other men who were now watching his every move. He was beginning to regret not asking for a weapon.

As he made his way along Hospital Street, a live band in the pub's lounge struck up and the sound of music, cheering and laughter filled his ears. At least some people were having a good time tonight, he mused bitterly.

Chapter Twenty-one

Later that night

Jamie lay in the darkness of his room and watched the illuminated hands of his alarm clock. It was just after eleven o'clock.

He had spent a little time in the hotel lounge bar but the noise and bustle played on his nerves. Even the barmaids, who flirted with him outrageously, failed to lift his spirits. He maintained the charade of the French visitor which seemed to give him extra appeal. One of the girls, a little on the plump side but none the less attractive, asked him if he would like to go dancing with her later when she would show him what Glasgow was really like. He got the impression she wanted to show him what *she* "was really like" rather than Glasgow, and the gold band on his finger wouldn't deter her. He declined the invitation graciously, feigned travel fatigue, and headed for his room just before ten.

He stretched out on the bed and eased his tired leg muscles. He had walked back from the Cleland Bar, taking the scenic route via the Suspension Bridge over the Clyde from Carlton Place to Clyde Street and up through St Enoch's Square towards the City Centre. It was reasonably early then and the City was still coming to life. Groups of young men and girls headed purposefully to their favourite haunts and the atmosphere was peaceful. He doubted it would stay like that. As the night wore on and more and more drink was consumed the Glaswegians' propensity for belligerence would surface and the A & E departments of the city's hospitals would start to fill.

At George Square, he toyed with the idea of taking a bus to Anderston but in the end decided to walk. It was a pleasant enough night. A night for thinking. He turned into George Street, crossed Buchanan Street at St. George's Tron Church with its tall tower and wonderful carvings, and then into West George Street.

As he climbed the hill towards Blythswood Square the street grew quieter. He was now passing mainly office buildings, a mix of ancient and modern, which, on a Saturday evening were shrouded in darkness. The street lights threw pools of light down onto the pavements and cast shadows against the stonework of the buildings. Occasionally, a car passed him heading down the hill to the bright lights of the city centre.

Just before Blythswood Square he spotted the first of the girls. It was still reasonably early but the ladies of the night were gathering. Theirs was one business that didn't shut down at the weekend though trade was often conducted in dark alleys and the back seats of cars.

At the corner of Blythswood Street he turned right, taking him past the Royal Automobile Club. Lights were on and the sound of music drifted out from the bright interior. Taxis stopped and disgorged passengers who tripped quickly up the stairs and into the warmth of the building. He passed by, crossed the road to the boundary wall surrounding the grassed square itself and continued on towards West Regent Street.

A group of girls had collected at the corner and others stood in the shadows along the side of the square. He watched as a car cruised slowly past, stopped, moved on and stopped again. A girl leant forward, spoke briefly with the driver, opened the door and slipped inside. The door banged shut and the driver pulled away, accelerating past Jamie as he turned into West Regent Street. He caught a glimpse of the driver; late middle age, overweight and bald with thinning hair swept over his shiny skull. Every young girl's dream, he thought with a wry smile.

He took a closer look at the girls as he passed. They came in all shapes, sizes and ages. Some were pretty, some not so pretty, but all were dressed provocatively in short, tight skirts, black nylons, high heeled shoes and heavy makeup, like it was some sort of uniform. What makes them do it, he wondered. Economic necessity, he mused, kids to clothe or a habit to feed. It was then he spotted a man lurking in the shadows of a doorway on the opposite side of the road, just down from number 1 Blythswood Square, the former home of the infamous Madeleine Smith. Madeleine was a lady of a different kind, a wealthy socialite, who escaped the hangman's noose in the late 1850s with a "Not Proven" verdict. Maybe the shadowy figure was the ghost of her murdered French lover, he thought with another smile, but the figure moved menacingly out of the gloom, his face illuminated as he lit a cigarette. No, not a ghost and not a punter, Jamie realised, it was pimp. He stared hard at the man who returned his look for a moment then sank back into the shadows. Economic necessity wasn't the only thing that brought the girls out, Jamie reflected. Arseholes like the one hiding across the road, had a lot to do with it too.

The street girls weren't much different from him, he thought darkly. They did what they were told, with veiled threats of unpleasant things to follow if they didn't. Sometimes the threats probably weren't even veiled, he mused. A girl stepped in front of him, smiling, though her eyes were dark and moody. He shook his head and walked on. Another, not much out of her teens, accosted him. She was pretty but in a few years she would be worn down and haggard... Old before her time. For a few quid he could use her as he liked right now... But he didn't like. He smiled, shook his head and sidestepped her, listening to the desultory comments and bawdy laughter of the others ringing in his ears. The look on the girl's face stayed with him for a long time.

Now he lay mulling over his current situation. Things were starting to look grim. The appearance Liam's fellow "soldiers" with him in the pub proved that. Nothing was simple any longer... but it had never been simple. He knew that. Nothing was ever simple where Brigadier Charles Redmond was concerned.

What had started off as a simple conduit job leading eventually to Liam Fitzpatrick's "disappearance" was being compromised by something else and he still didn't know what. That bothered him. It Really bothered him. All his instincts told him it was a game changer and his instincts were rarely wrong. It was a weight on Liam, he sensed that, and trust was an issue. He sensed that too.

The Brigadier, as always, was playing his cards close to his chest but he was behind it, whatever it was. With that in mind, it was unlikely to be a pleasant experience, he mused grimly.

Outside his window, a boisterous crowd was making its way westwards towards the Kelvin Hall, or Partick, or Byres Road... or maybe even the University Union, he thought. Memories flooded back. The laughter and the singing made him envious. He pushed himself up from the bed and walked over to the window. There were about ten or twelve in the group, young men and girls in their late teens or early twenties cavorting playfully on the pavement and spilling out into the carriageway. They were on their way to a party somewhere, he imagined. Lucky bastards, he thought... with probably not a care in the world to think about.

He thought of Kate and his children then. God, how he missed them. He had thought of phoning but with the hour difference in time thought better of it. Kate would need all the rest she could get. His eyes strayed to the bottle of Bushmills Irish Whiskey that sat, unopened, on the tiny bedside cabinet. He had found an off license in Argyle Street, not far from the hotel, and bought it on impulse. He had a feeling he would need it before the night was through. But not just yet. He could wait.

***

It was just before midnight when Liam Fitzpatrick spilled out of a taxi onto the pavement outside The Lorne. Jamie was watching from his bedroom window when the taxi pulled to a halt. He left the room and made his way downstairs to reception. The lounge was still open and some of the residents were growing rowdy. The attractively plump little barmaid who had chatted him up earlier caught his eye. She gave him a pained look, rolled her eyes, then smiled. He smiled back.

The night porter/receptionist was nowhere in sight. A radio played softly, the sound coming from the room just off reception. They were probably in there hiding, Jamie thought with a smile. He made it to the door just as Liam appeared, his eyes peering hopefully through the glass. Jamie opened the door and ushered him in. Surprisingly, the Irishman was still sober.

Without saying a word, he pointed Liam in the direction of the lifts and set off, Liam following in his wake. A couple, both the worse for wear, staggered unsteadily from the lounge and joined them as they waited for the lift to descend. The woman was almost wearing a long black dress that had given up trying to contain her enormous breasts. The guy was sporting a dinner suit and a black bow tie that hung loose at his neck and he had dribbled something down the front of his shirt. They were arguing, sniping away at one another. Jamie and Liam exchanged a look and suppressed their amusement.

One or other, it wasn't clear which from the slurred conversation, had been naughty and had been sharing their attentions with someone else.

Judging by the way the woman kept fluttering her eyelashes at the Liam, she was favourite.

Liam gave her a smile and the girl, taking it as an invite, swayed closer to him and took hold of his arm. Her man's face reddened and the veins stuck out on his neck. Never a good sign. Liam laughed and took hold of the woman. He said later he was only trying to steady her but her drunken boyfriend didn't see it that way. He drew Liam a dirty look from behind his blood-shot eyes. Liam simply gave him a shrug and smiled. That moved things up a notch. It was like waving a red rag in front of a bull.

Jamie sighed and signalled to Liam to back off. He wasn't worried about the Irishman's safety. He could handle himself and the other man could hardly stand. What did worry him was the prospect of having to referee a "square go" - that quintessential term for fisticuffs in Glasgow - in the hotel's reception, the inevitable result of which would be the arrival of at least two burly policemen. And "Sod's Law" would no doubt be invoked. For the uninitiated, Sod's Law states that if something can go wrong, it will, and that would probably mean Liam being arrested. He didn't want Liam spending the night on a hard bed in Partick Police Station. Apart from anything else, that would prompt too many awkward questions from his three pals.

He coughed loudly to attract the drunk's attention. The man turned away from Liam towards him, his eyes straining to focus.

'Don't even think about it pal,' Jamie said quietly. 'You'll just get yourself hurt. Take Mae West here off to bed before she gets you into more trouble.' His voice was soft and low but it carried menace.

The man stared at him belligerently at first, his face flushed. He drew in a deep breath and pulled back his shoulders. Here we go, Jamie mused unhappily.

It was a battle of wills now. The "stare" is something that has developed to a fine art in Glasgow. Jamie was an expert. The boyfriend, regaining temporary sobriety, tried to match Jamie's look, but failed. The man finally looked away and mumbled something derogatory under his breath that Jamie chose to ignore. He knew it for what it was; a face saving exercise, nothing more. You can't lose face in front of your woman, even at the risk of getting a good slap. Jamie just smiled in response but even that was intimidating.

All through the exchange, Liam watched, fascinated. The woman seemed confused now but at least she was taking more interest in her man again. He was probably on a promise if he could stay conscious when they got to their room.

At last, the lift arrived. There was a grating sound as the doors slid open. Jamie and Liam waited as the man took hold of the woman and pulled her into the lift with him, staring defiantly back at them. It was then that the reality of his situation dawned on him and panic flashed across his face. The thought of being trapped in a lift with these two didn't bear thinking about. He looked physically sick.

'Don't panic, pal,' Jamie said softly, his eyes settling on the man again. 'We'll take the stairs.' He could see relief flood the guy's face and heard the woman giggle. As the lift doors closed and the lift began its ascent, the argument kicked off again.

'Imagine bein' married to that floozy,' Liam chortled. 'Ah think she fancied me.'

Jamie was still laughing. 'I think that was the problem. She must have been tryin' to find someone to perform with tonight cos I don't think bugger-lugs will manage a hard on, the state he's in.' They both laughed aloud and headed for the stairs.

When the laughter died Jamie brought them both back to their own situation. 'What did you do with the three stooges?' he asked, raising an eyebrow.

'Ah left them in the pub. There was this nice wee doll... she was with a pal but her pal buggered off an' left her. Ah chatted her up an' she invited me back to her place.'

'There you go,' Jamie laughed. 'You are a Casanova, just like I said.' He paused a moment before going on. 'So how did your pals take that?' he enquired.

'They were pissed off,' Liam replied, grinning. 'It was envy, right enough,' he went on. 'Those three tossers could'na get a shag in a brothel. They were still in the Clelland when I left.'

'You're sure you weren't followed?'

'Aye, ah'm sure. Me an' the wee girl took a taxi to her place an' nobody followed us. We spent the next couple of hours shaggin'... took me all my time to get away from her,' he went on, giggling uncontrollably. 'Right nymphomaniac, she is. Gave it the petted lip when ah told her ah had to go out for a wee while. Ah said ah had a bit o' business to attend to but ah wouldn't be long an' ah'd be back to do the business with her. That cheered her up.' He was grinning salaciously.

It nodded and smiled. Liam was talking himself up but it was bluster. The poor bugger was wound up like a coiled spring and the grin and the big talk couldn't hide it. He hoped the Irishman could make it through.

'What about tomorrow, will your buddies be suspicious?' he asked.

'Nah, ah don't think so. Sex trumps everythin',' Liam replied. 'When ah turn up in the mornin' lookin' knackered an' smellin' of her the only thing those buggers will want to know is how many times ah shagged her... That's about as close to a ride as they ever get,' he finished, laughing uproariously.

Jamie shook his head. He knew guys like that. If they couldn't get their own leg over they liked to hear from people who had. It was a bit like watching a blue movie without the pictures. You relied on your imagination.

When he ushered Liam into the bedroom he saw the Irishman's nerves kick in again. He looked as if he expected someone to leap out of the bathroom or the wardrobe, armed to the teeth. He smiled grimly but not with amusement. He could understand how Liam felt.

'Don't worry, it's only you and me,' he said, reassuringly. He followed Liam into the room and made directly for the bottle of Bushmills, picking it up and breaking the seal. He hoisted the bottle and offered it over to Liam. The Irishman nodded gratefully.

There were no tumblers. Jamie passed Liam the bottle and waited as the Irishman took a mouthful of the whiskey and passed it back. Jamie followed suit and then pointed Liam to the only chair in the room while he settled down on the edge of the bed, the bottle still in his hand.

It was time to end the pleasantries. 'I think it's time you told me what the fuck is really goin' on,' Jamie started. 'As far as I was concerned my job was simply to be your contact for the intel on the attacks that are planned and then, when you've passed it over, get you out... But there's more, I know that now... I just don't know what the fuck it is an' that's making me angry.'

Liam laughed bitterly. 'Aye, Dermott, there's more,' he sighed. 'A whole lot feckin' more.' He pulled a small package from his inside jacket pocket and tossed it over onto the bed beside Jamie. It was an old, scuffed brown envelope, the type used by Civil Service Departments like the DHSS and the like. Jamie picked it up and examined it. The return address was just visible – DVLC Swansea – but he doubted the envelope contained anything to do with driver and vehicle licensing.

'Starin' at it won't help unless you've got X Ray eyes,' Liam said tersely. 'Open it.'

Jamie ignored him and weighed the envelope carefully in his hand. The flap was sealed with a thin strip of sellotape that was starting to curl at the edges. 'Why don't you just tell me what it is,' he said.

Liam held out his hand for the bottle of Bushmills and Jamie passed it over.

'It's a wee present for the man, so it is,' the Irishman said before taking a swig from the bottle. 'It's the first instalment of the feckin' "quid pro quo" you spoke about. You can look inside if you like.'

Jamie continued contemplating the envelope thoughtfully. He wasn't sure he wanted to know what was inside.

Liam took another mouthful of the whiskey and offered the bottle back to him again. This could turn into a session if they weren't careful, Jamie mused, and he had a feeling they both needed clear heads. He took a drink of the Bushmills and placed the bottle on the floor between his feet. Liam said nothing. He was waiting until Jamie's curiosity got the better of him.

Eventually, it did. Carefully, as if he were dismantling a bomb, Jamie prised the sellotape away from the envelope's flap and opened it, then tipped out the contents onto the bed. A small pile of photographs now lay on the bedcover, the faces of unknown men staring back up at him. He picked up the small bundle and flicked through it, discarding the photographs one by one back onto the bed.

The first one was of a hard looking man with a face that looked like it had been sculpted from granite. He was well dressed and his hair was neat and slicked back. He was holding a drink in one hand and he was smiling at the camera, but the smile didn't extend beyond his mouth. His eyes were hard and cold.

'James Flynn,' Liam announced. 'He's a 'Derry man. Your lot have been tryin' to pin somethin' on him for years... but they can't get anythin' to stick. He's a dangerous man, so he is. Ah don't know for sure but ah think he'll be in command of one of the other ASU's.'

Jamie nodded and placed the photograph back onto the bed. The second, third and fourth photographs were of the three men who had been with Liam in the pub earlier; Fionn Doherty, Eamonn Macari and Desmond Finnegan, the Irishman informed him. Doherty was the weasel faced little git who seemed to be paying him undue attention in the pub. He didn't look much, Jamie decided, but he knew better than to put store in that. Macari was taller, a little older, and, like the man in the first picture, well turned out. His face was set in a hard, unsmiling pose. The last of the three was the youngest... He didn't look old enough to be shaving yet, never mind volunteering, Jamie thought. He wondered if he was a baby faced killer or just another gullible kid who thought he was going to free his people. He would find out soon enough, he mused grimly.

'Doherty's the one to watch,' Liam said softly.

'Aye, he was giving me the evil eye in the pub,' Jamie replied thoughtfully.

Liam snorted coldly. 'Don't take it personal. He gives everybody that look... He's a queer fecker... and evil. You two have met before, right enough,' Liam added, adding an icy laugh for effect. He saw Jamie's head jerk up and smiled.

'You won't remember it... an' nether does he, which is just as well for both of us,' he went on, his voice edgy. 'That wee fecker wanted to pull out your finger nails and put you through the wringer at Kiltyclogher. He would have too if ah hadn't got to ye first.' That piece of information was accompanied by another nervous laugh. 'Thank feck it was a dark night. The fecker pissed on you... dirty wee shite that he is,' he added contemptuously. 'Do ye remember that?'

Jamie shook his head slowly. 'No, I don't remember any of that,' he said, smiling grimly. 'An' yet, I got the feeling I knew the little sod.' He reached for the bottle of Bushmills again.

'The wee fecker still has yer watch,' Liam went on. 'He tells everybody he took it from a dead Brit an' likes to give the impression he did the killin'.' He laughed coldly and seemed about to go on, then hesitated.

Jamie picked up on his uncertainty. 'Go on,' he pressed. He wanted everything. Liam shook his head angrily. He still seemed reluctant to go on. Jamie waited patiently and watched Liam wrestle with whatever it was that was giving him grief.

Eventually, Liam gave a nervous little cough. 'There's a lot of reasons why ah became an informer an' Doherty's one of them. He's a sick wee bastard... an' he got too close to home for my liking,' he said softly.

Jamie's brow furrowed. There was a cryptic clue somewhere in that last statement but what was it? He didn't have time to think about it before Liam was speaking again.

'Macari is hard as nails,' he said, 'but he can't think for himself. He needs someone to tell him when he can go for a shite,' he continued derisively. 'He's a psychopath, just like Doherty, kills for fun. Point him in the right direction an' he'll kill anythin' an' everythin' that gets in his way.' He paused and nodded down at the bottle of Bushmills.

Jamie picked it up and passed it across, waiting patiently as Liam downed another sizeable swallow. Liam wiped the back of his hand across his mouth and continued.

'Young Desmond there... he's new to all this. That wee boy volunteered months back but hasn't done much. Ah don't know much about him, right enough, so the bugger might be as bad as the other two for all ah know.'

'So, you four make up an ASU... who's in charge?' Jamie asked dourly.

Liam's grim lopsided smile said it all. 'Me,' he said guiltily.

Jamie nodded. It was no more than he expected. He picked up another photograph. 'So who's this?' he demanded, showing the picture to Liam. It showed a man in his early thirties. He was well built and good-looking and Jamie imagined he would be a big hit with the ladies. His dark hair was long and curly and his eyes seemed to sparkle, even in the photograph. He wasn't like the other men at all.

'That's John Cleary. He's a Dublin man... an intellectual, so ah'm told is. He's a planner more than a soldier. It's possible he's the man behind these attacks but ah can't be sure. He's a strange one, to be sure. He argues against the Leadership. They don't like him but they listen because some of them know he's got a point. He says that killin' civilians won't win the war an' he despises the buggers that carry out cowboy operations where the public get caught up in the crossfire. He says you Brits are masters of Public Relations and we need to learn from you. If I'm right an' he is the planner, the targets will all be military.'

Jamie dropped the photograph onto the bed beside the others and turned to the last one. It was a picture of a young woman. She would be around thirty, Jamie guessed. The photograph was in black and white and had been taken without her knowing. This picture was different from the others in just about every respect. It didn't fit.

'Who's this and what has she got to do with it?' he asked suspiciously.

Liam smiled conspiratorially and gave a little snort. 'Ah don't know who she is an' she's got feck all to do with anythin' as far as ah know,' he said, watching Jamie's reaction.

'Then why is her picture with this lot?' Jamie asked, sweeping his hand over the other photographs.

Liam sighed loudly and eyes the whiskey bottle. Jamie picked it up and passed it over. Liam took another generous swallow. 'It's there because ah have to give yer man a crumb. It's the last bit o' the puzzle, the bit your boss hasn't told ye about.' Jamie could hear the anger in his voice. 'An' it's the real price ah have to pay to get out o' this shit.'

Jamie gazed at him, a feeling of dread beginning to gnaw away at his inside. 'You're losing me, Liam,' he. What you say explains nothin'. Tell me.'

'He wants somethin' from me... Somethin' ah can't give him.'

'You're still talkin' in riddles... Spell it out.'

Liam stared at him bleakly and gave a resigned nod. 'It goes back to 1970,' he started. 'There was a bomb in Coventry that year... a big one. A lot of people were killed.'

Jamie nodded, wondering what was coming. 'Aye, I know about that one,' he murmured quietly. 'I've been to the bomb site.'

'The biggest atrocity to date, they call it,' Liam went on. 'The Militia was behind it. The Army Council knew feck all about it until it happened. They all condemned it... Christ, even the Provos condemned it.' He gave a cynical laugh. 'Bit ironic that,' he continued. 'Seein' as how they're doin' much the same thing now.' He shook his head sadly. 'Your man has been after the bomber ever since. He wants the bomber's head on a plate an' he expects me to deliver it, so he does. He never lets up.'

Jamie knew he was still missing something. 'And this is the thing you say you can't deliver?' Liam smiled enigmatically but said nothing. 'Is it can't, or won't?' Jamie probed.

Liam turned away from him. 'It's both,' he said softly.

Jamie's head was shaking disbelievingly. 'Why, for fuck sake?'

Liam was looking at the Bushmills again. Jamie handed it over. The Irishman held it up to his mouth but didn't drink. His eyes were on Jamie now, measuring him. 'Ah need to be sure ah can trust you,' he said. His voice was low and steady.

'I'm here because you told the Brigadier I'm the only one you trust and now you're questioning it?' Liam responded incredulously. 'Either you do or you don't. Make up your mind.'

Silence descended on the room. Jamie had said his bit. What happened now was up to Liam. The Irishman took a drink from the bottle and handed it back. Jamie held it loosely, swithering, then joined him. The whiskey burned his throat.

'I can't give him the bomber because she's family,' Liam murmured, his voice so low Jamie was struggling to make him out.

'Family,' Jamie repeated, adjusting to the shock. He thought back to his visit to the bombsite with the Brigadier, recalling the old boy's description of the bomber. It was a woman... A young woman, he said. Jamie remembered that clearly. The unthinkable was beginning to seem possible. He stared blankly back at Liam, struggling to find the words to take this forward. 'Roisin?' he whispered.

Liam looked away again. Jamie felt his world collapse around him.

'That's bollocks Liam; I don't believe it,' he spat angrily.

Liam looked grim, his face grey in the dim light. 'It's true,' he said. 'Ah wish to Christ it wasn't but it is. She planted the bomb... She didn't really have a choice.'

Jamie was still shell shocked. His problems had just gone off the scale and he was caught in a difficult situation... between a rock and a hard place, as the saying goes. And what was that about choice? Crap, he mused. 'Of course she had a choice,' he said angrily. 'We've all got a fuckin' choice, an' now you've left me with one.' His anger was reaching boiling point.

'It isn't that easy,' Liam replied. 'Some choices are harder to make than others. Some are even impossible. Like ah say, she had no choice.'

'Tell that to the families of the poor buggers that were blown to bits,' Jamie threw back derisively.

'You don't understand,' Liam replied, frustrated. 'She didn't want to do it; she was made to do it.'

That stopped Jamie in his tracks. His brow furrowed as he weighed up that statement. 'Made to, as in forced?' he queried

'Aye, forced, an' if ah had been in her shoes ah would have done it too... So would you,' he finished, staring Jamie out.

'Explain.'

Liam smiled forlornly. 'You're married... You've got kids. What would you do if somebody told you to blow up a pub in Glasgow or they'd kill your wife and children?'

Jamie looked at him with undisguised horror. 'I don't know,' he mumbled unthinkingly.

Liam laughed mockingly. 'Of course you feckin' know... You would plant the friggin' bomb.'

'I'd kill them,' Jamie whispered through gritted teeth.

'Aye, ah believe ye would,' Liam retorted. 'But ye'd plant the bomb first, so ye would.'

Jamie looked away pensively. Liam was right. The way Liam told it, he would have planted the bomb and then gone after the men behind it. 'Tell me it all,' he said quietly and saw Liam smile.

The Irishman took a deep breath and began. 'About a year after you were over in Belfast doin' that wee job for Brendan, Roisin met a young lad here in Glasgow. Trevor Evans, he's called. He's a nice lad... but not Brendan's cup of tea. There caused arguments between Roisin and Brendan.'

Jamie smiled coldly. That bit didn't come as a surprise. He probably wasn't Brendan Kelly's cup of tea either. He remembered the veiled threat Brendan had made when they met in Roisin's flat the morning he and Roisin had returned from Belfast. He hadn't taken it personally at the time. He just put it down to the man being over protective of his little sister. 'I take it Roisin stood her ground,' he said, remembering the girl's stubborn streak.

'Aye, that she did,' Liam agreed gloomily. 'When Roisin makes up her mind, no one will change it. Not even Brendan.'

Jamie shook his head and smiled; that was the Roisin he remembered. 'Aye, I know that well enough,' he agreed. 'But where is this takin' us?'

'Well, Roisin married Trevor... an' that upset Brendan an' a good few others, so it did.'

'You included?' Jamie threw in.

Liam looked hurt at the insinuation. 'No, not me an' not my Ma. We were at the weddin' but Brendan stayed away. Said he wanted nothin' to do with her.'

Jamie shook his head disbelievingly. 'Why, for fuck sake?' he asked

Liam smiled wryly. 'Oh, did I forget to mention?' he said. 'Trevor's English an' he's a Prod, like you.'

'Doesn't make him a bad person,' Jamie retorted with a quiet laugh.

'No, that's right... an' ah think Brendan could have lived with that,' Liam responded, confusingly as far as Jamie was concerned. 'But there was something else. Something Brendan couldn't forgive.'

Jamie hiked his eyebrows enquiringly and Liam's wry smile returned.

'The boy's a sailor in the Royal Navy,' he said, laughing. 'Can you imagine it?' he snorted. 'An IRA top man with a brother in law in the Royal feckin' Navy.' His laugh grew colder. 'It didn't do Brendan's reputation much good. People started to talk. Could he be trusted, they wanted to know. He needed somethin' to get him back on track... an' that's where the Coventry bomb came in. Brendan planned it an' he wanted Roisin to plant it. That would get the doubters off his back.'

Jamie stared back at him open mouthed. 'And Roisin agreed?' he asked, his voice mirroring his disbelief.

'Of course she didn't agree. Ah though you knew her?' Liam retorted irritably.

'So what happened?'

'Brendan had a word with some people an' Doherty and a couple of the boys had a word with her.'

'Here in Glasgow?'

'No, not here. Back in Belfast. She was over visitin' my Ma an' Brendan knew about the visit. He got the boys to meet her when she was leavin'.'

'The same Doherty that's with you now?'

'Aye, the very same.'

'Go on,' Jamie prompted. He had an idea what was coming but he wanted to hear it from Liam.

'Doherty an' his boys met up with her at the docks. Roisin had her kids with her...'

'Kids?' Jamie interrupted. 'She's got more than one?'

'Twins,' Liam replied, smiling. 'Two beautiful little girls with Roisin's red hair.'

'And where was Trevor at the time?' Jamie asked. He knew that the man wouldn't have come to Belfast. He would have been advised against it.

'He was at sea, as far as ah know.' He paused a moment and nodded at the Bushmills. Jamie smiled and handed it over. He needed a drink himself to help him deal with this. Liam drank and wiped his mouth before handing the bottle back.

'And they threatened to kill her kids?' Jamie said, moving things on.

'Aye, quite a persuasive argument that,' Liam replied, 'especially when it's delivered by a scumbag like Doherty. Everybody knows what he's like. Murder's a hobby wi' that wee shite.'

'How do you know all this?'

'Roisin told my Ma,' Liam replied. 'Reluctantly,' he added as an afterthought. 'She used to phone every week but after she went back that time she missed a few weeks. My Mammy was worried an' gave her a call. She knew something was wrong right away but getting' it out of Roisin was like pullin' teeth. Molly, my Ma, hasn't spoke to Brendan since. Says he'll rot in hell.'

'Aye, probably,' Jamie replied. And I'll probably meet him there.

'It was a stick an' carrot job,' Liam was saying, getting Jamie's attention again. The carrot was that it was to be just a wee bomb an' a warnin' would be given. They told Roisin the peelers would have plenty of time to clear the place an' there wouldn't be any casualties. The stick was that if she didn't do it, Doherty would kill her girls in front of her an' then he'd kill her man. He didn't say what he'd do to Roisin herself. The bastard left that to her imagination.'

'Does her man know all this?'

Liam shook his head sadly. 'No, he doesn't. Roisin was in hospital by the time he came home. She's still there.'

Jamie was shaking his head angrily as he listened. 'What about Brendan? Did he have anythin' to say about it?'

Liam laughed frostily. 'Brendan washed his hands of it. It was all for the good of "The Cause" he said. Sad bastard.'

'Does the Brigadier know?' Jamie asked. He wasn't thinking clearly.

Liam drew him a puzzled look. 'Don't be feckin' daft, Dermott. If he knew do ye think he would still be lookin' for her? She'd be dead.'

Jamie nodded apologetically, berating himself for his stupidity. Then he compounded it. 'Why not just tell him now?' he said.

'You are feckin' crazy,' Liam retorted, staggered. 'The old bastard wouldn't believe it. She's my cousin, for fuck sake. He'd just think ah was makin' it up. All he wants is revenge; simple as that,' he said, shaking his head resentfully.

'So why tell me?' Jamie asked, puzzled.

Liam gave a soft, bitter laugh. 'You didn't know her long,' he said, 'but from things she said, you two got close. Ah'm hopin' you had some feelin's for her; enough to help her. You're my last throw of the dice, Dermott. Ah want out of the feckin' mess ah'm in but ah don't want Roisin to be the price for that. Ah've got a fair idea what you do for that auld shitehawk... That's why ah wanted you involved. If ah'm wrong about you, ah've just made the biggest mistake of my life.'

They sat in silence for a while then. Jamie felt drained emotionally. The job was bad enough to start with but now it was a nightmare.

Liam started speaking again. 'If ah'm right, yer man is goin' to put you on the spot. He wants the bomber. He'll ask you to get her name from me and then he'll tell you to kill her. That is what you do for him, isn't it?'

Jamie's silence was enough of an answer but he felt the need respond. 'It's what I used to do,' he admitted. 'But I told him I'm finished with that.'

Liam looked up sharply. 'So he's already tasked ye with it, has he?'

Jamie held up his hands, palms out. 'No, he hasn't said anything to me about the bomber but he wants me operational again. I said no.'

Liam shook his head dejectedly. 'Seems he's got us both by the balls,' he said quietly. 'How did ye get involved with him in the first place?' he went on. 'You don't seem the type.'

Jamie gave a cold laugh in response. 'Much the same way as you, I imagine. He offered me a solution to a problem. I suppose you could say he made me an offer I couldn't refuse,' he snorted bitterly.

'Did he blackmail you?'

'Not really. He wouldn't call it that, anyway,' Jamie replied, smiling frostily. 'He just played on my fear.'

Liam laughed. 'Ah watched you in that lift... Ah didn't think you had any,' he observed.

'You'd be surprised,' was Jamie's only reply.

They sat in silence again. Outside in the street there were the usual noises associated with a weekend night in the city; laughter, loud voices shouting curses, squeals and giggles. In the hotel, the last of the guests staggered from the resident's lounge to their rooms and bawdy laughter filtered through the walls, bed springs creaked rhythmically and women faked orgasms. Jamie thought of the little barmaid and wondered if she was having fun.

'Will you tell him?' Liam found the courage to ask at last.

Jamie sighed. 'No, I won't tell him, but it won't end there; you know that.' He watched Liam nod disconsolately. The Irishman knew alright.

'So what can ah do?' Liam asked.

He didn't expect an answer, Jamie thought. He shook his head slowly as he thought it through. It struck him they had both been doing a lot of that; shaking their heads. 'I don't know,' he said at last. 'Unless we give him someone else,' he added pensively.

'Someone else?' Liam came back quickly. 'Like who?' A straw had been held out to him and he was grasping at it as any drowning man will do.

'I don't know that either,' Jamie admitted. 'But there's probably somebody that fits the bill.'

'What, some poor innocent lassie?' Liam retorted angrily.

'In this game there's no poor, innocent lassies Liam. Any girl involved with the IRA lost her innocence a long time ago... A bit like you an' me,' Jamie went on with a bitter laugh. 'Roisin was used by your lot, I'm bein' used by the other lot an' you're bein' used by both. We're just tools. There will always be people like us, people that can be chucked onto the scrap heap without a second thought.' He smiled again. 'But they always want results so let's give them one.'

'Meaning?' Liam queried, lifting an eyebrow.

'Meaning why don't we give him the people behind it... Your pal Doherty for a start and then there's Brendan,' Jamie added, his expression as cold as an Arctic wind.

'He knows the bomb was planted by a woman so he'll want a woman in the frame. Doherty's a lot of things, but a woman he's not.'

Jamie laughed quietly. 'We can get round that,' he retorted confidently. 'The bomber could be dead by now for all he knows. If he buys that, then we can sell him the men behind it. I'll happily give him Doherty's head on a plate. Is there anyone else you'd like topped while I'm at it?' he threw in flippantly.

Liam looked at him askance, wondering if that was a jest or not. 'You make it sound easy,' he said, eyeing Jamie carefully.

Jamie smiled and lifted the Bushmills. He took a mouthful and held out the bottle to Liam who nodded. The Irishman took the bottle and drank from it before handing it back.

'Familiarity breeds contempt,' he said. 'It also makes you a wee bit blasé.'

Liam was looking at him in a new light. 'When ah said before that ah thought ye were a killer, ah didn't really believe it, but now ye sound like one. Just how familiar are ye?' he asked.

'Too familiar,' Jamie replied, watching the Irishman's reaction.

'Is that why ye were at Malone's house in Kiltyclogher?'

Jamie laughed again. 'Kiltyclogher was a first for me,' he replied. 'The old boy wanted me to branch out. The job was in two parts: First, get everything I could on the arms shipment from him and then kill him. You beat me to it though, didn't you? Doherty's work I presume?"

Liam nodded. 'Aye, another example of Doherty's skill at gentle persuasion; the fucker was enjoyin' himself. Wouldn't stop. Malone pegged out before we got anythin' out of him.'

'Aye, I know. I found it.'

Liam looked up sharply. 'You found it?'

Jamie laughed at his reaction, nodding. 'He had it all written down. You wouldn't have understood it even if you'd found it anyway. It was in Cyrillic script.' Liam gave him a quizzical look. 'Russian,' Jamie explained, 'though he had a few notes scribbled in Gaelic in the margin. That stumped me,' he laughed. 'It was tucked inside one of the only two books you lot didn't rip the covers off; the big Family Bible in the bookcase beside that other bible, the one by Michael Collins,' he laughed again. 'What stopped you? Superstition?'

Liam snorted a laugh. 'Ah should have known,' he said. 'Ah remember seein' those... Fuck knows why we left them.' He grew serious then, the rest of Jamie's tale sinking in. 'How many men have ye killed?' he asked quietly.

A shadow passed over Jamie's face and Liam thought he had gone too far. He waited anxiously and sighed inwardly as the shadow turned to an expression of profound sadness. In all, the process had taken around a minute but each second had been a lifetime to the Irishman.

Jamie looked at him at last, an icy smile playing at the corners of his mouth. 'Too many,' he said finally, sighing softly. 'I console myself with the fact they all had it comin',' he went on. 'But every one of them took a little bit of me with them.'

'Ye didn't really tell me how ye got involved.'

'Yes I did,' Jamie retorted, nullifying the question. 'I told you; the Brigadier made me an offer I couldn't refuse. I accepted. End of story. Problem is, once you're in, it's hard to get out. It's a bit like breakin' free of a drug habit, I suppose. You know you shouldn't be doin' it but it's hard to resist, and the old boy keeps turning up, like a pusher with a bag of Speed.'

'How long have ye been doin' it?'

Jamie sighed. 'A couple of years. He got to me in seventy. Trained me for a year. My first kill was in seventy-one... My first for them, that is,' he added unthinkingly. Liam didn't pick up on it. 'Now he tells me I'm one of his best,' he continued. 'At least, I was, until I bumped into you an' your Merry Men at Kiltyclogher,' he laughed. 'One of the best,' he repeated pensively. 'Some accolade, huh?'

'Ye still haven't told me how many.'

Jamie fixed him with a steely stare. 'Enough,' he said simply. The tone made it clear he wasn't going to go any further.

'Right,' Liam conceded, nodding slowly. 'So, back to my problems; what do ah do about Roisin?' He felt Jamie's gaze boring into him as he waited for his response.

'I don't know... I need to talk to Roisin first.' Liam stared back at him and Jamie could see the uncertainty behind the Irishman's eyes. The whiskey clearly hadn't affected Liam's thought processes and Jamie knew what he was thinking. He held Liam's look and smiled. 'Bit late for doubts now, Liam,' he said. 'You've already told me enough to hang her and if I was going to do that, you're already too late to stop me.' He smiled to ease Liam's apprehension, shaking his head. 'Don't worry,' he continued. 'I'm not going to do that, I just want to talk to her.'

Liam hesitated. He knew he had already said too much, as Jamie said, but saying nothing would have got him nowhere. He needed help and his options were limited. Understatement, he thought ruefully. He had only one... Dermott Lynch. He returned Jamie's smile and nodded acceptance. 'Ah trust ye,' he said quietly. 'But there's another problem... Ah don't know if she'll talk to you.'

Jamie stayed silent but raised one eyebrow inquisitively.

'She's in hospital,' Liam went on. 'She was sectioned months ago. She's in Gartnavel Royal Hospital... Do you know it?'

Jamie nodded. 'Aye, I know it,' he said. 'What happened?'

'She's suffering from depression. What happened in Coventry got on top of her and...she...tried...' He stopped, his eyes filling up. Jamie didn't push him. 'She tried to kill herself,' he said finally.

'Jesus,' Jamie whispered, shaken. 'What did she do?'

'She took pills... Pills an' booze.'

Jamie struggled to come to terms with it. He thought about Lucie. He knew the torment she had suffered before she killed herself and could only imagine how Roisin had been. He remembered how he had felt when he learned that Lucie was dead. He had blamed himself then, he still did, and he thought then about Roisin's family. What were they going through? 'Who found her?' he asked.

'A neighbour... another sailor's wife. She lived, lives, in married quarters.'

Jamie shook his head in despair. 'Where was her man when it happened? Where were her kids?'

'He was at sea, the kids were okay. They were in nursery.'

'Fuck sake,' Jamie murmured. He sank his head into his hands. He was thinking earlier this whole carry on couldn't get worse but he'd been wrong. He should have known. No matter how bad things seem they can always get worse. 'It must have caused a shit storm,' he said. 'What happened to the children afterwards?'

Liam laughed frostily. 'Not too much of a shit storm,' he said. 'Apparently Navy wives get depressed a lot. Trevor's Ma came up from Liverpool an' she's lookin' after the kids now. Trevor's home now; he's on compassionate leave. Spends most of his time at the hospital.'

They sat quietly again. The bottle of Bushmills sat between them but neither man reached for it.

'Why won't she talk to me?' Jamie asked eventually.

Liam's smile was grim when he replied. 'It's not that she won't, she can't. She hasn't spoken to anyone. She doesn't eat... isn't takin' care of herself. You'll hardly recognise her if ye do go.'

'I want to see her Liam. I know what she's goin' through.'

'Aye, sure ye do,' Liam retorted cynically.

Jamie didn't take offence. He understood Liam's scepticism. 'Believe me Liam,' he said gently. 'I know. My first wife killed herself.'

Now it was Liam who was shocked. 'Your first wife... You've been married twice? What happened to her?'

'It's a long story, Liam, a long, painful story. Just take my word for it and tell me where she is.'

Liam sighed heavily. 'Ah'm sorry,' he said softly.

'You didn't know. Don't beat yourself up over it. Just tell me what ward Roisin's in and the best time to visit. I don't want to bump into her man.'

Liam nodded acceptance. 'She's in Ward 2 at Gartnavel. It's a secure ward but ye can visit any time ah think. Trevor goes up around eleven and stays till about six at night. The poor bastard's demented.' He looked down at his watch. It was just after one in the morning. 'Ye could go tonight,' he suggested.

'Aye, I could but I won't be here. I'm heading home tomorrow. I'll go this morning.'

'Remember Trevor visits about eleven,' Liam reminded.

'Don't worry. I'll be on my way long before then,' Jamie said with a smile, then he too looked at his watch. The hands told him it was ten past one. 'You'd better get back to your girlfriend,' he said, forcing a grin. 'Her bed will be getting' cold an' she might decide to look for someone else to warm it an' her up. Apart from anythin' else, you don't know who she might bump into.'

Liam grinned back and heaved himself up out of the chair. 'Don't worry, she'll still be waitin' for me,' he retorted, his grin widening.

Salacious thoughts seemed to be taking Liam's mind off his other problems. Lucky man, Jamie mused.

He walked with Liam to the lift and then decided to accompany him down to the exit. A couple of stragglers were drinking in the lounge and the wee waitress was still working. He caught her eye and she smiled invitingly. If he were like Liam maybe he could forget his problems for a while with her, he reflected... But he wasn't like Liam. Not now.

At the main door they shook hands. 'Listen, Liam,' Jamie said, holding onto him. 'We need to set up how we keep in contact. I'll phone you at your yard next week. Usual thing; say you're busy and call me back an hour later from a phone box. We'll fix up a routine then, okay?'

The Irishman nodded. 'Aye, that'll be grand,' he said quietly. 'Ah wish this was all over... and ah'm sorry ah got ye into it,' he continued apologetically. 'But ye're the only person I thought I could trust.'

Jamie smiled wryly. 'No Liam, thought doesn't come into it. I am the only person you can trust. Don't forget that.'

Liam nodded slowly and headed off, taking the steps from the hotel two at a time. Jamie waited on the top step, watching Liam's back disappear into the darkness. A black hackney cab passed the hotel on its way into the city. As it neared the point where Liam had disappeared it's brake lights came on, shining brightly in the darkness. The vehicle's interior lights came on as someone opened the door and a shadowy figure climbed in. Liam Fitzpatrick was gone.

Chapter Twenty-two

It was early. The taxi he had called to the hotel dropped Jamie in Great Western Road. Even this main thoroughfare from the city to the west was virtually deserted. He paid the cabbie and set off past the Pond Hotel towards the hospital. His head throbbed dully. He hadn't drunk as much of the whiskey as Liam but he was suffering none the less. Lack of sleep didn't help and what slumber he had managed to get had been filled with nightmarish dreams of the future. He imagined Liam's night would have been much the same but for the distraction of the "wee doll" he had managed to pick up in the pub. She would probably have worked off his hangover leaving him simply knackered instead.

He thought a lot about Roisin. There were so many questions queuing up in his head over her involvement in the bombing and so few answers. Visiting her was a way of satisfying himself of the truth about that though having met her brother Brendan and listened to Liam's graphic account of what had happened, he had little doubt. He just hoped the trip was worth it.

He skirted the tiny loch, Bingham's Pond, and headed towards the new NHS hospital, Gartnavel General. This modern multi-discipline hospital was in stark contrast to the old Gartnavel Royal that had overshadowed the place for years like a malignant growth. But then, all Victorian Asylums had that air about them, he mused as he walked. It seemed less forbidding now at least. He hated the word asylum. Asylum was a word that conveyed hopelessness and hopelessness was, paradoxically, what many of the inmates consigned to these places suffered from. It was an ironic twist, he mused grimly.

It sat atop a gentle slope, surrounded by mature trees and open parkland. Before the new general hospital was built, it and its patients were obscured from the view of the populace behind the screen of trees. Out of sight, out of mind, he meditated bleakly. Even now, mental illness was still a taboo subject, talked about in hushed tones if it was talked about at all. A bit like venereal disease, he thought with a wry smile. Things like that were not discussed in genteel society. He shook his head sadly. Things hadn't really moved on much since the hospital opened in the 1840s with the name "The Glasgow Royal Lunatic Asylum". When he was younger, he thought it was a rest home for royal lunatics, of which, his father assured him, there were many. He knew better now... about the place, that is. The jury was still out on the number of royal lunatics.

He skirted the hotel and turned into Shelley Road with the pond on his right. He knew the area well and memories of ice-skating on the frozen water of the pond in the depths of winter came to him. Happy days, he thought with a smile, when his cares were limited to what sweets to buy with his pocket money; Highland Toffee, a Sherbet Fountain or Penny Caramels.

The trees were almost bare of leaves after a storm some days earlier and the roadway and pavements were covered in a carpet of brown, yellow and red. Here and there, piles of the dead foliage had been swept into little mounds ready for transportation to a dump somewhere. He kicked his way through the mounds scattering a shower of red, gold and brown leaves around him as he walked. There was another storm on the way later in the day so his minor act of vandalism was of no consequence, he mused. The men would be back tomorrow to repeat their efforts and probably again by the end of the week. This was Scotland and this was autumn.

As he followed the road up through the trees the tall three storey red sandstone building that was Gartnavel Royal Hospital appeared before him. He looked at it carefully for the first time. In his youth it had always been there but it had never been a topic of conversation. Out of sight, out of mind, he thought again. The main block was an imposing structure with four corner brick chimneys rising ominously into the grey morning sky like accusatory fingers. It was like something out of an Alfred Hitchcock film, he thought, with knife-wielding murderer stalking its corridors like baddies in a horror movie. It had that feel about it.

He found the main door, a heavy slab of varnished wood set into the stone with glass panels at each side allowing the nurses to scrutinise callers before opening up. Brass handles, keyholes and a heavy brass doorknocker in the shape of a horned beast, all assiduously polished, added to the overall sense of doom. It displayed one concession to modernity, an electric bell positioned to the left of the door and an intercom system.

He pressed the button, leaving his finger on it for a second or two, and heard the bell jangling harshly in the interior. Almost instantly, a female face appeared behind the glass panel and a pair of alert eyes examined him. He smiled self-consciously and leaned forward towards the intercom. 'I know it's early,' he started apologetically, 'but I wonder if it's possible to visit Roisin Kelly?' he maintained his smile even when the nurse's brow knotted questioningly. He suddenly realised the cause of her confusion. Roisin had married so now she was Roisin something else and he didn't have her married name. He felt a little foolish. It wasn't a good start. 'At least, she was Roisin Kelly,' he started to explain when he heard the locks being thrown one by one and the big door swung open.

A pleasant faced nurse, plump and middle aged, was smiling at him. 'It was the Kelly bit that threw me,' she said, 'but as we only have one Roisin here just now it didn't take me long to work it out.' She looked at her. 'My goodness, you are early,' she said but it didn't sound like a reprimand.

'I only found out Roisin was here last night when I met her cousin and I'm leaving for London later this morning,' he explained. 'I hope it's alright.'

'Of course it is,' the nurse replied, still smiling, and stood aside to let him enter. 'Roisin doesn't get many visitors, apart from her husband and family,' she said, starting down the corridor with Jamie rushing to catch up. 'It might do her good,' she continued. She stopped suddenly and turned back to him.

'But I have to warn you, she isn't very communicative... she doesn't speak at all, really.'

She set off again and led him down a dimly lit corridor that did not improve on his first impression of the place. When they reached the mid-point of the long hallway a flight of broad stairs appeared on their left. The nurse swung to her left and began to climb, Jamie by her side. On the first floor another corridor ran off to both sides and the nurse turned right. There were signs of activity here, Jamie noticed, a nurse pushing a trolley laden with syringes, vials and pills was checking something against a list and another emerged from a room carrying a bedpan.

He couldn't help but admire them. They did a difficult job with little thanks from the public in general, but without complaint. It was more a vocation than a job, Kate always said. She was right.

This corridor was a little more brightly lit. It was an improvement but not by much. They carried on along the corridor until finally they reached a door with the number 4 on it in black on a white background. The nurse smiled encouragingly at him, knocked the door gently, and opened it, ushering him in. ahead of her.

It was bright in the room and Jamie screwed his eyes closed after the dim light of the corridor before focussing again. Roisin was sitting in an armchair by the window, rocking gently back and forth and staring vacantly outside. She didn't turn or give any indication she knew they were there. She appeared to be in a world of her own, Jamie thought... or a hell of her own, he reflected a moment later as he thought of what she had been through.

'You've got a visitor Roisin,' the nurse announced cheerily, tapping her gently on the shoulder.

Roisin turned to them, her sunken eyes dark holes in her wasted face. Jamie barely stifled a gasp of distress. He fought the urge to look away and forced a smile. This wasn't the Roisin he remembered and Liam's description of her hadn't prepared him for this. Her body was emaciated and her skin grey and mottled. Her bare arms, protruding from the rolled up sleeves of an old dressing gown, were no more than skin and bone. He looked at her hair. The vibrant red tresses he remembered now stuck to her head in greasy strands, limp and lifeless.

He smiled again. She was looking at him now, a knitting of her brow and a flicker of interest in her eyes, as if questioning some distant memory, and then she was gone, her curiosity abandoned. She turned away from him, her attention returning to the window and the world outside. She was like a prisoner, he mused, gazing out at the trees and sky that represented freedom, but it wasn't the walls of the room that confined her; it was her thoughts.

Jamie turned to the nurse in despair. She smiled sympathetically and her lips moved silently, mouthing the words "speak to her" as she nodded towards Roisin. Jamie nodded moved round the chair, positioning himself in front of her and sank down onto his knees. He reached out and took both her hands in his, catching her attention again.

'Have I changed so much Roisin?' he said gently, squeezing her fingers tenderly. She was looking at him intently now, memories flooding back he hoped. He gazed back at her, his smile broadening as he detected recognition. Her brow knitted again, almost as though in disbelief, and then tears began to gather behind her eyes.

'Yes Roisin,' he said gently. 'It's really me.' He pushed himself up and kissed her on the brow as her tears started.

Jamie turned to the nurse and saw what he took as a look of surprise on her face. Maybe there was hope there too, he thought.

'Can we have a few minutes alone?' he asked.

The nurse smiled again. 'I don't see why not,' she agreed. 'You're certainly getting a reaction from her and that's encouraging. It's a first, in fact,' she went on, still smiling. If you need me, just press this button,' she continued, pointing to a red switch on the wall. 'But don't stay too long, she'll tire quickly.'

'Thanks, but like I said downstairs, I can't stay long anyway.'

The nurse nodded and left, her footsteps fading down the corridor. Jamie turned back to Roisin. There was distress in her eyes now.

He knelt down before her again. 'I'm here to help you Roisin,' he whispered. 'Just listen to what I have to say. You don't have to talk if you don't want to but I want you to think and when I leave I want you to remember,' he continued gently.

'I know what happened to you,' he went on, keeping his voice low. 'And I know what you're going through.' He smiled as he said that, anticipating her disbelief. 'You might not believe that, but I do.'

She didn't believe it. He could see it in her eyes and knew what she was thinking; how could anyone know what she was going through. He might have a hard job persuading her but he had to try.

'Liam told me everything,' he continued. Tears began to flow. 'I know what you did and I know why,' he went on. Signs of distress showed in Roisin's face. Her nose was running and she sniffed, wiping a hand across it. He would have to tread carefully.

'I'm here because I want to help you,' he re-joined, talking softly in an attempt to alleviate her anguish.

There was another chair in the room, beside the bed. He left her a moment, pulled it over, and sat down beside her. Settled, he took hold of her hands again and felt tiny tremors running through her. 'You're blaming yourself for something that wasn't your fault,' he said. 'You had no choice in the matter. You didn't kill all those people... You were only the tool. Brendan killed them. The man Doherty killed them.' He paused a moment. He could see that she was still wrestling with the enormity of what she had been a part of but at least she was listening. He pushed on. 'I would have done what you did. I would have protected my family too.'

'But all those people died,' Roisin whispered. Her first words, so low he almost missed them. He could see it all in her eyes now. Confirmation of everything Liam had told him. He felt the anger build in him. Roisin had been used, just like he was used.

'Yes, people died,' he agreed gently. 'But if you hadn't done it they would still have died because some other poor man or woman would have been forced to do it... and you would have sacrificed your two wee girls and your husband for nothing Roisin,' he continued. It sounded harsher than he intended.

Tears were streaming down her face again. 'I killed fifteen innocent people; men, women and wee children,' she sobbed. 'How can you help me?'

'No, you didn't,' he replied forcefully. 'Your brother Brendan killed them, I told you. You were only the weapon he used to do it.'

She was shaking her head with despair, still struggling with acceptance of what he was saying. He wrestled with a dilemma now; how much to tell her of his own struggle. Confession might be good for the soul but it could lead to disaster.

'I've done some bad things too,' he said at last, choosing his words carefully. 'The only real difference between us is that I can justify what I do... You can't.' He smiled sadly and squeezed her hands again. 'But you're better than me,' he went on. 'You did what you did to protect your family; I do what I do to protect my own skin.' That wasn't strictly true but if it made he feel better the lie was worth it.

He watched her closely. She was thinking about it, trying to decipher the meaning behind his words.

She shook her head sadly. 'I don't believe you,' she said simply, still sobbing.

Jamie smiled bleakly. 'I'm going to share a secret with you, Roisin, just like yours has been shared with me,' he started hesitantly, watching her reaction. Her sobbing eased and he carried on. 'You knew why I agreed to go to Belfast back in 1967, don't you,' he said. Roisin said nothing but her crying had stopped and her expression confirmed his suggestion. 'And you knew what Brendan had promised me... He delivered it to me the morning we returned. We were in your place in Dixon Avenue, remember?' Roisin gave an almost imperceptible nod.

Jamie smiled again and carried on. 'It was a gun; a Walther automatic, and ammunition. I needed it for something important...'

'To rescue your wife,' Roisin interrupted, remembering.

Jamie's smile grew bleaker. 'Yeah, that was why I needed it and I used it... I killed seven men with it,' he went on, haltingly. 'Eventually, I justified it by telling myself they deserved to die. Maybe they did, maybe they didn't,' he added, almost as if thinking aloud. 'But I lived with it, shut it away, got on with my life.'

'But you saved your wife, didn't you, that's why you did it,' Roisin interjected. The look on Jamie's face told her she was wrong.

'Aye, that was why I did it,' he conceded, smiling wryly. 'But that wasn't how it worked out. I was too late. I killed the first six thinking I could save her but I knew she was dead before I killed the last of them. That was pure revenge. After that, I lost it for a while... Months of recrimination, self-blame, and trying to drink myself to death.' His smile turned bitter. 'I blamed myself for Lucie's death, but I had friends around me. They stuck by me, talked to me, argued with me... and eventually weaned me off the drink. The drink didn't work, Roisin. It deadened the hurt for a while but it didn't end it. It only ended when I stopped blaming myself for something that wasn't my fault... And you have to do the same.'

'I can't,' she whispered.

'Yes, you can,' he retorted, forcefully. 'You have to. You have to for yourself and for everybody else that cares about you... Kevin, your kids, Liam and your auntie Molly... because if you don't, Brendan has won.'

Jamie lapsed into silence. He felt exhausted and beaten. Roisin was away in her other world again. He hoped she was thinking about what he had said but wasn't holding out too much hope. He cast his eyes down at his watch, surprised at how the time had flown. He turned back to Roisin, took her hands again and pulled her to him, squeezing her fingers gently.

'I have to leave,' he said. Roisin seemed calmer now at least, he thought. 'Listen,' he went on. 'I know this is the probably the darkest time of your life, but you can beat it. You can,' he said again, emphasising the positive. 'Think about what I said. Think of your man and your wee girls. They need you, Roisin. Remember that... and remember this too; what happened wasn't down to you. Don't crucify yourself on their behalf for something they forced you to do. Fight it... and let me help.' And I'll crucify the bastards for you, he mused silently.

He pushed himself up from his chair and kissed her on the forehead again. 'Just think about what I've told you,' he said. 'That's all you have to do... and then try to believe in yourself again.'

He let go of her hands and made for the door. As he stepped out into the corridor, he turned and saw Roisin give him a tiny smile. That gave him hope. She had a long way to go, he mused, but the first step down this particular road was always going to be the hardest. He hoped she could finish the journey.

Chapter Twenty-three

Jamie returned to the Lorne, uplifted his bag and signed out. It was now 10.40 and there was a train leaving Glasgow Central for London Euston at 11.20. He intended to be on it. He still had one more thing to do before boarding the train but, after his visit to Roisin, he had something else on his mind. A call to the Brigadier would not change that.

He paid off the cabbie in Union Street at precisely eleven o'clock and bounded up the wide stair that led to the station concourse. He still had twenty minutes to spare - more than enough time. There was a bank of telephone kiosks at the far side of the concourse and most were free. He chose one at the railway end. Even today, Sunday, and in a busy railway station, it smelled like a public toilet. When he thought about it, he couldn't remember ever being in a telephone box from London to Aberdeen that didn't smell the same. Maybe someone came round regularly and sprayed them to keep them "fresh" – Eau de Pish sounded about right, he smiled wryly.

He wrinkled his nose as he fished coins from his pocket. Thirty pence should be enough, he though, and slipped three ten pence pieces into the slot. Sir Charles Redmond answered on the third ring.

'Raeburn,' the old man said gruffly, confirming Jamie's suspicion that this was a dedicated line for his use alone.

'Good morning Brigadier,' Jamie replied jauntily. 'Hope I'm not disturbing breakfast,' he added cheekily, knowing full well that breakfast at Hazelgrove House was long over and the house staff (the Brigadier refused to call them servants) would now be preparing for lunch.

'Good morning,' Sir Charles replied, sounding a little warmer. 'How did it go?'

'Your people didn't tell you?' Jamie threw back, adding a soft laugh.

'My people?' the old man replied, feigning innocence. 'I'm not with you.'

Jamie smiled. He could make a nuisance of himself over it, he mused, but there was nothing to gain by that. He had made his point.

'It went okay,' he said, giving nothing away. 'I'm catching the 11.20 train from here to Euston... do you want to hear my report now or wait till I get to London?'

'No, not over the phone,' Sir Charles responded tersely. 'Where does the train stop on route?'

Jamie stifled a sigh. His plans were about to be disrupted, he could feel it in his water. 'Where is the nearest stop to Hazelgrove, you mean?' he retorted with a snort. 'Watford Junction, I think.'

'Excellent. That's ideal. Get off the train there,' Sir Charles ordered. 'You'll be picked up.'

'You're not coming yourself?' Jamie threw back frostily. 'I intended catching a ferry at Dover tonight.'

'Catch another tomorrow,' the old man retorted. His tone brooked no further argument.

Jamie didn't hide his sigh this time. He might as well let the old bugger know he wasn't pleased but in the end he would have to comply.

'Okay,' he conceded frostily. 'But I'm not hanging about,' he added. 'I want to be home by tomorrow.'

'Understood,' Sir Charles agreed affably. 'I'll see you in a few hours then.'

Jamie still had the phone to his ear when the old man hung up. 'Not so much as a goodbye,' he murmured to himself and smiled bitterly. And Sir Charles thought he lacked social skills.

He looked out across the concourse towards the big four faced clock that hung from the steel roof girders. The time read 11.06. The call had been quick at least. He still had plenty of time to buy his ticket and board the train.

On impulse, he slipped more coins into the coin box and phoned home. After what seemed an almost interminable delay as the call was connected, the ring tone came back to him. There was no reply and he felt a mild panic seize him. He ended the call and dialled again, this time calling the only other place Kate might be.

Another long delay and then the ring tone. This time the call was answered almost immediately. 'Oui, bonjour, Hotel de la Place,' Sandrine Corbeau chirped cheerily. Jamie's anxiety evaporated immediately. Behind Sandrine he could hear a babble of voices and one he immediately recognised. The halting mixture of French and English could only be Kate.

'Bonjour Sandrine,' he replied. 'C'est moi, Jean-Luc Rochefort. Ma femme est la?' he continued quickly, speaking fluent French.

'Mais oui,' Sandrine replied happily and then Kate came on the line, her voice bubbling.

'Cheri,' she said, almost calling him Jamie in her excitement. 'Tu est ou?'

'I'm still in Glasgow,' he responded quickly. 'The train for London leaves in about ten minutes so I don't have long. I just wanted to let you know I won't be home until late tomorrow.'

'Why so long?' she asked, sounding dejected.

'I have to stop make a stop before London. I won't get to Dover tonight. I'm sorry, but you know how it is.'

'Uh-huh, I suppose I do,' she said forlornly. 'The children are missing you,' she went on.

Jamie grimaced. 'I'm missing them too,' he said, his guilt mounting. 'Tell them I'll make it up to them.'

'And me?' Kate asked plaintively.

'Yes, I'm missing you too sweetheart and I'll make it up to you, I promise.' He heard her laugh.

'You'd better hurry. I don't want you missing that train... and if you're any later than tomorrow you'll face the consequences,' she replied, still laughing.

'What consequences?' he said, playing the game.

'You'll be sleeping in the spare room with no one beside you to keep you warm.'

'Threat noted,' he replied. 'I love you,' he added.

'You can show me how much tomorrow,' Kate laughed. 'Go on, get onto the train.'

'I'm on my way he said,' and hung up. He missed her response. He was already out of the phone box and racing for the ticket counter when she told him she loved him too.

***

Later the same day.

The big black Rover 3500 swung off the A411, the Hempstead Road, and through the double wrought iron gates that guarded the driveway to Hazelgrove House. Jamie leaned back in the sumptuous leather rear seat and watched the trees flash past. It was just as he remembered it though now the trees were turning from the light green hues of early spring to the gold, yellow, brown and red of autumn. The verges were neatly tended and the fallen leaves had been swept from the drive.

He thought back to his time here. The gardens that surrounded the house had been bare and barren in March and he wondered what they would be like now. He wasn't disappointed. The blaze of that greeted him from late blooming plants and shrubs took his breath away. The house too, a brilliant white against the late afternoon sky and dressed in a coat of red leaved ivy was equally stunning.

It as an unfair world, he thought. People were living in shanty huts in some places and here one family owned all this. He had grown to like Sir Charles over time. They had their differences, sure, and this was one of them. The socialist in him baulked at it. There was no fairness and justice in this world. Greed rules, he mused bitterly.

As the car approached the house he saw Sir Charles waiting for him at the top of the wide flight of stone steps that led to the door. His customary briar pipe hung from his lips and a pale wisp of smoke rose into the cold air. The driver, the same man who had met him in Coventry almost a year earlier, pulled the car to a halt parallel with the stairway and climbed out quickly to open Jamie's door. Jamie beat him to it. Others would have waited but having someone rush to open doors for him ran contrary to every instinct he possessed. He was out of the car and smiling benignly before the man had straightened up.

'Glad you could make it,' Sir Charles called down to him, taking his pipe in his right hand and waving it ostentatiously in the air.

As if I had a choice, Jamie smiled ruefully.

'I'll show you up to your room and you can freshen up,' the old man went on, smiling jovially, as Jamie climbed the steps to him.

'Can't we just get on with it?' Jamie asked, trying to keep the pleading tone out of his voice. 'I've got a wife and kids waiting for me.'

'Good Lord, no, Raeburn... I should say Rochefort, Sir Charles responded, smiling conspiratorially. 'We'll be having dinner at seven thirty; drinks at seven. We'll talk afterwards.'

Jamie shrugged. There was no point in arguing. Heaving his bag over his shoulder he followed Sir Charles into the great hall and then up the wide, sweeping central stairway.

'Am I in my old room,' Jamie joked cheekily but the old man ignored him.

'Like I say, drinks at seven. Try not to be late,' Sir Charles went on, smiling disarmingly. 'I've arranged for clean clothes to be left for you in your room.'

Jamie suppressed an expletive and stared at the old man angrily. 'What's wrong with these?' he retorted irritably.

The Brigadier rolled his eyes. 'There's absolutely nothing wrong with them old chap. They're just not suitable.'

'Not suitable,' Jamie retorted, laughing. 'Let me tell you; this suit and coat are the best your money could buy,' he chortled. 'Do I look like some well-heeled spiv who's turned up here by mistake?' he carried on, still laughing.

'No, but they do make you look like a hitman and we don't want that, do we?'

Jamie stopped laughing.

I don't want it, that's for sure, but I'm not sure you don't.

He kept that thought to himself.

The house was quiet and they climbed the broad stairway side by side in silence. Jamie remembered it from months before and was having the same feelings now as then. He could have been in Cranston Hall in Derbyshire. The only real difference between both houses was that the gardens here at Hazelgrove House were much more extensive and the house itself was much quieter. But an additional thought came to him this time; were old man Kelman and Brigadier Sir Charles Redmond really any different, one from the other? One had been a criminal mastermind who acted outside the law; the other, the Brigadier, masterminded criminal activity outside the law too but the law turned a blind eye in his case. Worse, in fact, the lawmakers actively encouraged him. It's a strange old world, he mused, smiling drily.

Sir Charles escorted him up to the first floor and along the carpeted corridor and opened the door to a spacious room looking out over the gardens. 'Will this do?' Sir Charles asked as Jamie walked over to the big window and looked out. 'Your old room is being redecorated,' he added with a laugh and Jamie laughed with him. 'There's a telephone there by the bed should you want to telephone your wife. I'm sure she'll want to hear from you. And don't worry, the line isn't tapped,' he added with a smirk. 'Remember, drinks at seven,' he reminded Jamie again as he turned to leave. He paused at the door and turned. 'There is one other thing,' he said, doing his Machiavelli impression. 'There will be other guests at dinner. I will tell them you're French... You can play the part I hope, Monsieur de Rochefort?' he said as he closed the door behind him.

Jamie looked around the room and dropped his bag. 'You can play the part I hope, Monsieur de Rochefort,' he mimicked as he settled down onto the bed and reached for the telephone. When Kate answered his world was instantly better.

***

He made his way downstairs a little before seven that evening feeling distinctly uncomfortable. The dinner suit left for him was a good fit, certainly, but he didn't like dressing up like a mannequin and he wasn't James Bond. Still, with this suit on he could be anything, English, French or even bloody Chinese. His own clothes, the ones he purchased in Glasgow, were distinctly *not* French and his French clothes made him look a bit like a slightly disheveled anarchist. And tonight, by command of Sir Charles, the Lord of the Manor, he was French.

As he dressed in his room earlier he had heard his fellow guests arrive. Cars had driven noisily over the gravel forecourt, doors had banged closed and voices came to him, too indistinct to make out. He didn't spend any time worrying about who they might be. All he wanted was to see the night out, report to the old man and leave.

Now, as he descended to the ground floor, he heard laughter and conversation emanating from the dining room. There were women's voices and one man talking but it was not the Brigadier. The voices were the voices of the "Establishment"... upper class accents and shrill laughter.

Christ, what am I letting himself in for here, he wondered.

He hovered for a moment outside the door, building up his courage, when he heard a door open behind him. He turned to find the man himself.

'Don't be shy, old boy,' the Brigadier said, grinning. 'Go on in. Surprise them.'

'Surprise them?' Jamie retorted drily. 'What am I, the fucking cabaret?' he went on, keeping his voice low. 'If that's your game you forgot to leave the red fez in my room for my Tommy Cooper impersonation.'

'That's not it at all,' Sir Charles returned with a laugh. 'Don't be so touchy. You will, I'm sure, cause a bit of a stir, but you can handle that, can't you.' It was a statement, not a question and Jamie simply smiled.

The old man too was smiling as he leaned past Jamie and took hold of the door handle. He turned it quietly, pushed the door inwards, and then, with his hand on Jamie's back, eased him into the room.

The chatter ended spontaneously and an awkward silence fell on the little gathering as five pairs of eyes turned to face him. No matter what Sir Charles had said, he did feel like the cabaret act. It was surreal. The company, two men and three women, one of whom was Clara Whitelaw, stood with glasses in hand, smiling uncertainly at him. He hid his astonishment well.

Clara was standing a little behind the others, out of their line of sight, and was watching him furtively. She had clearly been expecting him, primed by the old man no doubt to prevent her giving the game away. Her smile was a little more nervous than those of the others.

He smiled warmly back at them, studying each of them more closely. The men, one older, around the Brigadier's age, and a younger man of about thirty-five were standing together slightly to the left of the women. They knew one another. All of them knew one another, he noted. It was in their body language. He was the interloper.

The two women with Clara were older. He recognised the Brigadier's wife, Lady Estelle. They hadn't been formally introduced during his enforced stay at the big house earlier in the year but he had seen from his window, strolling in the grounds. The other woman, judging by her refined looks and her smoky grey eyes, was Clara's mother. Both women were beautiful in their own right; beautiful and confident. It was a class thing, the confidence.

Jamie walked directly towards the women, smiling openly. Lady Estelle extended her hand. He heard the Brigadier introduce his wife and Jamie took her hand in his, letting his lips brush the back of her fingers. 'Enchanté Madame Redmond,' he said, gazing up into her bright brown, impish eyes.

She knows who I really am, he mused

Lady Redmond smiled graciously and turned to the woman beside her. 'And this,' she said, indicating the older woman, 'is my very good friend, Madame Ashcroft.'

Jamie repeated his act, taking the woman's fingers to his lips and kissing them softly. 'Enchanté Madame,' he said, maintaining the act. He only had time to say the words before he was presented to Clara. He smiled and looked her directly in her smoky grey eyes, seeing a mix of amusement, delight and fear. He thought fear predominated. She didn't want their secret laid bare, not in this company.

'And this,' he heard Lady Estelle say, 'is Clarisa Whitelaw, Clara. My husband tells me your paths have crossed before,' she continued, raising an enquiring eyebrow.

Jamie took Clara's long fingers in his and repeated the charade, kissing her hand and watching as a pale pink infused her cheeks. He laughed inside. The old boy had played it well.

'Why yes,' Jamie responded, every inch the Frenchman. 'We met in Belfast, I think?' Clara almost fainted. He hoped he hadn't overplayed it.

'Belfast!' Lady Redmond exclaimed. 'My goodness, what is it you do, Monsieur Rochefort?' The question was asked with just the right element of surprise in her voice but Jamie saw through it. She knew exactly what he did.

'Je travail pour mon gouvernement,' he whispered conspiratorially, and his hostess laughed. He had the good sense not to look at Clara.

Sir Charles took over quickly. He hadn't given out any information about his mysterious guest other than the fact that he was French and was in Britain on business. The one exception was his wife. He had let her into the secret earlier that day and she had chortled gaily. It would make the evening interesting, she said, agreeing to continue the deception. She was playing it perfectly.

But the next bit would prove more tricky, Sir Charles reflected, a little anxiously. The two men would not be impressed by Jamie's Gallic charms.

Their questions would be more pointed, more probing... Particularly Mark Whitelaw, Clara's husband, he thought uneasily. Mark was suspicious by nature and his discovery of Clara's affair had reinforced it. He smiled to himself. There would be fireworks if he found out that Monsieur Rochefort here was his nemesis. He decided it prudent to stay close to Jamie for a while.

He started the introductions with Clara's father. 'This, Monsieur Rochefort, is my oldest and closest friend, John Ashcroft. John is a Conservative Member of our Parliament. I won't bore you with the name of his constituency,' he continued with a laugh. 'It would mean nothing to you. John and I were comrades in arms during the war,' he continued.

Jamie took John Ashcroft's hand and felt the dry firmness of the man's grip. The man's eyes appraised him and he could see the shrewdness behind them. If Clara had inherited her mother's looks and beauty, it seemed she was the inheritor of her father's astuteness and intelligence. He wasn't unlike the Brigadier, Jamie noted; tall, broad shouldered and straight backed. He had quick, lively blue eyes set above a straight aquiline nose and a thin grey moustache that adorned his upper lip. He smiled easily but the eyes never stopped assessing.

John Ashcroft turned then to the younger man beside him. Jamie had already worked out who he was and what was coming. He sensed the man weighing him up, the penetrating look was enough. He was searching for something. 'This is my son-in-law, Mark Whitelaw, Clara's husband,' John Ashcroft said.

Jamie smiled and held out his hand. 'Monsieur Whitelaw. It is a pleasure to meet the husband of the charming Dr Whitelaw,' he said disarmingly, staring back unwaveringly at the man. Mark Whitelaw's grip was firm, perhaps a little too firm, he thought and smiled inwardly. He sensed what the other man was thinking. 'You are a very lucky man,' he added, quickly and flatteringly.

Mark Whitelaw continued to smile but the smile didn't extend all the way up to his eyes. 'I get the feeling I know you,' he said, his eyes narrowing slightly.

Jamie shook his head slowly. He dare not look at Clara. He knitted his brow, thoughtfully, keeping focused. 'No, I don't think so,' he replied slowly. 'I'm sure I would remember. What is it you English say... we do not move in the same circles, I think?' He smiled again, his eyes locked with the other man's. He would have to be very careful now in everything he said and did. This was not a game.

'Would you like a drink, Monsieur Rochefort?' the Brigadier said, intervening quickly.

'Jean-Luc, please, my name is Jean-Luc,' Jamie said with another smile. 'An aperitif would be lovely, thank you.'

'A dry sherry, perhaps? Or we can offer you Whisky, Pastis, Ricard... Suze even... or Armagnac.'

Jamie raised one eyebrow theatrically. 'Suze? You have Suze here in an English home?'

The Brigadier laughed. 'My wife, you may have noticed, is French like you Monsieur... Jean-Luc, and I myself spent some time in your country during the war. I acquired a taste for it then.'

'How do you say... good for you, Sir Charles. It is a special taste, no? Perhaps it is not patriotic, but I have never been able to acquire the taste for it. I do like your Scotch Whisky, however.'

With the mark Whitelaw episode over, Jamie was enjoying himself again and was playing his part to the hilt. He waited as Sir Charles poured him a malt, a Talisker, into a cut crystal tumbler and returned with it. He declined the offer of ice or water and sniffed the malt appreciatively.

'This is not one I have tasted before,' he said, sipping slowly at the golden liquid and letting his face light up. 'Formidable!' he said, raising the glass to the others. 'Santé.' He noticed that all the others raised their glasses and repeated the salutation. All except Mark Whitelaw, that is, who was still staring at him as though trying to place him. Jamie looked directly at the man and raised his glass again.

Whitelaw smiled guiltily and raised his glass. 'Santé to you too, Monsieur,' he said.

Jamie wasn't convinced. Mark Whitelaw was a man with a bad attitude, he decided.

When they finally reached the table after more minutes of small talk Jamie found himself sandwiched between Lady Estelle and Clara's mother. John Ashcroft, the Honourable Member for Essex Central, sat facing him on the other side of the table with Clara to his left and her, now sullen faced, husband on his right facing his mother-in -law. Sir Charles took pride of place at the head of the table. Poor Mrs. Ashcroft, Jamie mused.

It was all very cosy, Jamie thought, except for the fact that there was an undercurrent of suspicion. He smiled inwardly. Stick a group of spies and politicians around a table and what else could you expect, he mused.

He didn't know why but he was fairly sure Mark Whitelaw's problem lay with him. And that, he suddenly realised, was the problem. The man's mood was making everyone else uncomfortable. Morose sod, he thought.

The meal was delicious and after a couple of glasses of a particularly good French red wine, Jamie was chatting easily with the two older women. He kept a discreet boundary between himself and Clara. The last thing he wanted to do now was cause her more grief than he already had. And paying her too much attention might do just that, he deduced. She was unnaturally withdrawn and nervy. He felt for her. On a couple of occasions he caught her looking at him but he didn't return her looks. Discretion, he reminded himself, is the better part of valour.

Dinner finished at around nine thirty and the men retired to Sir Charles' study for "cigars and brandy". The ladies settled in the "drawing room". Jamie smiled to himself. This was how the other half lived, he reminded himself. And here he was, a pleb, at the centre of it. As the Brigadier handed round the cigars Jamie pulled a packet of Gauloise Bleu from his pocket. A nice touch, he thought, as he savoured the look of disgust on the old boy's face.

Conversation was stilted and seemed to focus on trivia. Jamie found himself fielding questions on the Continent's weather, the ordinary Frenchman's attitude to "England" joining the Common Market and the cost of living. He was tempted to remind them that it was the United Kingdom, not just England, that had joined the Common Market but that would have been strange coming from a "Frenchman". He did point out, however, that the ordinary Frenchman couldn't care less who was in it as long as it didn't cost him anything.

It was still relatively early when Mark Whitelaw announced that he was retiring to bed. He had an early start in the morning. The only surprise to Jamie was the fact that all the dinner guests were staying.

Mark Whitelaw's early night took some of the pressure off. Jamie could relax a little now, but he was finding the night tedious. He would rather be curled up, asleep, on a seat on the Calais to Paris train, heading for home.

The desultory conversation among the three remaining men continued for a while with more cognac and cigars before they rejoined the women. Clara, Jamie was surprised to find, was still there. He had expected her to have headed off to bed with her boorish husband. He remembered a feeling of irrational jealousy when that thought entered his head earlier. The change in her with her husband gone was dramatic and Jamie found it a little unsettling.

There was general chatter about politics among the older members of the group with Jamie and Clara on the sidelines. She manoeuvred herself close to him. There was a "professional" smile on her face but when Jamie looked closer he could see it was more than that. She was genuinely happy to see him... Happy that he was here. That too, was a little disconcerting.

'Charles tells me you want to be at Dover early tomorrow morning,' she said, looking at him over the rim of her glass. 'You will be missing your home, I imagine.'

'Yes,' he replied, holding her gaze. What was going on behind those beautiful grey eyes, he wondered. There was something there; he just couldn't work out what it was. 'My wife expected me home tonight,' he added, watching for her reaction. Why did he feel guilty?

The evening began to break up shortly afterwards. The Ashcrofts took their leave, wished "Monsieur Rochefort" a good night, and headed for their room on the first floor. Clara followed them shortly afterwards, holding on to Jamie's hand a little longer than necessary when wishing him good night. Her eyes lingered a little longer.

Sir Charles had disappeared somewhere, leaving Jamie alone with the shrewd Lady Estelle. The Brigadier was probably preparing the torture chamber, he mused, ready to extract all the information from him. He felt momentarily awkward. He needed a cigarette to calm his nerves but was reluctant to light up here in the confines of the plush drawing room.

It wasn't his impending debrief that bothered him. It was the domestic situation surrounding Clara and her husband. He had played a part in that and although he wasn't solely to blame, he felt guilty. He pulled his pack of Gauloise from his dinner jacket pocket and held them up for Lady Estelle to see. 'I wonder... do you mind if I go outside to smoke?' he asked tentatively.

She gave him a radiant smile. 'Pourquoi pas, Monsieur,' she replied in her native French. 'It is warm in here. Perhaps I could join you; do you mind?'

Jamie did mind but he wasn't going to say so to this lovely and gracious lady. 'Non, pas du tout, je serai heureux si vous joindre à moi,' he responded easily – 'No, not at all, I will be very happy if you join me,' he translated needlessly.

He escorted her to the French windows that led out onto the terrace, standing back to allow her to open the doors. He watched her admiringly. She was incredible, he thought, given her age. Her skin was smooth, her hair immaculate and her figure would have made many younger women green with envy. She took his arm and they walked slowly out onto the wide stone terrace. There was a hint of late blooming jasmine on the air.

It was a balmy night. A gentle breeze, still warm, eddied through the plants and shrubs and Jamie smelt the jasmine stronger now. He thought of Kate and his family and the complications that were taking over his life again. Why me? He mused sadly.

Lady Estelle led him across the terrace and stopped at the far edge, placing a long manicured hand on one of the stone balustrades. Jamie held up the pack of Gauloises again and watched, amused, as she giggled and looked to see if her husband was close. She nodded then, almost conspiratorially. 'Charles will be annoyed,' she laughed. 'It has been so long since I smoked one of these.'

Gingerly, Jamie teased one of the cigarettes from the pack and offered it to her. She took it carefully in her fingers, caressing it almost lovingly, before placing it between her lips. Jamie flipped open his battered Zippo and held the flame out to her. The light from the flame reflecting back from her face made her look angelic, he thought. When he brought the flame to his own Gauloises, he imagined the effect would be somewhat different. Demonic, perhaps, he mused dolefully.

'You played your part in there very well Mr. Raeburn,' Lady Estelle whispered softly as she blew out the first plume of smoke.

'So you knew all along,' he said with a quiet laugh.

'But of course. My husband and I have no secrets.'

'You're very lucky then,' he replied. 'Most couples have secrets,' he added and was sure he saw her smile in the darkness.

'Ne t'inquiète pas, don't worry; your secret is safe with me,' she responded, the smile still there.

Jamie regarded her pensively. And what particular secret would that be, he reflected, laughing inwardly.

'My husband thinks very highly of you,' she said, moving on. Her voice was still little louder than a whisper. 'You are, he says, the best of the best.' She caught Jamie's bitter smile and mistook it for amusement. 'You find that amusing?' she asked.

'Amusing?' he laughed. 'No, it certainly isn't funny, he said bitterly. Being "the best of the best" really makes me the worst of the worst, don't you think?' His bitterness surprised her. 'I'm not proud of myself,' he continued quietly. He turned away from her and looked out over the garden as though searching in the dark shadows.

She moved closer to him and he felt her hand placed on top of his. 'Are you talking about Clara now or the men you've killed?' she asked softly.

He turned back to her quickly. 'You know about that too?' he murmured, his disquiet growing.

Lady Estelle laughed disarmingly. 'I told you, my husband and I have no secrets.'

Now I know which of my secrets is safe with you, he mused.

'Were you ever in love with her?' she continued, watching him closely now.

Jamie gave her a grim smile. 'You don't miss and hit the wall, do you?' he retorted. She looked at him quizzically. Lost in translation, he realised instantly. 'You get right to the point,' he explained.

Her smile broadened and she nodded. 'Yes, of course, why not?'

Why not indeed, Jamie laughed to himself. Sir Charles had found a gem in this lady.

'Love is a strange phenomenon,' he responded. 'There was a popular song back in the 60s... It was by the Everly Brothers, do you remember them?' He wondered if pop music in the 1960s would be her scene. He was pleasantly surprised when her face lit up.

'Why yes... They were American... I remember them. "All I have to do is Dream" and "Bye, Bye Love" - that was them, no?'

'Yes, that was them,' Jamie confirmed, laughing aloud. 'And they also sang "Love is Strange" and that sort of sums up what I mean. Do you remember that one - "Once you've got it, you never want to quit, once you've had it, you're in an awful fit"? Love creeps up on you without warning, doesn't it?' She was still smiling, he noted.

'Yes, I remember that song too,' she said. 'And yes, it is strange... but you haven't answered my question.' She wasn't letting go.

Jamie gazed out into the darkness again, dragged deeply on his cigarette and wished that the night would swallow him up. This was getting too personal. There was almost complete silence broken only by the sounds of nature; the gentle hiss of the breeze in the leaves, the lonely call of an owl, the tiny squeaks of bats as they performed seamless aerobatics in the darkness.

'A bat,' Lady Estelle confirmed. 'We have a colony of them in the roof space. They're protected, you know.'

Jamie nodded absently, his mind still on her earlier question. 'I'm married,' he said.

'Yes, I know... but that still doesn't answer my question,' she persisted. 'Do your feelings scare you?'

Christ, she doesn't let up, Jamie groaned inwardly. But had she hit the nail on the head, he pondered? Did his feelings frighten him? He pulled deeply on the cigarette again, filling his lungs, and exhaled through his nose. He wasn't enjoying the Gauloises now any more than he was enjoying this grilling. He felt her fingers drumming lightly on the back of his hand.

'She's still in love with you, you know,' she said, opening the wound again.

'She's still got her husband,' he retorted automatically.

Lady Estelle smiled a little sadly. 'But they're not quite a couple, are they?' she remarked quietly.

Jamie acknowledged her comment with a sad little smile of his own. She had him with that one. 'Why is this important?' he asked.

The smile was still there when she replied. 'It isn't important to me,' she said.

Jamie got the impression she had anticipated the question.

'Clara will eventually get over the hurt,' she continued. She was still whispering. 'She and Mark might still weather the storm... But she'll probably always be in love with you, I think.' She paused, her fingers still playing lightly on the back of his hand, waiting for his reaction. She saw him look away towards the shadows again. 'The person this little chat is important to is you,' she said eventually, drawing his look back to her. 'Denying how you feel only makes you miserable. It is possible to love more than one person,' she went on relentlessly. 'It isn't exclusive. It's all a matter of degree.'

'You sound as though you're speaking from experience,' he said, still mulling over her words. He didn't add the question "are you?" – he thought better of it.

Lady Estelle's smile had turned enigmatic in the darkness. 'Maybe I am,' she said, giving a soft laugh. Her fingers still tapped gently on the back of his hand, creating a sense of intimacy.

Jamie was being drawn to her. He had never discussed his feelings with anyone like this before and yet, here he was, on the verge of confessing all. Even Frank Daly hadn't managed to get through his armour like Lady Estelle Redmond did. Confession is good for the soul, he thought for the second time that day. Maybe there was something in that... Assuming I have a soul, he mused. She was right, though. He had too many secrets and too many denials.

'Yes, I was in love with her,' he admitted at last, surprising himself. 'I still do, I suppose, but I can't give her what she wants.'

Lady Estelle nodded slowly. Getting him to open up had been easier than she imagined. Healing all the wounds – his and Clara's – might prove more difficult. 'How do you know what she wants if you don't speak to her about how you both feel?' she went on quietly. 'Until a few days ago, Clara thought you were dead. She was in mourning... even though you weren't together by then. She was, I think, getting over it - rebuilding her life – and then, out of the blue, she learns you're still alive. Imagine how that must feel.'

'She didn't know?' Jamie asked, his voice displaying his surprise at this disclosure.

'No one knew. Charles kept it from everyone.'

Except you, Jamie mused, smiling dryly.

'Clara turned up at your funeral and stood beside me, crying her eyes out.'

'And Mark... Was he there?'

'No, he wasn't there. He was licking his own wounds somewhere else, I imagine.'

'He doesn't know who I am, does he?'

'No. You're Jean-Luc Rochefort as far as he's concerned... But he's been let down before and you're a handsome young man. He's jealous, naturally.'

Jamie shook his head sadly. What a mess. 'What can I do?' he whispered, more to himself than Estelle Redmond.

'You can start by being her friend. She's not your enemy. She doesn't want to hurt you or punish you. She knew what she was getting into... She confided in me and she knows she can't have you – you made your choice – but she doesn't want to lose you completely.'

Jamie stared out into the night and pinched the burning tip of his cigarette between his thumb and forefinger. 'And is friendship enough?' he asked meekly.

'Only time will tell,' Lady Redmond replied gently. 'But it's a start.' She remembered a quote then – lovers who remain friends after their affair ends either were never in love or still were. Now wasn't the time to share it, she decided. She smiled. 'That wasn't so difficult, was it?' she said gently.

'No, it wasn't,' Jamie confessed.

'I knew what your answer would be all along,' she confided. 'It is in your eyes when you look at her... and in Clara's too.'

Jamie moaned inwardly. Was that what was behind Mark Whitelaw's mood? Had he too read those looks?

Estelle Redmond read his thought. 'He doesn't know it was you,' she continued reassuringly. 'Even though he saw you both together that night... Did you know that?'

'Saw us? What night?' Jamie blurted Christ, what else, he wondered?

'The last night you and Clara spent together,' she said, and felt him tense. 'He was outside when you left the house.' She went on quickly, anticipating his unasked question. 'He was further down the road. He saw a man leaving the house, that's all,' she said, explaining. 'He thinks that man is dead and he doesn't know it's you.'

'Why didn't he do something at the time?' Jamie pondered aloud.

'God knows... Only Mark knows that, I suppose.'

'I don't understand,' Jamie continued, mystified by Mark Whitelaw's inaction. 'I would have done...' He stopped, unsure where he was going with this.

Lady Estelle responded before he could go on. 'Yes, I imagine you would have,' she said. 'But you and Mark are two very different creatures.'

'But, Christ, if I thought someone was destroying my marriage...' He let his words tail off.

Estelle Redmond smiled a little sadly. 'Don't blame yourself... I think the marriage was on shaky ground before Clara came to you.'

Jamie ignored the blame bit. Yes, he blamed himself, but not in relation to Mark Whitelaw. 'But they're still together, aren't they?' he said, confused.

Lady Estelle's laugh took him by surprise. 'They still share the same house but they're not quite together. Not yet. They're working on it,' she went on. 'Your unexpected resurrection may be a setback to that but, as with everything else, only time will tell.'

'You like him?'

'Yes... or maybe I should say I used to like him. I would like the old Mark Whitelaw to return. He isn't good for himself these days.'

That, Jamie mused, was an understatement. But at least he now understood the man's apparent resentment of him. Every man that Clara came into contact with now would be suspect in Mark Whitelaw's eyes.

'Don't shut Clara out of your life,' Lady Redmond continued. 'You two still need each other, I think,' she said quietly, squeezing his fingers. They stood together for a moment in the darkness, enjoying the silence of the night, until a soft cough brought them both back to the moment.

'Ah, there you are,' Sir Charles called out as he strode towards them, two of the crystal tumblers in his hands. 'I'm afraid I have to take Monsieur Rochefort from you my dear,' he said, maintaining the pretense. 'We have things to discuss.' He handed one of the glasses to Jamie. The distinctive aroma of Talisker drowned the jasmine.

'Of course,' his wife responded immediately. 'It has been lovely talking with you Monsieur. Remember what I said, and bonne chance.' She stretched up and kissed him twice on both cheeks, kissed her husband on the lips, and left them alone.

Chapter Twenty-four

Sir Charles took his wife's place beside Jamie at the balustrade. If he was wondering what she and Jamie had been discussing, he gave no sign of it. Not that it mattered, Jamie mused, smiling inwardly. If he didn't already know he would find out all about it later. Sir Charles and Lady Estelle had no secrets, after all.

'I'm sorry about tonight,' Sir Charles murmured unexpectedly. 'I hadn't expected Mark Whitelaw to be here,' he added. 'I thought he was over in Ireland.'

Jamie shrugged, the gesture suggesting it was of no consequence to him.

Sir Charles caught the nuance and switched tack immediately. 'Do you want to talk out here or shall we go into my study?' he asked. 'The Talisker is in there,' he added, with a hint of a smile.

Jamie laughed softly. 'You certainly know how to manipulate me, Brigadier. The study sounds good. It is soundproofed I take it?'

The Brigadier shook his head and rolled his eyes. He led the way back into the house with Jamie following, sipping at his Talisker in a leisurely fashion as he ambled behind.

'Before we start, I have something for you up in my room,' Jamie said at the foot of the stairs.

'From our friend?' Sir Charles queried.

Jamie smiled. He doubted that "friend" was an appropriate description of Liam, but what the hell.

'You'd better bring it to me, then. I'll wait in the study,' Sir Charles went on. He waited a moment until Jamie set off, then walked off towards his study.

Jamie hurried up the stairs. It wasn't a desire to please that prompted his rush. He just wanted the night to be over with as quickly as possible. When he returned, the Brigadier was already ensconced behind his desk, his pipe lit. Jamie tossed the envelope with the photographs onto the desk and pulled out his Gauloises. He removed his bow tie - it was strangling him - and now stood, relaxed, in front of the older man.

Sir Charles picked up the package, weighed it thoughtfully in his hand much as Jamie himself had done, and nodded his consent to Jamie lighting up. Jamie took his time, lit the cigarette, and pulled up one of the Queen Anne chairs that were scattered haphazardly around the room, and sat down. He drew deeply on his French cigarette and sipped his Talisker.

The air was heavy with a throat burning concoction of pungent pipe tobacco and cigarette smoke. God alone knew what it was doing to their lungs, Jamie mused. He took another sip of the Talisker and sighed contentedly under his breath. He had lied to the assembly earlier. Talisker, the only whisky produced on the island of Skye, was a malt whisky he knew very well and liked even more. The Brigadier was going through the photographs a second time, the picture of the young woman now set aside from the others.

'I assume he told you who these people are?' Sir Charles said at last.

Jamie nodded. He leaned forward and picked up the photographs of the various men, identifying them one by one.

When he finished, Sir Charles leaned over the desk and lifted the photograph of the young woman. 'And what about this one?' he asked, his eyes burning into Jamie now.

Jamie shook his head slowly but kept his mouth shut.

Sir Charles eyed him suspiciously. 'Where did he get it, did he say?'

Again, Jamie shook his head.

'Did you ask?' Sir Charles asked, his voice rising in line with his frustration.

'No,' Jamie stated quietly.

The Brigadier puffed on his pipe and sipped his whisky. He seemed sceptical, Jamie thought. 'It's hardly a portrait, is it?' he said after a while. It wasn't exactly put as a question so Jamie avoided commenting. His warning to Liam was coming to pass. 'There's nothing remotely identifiable about her,' Sir Charles went on. 'The bloody thing is worthless, so why give it to us?'

Jamie shrugged. 'I'm sure you know the answer to that better than me,' he said.

Sir Charles put the photograph aside. His eyes locked onto Jamie's now, holding his look unblinkingly. He changed tack abruptly. 'Alright, let's get back to these men and what else Corkscrew knows about this attack,' he said, waving his hand over the other photographs.

Jamie gave another shrug. 'There isn't much to tell,' he started. 'Doherty, Macari and Finnegan are members of his ASU. As for the others, he thinks they're the men who will be commanding the other units. Their reputations precede them,' he added.

'Yes, I know of them,' the Brigadier acknowledged. 'The RUC and our own Security Services have been after them for years but have never been able to tie them to anything.'

Jamie smiled grimly. 'That hasn't stopped you in the past. I thought that was why you had people like me at your disposal... or has policy changed?' he asked acerbically. There was another possibility - one he didn't want to contemplate - maybe Ultra was running short of Archangels.

Sir Charles ignored his sarcasm. He was now deep in thought.

'There is one other thing,' Jamie continued. 'The attack, or attacks, will be carried out on 25 January next year and Corkscrew didn't come over to Glasgow alone... Doherty, Macari and Finnegan were with him. They met up with someone while they were over. He didn't tell me who, where or why. If he knows he's probably keeping it up his sleeve... as insurance,' he added with a grim smile.

Sir Charles looked up sharply. '25th January you say... did he say why that date particularly?'

'No, not at all. It is Rabbie Burns' birthday right enough... Maybe they're going to a big Burns' Supper,' he added sarcastically, before realising that suggestion might not be as stupid as it seemed. Burns' Suppers could be big affairs with lots of high profile guests all in one place at one time.

'Who did he meet with, did he say?' Sir Charles asked, his mind working overtime.

'No, I told you, he didn't say.'

The old man nodded pensively and began scribbling in a small notepad.

Jamie looked around the room as he waited. He remembered being here with the Brigadier just before his release back into the big bad world earlier in the year. It was about five weeks after the debacle at Kiltyclogher, and nothing had changed. The heavy, lingering smell of Sir Charles' pipe tobacco still clung to the curtains and furnishings and the desk was, as always, clear of paper. Tidy desk, tidy mind, the old boy had told him then.

The same bookcases lined the walls and, at a cursory glance, it looked to Jamie as if none of the books filling the shelves had moved; not even an inch. The old boy was obviously an aficionado of military history as most of the weighty tomes that filled the shelves were in that genre. "With Wellington at Waterloo", "Campaigns of Napoleon: Jena"... that was clearly an old one, its leather covers scuffed and its spine split. Probably worth a few bob, he mused. There was a whole set of "The Times History of The War Illustrated", volume after volume of that one, and another that he remembered from his earlier visit, General Charles De Gaulle's "Memoires de Guerre: L'Appel 1940 – 1942"... in the original French. A bit of light reading for her ladyship, or not, he smiled inwardly. It was still gathering dust with the others.

Sir Charles finished scribbling and rose from his desk to make his way to one of the big burgundy leather armchairs that sat each side of the room's ornate fireplace. He carried the bottle of Talisker in one hand and his tumbler in the other. Sitting down heavily, he waved Jamie to the chair opposite and waited until he had settled.

The cat and mouse game was about to start, Jamie anticipated. There was little point in trying to predict the questions that were coming just as there was no point in fabricating anything. Lying wasn't a good idea. It simply opened a can of worms that would lead to more questions, until he finally lied himself into a corner he couldn't escape from. When it came to interrogation, Sir Charles Redmond had few, if any, equals. He picked away at things relentlessly, like picking at an annoying scab until it bled.

So, lying was out of the question, but evasion, on the other hand, was not. The trick was to tell some of the truth, but not all of the truth. There was one proviso to that; if it came to questions about the bomber he would lie through his teeth but would keep it simple; Corkscrew didn't mention the Coventry bomber. End of story.

Sir Charles eased his bulk forward in his chair and leaned towards him with an offering of more Talisker. Jamie lifted his glass and nodded. The gurgling sound of the golden liquid filling his tumbler was strangely comforting.

'So how was Corkscrew?' Sir Charles started. Gentle probing to begin with.

'As you would expect,' Jamie replied, adding a grim little laugh. 'He's beginning to buckle... jumping at shadows.'

Sir Charles snorted. 'Understandable, I suppose. It wears you down,' he continued.

Jamie laughed coldly. 'Aye, I imagine the Grim Reaper turning up in your dreams every night has that effect.'

'He didn't give you much, did he?' the old boy went on. 'There was nothing he couldn't have left in a dead drop. Why insist on meeting you?'

It was a good question, Jamie mused. But it didn't come as a surprise.

'So what else was there?'

Jamie shrugged. 'I wondered about that myself,' he replied, avoiding a direct answer. This, he knew, was where things would start to get difficult. He sipped at his Talisker to give him a chance to think and thanked God he'd had the good sense to limit his alcohol intake earlier. The Brigadier was shrewd. There was no need to meet just to hand over these photographs and give a date. Logic pointed to there being something else and the old boy would work away at it until he got to the truth. Was it time for him to go on the offensive, he pondered.

'What aren't you telling me, Brigadier?' he asked, deciding the time was right. The old boy drew his brow together.

'I got the same vibes from Corkscrew,' Jamie went on. 'He was tip-toeing around something and I get the feeling you know what. He wanted to tell me but I don't think he trusts me enough just yet... So what is it?' he probed. He realised he was venturing onto thin ice but he had set out his stall quite carefully by stating his feeling that Liam was keeping something from him. He would soon find out.

'He said nothing to you at all?'

Jamie shook his head.

'Not even when he showed you the photograph of the woman?'

Jamie repeated his head shake but replied this time. 'No, he didn't, but that was when I realised there was something else going on. And you know what it is,' he accused.

Sir Charles sipped his whisky and puffed on his now dead pipe. He was thinking things through, Jamie knew the signs.

'Did he mention the Coventry bomb at all?' Sir Charles said quietly after a while.

Jamie smiled grimly. 'No, but I get the feeling that's what this is all about. Am I right?'

The old man looked through him. He was thinking again. It took a little longer for him to come to a decision this time. 'You made it clear you no longer wished to be an Archangel,' Sir Charles said after a while. 'Is that still the case?'

Jamie gave a soft laugh. 'It was a wee bit more than a "wish",' he replied brazenly. 'I said I wouldn't work for you again.'

'Semantics,' Sir Charles retorted. 'It amounts to the same at the end of the day. My question however is, do you still feel the same... Is that better?' he demanded caustically.

'Why? Does it matter?'

'It matters, old boy, because I have to make a judgement on how much to tell you.'

'And that would include whatever it is you've been keeping from me up till now, would it?' Jamie re-joined with a cold smile.

'Don't be obtuse, Raeburn. Just give me your answer.' Sir Charles was beginning to sound exasperated.

Jamie thought about it. He stared back at Sir Charles, trying to gauge what the old man was thinking and how far he would go with the story. One thing was certain, the Brigadier wouldn't go very far if he maintained his stand. And if I don't, and give in to him, he pondered, what then? There was only one way to find out, he decided.

'Let's say I've been giving it some thought,' he replied.

'Do share them.'

'I'm already back working for you... in a limited capacity. You haven't asked me to deliver the good news to anyone... Not yet. He paused.'

'And?' Sir Charles pushed.

'I've been sucked in again,' Jamie continued, smiling again. 'I'd be lying if I said I didn't miss it. What happened at Kiltyclogher gave me a fright; I had started to believe in my own immortality up till then.' His face was set hard now.

'My family comes first,' he went on. 'Until Kiltyclogher, you did. I went in there because of loyalty to you and because I thought it was important...'

'It was important,' Sir Charles protested. 'You stopped a major arms shipment.'

'And nearly got myself killed,' Jamie retorted. 'I spent a lot of time thinking about my family after that.'

'So what are you saying? You're not prepared to resume your role as an Archangel?'

Jamie snorted softly. 'No, I'm not saying that Brigadier. What I am saying is that I won't put my life on the line again the way I did at Kiltyclogher. I knew what I was walking into that night. I knew the bastards were there. I should have turned my back and walked away, aborted the mission. But I didn't, and do you know why? Because I thought I would be letting you down... Not the country, not the Queen, not my family... you. That won't happen again,' he said, shaking his forcefully. 'From now on my family comes first. I'll come back to work but I'll do it on my terms.'

Sir Charles smiled dryly. 'Strange,' he said. 'I thought that was always the case.' He waited a moment. Then – 'So, you will resume your duties?'

Jamie gave derisory snort. 'You're wasted in this line Brigadier... You should go into politics or acquire some of the bluntness you keep telling me I have. What you want to know is, will I'll kill for you again. You're spending too much time with your politician friends, Brigadier.'

Sir Charles smiled. This was the Jamie Raeburn he remembered. 'Alright,' he replied. 'Will you?'

Jamie nodded grimly. 'Yes, I will,' he said, a frosty smile on his face. He had thought about it since talking with Liam and meeting Roisin. He could do it for them. Yes, he could kill for them.

'I'll be your blunt instrument again, Brigadier,' he added with a heavy sigh.

Sir Charles gave a soft laugh. 'Don't belittle yourself, Raeburn,' he said. 'You are only blunt when talking to me. In every other way you're as sharp as a tack.' He leaned across, bottle in hand. 'Have another drink and I'll tell you what I want you to do.'

***

'It's quite simple, really,' Sir Charles said as he settled back in his chair, drink in hand.

Jamie laughed aloud. 'I've heard that before,' he said, 'usually from you. You know as well as I do there's nothing simple in what we do, so cut the bullshit Brigadier.'

'You're back to your insubordinate best, I see,' the old man retorted. There was no animosity in it. 'That's good,' he went on. 'I hope it extends to everything else.'

'Well I suppose we'll find out, won't we.' Sir Charles gave a slow nod in response. Jamie smiled in turn. 'So what is this thing that's really simple?' he asked.

Sir Charles re-lit is pipe and settled back. He drew Jamie a measured look and started with a question. 'Do you remember we met in Coventry earlier this year?'

'How could I forget?' Jamie retorted bitterly. 'It was just before Kiltyclogher.'

'Indeed... 5th February,' the Brigadier agreed. 'We went for a stroll.'

'You took me to the bomb site, I remember, but what has this got to do with Fitzpatrick?' Jamie queried, feigning ignorance. He knew exactly what it had to do with Liam.

'Everything, as it happens,' Sir Charles replied.

Jamie snorted derisively. 'You're telling me he was involved?' he said, laughing.

'Not involved, no, but he knows who was.'

Aye, he does, but he won't tell you, Jamie mused silently.

'So, this is all about the bomber?' he probed, trying to sound confused... 'And nothing to do with these attacks?'

The old man shook his head, smiling back at him. 'They are both part of the package I expect Corkscrew to deliver,' he said in reply. 'In return, he gets his freedom... his new identity and his new life.'

'And what if he doesn't know who the bomber is or who was behind it?'

'He does,' Sir Charles said. It had a ring of certainty.

'You've asked him, have you?'

The old man laughed softly. 'Oh yes, I've asked him. He denies all knowledge but he's lying. I know he's lying and I'm sure he knows I know.'

171

'And I come in to this where?'

The smile was still on Sir Charles' face but it lacked warmth. It was a bit like looking at a benign iceberg, Jamie mused.

'You are already in it, old boy,' the Brigadier answered. Jamie grimaced. He hated this "old boy" routine. 'Corkscrew asked for you... Dermott, remember? You are the only man he feels he can trust. That, I believe, gives you a somewhat privileged position. That trust gives you leverage. He will believe what you tell him... And you will tell him that without giving up the name of the Coventry bomber, he's going nowhere.'

Jamie held his look. 'But if he doesn't know who the bomber is that will gain us nothing,' he commented, taking another sip of the malt.

There was a momentary pause as Sir Charles framed his response.

'You're good at what you do, Raeburn,' he said finally. 'And you can take it that I'm good at what I do too. I've met with Corkscrew. I've interrogated him on this subject and I've listened to his denials, but, because I'm good at what I do, and I've been doing it for a very long time, I know instinctively when someone is lying to me.' He paused again, his eyes now locked on Jamie, watching him closely. He didn't see the shiver run down Jamie's spine but he knew he had caused on. He smiled frostily. 'When Corkscrew says he doesn't know the bomber, he is lying.' There was another pregnant pause. 'The way you do sometimes,' he went on, icy smile still in place.

Jamie smiled back innocently but he knew his card was marked.

'So you want me to betray him, is that it?'

Sir Charles laughed. 'There's that bluntness again,' he chortled. 'What I want you to do is persuade him that giving up the bomber is in his best interests. That way, I get what I want and he gets what he wants.'

'And when and if he tells me, what then?'

'Then you will tell me and you will bring him out, as promised. After that, you can bow out if you wish.'

'And the bomber?'

'She'll be picked up, she'll be interrogated, naturally, and she'll give us the names of the people behind the outrage.' There was no element of doubt in his voice.

Jamie smiled bitterly. The words "picked up" were significant. The old man hadn't said "arrested". Arrest would mean she would be in the system and there would then be a record of her. Her arrest would be come out in the press and the men who had planned the bombing would melt away. No, she would be picked up and then they would be picked up and then... Well, then they could be eliminated, and no questions asked. But he thought he would ask.

'And what happens to them then?'

Sir Charles stared back at him blandly. 'You're being intentionally obtuse again, Raeburn,' he chided. 'You know what happens to them then.'

Jamie sat back and took another mouthful of the Talisker. He swirled it around his mouth, savouring the different flavours He could taste the rich, dried fruit sweetness mixed with the smoke of the peat and the strong barley-malt. The peppery warmth hit the back of his mouth. He smiled contentedly and brought out his Gauloise again. Sir Charles wrinkled his nose but nodded consent. Jamie lit the cigarette and drew deeply on the strong tobacco.

'I'll do it for you,' he said softly.

The Brigadier cocked an eyebrow. 'That's a dramatic change of heart,' he commented warily. 'What brings this on?'

Jamie shrugged. He drew on his cigarette and took another drink of the whisky. 'The world's a shitty place,' he said. 'And someone has to clean it up. That bomb killed a lot of innocent people... women and kids, families... It could have been my family.'

Sir Charles topped up their glasses. He was quietly content. It had been much easier than he had thought and he wouldn't need to use Clara's powers of persuasion on Raeburn after all. That was a result... And yet, there was something troubling him. Something wasn't quite right with Jamie Raeburn's Damascene conversion.

'You've never killed a woman before,' he said softly.

Jamie smiled back coldly. 'You've never asked me to,' he said, matching the old man's tone.

'The question is; can you?'

The cold smile was still on Jamie's face. 'Man, woman, what's the difference? I work in pest control. It's a bit like working for Rentokil but the vermin and pests I exterminate are a bit bigger and more dangerous. As long as I think of it like that I can live with it.' He watched the old man carefully as he delivered this particular homily. He didn't want to overplay it.

They sat in silence for a while, summing each other up and filling the room with a toxic cloud of pipe and tobacco smoke.

'There is one other thing,' Jamie re-joined at last. The Brigadier raised a querying eyebrow. 'I want all surveillance on Corkscrew lifted,' he continued.'

'Why?' the Brigadier queried cagily. Jamie's demand did not sit well with him.

'He's scared. If he thinks he's coming under suspicion by his own lot he'll expect to be followed and watched. The boys in IRA Security are good. They can smell a tout at half a mile. They'll expect him to be watched by the Close Observation boys and RUC E4 but if they spot someone else keeping tabs on him it'll rouse their suspicions and he, we, can do without that. Pull them off,' Jamie argued.

'It's for his own protection,' Sir Charles countered.

'It could also be his undoing.'

The Brigadier stared at the ceiling, pondering Jamie's argument. There was, he had to concede, some merit in it but he suspected some ulterior motive behind it. 'I'm not happy with it,' he said at length. 'If we lose Corkscrew now we lose everything. I would prefer to keep eyes on him... For his own safety, as I said.'

Jamie gave a resigned shake of the head. It was a lost cause. Even if the old boy had agreed to his request, he knew he wouldn't stick to it. He would just have to live with it. That only left him then - 'I take it I don't need to keep looking over my shoulder?' he said.

Sir Charles laughed cynically. 'Keeping you under surveillance would be pointless, Raeburn. You'd simply lose them if you wanted to,' he said.

'Aye, like I did yesterday in Glasgow,' Jamie retorted, grinning in the face of the old man's earlier denial. Sir Charles gave a frosty smile in response but for jamie, that was enough.

'So, now that you're back on board, what will you need?' the Brigadier resumed, serious again.

'A new name, new bank account... I don't know what else until Fitzpatrick...'

'Corkscrew,' Sir Charles interjected irritably. 'Use his code name. Always.'

'Sorry,' Jamie acknowledged. 'I should have known better. I'm rusty,' he went on. 'It won't happen again. I was about to say that I don't know what else I'll need until Corkscrew comes up with the goods. Until then, all I can do is watch, wait and listen.' Sir Charles nodded thoughtfully. 'We don't even know the general location of the attacks,' Jamie continued.

'You will keep the name Michael,' the Brigadier announced. 'Michael Ferryman,' he added.

'Ferryman?' Jamie queried.

'Yes, it's appropriate don't you think?'

'Is it?'

Sir Charles snorted a soft laugh. 'Of course it is,' he replied. 'To get to Hades the dead have to cross the River Styx and who, but the ferryman, takes them across?'

Jamie smiled coldly. 'Aye, appropriate right enough,' he murmured.

'You still have the Messenger bank account, I presume.' Jamie nodded. 'Then take all the money out and close it. I'll set up a new account for you in the name of Ferryman. Do you still have the passport?'

Jamie nodded. 'Yes, amongst others,' he agreed.

'Destroy it. Keep the others. I'll arrange a new passport and other papers for you.'

'What about a weapon? I'll need one. Just give me a name, I'll do the rest.'

Sir Charles smiled. 'Bravo! You're even beginning to think like an Archangel again,' he said.

Jamie frowned. The old man was right. He was thinking like an Archangel again, but this time he would be his own Archangel.

'Jonathon Andrew,' the Brigadier said, breaking into his thoughts again. 'He can sort out your weapons.' He smiled again, icily. 'He goes by the name of "Jon" and some of his clients call him "the Godfather".'

Jamie laughed at that. He thought of Clara's relationship with Sir Charles and the irony was just too much. The Old Man didn't get it which was even funnier.

'The man is ex RAF, a Flight Lieutenant,' the Brigadier went on. 'Now, however, he's a solicitor practising in Glasgow.'

'With a side-line in gun running,' Jamie said, smiling wryly.

'He's a Criminal Lawyer which, I imagine, gives him a ready customer base,' Sir Charles continued. 'I'll let you have a letter of introduction but be careful when you talk with him. His customers also include PIRA and the Loyalists.'

'A true Capitalist,' Jamie retorted cynically. 'Happy to arm both sides in a war.'

'Not quite, Raeburn. He supplies but he tells us and we manage to intercept.'

'So he sells them a new shipment?' Jamie laughed. 'Great business.'

'Also very dangerous business,' Sir Charles commented, eyeing him disapprovingly. 'Anything else?'

Jamie shook his head then threw it back and drained his whisky glass. 'No, not now. If I do need anything else I'll get in touch,' he said. 'Now, I'm off to bed. I'm leaving first thing.'

Sir Charles nodded. 'I told Clara to get you to Dover as early as possible,' he said.

'Yes, I know; she told me,' Jamie replied, smiling easily. He placed his empty glass beside the fireplace and pushed himself up out of his chair. The business of the night was finished. What the morning would bring he could only guess.

Chapter Twenty-five

A weak sun was filtering through a gap in the curtains when Jamie awoke next morning. Outside, he could hear garbled voices and the slamming of car doors. *Déjà vu,* he thought groggily. This time though he was able to identify the participants; Mark Whitelaw and the Right Honourable John Ashcroft, Clara's father. It sounded like an argument but he didn't hear the women. Probably Ashcroft was giving his son in law a dressing down for the exhibition he made of himself at dinner, he thought, grinning. He recalled his conversation with Lady Redmond and smiled wryly. Mark Whitelaw had every reason to be sullen and moody and he was part of the cause. He shrugged the thought away.

He had slept soundly enough with the bedroom window open, waking briefly, earlier, to the sound of the dawn chorus. It was his first full night's sleep since leaving home on Thursday and he felt revitalised. He checked his watch. The hands said 07.05. He sprang out of bed and headed for the shower in the en suite bathroom. There was a train leaving Watford Junction to Euston just after nine and a train from London Victoria to Dover at ten thirty. He intended to catch both and be at Calais by early afternoon. If he did, he would be home by early evening. The transfer between Euston and Victoria might be tight and he had to build in a stop at some point to call Liam, but he would make it, he assured himself.

Refreshed after his shower, he hurried down to the dining room. The house was quiet; unnaturally so. Everyone appeared to have left, leaving him alone. The steady tick-tock of the tall grandfather clock that dominated the hall caught his attention and he checked the time, his eyes following the hypnotic swinging of the heavy brass pendulum. It was approaching eight o'clock. In the absence of Clara, he hoped Sir Charles had made other arrangements to convey him to Watford Junction.

He pushed open the dining room door and pulled up short. Sitting at the far end of the big rosewood table was Clara, smiling in a way that hadn't been possible the night before. He felt his pulse race before he managed to respond in kind.

'Hello Jamie,' she said softly. Her voice was like runny honey.

He could smell her perfume, the old familiar scent pushing up his heartbeat even further. She saw the surprise in his eyes.

'Charles asked me to take you to the station, remember?' she said.

Her eyes never left him. Jamie remembered that look and the effect it used to have on him. It was still potent. He would have to fight it.

'He asked me to give you these too,' she continued, holding out two thin, sealed envelopes in her long, sculpted fingers.

Jamie walked towards her and felt his knees wobble. Not a good sign. He reached out for the envelopes, hoping she couldn't see his hand shaking. 'Thanks,' he said simply as he slipped the packets inside his jacket. 'I thought you'd left', he said. 'I heard the commotion outside earlier.'

Clara pulled a face. 'Mark and my father,' she said. 'They both had to get back to London early and Dad decided to have a go at Mark. Not good for his blood pressure.'

Jamie nodded absently and turned his attention towards the large dresser behind her. It was like a hotel buffet... An expensive hotel buffet, he noted. Cereals, juices, coffee jugs and teapots, milk and sugar at one end and two large, heated trays with fried eggs, bacon, sausage and the usual accompaniments, fried tomatoes and mushrooms. He let out a low whistle. 'They don't do things by halves here, do they?' he said, laughing aloud. Clara smiled. He wondered if this was normal for her. It wasn't when they were together, he remembered. They usually skipped breakfast having more energetic pursuits in mind.

'The food has been out for a while,' Clara said, breaking into his thoughts. 'You'd better eat before it gets cold,' she continued. She tried to sound matter of fact while her heart raced at around 110 bpm.

Her eyes followed him as he went over to the dresser and poured himself coffee, topped it up with milk and dropped in two cubes of sugar. He ignored everything else and returned to the table, pulling up a seat beside her. She noticed the strange look in his eyes... It wasn't unpleasant or argumentative, she thought gratefully. He seemed more pensive than anything else. She thought back to happier times, realised she still hadn't got him out of her system and had to fight the urge to reach out for him.

'Are you okay?' he asked. He kept his voice gentle, considerate even. 'My Lazarus act came as a bit of a shock, I'm told.'

'I'm fine,' she answered hurriedly. She tried to sound convincing but realised she had failed miserably. She looked away from him and down at her hands. She lifted her eyes up again after a moment and fixed him with a sad little smile. 'No, I don't suppose I am, really,' she admitted.

Jamie pulled out his cigarettes and pulled one from the pack, offering it to her. Clara shook her head. 'No thanks, too early for me,' she said. She looked behind her at the food. 'Aren't you going to eat?' she asked.

'I'm not used to big breakfasts and "Full English" fry-ups any more,' he replied, laughing softly. 'I'm more into croissants and baguettes with butter and jam,' he went on. 'I would have thought Lady Redmond being French I might find some of those but it looks like she has adopted the English diet,' he commented, laughing. 'Looks like I'll have to settle for a Scottish breakfast today... my mother's staple; coffee and a fag. Anyway, after last night, I don't really feel like eating.'

Clara laughed with him before becoming serious. 'I'm sorry about last night,' she said. Her eyes watched him carefully.

'Not your fault,' he said, dismissively, taking a mouthful of coffee. 'You didn't do anything to spoil the evening as far as I recall. I'm the one who should be apologising,' he continued.

Clara shook her head slowly and let out an amused little laugh. 'We're behaving like children.'

Jamie saw the softness in her eyes. He remembered that look from way back. It was that look of vulnerability that had entranced and ensnared him once before. And she could do it again if he wasn't careful. Clara, he reminded himself, was anything but vulnerable.

'I've missed you,' she said in a whisper.

Jamie groaned inside. It would be easy enough to say the same but he fought the urge. It was bad enough fighting himself, he mused, without Clara saying that and adding to his problem. He opened his mouth to reply, to say something, anything, but was lost for words. But then, catching the look in her eyes, he realised words were no longer required. She was inside his head, reading his mind and viewing it all through his eyes. Her smile widened.

'I didn't really believe you were dead,' she continued quietly, 'even though the facts said you were.' Her eyes were still reading his thoughts but he could see big pools of tears gathering behind them. 'I was at your funeral,' she went on, giving a sad little laugh. 'Or what I thought was your funeral,' she went on.

'Was my wake good?' Jamie asked, laughing, unable to resist.

Clara drew him a hurt look and he immediately regretted his frivolous quip. 'I'm sorry,' he said softly. 'I've developed a talent for black humour... it gets me through the day.'

Clara smiled wanly. 'I still can't quite come to terms with it,' she said.

'What, me being back in the land of the undead?' he said, laughing again. 'Yes, I find it hard to believe myself, sometimes,' he admitted, reaching out at last to touch her hand.

'I missed you so much,' she whispered. 'I didn't even have a chance to say goodbye... not properly.'

Jamie smiled weakly. He knew what she meant. A vision of him standing alone by Jack's grave in the pouring rain filled his head. He hoped she hadn't felt like he did then.

The dining room door opened, the noise distracting them. Jamie turned to the source of the sound. Lady Redmond stood framed in the doorway, clearly reluctant to spoil the moment. She smiled warmly, her eyes moving from one to another, and then, without a word, she slipped back into the hall and closed the door behind her.

Clara was looking at him nervously, he noticed. Lady Redmond's reaction at finding them together seemed to have sent her a message. One she had misread, he thought. She expected anger from him.

He smiled and surprised her then started to laugh, amused. 'Lady Redmond and I had a long chat last night,' he said and saw her brow furrow enquiringly. 'We discussed lots of things,' he went on. 'But mostly, we discussed you... and me... and love. She's quite an authority on all of those,' he continued, laughing softly.

Clara blushed. 'I'm sorry,' she murmured. 'Estelle knew about us. Charles told her.'

Jamie laughed again. 'Oh, I know. They have no secrets, or so she says. Before I left for Ireland - that last time - the Brigadier and I had a wee set to about you. I remember he said something snide and that set me off,' he continued sheepishly. 'But then it struck me that he could only have made the comment if he already knew about us... and I didn't tell him.' He finished and lifted his eyebrows enquiringly.

'It was me; I told him,' Clara confessed quietly. 'I'm sorry.'

'Don't be. It's alright. I'd already worked it out. The only thing that still puzzles me though, is why? He would have given you grief. No?' He could see tears building again behind the grey eyes and eased off. She needed a moment to take control again.

Clara wiped away a rogue tear and sniffed. 'Mark came home unexpectedly that night,' she murmured. 'If you hadn't left when you did he would have found us together.' She shivered a little as she said it, her mind conjuring up the consequences of that.

'So I'm told,' Jamie threw in.

'Estelle again?' she asked anxiously. She saw him nod and searched his eyes again for signs of anger but, thankfully, he was still placid. 'It wasn't what you think,' she carried on quickly. 'I didn't tell blurt everything out in a fit of pique or anything like that. I had to tell Charles.'

Jamie raised one eyebrow but stayed silent. He was intrigued as to why.

'Mark and I argued that night,' she went on, eager to explain.

No surprise there, Jamie mused.

'When he came into the house I actually thought it was you coming back,' she said, laughing awkwardly. 'We had a blazing row.' She hesitated a moment. 'I thought our marriage was over, but he, strangely, didn't. I got a shock when he turned up in the office later that morning. I expected another blazing row but he was acting as if nothing had happened. I discovered then that he had 'phoned Charles and they had arranged to go for lunch. Over lunch, according to Charles at least, he didn't mention what had happened during the night. He simply told him he thought his army days were behind him and that he wanted out to spend more time with me,' she went on, adding a bitter little laugh.

'He even had the nerve to ask Charles if there was any possibility of him joining us in Ultra.' She accompanied that with snort. 'I wouldn't have known but for the fact that Charles was actually considering it and decided to tell me. He thought I would be pleased,' she added, smiling sadly. Her eyes, averted from him and directed down into her lap as she spoke, now lifted and locked onto his. 'I didn't want Mark anywhere near me just then... and it all just spilled out.'

Jamie nodded slowly as it all fell into place. Lady Estelle was the only loose end. 'And Lady Redmond,' he probed. 'How did she find out?'

'She called me. It wasn't long after... after I had told Uncle Charles about us. She invited me down here for the weekend and offered me a shoulder to cry on. I was feeling down and I didn't want to be alone. I'm sorry.'

As Jamie listened, his conversation with Lady Redmond the night before was still clear in his mind. He had felt guilty then and he felt guilty again now. He and guilt were becoming closely acquainted these days, it seemed.

What did it all this matter, he reasoned. So, she had told the Redmonds; so what? They were as close as family. It was no big deal. He had let Gerry Carroll in on it, after all, though he really hadn't had much of an option. The same could probably be said for Clara. They just had to move on. There was no point in raking over the ashes, he told himself, but there was only one problem with that... The ashes were still smouldering and could easily burst into flames.

'I wasn't very nice that night, was I?' he said. He saw her look at him questioningly, wondering where he was going with this.

'I took advantage of you,' he went on. 'It wasn't supposed to be like that, I'm sorry. I came to see you to tell you it was over...' He stopped, searching for words, and looked down into her big grey eyes. 'I shouldn't have done what I did...' he started again but quickly ran out of words. He looked away, remembering again his talk with Lady Redmond about feelings... and his were now showing. It was a simple truth; he had wanted her that night. He just hoped she couldn't read that in his eyes.

'Can we stay friends?' he asked, his voice dropping to a whisper.

'Friends?' she repeated the word as though she had misheard him and smiled a little forlornly. 'Just friends?' she added, for good measure.

'The situation hasn't changed, Clara. I'm still married and I love my wife.'

'And your children,' she added.

'Yes, and my children. They shouldn't be hurt by what we've done... none of it was their fault.'

Clara's sad smile was still etched on her face. 'It was nobody's fault, Jamie, it just happened... but you're right; they shouldn't be hurt.' She shrugged and forced a happier smile. 'I hear you've just become a father again,' she went on. 'How are they... Kate and the baby?'

Jamie was caught off balance by the question. They had been talking about them, not about his wife and kids, though he had brought them into it. Clara was still in love with him; it showed in the things she said and the way she said them... and it showed in her eyes. And now this question. He was lost.

'They're both fine,' he mumbled eventually, unable to think of anything else to say. But he should say something... 'Listen, Clara,' he started, but she silenced him with a finger across his lips.

'Ssssh,' she whispered softly. He imagined he saw the beginnings of another tear at the corner of her eye. She looked away for a moment, hiding it, before dabbing at her eyes and turning back to him. 'Tell me the truth Jamie; did I ever mean anything to you?' she asked quietly.

He held her eyes. She might as well read his as he answered, he thought. 'Yes,' he said at last. 'Too much, maybe,' he went on, surprising himself.

She smiled. It was a strange little smile; not happy, not sad. 'So where do we go from here?' she asked, her eyes still searching in his.

'Where can we go?' he threw back. That could have come out harshly but the look in his eyes softened it. 'I can't...'

She stopped him again, her fingers brushing his lips once more. 'I know,' she said hoarsely, her head shaking slowly from side to side. 'You had to make a choice... and you're right, we would probably have made each other miserable,' she went on. 'But at least I had you for a while. What is that poem by Tennyson? In Memoriam, I think... "I hold it true, what'er befall; I feel it when I sorrow most; 'Tis better to have loved and lost Than never to have loved at all". And I did love you Jamie.'

Jamie gazed back at her, forcing a smile. She had said it in the past tense but the lie to that was in her eyes.

'Don't shut me out, please,' she whispered. 'I couldn't stand that.'

'I won't,' he replied, his voice almost inaudible.

She stroked his cheek with her fingertips sending familiar shivers through him before breaking the spell. 'We had better hurry,' she said. 'Or you won't get home to your family today.'

Jamie looked down at his watch. Time had flown by. 'Christ,' he cursed. 'The train.' Shit!'

'Tch, tch,' she chastised him gently. 'Such language in front of a lady.' She smiled and took his hands, pulling him to his feet. 'Don't worry. My orders were to make sure you made it home. I'll drive you to Dover. Go and get your bag and I'll tell Estelle we're leaving.' She held onto his hands for a moment longer then leaned into him and placed a kiss on his cheek. 'Go on,' she urged. 'You're wasting time.'

Jamie left her and ran for the stairs, taking them two at a time. He picked up his bag from the unmade bed and checked the room. He had left nothing behind. Quickly, he closed the door behind him and raced back down the broad stairs to the hall just as Clara and Lady Edmond emerged from the dining room, their faces wreathed in smiles.

'You're leaving us then,' Estelle Redmond said as he came to a halt before her.

Clara kissed her on the cheek and left them. 'I'll get the car,' she said over her shoulder, 'and I'll wait outside.'

Left alone with Lady Redmond, Jamie was again lost for words. His awkwardness showed and Estelle Redmond laughed gently. 'My little chat with you worked, it seems,' she said, still smiling and showing a line of perfect white teeth. 'Clara looks happier than I've seen her in months.'

Jamie returned her smile, still uncertain. 'I hope she stays happy,' he said sincerely.

'Can I offer you another bit of advice?' she asked. Jamie nodded. 'Don't promise anything,' she went on. 'Just be yourself. Clara knows where she stands but she still loves you... Be gentle.'

The blast of a car horn split the morning air. 'I think she's getting impatient,' Estelle Redmond laughed. 'Come on.'

She took him by the arm and steered him towards the door, guiding him through and out into the sunlight. A Triumph Spitfire, pillar box red, stood idling on the gravel at the foot of the stone steps with its roof down. Estelle took him in her arms and kissed him on both cheeks, twice on each as on the night before. 'I hope you'll come back to visit us sometime. I enjoyed you being here... and everything I said last night was true. Remember that.' Finished, she released him and gave him a gentle shove towards the steps, waving down to Clara as Jamie climbed into the bucket seat beside her.

He barely had time to drop his bag behind his seat when the car sprang forward, wheels spinning and throwing up gravel behind it as it sped towards the driveway. Lady Estelle Redmond waited at the top of the steps until the little red dot disappeared from sight then returned to her home, a satisfied smile on her face.

Chapter Twenty-six

Jamie stood at the stern rail of the ferry and watched the ribbons of white from the ship's propellers stretch back towards Dover. He had lots to ponder. Staring at the famous White Cliffs, he thought they looked almost unassailable; a bit like his own problems, he mused. But for every problem there is a solution, he told himself.

And boy, did he have problems. Even more so now as a result of renewing his "friendship" with Clara. He had stuck to Estelle Redmond's advice and had promised Clara nothing but that had little effect on expectation, he suspected.

He took a final draw on the cigarette dangling from his lips and flicked the glowing butt into the air, following its progress as it tumbled over and over in the wind until it was swallowed up by the churning white wake.

He thought about Clara again. At the moment she wasn't so much a problem as a distraction but that wouldn't last. Their conversation on route to Dover made it clear that Sir Charles wanted her involved in the extraction of Liam Fitzpatrick from Northern Ireland which meant they would be working together... and that was what led to their affair in the first place. He would have to tread carefully, but for the moment he had other things on his mind.

Liam had placed him in a quandary - what to do about Roisin. Having gone to Gartnavel to see her he couldn't now just abandon her. Not that he would ever consider doing that, but it still left him with a dilemma; what could he do?

Liam's extraction was the easy part or, more accurately, the easier part, because none of what he was being asked to do was easy. He could probably arrange Liam's disappearance without help. The tricky bit was making people believe he was dead. He might have to kill the three other men in the ASU but que sera, sera, he thought, smiling grimly. He had already made up his mind earlier that Fionn Doherty was going to die and he would have no qualms whatsoever about bringing him the good news. The real problem was the disappearance of Liam. If three other bodies were left and Liam's wasn't with them questions would be asked and suspicions raised. He would have to think of a solution... and he would. Where there's a will, there's a way, his mother used to say. She was a wise woman, his mother.

Saving Roisin from the wrath of Brigadier Charles Redmond was something else entirely. It would take more than a wave of a magic wand and a crash course in prestidigitation from by David Nixon to achieve that. Now you see her, now you don't. Oh that it were so easy. If the Brigadier wanted her dead he would stop at nothing to make it happen. And he was a shrewd bugger. He wouldn't be easily fooled or led off the scent. The only plus point for the moment was that he had volunteered to do the job. That should give him an element of control but the old man would keep on top of him. He couldn't afford to let his guard drop.

Jamie had called Liam from Dover. The call had been brief, chiefly because Liam wasn't there and he had ended up speaking to a young girl. At least, she sounded like a young girl.

'Fitzpatrick Plumbers', she had answered in a voice about three scales higher than that of Mini-Mouse. If she ever hit top pitch the glass of the phone box would probably shatter.

Expecting the deep baritone of Liam, Jamie had been taken by surprise. But he recovered quickly, slipped into his thick Belfast accent, and asked if he could speak to Mr. Fitzpatrick himself. That was when he learned Liam wasn't around and wouldn't be back for about half an hour. He had decided to leave a message, suitably cryptic, that Liam should understand.

'Ye can tell Mr. Fitzpatrick that Dermott Lynch called,' he said. 'The job we spoke about is on. Ye can tell him ah've spoken wi' the customer an' ah'll call him again later in the week. Will ye do that?'

The girl, she gave her name as Concepta – what else, he mused – promised to give Mr. Fitzpatrick the message as soon as he returned. Was there a number he could call back on, she had asked?

'No, Ah'm travelling, ah'll get back to him,' was all Jamie said before ending the call.

So now he was back with his two problems; Liam and Roisin, in ascending order of difficulty. He had a feeling there were two more on the horizon, Clara and Kate, and Kate would not be pleased when she learned what was on his mind. They had moved to France to get away from all this shit, after all. Faced with his return to Ultra, she might prove to be the biggest problem of all.

***

By the time the ferry berthed at Calais, he had resolved some things. The logistics of Liam's snatch were simple enough. He had money... not a limitless supply, but the Brigadier would supply what additional funds needed. He had made a mental list – a things to do list – and high on it was a safe house, transport and a weapon. But he was in limbo until Liam identified the attack location. He could do nothing until then.

He felt the bulge of the envelopes Clara had passed to him in his jacket pocket. He pulled them out. One envelope was a plain brown A5 with the name William King scrawled across the front. He recognised the Brigadier's hand.

He tore open the seal and withdrew the document. It was a standard dark blue covered British passport with the emblem of the Crown embossed in gold on the front. The number shown in the slot cut in the top of the cover was 56653 but the slot at the bottom was blank. It had been aged a bit, scuffed and bent a little. He opened it and found a photograph of Liam Fitzpatrick staring back at him from page three. He smiled grimly and turned his eyes to the details on page two headed DESCRIPTION SIGNALEMENT. It made amusing reading.

The bearer, one William King, according to the first page, was listed as having the occupation "handyman" which covered all the bases, Jamie thought, grinning now. "Place of birth" was shown as Liverpool and "Date of birth" given as 23 August 1941. Country of residence was stated to be England, Height was 5feet 11inches and Eyes were green. There was nothing written down under "Special peculiarities" which amused Jamie further. He could think of a few. But the biggest laugh was in the choice of name. Sir Charles had a sense of humour after all. When Liam registered for anything in future and put his surname followed by his Christian name he would be referred to as King William. That would go down well!

He was about to slip the passport back into the envelope when he found a slip of paper tucked inside. It was a note, again in the Brigadier's spidery handwriting and it was addressed to him: Raeburn, keep this passport in your possession until Corkscrew fulfills his obligations to me. You can advise him that you have it in your possession but do not, I repeat, show it or give it to him. Funds will be allocated to a Swiss Bank account with details of how to access these made available to him on completion. R

He read it again then tore it into tiny pieces before throwing the scraps into the air and watching them drift away. That was Liam sorted. If he needed a new identity for Roisin it would prove a much more difficult task. He couldn't very well ask Sir Charles. But there were ways. There were always ways.

The second envelope, same size but plain white, had the name J Andrew on the front. This would be his letter of introduction. He decided not to open it.

He was happier in his mind when the ferry berthed and he followed the other foot passengers down the gangplank and into the terminal. The bustle, the noise and the rapid-fire French chatter brought him back into himself and he smiled happily for the first time in hours. He was almost home. With luck, he would be in Epernay by six tonight and home by half past. Then he could forget all this for a while.

***

It was two minutes to six exactly when the big SNCF locomotive came to a gentle halt at the Gare d'Epernay. Hoisting his bag up onto his back, he descended onto the sun-drenched platform and followed a party of nuns towards the exit. It was like stalking a waddle of Giant Penguins, he thought with a smile, as they shuffled silently along in line. A waddle of nuns, he laughed, attracting attention as people looked at him curiously. He grinned back.

He followed the nuns through the booking hall to the car park where a couple of taxis waited. His heart sank. There were only two taxis and seven nuns. That meant a wait for another taxi and at this time of night it might be a long wait. Serves you right, his conscience told him, for making fun of them.

He was resolved to his fate when suddenly, out of nowhere, a battered mini-bus swung into the car park in a cloud of nauseating black diesel smoke. It tilted dangerously on the access bend then screeched to a halt beside the nuns. Its engine clattered like an unhealthy as it sat idling, belching out more fumes. Jamie raised a protective hand to cover his mouth and nose, but to no avail. The stench of diesel was all-pervading.

And they say smoking is bad for you. Jamie smiled wryly.

But the arrival of the mini-bus signaled an improvement in his fortunes when the nuns piled in, directed with military precision by an older nun. This, Jamie presumed, was the Mother Superior, and clearly not a lady to be on the wrong side of.

With the nuns and their luggage packed in like soldiers setting off on on manoeuvres, the driver engaged the gears with a crunch that indicated the synchromesh was on its last legs. Without looking, no doubt putting faith in God and the presence of the nuns, he pulled out into the evening traffic to a chorus of blaring car horns. Seconds later, relative silence returned but a lingering blue cloud of diesel fumes still marked the vehicle's passing.

Jamie started for the taxis but lost out on the first one to an elderly couple. That left him with a choice of one; a run-down Peugeot with what appeared to be an equally run-down driver.

He opened the back door and slipped inside. The driver turned languidly towards him, an unfiltered Gitanes Brune dangling from his lips, and asked, sullenly, where he wanted to be taken. The man's breath reeked of garlic and foul smelling cigarette smoke. Jamie wasn't sure which was worse, the diesel fumes left by the mini bus or the smell of the Gitanes cigarette. The man's attitude brightened immeasurably however when Jamie gave him the destination. A trip out of town to Montmort, about 20 kilometres away, was a good fare to end the day.

It was hot in the car and Jamie wound down the window to allow a stream of cooler air to circulate. The driver scowled as his comb-over hairstyle was disturbed by the sudden draught, but Jamie simply smiled.

Within minutes the car had left the bustle of Epernay and was passing through Pierry. Open countryside lay beyond, vines on the left and fields of corn on the right. They followed the Voie de la Liberté, Liberty Road - the D951 - through the village of Vaudancourt and up the hill round the dangerous virages, sharp bends, to the flat plain of the plateau above. The car swung from side to side as the driver threw it into the bends with typical Gallic disregard for the safety of his passenger, himself and the other road users. It was, Jamie had decided long ago, a national trait. The guy should try Formula 1, he mused. He could give Jackie Stewart a run for his money.

The sun was over to his right and ahead the road began to stretch ahead, a long straight ribbon of tarmacadam that passed through dense forests on both sides. The hunting season was in full swing and great swathes of forest were blocked off from public access. Here and there, men acting as wardens, wearing bright, luminous cross belts and sporting a variety of hunting rifles, policed the boundaries. There wasn't a shotgun in sight, he noted. When it came to killing, these boys didn't use the blunderbuss approach. He felt sorry for the Sanglier, the wild boar, and the deer that roamed the forests, though death usually came to them quickly.

Soon, the driver was coasting down the steep incline to the valley of the Surmelin with the roads to Mehart and La Chaude Rue to right and left respectively. The imposing Chateau of Les Castaignes sat behind a band of trees to his left and ahead of him the Chateau de Montmort shimmered in a late afternoon heat haze. It was breath taking. How could he even be thinking of taking his family away from this Garden of Eden, he thought gloomily.

He checked his watch. It was just approaching twenty past six and Kate would be preparing dinner while Lauren, young Jamie and Lucy would be doing their homework. He wondered if his baby son would be asleep.

As the Peugeot swung round the bend at the entrance to the village Jamie barked instructions and the driver braked hard before turning, a little too fast, into the Cour des Gentils and down towards the house. A cloud of dust rose behind them. Jamie grinned as the man cursed loudly and screeched to a halt. Roads here were not like the roads in the town; tarmacadam hadn't reached this far yet and a fine coating of dust settled on the car's windscreen and bodywork.

He ignored the man's scowl and peeled off several franc notes from a wad, adding a generous tip, which was unnecessary, but he was in a good mood. He didn't care if the Frenchman thought he was being flash tipping like that. But the man suddenly seemed cheerful too, he noticed.

His return had gone unnoticed. The village was still its sleepy self. With his bag over his shoulder, he began the short walk down the impasse, or cul-de-sac, towards his home. All around him, flowers provided a kaleidoscope of colour. He breathed deeply on the scent. God, it felt good.

But even here, in the midst of peace and beauty, he was beset by dark thoughts. He would have to leave here soon, perhaps for the last time. What then for his wife and family, he thought despondently. He shrugged the thought away. This wasn't a time for depressing thoughts like that. It was a time for happiness and fun.

Chapter Twenty-seven

Kate Raeburn rolled over in bed, her arm sliding out her side, reaching... and then she woke with a start, rubbing sleep from her eyes. Had she been dreaming? No, it was not a dream. Jamie had been there beside her, his arms around her. She could still smell the scent of him.

She sat up, listening for sounds of him, but there were none. Her eyes slowly adjusted to the semi-darkness of the room and settled finally on a pale glow coming from the hallway beyond the partly open bedroom door. All the outside shutters were closed but the windows inside were open, allowing cooler air to seep into the room. A gentle draught eddied through the gaps in the shutters and rustled the curtains.

She stretched languidly and smiled at the memory of the night. Slowly, she pushed herself up from the bed. The tiled floor was cold against her feet and she quickly slipped on her slippers before wrapping her dressing gown around her naked body. Silently, she made her way along the landing and down the curved wooden stairway to the hall below. The door leading to the terrace and garden behind the house was ajar and she pulled it towards her, opening it wider. Jamie was standing on the terrace, his dark silhouette picked out against the pink of the rising sun. She picked her away across the stone-topped terrace and wrapped her arms around him, pressing her body against his back.

'I thought I'd been dreaming,' she murmured, nuzzling against his neck. 'I woke up and you weren't there... and here you are standing all alone in the darkness. Don't you love me anymore?'

Jamie laughed softly and turned to her, pulling her close and kissing her open mouth. 'That's a stupid question,' he whispered as they moved apart.

'Yes, so I feel,' she giggled, allowing her hand to slide down to his groin. He groaned teasingly and Kate laughed softly. 'Come back to bed.'

He slipped his hands down to cup her bottom and pulled her close. 'In a minute,' he whispered. 'There's something we have to talk about,' he continued.

Kate tensed. The anxiety in his voice was clear. She eased back from him, searching his eyes. He turned away but held onto her, his grip, if anything, tighter than before.

'What's wrong?' she whispered. Her hands now cupped his face.

'You're not going to like it,' he murmured, holding her look now. 'But I have to go back over to sort all this mess out,' he continued.

They stood still, like statues, gazing at each other.

The sun was rising slowly above the horizon to the east and the world was coming to life as the darkness retreated. The moon still shone, cold and white, among the stars but soon it too would disappear. They missed all that beauty, engrossed as they were in each other.

Kate's mind raced over what he had told her about his visit to Glasgow. He had explained it all before he left, or she thought he had. They hadn't spoken about it since his return, they had had other things on their minds, but she had noticed he was quieter than usual. She had put that down to tiredness but now she knew it was something else. Something had changed. She could feel it in her bones.

'When?' she asked, forcing herself to stay calm.

'I don't know exactly,' he admitted. Then he carried on, surprising her with his candour. 'There's been a change of plan,' he said softly, pulling her close and nuzzling his mouth against her ear. 'It isn't as straightforward as the Brigadier hoped.'

Kate gave a bitter little snort of derision. 'Why doesn't that come as a surprise?' she retorted, shaking her head sadly. 'Nothing that man has asked you to has ever been straightforward, has it?'

Jamie smiled sheepishly. 'No, I don't suppose it has,' he agreed. 'But this time I'm changing the plan and he doesn't know about it.'

Kate knitted her brow and gently stroked his cheek with her fingers. 'Will it be dangerous?' she probed anxiously.

'Maybe...a little,' he conceded reluctantly. 'If the old boy finds out what I'm up to.'

Kate didn't ask what it was. He would tell her when and if he could. 'How long will you be away?' she asked instead.

Jamie shook his head from side to side, his message clear. 'I don't know,' he said. 'But it will be a while before it happens.'

Kate sighed heavily. She didn't argue and she didn't cry, but her stomach was churning, tying itself in knots. Yet the truth was, she had half expected something like this all along. She had thought about this moment. It had a certain inevitability to it. 'We'll have time to arrange things then,' she said.

'Arrange things?' Jamie asked, confused.

'This place,' she replied. 'And where we're going to live when we go.'

'When we go,' he repeated.

'I'm not staying here alone Jamie,' she said and he could see she had thought about it. 'If you're going back we're all going back.'

He gazed into her big green eyes and realised there was little point in arguing. Her look convinced him it was an argument he wouldn't win.

He smiled wryly. 'We'll talk about it later,' he said softly.

'I'm not staying here without you,' she carried on, ready to argue before picking up properly on his reply. 'You're not angry?' she asked uncertainly.

Jamie smiled and pulled her close again. 'No, not angry. I don't really want to be away from you and if you want to come, I'm happy. I just thought you would insist I stay here... This was supposed to be our bolt hole, after all,' he said, sweeping his arm around the landscape.

'It still will be, when this is all over,' she said. 'How long do we have?'

Jamie smiled. 'A couple of weeks, maybe a little longer,' he said. 'Enough time to tidy up and say goodbye to everyone.'

She rose on her tiptoes and kissed him. 'Okay, that's long enough,' she said. 'Now, come back to bed.'

***

It was later that day when Jamie finally told her everything. They had returned to bed at around half past five that morning and made love again, coupling frantically, taking each other to familiar places. They would probably have remained in bed all day but for the plaintive cry of baby Jack and the stirring of his siblings.

It was mid-afternoon now. The baby was asleep and Jamie and Kate were sitting together on the terrace. They had avoided all talk of returning home until now, both of them conscious of the fact that taking that step might be irreversible. But they could not avoid it forever. Kate broke the silence.

'I missed you when you were away,' she said, taking him by surprise. 'It was worse this time. I was afraid.'

'This time?' he repeated, laughing softly and trying to make light of it. 'Are you telling me you weren't scared before?'

She squeezed his hand. 'Yes, of course I was, but it was worse this time. I used to worry about you when you were away...this time I was really frightened.'

'That's because of what happened last time,' he counselled, trying not to sound dismissive but reassuring. 'That won't happen again.'

Kate smiled sadly. 'The same old Jamie,' she replied. 'You say that, but you don't know.' She paused a moment, reluctant to go on. 'Will you have to...?' She stopped again, abruptly this time. She could not finish the question.

Will I have to kill someone, you mean, he mused silently.

'Yes, probably,' he admitted, avoiding the whole truth. He had already chosen his victim.

Kate's eyes sank to her lap. 'And afterwards...will it be more of the same?'

'No, love, this time really will be the last,' he said sincerely.

She held his gaze for a moment, searching for the lie. She wanted to believe him, but the last four years had hardened her to what he did. Could he ever give it up, she wondered?

More to the point, would he be allowed to?

Jamie read her searching look. There was no point in lying to her. He knew that from experience. She was a living, breathing, lie detector. 'Okay,' he conceded quietly. 'The job at Kiltyclogher was supposed to be my last,' he said. 'I'm only back in the game because of Liam Fitzpatrick.'

'And once you get him safely out, that's it is it?'

Jamie looked at her. To lie or not to lie, he mused. 'Not quite,' he said, choosing the latter course. 'It's not just Liam's escape.'

Kate raised an enquiring eyebrow.

'There's someone else,' he responded, still reluctant. Kate said nothing. She was waiting and she would wait until he told her. There was no avoiding it. 'When Liam comes out he wants to bring a friend with him,' he said. 'And just like him, she too has to disappear. It'll be tricky, but it can be done.'

'But there's more,' Kate interjected shrewdly.

Jamie smiled sheepishly. Why do I even try, he mused?

'Aye, there's more...and that's where it gets complicated.'

'And are you going to tell me?'

Jamie nodded slowly. 'I don't really want to but I suppose I have to,' he replied, his voice dropping.

'Why the reluctance?'

'It concerns another woman. She's Irish too; someone I know from the past,' he started, seeing the look of suspicion grow in Kate's eyes. 'Before we were married,' he added hastily, trying to dispel her anxiety. 'I did a job in Belfast... it was back in 1967, after you had headed home to Calverton.'

Kate nodded slowly. 'I remember, didn't you tell me a bit about it once,' she said hesitantly.

Yes, I told you a bit about it, but not all about it.

'The woman in question is Liam Fitzpatrick's cousin. She's the reason he wants me involved in this and no one else,' he continued.

'Why?'

'Because she's in trouble... and because I'm the only one he's prepared to trust,' he replied. He was still avoiding the issue. He knew it and Kate knew it.

'How much trouble is she in?' Kate probed.

Jamie sighed. He was going to have to come clean. 'Serious trouble,' he said. 'She was forced to do something and now her life is hanging by a thread. Liam asked me to help,' he finished with a shrug.

Kate laughed. She sounded bitter. 'And Sir Galahad can't refuse?'

'I could, I suppose,' he said, shrugging again. 'But you know me.'

Kate's bitterness evaporated and she and she looked at him lovingly. Yes, I know you, she mused, and the man I fell in love with doesn't walk away. Sometimes I wish you would.

'What did she do?' she pressed on and saw his features darken.

Jamie looked away from her over the fields. Now was the moment of truth. Would she understand? There was only one way to find out. 'She planted a bomb that killed and injured a lot of people,' he said quietly, turning back to look at her.

Kate's jaw dropped and her eyes widened in shock. 'Isn't that the kind of person you're usually sent to deal with?' she stammered. She didn't mean it as a question. It just came out that way.

'Aye, it is,' he agreed, nodding. 'And I suspect the Brigadier will ask me to do just that,' he continued coldly. 'But I'm not going to,' he added after a moment's hesitation.

They were silent for a while. Everything continued as normal around them. Birds sang, insects buzzed and the sounds of human activity, voices, laughter and a chain saw whirring in the distance, drifted to them on the warm afternoon air.

'Why did she do it?' Kate asked after a moment, taking hold of his hand.

Jamie laughed bitterly, disconcerting her. 'It was either do it or watch her kids and her husband being murdered in front of her,' he said, anger simmering in his voice. 'Faced with that choice, I would have planted the fuckin' bomb too,' he continued. There was another moment's silence before he spoke again. 'Sorry,' he murmured. He knew she didn't like him swearing.

If Kate was shocked by his initial revelation, she was completely stunned now. She did not know what to think. If it was true, she had no doubt Jamie would have done what the woman had done. There was only difference, she mused. Jamie would have done it but he would not have stopped at that. If it's true, she repeated to herself.

'How do you know that's the truth?' she delved carefully.

'Liam told me,' he said.

'And you believed him?' Her voice registered her own disbelief.

He smiled at that. 'Not at first,' he replied. 'I'm not entirely gullible, Kate. I told him I wanted to talk to her. I asked him where I could find her...and then I went to see her...on Sunday morning before I left Glasgow.'

'Where does she live?' Kate continued digging.

The bitter laugh came again. 'To be honest, she's not living anywhere. She's in Gartnavel Royal,' he said.

Kate knitted her brow.

'You know it,' he said. 'It's the mental hospital behind the pond on Great Western Road...where the big new hospital is. Remember it?'

She nodded slowly. It came back to her. 'Yes, the old building hidden by the trees,' she concurred. 'What did she say?'

'Not a lot. She cried most of the time. She's clinically depressed according to what I've been told. The nurse I spoke to said she hardly ever spoke and has no interest in herself. She looked a mess, to be honest.'

'Catatonia,' Kate suggested.

Jamie knitted his brow. 'What's catatonia, when it's at home?' he asked.

'It's associated with severe depression,' Kate explained. 'The person can suffer from extreme sadness most of the time. They feel worthless, lose interest in themselves, think of self-harming or suicide, don't eat, don't talk...'

'Aye, that about sums her up, I think,' Jamie interjected. 'She isn't eating. One look at her told me that. She just sat staring out of the window at first...didn't seem to recognise me at all. She wouldn't speak...just rocked backwards and forwards, slowly, all the time.'

'Did she speak to you at all?'

He smiled grimly. 'Aye, eventually. A few words. Nothing meaningful. She said she had done something terrible and I told her she wasn't the one to blame... And she isn't,' he added defensively.

They reverted to silence for a while as Kate took stock and Jamie remembered.

'Can you help her?' Kate asked at last.

'I don't know,' he said, shaking his head. 'She needs to help herself first, I suppose. I just kept telling her she had two little kids who needed her and that I would have done what she did. The people who forced her into it are the ones to blame. Her feeling the way she does just lets those bastards off the hook. She's shouldering all the blame,' he persisted, his ire coming out again.

'So you believe her story?'

'It's not a story, Kate,' he retorted angrily.

'I didn't mean it like that,' Kate came back quickly. 'I'm sorry.'

'So am I. You're the last person I should be falling out with over this,' he said contritely. 'It's just...I don't know; the poor girl's helpless.'

'What is it Liam wants you to do?'

He smiled his grim smile again. 'It's more what he doesn't want me to do,' he murmured. 'He doesn't want me to kill her.'

'But that's not enough?' Kate queried shrewdly.

'No, not really; if I don't, someone else will,' he retorted.

Kate pulled herself close to him and wrapped her arms around him. They stayed like that for a while, drawing strength from each other. At least they weren't arguing, Jamie mused thankfully. Arguing about anything with Kate, even debating, was like playing chess against Bobby Fischer, the American Grand Master. No matter how well you planned your moves, you always knew you were going to lose.

'You won't be able to do it on your own,' Kate said eventually, having thought about it. 'Does it mean you'll have to go over to Ireland?' she asked then, suddenly anxious. 'Didn't that horrible man say you couldn't go over there again...not for a while anyway?'

Jamie smiled again. She had a good memory, did Kate. Yes, "that horrible man", also known as Brigadier Charles Redmond, had indeed said that, and she had stored that little gem away for a rainy day. Metaphorically speaking, it had just started to pour.

'I don't think so,' he said, trying to allay her mounting anxiety. 'Whatever it is that Liam is involved in is taking place in England. I won't go over to Ireland.'

Her eyes told him she didn't believe him, but she said nothing. He could not leave it like that. If he did, it would fester. 'I won't,' he repeated.

Kate nodded slowly, reluctantly accepting him at his word. 'So what about this poor girl?' she asked, switching her thoughts back to Roisin. 'Does she have a name?'

'Yes,' he replied simply.

'But you'd rather not tell me what it is?' she laughed quietly.

Jamie pulled a face.

'Should I be jealous?' Kate carried on mischievously.

Jamie laughed. There was no tension. 'No, you shouldn't,' he said. 'You know I'm a one woman man,' he added.

'Oh yes, and who is she?' Kate giggled.

'Come up stairs and I'll show you,' he laughed, but his mirth was interrupted by the cry of baby Jack. Kate pulled a sorrowful face and rose from her seat.

'Okay, later,' Jamie said, as she disappeared into the house.

Chapter Twenty-eight

16 October 1973, County Armagh - Northern Ireland

Kevin Sparke drove sedately along the A3 heading south towards Armagh, his final destination the hamlet of Darkly, nestling in the border countryside near the village of Keady. He whistled tunelessly, a man happy in his work. He liked Ireland; the whole of the country, not just the North, and he felt a certain empathy with the people. They were just like his people, struggling against Imperial domination, just as his father and his friends had struggled against the Czar and his cronies a mere fifty years earlier.

His identification with the Irish people, however, stretched way beyond their struggle. He loved the way of life here and the ordinary things... like Guinness and Irish whiskey. Oh, and the women...yes, he loved the women.

There was Religion here of course, that was one thing he didn't take to. Marx had it right, he mused; the opiate of the masses Karl called it. It was a tool, nothing more, in the hands of the unscrupulous. It could be manipulated and used to control the the population, the masses. And here in Ireland the church was powerful. Take abortion, for example. Britain had made it legal a few years earlier, 1967, but there was little chance of it happening here. Then again, you could probably break the law on it and then go to confession. That intrigued him. No matter what you did you could trot along to confession, admit your sin to the priest, and he would forgive you. Not only that, God would forgive you, because the priest had a direct line to Him. Simple really, admit your sin, pay your penance, and forget about it. Great. Nobody need worry about having a conscience. It made him wonder sometimes why Marx had not seen the value in it.

Kevin Sparke was not his real name, of course, but it had served him well over the years; since before since his arrival in Dublin from East Berlin, in fact. He spoke perfect English, though anyone listening carefully might detect a slight American accent. That did not matter. It was at one with his legend, his background story.

That had been well researched by the KGB long before he became the man he now was. Kevin Sparke was real. If anyone checked they would discover that Kevin's father was an Irishman from Dublin who had served with the British Army during the Second World War and had been with the Allied occupying forces in Germany when the war ended. His mother, according to the story, was Giselle Mannheim, a German refugee from Frankfurt who had fled the Red Army's advance. She was one of the lucky ones... she reached the west unscathed. Then the beautiful German girl had met the handsome Irishman; they married, had Kevin, and immigrated to America in 1949.

Sadly, they had died together along with Kevin's younger sister, Erin, in an automobile accident in 1961 when young Kevin was 15 years of age. He was fostered after that with a family in Denver until he was 18 years old. He had a penchant for journalism and worked with a local paper for a few months before joining the US Army in 1964. He was shipped out to Vietnam in 1965. Nineteen sixty-five was a bad year for Kevin. At least, it was a bad year for the real Kevin. He was badly wounded when his unit engaged insurgents near the Laos border late in '65 and was brought back to the States for treatment.

All of that was true and verifiable. There was a Kevin Sparke whose parents and sister had died in a car accident in 1961, who had been fostered to a family in Denver, Colorado, and who had joined the US Army in 1964. It just was not this Kevin Sparke. The real Kevin was dead.

The new Kevin could speak both English and German fluently, as well as Russian and Polish, though he did not boast of the fact. Born in 1946, his age fitted the profile of the real Kevin. His father, however, was not Irish and his mother was not West German. His father was Russian, a Major in the old NKVD – now the KGB - and his mother, whilst German, was the daughter of an East German communist. Both were still alive and living happily in Moscow. Kevin's real name was Igor Bushevesky, though it was so long since he had used that name he had almost forgotten it.

He had been groomed for this job from an early age. Educated and trained for it. And all of the years of preparation and training had been worthwhile. Now he was a deep penetration agent dedicated to the final victory of his motherland.

His posting to Ireland had been a disappointment to Igor. He had expected more from the years of schooling...New York or Washington, maybe. His legend was that of an American citizen after all. However, as a dyed in the wool communist, he accepted his lot, content that he was doing his bit for his country. It was not long, however, before he understood the great plan behind his posting. Ireland in the late 1960s was a country bubbling under with dissent. In the North, the Catholic population felt disenfranchised and oppressed, and in the South there was a ground swell of sympathy for their Northern neighbour's plight... but no more. The country was a melting pot of dissent and Kevin's job was to keep stirring that pot.

Igor, or Kevin, arrived in Dublin in 1967 at the tender age of 23. Now, a mere six years later, he was a major player in the supply of weapons and explosives to the warring factions in the North. But that was only part of his role. As his contacts list grew so too did his knowledge of people; their likes and dislikes and their political leanings... and, of course, their greed. If a man would not sell himself for his principles he would, most likely, sell himself for money.

On that basis, he now had access to people who mattered. Some, very few it had to be said, knew him for what he was... a Russian agent. The others, and that included the IRA and a smattering of politicians North and South of the border, knew him only as Kevin Sparke, foreign correspondent for a syndicate of newspapers in the United States. Only his "customers", the IRA – in all its colours - knew of his side-line in procuring arms. To them he was exactly what he appeared to be, an Irish American sympathiser, with contacts in continental Europe who could supply them with virtually unlimited quantities of guns, ammunition and explosives.

That gave him an in. It gave him their ear and allowed him to suggest targets. And that was what today was about. The UNM, a splinter group of the IRA, wanted a headline grabber. They wanted to thrust themselves to the forefront within the organisation. He had already suggested he knew a target that would get them the kudos they craved though, in truth, it would gain them only notoriety. The gain would all be his and Mother Russia's.

Today was about the detail... at least, some of it. He knew what he had to do. Keep the fish on the hook and not lose it.

He passed through the city of Armagh without incident and watched the British Army carrying out stop and search patrols with the RUC. That was part of daily life, particularly here in the predominantly Roman Catholic border country. He was proud of the part he had played in that.

He didn't worry about being stopped. His papers and his cover were perfect. His job as a freelance reporter was perfect cover. He had been stopped in the past, his papers checked, and had been ushered onwards with a friendly wave. He smiled to himself. One of the KGBs top spies in England, Kim Philby, had posed as a reporter when he worked with MI6. Igor was simply following in that great man's footsteps.

And, as a foreign correspondent, he had reason to travel throughout the land gathering "news". No one questioned that. He had carte blanche; even today when he was "interviewing" Pearce Duggan. The result of this "interview" would appear in The Washington Post in a few days' time, proof, if any were needed, of his role.

Pearce Duggan was an Irish businessman. He ran a haulage company and his fleet of trucks carried goods all over Ireland, to the far reaches of North and South, as well as to mainland Britain. Fruit, vegetables, beef stock and sheep...the staples of life. They also carried, from time to time, some more unhealthy cargo...the staples of death, you might say. That brought a smile to his face.

Kevin had already written the article and would send it off later today or tomorrow. The Washington Post was waiting for it. It was a good piece, he mused, setting out as it did the difficulties faced by Irish business in these troubled times.

It would go down well with the Irish in the United States. It might even end up being syndicated over to Britain itself. His pieces sometimes did, after all, and he was forging a reputation for himself. That tickled him. He was becoming "accepted" and being "accepted" was good. He smiled again. It made his job so much easier.

He was near to Keady now with Darkly only minutes beyond. A strange name for a village, he reflected, but the Irish were a strange people. He was looking forward to the meeting. The "businessman" he was meeting with was a veteran of the struggle. Pearce Duggan was old school IRA but he was also involved with a group that made the Provos look like choir-boys. The Official IRA would baulk at this job and even the Provos, who might think twice, would probably reject it. For both of them it would be a step too far. The UNM, on the other hand, would embrace it with open arms.

Duggan was an unusual Nationalist. He wanted his country to be free but he didn't allow that desire to interfere with his entrepreneurial spirit. His family had worked a smallholding near what was now the border with the Free State for generations, but eking out a meagre living from the soil growing cereals, turnips and potatoes was not enough for Pearce.

He had seen an opportunity early on and he had grabbed it. He started small, buying one lorry to take his produce to the markets in Belfast and 'Derry. Gradually, word spread amongst his neighbours about the money that could be made in this way, and his farm became a staging post for produce of all sorts from the surrounding farms, including livestock. He built barns and storage units as the business expanded and now his fleet of waggons delivered produce throughout the country, North and South, and even across to the Mainland via Stranraer in South West Scotland, Hollyhead in Wales and, occasionally, even via Liverpool.

Most of the time his lorries carried produce; vegetables and livestock, but now and again they carried more lethal cargo amongst the cases of turnips or the cattle destined for the abattoirs in Glasgow and Liverpool. On these occasions, specially adapted lorries transported guns, ammunition and explosives...the staples of death he had reflected on earlier.

Pearce Duggan, as well as being a Senior Brigade Commander in the IRA, was involved in the UNM. He was also the principal conduit for most of the weaponry and military hardware that ended up in the hands of the IRAs Active Service Units in the North and on Mainland Britain.

Kevin knew that today's meeting had come as a surprise to the Irishman. It was not a pleasant one, though, judging by his grudging acceptance of the "interview". But Duggan was also intrigued. He had sold the operation to the big Irishman on the basis that it was so big it could end the struggle. That had been met with a degree of scepticism but Kevin's enthusiasm, the fact he dropped in the name of Brendan Kelly and the fact that he always delivered, had swung the man behind him.

Today, Pearce was expecting to learn the target but he would be disappointed. Today wasn't about that at all. It was about some fine detail and about reassuring Kevin that Pearce Duggan and his men were up to it. This attack wasn't just about Ireland asserting itself; it was about striking fear into England and her loathsome American ally, Igor ruminated joyfully. But, as with every gamble, the higher the stakes, the greater the risk... and this operation was highly risky.

Approval had come from the very top in Moscow but with the approval came the warnings. If Russian involvement came out there would be hell to pay and he, Igor, instead of basking in glory, would be breaking rocks in a Gulag in Siberia for the rest of his life. It would be a miserable life but, thankfully, short. A bullet to the back of the head would be preferable but he doubted he would get the choice. He did not dwell on that. It was not going to happen, he assured himself.

His cover was tight. If the operation went wrong, no one, including Pearce Duggan and his fiery daughter, could identify him as anything but an American. Even better, they thought he was an Irish American, and he intended it should stay that way. In all of his dealings with the IRA he was careful to maintain that cover and protect it. The guns he supplied came via Holland and Spain, and even Libya. Nothing was traceable back to Russia... not directly, at least.

He passed through Darkly and reached the service road leading to the farm. It was time. He put on his big toothed, American grin and prepared for the meeting.

***

Pearce Duggan stood in the doorway of a steel container unit and watched the little red car turn off the main road and onto the heavily rutted track that led to the farm. His drivers grumbled constantly about the state of the access road, but it served a purpose and he ignored their complaints. That purpose was amply demonstrated by the way the little red car crawled forward on the rutted and pot holed track. It came to a stop from time to time and, when moving, swayed and bobbed, from side to side and up and down, as it negotiated its route.

The drivers of the Royal Ulster Constabulary Landrovers that called, unannounced, from time to time faced the same problem, but they were a bit more cavalier and reckless in their approach. None the less, the road slowed them enough to let him prepare for their arrival. These bastards, and their Brit Army chums, visited often but they always left empty handed. He intended to keep it that way.

He turned slightly and looked in the direction of the wood sitting on the ridge of high ground overlooking the farm and depot. A smile played at the corners of his mouth. He knew he was being watched. The bastards were dug in up there, living in their makeshift hides on cold rations, and crapping into plastic bags. Poor sods, he grinned. They thought he didn't know they were there.

So, his visitor today, like all his visitors who arrived in daylight, would be photographed and documented. His car would be checked; the Dublin number plate noted and traced through Garda records and, in the fullness of time, it would be shown to belong to one Kevin Sparke, Journalist - American journalist. The bastards could photograph and document all they liked, he grinned. They certainly wouldn't get anything from him, and the American was squeaky clean.

The phone call arranging the meeting said he was coming for an interview about an article he was writing on the difficulties of cross border trade in these dangerous times. That was a good laugh. As far as Pearce was concerned, trade had never been better.

The American's call had irritated him but, at the same time, he wanted to know what the target was. The American was playing that cagily. He kept going on about security as if he, Pearce Duggan, was a fucking novice. Fair enough, security was a problem in some Brigades. Some of them leaked like sieves with bloody touts everywhere, but not in his Brigade. There were no touts in his circle, he had assured the Yank, but the man simply smiled.

Still, it was getting near to the date and he needed the target. All he had been given up to now was the date and the general location. That, he had to admit, had brought with it sleepless nights. Scotland, particularly the West of Scotland, was neutral territory. The Army Council forbade operations there. Even the Loyalists wouldn't dare start anything there. There was too much to lose. They trained there, had arms caches there and recruited there and it was one of the main weapons routes into the Province, for both sides. He heard someone once call it the IRA's Ho Chi Min Trail. Pearce liked that. His boys were just like the Viet Cong. But operating in Scotland was a big gamble so the target had better be worth it.

In one respect, he agreed with the American. Security had to be watertight. If word leaked out about an attack in Scotland there would be hell to pay and it wouldn't just be the Brits he would have to worry about. His own lot wouldn't be pleased either and he could end up with a bullet in the back of his head, if the feckin' SAS didn't get to him first.

He planned to keep the target to himself until just before the attack took place. That way his men couldn't talk about it. He gave a quiet snort. It wasn't that difficult to keep it a secret when he didn't feckin' know it himself. All he had was the date, 25th January, not the 24th or the 26th or any other day come to that. He wondered what the Yank knew and how he knew it.

He had planned as best he could given what little he knew. He had picked his men, sixteen in total in four teams of four. Three would take part in the attack and one would be held in reserve. They were all good men and they would do what they were told. The plan was to send them over to Scotland at the beginning of January. Three weeks on the ground would be enough. The ASU's would arrive separately and would meet up only 48 hours before the attack. That way, if one of them was taken down, they couldn't compromise the others and the reserves could be sent over. Up until the final rendezvous each ASU would think it was carrying out a separate attack. The yank insisted that was crucial to the success of the mission because they wouldn't know the real target, and who was he to argue? I don't even know the feckin' target.

There was a scraping sound behind him and he turned to find his daughter, Orlagh, watching the car's approach over his shoulder. He gave her a smile but all he received in return was a sour faced grimace. Orlagh did not like Kevin Sparke, a fact she had made crystal clear to the man on several occasions. It didn't seem to deter him and he still tried to flirt with her. Pearce grinned. He knew his daughter better than the Yank. If Orlagh didn't like him he could flirt with her and try to impress her till the cows came home; it wouldn't work.

'Do you want to sit in on this?' he asked her over his shoulder.

Orlagh was his sounding board. He couldn't discuss things with anyone else; wouldn't discuss things with anyone else. He trusted no one else, not even this Yank.

At 31 years of age Orlagh Duggan should have been married and away from home but since her mother had died six years earlier she had taken more and more of an interest in the "business". She was Pearce Duggan's guide and his conscience, just like her mother had been. She was also a hardliner, prepared to do anything to further "The Cause".

'Why is he here?' she enquired. 'It should have been another month at least. We don't need anything yet and we can do without surprise visits from the likes of him with our guests up in the woods watching,' she added bitterly.

Duggan smiled. His daughter was as cautious and as suspicious as he was. 'Don't fret, girl,' he said quietly. 'The boys up there will be expectin' him; his telephone call will have been relayed back to them but his cover's watertight. We'll be all over the newspapers in America in a week or so. He'll just be lookin' for an update on how things are progressin' and that has to be face to face. The phone's out of the question.'

Orlagh nodded. 'Did he ask for me to be here?' she asked.

'Oh aye, doesn't he always,' her father replied with a wry smile.

Orlagh's sour expression grew even sourer. She wondered if her father, like her, had sussed out why the American always asked that she be present. It certainly wasn't for her scintillating chat; she usually insulted him from the moment he arrived. No, it wasn't that. It was her red hair, her long shapely legs that even the old dungarees she habitually wore couldn't hide, and her breasts. The man could not take his eyes off her, her breasts in particular. He made her squirm.

Orlagh nodded again and ran her fingers through her long red hair. She gave him a lazy smile and Duggan saw her mother in it, the way she used to smile at him when they were younger. Orlagh was a younger version of the most beautiful woman Pearce Duggan had ever set eyes on. She had her mother's beauty but his nature, he thought proudly.

'I'll go and change,' she said quietly. She did not like Kevin Sparke, detested him in fact, but she enjoyed winding him up. She headed off to change into something that would present him with a vision of something he would never have.

As she disappeared behind the storage unit, the red car finally extricated itself from the ruts and sped towards Duggan in a cloud of dust. Duggan lit a cigarette and waited. The car raced towards him, not slowing, but Duggan refused to be unnerved and remained stock still, waiting. At the last moment, Sparke applied the brakes and spun the steering wheel, sending the car into a broadside skid that ended about ten feet short of the Irishman. Dust rose in a cloud around him but still he refused to move, drawing nonchalantly on his cigarette instead.

Kevin Sparke threw open the car door and emerged with a broad grin on his face. 'When you get that road of yours fixed, I'll stop playing that little game,' he drawled, brushing the settling dust off his jacket.

'You'll have a long wait, then,' Duggan replied laconically. 'Dust and dirt is a lot easier to get rid of than the Brit Army and RUC Peelers. So, what have ye come all the way out here for, Kevin? There's three months to go yet before the big day; are ye checkin' up on us?' the Irishman asked with a quiet laugh, taking another pull on his cigarette.

'Can we go inside?' Sparke asked.

Duggan laughed aloud. 'Why, do ye think someone's listenin' to us? Sittin' over there in the woods with some of that new-fangled listenin' equipment yer always tellin' me about?' His laugh grew louder, mocking. 'Oh, they're there alright, Kevin,' he continued. 'But the only equipment they've got is bins an' cameras. Believe me son, if they had anythin' else up there, I would know about it.' He smiled to himself as his visitor visibly paled. 'Ach, come away inside if it makes ye feel better,' he conceded at last.

As they made their way to the house Duggan saw Sparke turn furtively up towards the treeline. The Irishman took hold of him firmly by the arm and turned the American's attention back to him. He forced a smile as he spoke. 'Don't keep lookin' up there like a frightened rabbit, son; you'll convince the bastards think you've got somethin' to hide,' he said, still smiling, but his eyes were hard. 'I know they're there and they know I know. It's a little game we play, an' now you're in it with us...so play your part. An' relax. As far as I know they haven't got a lip reader on their books,' he finished, laughing uproariously.

Kevin nodded nervously and smiled inwardly. He was playing his role to the hilt. He wasn't a spy after all, he wouldn't know about things like that. Would he?

Duggan pushed open the door of the single storey house and ushered his guest into the kitchen. All business was conducted there and no one was allowed into any other part of the house. That was the private domain of Duggan and his daughter and it was sacrosanct. He indicated a chair by the table and bid Sparke sit while he filled a kettle with water and lit a gas ring on the stove. Water dripping from the kettle hissed as he placed it on the now flaming ring.

He made his way to the table and pulled out another chair, sitting down to face the American. Nothing was said. Sparke knew the ritual. Discussion would not start until the kettle was boiling, the tea was made and Orlagh had joined them. Duggan could hear his daughter moving about in her bedroom and watched the hunger build in Sparke's eyes. It was the sort of look that might, in other circumstances, encourage Duggan to take his shotgun down off the wall, but he knew that Orlagh could handle the man without his help. She had proved that with other men before this, an' better men than this prick. It was a shame that fighting the good fight brought them into contact with arseholes like Kevin Sparke, he reflected, but needs must.

Orlagh entered the room just as the kettle began to bubble and a white cloud of steam issued from the spout. She said nothing but moved past the men to the stove and made a pot of tea. Her father looked at her admiringly but there was only naked lust in Kevin Sparke's eyes. She had changed out of her work clothes of denim dungarees, wellington boots and shapeless woollen jumper into a dress that clung to her shapely body and accentuated all her curves to perfection. The hem sat about six inches above her knees and her perfectly muscled legs tantalised. She had tied her hair back in a ponytail and had applied a touch of blusher to her cheeks. Her lips were a dark crimson, painted on flawlessly and her emerald green eyes sparkled. The finishing touch was a hint of perfume; something French she had told him once. The picture was appealing and Duggan could understand the younger man's lust, he just didn't like it.

Orlagh poured tea into three cups and placed them on the table. A milk jug and sugar bowl were already there. She dispensed with biscuits. If it had been anyone but Kevin Sparke she might have pushed the boat out. Finished, she sat down beside her father and fixed their guest with a smile. Little did he know what she was thinking behind it. The smile turned to one of naked disgust as the American added four heaped teaspoons of sugar to his cup and began to stir. He missed the look. He was too busy preening himself in front of her. She smiled knowingly.

You can't make a silk purse out of a sow's ear, Kevin, she mused.

She could have said it but it would have made no difference. The man was so far up his own backside he would never see the light. He believed he was special but she knew the truth. At least, she thought she did.

Pearce Duggan sipped his tea and kept his eyes on Kevin. Apart from the obvious, the man had something on his mind. He was excited, like a man with a secret he could not wait to share but, at the same time, cautious about whom he could share it with. Duggan had a sudden bad feeling and a quick glance at his daughter told him her thoughts were on the same track. But there was no point in delaying further, he decided.

'Well Kevin, we're inside now, away from the eavesdroppers and lip readers,' he said derisively. 'Why are ye here? Ye know we don't like surprises and we don't like ye turnin' up here too often. Our friends in the woods might get suspicious.'

'There's three months till the big day,' Kevin retorted, shrugging the criticism off. 'I just want to know you're ready and that you've got your teams in place,' he continued testily. Duggan's thinly veiled animosity had thrown him. He had expected a warmer reception.

He turned his attention to Orlagh, hoping for a more reasonable reaction, but her stony eyes matched those of her father. She was wearing that superior look that annoyed him so much. If he had her for an hour alone he would wipe that supercilious smile off her face, he fumed. But this wasn't getting him anywhere. He had to control these emotions.

'So what is it... the target?' Orlagh asked, taking over from her father for a moment.

Sparke's eyes darted to Pearce Duggan, his brow knotting.

'Orlagh is my right hand,' the Irishman said quietly. 'If anything happens to me she will carry on. The men know that.'

Sparke nodded slowly, turning his attention back to the woman.

'It will strike fear into the English,' he said. 'And it will bring them to their senses about this place,' he said.

'Yes, so my father said after your last visit, but what is it?' Orlagh retorted irritably.

The American smiled coldly. 'Not yet,' he said. 'You don't need to know just yet,' he added, prompting frosty laughter from father and daughter.

'Is that a fact, Kevin?' Pearce Duggan snorted sarcastically. 'Ye want us to prepare men for a big attack but ye refuse to tell us what the target is. How do ye expect us to prepare them?'

'That's why I'm here,' Sparke retorted. 'I'll tell you what you need to know to prepare them but the target stays with me. Like I told you, this will be big.'

'Yes, we get that,' Orlagh re-joined. 'You keep telling us that it's big, but you still haven't told us what it is. We need the target, so either tell us what it is or get back in your little red motor car an' piss off. We've got work to be doin' here.'

Sparke looked as though he had been slapped in the face. This bloody girl would have to be put in her place, but now was not the time. He bit back a retort and forced a smile. It was make or break time. He turned to Pearce Duggan, cutting the girl off. 'Well, that's fine by me,' he said. 'If you don't want this chance I'll leave now,' he continued, but made no move.

Duggan stared back at him, torn between the unknown opportunity and his daughter's animosity towards the man. He turned his eyes to Orlagh and gave an imperceptible little shake of the head. 'Tell us what ye can,' he said, shrugging. 'We can wait a bit longer to know the target... but not too long, mind,' he added.

Kevin Sparke smiled but kept his eyes away from Orlagh. His time with her would come. He only had one worry about the whole operation and it was that worry that stopped him naming the target. When he did, the sheer enormity of it might scare them off. Then again, maybe not, he reflected; these people were fanatics, after all. The irony was wasted on him.

'The attack will be co-ordinated. Your three ASUs will carry out separate tasks. It involves hi-jacking a vehicle and that vehicle the ace in the pack. When you have control of that lorry, you have total control over what happens next. I have arranged for uniforms and weapons. These will be kept safely near the target. I will let you know where nearer the time.'

'Everything seems to be nearer the time,' Orlagh Duggan interrupted testily.

Sparke smiled coldly. 'True,' he admitted. 'But for good reason. If any of this gets out, the consequences will be fatal.'

'Is that a threat Kevin?' Orlagh retorted icily.

'Yes,' he said, his smile widening. 'It is... But believe me, you will not be the only ones to suffer. I will be first in line.'

'Well, whoop-di-doo,' Orlagh laughed sarcastically, stifling it immediately on catching her father's withering look.

'So the lads dress up an' hi-jack a lorry,' the Irishman continued, bringing his daughter and Sparke back to the subject in hand. 'Then what?'

'You threaten to blow it up.'

'Threaten?' Pearce responded. He was confused.

'Yes, threaten. You will not actually have to blow it up. The threat will be enough, believe me.'

'An' how do our lads get away? What yer suggestin' sounds like it will end in a stand-off.'

Kevin Sparke laughed. 'It will Pearce, it most certainly will... but your men will walk away from it.'

Pearce Duggan shook his head slowly. 'Yer askin' us to take a helluva lot on trust, Kevin,' he said slowly.

'I know,' Sparke responded, sounding suitably apologetic. 'But that's the way it has to be... for now,' he added, after a moment's pause. 'Do you want me to go on?'

A quick nod from Pearce Duggan. Stony silence from Orlagh.

Kevin sipped at his now cold tea and smiled. He couldn't push his luck much further and he knew it. If he didn't give them the target soon they would walk away and he could not let that happen. But for now, they were still in. Slowly and meticulously now, he outlined the logistical details; the uniforms, the guns, the explosives. That should buy him some time.

***

As they watched the little red car weave and bob back down the track to the main road and beyond, Orlagh Duggan shivered involuntarily. They were committed for now but she still had her doubts. Something niggled at the back of her mind. Alarm bells were ringing but she couldn't pinpoint the danger. Maybe it was simply her distaste for Kevin Sparke himself. Maybe she was letting her personal feelings interfere with her judgement. Maybe; lots of maybes, but something about the bloody man didn't ring true.

When Sparke's car turned north onto the main road and disappeared from sight, she placed a hand on her father's arm to get his attention. 'Do ye trust him, Da?' she asked, her voice soft yet serious.

Pearce Duggan turned to her, a cold smile in his heavily lidded eyes. 'Ye know me better than that, me darlin,' he replied softly. 'The only person I trust in this world is you, and that man there doesn't even appear on a list of possibles. No, we need to keep an eye on that one, so we do.'

He put an arm around her shoulders. 'For now, we'll carry on plannin' an' get the boys ready. But yer right, we need to have the target. We don't want Kevin springin' somethin' on us at the last minute when the lads are committed. Two or three weeks... if he hasn't told us by then we're out.'

Orlagh smiled. 'He won't like it,' she said.

'Well he'll just have to lump it then,' her father replied, patting her arm.

Chapter Twenty-nine

Same Day, London.

Clara Whitelaw leaned back in her chair and rubbed tired eyes. She had been staring at these bloody photographs for what seemed hours now and she was getting nowhere. Just over a week had passed since her reunion with Jamie and she was coming to terms with it.

She now had other things on her mind, but these "other things" still involved *him* so she found it impossible to shake him from her thoughts. Sir Charles had made it clear to her what he wanted, and what he wanted he usually got. What *she* wanted was to keep Jamie out of it but that, she fretted, was nigh impossible.

She turned back to the photographs on her desk. Of the bundle lying there, only one was of any importance. She leaned forward and picked it up, staring at it as she waved it gently in front of her. 'Who are you?' she pondered softly to herself.

This photograph had been puzzling her since Charles had laid it on her desk the day after Jamie's departure. She remembered looking at it at the time and laughing aloud. For identification purposes, it was worse than useless, and that made her question why it had been included with the other pictures at all.

The others she understood. They were snaps of the men Corkscrew had identified as being involved in the Active Service Units chosen to carry out the threatened attacks. The men in these were all clearly identifiable. This snap, on the other hand, showed an anonymous figure in an equally anonymous location... and the Irishman hadn't given any clues as to the identity of either. That too baffled her. Why provide a photograph and nothing else?

'What am I missing?' she asked herself for the thousandth time. Something niggled at her... a feeling, no more than that, that Jamie Raeburn knew something about this but, like Corkscrew, he was keeping it to himself. She found that disturbing.

Concentrate, she told herself, push him away.

'Okay, what am I missing?' she murmured again, through clenched teeth.

She studied the photograph closely once again. She had lost count of the number of times she had done that. What was she looking for? A clue, any clue, that would tell her where or who the woman was. Wasn't that the definition of insanity, doing the same thing over and over and over again in the vain hope of getting a different result? Maybe she was insane, she mused bitterly. It was a bland, unspectacular photograph of a bland, unspectacular girl. So, what did she have?

The woman in the photograph was around thirty, she estimated. She was average height and average build. The photograph was in black and white but that was neither here nor there other than her hair was long and dark. The description of the suspected bomber described a young woman with medium length blonde hair. The hair didn't matter. Hair colour could be changed as could style. Dyes and wigs were plentiful.

The picture had been taken covertly, that much was clear. The woman was unaware that she was being photographed. Her posture and movement showed that.

She turned her attention away from the woman to the background. The landscape, cityscape more like, was familiar. The big spire in the background stood out like a beacon. It was Belfast without a doubt but it was the city, not the suburbs and there was no way of identifying where the woman had come from or where she was going. It was useless. Just what was Corkscrew up to, she pondered.

Okay, Charles was putting pressure on the Irishman to give up the bomber. It was a condition of his disappearance with a new identity. So the identity of the bomber was as important to Corkscrew as it was to Charles, she mused. Was that what it was, a simple lure to keep Charles on the line? Corkscrew didn't know who planted the bomb but felt he had to give Charles something or his escape route would be cut off. Possibly.

She sat back and closed her eyes, rubbing at her temples. Another thought began to form in her mind. Maybe it was a smokescreen. Maybe Corkscrew was carrying out a double bluff. Maybe he did know who the bomber was and this was designed to throw Charles off the scent. In this game anything was possible. But now Jamie was involved. Did Corkscrew really trust him and how close had they been? Questions, questions and more questions... and no answers.

She fixed her eyes on the younger woman in the photograph. 'Who are you?' she murmured again. 'Bomber or can carrier?'

Working back to her earlier thought she opened her desk drawer and rummaged through the files. Under 'C' she found the one she was looking for and withdrew it. She had read it before but it was worth reading again, she decided. The file contained everything Ultra and the other Security Services had on agent Corkscrew, though to Five and SIS he was simply Liam Fitzpatrick. Taking a sip of now cold coffee from the mug on her desk, she began to read:

"Liam Fitzpatrick, born 1st May 1940" - which would make him 33 years old now, she computed. "Second oldest of a family of four children, his siblings all girls. Father, Eamon Fitzpatrick, deceased - killed on active service" - She read that with a wry smile, Fitzpatrick Senior hadn't been fighting for King and Country, he'd been fighting against them. He had been part of an IRA Active Service Unit that had carried out an attack on an RUC police barracks in County Antrim. Someone, maybe just like his son now, had tipped off the authorities and Eamon and a few of his friends had been shot dead for their troubles. That, she mused philosophically, is how terrorism is perpetuated; like the circle of life. You kill a father and you end up fighting the son. It feeds on itself.

She shook her head slowly. The more she read the more she was amazed that Sir Charles had managed to turn Liam Fitzpatrick. Touting was anathema in the Nationalist community. Most of them would rather die of cancer than turn informer. Getting a man like Fitzpatrick to tout was quite a feat. Fitzpatrick's freedom fighter father would be turning in his grave, she thought, laughing at the alliteration.

She turned her attention to the women in the family. The bomber, after all, was a woman. Witnesses described a young blonde woman and, according to Charles, Fitzpatrick had never disputed the fact. What did that tell her? It could be more smoke and mirrors and she might be wasting her time but she had nothing else.

When it came to the female members of the Fitzpatrick family, the information in the file was scant. "Mother, Mary (aka Molly) Theresa Fitzpatrick, m/s Kelly, born Tralee, 24 April, 1921. Father; Eoin Kelly, deceased. Mother; Mary Bernadette Kelly, deceased". Clara smiled harshly. Molly's was a birthday no one in the family would ever forget, falling as it did on the fifth anniversary of the Easter Uprising. Information on Corkscrew's sisters was equally meagre, restricted to names, dates of birth and last known addresses. She read them out, murmuring each under her breath, as though they might hear her and respond.

'Mary Ann Fitzpatrick (Thomas), d o b 10 May, 1939, l k a – last known address - , 83 Railwayview Street, Bangor, County Down, n k a - no known associations.

Ann-Marie Fitzpatrick (O'Neil), d o b 13 September, 1945, l k a, 179 Constitution Street, Belfast, n k a.

Siobhan Brigid Fitzpatrick (Flaherty), d o b 1 February, 1947, l k a, 79 Arran Street, Short Strand, Belfast, c w a – shorthand for current whereabouts unknown – and, like her sisters, n k a, no known address.'

She took another sip of the cold coffee and pulled a face at the bitter taste. She ran over in her mind what she had read. Corkscrew's mother was too old to be the bomber but all three sisters were in the right age group. It would be worth following them up, she decided. The "no known associations" against their names meant nothing.

With a long, drawn out sigh, she leaned back heavily in her chair. Her eyes were nipping and she rubbed at them gently with the tips of her fingers in a vain attempt to ease the strain. She closed them, and immediately a picture of Jamie formed before her. She wondered how he was and when he would make contact again. She wondered too if, like her, he found it difficult to shut her out of his mind. She shrugged mentally and forced her thoughts back to Liam Fitzpatrick and the Coventry bomber.

She started with the premise that the bomber actually was the young blonde woman seen by witnesses in the pub. The UNM, an extreme splinter group of the IRA, had claimed responsibility for the atrocity so, logically, the bomber was a member. If that was the case then Corkscrew, also a member of the UNM, had to know who she was. So, run forward to the present: Corkscrew was still involved with the IRA/UNM but was now an informer.

He was passing on intelligence about a major attack being planned on Mainland Britain. That intel, if the attack or attacks did go ahead, would lead to the arrest or death of men who thought of him as a friend, and yet, she mused thoughtfully, he seemed to have no qualms about that. What did that tell her, she queried. If Corkscrew could so easily inform on the men in the active service units now why did he not simply give up the bomber? There were only two possible answers, she concluded. One, he didn't know who the bomber was or, two, he did know but she was more than just another member of the IRA to him. He was close to her... maybe more than just close. Family? Lover?

She thought again about his sisters. If Corkscrew's motivation for joining the IRA was his father's death then the same could be said for them. And what about Mary or Molly Fitzpatrick? She was too old to be the bomber but that didn't exclude her from involvement. The children had lost their father; she had lost her husband.

But wasn't that all too obvious? The Fitzpatrick family had been checked. The names of the women were in Corkscrew's file. If there had been more on them it would have been shown in the file or at least referred to. And Corkscrew wasn't stupid. He would expect his immediate family to be investigated thoroughly... so logic pointed to the fact that they were not involved.

She smiled grimly to herself. In the normal world, it was usually safe to apply logic. The definition of the word came back to her instantly, the benefit of a good university education, she reflected wryly – (Logic) that branch of philosophy concerned with analysing patterns of reasoning from which a conclusion can be properly drawn from a set of premises, without reference to meaning or context.

Yes, that was it, she laughed. But I'm not dealing with the normal world, she mused, so logic doesn't necessarily apply and now I'm going round in circles.

None the less, she tossed it around in her mind for a while, determined to consider all the conclusions. She laughed aloud after a while. There were no conclusion to consider, nothing tangible at least. All she had was instinct; a gut feeling. Thinking about it logically, she smiled again, it was unlikely that his sisters and his mother were involved, though not impossible. So, if not one of them, who?

All her instincts told her that the man's obfuscation pointed to the bomber being someone not just known to him, but someone close to him. Girlfriend? Did he have one or was she an ex? God, that would take some digging and Five would want to know why. And what about other relatives? Aunts, cousins, she wondered, what about them? There could be many of those and that was without looking at close friends. Checking all of them would be a nightmare and could tie her up for months... And she didn't have months.

The easy way was to wring the name out of Corkscrew; the old-fashioned way, that is, she smiled coldly. But that wasn't an option just now. Only one person was likely to get to the truth and that was Jamie. He had said he would do it, even said he would kill the bomber, according to Charles, but she wasn't so sure. Everything she knew about him told her he wouldn't play ball. She thought maybe Sir Charles felt the same and that was why she had been ordered to stay close to him. She thought about him again now, obliterating everything else. She wondered if he had ever killed a woman before. The thought made her shudder. God, where would this all end, she mused sadly?

She rubbed her tired eyes once again and yawned. She needed a stiff drink and a good night's sleep. 'Maybe then I'll find myself closer to the truth,' she murmured quietly to herself before a grim smile settled on her lovely features. 'Who am I trying to kid?' she laughed harshly as she cleared the photographs and the file from her desk.

Chapter Thirty

25 October 1973, North East France

Jamie stood by the window watching the rain sweep across the fields to batter the house, beat the grass flat and twist and bend the trees. A fork of lightning, brilliant white against the dark grey sky, lanced down through the firmament. He watched, fascinated, as it earthed on a spot on the hillside opposite, about a mile away.

The flash illuminated the room around him with an eerie glow, and seconds later the windows of the house rattled with the force its power. The storm had started about an hour earlier, off to the north, and had been moving steadily towards them ever since. Soon it would be right over them and the house would shake even more. The power of the storms here always awed him...it was like a regular re-run of the apocalypse.

The rain fell heavier, battering off the ancient roof tiles. It was like sitting inside a drum played by some manic percussionist. The roads would flood soon as the drains filled to overflowing, he mused, as he watched the rainwater flow in sheets down the windowpane. Even though the village sat on top of a plateau, it didn't entirely escape the inundations that usually accompanied the storms.

He thought nostalgically of home. Glasgow rain, the rain he was used to in the past, was fine and persistent. People talked about "a wee smir"... as though they were walking through a cloud rather than standing below one. It was so different here. When it rained here, it was like standing beneath a waterfall. The Gods, it seemed, played games on them, dumping giant pails full of icy water down onto the countryside below to see how quickly they could cause drains to overflow, streams to burst their banks and rivers to form in the roadways. Maybe they ran a book on it, he mused irreverently...like betting on the horses or a football match. Well, for amusement, it probably beat listening to millions of harpists playing melancholy music all day.

But there was one thing he could be sure of here. Eventually, sooner rather than later, the storm would pass and the sun would shine again. The floods would clear and steam would rise from the roads as they dried quickly in the heat. That didn't happen in Glasgow, he mused, as he turned away from the window, depressed now.

He was letting things get on top of him. Time was running out. He had plans to make and decisions to take. He heard laughter from another part of the house and his wife's voice as she played with the children, taking their minds off the storm. What would he do without her, he mused? He shook his head slowly. The answer to that was obvious; he would sink like a stone.

At least one of his problems had been resolved. Kate's insistence that they all return "home" with him had come as a relief. He had not wanted to leave them here in the first place, even though Kate had it in her mind that he would. There was, however, one minor difficulty with the plan. He didn't want her and the kids anywhere near the action when it took place. If anything went wrong the fallout would be unimaginable. Perhaps he could get her to stay with her parents until the operation was over. Aye, maybe, but he doubted that staying in Calverton near Nottingham wasn't on her agenda.

Thinking like that turned his mind to Roisin. Her family too was causing him problems. He laughed inwardly; "problems" didn't come close. If Roisin had to be spirited away, like Liam, she would need a passport... just like Liam. But it didn't stop there. Liam was on his own, Roisin had a husband and two kids. He hadn't even broached the question of whether she would leave them but he doubted if that would be on her agenda either.

That would mean making four people disappear and he didn't hold out much hope of achieving that. He still didn't know if Roisin's mental health was up to it and there was another huge problem that scared him to death. Her husband was in the navy... the Royal fuckin' Navy, which, on its own, was bad enough but the guy was a Petty Officer on board one of her Majesty's Polaris carrying nuclear submarines, HMS Aegaeon. Ironic, he thought, smiling then, Aegaeon being the Greek God of storms. If Roisin's husband "disappeared" suddenly there would be one hell of a storm. The Navy and the Security Services would search high and low to find him. He was getting ahead of himself, he decided; he didn't even know if her man would go along with it. If not, what then?

He couldn't think like that, he decided. He had to deal with it as if he would. That would mean new passports for both. The twins weren't a problem; they could simply be added to Roisin's or Trevor's passport. Two passports and new identities. It could be done. He knew who to ask, but, and it was a big but, he didn't really want to involve him. And if he didn't? There was no answer to that. He would have to make the call.

Kate entered the room, breaking his concentration. He turned to her and smiled wanly. She hugged her baby close to her, asleep in her arms, and Jamie felt a stab of guilt. What was he doing to them? He should have taken the way out when Liam offered it; left him to his own devices. All he would have had to deal with then was his conscience. He pushed the thought from his mind and pulled Kate and their new baby to, nuzzling his head against the child.

'It's weighing heavily on you, isn't it,' Kate said quietly. It wasn't a question. She was reading his mind again, he mused.

'Yes, it is,' he conceded reluctantly, stroking the back of her neck.

'Don't torment yourself,' Kate went on. 'Whatever it is that's bothering you isn't going to change by worrying about it. You'll have to deal with it eventually, so just do it.'

He laughed softly. She was reading his thoughts. 'I thought you were against all this?' he retorted.

Kate smiled emotionally. 'I am,' she said, 'but that's not going to change anything, is it? You're committed.'

He smiled back lovingly. 'Yeah, maybe I should be... in a locked ward with no key.'

She gave him a worried look. 'Is it so bad?' she probed.

Jamie nodded slowly but forced a smile. 'Bad enough,' he admitted. He pushed back from her and kissed her brow. 'Listen, I'm going into Epernay,' he said. 'Do you need anything?'

Kate wasn't diverted. 'Why do you need to go?' she asked quietly.

'I've got a couple of phone calls to make.'

Kate furrowed her brow. 'We have a phone here; why not use that?' she went on, not entirely sure she wanted to hear the answer. Jamie said nothing, just looked awkward and shook his head.

Her worried expression became more anxious as the implication of what he hadn't said struck her. 'This is a joke, right? You think the phone is bugged?' She laughed at the notion but it was a nervous laugh. She knitted her brow. 'That's absurd,' she continued. 'This is France.' She still didn't believe.

Jamie smiled slowly. 'You're right, it is absurd... and maybe I'm just paranoid, but this whole thing is crazy.' He paused a moment. 'The Brigadier was here during the war. He worked with SOE.'

'Who?'

'SOE, Special Operations Executive,' he explained. 'He was a British agent then. He'll have friends here... and his wife is French,' he added. 'Maybe I'm over-reacting, but I just don't want to take the chance.'

He felt Kate shiver and her face lost its colour. He pulled her close again. 'When this is over sweetheart, I promise, I'm out,' he whispered softly.

Kate gave him a wan little smile. That would be a hard promise to keep.

Chapter Thirty-one

Jamie drove out of the village less than an hour later. It was just before two o'clock in the afternoon. The thunderstorm had passed and the rain had stopped but, unusually, the sky was still a sombre grey. The sun was battling to find a way through the cloud layer but he thought it would be a while before it bathed the land in its heat.

The elderly, late model, Citroen Traction Avant 15CV 6H, glided along the Epernay road, its 6 cylinder 2,866cc responding to Jamie's gentle touch on the throttle. He loved this car. The black paintwork still gleamed like new and the chrome of the radiator grill with the distinctive double inverted Vs filled him with pride. He had spent hours of dedicated work on it. He treated it with the respect he had shown to his beloved Triumph Bonneville 650cc bike and it repaid him handsomely. It might be old but it ran like new and when he drove it he felt a sense of exhilaration.

But not today, not now. The image of Kate standing forlornly at the window as he left home, with baby Jack in her arms, was still with him. He had given her a wave and she had smiled, moving Jack's tiny hand up and down to mimic her own wave. It made him feel wretched but with it came a determination to see the thing through as quickly as possible.

Once clear of the village and onto the open road he put his foot to the floor, and pushed the big car to its limit. The forest fringe flew past in a blur on both sides as he raced along the long, straight road. There was little traffic but what there was soon disappeared from his rear view mirror as the Citroen ate up the kilometres like an avaricious beast. Soon, he was clear of the forests and fields, great expanses of turned earth, spread out on both sides.

The villages of Brugny and Vaudancourt were close now. He eased back on the throttle and gently applied the brakes before throwing the car into the first of the series of sweeping curves that lead downhill to Vaudancourt and then on to Pierry. The bends were notoriously dangerous, especially on the downhill route, and more so when the road surface was wet like today. Braking harshly before the bends only added to the danger, something he had learned the hard way on his first attempt. He eased his speed again, applying cadence braking – lightly tapping his foot repeatedly on the pedal - to prevent lock up and an inevitable skid. He was facing enough danger in the coming weeks without adding to it.

At the foot of the hill he swept into the final bend and entered the village of Vaudancourt. The road stretched out straight ahead of him now. Autumn was closing in and the colours around him were magnificent. The vines, once vibrant green in summer, were now a brilliant melange of browns, reds and yellows. He wished he had time to appreciate the season, his first autumn here, but circumstances were conspiring against him.

That didn't help his mood. Even the excitement of his high-speed drive had failed to lift his spirits. He should be spending time with his family; taking his children on expeditions to explore the countryside by day and making love with his wife at night. Instead, he was off tilting at windmills again. He cursed himself silently.

He parked the Citroen in the centre of Epernay, a short walk from the Place Hugues Plomb, the main square. There were public telephone boxes sited outside the Post Office and he headed for these. The air was still heavy and muggy and another storm threatened. He visited the Post Office, bought some stamps with a Twenty Franc note and asked for the change in coins. His pockets now bulging with One Franc, Fifty, Twenty and Ten Centime pieces, he returned outside to the public telephones.

The time was now two fifteen in the afternoon. In Belfast, it would be one fifteen and in Washington, it would be seven fifteen in the morning. He doubted that Conor Whelan, workaholic though he was, would be at his desk at this hour. That made Liam top of the list.

He fed coins into the apparatus and dialled, waiting patiently as the call routed through the various telephone exchanges and trunk centres on route. Liam himself answered and Jamie let out a quiet sigh of relief. He wondered briefly if young Concepta had outlived her usefulness, or if her voice had finally driven Liam insane.

The call was unexpectedly brief. Liam apologised, made an excuse and said he would return the call in a few minutes. Something in the Irishman's voice triggered caution and Jamie remembered the arrangement they had made. He read off the number of the phone box, reversing the sequence of digits, and hung up. He didn't remind Liam to add the international code. He would know.

He turned to look outside the box and met the angry glare of a well-dressed, middle-aged woman who was obviously keen to use the phone. He ignored her and turned back to the instrument, lifting the handset and placing a finger on the cradle to allow Liam's call to come through. As a deception, it wasn't much but it worked. Out of the side of his eye he saw the woman stomp off angrily before suddenly picking up speed to grab another box that had become free.

When his own phone rang, he answered immediately. When Liam spoke Jamie could hear a steady hum of background noise; traffic noise, and a vehicle horn being sounded repeatedly. The penny dropped immediately. Liam was out of his office.

'Your phone being tapped?' Jamie asked.

'Don't know for certain,' Liam replied breathlessly. 'But it stands to reason. They watch me every other bloody way. Ah'm not takin' any chances.'

'Fair enough, neither am I,' Jamie replied, smiling coldly. 'Let's keep this short. Anything new?'

'Oh aye,' Liam responded expressively. 'Quite a lot, as it happens.'

'Alright, let me have it,' Jamie retorted brusquely.

'First off, that young lass, the one we spoke about... the one that's in hospital?'

'Yes, I remember.'

'Seems she's on the mend, so she is. Long way to go, right enough, but reports from the hospital are good. My Ma thinks it's a miracle. Ah didn't want to busrt her bubble,' he laughed. 'Ah don't know what ye said to her but whatever it was, it must have worked.' Liam laughed as he said it. 'Ye must have got closer to her in Belfast that she let on.'

Jamie ignored that. 'That's good. I'm pleased. What about her man, any word on him?'

'No, his compassionate leave was cancelled an' he' back at sea. He's not due to return until the middle or end of December.'

'So he still doesn't know the score?'

'No, he doesn't... an' I don't know that it's a good thing tellin' him.' Liam replied, doubtfully.

'If we're getting Roisin out, he has to know and he has to go along with it. She doesn't have a choice.'

'Ah don't like it,' Liam persisted.

'Okay, we'll leave it just now. Her man's not back for a while anyway so we have time. What about the other thing? Is it still on?'

There was a brief pause before Liam replied. Now they could only be talking about one thing. 'Aye, it's on... same date, but...' There was a moment's hesitation before he went on. 'Ah thought it was three attacks but ah was wrong. There will only be the one.'

'So just the one ASU?' Jamie pressed on, hopefully.

'No, still three... twelve men.'

'Shit!' Jamie hissed. He didn't need to enlarge on it. Liam would know what he was thinking. 'You'd better tell me the rest.'

'One big job, three ASUs in a co-ordinated attack.'

'Where?' Jamie pressed.

There was another momentary hesitation before Liam came back. 'Ah still don't know,' he admitted. 'The security on this one's as tight as a duck's arse.'

'The Brigadier won't be pleased,' Jamie retorted dryly. 'He wants this out of the way.' He allowed a moment's silence before going on. 'It makes things a damn sight worse for us too,' he said quietly, voicing his own thoughts.

'Aye, ah know that... it makes it more difficult.'

Jamie laughed. 'Difficult doesn't come close, Liam.'

There was silence for a moment as both men considered the change. It was Liam who broke it.

'Ah take it ye've spoken to the man?' he asked.

'Right after our meeting... next morning, in fact. He wanted chapter and verse.'

'Anythin' else?'

Jamie's cold laugh didn't throw Liam. It wasn't unexpected. 'Did he ask me to do anything about the bomber, you mean?'

'Aye, that's what I meant,' Liam conceded gruffly.

'Of course he did,' Jamie retorted. 'You knew he would.'

'An' what did ye tell him?'

'I told him I would.'

The silence that followed was almost palpable. Again, it was Liam who broke it.

'Ye said ye would... would what exactly?' he asked, sounding nervy.

'Get the bomber's identity out of you and bring her in,' Jamie said without batting an eyelid.

Liam wasn't quite so calm. He exploded. 'You bastard! Ah trusted you...'

'Would you rather he got someone else to do it?' Jamie interrupted, stopping him in his tracks. 'What do you take me for Liam?'

There was silence and then contrition. 'Ah'm sorry. Ah didn't think.'

'Forget it. But things are still going to be difficult. He's got other people working on it as well as me and they'll come up with the answer eventually.' He knew that would come as another kick in the balls to Liam but that was life.

'Ye're a right feckin' ray o' sunshine, so ye are,' Liam responded, confirming it.

Jamie laughed coldly. 'I'm just a realist, Liam... or, if you prefer, a cynic. It just means we have to find an answer to the problem before they come up with theirs.'

The pips sounded and Jamie waited as the Irishman fed more coins into the box. That would give them a few more minutes, Jamie estimated.

Liam came back to him as the coins registered. 'So what do we do now?' he asked.

'You keep me posted on developments. I'll put my mind to the problem of Roisin... I've got an idea.'

'What idea?'

'I'll keep that to myself just now... don't want you getting' your hopes up. I have to talk to someone.'

Liam accepted that without demur. 'How do we keep in touch?' he asked instead.

'I'll phone you next week... just like today. I'll ask about a job. If you've got anything to tell me, call me back later from a phone box. You've got my home number. When I answer, just hang up... don't say anything... then call me on this number, 0033625782173, ten minutes later. Okay?' he replied, giving Liam the number of the Hotel de la Place.

'What if ah need ye in a hurry?'

'Same routine. Phone me at home, hang up then call at the number I gave you ten minutes later. If I'm not there, call me again an hour later.'

'Aye, okay,' Liam responded. He hesitated, scared to pose his next question, but he needed to know. 'Ye are still up fer this?' he asked. 'Ah mean... can ye do it?'

Jamie laughed frostily. 'Don't worry, Liam, I'm in. Just you keep feeding me with information and I'll handle this end. Anything else?'

'No, nothin' else.'

'Right, I'll call you next week. Watch your back,' Jamie said, finishing the call. He hoped he sounded confident... more confident than he felt, at least.

Chapter Thirty-two

He remained in the phone booth and made his second call. There was no chance of anyone listening in this time. Ultra's offices were swept for bugs every day. The Brigadier answered gruffly on the second ring.

'Good afternoon Brigadier,' Jamie started affably.

'Ah, Raeburn, at last,' the old boy replied, making it sound as if Jamie had been out of touch for too long when it had less than 10 days. 'I hope you have some news?' he demanded and carried on. 'I've been thinking about our last conversation and I've decided that Dr Whitelaw should be your case officer on this. She's working on the identity of the bomber in tandem so it makes sense. Be a good chap and fill her in. She's still on the same number as before... I'm sure you won't have forgotten it.'

Jamie had no time to respond to the jibe before the call ended. He stared angrily at the instrument in his hand, his frustration finally ebbing away. He fed more franc coins into the coin box and re-dialled. Sir Charles was right on one thing with his snide remark. He did remember the number.

Clara Whitelaw answered quickly. She recognised his voice instantly and reacted happily. 'Jamie,' she said. 'What a pleasant surprise.'

'Really?' he retorted. 'According to his nibs you were expecting a call... But it is nice to talk to you, even if it is all work.' He could see Lady Redmond in his mind's eye, reminding him to be nice. 'You've been given the dubious honour of being my case officer, I'm told. Care to tell me why?'

'Charles thought it best as he has landed me with the task of identifying the bomber from whatever Corkscrew passes on.'

'Yes, he said,' Jamie replied thoughtfully.

'You sound suspicious,' she said, covering the query with a laugh.

'Do I? Maybe I'm just paranoid. Does he expect you to keep tabs on me?'

'Good Lord, no,' she responded quickly. Too quickly, Jamie reflected. 'He simply wants the bomber. You're Corkscrew's contact. It will save me a lot of grind if you can wheedle the name out of him, that's all.'

'I've asked this before,' Jamie responded. 'What if he doesn't know who the bomber is?'

'He does... there's a connection between him and the bomber, I just haven't worked out what it is yet.'

Jamie felt the hairs on the back of his neck stand on end.

Connection between them; where the fuck did that come from?

He laughed to cover his consternation before replying. 'Bit of a leap, don't you think? How did you work that out?' he said, playing it down.

'No, not really,' she threw back quickly. 'I've been pondering why he gave you a photograph. If he doesn't know her, how did he get a photograph? Then I asked why it was such an anonymous picture, taken when the girl was unaware of it. It could be anyone... and it probably is,' she added tellingly. Jamie could see where her mind was leading her. 'I think he knows her... not just knows her, he's close to her in some way.'

'How close?' Jamie asked, his heart sinking.

'Girlfriend, maybe or relation,' she came back, flooring him completely. 'He's protecting her. That's the only logical conclusion.'

And that was the final nail in the coffin. Roisin's position had just become worse... exponentially, he reflected anxiously. Clara was sharp. She would work it out. It might take time but she would get there. Determination was something she had in abundance; he knew that from experience... Not bitter experience, just experience.

'I take it you've been in touch with Corkscrew again,' she started again.

'Yes, how did you guess?' he retorted mordantly.

She ignored that. 'Any news then?' she enquired.

'Some. The three attacks have now become one.'

Clara's brow furrowed questioningly. 'Is that good or bad?'

Jamie laughed coldly down the line. 'It would be good if it was only one ASU taking part but according to Corkscrew it's still the three. He doesn't know who the others will be but his best guess is still the guys in the photographs I passed to the Brigadier.'

'And the target?'

'There's still no intelligence on that. Only the date... that's still 25 January.'

'So we still don't know if it's in the Province or here on the Mainland?'

'No.'

'But he still believes the target is military?'

'He hasn't said anything to the contrary.'

'And that's it?'

'Aye, that's it,' Jamie confirmed. He smiled wryly. She was being very formal now.

'Is it definitely here on the Mainland? Not Belfast or Derry?' Clara probed.

'He hasn't been told anything different. The ASUs have been told they're coming over at the beginning of the year...just after Hogmanay.'

'Hogmanay?'

'New Year,' he explained, patiently, making allowance for her upper middle class English background.

'And he still believes it's a military target?'

'He didn't say anything to the contrary.'

'And that's it?'

'Aye, that's it,' Jamie confirmed, smiling wryly. She was being very business-like.

'It isn't much, is it?' she continued.

'No, not much,' he agreed. 'But he can only pass on what he's told. I'll keep on top of him, get as much as I can, and I'll press him about the bomber.'

'Yes, make sure you do,' she retorted. 'Phone me again as soon as you have anything. I'm about to start pouring through his family record. There has to be a link somewhere... If you can get it out of him it'll save me a slog.'

'Okay,' he concurred, trying to sound positive. 'I'll call you again next week.'

Clara brightened again. 'Good. Maybe we can have a happier chat,' she said.

Jamie wasn't sure if she was joking or serious but no matter, his next call had taken on even more importance. He finished the call with that thought in his mind, promising again to get what he could from Liam. He had a feeling Clara didn't believe him.

Chapter Thirty-three

Jamie left the bank of phone boxes in the Place Hughes Plomb and made for Le Congress, a bar he and Kate had visited on a few occasions. He needed time to think. He could do that over a drink and the bar would be quiet at this time in the day. His third phone call was the one he really did not want to make but Clara's voiced certainty about a link between Liam and the bomber made it unavoidable.

He ordered a pastis and sat at a table near the window. The golden liquid turned a milky yellow as the waited added water and ice and Jamie swirled the mixture around the glass, listening to the clunk of the ice on the side of the glass while contemplating his approach. He wondered what sort of response he would get... After Conor got over the surprise, that is. Maybe he was asking the impossible, he mused disconsolately. His request wouldn't be easy to fulfil, even for someone with limitless resources and he doubted that Conor Whelan fell into that category.

But that would come after the shock. It was another Lazarus moment. Explaining what had actually happened would take some time but it would probably help with his appeal. The reason behind it would be clearer.

He nursed his drink and checked his watch. It was just leaving three o'clock in the afternoon, which, by his reckoning, made it just after 09.00 in Washington. Conor should be behind his desk in his office by now and there was no point in putting off the call. It was time to face it.

He sorted out his money, leaving aside sufficient coins for the call which, he knew, would have to be routed through the operator. Satisfied he had enough, he paid his bill and left the Restaurant. Slowly, almost reluctantly, he retraced his steps to the bank of phone boxes in the main square. The sky was clearing at last and he could feel the sun on his back, warming him. He still felt cold on the inside though.

The phone box he had used earlier was vacant and he slipped inside, placing his coins on top of the apparatus. It took an effort of will to pick up the handset but finally he did, placing the receiver against his ear. He dialled "0" and waited. The operator answered almost immediately. Her voice was deep and sexy and she sounded young but he had been fooled before, he reminded himself. She was probably in her fifties with a face that would turn milk, he mused. It took his mind off what he was about to do at least. He asked for a trunk call to America, gave her the code and slipped coins into the box as directed.

The connection seemed to take forever but, finally, the ringing tone echoed back over the line. One ring, then two before he heard Conor answer. His voice sounded robotic, metallic even, but it was definitely Conor.

'Hello Conor,' Jamie said softly. 'Guess who?'

There was silence for an instant and then Conor exploded. 'Jeeesus, Jamie, is it really you?' the American responded, clearly startled. 'Where the hell have you been, kid? I thought you were dead... did a search through intel from your neck of the woods,' he went on. 'Discovered that a Captain Messenger was killed in a SNAFU in Ireland...'

Jamie interrupted him with a laugh. 'A what?' he asked, amused.

'A SNAFU, kid, it's an acronym – stands for situation normal all fucked up.'

Jamie laughed louder. 'It was certainly that, big guy,' he chortled.

'Hey, it's no laughing matter. Shit, I panicked when I read that, kid. I managed to contact your Mom a few weeks back but she couldn't tell me much either other than you were still alive. I don't know if she really believed it though; she didn't sound happy. Where the hell have you been?'

Jamie laughed quietly, his mood lifting. 'I hope she believes it Conor,' Jamie replied, old friend "Guilt" nodding hello from the corner. 'It has been difficult.' Now there was an understatement if ever there was one, he mused.

'What about Kate and the kids?' Liam continued, a note of anxiety creeping in.

'They're good, Conor... and we've got another boy,' he added, laughing merrily. He knew what to expect from the American.'

'Jeeze kid, what you trying to do, repopulate the planet single-handed?'

The laughing continued. 'And what about you and Mary? Are you doing your bit to save the world?' he teased.

'Hell, yeah... that's why I was trying to get in touch with you,' Conor responded in a rush, his joy almost palpable from the other side of the Atlantic. 'Mary presented me with twin girls six months ago,' he added proudly. '3rd March.'

Coincidence...or something spiritual, Jamie mused. 'I didn't even know she was pregnant,' he said, returning to the conversation. 'You kept that quiet.'

'Yeah, well... she had a couple of miscarriages... they cut us up a bit so we decided to keep it to ourselves this time.'

'I'm happy for you, Conor, truly... for both of you... all four,' he laughed and Conor Whelan joined him.

When the laughter died down it fell to Conor to open the conversation. The real conversation.

'So what the hell happened and where are you now?' he asked bluntly, just as the operator broke into the call telling Jamie to insert more money.

The sound of the coins dropping into the box fed back down the line before Jamie could answer. 'It's a long story, Conor. Short version is that an operation in the Irish Republic went badly wrong. There was a reception committee waiting for me. Really, I should be dead, but here's the crazy bit... One of the IRA men recognised me. He maybe even knows you... or of you,' he went on. The silence at the other end of the line told him he now had Conor's undivided attention. 'It all goes back to that wee trip I made to Belfast in '67, remember?'

'Yeah kid, I remember. How could I forget?'

'Yeah, well, I met this man when I was over there...'

'I can't figure how he would know me,' Conor announced dubiously.

'He's Brendan Kelly's cousin,' Jamie replied as if that explained everything. It did, more or less.

'Holy shit!' Conor exploded. 'So what happened?'

'Like I said, he recognised me. Shot me but missed... though not completely,' he added, laughing coldly. 'The bugger faked my death, pulled the others off. The SAS brought me out.'

'So what was all that shit about Captain Messenger buying the plot?'

Jamie laughed again. 'The IRA thought they'd topped a Brit agent over there so the illusion had to be maintained. Captain Messenger had to die. He had a good funeral, apparently, full military shit, though I don't think many of the mourners actually knew him... or me, come to that. I didn't attend,' he added, laughing wryly. 'Afterwards, I had to disappear.'

'And now you're back! Jesus, Jamie, you've had more resurrections than Lazarus.'

Jamie laughed again. 'Aye, it has been said more than once,' he agreed.

'So what now?'

'It gets better, Conor... or worse, depending on your point of view, but I don't have enough time or money to explain it all just now. Thing is, I need your help.'

'You got it, you know that,' Conor Whelan replied without missing a breath.

'Yes, I know, I only need to ask... but this time it might be too big an ask. It's complicated.'

'Give me a number where I can reach you,' Conor stated, taking charge. 'You still haven't told me where you are,' he added.

'We're living in France, a village north east of Paris. I'm Jean-Luc Rochefort and Kate is Karine Rochefort.'

Conor let out a low whistle. 'Rochefort, nice name; I like it. Like the Duc de Rochefort?' he said.

'Who?' Jamie fired back, puzzled.

'Don't you read classic literature, kid?' the American teased. 'He's a character in The Three Musketeers by Alexandre Dumas. He's one of the bad guys. You should have picked one of the musketeers... Aramis, probably,' he added laughing. 'He was quite a ladies' man.'

'Haven't read it and haven't heard of the Duc de Rochefort either. I went for names with my initials. I could just as well have been Jean Renard or Jacques Rocquefort, like the cheese.'

Conor chuckled. 'And what's the name of the village?' he asked.

'It's called Montmort...'

'Dead mountain!' Conor laughed, translating the name literally. 'Sounds dark and dramatic.'

'It's the polar opposite,' Jamie assured him, still laughing. 'I'll give you two numbers,' he went on, dragging the conversation back on track. 'The first one is our house, but don't use it for anything to do with this. The second is the local hotel. I'm there most nights from six till seven... that's French time; remember you're six hours behind.'

Conor acknowledged that with a grunt but his anxiety had resurfaced as he thought about what Jamie had said. 'Your phone bugged?' he queried. 'Is that why you're calling from a cabin?'

'I don't know, Conor, I'm just not taking the chance, not with what I'm into. You ready?'

'Yeah, right, gimme the numbers,' Conor retorted but his mind was on what Jamie had just said.

Jamie rhymed off the numbers and Conor repeated them back to him.

'I'll call you tonight... can I let Mary know you and Kate are okay?

Jamie laughed before replying. 'Can you keep anything from her?'

The big American chuckled. 'Not a lot... Some spy, huh?

'It would be great to see you both again,' Jamie continued nostalgically. 'We never did take you up on that offer to visit you in the States, did we?'

'Maybe we'll come visit you soon,' Conor replied, serious again.

'Well it won't be in France, my friend. We're heading back home in a few weeks.'

'Is that wise?' Conor cautioned, anxious again.

'Probably not, but there's something I have to do... and part of it is why I need your help.'

'Like I said, you got it, kid. I'll call you later.'

Conor's timing was perfect. The operator came on the line to indicate time was running out. They had just enough time to say goodbye.

As Jamie headed back to his car he felt more confident than he had for a while. Conor Whelan, on the other hand, was worried.

Chapter Thirty-four

Conor phoned, as promised, at five minutes past six that evening. The bar of the Hotel de la Place was busy with regular patrons enjoying a drink and a smoke before returning to their homes for dinner. Sandrine, working as usual behind the bar, scurried through to Reception and moments later Jamie heard her call him.

'*Jean-Luc, c'est pour toi,*' she shouted at the top of her voice for all to hear. Not that it mattered; Jamie was like a piece of the furniture in the place now. She left the handset on the Reception counter and made her way back. As she passed Jamie, she whispered. '*C'est un homme, je pense il est Americain,*' she said, rolling her eyes.

Jamie smiled. It would indeed be an American. He lifted the handset to his ear and spoke quietly. '*Conor, c'est toi?*' he asked.

'Of course it's me you dumb Jock... who else would it be? And give over with the Francais, I don't speak the lingo.'

Jamie laughed. He could hear noise in the background, children he thought, very young children. 'Where the hell are you?' he asked, still laughing. 'The local kindergarten?'

'No, kid, I'm at home. Mary sends her love,' he continued, and Jamie could hear his friend's wife in the background. 'After your call, I decided to have an afternoon off. I couldn't concentrate. You've got me worried kid.'

'Hey, don't worry, you know me Conor. It's more awkward than dangerous.'

'Yeah, I know you,' the American drawled. 'That's why I'm worried. So tell.'

Jamie launched into his explanation without concern. It did not matter if anyone heard him. He knew everyone in the bar and, conversely, they knew him; and none of them understood English.

Conor listened in silence as Jamie ran through the story about Kiltyclogher again and his eventual disappearance to France. He made no comment. Up to that point, it all made sense. Jamie had not identified Liam Fitzpatrick as the man who had saved his life but that was about to change.

'About a month ago I had a visit from Sir Charles Redmond...'

'The old dude who runs Ultra?' Conor interrupted, clearly unimpressed.

'That's him,' Jamie replied with a smile.

'How the hell did he know where to find you?'

'It was part of the deal I struck with him. Anyway, he turned up one day asking for my help.'

'And you agreed?' Conor retorted disbelievingly.

'Not exactly, not right away anyway. I told him I was out, finished with Ultra, but...' He hesitated... he was coming to the crux of it now.

'But what?' Conor pressed him.

'Saying no left me with a bad feeling, that's all.'

'Shit Jamie, saying no and living with a bad feeling is better than working for that crazy old dude again. That sort of work can get you killed and by my count you've already used up all of your nine lives.'

'Yeah, I know that, but it isn't that simple.'

'Sure it is. You just say no... N O,' he said, spelling it out.

'No, it isn't, Jamie said, laughing bleakly. 'The person wanting my help is the guy who saved my arse.'

'The IRA guy? Conor queried. 'Brendan Kelly's cousin?'

'Yeah, that's the one.'

'Kelly is one bad ass son of a bitch,' Conor threw in. 'Why does this other dude need your help?'

'He wants out of a bit of trouble he's in. He's not like his cousin; he's no angel, but he's not Brendan Kelly. He's got a conscience.'

Conor laughed. 'Hey, that's new,' Conor laughed. 'A terrorist with a conscience. What's his angle?'

Jamie hesitated but only for a moment. 'He's been working for the Brigadier for a couple of years. He wants out of it.'

'He been doing what you were doing?'

'No, nothing like that. He's been passing on information.'

Conor let out a low whistle. 'He's an informer?' Conor went on, questioning the obvious.

'Yes, but he's special.'

'What way, special?'

'Nobody other than the Brigadier knows about him. Everything he passes over stays with Ultra until the old Man decides it's safe to pass on.'

Conor let go another low whistle. 'Your Brigadier plays hard ball,' he commented dryly. 'But why do you need to be involved. They could pull the guy out easily enough, surely?'

Jamie laughed sardonically. 'True enough,' he said. 'But there's a complication...'

Conor laughed irreverently. 'There's always a complication. What is it?'

'There's two, actually. The first is straightforward enough. The IRA are planning a big attack, maybe even more than one, somewhere on the Mainland. It isn't known where yet. The Irishman has to stay in place until he gets that information.'

'Do your MI5 know about these attacks?'

'No, they don't.' That released another whistle from Conor. He had quite a repertoire, Jamie mused, smiling. He sounded like Ronnie Ronalde, the happy whistler... Probably start yodelling next.

'Your Man sure takes risks.'

'Yes, but he has good reason,' Jamie qualified. 'Anything he passes on could be the death of his tout. He doesn't want that.'

'How come?'

'The IRA are keeping these attacks completely under wraps. Only the men picked to take part know about them. If word gets back to the Organisation that the British are onto their plans IRA Security will start digging for the tout... and they won't have to look too hard to find him.'

'But how would they know?'

Jamie laughed coldly. 'The Organisation might have someone inside MI5 or Special Branch,' he disclosed. 'That's how we think they got to me back in February.' There was no whistle from Conor this time, just stunned silence.

It took the American a moment to gather his thoughts again. Finally, he did. 'You said there were two problems,' he re-joined. 'What's the second one?'

'It's a bit more complicated,' Jamie started, bringing out an incredulously laugh from Conor.

'Number one ain't complicated enough? He retorted scornfully.

'Yeah, but number two is worse.'

'Jesus H Christ,' Conor exclaimed irreverently. 'Life sure is exciting when you're around, kid. Okay, I'm sitting comfortably, shoot.'

'It goes back to my visit to Belfast in '67 as well.'

'Ah, the infamous Brendan Kelly again,' Conor interjected.

'Not exactly,' Jamie hedged. 'The problem isn't him, it's his sister. I told you about her at the time, didn't I?'

Conor laughed softly. 'Oh yeah, the little broad with the flame red hair, green eyes and a liking for night-time snacks... she the one?'

'Yes, that's her,' Jamie confirmed, regretting having given Conor quite so much information at the time.

'So what's her problem?'

'There was an IRA bombing in Coventry a couple of years back... A lot of people were killed and a lot more injured.'

'Yeah, I remember that,' Conor responded reflectively. 'It made the news over here.'

'Roisin Kelly planted the bomb,' Jamie said, dropping his bombshell. He heard Conor's gasp so a bombshell it was. 'It's complicated, like I said,' he continued, regardless, 'and she needs my help.'

'She needs your help?' Conor repeated incredulously. 'Why, for Christ's sake, do you want to help her? You didn't get to know her that well,' he spat back. 'She plants a fucking bomb and now she wants your help.' He was having difficulty keeping his voice down now.

'She didn't have a choice...' Jamie threw back at him.

Conor's sarcastic laugh stalled him. 'Didn't have a choice? Of course she had a fucking choice. What's the matter with you?'

'You have to trust me on this, Conor...'

'I do trust you; I just think you've lost your fuckin' mind.'

Jamie grimaced. Conor, it seemed, was going to take some convincing.

'Okay, you're right,' he said. 'She did have a choice, but faced with the choice she had I would have planted that bomb... And I think you would too.'

'You think?' Conor retorted disdainfully.

Jamie paused for a moment, marshalling his thoughts. 'Okay, hear me out,' he started. 'Imagine someone turns up at your door one day. You know them, not well, but someone in your family knows them, so you invite them in. Remember, this is the IRA we're talking about. Your visitor tells you that your brother is upset because you haven't agreed to help him out with a little job and he's asked him to have a word with you. He tells you that you really have to plant that bomb...'

'Yeah, and I tell him to fuck off,' Conor interjected angrily.

'Of course you do. So would I... And so did Roisin Kelly,' Jamie retorted. 'But then your visitor says; okay, if you won't do it I'll need to convince you some other way so how about, for starters, I kill your kids - Roisin's got twin girls too, just like you, by the way - and then I'll kill your wife and then, when you've watched me do all that, I'll kill you too.' Jamie paused a moment for effect, then. 'You'd still say no?' he posed softly.

There was silence. Jamie couldn't even hear Conor breathing, and then: 'Is this shit for real?' the American asked.

'As real as it gets... And guess what, old friend Brendan was behind it.'

'Bastard!' Conor swore viciously. 'It's hard to believe. I mean, that could all be bullshit, right? How do you know it's the truth?'

'Yeah, it could be bullshit, but it's not. Like I said, you have to trust me.'

There was another pregnant silence. Jamie knew there was nothing more he could say. He had played his last card. It was up to Conor now.

'Who fed you this?' the American asked at last.

'The same man who wants me to get him out. His name is Liam Fitzpatrick.'

'The girl's cousin?'

'Yes.'

'And you believe him?' There was doubt in his voice but not too much.

Jamie smiled at his end of the line. Trust was kicking in but it wasn't fully there yet. 'Not at first,' he admitted. 'I was sceptical, just like you... so I went to meet her.'

'You went to Ireland to meet her? Are you out of your mind?'

Jamie laughed. 'I'm crazy Conor, but I'm not that crazy. She lives in Glasgow... though she's locked up in a mental hospital just now.'

'Yeah?'

'She's suffering from severe depression...'

'So am I kid, listening to this,' Conor chipped in, immediately regretting it. 'Sorry,' he added quickly. 'That was out of order.'

Jamie skipped over it and carried on. 'She's in a bad way, Conor. Catatonic, the nurse said. She's lost all interest in life; blames herself for what happened, I think. I was with her for half an hour but she didn't say much... just rocked backwards and forwards in her chair. The nurse who took me to her left us alone for a while. That gave me a chance to open up with her. I don't know if I got through or not but word back through Fitzpatrick is that she's a bit better.'

'And you believe her story?'

'Yes, I do, but I've got an added reason for believing her.'

'Yeah?' Conor probed, his cynicism gone.

'I've met her "visitor". He's an animal... a psychopath by the name of Doherty. Fionn Doherty. He was one of the men with Fitzpatrick the night I was taken down. I met Fitzpatrick in Glasgow a few days ago and the little shite was with him then too.'

'Woah, woah,' Conor jumped in. 'This dude was with Fitzpatrick in Ireland when you were hit and with him again in Glasgow days ago. Did he recognise you?'

'No,' Jamie responded immediately, laughing coldly. 'If he had, one of us would be dead.'

'So this son of a bitch is bad news?'

'The worst; I saw what he's capable of at Kiltyclogher. He could teach the boys in the Lubyanka a thing or two.'

'Okay,' Conor conceded at last. 'I get it. The girl's a victim like the rest of the poor bastards blown up by her bomb... and you've decided to get back on your horse and go tilting at windmills again.'

Jamie laughed. 'You and Kate think alike,' he chortled. 'She said much the same thing.'

There was a moment's quiet. Jamie waited anxiously for the American's decision, his breath held in his throat.'

Conor let out a little cough as though clearing his throat but, in reality, he was clearing his mind. 'Okay, tell me what you need,' he said. 'I'll see what I can do.'

Jamie's held breath came out in a rush followed by a sigh of relief. 'I don't really know how to go with this,' he admitted. 'If it were the girl alone it would be less of a problem. Her man and her two kids complicate matters.'

'And some,' Conor agreed. 'It seems to me your options are limited.'

'I might need passports and a safe haven for them... but a lot depends on her husband.'

'He doesn't know?' Conor queried perceptively.

'No, he doesn't. If this goes ahead he'll have to know but there's another wee problem with that.'

Conor laughed humourlessly at that news. 'Why am I not surprised? Problems seem to follow you around, kid. So what is this other "wee problem"?' he asked, mimicking Jamie.

'He's at sea...'

'So he's a sailor, why is that a problem?'

'He's a special kind of sailor, Conor. He's in the Royal Navy... he's a Chief Petty Officer... on submarines...Polaris submarines, based on the Clyde.'

'Sweet Jesus!' Conor exclaimed. 'Guy's like that can't just disappear. All hell would break loose.'

'Like I said, it's a wee problem,' Jamie laughed wryly.

'What you've got in mind won't work, Jamie. You need another solution; a substitute.'

'A substitute?'

'Yeah. A patsy, somebody to take the fall for her. Think about it. If your people don't know who she is then give them someone else. Find a woman who's already dead who fits the profile. They can't kill a dead woman,' he went on with a soft laugh. 'If you can't find somebody like that then fit up some bad ass for it... there must be plenty who fit the bill. That's your answer.'

'You think?' Jamie queried thoughtfully.

'It worked for you, kid, didn't it?' Conor retorted casually.

Jamie smiled. It had worked for him so there was no reason why it wouldn't work for Roisin. All he had to do was find someone who fitted the general description of the bomber and convince Clara Whitelaw and the Brigadier. It sounded simple but the person would have to be pretty special. Age, height and build wouldn't be enough. She would need to be a player and her movements at the time would have to be obscure. If Clara could place his scapegoat somewhere else when the bomb went off, it wouldn't work... And Clara would dig all around her.

They finished the call shortly after that, Conor promising to keep in touch and Jamie likewise. The important thing was they were in contact again and both of them felt the better for that.

Jamie returned to the bar and finished his drink before returning home. His mind was on the challenge set by Conor. Where could he find a substitute for Roisin?

Chapter Thirty-five

Friday 2 November 1973, South Armagh

Liam Fitzpatrick sat uncomfortably in the back of the little white minibus and chain-smoked nervously. The telephone call earlier in the afternoon had taken him by surprise. There was a "darts match" in Armagh and the team needed him. In other words, Pearce Duggan wanted to see him. That was the first unpleasant surprise of the day. The second was the discovery that that Doherty, Macari and young Finnegan were accompanying him. He didn't like surprises like that.

Fionn Doherty sat facing him, a contemptuous smile on his face. The man never changed. He did not like Liam and Liam knew it. It all had to do with Brendan and Roisin, Liam supposed, and the bomb in Coventry. The man couldn't understand why he had never challenged him about his part in Roisin's coercion. Probably thought he was afraid, he mused.

Well, don't worry Fionn, everything comes to him that waits...an' your time's comin'.

The other two men, Macari and Finnegan dozed fitfully as the little bus negotiated the bends and struggled up and down the hills through the border countryside. If they needed to make a quick getaway, they would not be doing it in this jalopy, Liam mused unhappily.

He dropped his cigarette stub on the floor and ground it into the metal, immediately fishing another from his pack and lighting it. Doherty's contemptuous smile broadened.

'Nervous are ye, Liam?' the weasely little man laughed.

'An' you're not?' Liam retorted, derisively. 'Drivin' about this place, tooled up, in a banger that couldn't outrun a boy on a feckin' bike, inviting the attention of the Brits, the Peelers an' the Prods, that's your idea of fun, is it?'

The smile disappeared off Doherty's face. Liam looked at him and shook his head slowly. The sooner he got rid of this ganch the better because if he didn't, Doherty would get rid of him. He was in no immediate danger. If Doherty was fool enough to do anything to him now he would incur the wrath of Pearce Duggan and, even though he was a ganch, a fool, he was not that stupid.

The bus entered the outskirts of Armagh on the Portadown Road and slowed, the driver making his way carefully towards the centre of town. Liam smiled. He hadn't imagined the driver could drive much slower without the bus coming to a complete stop, but it seemed he was wrong. He gave Finnegan a gentle kick with the toe of his boot and nudged Macari. 'Wakey, wakey lads, we're there,' he said, stubbing out what remained of his cigarette on the metal floor.

Both men came awake slowly, rubbing their eyes. If they had been stopped or ambushed on the way down, neither would have known a thing about it until it was too late. They were little better than useless, in Liam's opinion. Still, he shouldn't complain, he mused, better to deal with somebody useless than someone like Doherty. Doherty is dangerous, these lads are not.

The mini-bus pulled to a stop outside O'Driscoll's pub in College Street, their arrival announced by a squeal of brakes. That, Liam mused, said much for their efficacy. He grinned. The brakes didn't need to be efficient, the bloody bus never built up enough speed to need them.

He slid back the sliding door and stepped out onto the pavement. It was a cold, wet night and he shivered. He turned towards Doherty who was immediately behind him, awaiting a snide comment, but the man was too busy surveying the street and the pub. It was early evening, just after seven thirty, and the journey had taken them a little over an hour.

Light spilled from the pub and laughter and loud talk could be heard from inside. Liam looked around. The instructions were to wait for Duggan before venturing into the pub but he thought it unwise to linger for too long in the street. Unwise was probably understating it; criminally insane was closer.

He turned uneasily, searching for any sign of Duggan, but there was nothing. Even Fionn Doherty, normally blasé, was showing signs of nerves. Suddenly, a car appeared from the direction of Upper English Street and flashed its headlights, twice in quick succession. Liam began to breathe easier.

The car pulled into the kerb on the opposite side of the road and both front doors swung open. Orlagh Duggan was first out, her eyes sweeping the street automatically before her father emerged. Liam smiled grimly as his three companions straightened up. The guard coming to attention, he smiled inwardly.

Duggan strode quickly across the road and stopped in front of Liam. Orlagh circled them, her eyes still ranging up and down the street while the eyes of the three men ranged up and down her. Liam had to admit she looked good but beauty, he reminded himself, is only skin deep and beneath the surface, Orlagh Duggan was one ugly bitch.

'I've got a meeting in the pub at eight. My visitor will be coming by car...a small red car. His name is Sparke. Watch for him and when he arrives, bring him to Orlagh an' me in the back room. Come in with us out of the cold just now an' I'll show you the room. The landlord is one of us, but I can't vouch for the customers. That's why youse boys are here. I want two of youse by the door to the room an' the other two at the entrance. You see anythin', raise the alarm an' we'll all leave by the back door. Our guest can fend fer hisself.'

Liam raised an eyebrow. 'Is that wise? Is it not better to take him along?'

'No, it isn't,' Duggan spat back. 'You just do as yer told. The peelers won't bother him, believe me son. Right, come on,' he finished. 'Come in an' get yerselves settled.

With Orlagh in front and her father bringing up the rear, the little band pushed into the pub. It was like walking into a Turkish hashish den, Liam mused. The air was heavy with blue tinged smoke and a wall of noise battered their ears. At the sight of Orlagh Duggan, a channel appeared through the throng and the group made its way to the bar. Duggan pushed his way to the front and the barman, a balding man with a fat stomach hiding behind a badly stained shirt, leaned across the bar to shake his hand. Liam gave the man a cursory look. The fat stomach and the stained shirt were not the man's only minus points. His nose was prominent and red, pointing to a man who sampled too many of his own wares, and his teeth were tobacco stained and uneven, standing like tombstones in an old cemetery. He smiled at Orlagh, a smile that simply made him look even more macabre. Orlagh, as far as Liam could determine, wasn't impressed.

'Is the room ready?' Pearce Duggan asked, his face serious.

'Oh aye, that it is Mr Duggan,' the landlord replied.

'An' the back door into the alley?'

'Unlocked, just like you said,' the man confirmed. 'Now, can I get youse a drink?'

Duggan smiled at last. 'That's good of you Sean,' he said. 'I'll have a Bushmills an' Orlagh will have her usual.' He turned, still smiling, to face the four men. 'The lads won't be drinkin' just yet... they're on duty,' he laughed. 'Give them a bottle of Bushmills when they're leavin' and a few beers... but not before,' he added menacingly. 'If I smell even a hint of booze off any of ye when I come out of that room, ye'll regret it.'

He waited as the landlord poured his and Orlagh's drinks and then turned to Liam. 'You're in charge,' he said. 'Keep these bastards on their toes. When our friend arrives, bring him straight through... an' nobody else comes into that room, got it?'

Liam nodded. 'Got it,' he said.

Duggan turned back to the barman. 'Can ye get a couple of chairs for the lads? Just outside the back room will be fine. The lads at the front door can stand.'

He swung back to the others, lifted his drink and headed off in the direction of the back room with Orlagh swaying along behind him. When the girl's bottom finally disappeared from sight behind the back room door, there was an almost palpable sigh as most of the men watching scratched at their groin.

'Right,' Liam said, addressing the other three. 'Ye heard the man. Finnegan, you an' me will guard the door there. Fionn, you take charge at the front. You two make a good team,' he continued, smiling at Eamonn Macari. 'You two are the front line. Ye see anythin' suspicious ye tell me right away. Right?'

Both men nodded, Doherty a little more reluctantly than his partner.

'When the man Park arrives, give me the nod. I'll come for him and bring him through. An' no drink, remember. Duggan will flay the skin off yer backs if he even thinks ye've taken any. There'll be time for drinkin' on the bus back to Belfast.'

Fionn Doherty stared back at him. Liam held his look, unblinking, until the smaller man looked away and headed for the door. Liam gritted his teeth. He had to put up with the wee shite for now.

***

Kevin Sparke arrived promptly at eight. It was Macari who spotted him first as he stepped from his car and made his way towards the pub. He nudged Doherty. 'Is that him, do ye think?' he asked.

Doherty laughed under his breath. 'If he came out of that wee red car then who else could it feckin' be?' he relied scathingly. 'Let Fitzpatrick know.'

Macari pushed back into the pub and caught Liam's eye through the crowd, nodding vigorously.

Liam pushed up from his chair. 'Stay here,' he commanded, his eyes meeting those of Finnegan. 'An' keep yer eyes open.' The young man nodded, his hand moving unconsciously to the revolver in his jacket pocket.

Liam shook his head and headed off through the crowd to the door. Unlike Orlagh Duggan, he did not have large breasts and hypnotically swaying hips so he had to force his way through. An' they say chivalry is dead, he smiled to himself.

He met the visitor at the door, Fionn Doherty close behind him. 'Mr Park?' he queried.

Kevin Sparke nodded. Park was as good as Sparke as far as he was concerned. Better, in fact.

Liam took him by the arm and started through the crowd again. The man followed. Young Finnegan rose from his chair as they approached and knocked on the door. Even above the noise in the pub, Liam could hear the command to enter shouted by Duggan. He pushed the door open and allowed the man to pass him. Duggan said nothing but his eyes told Liam to close the door and stay out until the meeting as over. He wasn't going to argue.

He settled down in his chair again and smiled over at Finnegan. The youngster was enjoying every minute of this. He was filled with self-importance now he was one of Pearce Duggan's Praetorian Guard. Poor little shit that he was. If he lived longer than the next three months, Liam mused, he would be lucky.

***

The meeting lasted about forty minutes. Liam did his best to listen for clues as to what was going on behind the door but the noise in the pub made it impossible. The darts match that was their cover was well under way and the copious amounts of beer and spirits being consumed by players and spectators alike, was ramping up the din. Liam sat nervously throughout, his eyes roving around the room looking for anything out of place. He smiled grimly to himself. It was unlikely he was the only tout in the pub tonight. All it needed was someone to make a quick call to the RUC or the Brits and they would arrive mob handed. If that happened, he could say goodbye to his new life and would probably end up on the run like Brendan.

The door opened suddenly, taking him by surprise, and Pearce Duggan stood in the opening. He looked pleased with himself.

'We're finished here,' he said brusquely. 'Make sure our visitor gets to his car safely, will you,' he continued, directing the order to Liam.

Liam was already on his feet. The visitor was moving towards the door, hand outstretched and Duggan was turning back to him. Orlagh Duggan hung back. Her face was a picture, Liam mused. Something told him she did not like the man.

'It has been a pleasure, Pearce,' the visitor said, his American drawl evident to all. 'As things develop I'll keep you up to date in the usual way,' he said, smiling to show a set of perfect teeth.

Smarmy bastard, Liam thought.

'Aye, Kevin, that'll be fine so it will,' Pearce Duggan replied, taking the outstretched hand and pumping it strongly. 'The boys will be ready,' he said, then stopped abruptly, conscious of breaking one of his own sacrosanct rules. Even a slip like that could be fatal.

Liam watched as the American turned back to Orlagh with a little wave of the hand. The girl's expression remained stonily neutral. She was still staring at the man's back as Liam escorted him through the drinkers and darts players to the door and handed him over to Doherty.

'Take him to his car an' make sure he's safely away,' he ordered.

Doherty gave him an insubordinate look but said nothing, simply spun on his heels and lead the man away, Macari following.

Me an' my shadow, Liam mused with a laugh. Al Jolson could have been singing about those two. Where Doherty went, Macari followed, so getting shot of Doherty would mean getting shot of his shadow, Macari, as well. But so what? Both were a waste of space and the world would be a better place without them.

They congregated in the back room after that, Pearce and Orlagh sat at the table that dominated the room, finishing their drinks, and the four men stood in a tight group by the door.

'The big operation is on,' Pearce Duggan informed them. 'Ye'll be travellin' over to Scotland at the beginnin' of January an' ye'll be back home by the end of the month. Ye'll be heroes, so ye will. This will bring the Brits to the negotiatin' table an' end this feckin' war,' he continued, his excitement bubbling over.

'What are we attackin' that's so feckin' important?' Fionn Doherty asked.

Liam smothered a smile. Thank you Fionn.

Duggan drew the man a suspicious look, his eyes boring into Fionn until the weasel turned away. 'Ye don't need to know that yet. Just take my word for it; it's feckin' big. The Brits will shit themselves.'

The men said nothing. No one was willing to ask anything. Pearce Duggan was paranoid about security. Asking questions made the man distrustful and if anything went wrong he would remember who had asked the questions and that person's life span would be dramatically shortened.

'There's somethin' else,' Duggan went on. 'You all know it's one attack now but ye'll still be actin' separately. Three units, one target.'

'Which Brigade's are providin' the other ASU's?' Fionn asked, his reward a scowl from Duggan.

'Youse don't need to know that,' the big man spat out and Fionn shrivelled. Liam sat back, amused.

'Why would ye?' Duggan went on, suspiciously.

Bad move Fionn, Liam mused happily. Every time ye ask a question ye make Pearce more suspicious. Keep it up.

'All youse need to know is that this will be the biggest fright the Brits will ever get an' they won't see it comin'.' He was still staring at Fionn as he spoke, his message clear. If the Brits did see it coming he knew who to blame.

Fionn Doherty was beginning to see the light and his face paled. 'Ye can trust me, Pearce,' he said, fawningly, trying to hide his fear. It wasn't often that happened, Liam reflected, so tonight had turned out much better than he had expected.

'There's one other thing,' Pearce Duggan continued, clearing his throat. 'Orlagh will be co-ordinatin' the attack. Yous will take yer oders from her, right?'

Liam smiled to himself. That was a question that only had one answer. Duggan's next words confirmed it.

'What she tells ye comes from me. If you let her down ye'll be lettin' me down.' Nobody needed to be reminded of the consequences of that.

'Right, away back to Belfast wi' ye. An' not a word to anyone,' he ordered, his eyes lingering on Fionn Doherty.

Four heads nodded in unison. Oh aye, they would keep it to themselves alright; well, at least three of them would.

Chapter Thirty-six

Sunday 4 November 1973

'His name's Pearce Duggan,' Liam Fitzpatrick murmured down the phone. He sounded scared, Jamie thought, but that was hardly a surprise. 'The name probably means nothin' to ye,' the Irishman continued. 'But it will to yer man.'

'Okay, I'll pass it on,' Jamie agreed. 'Why is *he* so important?'

There was a slight pause, just enough for Jamie to pick up on. 'Duggan's runnin' the operation,' Liam mumbled guiltily. He knew what to expect.

'And you didn't think to tell me before now?' Jamie exploded. 'What the fuck are you playin' at Liam?'

There was a silence for a while before the Irishman answered. When he did, he was contrite. 'Alright, ah know. Ah'm sorry, ah should have told ye but ah was afeared your lot would take him out. That happens, ah'm in the shit. The hard men from Security would take the unit apart. It wouldn't take them long to get to me an' ah don't fancy a bullet in the back o' my head.'

Jamie calmed a bit. In the same circumstances, he might have done the same. 'So this Duggan is big in the Organisation?' he probed.

'Aye, he's big,' Liam agreed. 'There's somethin' else,' he went on.

Jamie's ears pricked up. 'Go on,' he instructed.

'There was a meetin' on Friday night; Pearce, his daughter Orlagh, and a Yank. The Yank's name is Kevin Clark or Park, ah'm not sure of his second name but it's somethin' like that.'

'What about?' Jamie prodded.

'The attack, ah suppose. Duggan was all excited afterwards an' that's when he telt us the attack is definitely goin' ahead.'

'Why would an American be involved?'

Liam snorted a laugh. 'Irish Americans, if that's what he is, are more Irish than us feckin' Irish ourselves,' he giggled. He was still nervous. 'From what ah gather, he's a reporter for some Yank newspaper... but ah think he's somethin' else.'

'Like what?' Jamie delved.

'Ah don't know,' Liam admitted. 'But he's not what he seems, ah'd stake ma life on that.'

Jamie gave a snort of derision. 'Given your current position that's not much of a bet.'

'Aye, very funny!' Liam retorted caustically, before he saw the funny side. 'Ah suppose ye're right,' he said. 'Ma life's already on the line isn't it.'

Jamie decided not to confirm that. 'How did you get all this?' he asked instead.

'Ah was at the meetin'... well, no' exactly at it, Duggan wanted his back watched when he was meetin' the Yank. It was down in Armagh. Ah had to spend the night wi' that wee shite, Doherty an' those other two pricks,' he added disgustedly.

'What else did you find out?'

'Ah didn't get much. There was a darts match on in the pub an' a lot of noise. Duggan's a dangerous fecker an' his daughter is a real piece o' work; a chip off the old block, so she is. She's suspicious as feck. The three of them were shut away in a back room for about an hour. When they finished they all came out together. Duggan an' the Yank were shakin' hands an' Orlagh was holdin' back. Ah don't think she likes him much but Pearce an' the Yank were elated.'

'Have they met before?' Jamie went on.

'Ah don't know fer sure, but they were pally enough.'

'An' you think this American is involved?'

'Definitely... Pearce an' Orlagh were excited afterwards. That's when he told us the mission was definitely on an' Orlagh's in charge.'

'Still the 25th of January?'

'He didn't spell it out. Said we would be travellin' over to Scotland at the beginnin' of January an' we'd be back before the end of the month. As heroes,' Liam added with a cynical laugh. 'Ah suppose it must still be the 25th.'

'Scotland, you said?' Jamie fired back. 'You're sure.'

'Aye, ah'm sure. It makes sense. Why would Duggan have us meetin' that guy in Glasgow at the beginnin' of October if it wasn't Scotland?'

Jamie was quiet for a moment, thinking things through. It was all falling into place but it wasn't getting any better. In fact, it kept getting worse. He had a bad feeling about it. 'Tell me that's everything,' he asked hopefully.

Liam gave a short laugh. 'Well, that's all there is about the attack but there is somethin' else your man will be interested in,' he said.

'Go on,' Jamie pressed.

Liam hesitated, as if unsure where to start. 'A couple of weeks back ah was called out to unblock the toilet in a house on the Bangor Road...'

'What an interesting life you lead, Liam,' Jamie interrupted sarcastically.

'Shut up an' listen,' Liam spat back. 'The toilet wasn't blocked. It was all a set up to get me there so ah could pick up a bit of information.'

'What sort of information?' Jamie pressed on, intrigued now.

'It was a cassette tape. Ah don't know what was on it. Ah picked it up an' delivered it to Duggan. Everythin' kicked off after that.'

'Whose house was it?'

Liam's laughed. He felt like a magician about to pull a rabbit out of a hat. 'It belongs to the MP for Belfast East... Sir Rodney Calder.'

'If he's Sir Rodney Calder then I take it he's not SDLP,' Jamie retorted mordantly.

'No, Unionist,' Liam replied, missing Jamie's jest. 'The old fart doesn't have a clue,' Liam pressed on. 'Bugger is never there; spends most of his time in London. He's got a woman who looks after the place for him... as well as a gardener an' a handyman.'

'Do they live in?'

'Nah,' Liam advised, 'but they all have access.'

'For a dead drop it's something else. It's the last place anybody would think to look,' Jamie mused aloud.

'There's somethin' else,' Liam went on hesitantly. He sounded uncomfortable, Jamie noticed. 'Ah visited the house two days before you turned up in Kiltyclogher. Same routine. Ah took back a tape that time as well.'

Jamie was stunned into silence for a moment. He remembered his gut feeling as he approached the farmhouse at Kiltyclogher that night. The bastards knew he was coming. 'You think that's how I was blown?' he asked.

'Don't know; could be a coincidence,' Liam replied hesitantly again. 'But ah don't believe in coincidences; do you?'

Jamie laughed coldly. 'No, not in this game,' he murmured. 'You're right, the old man will be interested. I'll pass it on.' It was time to end the call, he decided. 'Right,' he continued. 'We'll stick to the same routine. You get anything, call me. Don't use the same phone twice and don't phone from a coin box near your work.'

'If ah'm seen doin' that they'll know ah'm up to somethin',' Liam retorted unhappily.

'Aye, but they won't know what,' Jamie laughed.

'One last thing...'

'What?'

'Roisin... What do we do about her?'

'I'm working on it,' Jamie said.

'Aye, okay,' Liam acknowledged with a sigh. 'Christ, ah'll be glad when this is over.'

Jamie laughed bitterly. 'You an' me both Liam,' he said. 'Just keep the faith,' he added as he replaced the handset.

He looked around the hotel reception. It was empty but for him with all the activity taking place in the bar. He was using the phone in the hotel a lot these days and suspected that was causing some ribald comment. He had seen the winks and gestures. The men thought he had a mistress. Why else would he be phoning from here when he had a phone at home, they argued, not unreasonably. He would have to keep them guessing, he smiled wryly... and he still had two more calls to make.

***

Conor Whelan leaned back in his chair and dragged on a cigarette, purging the smoke out through his nostrils as he listened to Jamie's information while, in the background, Mary Whelan made cooing noises to their children.

'He's Irish American, like you,' Jamie told him. 'He's a reporter for one of the big newspapers in the States, apparently, but Liam Fitzpatrick has doubts about him.'

'And he says the dude's name is Park, or Clark?'

'So he says... but he wasn't sure.'

'Did he say which newspaper?'

'No... I don't think he got that.'

Conor sighed heavily. 'Okay kid, it isn't much to go on but I'll have my people check him out. What about the other matter, the girl?' he went on without missing a beat. Jamie's silence gave him his answer.

'Have you thought about what I said?'

Jamie laughed frostily. 'Yeah, I've been thinkin' about it, but that's as far as it goes.'

'You can't do it alone, Jamie,' Conor continued. 'You need help.'

'I know that Conor,' Jamie laughed. 'But reinforcements are thin on the ground.'

There was a lengthy silence between them after that. Jamie was about to end the call when Conor spoke again. 'I was thinking of coming over,' he announced. 'Mary hasn't seen her folks for a while and they keep asking to see the children.'

'No, no, no, Conor,' Jamie shouted adamantly. 'This is my problem.'

'Yeah, like that Cranston Hall place was your problem... Two heads are better than one, kid.'

Jamie sighed heavily. 'This isn't your fight,' he said.

'And the night I was getting the crap kicked out of me in Glasgow wasn't your fight either.'

'I don't want you involved. This is getting messy.'

'Yeah, I know, but I'm coming over to Scotland anyway. Mary has already called her folks and I've cleared it my end. If you don't get in touch, I'll come find you,' Conor stated defiantly.

Jamie heard Mary Whelan in the background throwing her weight behind her husband. He lifted his eyes to the ceiling and pulled a face. God knows, he didn't want this, but Conor Whelan was like Kate; when he made up his mind to do something there was no shifting him. It was better to give in gracefully than fight a battle he couldn't win.

'Okay,' he sighed. 'Give me Mary's folk's number.'

Conor sounded happier as he reeled off the digits. Jamie read them back to him and promised to call. He would, but whether he would involve Conor in this shambles was another matter. They finished the call on that note.

He replaced the handset and checked the time. It was four o'clock on a grey Sunday afternoon in France so it was three o'clock in London. There was some laughter and shouting through in the bar and Kate was waiting for him at home. Just time for one more quick call, he decided, a little guiltily. He lifted the handset again and dialled for the operator.

**

The weather in London was similar to the weather in France only different. It was raining in London. Clara Whitelaw sat in the lounge of her Kensington town house poring over The Sunday Times, a task she started every Sunday morning and usually finished by Tuesday... if she ignored the magazine.

The phone ringing in the hall was irritating. She looked up from the paper and saw her husband draw her a challenging look. It was a battle of wills as to who would break first and answer the infernal thing. It was usually her, she mused, and it probably would be again now, but she would push him as far as she could.

Finally, with an exasperated groan, she pushed herself up from her chair and stomped out to the hall as a satisfied little smile drifted across her husband's face. He could be such an arse, she thought angrily.

She was still angry as she lifted the handset and almost shouted the number down the line.

'Aye, that's the number I asked for,' she heard a familiar voice say and suddenly she was relieved she had answered. 'Have I called at a bad time?' he went on, laughing.

'Jamie? What are you doing?' she whispered urgently. You shouldn't be calling me here,' she added, half scolding, half pleased.

'I couldn't wait,' he replied, tongue in cheek. 'I take it Mark is around?'

'Yes, of course he is. Why else would I be whispering?'

'So you're still patching things up. That's good.'

'Is it?' she murmured, sounding disappointed.

Not a good sign, he thought. 'Listen,' he said, quickly pushing on. 'I need you to get something to the Brigadier...'

'So that's why you called?' she cut in petulantly. 'That's why you couldn't wait.'

Of course that's fucking why.

'Come on Clara,' he retorted. He tried to sound apologetic. 'This is hard enough without you going off on one.'

'I'm not going off on one, I'm hurt, that's all. I thought we could work through our... problem.'

So now I'm a problem. 'We can, Clara,' he said as gently as possible. 'But there are things happening that we have to deal with.' He waited for her response, the seconds ticking past.

'Okay,' she said at last. 'Tell me.'

Jamie relaxed. 'I've got a name; Pearce Duggan. He's the man behind the planned attack. He's probably got a file six inches thick at Five but from what Corkscrew says, they haven't been able to pin anything on him.'

'When did he learn this?'

'He has known for a while...'

'So why is he only telling us now?' she interrupted angrily.

She was reacting as he had, Jamie reflected. He laughed frostily. 'I'll get to that,' he said. 'But before I do, there's something else. Duggan met with an American a couple of days ago. Corkscrew says this man is involved in some way so I want a check run on him. He's supposed to be a news reporter. His name is Kevin Park or Clark or something similar; Corkscrew isn't sure.' He didn't tell her about his conversation with Conor. That he would keep to himself.

'Okay, I'll pass that on too,' Clara agreed. She sounded a little more interested now. 'So the attack is still on?'

'Yes, 25th January, but it's one attack now, not three. The ASUs are coming over at the beginning of January... to Scotland,' he added.

'You said ASUs.'

'Uh-huh, three of them., the original complement.'

'It's not just one attack, it's one big attack... and not a bomb,' she added thoughtfully.

'Surely Five have had a sniff of it,' Jamie probed.

'No, not a whiff,' Clara advised. 'The Paddies are really keeping this one tight... or maybe Five are keeping it to themselves.'

Jamie smiled bitterly. The Official IRA didn't trust the Provisionals and MI5 didn't trust SIS and neither of them trusted Ultra. What a way to fight a war, he mused. If they all talked among themselves a bit more the bloody war would be over already though who would have won was open to debate. He didn't pass comment. Clara already knew his thoughts on the subject.

'There's more,' he said, deciding on a change of tack. 'Duggan has a daughter... her name is Orlagh.' He spelled it out for her before going on. 'She's involved in the attack too in some way. Corkscrew hasn't said how but she was at the meeting with the American.'

'Interesting. Does she have form?'

'According to Corkscrew she's been an active volunteer since the beginning. I imagine she's her old man's lieutenant. There will be a file on her too, I suppose.' As the words came out of his mouth, a light came on in his brain.

"They can't kill a dead woman... If you can't find somebody like that then fit up some bad ass for it." The answer to Roisin's problem could be staring him right in the face. Orlagh Duggan might be that bad ass. But he needed more than just a name... she had to fit the profile. His excitement almost made him miss Clara's next question.

'Could she be our bomber?' she asked softly. Jamie smiled. Clara was much quicker on the uptake than he was.

'Did Corkscrew say anything?' she went on digging.

'No, nothing,' Jamie replied. His elation at this turn of events was hard to hide. If Clara had been facing him she would have seen it plastered all over his face. He forced himself to stay calm. He paused, as if grudging something up from memory. 'He did say she's a "real piece of work" though. I think she must have blood on her hands.' He sat back and waited. Last thing he wanted to do now was overplay it.

'Really?' Clara came back thoughtfully. 'Maybe I should check her out,' she said, almost to herself.

Yes, you do that.

Jamie was smiling broadly now. He decided to push his luck. 'How are you getting on with the photograph? You were looking into Corkscrew's family.'

'I haven't found anything yet, other than motivation,' Clara replied, sounding discouraged. 'The family is like a bloody dynasty... There are siblings and cousins galore. It's going to take a while.'

Jamie allowed himself another satisfied smile. He still had time. But now he had to find out more about Orlagh Duggan; and quickly. 'Shame,' he said solicitously. Again, thank God, Clara was at the other end of a telephone line and not looking him in the eye.

'You said there were a couple of things,' Clara reminded him then. 'And you still haven't told me why it took Corkscrew so long to tell us about Duggan.'

'I'm coming back to Britain,' he announced. 'Tell Sir Charles I'll need the new account he promised and an injection of cash.'

'Okay, I'll do that. Where will you be staying?'

'Calverton... the Midlands.'

'I know where it is,' she threw back. There was a moment's hesitation, then: 'That's where your wife's family live, isn't it?'

'Yes, you know it is. You've read my file.'

'You're bringing the family?' she asked. He could hear something in her voice; disbelief or disappointment, he couldn't say which. 'Is that wise?' she asked though he thought it sounded more like a suggestion that it wasn't.

Jamie gave a wry laugh. 'When was the last time I did anything wise?' he retorted. 'But you're right,' he conceded. 'It wouldn't be wise to have them anywhere near me when I'm bringing Corkscrew out so they'll be staying in Calverton while I go up to Scotland.' He paused a moment, then added: 'If anything goes wrong with this and I don't make it, it's better she's with her family than stuck in France.'

'Uh-huh, I suppose it is,' Clara agreed thoughtfully. 'Will I see you?' went on hesitantly.

'Of course you will,' he said, forcing a little laugh. 'You're my controller, we're working together on this, remember?'

'I meant...'

'I know what you meant, Clara,' he cut in quickly, stopping her from going on. 'Yes, you'll see me,' he continued, a little softer now. She could take it whichever way she wanted, he thought. It was time to finish the conversation. 'I have to go,' he said. 'People here are starting to talk about all the calls I'm making.'

'People talking? Where are you phoning from?' she asked. She sounded horrified.

'The local hotel... but don't worry; they think I've got a mistress,' he laughed. That might cheer her up.

He was about to hang up when he remembered the other snippet Liam had delivered. 'Oh,' he said, ' before I go there's another interesting little matter Corkscrew has come up with.'

'Go on.'

'A dead drop... actually, an ingenious dead drop.'

'Oh yes? And where would that be?'

'The last place you would think of looking,' he laughed, unable to hide his amusement. 'It's a house on the Bangor Road, Belfast. I don't have a number but it shouldn't be hard to find. It belongs to Rodney Calder, Sir Rodney Calder, Ulster Unionist MP. Your father probably knows him,' he finished, chortling.

'Seriosly?'

'Yeah, seriously. I'm not in joking mode. Corkscrew thinks that's where word of my trip to Kiltyclogher was delivered to the bhoys.' He heard her gasp.

'Why does he think that?' she delved.

'Simple deduction. He picked up a message there before Duggan's meeting with the American reporter last week and that was the second time he had been there. The first time was two days before I turned up at Malone's cottage.'

He heard her suck in her breath again and then she was quiet for a moment. 'This is all getting very complicated,' she said at last. 'Please be careful.'

Jamie smiled. Understatement seemed to be the order of the day between her and Liam. 'Oh, don't worry,' he said 'I'll be careful. Very careful. I'll call you again if and when I get more,' he added, finishing the call.

If Clara said anything in response, he missed it. He had already replaced the handset back in its cradle.

Chapter Thirty-seven

Monday 5 November 1973, London.

'Pearce Duggan,' Sir Charles said thoughtfully. 'Yes, the name rings a bell... runs a haulage business somewhere down in "Bandit Country" if memory serves. Our friends in Five and SIS suspect he traffics guns and explosives in amongst livestock and farm produce.' They were in Clara's office.

Clara smiled, awed by her mentor's ability to recall the detailed content of files he had read in the past. 'And the daughter?' she asked.

'Yes, Orlagh... Quite a lady, by all accounts, though I use the term "lady" loosely. Thought to have been involved in the killing of a Garda Special Branch officer in Tralee a couple of years back...'

'She ordered it?' Clara broke in, probing.

Sir Charles smiled frostily. 'No, my dear; she did it. Led him on, took him to an isolated spot and slit his throat while his trousers were down... at least, that's what the Garda think happened. They couldn't prove it.'

'Good God!' Clara exclaimed, shocked.

'I sometimes wonder about that,' Sir Charles retorted with a wry laugh. 'Is He good? I'm beginning to think like Raeburn, it seems,' he added, chuckling. 'And the American; What have you done about him?'

'I've asked Box to have a look into his background,' she advised, using the shortened colloquial name for MI5 after its wartime address of Box500. 'As he's a foreign national I've asked SIS to have a look at him too.'

Sir Charles nodded. 'Have they asked why?'

Clara laughed. 'Naturally,' she said and watched her mentor raise one eyebrow. 'I told them it was a vague report he might not be what he seems,' she went on.

'Good. If he is linked to this attack, we don't want things going off half cocked.'

'No, of course not. I'll let you know as soon as I hear anything.'

'Yes, do,' Sir Charles replied. 'My instincts tell me he is not what he seems,' he mused aloud. 'I might be wrong, but...' he finished, letting it hang in the air.

'Yes, I know. Corkscrew's of the same opinion, apparently.'

'Yes, Corkscrew,' Sir Charles murmured thoughtfully. 'Why did he take so long to come clean about Duggan? Makes one think, doesn't it?'

'Yes,' Clara agreed. 'I did ask Jamie about that but didn't get an answer.' She hesitated a moment. 'I think he has one though,' she added.

'Well, when he gets back in touch with you ask him again and this time, make him answer.'

Clara nodded pensively, her thoughts already moving on. 'What more do you know about Duggan's daughter?' she asked.

'Not a lot, to be honest, but there is a file on her at Thames House. You could ask them to have a look.'

'Won't they wonder why?'

The Brigadier knotted his brow. 'Of course they will. I'm sure you can come up with something plausible. You could even tell them the truth.'

'The truth?' Clara responded, confused.

'You're looking into the possibility of her being the Coventry bomber,' the old man answered, smiling shrewdly. Clara reddened. 'The same thought had occurred to me,' Sir Charles went on. 'Though it does seem a little obvious. Did Raeburn suggest that?' he probed.

'No, not at all, in fact. He was only passing on what Corkscrew told him; she's involved in the attack we're trying to thwart.'

'Right,' the Brigadier acknowledged pensively. 'Okay. Have a look at her. Anything else?'

'Yes, two things. First is a dead drop Corkscrew has identified. Sir Charles' eyebrows rose fractionally, prompting her to continue. 'Jamie thinks it's ingenious and I have to agree,' she resumed. 'It's in the last place anyone would think of looking... the home of a sitting Ulster Unionist MP.'

The Brigadier's eyes narrowed to slits. 'Who?' he demanded.

'Sir Rodney Calder, the Honourable Member for Belfast East...'

'Yes, I know who he is,' Sir Charles interrupted coldly. 'Not one of my favourite people... Rumours abound about his private life. Sordid rumours, I hasten to add. Did Corkscrew say how he came by this information? It could be a plant.'

'It could,' Clara admitted, 'but something tells me it isn't. He says he has picked up information from the house on two occasions and the first time was just before Jamie arrived in Kiltyclogher.'

'Jesus,' the Brigadier murmured uncharacteristically. 'Pass it on to Five,' he instructed. Clara nodded but noticed a troubled look in the old man's eyes.

'Is there a problem?' she asked.

'Yes, I'm afraid there is. Michael has always insisted the IRA knew he was coming even though there was no evidence to substantiate it. Nothing like that has happened since; no other Archangels have been compromised. That led me to believe that what happened to Michael was just bad luck. Now, I'm not so sure and therein lies the problem.'

Clara shook her head, looking confused. 'You've lost me,' she said.

Sir Charles' smile was like an Arctic wind. 'Other than me, no one in Ultra knew where Michael was going,' he explained, his voice low and thoughtful. He had reverted to using Jamie's old Ultra codename, Clara noted. 'That means, if there was a leak, it came from Box or SIS.'

Now Clara understood. Protocols in place forced Sir Charles to inform his counterparts in the other services when an operation was taking place. If there was a leak and it was coming from MI5, by reporting the dead letter drop they could be warning the mole that the drop was blown and there was another problem. A bigger one. If the mole learned the drop was exposed, he, or she, would start looking for the source. That would be bad news for Corkscrew.

'I will have to think carefully about this,' Sir Charles continued contemplatively. 'Meantime, disregard my earlier instruction. Keep this to yourself.'

Clara did not bother to acknowledge. He knew she would keep it to herself, he just said things like that sometimes.

'What was the other thing?' her mentor asked, moving on.

'Jamie is returning to England in a week or so. He's asking for his new identity and funds.'

'Fine, I'll arrange it. When is he calling you next?'

'He hasn't set a time. He calls out of the blue, like yesterday. He's using the phone in the local hotel.'

Sir Charles laughed aloud but there was little amusement in it. 'Not very trusting, our boy, is he?'

Clara smiled, hiding her thoughts. It goes with the job. Then an altogether darker thought formed in her mind. 'You haven't had someone tap his phone, have you?' she asked incredulously, letting the thought escape.

Sir Charles gave her one of his best "how could you possibly think that" looks before responding. 'Good God, no,' he said, sounding hurt. 'I don't have that sort of pull any more.'

Clara eyed him sceptically. She did not believe that for a minute. He was cosy with people working in similar positions to his own in most of Europe's governments, and most certainly in France. That sort of "pull", as he put it, went with the job.

'When he does eventually call you, tell him from me that I want regular updates, even if that means he's telling you he has nothing to report. I want you to keep on top of him,' he continued, her accusation already forgotten.

Keep on top of him, Clara mused. That would be nice. She smiled and kept the thought to herself.

'And press him about the bomber. He's the best man for the job.'

'I don't think so Charles,' she disagreed tentatively. 'Didn't he say he wanted nothing more to do with Ultra.'

'Yes my dear, he did, but when I spoke to him at Hazelgrove last month he had changed his mind.'

Clara forced a smile. 'I don't believe it,' she said.

'Neither did I,' Sir Charles responded, smiling coldly. 'That's why I want you to keep him in line. If anyone can, it's you.'

Clara forced another smile. She thought his trust in her in that respect was misplaced. The control she once had over him was gone. 'Okay, I'll try,' she agreed, hiding her reluctance.

'While we're discussing the bomber, how are your enquiries into her identity going?' the Brigadier asked, waiting expectantly.

Clara frowned disgustedly. 'They're not going,' she retorted. 'There are sisters and aunts, cousins, and cousins of cousins, and cousins of cousins of cousins,' she went on, her exasperation coming out. 'Honestly, it goes on forever... there are scores of them. Some I can eliminate quickly, some not.'

'That's the scourge of Catholicism, my dear,' Sir Charles laughed sardonically. 'No contraception. If you do identify any possibles have Five follow them up. I still think our best hope is in Raeburn wheedling it out of Corkscrew, but don't give up your digging.'

He paused for a moment and Clara anticipated the end of the meeting. She shuffled her papers together on her desk in expectation, ready for his departure, when he started to speak again.

'Keep pushing Box and SIS on this American fellow,' he said. 'Dead drops and American newspaper reporters are a strange combination. I want everything they can get on him as quickly as possible.'

He rose from his chair then, gave her one of his encouraging smiles, and left her alone with her thoughts. Jamie Raeburn, he suspected, would figure prominently in those.

Chapter Thirty-eight

The next two weeks were frenetic. Kate phoned her mother and spent a lot of time crying down the phone asking forgiveness. It wasn't long in coming. The news that the family was coming home and had an addition ensured her mother's acceptance. And what Kate's mother accepted, the rest of the family accepted. She was the *matriarch*.

Jamie's resurrection was a little more fraught. Before calling his mother he had recalled Conor's comment of days earlier - *"she couldn't tell me much... other than you were still alive. I don't know if she really believed it though"* – and so it transpired. It took a while before she did believe and then the tears came followed by the anger and then, finally, the reconciliation. It didn't help his cause that he couldn't tell her why his disappearance had been necessary.

In two weeks they arranged their travel, complicated by the fact that young Jack was born in France. To all intents and purposes, he was French and so were they. When they finally departed for home it would be as *la famille Rochefort*, there was no alternative. The Brigadier would have to sort out baby Jack's Birth Certificate when they arrived.

They packed what clothes they needed, deciding to travel light. They would need to buy new anyway. Arranging travel, closing up the house and disposing of things they couldn't take with them or keep was a wrench but they, all of them, accepted it philosophically. Jamie's much-loved Citroën was the last to go.

He spent much time on the telephone in the hotel. With word of the family's departure common knowledge the gossip was more refined now. His fellow drinkers had decided he didn't have a mistress after all and spent all their time trying to work out what he was up to. It was fortunate none of them could speak a word of English.

During the last two days he contacted Conor, Liam and Clara. Conor, he learned, was arriving in Scotland with his family in mid-December. The plan was to spend Christmas with Mary Whelan's family in Dunoon but Jamie suspected their stay could extend well into the New Year. He knew Conor too well now.

Liam had little to pass on. He had not had any contact with Duggan or his co-conspirators since the night of the "darts match" in Armagh on 2 November. With nothing to report, Jamie had not contacted Clara Whitelaw again since his report of the American and the dead drop. As a result, his call to Clara proved to be the most difficult but also, in some ways, the most rewarding.

After a tirade about his failure to keep in touch she got right down to business. Apart from the usual undertones, her questions were all about Corkscrew and the bomber.

'You never *did* tell me why Corkscrew kept Duggan from us,' she said. It was her opening salvo.

'No, neither I did,' he replied, his tone matter of fact.

'Well tell me now,' she ordered. 'Charles wants to know.' She heard Jamie's laugh echo down the line. 'Well?' she pressed.

'He was scared,' Jamie replied at last.

That gave Clara an opportunity to get her own back. She laughed mockingly. 'He's a big boy,' she chortled on. 'What's he afraid of?'

'Us,' Jamie replied simply. It didn't stop her.

'I thought we were on his side?' she responded, still amused. It was a rhetorical question but Jamie rose to it anyway.

'Are we? Really?' he said. 'I don't think he sees it quite like that. He thinks he's a pawn in Charles' game... and you know what happens to pawns; they get sacrificed when the need arises.'

'That's ridiculous,' she retorted. She wasn't laughing now.

'No it isn't. He thinks he's expendable and, know what, I feel the same sometimes.'

'That stopped her for a moment... but only for a moment. 'He expects us to bring him out and save his skin,' she said coldly, 'Yet he wants to play games,' she threw in for good measure.

Jamie sighed, just loud enough for her to hear. 'Okay, he wants brought out to safety but it's a matter of cause and effect. He's in the mess he's in because the Brigadier has him by the balls. That's the cause. And now he wants out because he's scared shitless; that's the effect.'

'This is getting us nowhere,' she retorted angrily. 'And it still doesn't explain why he didn't tell us about Duggan.'

'You think not?' Jamie replied. 'Think about it,' he carried on, patiently, 'and put yourself in his shoes. He tells us about Duggan and next thing he knows, Duggan is lifted by the RUC. Naturally, these boys grill him about this big operation he's planning on the Mainland. It doesn't take brain of Britain to work out what happens next, does it?'

'We wouldn't lift Duggan,' she retorted derisively. 'We would watch him, certainly, but we wouldn't pick him up.'

'No, I accept that,' Jamie replied, maintaining his. 'You wouldn't. The Brigadier wouldn't, because he's his man, but Five might... or Special Branch. They don't always see things the way Sir Charles does. And who's to say they wouldn't find out? Charles has to pass on intel of that nature, I imagine.'

He wasn't entirely sure if the Brigadier did have to pass on intelligence but he would be taking a hell of a risk if he didn't. Clara's silence told him she was thinking about it.

He could picture her running it through her mind. They both knew there was rivalry and jealousy in the Security Services. Five and SIS were constantly at odds and neither of them were happy with Charles Redmond's cosy relationship with the Prime Minister. When you added in the inevitable cock-ups that plagued them all, Corkscrew had a point. He hoped Clara saw it that way too.

'What about the bomber?' she asked. Jamie smiled to himself. She had moved on and Liam's explanation had been accepted. 'Has Corkscrew given you anything yet?'

'He's working on it,' Jamie responded.

'I'll take that as a no then, shall I?' she answered tartly.

Jamie ignored her and asked a question of his own. 'What about your research... made any progress?' He hoped the answer to that was no.

'He comes from a large family,' she said, frustrated. 'I've managed to eliminate some,' she said.

Jamie laughed. 'I thought that was my job,' he threw in before she could go on.

'Very funny,' she retorted dryly. 'Anyway, the list of female members of the Fitzpatrick clan is endless. I'm still working through it sorting the wheat from the chaff.'

That wasn't really what Jamie wanted to hear. If Roisin were on that list then Clara would find her. He was still agonising over that possibility when Clara continued.

'What about the Duggan woman?' she asked. 'Did he say anything more about her?'

Jamie recognised a straw when he saw one. He wasn't quite drowning yet but he grasped it all the same. 'No, he hasn't mentioned her. You don't think she's involved, do you?' he asked, trying to sound casually dismissive.

'I don't know but she does fit the profile.'

'What profile?' Jamie asked, keeping the pretence going. He knew what profile; he just didn't want Clara to know he knew.

'The profile of the bomber, silly,' Clara retorted with a snort that fell just short of derision. 'Age, build and motivation... and she has killed before,' she went on. 'She could be the one.'

Hallelujah! Thank you God.

'You think so?' Jamie asked, continuing with his obtuse questions while his pulse raced.

'Yes, I do. But I need to know where she was at the time and that's a bugger,' she went on, her swearword taking him by surprise. It was so unlike her. She was under pressure. 'I have to be careful who I involve. The plods are out, even Special Branch is tricky and I'm worried about asking Box. They might start asking questions about her father and upset the applecart.'

So she had thought about Liam's excuse about Duggan, he mused, satisfied.

He heard her speaking again. 'Have you set up regular contact with our boy?' she enquired.

'No, we are still contacting each other as and when necessary. It's safer that way. Why?'

'Charles wants regular updates. The attack, if it is going to take place, is only two months away.'

'Having doubts?'

'Some,' she admitted. 'Who's to say this isn't just something he has dreamed up to get himself out?'

'Seriously?' Jamie countered, stifling a laugh.

'All we have is his word on this. Nothing is coming through from other sources.'

'Has the Brigadier said that?'

'No,' she admitted, 'but he must have doubts.'

'Corkscrew is his man. He knows him much better than you do, Clara. If he had doubts, he would say so. If he hasn't said, he doesn't have any. And neither do I for what it's worth.'

'Okay, you're right,' she conceded. 'We have to take it seriously so set up regular contact with Corkscrew. I'll leave the frequency up to you but every seventy-two hours is probably best.'

Jamie laughed. 'So you're leaving it up to me as long as it's every seventy-two hours.'

His sarcasm was wasted on her. 'Just do it Jamie,' she ordered curtly. 'And while you're at it, pump him some more on Orlagh Duggan. I've seen the photograph of her in her file. She's an attractive young lady. Maybe he's closer to her than he's letting on. I want to know where she was and what she was doing in August '71.'

Every cloud has a silver lining.

Jamie allowed himself a cautious smile. Maintaining regular contact with Liam increased the danger. Awkward questions might be asked about why he was making phone calls from coin boxes dotted around Belfast when he had perfectly good telephones at his work and his home. On the other hand, Clara was now thinking about Orlagh Duggan being the bomber. That was the bonus..

'Okay,' he said, drawing the word out to sound 'But I still think you're wasting your time.'

'Maybe,' she acknowledged. 'But I still think Corkscrew's holding something back so will you do that for me?'

'Of course I will. For you, Clara, anything,' he replied and heard her laugh. She sounded amused and sad at the same time. That was the wrong thing to say, he reflected, a little too late. Why was it, when he was around her or talking to her like this, he had a bad habit of speaking without thinking?

'How I wish that were true,' he heard her say as her laugh subsided. She did not give him a chance to respond. 'Right,' she continued decisively. 'When you set up your routine with Corkscrew call me back and let me know. I'll expect a report from you after each contact.'

'Understood,' Jamie confirmed. There was nothing else to say. Now he had to call Liam.

Chapter Thirty-nine

Later that day

'It's that mawn, again, Mr Fitzpatrick,' Concepta shouted out in her thick West Belfast accent.

Liam, who was tidying up in the yard shouted back angrily. 'What man?'

'That Mr Lynch ye spoke to earlier,' the girl replied.

Liam dropped an armful of copper piping onto the cobbles with a loud clattering noise and ran for the office. 'Put him through to me in here,' he said, pulling the door to his private office closed behind him. It wasn't much of an office, just enough space for an old, badly misused desk, a chair and a battered and scuffed metal filing cabinet that was once a uniform light grey colour and was now all shades of that hue. The walls were thin but that was the least of his problems.

'Aye, what is it, Mr Lynch? Did ye forget somethin'?' he said as he picked up, running the mantra through his head. Don't give any fucker listening anything to get suspicious about,

'Aye, sorry to bother ye again, Mr Fitzpatrick,' Jamie replied, playing along. 'I spoke to the customer about that job we were discussin'. He's happy to go ahead but he would like regular updates... every two or three days. Are ye alright wi' that?' Anyone listening could make what they liked of that. He heard Liam curse quietly under his breath.

'Aye, ah daresay, if that's what it takes to get the job.'

'That's grand,' Jamie replied, full of bonhomie. 'I'll let the customer know.'

'Ye just caught me there,' Liam went on. 'Ah was just heading out for an hour or so. Just as well ye phoned when ye did.'

Jamie smiled. Liam would call him in an hour. 'Well, don't let me hold ye back. All the best,' he said, finishing the call. Liam already had his number.

***

The phone rang in the Hotel de la Place precisely one hour later. When Jamie put the receiver to his ear, everyone in the bar could hear Liam's roar down the line from Belfast. Jamie grimaced and some of the customers grinned. The caller wasn't happy.

'What the fuck's goin' on, Dermott?' Liam screamed. 'If ye keep callin' me at the feckin' yard the snoopers will get suspicious,' he complained.

'Sorry, Liam,' Jamie replied calmly. 'I had no alternative but I won't do it again... unless there's an emergency,' he added after a slight pause. 'London wants regular contact. They want reports from you every three days.'

'What the fuck for?' Liam snapped, quieter now.

'They're getting nervous. 25 January is only two months away and they've got nothing worthwhile yet. If you've got nothing to tell me, just phone and say that you're still waiting for prices for some of the bits for the job.'

'Bits for the job?' Liam repeated, laughing sarcastically. 'Like what?'

'Christ, Liam. You're a plumber. Use your fuckin' imagination. It's a big job... new kitchen and bathroom. You're waitin' for a sink, or taps, or anything, I don't know. If you do have anything worthwhile to pass on say you'll call me again in a day or two days and then go to a call box and call me just like we're doing now; one day means one hour and two days means two hours. You'll be fine.'

'Aye, ah can fuckin' work that out,' Liam replied caustically. 'But "ye'll be fine" is easy for you to say How long do ye expect me to keep this up?'

'As long as necessary,' Jamie replied shortly.

'An' was that all ye called for?' Liam was still angry; it was in his voice. 'Ye could have arranged that next time ye called.'

'No, there is somethin' else,' Jamie re-joined. 'How well do you know Orlagh Duggan?'

'Why?' Liam queried suspiciously.

'Just tell me, Liam,' Jamie retorted, irritably. 'How close are you to her?'

'How close? As in, have I been shaggin' her, ye mean?' Liam laughed bitterly. 'Fuck sake, ah'm no' that desperate, neither ah am. She's a fine lookin' doll, right enough, but ah would'na take the chance. She's got a reputation... the Black Widow some folk calsl her... like the spider... ye know, the one that kills its mate after shaggin' him. Ye widna want to suffer wi' premature ejaculation wi' Orlagh, if ye catch ma drift,' he continued, laughing. A little manically, Jamie thought.

'Aye, I get you,' Jamie replied. 'So, she means nothin' to you?' he went on.

'Are ye deaf or what?' Liam shouted down the line, exasperated. 'Look, what is this? She's Pearce Duggan's daughter an' that's the only reason ah know her. Ah would steer well clear o' her otherwise.'

'That's good. That's all I need to know.'

'Ye still haven't told me why, Dermott.'

'Simple answer is that our friends think you're protecting her. Think maybe you an' Orlagh had a thing goin'... so now I can assure them you haven't. That leads on to the next bit. They want to know where she was an' what she was doin' in summer '71, if you can find out without dropping yourself in the shit.'

Liam responded with a frosty laugh. 'Ah'm already in the shit, or had ye forgotten that Dermott?' The laugh went on for a while longer, then. 'Summer 1971?' he said.

He was working things out in his head, Jamie realised. He was Irish but contrary to common folklore, he wasn't stupid. If he reached the right conclusion he didn't say.

'Alright, ah'll see what ah can find out,' was all he said. 'Anythin' else?'

'No,' Jamie confirmed. 'That's all I need.'

'Right, ah'll be away then,' Liam said, finishing the conversation. 'I'll phone ye again in three days, six o'clock.'

'No, make it four days. I'm travellin' back home on the third day. Call me on this number,' he said, reeling off the number for Kate's parents.

'Right,' Liam acknowledged. 'Bon voyage,' he added sarcastically.

***

Clara was surprised to receive the call. 'My, my, twice in one day,' she said as his voice came to her down the line.

'You told me to call when I'd spoken to Corkscrew again; that's what I'm doing,' Jamie replied, a little too sharply.

'So I did,' she said. Her voice told him he was getting off on the wrong foot again and that was not good. He needed to keep Clara on side.

'Sorry,' he threw in quickly. 'I'm just getting a bit edgy, that's all.'

'So, you've set up regular contact?' she asked. She sounded mollified, a little at least.

'Yes, every three days, just as you asked,' Jamie confirmed. 'Though our next contact will be in four days, Saturday at six, British time; I'm travelling home on Friday. I'll call you immediately afterwards.'

'So I'm working overtime again, am I?' she said, laughing.

'I could call you on Monday morning if you prefer,'

She laughed again. 'You know that's not a good idea, my darling,' she countered. 'Charles wants his updates.'

'So it's okay to phone you at home?' he retorted impudently.

'This time, yes.'

'Mark won't get miffed?'

'Not if we keep it short and to the point.'

Jamie laughed. 'That's not what you usually say.' He immediately regretted it. He'd done it again... spoke without thinking.

'Yes, well...' she said, drawing the "well" out, before letting him off the hook. 'And what about Orlagh Duggan; did you ask him?'

'Yes, I did. You can relax. He hasn't had a thing with her. He says he'll try to find out where she was and what she was doing in the summer of '71. I didn't say why you wanted to know but he will have worked it out.'

'Okay, that's good, thanks,' she replied. There was a moment's silence and then she continued. 'How are you bearing up?' she asked. 'You said you're getting edgy.'

'Assessing my mental state again, are you?' he retorted.

'No, just worried about you. I still care; you know that. I don't want you to get brought down by this.'

'I won't,' he said. 'But thanks for your concern.' He was sure she had more to say on the subject but he didn't really want to hear it. 'I'll need to go,' he said, cutting things short. 'I'm running out of money for the phone. I'll call you on Saturday, about six thirty.'

He replaced the handset and let out a sigh. Clara could still turn out to be his biggest problem, he mused, her words "my darling" still bouncing around in his head.

Chapter Forty

They left France on the morning of Friday 16 November. It was a sad affair. There was a big turnout of their friends and neighbours, all of them insisting that they return soon. Kate had a tear in her eye, as did Lauren, and Jamie felt low... but he didn't show it.

They kissed their friends and said their farewells, assuring their new found friends that they would be back, but, deep down, Kate and Jamie both knew it was unlikely.

The trip was long and tiring and it was late evening before they arrived in The Midlands. Calverton hadn't changed much. Kate's family was out en masse to greet them and their tiredness evaporated. They laughed and joked, ate and drank, and new baby Jack was the star attraction. The baby smiled and made little noises as he was passed around from grandmother to grandfather and then to aunts and uncles. Jamie smiled proudly. To all those there it seemed he didn't have a care in the world. Only Kate knew the truth. Behind his calm exterior, worries about the future were gnawing away at his insides relentlessly.

He hadn't spoken to Kate much about it in the preceding weeks. Or she to him, some to that. They weren't avoiding it as such; they simply accepted it. They were both aware of what he faced and although Kate said little, Jamie knew it was a heavy burden on her. It seemed to follow her around, like a cloud or some ghostly apparition, always lurking in the background.

It was just after midnight when they finally escaped the attentions of the family and made it to bed. Fatigue had evaporated with the enjoyment of seeing family again and, as they lay close together, Jamie began to outline his plans. It was time, he decided, to give her the detail.

Kate listened in silence, gripping his hand, saying nothing until he finished. 'It's worse than I imagined,' she whispered softly. She knew he was anxious, as much about her reaction as anything else. She lay curled against him, soft and warm. 'What if something goes wrong?' she asked, after a pause. 'And this woman, Roisin Kelly, how do you know she's telling the truth?' she went on, lifting up her head to look at him in the semi-light.

He smiled down reassuringly. 'Nothing will go wrong, baby. If anything comes up I'll deal with it,' he whispered soothingly. 'As for Roisin, she's Roisin Evans now,' he carried on. 'I know it's the truth because I spoke to her. The mention of her brother's name and the name of the man who threatened her frightened her... badly. No one could fake what I saw.'

'I don't know how much more of this I can take, Jamie,' Kate replied, her voice breaking. 'These men, they're evil, and there are so many of them. I think I'm going to lose you. I don't want to be alone.' A tear ran slowly down her left cheek.

Jamie leaned close and kissed it away, cupping her chin in his hand and tilting her head up to look her in the eyes. 'You'll never be alone. I'll always be with you,' he whispered, sliding his body lower to kiss her softly. He felt her lips part and her tongue come alive in his mouth as she returned the kiss. Her fingers gripped him tightly.

And then the dam burst. Months of pent up desire and emotion flooded out, engulfing them in its wake. Kate reached for him eagerly, her fingers encircling his now erect penis, arousing him further. She heard his breathing loud in her ear, faster now. She could feel his heart beat frenziedly against her breast. And then his fingers opened her, teasing her labia apart. She moaned softly as his fingers caressed her clitoris. It had been so long. She was losing control. Her body tingled with excitement as she felt his hips move in time with her arousing hand. He was ready. She felt it.

She eased him over onto his back and straddled him. His eyes gazed longingly up at her and she saw his burning, all consuming desire. She smiled happily and lowered herself onto him, impaling herself on his sex. She felt his hands on her breasts, his thumbs and fingers kneading her already swollen nipples, taking her further. She began to move, slowly at first, rising and falling on him, feeling him fill her. She moaned softly, oblivious to everything else. Nothing else and no one else mattered. Only them as it always had been.

The pace of their coupling increased, her downward thrusts met by his surging hips as he pushed deeper and deeper into her. Her control was finally going. She was almost there. She let out a long soft moan and her back arched suddenly, her body rigid as the orgasm took her. His pulsating thrusts continued, on and on, pushing her to a second climax. Her body felt as though it were on fire. She tightened the muscles of her vulva around him and cried out, stifling the sound with the back of a hand.

'Come!' she whispered urgently. 'Come, pleeease,' she repeated.

She felt him thrust upwards, swelling inside her. He held himself there, gripping her tightly with his hands, and then the spasms of his ejaculation filled her. It seemed an age before she felt him sag slowly beneath her. His big, brown eyes looked up longingly at her. She laughed quietly and lowered her body onto his, pressing her still swollen nipples against him. She felt his hands encircle her bottom, pulling her closer still, and felt him expand and contract inside her.

'I love you so much,' she whispered. 'I don't know what I'd do if...' she started, but he cut her off with a kiss.

'It won't,' he said softly as the kiss ended. 'I'm going to grow old with you.'

They lay together in comfortable silence for a while, their bodies melded together. Jamie nibbled at Kate's ear and ran his tongue tantalisingly down her neck. He could taste the salty sweat on her skin. She was everything to him. There had never been anyone like her in his life. There never would be. When they made love he was carried away, transported. He savoured the seconds; the touch of her fingers and the hunger of her kisses lingered in his mind long after the moment had passed.

He felt the hunger grow in him again. He wanted her again. Now. Gently, he turned her onto her back and knelt over her, easing her legs apart. He licked at her breasts and sucked hungrily on her nipples. He felt the touch of her skin against him as her arms encircled his neck and he felt the heat of her breath in his hair. He pulled back, kneeling now, with his back erect. Gently, he slid his hands beneath her bottom and raised her hips up towards him. He saw her smile, saw his own anticipation mirrored in her face. He eased his body forward and entered her. They coupled furiously, their bodies moving in unison as they rose and fell together. He felt the climax start deep inside him as it always did, like a volcano about to erupt. Suddenly, the heat of it coursed through him. He heard her moan, felt the muscles of her tighten around him, and her fingers grip him. It was engulfing them both. Finally, he sighed and sank slowly down onto her, this time completely spent.

He thought about Kate's worries then. Her fear of losing him... as he feared losing her. He couldn't go on like this. Kate and his children were all that really mattered. Their time in France had been idyllic but behind it there was always the fear that the past would come back and haunt him. And that had always been there. He had to rid himself of it, once and for all. France had been an interlude, a pleasant interlude, but nothing more than that. It was simply a stop-off point. Their life was here with their families and his life was here with Kate, not charging all over the place for Charles Redmond.

He felt the thoughtful touch of Kate's fingers as she teased them through his long, unruly hair. Her long nails traced the jagged line of the scar on the left side of his head and he knew what she was thinking. He lifted his head and looked into her sparkling green eyes.

'I won't be that stupid again,' he murmured quietly. 'When this fiasco is over we'll still be together. Just us... you, me and the kids. No more crazy jobs like this. I promise.'

Kate smiled happily. The look in his eyes confirmed his words but a doubt remained. Would he ever be allowed to simply walk away, she wondered fretfully? Only time would tell, as always, but for now, at least, she could be happy.

Part III

Chapter Forty-one

1 January 1974, Calverton - The Midlands

The telephone was ringing, jangling annoyingly through the sleeping house. Jamie lay awake, Kate asleep beside him, warm and comfortable. Coming home had been good for her.

He heard a door creak open and footsteps make their way along the hall then pas softly down the stairs. More creaks as the old stairs gave under the weight of the human descending them and the ringing went on, and on.

Finally, a moment's silence followed by a sleepily mumbled "hello" from Emily Edwards, Kate's mother. There was a short flurry of conversation that Jamie couldn't make out and then the creaking of the stairs and the padding feet on the landing, stopping outside the door. Then a gentle knock.

'Jamie, are you awake?' the woman's voice whispered.

He pushed himself from the bed, grabbed for his pyjama trousers and pulled them on, shivering in the cold. He made it to the door in three short steps and eased it open.

'What's wrong?' he asked.

'Nothing's wrong,' Emily Edwards replied, still whispering. 'Other than the fact that it's eight o'clock on New Year's morning and some gentleman has to call you to wish you a Happy New Year.' The way she said "gentleman" indicated she didn't think he was.

'Sorry,' Jamie mumbled as he pushed past her. 'Who is it... did he say?'

'No, but he's Irish,' she responded as she made her way back to her bedroom.

Jamie's heart sank. It could only be one person on the other end of the line and that meant it was urgent. He had spoken to Liam two days earlier and there had been no change. They had agreed to forego the three-day rule and make contact again on 2 January. He made his way quickly down to the phone in the hall, his heart pumping.

'Liam,' he hissed quietly. 'What's up?' Then, raising his voice a little. 'Happy New Year,' he said, adding a little laugh for the benefit of Emily if she was listening.

'It's on,' Liam came back, ignoring the greeting. 'Ah'll keep it short. We're leavin' tomorrow. We're all goin' by different routes to the mainland and meetin' in Liverpool on the third.'

'So the attack is down there?' Jamie whispered, looking nervously back towards the stairs.

'Nah, we come up to Scotland after that. A place called Alexandria. Do ye know it?'

'Yeah, well enough,' Jamie acknowledged. 'All 12 of you?' he went on.

'Don't know. Ah only know the details for the four of us. How will ah keep in touch wi' ye now?' Liam went on, nervously.

'I wish I knew,' Jamie retorted. 'I'll come up to Glasgow. I'll think of something, don't worry. Anything else?'

'Aye, just one thing. Remember ah said Orlagh Duggan is co-ordinatin' the attack?'

'Yeah?' Jamie replied, his question clear.

'Well she's comin' over to Glasgow later. Takin' command on the ground, her father says.' He finished with a bitter laugh.

'You're sure?'

'Oh aye, ah'm sure, so ah am. She'll be over.'

'Okay, thanks Liam. I'll fix up a way of meeting you. Watch your back.'

A cold, frightened laugh was all Jamie got in response before the line was dead.

***

Kate was awake when he returned. She shifted nervously in the bed and wrapped her arms around him as he slid beneath the covers. 'Who was it?' she murmured.

The house was still quiet, everyone still asleep with the possible exception of Emily Edwards, and Kate was astute enough to know that whatever the caller had said had to be kept between them alone.

'It was Liam. He's on the move. It's going ahead,' he said. He sounded guiltily excited, Kate thought.

'Did he say where?' she asked hopefully. If they knew where the attack was to take place then surely they could finish it all quickly, she reasoned.

'No, he doesn't know yet,' Jamie murmured. 'He's staying in Alexandria though.'

'Where?'

Jamie smiled. 'It's a small town about twenty miles from Glasgow... near Loch Lomond. Where we went on the bike years ago, remember?'

Kate smiled now. 'Yes, I remember,' she said, the memory warming her. 'We made love outside, beside the loch,' she giggled happily, forgetting her problems for a moment.

Jamie broke the spell. 'I'll have to go up to Glasgow,' he announced.

'How long for?' She tried to keep the misery out of her voice but didn't really succeed.

'I don't know love. It could be a week, maybe longer.'

'What are we going to say to my mother and everyone else,' Kate asked. She was always practical.

'I'll say I'm going to a funeral; say that's what Liam's call was about – and while I'm there I can look for a house for us.'

'I want to come with you,' she said plaintively.

'You can't sweetheart, you know that,' he replied gently. 'I need to be able to do things without thinking about safety.'

'About my safety, you mean.'

He smiled apologetically. 'Yes, about your safety,' he agreed.

She pulled him to her and placed a kiss on his mouth. He wrapped his arms around her and pulled her closer. Her heart was beating furiously against him, her fear showing. 'I love you,' he said softly. 'I'll always love you.'

Chapter Forty-two

Friday 4 January 1974, Dumbarton

Four men stepped stiffly from a battered Morris van and made their way into a derelict tenement building in Castle Road, Dumbarton. The time was five fifteen on a dark, wet morning.

They had driven through the night from Liverpool, stopping off in Glasgow on a vacant piece of ground in Gorbals to sleep, shivering in the cold for two hours. In reality, they had slept little. Even surrounded by crumbling, derelict buildings where no one in their right mind would venture, they felt insecure and nervous.

The building they entered now was exactly as described to them but even so it had been difficult to find. Demolition was in progress and street names and numbers had been removed or obliterated making their task doubly hard.

The site itself had been easy to find. The scribbled note detailing their route had been accurate to a T. The blocked off road was where it should have been and, when the makeshift barrier had been removed, the van had been able to gain access to the site.

Once on the site, negotiating huge potholes and enormous piles of building rubble, four pairs of eyes had strained to find their destination. Tall street lamps, stripped of their high-pressure sodium bulbs, stood like sentries at the edge of what had once been pavements, the van's headlights sweeping over them and casting long shadows against the remaining buildings. A crack of light peeking from behind a boarded up window guided them to it eventually.

Liam Fitzpatrick edged around an old Ford Cortina and brought the van to a halt. The building they were now entering stood like a gaunt skeleton, towering up into the darkness. They moved forward in single file, crunching and stumbling over broken slates and glass in the darkness, jumping at every unexpected sound.

Liam checked his watch. They were right on time. His instructions were to be get them here between five and five thirty and he had made it with ten minutes to spare. He pushed on into the tenement close. The once tiled walls had been gouged and scratched and broken pieces of ceramic littered the floor. Graffiti had been scrawled on the walls, barely visible in the now almost total blackness. As with the boarded up window, a tiny sliver of light appeared below a door on their left. Liam stopped, hesitating to knock. He gave an involuntary shudder as the cold ate into him.

Fionn Doherty, standing immediately behind him, felt him tremble and laughed cruelly under his breath. 'Shittin' yerself already are ye, Liam?' he murmured sarcastically, loud enough for the others to hear. 'Or did somebody just walk ower yer grave?'

Liam turned to face him, the man's face barely visible. He could hardly see him but he could smell him. He smiled coldly at the man.

No, but ah'll be dancin' on yours soon, you psychopathic little shite.

Doherty laughed and Liam joined in, playing the man at his own game. The others waited, wondering what would follow.

'The only reason ye'r no' shiverin' wi' the cold yerself Fionn is because ye filled yerself with whiskey, ya quare wee eejit.'

Fionn glowered at him but held his tongue. Confrontation wasn't a good idea. Fitzpatrick had Duggan at his back but he would make him pay for that insult one day. No one called him a stupid wee idiot and got away with it, and that included Liam feckin' Fitzpatrick.

Liam turned back to the door and knocked. Three heavy, regular knocks. Seconds later, the door swung inwards and a large, ruddy faced man appeared in the doorway. 'Ye're expectin' us, ah hope?' Liam said, without bothering to introduce himself. The man didn't need a name.

The big man gave them a perfunctory look. 'Aye, you'll be the Paddies,' he said with a laugh and opened the door wider. His accent was all Glasgow.

'Aye, that would be us, so it would,' Liam retorted, smiling through his anger. The stereotype annoyed him. He pushed past the man into the apartment, the others following, and left their host to close the door. He did, slamming it shut with a force that shook the place.

Fionn Doherty jumped nervously, turning angrily on the man. 'Ya feckin' eejit,' he shouted. 'Are ye tryin' tae waken the feckin' dead?' He moved towards the man, reaching out for the other man's jacket, but the big man brushed him off easily.

'The fuckin' buildin's empty, wee man,' the Glasgow man said with a grin. 'The whole fuckin' place is empty. There isnae a livin' soul within' a mile o' here so the only folk ah might waken are the dead. Jist cool yer jets, Paddy.' The Glasgow accent made him sound menacing... menacing enough to make Fionn back off.

His temper had reached boiling point but Fionn Doherty was a pragmatist, if nothing else, and the Glasgow man in front of him was bigger and broader than he was. Not only that, seeing him in the naked light, the man looked as if he had been in more than a few brawls in his time... and survived. As with Liam, Fionn decided it could wait. The others laughed and that made him angrier. If there was one thing Fionn Doherty hated more than anything else, it was people laughing at him rather than with him. Well, he would show them.

Liam read what was in Fionn's mind as he discretely studied the Glasgow man. He was big, topping 6 feet. His cropped hair was a steely grey, which matched his pallid skin. His eyes, wide set, were an ice cold blue, so cold you could almost feel the temperature drop when you looked into them. This, Liam decided, was not a man to mess with. The skin on his face was taut, not puffy, and a jagged scar ran from below his left ear to finish under his chin. His jacket was tight across his chest, fastened with one button that was straining under the pressure, and his arms looked strong enough to crush anyone who had the misfortune to be caught in their grip. Fionn had made the right decision, Liam mused, quietly amused.

'Make yersells at hame,' the big man said, laughing coarsely as he watched the four Irishmen eye the surroundings with disgust. 'It might no' be 5 star an' aw the other guests have goat four legs an' long tails, but they'll no bother ye.'

'Are we feckin' stayin' here?' Macari asked angrily, a look of disgust spreading across his face.

Pearce Finnegan, the youngest member of the group, simply looked bemused. Overawed might be a better word, Liam thought. The boy had not known what to expect and being in the company of these three hard men made him quieter than usual... and jumpier.

The Glasgow man laughed aloud. 'Whit's up? Dae ye no like it? Is it no' up tae the high standards yer used tae in the bogs?'

Macari stared back at him maliciously. Doherty's look was one of pure malevolence. The big man smiled back at them, challengingly. Liam broke it up. 'No, we're not stayin' here,' he broke in.

'So why the fuck are we here?' Macari fired back. 'It can't be for this ganch's scintillatin' conversation, that's fer sure.'

The big Glaswgian looked on in amusement. How anyone in their right mind could think they would be staying in this shit hole beggared belief. It was a weapons cache, nothing more. He looked over at Liam who was clearly in charge, lifting an eyebrow.

Liam saw the gesture and nodded. 'The weapons for the job are here,' he said.

Doherty's eyes lit up. To Fionn, in the words of John Lennon, happiness was, indeed, a warm gun.

'And the uniforms,' Liam added.

'Uniforms? What feckin' uniforms? First time I've heard a knitted balaclava called a uniform,' Macari retorted, looking around the group and drawing a laugh from Doherty.

'We'll be wearing other uniforms on this job,' Liam said, smiling back at him. 'That's why we were measured up back in October, remember? Or did ye think it was fer a coffin?' he laughed. Macari smarted at that. He hadn't remembered. 'So now we try them on now and make sure they fit,' Liam went on. 'They'll stay here with the guns until we need them.'

Doherty looked disappointed. He was about to protest when Liam cut him off. 'We pick everythin' up just before the job – Boss's instructions,' he added, meaning Duggan, but avoiding the use of the man's name. 'He doesn't want us wanderin' around for three weeks tooled up. They stay here.' He eyed them all, one by one, and one by one they nodded their agreement, even a reluctant and disappointed Fionn Doherty.

'Once we've tried on the uniforms and picked out weapons we'll head for the safe house. It's near here, isn't it?' he said, directing the question at the big Glasgow man.

'Aye, that's right... Ye're stayin' wi' "friends" in Alexandria,' the man replied. He smiled. Judging by the expressions on these Micks' faces, it could be on the far side of the fuckin' moon for all they knew. 'It's only a few minutes' drive,' he added, looking pointedly down at his watch. 'Ah don't want tae rush ye,' he said, making no effort to hide his o subdue his natural sarcasm, 'but ye'se hud better get a move on. The men start work at seven.'

'What feckin' men?' Doherty retorted, alarmed.

The big man snorted derisively. 'You're even thicker than ye look, pal,' he said. 'Look around ye. Ye're in the middle o' a fuckin' demolition site an' the gang starts at seven. Ah want you lot well away tae fuck long before then.'

'But what about the gear?' Fionn went on anxiously. 'Is it safe here?'

That brought another laugh from the big man. His opinion of Fionn Doherty's stupidity was hardening. He shook his head dismissively. 'Dae ye think yer boss man wid want ye tae leave it here if it wisnae safe?' he replied mockingly. 'This buildin' isnae due tae come doon until the middle o' February. It's been stripped oot completely so naebody comes in here except me an' the other security man, an' he'll no' say a word. Ah'll look efter yer wee toys fur ye,' he continued, grinning in the face of Fionn's anger. 'Now, get a fuckin' move on. Everythin's beneath the flair in whit wis the kitchen in the flat opposite.'

'Right, let's get on wi' it,' Liam said, nodding to Pearce Finnegan. 'You come wi' me, Pearce. We'll go first. You two wait here until the big man here comes fer ye,' he ordered. Both men nodded. Fionn was still sullen.

Liam and Finnegan followed the Glasgow man across to the flat opposite. The door appeared to be wedged shut with junk and boxes piled in front of it. The big man moved boxes aside and produced a torch and a key, inserting the latter into a keyhole that had been obscured by the accumulated rubbish. He turned the key with a loud click and pushed the door inwards on well-oiled hinges. Liam smiled appreciatively.

The big man led the way. The flooring in the hall had been stripped out and he stepped carefully from joist to joist with Liam and Finnegan following. At the end of what had been the hall, an opening faced them with two more to their right. These led to what had once been the living room and bedrooms. The doors were gone, as was everything else.

Strangely, Liam noted, one door remained, this one leading off to their left. It was damaged and, like the main door, it appeared to be jammed shut. It led, he presumed, to the kitchen. Their guide leant against it and a small gap appeared. He pushed harder, straining against the door's inertia, and slowly a gap appeared. With a final effort, and a loud scraping noise, the door moved inwards. Here, the flooring planks remained in place, but, just like the other rooms, everything else had been removed. A number of holes in the walls showed where kitchen units had been attached and larger holes in the floor indicated were where the water and waste pipes had been. It was no more than a desolate shell in the pale light now filtering through the filthy, broken windowpanes.

With the toe of a boot, the man cleared a small pile of rubbish from the floor and bent down. He felt around for a moment, his fingers scraping through the debris, until he found what he was looking for, and then pulled hard. A section of flooring rose, protesting, in a cloud of dust. Beneath the floor lay a number of canvas bags. One by one, he hauled them up and passed them to Liam who was waiting patiently.

Between them, Liam and Finnegan spread the sacks out and opened them. Inside one bag were the uniforms. A second bag contained handguns, machine pistols and ammunition. The third bag intrigued Liam. What else was there, he wondered. There was already enough to arm an entire Brigade, he mused grimly. He opened the sack tentatively. Inside were two long metal tubes with flared ends. He pulled one out. It had two handgrips, one fitted with a trigger mechanism. He had seen one of these before but had never handled one.

'What is it?' Finnegan asked, looking over his shoulder, curious.

Liam smiled grimly. 'It's an RPG-7 Pearce... Russian.' He pointed to the Cyrillic lettering stencilled on the side, РПГ-7

'What's it for?' the youngster went on, intrigued. Unlike Liam, he had never seen anything like this before.

'Rocket propelled grenade launcher, fires heavy duty stuff at tanks an' armoured cars.'

'Jesus, Mary an' Joseph,' Finnegan muttered, scared now. 'What the fuck are we goin' up against?'

Liam shook his head. 'Ah don't know son,' he said cruelly. 'But ah don't think it'll be a Morris Minor. Whatever it is, it's armoured.' He turned to the last bag then. This, he assumed, contained the projectiles. 'This the rockets?' he queried, directing the question at the Glasgow man who was staring back impassively.

The man shrugged. 'Ah've nae idea, pal,' he said. 'The bags wur delivered like that. Ah didnae open them... ah'm no' that daft.'

Liam smiled coldly and unsealed the bag. Inside he found what he expected; four thin tubes with bulbous heads. These looked different from the ones he had seen before; more powerful, he thought. He didn't like the look of them.

'Armoured vehicles,' Finnegan muttered, not coming to terms with it.

'Aye, that's whit ah think, Pearce. Ye still glad ye volunteered? Ye always wanted tae be a hero, didn't ye?'

'Shite,' Pearce murmured.

The Glasgow man sniggered but he too was looking worried now. It wasn't the weapons themselves that bothered him, it was the chance of them being discovered by the police before the Micks removed them. If that happened, he was looking at a long stretch in Barlinnie or even Peterhead, and he didn't like prison food.

'When will ye be comin' back fur them?' he asked, he asked anxiously.

'A couple o' weeks, ah imagine,' Liam replied, grinning. 'Think ye can handle it?' he went on. He knew what was on the man's mind.

'Ah'll jist huv tae, ah suppose,' the man retorted. 'Mind you,' he added, grinning back at Liam now. 'It could be worse... Ah'm no' the wan that hus tae fire them.'

Liam nodded thoughtfully. The big man was right and it made him wonder who would be firing them. He hoped to God it wasn't him before remembering there was no chance of that. He'd be "dead" by then. He forced a smile and turned to Finnegan.

'Right, Pearce, let's you an' me try on these uniforms,' he said, handing a tunic, trousers and boots to Finnegan and selecting one set for himself. They were a good fit, right down to the heavy black leather boots and the shiny black cork helmets.'

'A' we need now is a fire engine,' Finnegan said, laughing again. He was still nervous.

'Ah think yer wish will be granted, Pearce,' Liam grinned. 'Now, get changed back intae yer own gear and pick a weapon,' he instructed.

They both peeled off the uniforms and dressed again in their own clothes. Liam was first and had already chosen a heavy Browning automatic from the weapons bag before Finnegan got round to it. He folded his uniform and laid the heavy gun on top. 'That's me,' he said, turning to the younger man who was examining the selection of pistols. 'Have ye fired a handgun afore?' he asked him.

Finnegan shook his head.

'Jesus,' the Glaswegian murmured, still looking out through a crack in the hoarding on the window. 'A lamb tae the fuckin' slaughter, eh?'

'He'll be fine,' Liam retorted shortly. 'Wi' any luck we won't need t' fire them,' he said, trying to reassure the younger man.

'Aye, wi' any luck,' the Glasgow man laughed. The conversation was clearly getting to Finnegan.

'Leave it,' Liam spat angrily. 'Go an' get the others,' he instructed, 'while we pack our stuff away.'

The man gave him an insolent grin in response and headed off, kicking viciously at the outside door as he passed.

'Ignore him, Pearce,' Liam said when the big Scotsman was out of earshot. 'If ye stick close tae me, ye'll be fine. Forget Macari an' Doherty, they'll be lookin' after themselves, not you. They've done this sort o' thing afore. Jist stick wi' me, right?'

Finnegan swallowed hard and nodded nervously.

'An' don't pay any attention to the feckin' Jock... He's probably no' fired one o' these before either,' he went on, laughing confidently though he didn't actually believe that. 'If ye do have tae fire the bloody thing, just point it an' pull the trigger. Ye've as much chance o' hittin' yer target that way as aimin' it. Right, let's get out o' here an' give the others room,' he finished. As they headed back they heard the front door scrape open again.

They passed Doherty and Macari in the narrow hall, squeezing past them face to face. Doherty gave them both a sullen smirk.

Back in the main flat, they waited silently. The Glasgow man busied himself tidying up until the others returned. The time was now six twenty.

'There's a wee dairy back there on Glasgow Road,' the big man told them. 'It's open fae six an' ye can get a cuppa tea or coffee an' somethin' tae eat.

Wait fur me there. Ah finish at seven an' efter that ah'll take ye tae yer digs.' He opened the door out into the close mouth and ushered them out. 'Move yer arses,' he said, harshly. 'Ah don't want anybody tae see ye here.'

Liam led them out and they climbed back into the old van. He settled into the driver's seat as before with Finnegan beside him while the others, grumbling again, climbed into the back. The van coughed into life in a cloud of black fumes and Liam reversed back along the still dark road before turning and squeezing the van back through the gap. It was finally coming together for him but he now had one major problem. He had no idea how Dermott would make contact with him and without Dermott he was fucked.

Chapter Forty-three

Same Day, Glasgow

The city hadn't changed much. Gordon Street was still Gordon Street and the population was still its cocky, self-assured self. It felt strange to be back here alone, without his wife and children, but that was unavoidable... or so he kept telling himself. This was the final stage. One month, maybe less, and it would all be over. There was only one problem, he still didn't know what "it" actually was.

He had spent New Year's day wound up like a coiled spring after Liam's early morning call. Emily Edwards had been curious, commenting and questioning. Jamie had started off by telling her Liam was an old friend from Glasgow. That prompted the reply "but he's Irish" to which Jamie had simply laughed and told her that Glasgow wasn't an Irish Free Zone and they had lots of different people living there; Indians, Pakistanis, even Poles and there was a big Polish Club in the West End. That earned him a scolding look from Kate and a dismissive snort from Emily.

His announcement that another old friend had died and he would be travelling up to Glasgow for the funeral quietened Emily down. She became a little more understanding and put his mood down to that. She brightened up when he announced he would stay a little longer and do a bit of house hunting. Until then, she had been convinced he would take Kate and the children back to France. Scotland she could live with, she had announced... as long as they had a house big enough for when she visited. Jamie took that on board.

He had called Clara on 2 January to confirm that Liam, Corkscrew, was on the move. That eased her doubts about the whole thing but the fact that the target was still unknown still had her on edge. Everyone, she told him, was fretting now. One by-product of Liam and the other men leaving Ireland was that alarm bells would start ringing. The disappearance of 12 active volunteers presaged something big and all the security services would be on the alert. Whether they would be looking for them in Scotland was another matter, Jamie had mused. Scotland was regarded as a backwater and no one seriously believed that the IRA would ever carry out an attack there.

The news on her investigations into the identity of the woman in the photograph was equally bad. The list of "possible" links to Corkscrew was shortening. He had been able to take a little pressure off Roisin by telling Clara that Corkscrew had been unable to find out anything about Orlagh Duggan's whereabouts during 1971. He embellished it a little by adding that Liam had spoken to a number of people who knew her and her comings and goings at the time were shrouded in mystery. That was probably enough on its own to tip Clara further towards Orlagh as the bomber. The news that the woman was coming to Scotland to co-ordinate the attack was the icing on the cake as far as Jamie was concerned. He didn't need to suggest anything else.

Clara finished the call by telling him to take care. She meant it; it was in her voice. He was still figuring in her thoughts.

So now he was in Glasgow, without a clue as to what was happening. The only certainty was that the attack was going ahead, probably somewhere in the Central Belt of Scotland, but even that was far from certain. The whole thing was a shambles. He had to find some way of contacting Liam. Without that, everything would come unstuck.

Conor was still in Scotland. He and his family had arrived during the second week in December and they were still with Mary Whelan's family in Dunoon. They were meeting tomorrow, at Conor's insistence, and pressure was being piled on Jamie for the "girls to meet up". It was something he knew he couldn't resist for long... he didn't want to. They were family or as good as. But Jamie could see Conor's machinations working away in the background. Conor wanted to help, but did he really want to involve him at the sharp end of this? Asking for help with new identities was one thing, asking him to cover his back when bullets started flying was another. But he had no one else, no one he could trust. He knew he would probably give in to his friend's plea and consoled himself with that thought. Trust was everything.

It had seemed a long way off when they arranged the meeting. Not so distant now, Jamie mused. But the thought of being with the big American again, even in these circumstances, lifted his spirit. He had to think positively, he thought grimly.

Conor Whelan was no fool. They had discussed Liam's escape plan and, even with luck on his side, they both knew it would not be easy for Jamie to carry out. He was pitting himself against anything between four and twelve hardened IRA men, not to mention the "Black Widow" who would be there too.

Conor had shared his opinion of the whole thing with him. Paraphrasing it down, he told Jamie he was crazy. He threw in a few expletives along the way. He pointed out what he thought was obvious; Jamie couldn't do it alone. Jamie's response was that he wouldn't be doing it alone. That momentarily raised Conor's hopes, until Jamie reminded him that Liam Fitzpatrick had a part to play in his own escape. Conor's response was simple. Two was better than one, sure, but three was better than two. And that discussion would take place again tomorrow.

Now, however, he had other things to worry about. He had toyed with the idea of staying with his own father and mother while he was here but he didn't want them caught up in any crossfire. He decided to compromise. He had phoned to say he was coming to Glasgow for a few days and wanted to stay. His mother was delighted, less so when she discovered that Kate and the children were staying in Calverton, but he mollified her with the news that he would be house hunting for them all to move back.

He didn't lie. He would be house hunting but the first house he would be hunting for was a safe house. The family home would come second.

. Eight weeks would take him to the end of February, more than enough time. By the end of January, everything would be back to normal and he would be back with his family... or he would be dead. He tried not to dwell on that.

***

The sky was leaden. It was a typical January day, grey and damp, with a hint of sleet in the air. The streets and pavements were wet with the remnants of an earlier snow shower, the white slush collecting in the gutters and clinging tenaciously to walls. Jamie stood under the canopy of Glasgow Central, his holdall slung over his shoulder, and shivered.

He checked the time. Not yet two o'clock. That gave him time for a fortifying drink before facing his mother. She had forgiven him but she would still have a go. He decided on the Horseshoe Bar in Drury Street. It was close and, from memory, he could get something to eat there as well. He had missed breakfast. There had been a choice on offer; eat breakfast or make love with Kate. That was no contest. Food, he had decided, could wait... but that was this morning. Now his stomach was telling him his throat was slit.

The Horseshoe Bar is famous. It sits wedged in a narrow canyon of high sided buildings in a side street between Renfield Street and Mitchell Street. Its popularity meant it was still busy with lunchtime drinkers when he arrived. He scanned the pub, more in hope than expectation, and was surprised to find a space at the bar. He pushed through the drinkers and dropped his bag heavily at his feet before scanning the array of beer pumps.

Memories flooded back - Tennent's Lager, McEwan's Export, Guinness, Usher's and Maclay's and Younger's beers. He smiled. He had dreamed about these sometimes in the last few months when the sun was beating down on his back. He ordered a pint of "heavy" and a Scotch Pie and beans. After months of eating French food, he wondered if his stomach could take it. There had been times when he longed for a Scotch Pie and a pint and just thinking of them now made him salivate.

He waited patiently and cast an eye around the pub while the barman poured his drink. It was just as he remembered it. It hadn't changed at all. Then again, it probably hadn't changed in a hundred years, he mused, smiling wryly. Looking at the wrinkled and lined faces of his fellow imbibers, he thought they had been drinking here for most of that century.

He searched for a seat and his luck was in. An elderly couple, a little unsteady on their feet he noticed, rose from a small table next to the wall. They weaved precariously through the tables and the drinkers. Jamie lifted his bag and his pint and headed for the vacated space, catching the barman's eye as he moved off. The man nodded and told him his "lunch" would follow shortly.

As he worked his way through the people and tables he realised he was attracting attention. The reason was obvious. After all the months in France his skin had acquired a deep, dark bronze colour that even now, in January, hadn't faded. That made him something of a freak here where the population was a pasty white and the nearest they got to a tan was the nicotine stains on their fingers. His long hair and his expensive clothes added to his mystique, he thought. It amused him. He wondered if they were trying to place him – a game of spot the personality, he mused. But it struck him that could be a problem, given what he was here to do. He would need to think about that.

He reached the table and sat down, moving an abandoned newspaper from beneath him. It was the Daily Record. The banner on the front page, red with the name in white, identified it. He picked it up and began to read, turning to the back pages first. Old habits die hard and in this city most men started reading at the back. Sport to Glasgow men - football really – is more important than life itself. It's more important than religion. In fact, it is a religion.

He checked the league tables. In the First Division, Celtic sat top with Edinburgh's Hibs and the other half of the "Old Firm", Rangers, tied in second place. That hadn't changed either, he mused. But he had. He had lost interest in it. Jack's death had taken the fun out of it. He missed the banter between them. He tried to remember the last match he had been to but failed, other than the Celtic, Motherwell game in October and he had only been there to meet Liam. He was getting old, he mused, old and boring.

Twenty-eight years of age and already I'm behaving like an old fart.

The thought made him laugh aloud and that attracted more attention. He looked around him, meeting the strange looks, and gave them a smile. The drinkers went back to their drinks. He was just another bam-pot.

The sound of approaching footsteps distracted him and he looked up to find a girl in her early twenties standing over him. Her hair was pulled back in a severe bun and she had a little too much makeup on an otherwise pretty face. She smiled tentatively and held out a plate laden with a pie and a steaming mound of baked beans. Jamie nodded happily and she placed the plate carefully on the table in front of him, following up with a paper napkin and utensils. Given the steam rising from the plate, her warning to "be careful, it's hot" was somewhat superfluous.

He thanked her, received a radiant smile and a fluttering of eyelashes in reply, and set about his meal, breaking the crust and forking out some of the pie's meaty innards. Manna from Heaven, he thought appreciatively.

As he raised a heaped forkful of the juicy meat to his mouth, his eye caught the headline on the front of the paper. "Uproar over Nuclear Waste Convoys," it read. Intrigued, he began to read. Apparently, according to the paper at least, the good citizens of Helensburgh and Dumbarton were outraged over convoys transporting nuclear reactor waste from the Royal Naval Base at Faslane on the nearby Gareloch to reprocessing plants in England. The paper made a big thing about the potential for accidents and resultant radiation leaks. The Ministry of Defence, it went on to say, was defending the procedure. It was "perfectly safe", a spokesman said.

Well, they would say that, wouldn't they?

He read on.

"The convoys, usually consisting of two or three heavy trucks, accompanied by a MOD Police escort, travel by night to avoid the heavy traffic in the Central Belt. The MOD spokesman told the Record that the practise has been in place for a number of years without any reported incidents. The spokesman added that the MOD acknowledges the concerns of the local authorities and the people of Helensburgh and Dumbarton, as well as those in Clydebank and Glasgow. However, the MOD takes the issue of public safety very seriously and assures the public that all necessary steps to prevent accidents are taken and that safety procedures are reviewed on a regular basis."

Jamie smiled. Accidents happen because people make mistakes, he mused. It didn't matter that the MOD reviewed its procedures regularly. They could do that every day and accidents would still happen. It was that old fate thing... if it was going to happen, it would. He smiled dryly and made a mental note not to look for a house in Helensburgh or Dumbarton.

He finished his pie, scraping the last of the beans off his plate with the edge of his knife, and downed the last of his pint. The "last orders" bell was ringing as he stepped out into Drury Street and turned towards West Nile Street. It had started snowing again, flakes settling on his clothes and his hair. The wind was picking up and the thought of standing in the open at a bus stop in St. Vincent Street waiting for a bus to take him to Knightswood was gloomy. Suddenly, and not for the first time, returning to France seemed a much better option.

He looked for a taxi and luck was with him. As he walked, head down, up West Nile Street a taxi was disgorging passengers onto the pavement. He lifted his head to look. Two young girls in long coats, unbuttoned to reveal shapely legs sheathed in thigh high black leather boots, stepped, giggling, onto the concrete. An older man, in his thirties Jamie guessed, and wearing an expensive double-breasted pin-stripe suit beneath a fawn coloured trench coat followed them.

Jamie rushed forward, eager to catch the cab before it pulled away again, just as the final passenger eased himself out. This one was a portly older man sporting a heavy woollen overcoat that smelled faintly of damp or mothballs. Jamie smiled as the man hurried past him to catch his younger companions. It was an unusual pairing, he mused. If the men were hoping to get lucky they were in for a disappointment, he suspected, but only after spending a lot of their money.

The cab driver caught Jamie's look and read his thoughts. They laughed together.

'Nae chance,' the cabbie commented with a wide grin.

Jamie brushed the snow from his jacket and gave him his destination. The driver nodded, slipped the cab into gear and executed a tight U-turn. Seconds later they passed the foursome waiting at the lights at St Vincent Street, the men clinging desperately to their younger escorts. They would have a hard job keeping them, Jamie guessed.

Ten minutes later, the taxi was in Dumbarton Road passing Partick Cross. The snow had stopped again but the wind was still bitingly cold. The sun was fighting to break through the gloom but it was losing the battle.

Jamie lounged back in the seat and watched the buildings flash past. It was all so familiar. Nothing seemed to have changed here either. The Subway entrance, leading down to the tunnels that ran round Glasgow, was exactly as he remembered it. Next to it was Catherine's of Partick. The shop was famous the city over, he remembered. Not that he was an aficionado of haute couture; it was simply that Catherine's was where his mother had bought her "frock" for his wedding. She regaled everyone with that fact and it drove his father insane. He saw it as working class snobbery. She ignored him.

Right enough, his father had no right to complain, Jamie recalled with a grin. This was the man who refused to buy his wedding clobber "off the peg" and insisted on going to Hector Powe in Gordon Street instead. He had teased his father for weeks after that – a "champagne socialist" he had called him.

Happy days, he mused sadly – before Sir Charles Redmond snared him. He shook his head gloomily. Were they really happy days, he reflected? Hadn't it all started to go wrong long before that? The ghost of Max Kelman sauntered through his mind. He shook the thought away, remembering Frank Daly's advice - "don't look back, the past will destroy you".

Good advice, that.

He concentrated on the scenery flashing past the car window, if you could call grey, grime stained tenements and small shops, scenery. Everything was predominantly grey, offset by the sprinkling of white snow that now covered the roadways. Occasionally, a garish display in a shop window or a red and white striped barber's pole gave a splash of colour to the otherwise uniform drabness. He recognised familiar and comfortable landmarks, mostly pubs. He had partaken of the odd libation in most of them, he smiled vacantly, but that too was way back in the past.

On his left, Partick Pubic Library filled his view. A square block of a building built just before the second war, in 1935, its single storey structure sits diagonally off the line of the Dumbarton Road. It is, in its own small way, quite imposing with its balustrade parapet along the top and its protruding corner bay with the coat of arms of Glasgow emblazoned on both sides. Another reminder of the city's former greatness.

This area had once been prosperous, he remembered. The old buildings that remained told the story - Partick Burgh Hall and Partick Police Office to name but two – and even the famous Partick Thistle football team had played here. Their park had been just off Castlebank Street until the early 1900s before they moved to Maryhill. Aye, he mused, maybe the old buildings were still here but the prosperity had melted away.

Minutes later and the cab turned right into Crow Road. There were more remembered landmarks here for Jamie and more memories. The Rosevale Bar and the now derelict Rosevale Cinema flashed past on his left just before the turn. He had spent nights there, usually in the back row with a girl and that girl had usually been Carol Whyte. He wondered, idly, what she was doing now. She could have been with him, he reflected. Sometimes the memories were not of better times. This trip down memory lane was depressing, he decided. Think of the future, he told himself.

Aye, think of the future... like that's not depressing.

The taxi passed Broomhill Cross and headed on towards Jordanhill and Anniesland. The grey began to disappear and the houses and flats became more substantial. This was the suburbs where the middle classes multiplied and prospered. It gave the workers something to aspire to.

They passed beneath the railway at Jordanhill Station and swung left into Southbrae Drive. The houses were even bigger and better here. Large red sandstone terraced and semi-detached villas lined the road on both sides before Jordanhill School appeared on the right. Its size and stature gave it away. He could never have gone there. His father's pockets weren't deep enough.

Beyond the school the houses on the left were more modern but still substantial. It was nice here. Peaceful too; not unlike where they had lived before on the Bearsden Road.

As the taxi approached Anniesland Road the houses changed again. Big Victorian and Edwardian Villas with high hedges were the norm here. That would all change in a minute or so. He pictured his route; left into Anniesland Road and then right into Lincoln Avenue past the telephone exchange and the post Office sorting office and into the edge of Knightswood. He was almost home... but it wasn't home any longer..

Everything flashed past now as he prepared himself for the reunion: Alderman Road, the gold course, the high flats, the gravel football pitches, Archerhill Road, and then he was there. The taxi stopped outside the house and he saw a curtain twitch. The driver slid back the little connecting window and pointed to the meter. Jamie found a Five Pound note and slipped it through. He made the cabbie's day when he told him to keep the change.

And then he was out on the pavement. He felt apprehensive. Like a small boy coming home with a rip in his best trousers and his shoes covered in mud. He stood by the gate, memories flooding back, almost overwhelming him and then the door opened and she was there. A little older, her hair a little whiter, but the smile on her face was the same. He pushed through and ran up the path, dropping his bag and catching her in his arms, sweeping her off her feet. 'Hello Mum,' he said. He held her close, felt the anxiety flow from her, and knew, immediately, that he couldn't stay. He would have to find somewhere else and think of an excuse.

Chapter Forty-four

Conor Whelan stepped down from the Gourock to Glasgow train onto platform 10 at Glasgow Central at eleven-five am. Here, under the high canopy of the old station, the air was reasonably clear, only hint of thin fog seeping in from the outside. He looked down the length of the platform, searching for Jamie at the ticket barrier. He didn't find him; not immediately anyway.

His eyes roamed over the faces. There were a couple of men of Jamie's build but one was an older man, probably in his late forties or early fifties, and the other had long hair and a beard. This man was wearing a heavy Parka, the hood covering most of his head with his. His eyes roamed over the man then checked and returned. As he cut the distance between them, he saw the man smile and then start to laugh. Conor's eyes opened wide in surprise. Jamie, for it was him, had changed dramatically.

He quickened his pace, trotting now, his heavy coat flapping around his legs. He fumbled in his pocket, searching for his ticket, and thrust it in front of the ticket collector. The man gave it a perfunctory glance and waved him through.

Jamie stepped forward, his arm open. Conor gripped him in his customary bear hug and grinned. Other travellers, hurrying through the barrier, were caught unaware by their antics and swerved to avoid them, drawing them pained looks. The looks were wasted.

Finally, they broke apart and looked at one another. It had been a long time, Jamie realised, and his appearance had changed. Conor, on the other hand, looked no different. He waited for the big American's reaction.

Conor shook his head slowly in amazement, his hands on Jamie's arms as he looked him up and down. 'Jeeze, kid, you look prehistoric,' he said, laughing. 'What's with the hair and the beard? Disguise?'

Jamie grinned back at him. 'More like camouflage,' Jamie retorted. 'I'll tell you all about it later. Let's get out of here.'

They walked together down past the old timber booking office, past the big World War 1 shell that stood in the middle of the concourse, collection point for donations for the wounded and disabled, and out into Gordon Street. 'Where are we going?' Conor asked as they stepped out into the fog.

'We need to have a quiet chat,' Jamie replied, sounding serious now. 'We could go to The Horseshoe but it'll be busy... and noisy. The Pot Still is just up the road in Hope Street,' he said. 'It'll be busy too, but quieter... whisky drinkers are more refined,' he went on, laughing quietly. 'It claims to have the biggest collection of malt whiskies in the country.'

'Sounds good to me,' Conor enthused. 'What are we going to chat about?' he said, using the English "chat" rather than talk.

'You know what we're going to chat about,' Jamie threw back, smiling a challenge at his friend. The American returned it.

The Pot Still sits at the corner of Hope Street and West Regent Lane, a throwback to the 1800's. Conor marvelled at the place as they pushed through into its warm, cosy interior. The solid dark wood bar with shelved walls on three sides beneath the magnificently corniced ceiling supported by enormous pillars took him back in time. The range of whiskies on display behind the bar took his breath away.

Jamie grinned at him. 'Things might be bigger in America but they don't get as good as this, eh?' he laughed, guiding Conor to a seat near the back. 'What's your poison?' he went on, sweeping his arm demonstratively towards the shelves of bottles.

'You choose, kid. You're the native. I'm just a visiting colonialist,' he joked, still staring in awe at the display.

All around, the other patrons were sniffing glasses and sipping at strangely named whiskies. Conor gazed through the smoke filled atmosphere. Why had he never found this place before, he wondered. It was full of people enjoying a drink but the ambiance was sedate and relaxed. It wasn't your average bar.

Jamie returned from the bar with two glasses of golden sunshine filled liquid and a small jug of water. He pulled a seat out from the small table with the toe of his shoe and sat down, placing the glasses and jug carefully on the highly polished surface.

'No Coke?' Conor queried, straight faced.

Jamie drew him a look of abhorrence. 'That could get you thrown out on your ear, Jamie said beneath his voice. That is sacrilege. Only heathens mix malt whisky with anything other than more malt whisky... or a wee drop of water.' He saw the smile at the corner of Conor's lips and realised his leg had been well and truly pulled.

'So what did you get me?' Conor asked, raising the glass and sniffing the whisky like a connoisseur.

'It's a Knockdhu 12 year old,' Jamie reported, sniffing the aroma appreciatively. It smelled aromatic with a touch of honey and lemon coming through. He swirled it in the glass, watching the yellowy amber liquid cling to the glass. Conor watched him, slightly amused. Jamie saw him watching and grinned. 'Well, are you just going to sit there watching me or drink it?' he chided teasingly.

Conor raised his glass and sipped, his face lighting up as the initial sweetness of the malt took him by surprise. 'Wow,' was all he said as he replaced the glass on the table.

They spent the next few minutes talking about family. Photographs were brought out from wallets and shared. Happy memories remembered. With those out of the way, it was Conor who brought them back to the serious business.

'So what's with the camouflage?' he asked, nodding in the direction of Jamie's beard and long hair. Jamie said nothing but simply raised his hand to his temple and lifted his locks, turning his head to the right.

'Jeeeesus,' Conor whispered, his eyes widening.

'He missed,' Jamie smiled grimly. 'But only just.'

'The guy who wants brought out?' Jamie nodded and sipped at his whisky, waiting for the next question. 'Have you worked out how you're going to do it?'

Jamie shook his head this time. 'I can't; not yet,' he said. He looked around. They were in their own little bubble, like everyone else in the pub. People were interested in their own company, not anyone else's. 'Last time I spoke to him was New Year's day. He was leaving on the second; should be here by now.'

'Where?' Conor asked.

'That's the problem, I don't know exactly. He's staying in a place called Alexandria... it's near Dumbarton, but I don't have an address. What makes it worse is he'll be with the rest of his ASU, including Doherty. The wee bastard might not have recognised me last time but if he sees me again talking with Liam Fitzpatrick he'll start to wonder.'

Conor nodded thoughtfully. 'I told you this is too much for one man,' he said softly. Then: 'What were you thinking of doing?'

Jamie smiled wryly. 'Alexandria isn't big. I was going to head down there for a few days...'

'You're joking, right?'

'No, not at all; do you have a better idea?'

'Any idea has to be better than that, kid. Apart from the fact that finding your boy will be down to luck, what happens if he's with this Doherty? Think Doherty will just put it down to coincidence?' Jamie shrugged in response. The same thought had crossed his mind. 'No, I don't either,' Conor continued. 'From what you say, if that guy sees you again anywhere near that place, you're blown.' He waited a moment, letting Jamie digest that, then added: 'He doesn't know me, though.'

Jamie shook his head dourly. 'I've told you before Conor, I don't want you involved...'

'And I've told you before, I don't care. You need a hand with this. You got anyone else in mind?'

'Clara Whitelaw,' Jamie answered, averting his eyes.

'The doctor lady from Ultra?'

'Psychologist,' Jamie corrected.

It was Conor's turn to shake his head. His reason, however, was disbelief; not refusal. 'You think she's up to it?' he demanded.

Jamie smiled back at him. 'She's no angel,' he said.

'You know this for a fact, do you?' Conor fired back. He saw Jamie's cheeks redden, and rushed on. 'Okay, don't answer that,' he said, smiling himself now. 'It's still better if I do it,' he continued. 'It's harder for a woman to make contact unless she's expected. She can't just walk up to your boy, can she? And come to think of it, does she even know him? Is she in on the old dude's shenanigans?'

'She knows him; she's seen photographs. He's on the Army and MI5 watch list. She's got that advantage over you.'

Conor pushed his chair back and lifted his empty glass. 'Time for another,' he said. 'What do you want?'

Jamie took a cigarette from his packet of Gauloise and offered the pack to Conor. The American wrinkled his nose in disgust and took a pack of Lucky Strike from his own pocket. 'I'll stick with these,' he said, grinning. 'Now, what do you want to drink?'

'Surprise me,' Jamie replied, flicking open his Zippo to light the Disc Bleu.

While Conor was at the bar, Jamie thought through his options. It didn't take long. He didn't have many. Conor was right on almost every count. He couldn't afford to be seen by Doherty; finding Liam was down to pot luck; and Clara would stick out like a debutante at a Gypsy wedding. When she opened her mouth to speak her accent would drop her in it. She could disguise it, sure, but one slip would be one too many. And how would she make contact with Liam, anyway, he mused... walk up and say, "hi stranger, want to buy me a drink?" No, it wouldn't work. So what was he left with? Conor's offer. And even that was full of holes, the biggest of which was that Conor wouldn't recognise the Irishman even if he walked up and slapped him.

Conor returned and placed two fresh glasses on the table. 'Worked it out yet?' he asked as he sat down. 'You were sure giving it a lot of thought.'

Jamie smiled and lifted the whisky to his nose, drawing in the aroma. He followed the ritual as before, swirling the deep golden liquor around the glass and sniffing it again. He could smell hints of peat with toffee, liquorice and flowers behind it. The taste was intense but sweet and peaty. He drank some down, a taste of ripe fruit and honey lingering on his palate. 'Islay?' he asked thoughtfully.

Conor smiled. 'Bunnahabhain, 12 Year Old Single Malt,' he replied. 'Is that Islay?'

'Yes, that's Islay. You can tell the Islay whiskies by their peaty nose.'

'Lots of them, are there?'

'For a small island, yes, lots,' Jamie confirmed, laughing. 'There were 23 distilleries operating on the island at one time. It's down to 10 or 11 now, I think.'

Conor grinned. 'Wow. Guess it'll take us all day to go through them all then,' he suggested.

'That would certainly take our minds off things,' Jamie laughed. 'Maybe better to come back another time.'

'Yeah, sounds like a plan. So, back to your problem; what have you come up with, if anything?'

'I've decided you're right. I can't be seen and Clara Whitelaw would have a hard job making contact.'

'So that leaves me,' Conor retorted, smugly.

'Yes, that leave you but there's still a problem. You don't know him and he doesn't know you. What you going to do; walk around asking everyone you meet if they're Liam Fitzpatrick?' Jamie suggested sarcastically.

Conor drank some of his whisky and looked crestfallen. He lit a Lucky Strike and both men sat for a while drawing on their smokes and sipping the whisky.

Two men entered the pub, both dressed in leathers and wearing motor cycle crash helmets. No one paid them much attention, least of all Conor and Liam, until that is, they removed their helmets. It wasn't two men but one man and a stunning girl with long blonde hair that tumbled down over her shoulders. Until that moment, she had been just an anonymous shape. Now every pair of male eyes in the pub turned to admire her. But Jamie was off on another track.

'That's it,' he said, looking over at Conor.

'What's it?' Conor asked, still eyeing the girl appreciatively.

'We both thought she was a man when she walked in. It was only when she took off her helmet we saw it was a woman. Wearing a helmet with the visor down makes you anonymous.'

Conor looked at him, the idea finally taking hold. 'So you go down wearing leathers and a helmet,' he said. 'But you still have to make contact with your boy and to do that you need to take the frigging helmet off.'

'No I don't. You can do that for me.'

Chapter Forty-five

Jamie and Conor left the pub just after half past two as the door was closing, Conor bemoaning the city's licensing laws. They had managed to sample three more malts, a Highland Park 18 Year Old from Orkney, a Mortlach 16 Year Old and finally, a Laphroaig 30 Year Old which, Jamie remarked with a laugh, was even older than he was. The long, succulent flavour of it remained with them as they headed back into the centre of the city, looking for somewhere to eat.

They had resolved a lot in their three hours in the Pot Still but Jamie still had one thing on his mind. They found a Steak House in George Street, The Georgic, sitting between Montrose Street and North Portland Street, just across from Albion Street and the Daily Express office, and settled down for a late lunch.

Jamie didn't waste any time raising his outstanding problem, assuring Conor that it wasn't a problem as such before he started. He doubted Conor could help in any event. This was more personal than anything else.

'We were talking about my folks earlier,' he said as he forked a chunk of rare steak into his mouth. Conor looked up, waiting for the anticipated follow up. 'I'm staying with them just now.'

'Yeah, you said. You got a problem with that?' Conor delved perceptively.

'It's not a problem... it's more...' Jamie found himself stumbling over the words. 'I don't think I should have landed myself on them. My mother worries...'

'Sure she does. All Moms worry about their sons and daughters... and you give yours more cause than most,' Conor stated bluntly. 'Same could be said for Kate,' he went on, relentlessly.

Jamie didn't respond to the accusation but his eyes betrayed him. Guilt, always his companion these days, was waving out from behind them.

'I'm going to move out,' he announced. 'This thing I have to sort is going to cause more worry than it's worth. I don't want to pile more onto her. I start staying out at night or coming home late she'll lie awake all night.'

'What about your Pop?'

Jamie smiled at the Americanism. His father would hate to be called "Pop". 'He's got a vague idea of what I do,' he said. 'He knows I'm here for a purpose other than house hunting... but he keeps it to himself and tries to keep my mother calm.'

'You got a place to go?'

'No, not yet. I need to make contact with Liam Fitzpatrick first... find out where the bloody attack is taking place,' he said softly, looking around the restaurant cautiously. The place was empty.'

'Some of the guys down at Holy Loch have places up here they use when they're on leave. You want me to ask around?'

'Really?' Jamie retorted, interested.

'I'm not saying these places are five star, kid... They might be knockin' shops,' he added, laughing. 'But at least nobody would go looking for you there... or would they?' he added, laughing louder.

'If you can find out for me that'll be great. You're right, no one important would look for me there... can't speak for my "Pop" though,' he threw in, grinning now.

'Okay, consider it done. So what do we do now?'

Jamie looked around the restaurant again. A young couple had come in but were seated well away from them and the waiting staff were busy serving. He turned back to Conor, keeping his voice low none the less. 'I need to arrange for a weapon...'

'Weapons,' Conor corrected. 'I'm coming too, remember?'

Jamie sighed. 'Yeah, I remember. It's against my better judgement, but I need you... So, weapons. I've got a name and a number. I'll check it out on Monday. Before that I'll look for a bike and some gear. My old leathers are still at home... they should fit me still, but I'll need a new helmet. One that hides my face.'

'Your old bike is down in Dunoon,' Conor said thoughtfully. 'I saw it a couple of days ago.'

Jamie's face lit up nostalgically. 'You're kidding,' he said. 'The Bonneville?'

'Yep, the "Beast",' Conor replied, smiling at Jamie's delight at mention of the big Triumph 650.

'I sold it on to one of the guys when I was shipped back home. Don't think he's getting much use out of it now, though. You want me to ask if he'll sell it back?'

Jamie grinned happily. 'Would you? The sight of me on that bike again will frighten the life out of my mother every bit as much as my late nights, right enough, but yeah, get it back for me if you can.'

'No guarantees, but I'll ask,' Conor agreed cheerfully. 'Is that everything then?' he asked. 'Cos if it is, what say we head back to that Pot Still place when we finish up here and you can continue my education.'

Jamie laughed again. Conor Whelan was great medicine. 'Sounds good to me,' he quipped. 'Just don't be falling overboard from the Dunoon ferry on your way back home.'

Conor pulled an insulted look. 'I'm an officer, kid. Officers don't fall overboard, they just lie down and get someone to carry them off.'

They finished their meals in a better mood than when they started, and left The Georgic for the Pot Still at twenty minutes to five. Conor wanted to be first in the queue when the doors opened at five. His "education" would recommence at five minutes past.

Chapter Forty-six

Monday 7 January 1974

Jamie left his parents' house just after 9am and walked up Great Western Road to Knightswood Cross. He had a phone call to make and his inbuilt caution, maybe even paranoia, prevented him using the home phone. It was a ridiculous thought, he knew that, but his world revolved around ridiculous thoughts and the Brigadier knew where he was staying while he was here. That was another good reason for moving out.

The trees were bare, their leafless branches pointing skywards like extra-terrestrial limbs pointing to home. The sky was its usual grey... all shades of grey this morning, he noticed from light, almost white, to dark, almost black. The ground was hard and frost sparkled in the feeble light.

His thoughts drifted to Kate. They had spoken on the telephone the night before but his mother had got in on the act, hogging the line to talk about her grandchildren for almost forty minutes. He couldn't complain; not after what he had put her through. But he still missed Kate and there was an emptiness inside him that simply talking with her didn't fill. It outweighed everything, even the excitement and adrenalin rush of his "work".

His mother had seen the loneliness showing in his face when the call had ended. Guiltily, he knew that would make it easier for him to leave. His mother would accept his missing Kate and his children without question. That was how normal people were. His guilt was there because he wasn't really normal.

The red call box at the cross was vacant. He pulled open the door and accepted the familiar smell. The road outside was busy, traffic heavy in both directions, and it made the call difficult. He pressed the receiver against his right ear and pushed the digit finger of his left hand into his left ear as the ringing tone came back to him.

'J. S. Andrew & Company, good morning,' a young woman welcomed politely.

'I'd like to speak with Mr Andrew, if possible; my name is Ferryman' Jamie replied, equally polite.

'He's rather busy,' the voice came back, protectively.

'I don't think that will be possible at the moment.'

Yes it will.

'I'm an associate of an old friend of his, Charles Redmond. Charles asked me to call. If you could just pass that on to Mr Andrew I'm sure he'll give me a moment.' There was just enough in Jamie's tone to suggest that it would be better that she ask Mr Andrew than not.

'Hold on a moment,' the girl responded. Jamie smiled blithely.

A moment passed and then, with a click, a man's voice came to him. 'Jon Andrew,' the voice stated. 'How can I help you, Mr Ferryman?' His tone conveyed curiosity with just a nuance of apprehension lurking behind it.

'Good of you to spare a moment to talk to me, sir,' Jamie replied. 'Charles did say you are a very busy man. However, I have a small problem of some urgency and he did say you were the man to see.'

'Is it a police matter, Mr Ferryman?'

'It's somewhat more delicate, actually. I wonder if it would be possible to meet with you... say this afternoon?'

There was a moment's hesitation and then Jon Andrew spoke again. 'I do have a slot at three-thirty today; does that suit?'

'Perfectly,' Jamie replied. 'I'll see you then.'

'Yes, I look forward to it,' the solicitor said unenthusiastically.

Jamie smiled again. No, you're not. 'Goodbye then, until this afternoon,' he said and replaced the handset.

***

'We're on... this afternoon, half past three. Can you make it?' Jamie said as Conor came on the line. He had spent a few minutes chatting with Conor's wife, Mary, before the big man himself arrived. Her voice told him his call was expected.

'Where?' Conor enquired, speaking normally.

'Glasgow. The man's office in Hope Street.'

'Have you checked it out?'

Jamie laughed. Conor was the consummate professional spy. 'Not yet,' he retorted. 'But I will, don't worry. So, back to my question... Are you coming.'

Yeah, I'll be there. I'll pick you up at your Mom's place before three. That do?'

'Sure, that's fine... You've got a car?' he added, almost as an afterthought.

'No, a magic carpet; of course I've got wheels,' Conor retorted sarcastically. 'Mary's Dad has said I can use his. Not what I'm used to but it'll do.'

'Okay, see you later... And Conor, thanks.'

'Don't embarrass me,' Conor laughed and cut the line.

Jamie stepped out from the call box and filled his lungs with cold, fresh air. A long way back down Great Western Road he spotted a green, white and gold Corporation bus coming from the direction of Drumchapel. He thought about the question Conor had thrown into the conversation and, without a second thought, made his way across the busy junction at Knightswood Cross to the bus stop to join the short queue already there.

The bus, a Number 2 destined for Cathcart on the city's south side, finally pulled to a halt at the stop and disgorged passengers. As the last of these stepped down from the platform, the green, white and gold monster swallowed the next lot, Jamie among them.

He climbed the stair to the upper deck and made his way up the centre aisle to the front. There was a spare seat beside a heavily made up lady of indeterminate years and he plumped himself down beside her. She turned slowly towards him with a disapproving look then turned her attention back to the world outside, peering through a small circular spot on the window that she had cleared on the condensation. He studied her for a moment. Her expensive clothes, and they were expensive, did nothing for her. A big fur coat made from God knows how many poor animals was wrapped around her and she had a matching hat on top of her dry, frizzy hair. The makeup didn't cover her poor skin and she had skinny hands with arthritic fingers. He thought she was trying too hard to hold onto youth but it had escaped long ago.

He switched off from her and looked around, taking in the familiar sights, sounds and smells of Glasgow's public transport. All the windows were, as usual, steamed up with little patches wiped on each to allow people to see where they had been and where they were going. On the front window, someone had cleared a large chunk and little pools of water had gathered on the bottom edge, trickling down the window like tiny worms.

Ahead of him, through the patch of clear glass, he could see the traffic backing up at the lights at Anniesland Cross. All around him, people shrunk into heavy coats and wrapped scarves around their heads and mouths. Red eyes and runny noses the order of the day. There was a background noise of the bus engine, chatter, sneezes, coughs, noses being blown into soggy handkerchiefs, and throats cleared. Where did all that phlegm go now, he wondered vacantly. Roll on summer.

The smells were, if anything, worse. Diesel, damp, sweat and cigarette smoke mixed with a range of perfumes, cheap and expensive... A cocktail to give the faint-hearted the dry-boak. He pulled out his cigarettes to add to the fug and received a censorious look from his companion. He smiled disarmingly back at her but his youthful charms were having no effect other than a pointed wrinkling of her nose to convey her distaste. A vision of Roger Daltry of The Who came to him then. He smiled wryly. The way things were going he wouldn't have a problem; he'd be dead long before he got old. He looked at the woman again, a new thought forming; If you don't like smoke you should have sat downstairs. He kept smiling to hide it.

He flicked his Zippo and drew on the flame. The aroma of the French cigarette filled the space around them and he waited, hopefully, for the woman's complexion to turn green. Disappointingly, it didn't. She just stared stonily ahead.

The bus made its way past Anniesland and the big mansions on Great Western Road slid past on the right. Next, Bingham's Pond appeared through the murk and his thoughts turned to Roisin. What was he to do about her? Could he manoeuvre Orlagh Duggan into the frame for the bombing? It wouldn't be easy... not with Clara Whitelaw on the scent, but he had to try.

The bus took nearly forty minutes to reach the city. He got off in Renfrew Street. It was a little milder here, but not much. People still hurried by, eager to get from point A to point B as quickly as possible, to escape from the cold. He pulled his Parka tightly around him and zipped it up to his neck. He left the hood down.

He made his way along Renfrew Street and turned right into Hope Street past the site of the old Majestic Ballroom. A new shopping centre was taking shape from the rubble. A big sign fixed to the security fence around the site announced the opening of the new Savoy Centre later in the year. At least they were keeping the old name, Jamie mused cynically. Glasgow, city of change... Aye, right!

He sauntered down Hope Street, taking in the shops and offices dotted along its length. He crossed over Sauchiehall Street and window shopped for a while at the Watt Brothers store that stretched all the way to the corner of Bath Street. He was on the downward slope now, heading towards West Regent Street, West George Street, St Vincent Street and, finally, Bothwell Street. The Central Station and the Central Hotel were just beyond.

His destination, Carswell Chambers, sat at 135 Hope Street, the same side of the road as Watt Brothers. He crossed over to the other side of the road. He wasn't visiting the place, he just wanted to look. He carried on down the hill past the Pot Still. The door was still locked but the shutters were up and he could see staff inside preparing for opening at eleven o'clock. He smiled at the memory of "educating" Conor a few days earlier. They still had a few hundred whiskies to sample from the pubs colossal range. He hoped they had the chance to do that.

Carswell Chambers sat a little further downhill from the Pot Still. He stopped at the corner of West Regent Lane and looked across at the building, taking his time to light another cigarette. His Gauloise were almost finished which, he imagined, would cheer up his mother a bit.

He studied the building carefully. Six floors of office accommodation, seven if you included the ground, rose majestically up into the grey sky. He let his eyes wander up the façade. He could make out small spires set at each corner and arches and balconies encasing the windows of the top two floors. In its day, it was probably considered architecturally outstanding, he imagined, but its day was long past.

The red sandstone exterior was dark, almost black. Years of industrial grime, soot and birdlime had taken their toll, and the windows were covered in several layers of Glasgow filth. The people in the offices would probably need the lights on all day to see anything, even in summer.

He lounged on the pavement outside the Pot Still for a while and took it all in. Two pillars, topped with an ornate frieze, flanked the entrance. The frieze depicted a shield with the number of the building in the centre and a couple of chubby Cherubs, one on each side, facing to right and left. Just above those two little fat boys were two lions sitting on their haunches, shields between their paws. It was a statement of some sort, he imagined, but, with the passage of time, he doubted if anyone could remember what that statement was.

He crossed over Hope Street to the building and stood outside the entrance. There were high wrought iron gates that closed at night, enclosing a small inner space, a vestibule, and beyond that were heavy, wood panelled doors opening up into a big reception area. Bright fluorescent lights, suspended from the high ceiling, illuminated the area but he could see nothing of interest.

There was a business directory fixed to the wall. He scanned the list looking for J. S. Andrew & Company, Solicitors. He found the firm on the third floor. It seemed they shared the floor with an Asian Import/Export business, Iqbal and Company, and a firm of Theatrical Agents, Samantha Wolf and Associates.

He wondered about emergency exits. There would be some, he knew that, he just wanted to know where. He didn't expect to have to use them but he liked to be prepared... just in case.

Chapter Forty-seven

Same day

Conor, as promised, arrived before three. He spent a little time in the house saying hello to Jamie's folks and making an excuse for taking Jamie away for a while. Jamie was grateful. His mother liked Conor a lot and the excuse was all the more convincing coming from The American.

They drove into Glasgow in silence and left the car in West Nile Street. The car was a compact little Austin 1100. It wasn't the sort of car Conor normally drove but it was certainly more suited to driving in Glasgow with its narrow roads. It wasn't Boston or New York. They stepped out from the cramped little Austin and Jamie pulled change from his pocket to feed the parking meter.

'Head on down to Central Station and wait for me in the tearoom,' Jamie instructed as they arrived at Carswell Chambers. 'I shouldn't be too long.'

Conor regarded him placidly. He decided there was no point in arguing. He reminded himself he was lucky to have been allowed this far. He was nervous. Jamie, on the other hand, seemed totally relaxed. 'Don't you ever get anxious?' he asked, eyeing his friend up and down.

Jamie returned his look. 'That's like asking me if I don't get scared,' Jamie laughed, drawing hard on the cigarette he was smoking. 'Of course I am, I just don't let it show.' He blew out a plume of white smoke mixed with condensed breath. The day wasn't getting any warmer.

The big American shook his head uneasily.

'Relax Conor, this is an easy bit,' Jamie continued lightly. 'Nothing is going to happen to me in here. Go and get a coffee.'

With another shake of the head, Conor sloped off down the hill towards Bothwell Street. He didn't look back but he could feel Jamie's eyes on him the whole way. He went reluctantly but, he had to concede, Jamie had a point. Nothing was likely to happen to him in there. He, himself, was probably in more danger from drinking the foul coffee they served in the station tearoom than Jamie was in visiting this schmuck lawyer.

Jamie watched Conor until he had crossed Hope Street and turned left into Gordon Street. The streets were reasonably quiet. There were few pedestrians about and what traffic there was, was light. There were no suspicious characters. Other than me, he thought with a cynical smile.

Satisfied that Conor was doing as he had asked, Jamie took a final pull on his cigarette and tossed the butt into the roadway. It sizzled in a pile of slush before dying. Turning, he entered the small vestibule he had viewed earlier and climbed the short flight of steps to the main door. He didn't need to look at the address board again, he knew exactly where he was going.

Beyond the outer was the larger reception area. An "Enquiries" desk sat unmanned on one side with a narrow stairway behind it leading to the upper floors. In the past, there would have been a uniformed commissionaire on duty here but the big companies that had occupied the place in those days were no longer here. Now, there was just a mix of small businesses surviving on a shoestring. A commissionaire was an expense they could well do without.

There was a ramshackle lift. One of those wooden oblong boxes, a bit like a coffin stood on end, with two sliding grill doors. He decided to take the stairs.

Here too there were signs of former grandeur. A quality carpet covered the stairway. The quality still showed around the edges of the treads but the centres were threadbare and, in some spots, the wood below showed through. The wood panelling on his right was dark with years of neglect but its quality was obvious. On his left, the latticed metal framework of the lift shaft was gathering dust.

On the first landing, a double half glass panelled door faced the lift grill. A plaque on the wall at the top of the stair announced the occupiers of the floor and their room numbers. Behind the door, Jamie could hear the staccato clicking of typewriters, muted conversation and female laughter.

He climbed on. The carpet seemed a little better between the first and second floors. Below him, he heard the clatter of the lift doors as they opened and closed, and then there was the hum of the electric motor. The heavy cables in the shaft began to move and the lift started to rise. It passed him just as he reached the second landing, continuing its ascent... the coffin on its way up to the Pearly Gates, he thought with a smile.

The second landing replicated the first. There were no sounds behind the door now though. He chanced a look beyond the door. A dark corridor stretched away to left and right with doors off on both sides. Some of the doors had glass panels on their upper half that allowed some meagre light to filter through into the corridor. Without those lights, the corridor would be in darkness. No one home, he surmised.

He closed the door and started his final climb. Again, the carpet seemed better here. People were lazy. No one, it seemed, was prepared to climb higher than the first floor landing.

There were sounds of activity on third floor. Typewriters were clicking and voices carried to him. As he reached for the door, it swung inwards and an attractive woman and a garishly dressed man emerged onto the landing. Their conversation was interspersed with numerous "darlings" and gestures. Jamie smiled and stood back to allow them access to the lift call button. They ignored him. It was then he remembered who shared this floor with the lawyer... Samantha Wolf and Associates, Theatrical Agents. He wondered if this was Samantha and the man, if it was a man, was one of her associates. It was either that or they were a couple of out of work thespians. Between jobs, as they say, he recalled with a smile.

He pushed past them and into the corridor. J. S. Andrew, Solicitors, was third door down on the right according to the wall plaque outside on the landing. There was more activity here. Muffled voices behind doors and the clicking of numerous typewriters interspersed with the sharp tinkle of their bells as they reached the carriage return point. It was musical in its own way, like some manic symphony, he mused.

Further down the corridor, a door opened and a dark skinned man stepped out into the corridor, glanced in Jamie's direction, and pushed through into a facing room. That would be the Asian Import/Export offices down there.

A small oblong plaque outside the third door on the right told Jamie he was in the right place. There were two names in gold lettering; Jonathon S. Andrew LL.B.(Hons) and Evelyn Trott LL.B. He gripped the handle and pushed the door open. It fed into a bright reception area with a scattering of chairs and a small coffee table with a selection of magazines and some newspapers.

A young woman appeared at the reception desk, alerted by the tiny bell that rang as he opened the door. She was well dressed. Presentable, just right for the job, Jamie imagined. She smiled at him enquiringly and he smiled back.

'Good afternoon. My name is Ferryman, we spoke this morning I think,' he announced with a smile. 'I have an appointment with Mr Andrew at three – thirty,' he continued, sneaking a glance at his watch. It was now 3.25pm.

He watched as the girl looked down at a diary in front of her and then smiled again. 'Please take a seat,' she said. 'Mr Andrew won't be long.' Mr Ferryman was on the list.

Jamie chose a chair and sat down, unbuttoning his coat. The girl disappeared and there was only the faint smell of her perfume to announce that she had been there. Once again there was the sound of muffled voices and the clatter of typewriters. One day, someone would invent silent typewriters, he mused. The noise was deafening.

He flicked through the selection of magazines and newspapers. Cosmopolitan and Woman's Own figured in a minor way... Mr Andrew didn't get many female clients it appeared, along with Punch, Practical Motorist and a couple of well-thumbed Mayfair magazines for the men. He pushed the glossy offerings aside and picked up a newspaper. It was the Daily Record.

He flicked through it, not particularly interested, until an article on page three caught his attention. A picture of a submarine and below that another of two heavy lorries. Protests at Faslane, the by-line read. It was the same story he had read a couple of days earlier but this time it took the story further. Local people were organising a protest against the transportation of the Polaris submarines' nuclear waste from Faslane to the waste reprocessing plant at Windscale in Cumbria. CND had promised support and people were being rallied from all over the UK. The next shipment of the lethal waste, according to the paper, was due at the end of the month and the forces of opposition were gathering. Everything, it seemed, was happening at the end of January.

He heard a door open and looked up. The girl was back, smile fixed on her face. 'Mr Andrew will see you now,' she said, standing back to allow Jamie through into the inner sanctum. Jamie tossed the paper back onto the small table and rose to his feet, the girl's eyes watching his every move.

He walked past her into an outer office. Three other women, headphones attached to their ears, slaved over typewriters while a fourth, older, seemed to be working from a lengthy document opened in front of her. None of them paid him any attention. His escort ushered him to a solid wooden door and opened it without knocking, keeping hold of the handle as he passed and closing it behind him.

Jonathon Andrew rose from behind his desk and came forward to meet him, hand outstretched. He was not what Jamie had expected. Nowhere close, in fact. He was small, about five foot six, with dark hair, greying slightly at the temples, swept back from his forehead. He was wearing a charcoal grey chalk stripe suit, a white shirt with what Jamie took to be a Royal Air Force tie, and gleaming, expensive, black leather shoes.

Jamie took the hand and shook it. There was strength there.

'Well now, Mr Ferryman,' the lawyer started. 'What can I do for you? Your call was cryptic, to say the least,' he continued with just a hint of amusement.

Jamie decided he liked him. First impressions were usually right and he was picking up the right vibes. He released the man's hand and slipped his free hand into his inside jacket pocket, pulling out the envelope containing the letter of introduction. 'Perhaps you should read this first,' he said. 'It will make things easier in the long run,' he said, returning the man's smile. 'We'll both know where we stand.'

The solicitor took the envelope and turned it over in his hand, his brow knitting a little at this unexpected development. He returned to his chair and picked up a thin red leather handled letter opener from among the papers on his desk. Carefully, he slid the blade into the tiny gap at the fold of the flap and slid it along. Stealing a glance at Jamie, he extracted the folded sheet of paper from inside and opened it. Almost unconsciously, he took a pair of pince-nez spectacles from the desk and slipped them on, beginning to read.

Jamie sat in a chair facing the man across the big desk and looked around. He hadn't been in many lawyer's offices... none in fact, but it held few surprises. He doubted that Mr Andrew was stupid enough to keep the hardware here, but you never know. A quick look round more or less confirmed it. The office was utilitarian, the furniture basic and functional. There were files everywhere. Mounds of them; in piles on the floor and scattered across the desk. Three grey metal filing cabinets were set against one wall and a bookcase filled the other. Dusty legal tomes ranged along the shelves but none seemed to have moved in quite a while.

Finally, the lawyer stopped reading and looked up. 'So you work for my friend Sir Charles,' he said, the humour now gone from his eyes.

'I didn't realise you two were that close,' Jamie retorted cheekily. 'You must be one of the exalted few,' he continued. 'He hasn't got many friends.'

The man smiled again. 'Maybe "friend" is the wrong word,' he laughed. 'I take it you're not one of those either?'

'No, I can't say I am.'

'So you're one of his shadowy associates?'

Jamie smiled coyly. He wasn't an associate but it was good enough for the moment. 'In a manner of speaking,' he said. 'I do the odd job for him.'

That brought out a genuine laugh from the other man. It didn't take much imagination to work out what multiple sins that could cover.

'So what is it you want?' the lawyer asked again.

'Doesn't it say in the letter?'

'No, it doesn't,' Jon Andrew smiled equably. 'It said I should give you whatever assistance you need; no more, no less... Which brings me back to my question; what is it you want?' The solicitor leaned back in his chair and watched Jamie carefully.

'I need two handguns and ammunition,' Jamie stated bluntly.

The lawyer stared back at him impassively. He thought about asking Jamie what made him think he was in a position to supply them but discarded it. He wouldn't be here with an introduction from Sir Charles Redmond otherwise. Better just to give him what he wanted and hope that was the end of it. There was, of course, the question of payment.

'They'll cost you,' he said, picking up a pencil from the desk and chewing the end of it.

'Of course they will,' Jamie said, smiling now. He patted his jacket. 'Don't worry, I won't short change you.'

'Do they need to be untraceable?'

Jamie laughed frostily. 'As long as they can't be traced back to me at the end of the day, I don't really care.'

The lawyer hesitated a moment, clearly thinking it through. 'Do you have any particular item in mind?' he asked eventually.

'Not particularly, though I want reliable models. A Walther PPK or a Browning, a Beretta... a Makarov even, any of these... with sound suppressors, any of these would do.'

'I think we can manage that,' the lawyer replied. 'When do you need them?'

'Now,' Jamie responded, holding the man's eyes. He saw the lawyer smile again.

'Let me see the money,' the older man said, leaning forward in his chair, hand outstretched.

Jamie withdrew the money from inside his jacket. It came in the form of a large wad of £20 notes in a roll bound with a rubber band. 'There's a grand there,' he said. 'I'll expect change.'

The lawyer took the bundle. Carefully, he slipped the rubber band from the roll and began flicking through the notes.

Jamie knew what he was doing. He didn't blame him. He was just being careful. Fakes or marked notes would not show good faith and a transaction like this depended on that above all else. He smiled as the man finished checking. 'Satisfied?' he asked.

The lawyer nodded. His eyes didn't waver. They remained fixed on Jamie throughout the transaction. 'Satisfied,' he confirmed. He placed the rubber band back onto the roll of notes and returned them. They both now knew where they stood.

'£450 for the two, with silencers and two boxes of ammunition, whichever calibre you choose,' the older man said. 'No haggling.'

Jamie grinned. He liked the man's style. 'You want the money now?' he asked.

'If you trust me,' the lawyer replied, returning his grin.

'What's not to trust?' Jamie retorted. 'You don't come across with the goods, I come back.'

The lawyer laughed. 'I don't doubt it,' he said. 'Do you know Glasgow?' he asked.

'Don't let the tan fool you,' Jamie replied, grinning widely now. 'I might look like a foreigner but I was born and brought up here.'

'You'll know Springburn then,' the man continued.

Jamie nodded. 'Well enough,' he said.

The solicitor leaned forward again and picked up his phone. As he dialled, Jamie undid the roll of notes and peeled off half of them. He laid them carefully on the desk in front of the man.

Jamie could hear the ring tone echoing down the line before a man's gruff voice answered. 'Mungo,' the lawyer said. 'How are you?'

The man's response was muffled but Jamie took it he was saying he was alright because the lawyer's expression remained positive. The small talk went on for a while before the lawyer got to the point. 'I'm sending someone over to see you,' he said. 'He's looking for a couple of small hand tools and the bits and pieces to go with them.'

Again, Jamie heard the man's muffled response but couldn't make it out. The lawyer looked over at him. 'When can you go to pick up the goods?' he mouthed quietly.

'Now,' Jamie responded. 'I can be there in half an hour.'

The lawyer returned to his conversation with the man on the phone. 'The customer will be over in an hour, Mungo. You can show him the full range. He has already paid.'

There was another muffled response. The lawyer's sanity in suggesting the man show Jamie "the full range" was probably being questioned, Jamie imagined, smiling inwardly.

'Yes, I'm sure,' the lawyer retorted. 'His credentials are impeccable. Just do as I say, there's a good lad,' he continued, and hung up. He turned his attention back to Jamie, his smile still in place. 'You're going to the Balgray Vaults in Palermo Street... that's just off Atlas Road. Ask for Mungo Mellis. You can't miss the place... or Mungo, come to that.' He said the last part with a wry smile.'

Jamie checked his watch. 'I'll be there in an hour,' he confirmed, pushing himself up from his chair and holding out his hand.

The lawyer took it firmly and shook it. 'I hope your venture works out,' he said. 'Whatever it is.'

Jamie smiled again. 'So do I,' he replied.

Chapter Forty-eight

Conor was on his second cup of coffee when Jamie strolled into the tearoom. He was nursing it, determined not to buy a third. 'Everything go okay?' the big American asked casually, hiding his relief.

Jamie nodded. 'Aye, it went well. We need to go somewhere else now. You ready?'

'Did you just say "we"? You're letting me tag along?'

'This is the good bit,' Jamie laughed. 'We're going to pick up the equipment.'

Conor pushed back from the table and stood up. 'In that case, let's go,' he said.

'Not finishing your coffee?' Jamie asked, laughing.

'That isn't coffee,' the American murmured under his breath. 'It's what they wash the dishes in. The things you make me do.' They left the tearoom laughing.

'Where now?' Conor asked as they made their way back to the car.

'Springburn,' Jamie replied.

Conor gave him a quizzical look.

'It isn't far,' Jamie continued. 'North of the city... Just follow my directions.'

'Yes, boss,' Conor laughed.

They drove down to the corner with Hope Street and turned north, up the hill past Bath Street and Sauchiehall Street and then turned right at the top of the hill into Renfrew Street. Conor knew this part of the city reasonably well. Buchanan Bus Station appeared on their left and then they turned left into North Hanover Street. He was less familiar with the area now and concentrated on his driving while Jamie called out the directions. At Dobbie's Loan they cut across into Kyle Street and then Baird Street before turning north again on Springburn Road.

This was new territory as far as Conor Whelan was concerned. He absorbed it, committing it to memory. He would find his way back with or without Jamie.

A cemetery appeared on their left, rising up behind a high wall.

'Sighthill Cemetery,' Jamie commented, seeing his friend's quick glance. 'I've got some distant relatives buried in there,' he added.

'Yeah?' Conor laughed. 'Well let's hope you're not joining them soon,' he said.

Jamie joined his friend's laughter but wondered if that was tempting fate.

A little further on, a side road climbed up on their left, high tenements lining the skyline while they continued on the main road below. There were factories off to the right, thick smoke, ranging in colour from white to black and all shades of grey in between, rising from their chimneys. Conor's eyes took in the tenement houses built close to them. Health hazard, he thought with a shudder.

'We're turning right up ahead,' Jamie advised. 'You'll see a fire station on your left just at the junction. Turn right there.'

Conor drove on, the fire station appearing on his left seconds later. With a crunch of gears, he slowed, indicated and pulled into the right hand lane and then hard right at the junction into Atlas Road. Mirror, signal, brake had just gone out the window, Jamie mused.

They were in the midst of tenement houses and shops now. It was busier here. People, mostly women well wrapped up against the cold, were out shopping. There were few cars. It wasn't the most prosperous of the city's suburbs, Conor surmised.

'Stop anywhere here,' Jamie instructed. 'We'll walk the rest.'

Conor pulled over. There was plenty of room with only a couple of vans and a lorry parked on the long stretch of road.

'Is it safe here?' he asked.

Jamie gave a sly grin. 'For us or the car?' he asked.

'The car... I don't think I can face the wrath of Mary's mother if anything happens to it,' Conor replied nervously.

'Relax. It's safe. They're good people around here.'

Conor accepted his assurance and stepped out of the car. The cold hit him immediately after the warmth of the Austin and he pulled his coat tightly around him. Jamie did likewise.

The American waited, shivering, until Jamie gave him a nod and they set off along Atlas Road, past the junction with Flemington Street, towards Palermo Street.

Conor kept time beside him all the way, his eyes taking in everything like an interested tourist. They passed a pub, its doors wide open, and the sound of Glasgow banter filtered out to them. With the best will in the world, Conor couldn't understand a single word. Glaswegians spoke a language he had never mastered. 'What's a scunner?' he asked Jamie as they passed two women conversing loudly.

Jamie laughed. 'Something shitty,' he explained. 'Like the weather today... that's a scunner. Losing your wages in a card school, that's a scunner too... get it?'

'Yeah, I get it... like what we'll be doing soon, that'll be a scunner?'

'Aye, if it goes wrong. But if it comes off, it'll be pure dead brilliant,' Jamie laughed.

Conor shook his head. 'Pure, dead brilliant,' he muttered. What language strung those three words together? He surely had arrived in a different world.

They turned left into Palermo Street after a couple of minutes' walk and the pub was facing them. Just as "the Godfather" had said, you couldn't miss it. It formed the ground floor of a four-storey tenement building and was painted white with dark blue window frames and a dark blue door. It stood out against the otherwise grey background like a lighthouse in a fog.

'We're there,' Jamie announced. He stopped and turned to Conor, his voice dropping 'This is where we're picking up the guns. Leave the talking to me. If you open your mouth, the natives will be inquisitive. They don't get many tourists around here,' he said with a laugh. 'And the natives getting' nosy isn't good.'

'Okay kid, I get it. Now can we just get on with it? The cold is freezing my nuts off.'

They crossed the road and pushed through the blue door. It was warm inside. A few men stood beside the long bar drinking pints of beer, but the place was far from busy. Then again, it was just after noon. Still early, Jamie reflected.

He looked around, conscious that their entrance had killed conversation. Eyes turned to watch them. There was no hostility, just curiosity, but curiosity could be dangerous. He smiled amiably, trying to put the locals at ease. He was looking for Mungo, the man he "couldn't miss", but no one stood out. The men in here were all the same; all vertically challenged, pale skinned and worn down by life.

There was a commotion at the end of the bar and Jamie turned towards it. A big man appeared, seemingly out of nowhere, but closer inspection showed there was a door set into the wall, hidden between two gantries of bottles. The man had unkempt salt and pepper hair and a big red beard. The muscles of his arms bulged beneath his bottle green shirtsleeves and his chest strained at the buttons. You certainly couldn't miss him, Jamie thought smiling to himself. This had to be their man.

Conor let out a soft gasp. 'Jesus, where did the jolly green giant come from?' he muttered under his breath. Jamie drew him a wry look.

The big man was watching them warily. Jamie smiled and started towards him. 'Mungo?' he enquired, watching the man's eyes.

'Who's askin'?' the giant threw back.

'My name's Ferryman,' Jamie replied. 'I think you're expecting me.'

'Ye're early,' the man responded, his eyes leaving Jamie and moving to Conor. 'An' who ur you?' he asked.

'He's with me,' Jamie cut in. 'He's a pal,' he added, laughing quietly.

The punters around the bar were watching expectantly now. They knew Mungo Mellis but the two strangers were, well... strangers. They knew what Mungo was capable of... but these two? There might be some fun. They watched the procedings attentively, their drinks forgotten.

Jamie stood his ground, watching the big man unblinkingly.

'Ah wis telt aboot you, no' him,' Mungo said belligerently. 'Wan man, ah wis telt.'

'An' I'm that man... I don't like the way this is goin' Mungo,' Jamie went on, lowering his voice. 'I don't like discussin' business in public.' He turned and eyed the other drinkers. They knew a challenge when they heard one.

A frisson of excited anticipation ran around the bar as the punters waited for the fireworks to start. Wee disagreements were commonplace around here but nobody, in living memory, had fronted up to Mungo Mellis. This should be good, they all thought.

But they were disappointed. Mungo wilted first. He saw something in Jamie and heard something in his voice the others had missed. It was in his eyes. There was an implacable hardness lurking there, just behind the pupils. 'Come on through tae the office,' Mungo said, lifting the access flap in the bar top to let the two men through. Jamie turned to Conor and smiled.

The American let out his pent up breath, relieved. This was the Jamie Raeburn he remembered; the Jamie Raeburn he had travelled with to Derby years before, but with a harder edge. He had always been confident, bordering on brash even, but what he had just seen took it to a new level.

Around them, the customers returned to their drinks and their conversations. The excitement was over. There would be no blood spilled on the rough wooden floor of the Balgray Vaults today... at least not now. The sense of disappointment was almost palpable. They consoled themselves with their beer and the knowledge that it was Friday and the weekend usually brought out the worst in people.

The "office" was a small square room with a table, a couple of chairs, a telephone and a battered olive green filing cabinet. The air was heavy with stale cooking odours; fried bacon, square sliced sausage and black pudding, all fried in over used lard. It was strangely appealing to Jamie thought to most it wouldn't be the most pleasant smell in the world.

A middle-aged woman, old before her time, with peroxide blonde hair and an abundance of wrinkles, sat at the small table attacking a roll and "something" and drinking from a chipped mug. Lunchtime at the coalface, Jamie thought.

Mungo drew her a hard look. 'Away an' mind the bar, Agnes,' he said in a voice that brooked no argument. 'Ye can take yer piece an' yer tea wae ye,' he added, softening the blow. Jamie smiled. He wondered how many people, if any, argued with Mungo Mellis... But the man had a soft side too, it appeared.

The woman rose grumpily from her chair, picked up her cup and her filled roll and made for the door. As she passed Jamie, the smell of Lorne sausage filled his nostrils, solving the puzzle of what was in the roll. Her life wasn't all bad, he mused.

When the door closed behind her, Mungo locked it and turned to Jamie. He gave Conor a cursory glance, still suspicious. 'Mr Andrew said ye wiz lookin' for some hand tools,' he started.

'Two,' Jamie confirmed.

Mungo nodded. 'An bits an' pieces tae go wi' them,' he continued.

It was Jamie nodding now.

Mungo still seemed reluctant to proceed.

'What's up Mungo?' Jamie asked, keeping it friendly.

'Nuthin', the big man retorted. His look contradicted it; that and his suspicious glances at Conor..

Jamie smiled again. 'Listen,' he counselled. 'If you're still unhappy about showing us the goods, phone your boss. I've paid him. You don't trust me, I understand that, but he does... and he calls the shots. So call him or show us. We'll be out of your hair quicker that way.'

Mungo wavered, his eyes darting between both men, and then pushed the table aside. There was a stained and threadbare rug on the floor beneath it. He knelt down and pulled the rug aside to reveal a trapdoor with a heavy metal ring pull set into the wood. He heaved and pulled the trapdoor clear of the floor. A black void appeared.

The big man eyed them cautiously then bent down into the opening. There was a loud click and light filled the void. A wooden stairway led down and a musky smell of stale alcohol wafted up to meet them.

'Everything is down there,' he said, straightening up before starting the climb down. 'Follow me.'

Jamie and Conor exchanged a look before Jamie followed Mungo with Conor bringing up the rear. They found themselves in a cellar with racks of bottles and kegs of beer lining the walls. The floor was of compacted earth and crumbling concrete and the walls were of brick, painted white. A steel access flap in the ceiling near the exterior wall allowed cracks of faint light in. This, Jamie assumed, was the hatch used by the draymen when delivering beer. There was the faint sound of talk and traffic from outside. But there were no guns.

Jamie looked enquiringly at the big man. Mungo grinned and reached out to one of the racks filled with bottles. There was a click and the rack slid sideways, revealing another trap door.

'What now?' Conor muttered. 'The catacombs? White bones and spiders?'

Mungo laughed. It changed him. He was enjoying himself. He lifted the trap door easily and a light came on automatically. Another stairway appeared. They descended as before, Mungo first, Jamie second and Conor last.

At the bottom, Jamie barely suppressed a gasp. Racks lined the walls here too but this time the merchandise wasn't alcohol, it was guns. Rifles, handguns, automatics, semi-automatics, revolvers, machine pistols, some of them recognisable, some not, lined the walls.

Mungo stood back and allowed the two men to examine the wares. Jamie made straight for the rack containing the handguns, his hand reaching out for a Walther PPK, the dull metal gleaming evilly in the ceiling light.

'The old favourite, kid,' Conor murmured behind him. 'The one you started with.'

Jamie nodded slowly and hefted the weapon in his hand. As Mungo watched, impressed, he stripped it and rebuilt it. 'I'll take this one,' he said, satisfied.

Conor walked down the rack. The range of weapons available was staggering. There was enough firepower here to start a small war, he mused. Finally, he stopped wandering and reached out for an automatic. It was a Browning, bigger and heavier than Jamie's Walther, but he liked the feel of it. 'What do you think?' he whispered, showing it to Jamie.

Jamie took it from him and did as he had done with the Walther, his fingers nimbly stripping the weapon and rebuilding it.

Conor was doubly impressed now. He could fire a gun with the best of them but the kid was on a different level. He shuddered to think how he had developed these skills... and what he did with them.

'Yeah, it's good,' Jamie said with a smile as he handed it back.

He turned to Mungo who was lounging at the foot of the stair. 'Ammunition and spare magazines for both,' he demanded. 'And where are the silencers?'

Mungo nodded to a rack containing small wooden boxes. Jamie sauntered over and rummaged, selecting two of the sound suppressors and slipping them in his jacket pocket.

Mungo retrieved boxes of 9mm ammunition from rack at the far end of the wall, selected the spare magazines for each gun, and returned to Jamie, holding them out. 'Is that it?' he asked.

'Aye, that's it,' Jamie confirmed, smiling coldly. 'You can let your boss know I'm satisfied with the service.'

Minutes later, the two men left the bar and strolled back down Palermo Street, their pockets weighed down with the lethal cargo. They both had different thoughts but neither voiced them. Conor hoped he wouldn't have to use the Browning tucked into his coat pocket. Jamie knew his use of the Walther was inevitable.

Chapter Forty-nine

They drove back into the city. They were talking now, the practicalities of contacting Liam Fitzpatrick the main topic of conversation. That still posed difficulty. Conor, however, did have one bit of good news; the Triumph Bonneville was available and he had agreed to meet the price. He was picking it up next day.

That was a boost for Jamie. With the right clothes and the big bike, he would be virtually anonymous... *Virtually*, he reflected, because the bike itself would attract attention.

It was too early to fit in a couple of drinks in the Pot Still so they settled for coffee in a small Italian café at the bottom of Hope Street, opposite the Central Hotel. The coffee here was much more to Conor's taste. As before, the talk returned to Liam Fitzpatrick. As they talked, Conor reflected on what he had seen earlier. He had questions and, being professionally inquisitive, he had to ask them. It became a voyage of discovery for the American, one he sort of wished he hadn't embarked on. He learned things he wished he hadn't.

Having watched Jamie operate earlier in the day, much of what he learned hadn't come as too much of a surprise. The confidence and control he had shown when dealing with the big man, Mungo, had amazed him. Mungo had been wary of him; maybe even afraid. It had been there in the giant's eyes... and not many men would frighten Mungo, Conor suspected. So what had, he wondered. There had been nothing overt; no threats, physical or verbal, and yet Mungo had caved in. In the end, he put it down to animal instinct... Both men were predators and one of them sensed that the other carried more treat than he did.

And there was the thing with the guns. He had watched, almost in awe, as Jamie stripped them down and rebuilt them. Jamie clearly knew exactly what he was doing. He knew his way around guns. The word "professional" had jumped into Conor's mind at the time and it disturbed him. It wasn't just because of their friendship, it was more than that - much more than that - and he wanted to know what it was. That was why he asked the questions and that was why he was even more anguished now. If he hadn't arranged that meeting between Jamie and Brendan Kelly back in '67, if he hadn't written up the security evaluation on him, then maybe Jamie wouldn't be in the situation he now was. All things considered, it was his fault.

'What's wrong?' Jamie probed, sensing the American's misery.

'I blame myself for what has happened to you,' Conor replied, gloomily.

Jamie gave a short laugh and patted his friend's arm. 'Stop beating yourself up... it wasn't your fault.'

'I put you in touch with Kelly. I wrote the report on you.'

'Yeah, you did,' Jamie conceded. 'But I killed Max Kelman, you didn't. If you hadn't introduced me to Brendan I would have found someone else to provide a weapon. It all started with Kelman, not your report.' He smiled easily as he finished his coffee, the matter closed. 'It's about time you were heading back to Dunoon,' he said.

Conor laughed self-consciously. He loved Jamie like a brother and still felt he had let him down, no matter what Jamie said. He decided something else then. He wouldn't call Jamie "kid" ever again.

'What about Fitzpatrick and the girl?' he asked, conscious that they hadn't resolved either problem.

Jamie smiled wryly. 'I don't know,' he said. 'But I've got a feeling they'll resolve themselves. I feel it in my bones.'

Conor knew all about gut instinct. The only question was *how* they would resolve themselves.

Chapter Fifty

Same day, evening

Clara Whitelaw reached across the dining room table in her Kensington home and lifted the decanter. Her husband, Mark, watched her, raising an eyebrow in mild rebuke. She ignored him. She had already drunk too much of the Bordeaux, she knew that, but another glass wouldn't hurt, she decided. She had been wrestling with a dilemma for most of the day, one she had to face but didn't particularly want to. The wine would also help with the mind numbing normality of married life and that, on its own, was as good a reason as any. Normal service may have resumed in the Whitelaw house but life was still strained and difficult. Mark wasn't the type to forgive and forget.

Suddenly, the telephone in the hall shattered their fragile peace. Once, twice, the tone grated shrilly in their ears before Mark pushed himself up from the table, a dark scowl on his face. 'It's eight o'clock, for God's sake,' he muttered. 'Can't we get any peace?'

Clara smiled up at him demurely as he passed her. *Not in our chosen lives, no,* she was tempted to say, but she kept the thought to herself. Like so many of her thoughts these days - the private ones – it was for her and her alone.

She heard her husband's voice carry down the hall as he answered the call. He sounded irritable. Then the noise of his stomping footsteps came to her. Irritation had clearly turned to anger. 'It's for you,' he announced tetchily. 'One of your hired help,' he continued, edging into sarcasm. 'It's the one who is on to you a lot these days; can't he even wipe his behind without getting your permission? And it's eight o'bloody clock!' he went on, repeating his earlier gripe.

Clara understood his anger and she knew she shouldn't rise to it... but. 'We're in the middle of a big operation,' she said. 'You, of all people, should know what that's like; we don't work nine to five.' She could be irritable too.

Her husband gave a derisory snort. 'No, don't I know it,' he retorted irritably, but her response had stirred another thought. He knew she was working on something important, but "big operation" came as a surprise. If Ultra was involved in a "big operation", why didn't he know about it? Protocol dictated that major operations were intimated to the other services and this one obviously had not. If it had been, he would know about it. So what the hell was it? He covered up his thoughts with another derogatory comment. 'I'd forgotten you work with nutters who love their work... it's twenty-four seven for your boys.'

Clara gave him a frosty look but she was smiling inside. *No, not this one.* That was another thought best kept to herself. She rose quickly from the table and headed for the phone.

'Sorry,' Jamie started before she had a chance to speak. 'I don't want to cause you grief but it's important.'

'It's alright. My husband gets a little suspicious when I get calls from strange men,' she said jokingly, just loud enough for her husband to hear. 'Where have you been?' she continued, dropping her voice. 'You were supposed to call yesterday. Have you managed to make contact with Corkscrew?'

'No, not yet; it's difficult.'

'So why are you calling?'

'An update,' he said simply. 'One, you can tell Sir Charles I've spoken with Mr Andrew and sorted out my hardware. Second, I want to know if you have anything back on the American journalist.'

'Not a lot, to be honest,' Clara replied. 'The Cousins aren't sharing much with us these days,' she said, referring to the American Intelligence Services. 'They're in a huff because we're not with them in South East Asia getting our noses bloodied. Why do you ask?' Her interest had piqued now.

'He might not be what he seems,' Jamie replied.

Clara laughed. 'A little bird tell you that, did it... a little *American* bird?' she said. 'I'd forgotten your link to them.'

He laughed now. 'Yeah, I asked him to have a look at the guy.'

'That was naughty. Charles wouldn't be pleased,' Clara said. He detected a hint of amusement in her voice.

'Well, he doesn't need to know, does he?' he replied. It was a suggestion more than a question.

Clara hesitated a moment before responding and when she did she ignored his last remark. 'What did your friend tell you?' she asked.

Jamie smiled again. He could rely on her to keep it to herself though, in this case, it didn't really matter. The Old Man probably expected it anyway; expecting him, as usual, to do things his own way.

He returned to the matter of Sparke. 'The real Kevin Sparke is a Vietnam veteran, one of the guys who got his nose bloodied, as you put it. Whether it's the same guy or not is another matter. Kevin Sparke, the vet, was badly wounded in some fucked up operation in Laos. He nearly got his head blown off, apparently. He was brought back to the States for surgery - they had to rebuild most of his face. He spent time in hospital before being invalided out of the Marines in sixty-five, and then went into rehab. He disappeared after that. Nothing was heard of his for a couple of years and then he resurfaced with a job as a journalist working for a newspaper in New York. He voices some extreme right wing views and allies those to some inflammatory statements and comments. Those got him noticed. His career took off then. He works freelance now but he's never short of takers for his articles. He moved to Europe a while back and that's about it. They don't have anything on him after that.'

'That all sounds normal. Why the suspicion now?'

'Gut instinct, I think. When Sparke resurfaced, he didn't want anything to do with his old buddies - shunned them, in fact. His former friends in the

Marines found that strange. He had been a bit of an extrovert... drinking and whoring were his main hobbies,' he added with a laugh. 'They say he became reclusive, kept himself to himself and acquired a pathological dislike of photographers... at least, photographers who wanted to take pictures of him. Anyway, the bottom line is that they think something smells. One of my friend's people is following it up but with Sparke out of the US at the moment, it isn't a priority. I just wondered if we had anything.'

'Like I said, not much... but you're right, it sounds wrong. What is a right wing journalist doing talking to the IRA? They're political opposites,' Clara mused thoughtfully. 'I'll have him looked at again,' she went on. 'There is one thing though; MI5 checked out the house in Belfast. They spoke to Sir Rodney and his staff. The checks all came back clear... But when they went on to ask Sir Rodney about strangers visiting the house, he got a bit cagey. Not surprising with his reputation,' she laughed coldly. 'What he did in his own time was his own business, he told them, but he did say that he had been visited by a journalist a few times, both in London and at his house in Belfast. He didn't give the journalist's name but said he was doing a political piece. The Inquisitors got more from the housekeeper. She could remember the man's name and it is Sparke... and he is American, she was sure of that. She also told them that Sir Rodney had given the man permission to visit the house in his absence to use the library. He has quite a collection on Ireland, past and present, it seems. The housekeeper didn't like him.'

'It has to be him,' Jamie retorted.

'Yes, I suppose he is in the frame, but we need proof. The fact he visited to use the library doesn't mean he left a message Corkscrew picked up.'

'No, but it doesn't mean he didn't either,' Jamie replied tetchily. 'Maybe we should be keeping a closer watch on Mr Sparke.'

'Yes, maybe, but there's a problem with that.'

'What?'

'If we ask Five to put Section 4 onto him they will want to know why. If we tell them it concerns a suspected IRA attack they'll start jumping up and down and it might blow Corkscrew.'

'Ah, that's the thing about intrigue,' Jamie answered, laughing frostily. 'You just don't know who your friends are.' He heard Clara give a little snort.

So we still don't know the target?'

'No, but we know the troops are here so it's definitely going ahead.'

'And that's all we have,' she responded dispiritedly.

'Not quite all,' Jamie came back softly. 'There's something else.'

'What?' she demanded, interested again.

'Orlagh Duggan... She's coming over.'

'Why? I thought Corkscrew was running the show.'

'He's only in command of his own ASU. There are three ASU's and Orlagh Duggan is running the whole thing.'

'You're sure of this?'

'Absolutely,' Jamie confirmed. 'Duggan himself told Corkscrew on Thursday morning, just as he was setting off for the Mainland. Orlagh is in charge.'

'Interesting,' she mused aloud. 'She's getting her hands dirty this time.'

Jamie hesitated. 'That assumes she hasn't dirtied her hands with something like this before,' he said quietly.

'Yes, it does, doesn't it,' Clara replied enigmatically.

She wasn't ready to front up to her dilemma. Not yet. Not until she knew the target.

'When you make contact with Corkscrew I want to know immediately,' she continued.

'Okay,' Jamie acknowledged carefully. He decided not to ask about her investigations into the bomber. Something told him he wouldn't like the answer.

'Right, I had better get back to Mark,' she said quietly, finishing the call. 'He's suspicious enough without me whispering to you all this time. But remember, I want to know as soon as you re-establish contact with Corkscrew.'

'I'll remember,' he replied just as the call disconnected.

Chapter Fifty-one

Tuesday 8 January 1974

Making contact with Liam turned out to easier than Jamie anticipated and came about unexpectedly. It was probably a desperate measure on Liam's part and it caused Jamie some mild aggravation, but it resolved what until then had seemed an intractable problem.

Jamie received a call from Kate early that morning. She was nervous and worried, he could tell, and she was whispering down the line. That wasn't normal. His mother was hovering in the background, waiting for a sign. She had answered the phone and had picked up on Kate's anxiety so, naturally, she was worried too. She said as much when she handed him the phone.

'Calm down love,' he said, as Kate garbled her news. 'Just start at the beginning and tell me again.'

'Your Irish friend phoned here,' she said, slowly and deliberately now. 'My Mum answered the phone. He said he knew you weren't here but he needed to contact you urgently. Mum said he sounded edgy. He left a telephone number and asked if she could pass it on to you. He said the best time... and he kept stressing that, the best time to call him is tonight, or tomorrow night, at half past six. Are you okay?' It wasn't Liam she was worried about, it was him.

'I'm fine, don't worry,' he said reassuringly. 'He's come over to Scotland and we don't have each other's numbers, that's all.' He knew she didn't believe him. 'Are you and the kids okay, that's more to the point,' he continued, speaking a little louder now.

'They're fine... I'm fine... it's just...'

'I know,' he said gently, cutting her off. 'It won't be long... and Conor is helping me.' He hoped that, at least, would settle her. 'I'll be back with you as soon as possible.'

'And what about Liam? What will I tell my mother?'

'I'll call him tonight,' he replied. 'It'll be about the funeral, that's all.' She knew the story he had given her mother. He hoped she took the hint.

'Okay, I'll tell her,' she said. He managed to avoid sighing with relief. 'You'll need the number,' she went on. 'It's 01389 -275572...' She paused a moment. 'I love you. Be careful,' she said softly.

'I love you too, and I will... promise,' he said. 'I'll phone you again later,' he added before hanging up.

He turned to his mother, smiling again. She still had a worried look on her face but she had heard him ask about the children. She should be less anxious now but she would know there was something. 'Kate and the kids are fine,' he said.

'Kate sounded worried.'

'Just a call from a friend about a funeral I'm going to. He gave me the wrong time, that's all.'

'When is it?'

Jamie sometimes thought his mother had given Sir Charles lessons in interrogation techniques. 'Tomorrow,' he lied.

'You didn't say. Where is it?'

'No, sorry, I should have mentioned. He wasn't a close friend, just a lad I worked with at Brown's years ago.'

'Where, you haven't said.'

No, because I didn't want to. The more I lie the bigger the chance you'll catch on.

'Clydebank Crematorium... tomorrow morning.'

Don't ask his name and don't ask the time... pleeeease.

'You'll need a white shirt and black tie,' she said finally.

Jamie nodded. 'Yes, so I will,' he said. 'Thanks, I'll buy them today.'

She smiled at him a little sadly. She still didn't believe him but the truth would hurt her more. That consoled him somewhat, but not a lot. He didn't like lying to her. But he had another worry on his mind. Kate had called him here. She hadn't mentioned Liam by name but she had given the contact number and the contact time. He prayed the line wasn't tapped.

***

At about the same time Jamie was talking to Kate, Orlagh Duggan boarded an Aer Lingus Boeing 707 at the new Terminal 1 of Dublin Airport en route to Amsterdam. Amsterdam wasn't her final destination. That was Glasgow but, at her father's insistence, she was following an obscure and convoluted route rather than take a direct flight. At Amsterdam's Schiphol Airport she transferred to a British Airways flight to Heathrow, now travelling on a British passport under the name Olivia Dunlop. At Heathrow, she changed again, this time to another British Airways flight, arriving in Glasgow in mid-afternoon. Her father's warning about security appeared to have been superfluous. No one, as far as she could see, was watching her departure. The Brit Security Services, it seemed, were still blissfully unaware of the impending attack.

Still, it was better not to take chances, she mused. When it came to security, she was her father's daughter. Perhaps not quite as paranoid as him, but she trusted no one. And this attack deserved nothing less than total secrecy. It would go down in history. The Organisation could kill soldiers and RUC men and blow up pubs and restaurants but after the initial horror, the public quickly forgot. If it did not touch them in their own homes, it soon became yesterday's news. And the British Government would carry on regardless, sending in more soldiers, interning more good men and killing more volunteers.

But this attack would change all that. The bastards wouldn't be able to ignore this one. It would cause panic... real, lasting panic, and they would have to pull out the troops. She smiled contentedly. Ireland would be reunited and she and her father would have played a major part in it. It was a shame her countrymen could never know. The Brits might pull out their soldiers and sue for peace but they would never forget. She, her father and every man of the ASUs wouldn't live long if the truth came out. She was not going to let that happen. She didn't fancy being a martyr no matter how great the cause.

The flight to London was uneventful. The British Airways BAC111 was filled to capacity, all 89 seats occupied, and she sat wedged between a portly Englishman and an equally portly American woman who chain-smoked constantly while the cabin light was lit. Orlagh pretended to sleep. The last thing she needed was conversation.

At Heathrow she transferred onto another British Airways flight to Glasgow and touched down at Abbotsinch Airport at three forty in afternoon, about ten minutes late. No one was waiting to meet her at the terminal for the simple reason that no one knew she was coming, not today at least.

She stepped out from the terminal into a bright winter afternoon. Knowing Glasgow's reputation for abysmal weather, she took it to herald good fortune. Her confidence rose, not that it had been low, but she felt more secure now.

She joined the queue for taxis and listened into the conversations taking place around her. There were accents from all over the world; English, naturally, American, Indian and Pakistani, as well as native Glaswegian. She didn't hear any of her countrymen or women. They were here, though, and that saddened her a little. When the attack took place, they would suffer.

The snippets of conversation were mundane. Everyone, it seemed, lived in a bubble, concerned only about themselves. She searched for a word to describe the mood around her. Carefree, she thought, that was it. She even felt caught up in it. But that would change in less than three weeks and then it won't be safe to be Irish around here, she mused.

As she settled into her taxi she thought about what lay before her. The three men leading the ASUs now knew she was taking charge but the others should still be oblivious. Men being men, that might prove difficult but she shrugged it off. She was there with the authority of her father and no man, least of all these men, would challenge that. They might not like it but they would do what they were told.

Then there was the enforced rendezvous with Kevin Sparke. That *did* annoy her. Her father had sprung that on her the day the ASU's left. She had railed against it but he was unapologetic. You have to meet with Kevin, he said. Why, she had asked. Because he's bringing the explosives you'll need to carry it off, that's why, he explained, and that was that.

She could deal with it. On the one hand, she had operational control over the attack. She relished that. On the other, she had to meet with slimy Kevin. That she didn't relish at all. She didn't trust him further than she could spit into a gale. It wasn't the fact he wanted to screw her, she could cope with that, it was something else... something undefinable but nasty.

She smiled wryly. She knew exactly how to deal with men like Kevin Sparke... And when the time came, she would.

Chapter Fifty-two

Same Day

Jamie left the house in mid-morning. He told his mother he was off to buy a shirt and black tie and then, with Conor's help, he was going to do a bit of house hunting. She accepted it but he wasn't sure she believed it. One thing was certain, he had better return with a shirt and tie.

He followed his routine from the day before, walking first to Knightswood Cross and catching a bus into the city from there. He called Conor from the call box at the Cross and got his first bit of good news for the day... or second, if Conor's call to Calverton could be classed as good news. Conor had the Bonneville. All Jamie needed was leathers and a new helmet. The leathers were no problem. He already had these lying in a wardrobe in his mother's house. She hadn't thrown them out. She was a hoarder. He had checked them the night he had come up with the idea. He didn't bother trying them on. His build hadn't changed much.

He did need a helmet though. His old helmet was still there, battered and scratched, but it was his "old" helmet in more ways than one. In the days when it was made visors were unheard of... and he needed a visor. It didn't matter that he could now make contact with Liam, he still had to meet him or take Conor to meet him, so his face had to be covered.

From memory, he knew there was a motor bike dealer in Great Western Road near St George's Cross. He would go there. He arranged to meet Conor later in the afternoon to pick up the Triumph. His mother wouldn't like it and would give him grief but he would grin and bear it. It was for the greater good.

He caught a Number 11 bus into town; different route but much the same scenery. His first stop was Watt Brothers; the Men's Department. A white shirt, plain, and a black tie were purchased in short order. It was still early so he wandered around the shops in Buchanan Street for a while, ruminating. The Christmas decorations and lights were being removed. Soon, the city would return to its usual drab grey. One day, who knows, it might be as bright as Paris, he mused... but not for a while.

He felt unnaturally nervy. Something niggled at the back of his mind, something important, but it eluded him. It was something he had read, or heard... or sensed. He wrestled with it on and off, trying to identify it, then pushed it away. It would come to him. There were other more important things to deal with, and one of those was the feeling that Clara hadn't been entirely truthful with him when they had spoken the night before. There had been something in her voice, as if she was holding back on something that was bothering her. Maybe he should ask her, he mused thoughtfully. Better to have whatever it was out in the open than sprung upon him when he was least prepared to deal with it. It might be personal, though he doubted that.

On impulse, he headed for the Central Station and the telephone boxes there. He had time and it was better to bring it out now than wait. He dug out some coins and fed the box, dialling quickly. Clara answered almost immediately with her usual curt "hello" and the number. She never gave her name.

'Hello Clara,' he said.

'Jamie,' she retorted, sounding a little happier... but only a little he noted. 'I was just thinking about you,' she went on. 'You must be telepathic.' A nervous little laugh accompanied that.

'Spooky,' Jamie replied, giving a laugh himself. 'I was thinking about you... hence the call.'

'That's nice. What were you thinking?'

He hesitated. Should he go for it or navigate round it? He decided on the sledgehammer approach. 'I was thinking you weren't being straight with me last night,' he said. 'There was something bothering you... something I think involves me, and you were keeping it to yourself.' He left it at that. His question was implicit; he didn't need to spell it out.

Clara gave a little snort of laughter. She was trying to write it off but she wasn't succeeding. 'I don't know what you're talking about,' she said but it sounded defensive rather than dismissive. 'I just have a lot of things on my mind, you included.'

'Uh-huh,' Jamie responded. 'Okay, I'm sorry.' He didn't sound sorry.

'Was that all you called about?' Clara went on, tentatively.

'No, there is something else. Corkscrew made contact.'

'Did he have anything for us?' she threw back immediately.

She was keen to change the subject, he thought. It only served to reinforce his suspicion that something was amiss. 'I don't know yet; I'm calling him tonight.'

'You haven't spoken to him? So how did he make contact?'

'He phoned and left a message for me. Left a number. Said to phone tonight or tomorrow night... six thirty,' he retorted shortly.

'But how? Who with?' she asked. She sounded confused.

'My mother-in-law... her's was the last number he had for me. Not the best plan in the world but at least he made contact.'

'I'm sorry,' Clara said quietly. 'I know you didn't want your family involved.'

She sounded genuinely unhappy, Jamie thought, but it wasn't her fault; it was his. 'Forget it,' he replied dismissively. 'I should have foreseen the problem. I'll phone you again later, after I've spoken with Corkscrew. Maybe then we'll know where we're going with this.'

'I hope so...'

'Aye, so do I,' he retorted, cutting her off. 'Will your husband be home when I call?'

'I don't know; probably. It depends when you call. Why?'

Jamie laughed softly. 'I don't want him getting the wrong idea, that's all. Talk to you later.'

He ended the call before she had the opportunity to ask him what was the wrong idea. The fact she was thinking like that made her predicament even more difficult, she reflected. She smiled sadly and returned to her work.

Chapter Fifty-three

Same day, early evening

Conor turned off the B857, Renton Main Street, into Station Street. There was a thick mist hanging over the ground, the nearby River Leven the cause of that. Jamie sat quietly beside him, speaking only when directions were necessary, deep in thought.

They had met, as arranged, that afternoon, Conor transporting the Triumph Bonneville from Dunoon on a trailer borrowed from a neighbour of his in-laws. Jamie had been outwardly delighted but his friend detected something else behind the smiles. He had quizzed him gently but his efforts gained him nothing. Whatever was bothering him, he wasn't about to divulge it.

They had eaten with Jamie's parents at five o'clock, Jamie's mother pulling out all the stops to feed the big American. She had reacted enthusiastically when Jamie phoned to say he was bringing Conor home for "tea", even when he went on to tell her they had to leave the house by six. He didn't say why and she didn't ask. The fact that Conor Whelan was with him made all the difference as far as Mary Raeburn was concerned.

Her confidence in the American was shaken a little when she saw the motorbike being unloaded from the trailer. She had a pathological dislike of motorbikes, especially motorbikes that Jamie brought home. She had unhappy memories of Jamie's father coming off one years earlier, before Jamie was born even, but his many weeks in plaster with broken fibula and tibia bones of his right leg remained with her. She had sometimes wished it had been his neck he had broken but she would never admit it.

The meal had been excellent and Conor's profuse praise restored her faith. Talk had been of family and children but even then, Conor noticed Jamie was unusually quiet. If his father or mother noticed, they didn't say, and Conor shrugged it off.

When Jamie announced they were leaving just before six o'clock and that they were taking the Austin, Mary Raeburn breathed a sigh of relief. It was bad enough riding a bike in summer, at this time of year she considered it madness. She trusted Conor's driving skills more than Jamie's biking skills but then, she had never sat in the front passenger seat of a car being driven by Conor Whelan. That might have changed her mind.

The drive down to Renton had taken just over twenty minutes. The road was straight and reasonably quiet as far as Bowling and Conor had pushed the little car along at speeds it had probably never achieved before. It roared a little, but the gauges, oil pressure and temperature, remained comfortably constant. It was only after skirting Dumbarton that Conor sought help and Jamie had furnished him with directions.

It was approaching Liam's stipulated time when Jamie instructed him to make for the railway station. There should be a telephone box there, he reasoned, and he was right. Conor pulled the car to a halt in front of the station building and eyed Jamie questioningly.

'Wait here,' Jamie instructed. 'I'll make the call and we'll take it from there.'

'You think he might want to meet?'

Jamie shrugged. 'Don't know,' he said. 'You got your Browning with you?' Conor smiled grimly and tapped the front glove box of the car. His expression seemed tortured in the diffused orange light of the streetlamps. Jamie nodded and stepped out into the slowly drifting fog. His heart was pounding.

***

Liam Fitzpatrick nipped the tip of his cigarette and tucked the remaining stub behind his ear. Eamonn Macari watched him dispassionately, pulling his overcoat around him and drawing heavily on his own cigarette. It was cold and he wished he was back in the safe house in the heat but orders were orders. No one was to leave the house alone, the old woman living there had said, "orders" she had added. No one questioned who had given the "orders", they all knew. And now Fitzpatrick was making a phone call and he had drawn the short fuckin' straw while Doherty and Finnegan sat back in the nice warm little house drinkin' beer. 'Bastards,' he mouthed under his breath.

Liam heard him and grinned. 'Ah won't be long Eamonn,' he said with a laugh. 'Ah'll have ye back with a beer in yer haun in no time, so ah will, but it's Duggan's orders.'

He checked his watch and walked over to the phone box at the corner of Main Street and Gilmour Street, Alexandria. It was precisely six twenty-nine. He pulled the door open and stepped inside, placing a handful of change on the top of the telephone unit. Quickly, he sneaked a glance back at his reluctant companion. Macari was too busy trying to keep warm to pay him much attention. He was a few yards away and the fog, though thin, was helping Liam. He turned back to the box, lifted the handset and placed a finger on the cradle. He started counting down the seconds. At forty-three he felt vibration through his finger and released the cradle just as the ringing started. He looked back at Macari. The man was lighting another cigarette, his head tucked close to his chest, oblivious to everything else around him. Liam turned his back on him.

'Don't say anythin', just listen,' he started urgently, keeping his voice low. 'Ah don't have time fer explanations an' ah've got a pal outside. 44 Margaret Drive, Alexandria; that's where we're holed up. The weapons are in a derelict building off Castle Road, Dumbarton... ah don't know the number but it's the only occupied buildin' in the street. The place is about to be demolished... an' there's enough firepower there to start World War feckin' three.'

'Explosives?' Jamie interrupted.

'No,' Liam retorted curtly. 'Uniforms... peeler uniforms an' firemen gear.' He hesitated only a moment then carried on. 'Ah need to go. Give me a number ah can phone ye on. Ah don't know when ah'll get the chance but when ah learn the target ah'll call. Then it's up tae you.'

'01369 – 355779. Ask for Conor an' say you're a friend of Jamie.'

'A friend o' who?'

'Jamie, they'll know who you mean.'

'Right, ah'll be in touch... Oh, an' one other thing; Orlagh Duggan arrived in Glasgow today. God be with ye.'

Jamie stood with the phone against his ear. His nervousness was still with him but Liam's parting words made him laugh... "ah'll be in touch", like he was considering an offer, not playing with his life... and with Orlagh now here, he surely was. Jamie was still laughing wryly when he replaced the handset and stepped out into the cold.

***

In Alexandria, Liam pressed his finger on the phone cradle and slipped money into the coin slot. Dial tone buzzed in his ear and he started to dial, afraid to turn and look at Macari. The phone at the other end of the line rang and he waited patiently.

'Hello, who's this? the voice of Molly Fitzpatrick echoed down the line.

'Hello Ma, it's me, Liam.'

Molly Fitzpatrick gave a little chuckle. 'Did ye think ah wouldn'a recognise ma own wee boy's voice,' she replied. 'Are ye okay? Where are ye?'

'Ah can't tell ye that, Ma, ye know that, but ah'm fine. We arrived in Liverpool on the third an' drove south. We're stayin' in a flat... proper shithouse...' He stopped, biting his tongue. 'Sorry, Ma, it's a dump, that's what ah meant t' say. Ah just wanted ye t' know ah'm alright.'

'That's fine son. Will ye phone again?'

'Aye, if ah can. Ah don't know if we're stayin' here or movin' on... might be goin' further south, least that's what we've been telt.'

'Okay son, take care an' watch yerself.'

'Ah will, never fear. Ah love ye Ma.'

'Love ye too son.'

They both ended the call at the same time. If Liam had stayed on the line he would have heard the tell-tale click as the recording device in Belfast disconnected... But he didn't need to hear it to know the call was monitored. That was a fact of life for a man on MI5s Watch List.

He pushed open the door and saw Macari looking at him belligerently. His heart missed a beat as he waited. 'What the feck kept ye?' the man spat angrily. 'It's feckin' freezin' out here.

Liam smiled apologetically. 'The line was busy,' he said. 'Feckin' women, eh?' he added with a laugh.

Macari simply growled and stomped off. Liam smiled again, happy this time, and followed. Another hurdle crossed and he was still in the game.

***

Less than two miles away, Jamie stood outside the Austin and lit a cigarette. Conor joined him and he handed over his packet of Embassy, waiting with his Zippo ready as the American pulled a cigarette free. No one was allowed to smoke in Conor's father-in-law's car. They stood for a moment, drawing on the tobacco before Conor's curiosity finally got the better of him. 'Well?' he asked, blowing out a cloud of smoke.

Jamie drew on his own cigarette before answering. He anticipated an angry explosion. 'He asked for a contact number... I gave him yours,' he said calmly.

'You gave him mine?' Conor retorted, equally calm... on the outside at least.

'Yeah, listen, I'm sorry... there was no other number I could think of.'

'Clara Whitelaw, maybe?' Conor responded.

He was controlling himself well, Jamie thought. 'Yeah, maybe.'

'And that's it... "Yeah, maybe"?'

'I said sorry... all he's going to do is phone and ask to speak to you. He'll say he's a friend of mine. He'll only call when he has the target... one call, that's it.' The anger was still there in Conor's face but it was subsiding.

'And what then?'

'Well, then I suppose I have to come up with a plan.'

'Don't you mean *we* have to come up with a plan?'

Jamie grinned sheepishly. 'Yeah, you're right, *we* have to come up with a plan.'

'So what else did he tell you?' Conor probed.

'The address of their safe house and the arms dump.'

'Which are?'

Jamie gave a quiet laugh and sucked on his Embassy cigarette. 'The safe house is in Aleaxandria... about a mile and a half down the road, that way,' he said, pointing west. 'And the guns are stored in Dumbarton, a couple of miles back that way,' he continued, turning and pointing back the way they had come.

They were silent for a while, enjoying the peace and their cigarettes. Conor had calmed down. He was thinking of the end game now.

'So why don't we just head down to the safe house now, while we're here, and finish it tonight?' he asked pensively.

'Because that probably wouldn't finish it. There are three Active Service Units of the IRA over here... that's 12 men. There are only four in the safe house. If we take out Liam's boys that still leaves eight and they probably have a contingency in place.'

'You make them sound like the US Marines,' Conor interrupted with a laugh.

Jamie drew him a look. 'Nah, they're not like your marines... they're much more committed... and dangerous.'

Conor returned his look, unsure whether he was joking. He decided he wasn't. 'So what do we do?'

'We wait. When we know the target we pass it on. We will take out Liam's group and the Brigadier can organise the rest... Probably the SAS.'

Conor nodded, thinking it over. It made sense. Everything done in one fell swoop. He doubted there would be any survivors. That made sense too. 'What do you want me to do until then?' he asked.

'I want you to stay in Dunoon and wait for Liam's call. Spend time with Mary and your kids... enjoy them.'

'And you?'

Jamie smiled bitterly. 'I'll be here, working away behind the scenes,' he said.

'The girl?'

'Aye,' Jamie nodded. 'The girl.' He didn't tell Conor that Orlagh Duggan had arrived. He didn't need to know. 'I'll be moving out from my mother's house in a day or two so you won't be able to call me there. Did you ask around for me?'

'Yeah... got a couple of addresses. I'll phone you with them tomorrow.'

'No, I'll phone you.'

Conor looked at him sharply. 'You still think...'

'I don't know,' Jamie interrupted. 'I'd just rather be sure no one knows where I'm moving to, other than you. There's an old Irish saying; "It is not a secret if it is known by three people". Let's just keep it to ourselves and I'll phone you. Better safe than sorry. Right, take me home James,' he quipped, his mood changing. 'Stop at another phone box on the way,' he went on. 'I've got another call to make... and you can stay the night at our house if you like. I've got a good bottle of malt,' he added, temptingly.

Conor grinned. 'In that case, I will. I'll phone Mary when we get to your place. Now, get your butt into the car and let's get out of here.'

Jamie smiled, drew his last mouthful of smoke and threw the glowing cigarette end away.

Conor followed the route back to Glasgow, almost forgetting to stop at a call box. Jamie reminded him then suggested he pull into the car park behind The Lincoln, a pub on Great Western Road not far from his parent's house. They left the car and went inside. There were a few drinkers in the public bar, all men, and fewer in the lounge. The drinkers here were mostly women. The public phone was in the lounge so they settled there.

Jamie ordered two pints of Tennent's Lager and carried them over to a table away from the bar. They were the only two men in the lounge and found themselves the centre of attraction. Conor returned the stares, smiling. 'Some good looking broads in here,' he said under his breath.

'Aye, but some of them know where I used to live so keep your carnal cravings to yourself. I've got enough worries,' Jamie joked. 'Look if you like but there's a bottle of malt waiting for us, remember. I'll be back in a minute.'

He took a swallow of the lager and pursed his lips. It wasn't his favourite but he was only having one. He placed the tumbler on the table and headed for the phone, some eyes following him while some stayed glued on Conor. He smiled to himself; most of the women were married and their men were probably in the bar. He hoped Conor took his advice.

Clara answered the call immediately. She had obviously been waiting. It was now after seven so she would be in a mood no doubt.

'It's me,' he said as she gave the number.

'I wasn't expecting anyone else,' she replied tetchily. She was in a mood. 'You're late.'

'Sorry; you going out or something?' he retorted cheekily. 'I can phone back tomorrow morning at the office if you like. Is Markey boy listening, is that it?' he went on, laughing now.

'No, he's not in. He was called back to Century House. There's a big flap on... probably the one we know about but they don't,' she said.

'So why the mood?'

'I'm not in a mood. I've got something on my mind, that's all. Anyway, get to the point. I take it you've spoken to Corkscrew... what does he have for us?'

'I'm fine thanks,' he retorted. Two could play. Clara, however, wasn't in the mood to play.

'Get on with it Jamie,' she said, and alarm bells began to ring.

'I've got the address of his safe house and the location of the arms dump. The safe house is in Alexandria... that's the one near Dumbarton, not the one in Egypt.' Clara didn't appreciate the joke. Her stony silence evidenced that.

'The arms dump is in Dumbarton itself,' he went on.

'Where?'

'It's a derelict building on a demolition site... off Castle Road.'

There was a pause before Clara posed her next question. 'What is there in Dumbarton worth attacking?' she asked. Nothing sprang to mind.

Nothing sprang to Jamie's mind either. 'A big rock with a castle on top and a very large whisky bond,' he told her. 'The castle will be garrisoned, I suppose, so it falls into the category of "military target". The bond isn't military and it's guarded by a flock of geese anyway.'

'Geese?' Clara queried, incredulous.

'They make great guards... make a racket if anyone comes near the place,' he replied seriously, only to be dismissed with a laugh.

'Well, I doubt they're going to attack a whisky bond so we can score that off the list. Anything else?'

'There is the submarine base at Faslane... and naval shipyards in Glasgow on the Upper Clyde.'

'The nuclear subs at HMS Neptune?'

'Yeah, the Polaris subs. They're at Faslane, aren't they?'

Clara laughed. She sounded amused by the thought. 'They wouldn't dare. The security around that place is impenetrable. It is on alert 24 hours a day. They would be committing suicide and they wouldn't get near the warheads.'

'How do the warheads get there?' Jamie asked out of simple interest.

'By road and rail. They're shipped up from the Atomic Weapons Establishment down here, in Berkshire, to the submarines but they're guarded the whole way... MOD Police – Special Escort Group – and Royal Marines, Fleet Protection Group as well as local plods on route. They wouldn't get close. They'd need a lot more than three ASU's and even then it would be suicide.'

'It was just a thought.'

'I know, I'm sorry. I shouldn't be biting your head off but...'

There it was again. The "but". *There is something going on and it involves me. What the hell is it?*

'It's okay,' he said. 'I get it. We're all under pressure with this mess. Just to add to yours, Orlagh Duggan arrived in Glasgow today.'

'Did she? The one you think is the bomber?'

'Woah,' he threw back. 'I never said that.'

'No, you didn't,' Clara said but she didn't sound convinced. 'We need to talk a bit more about her,' she continued.

The hairs on the back of Jamie's neck stood on end. 'Why?' he queried, trying to keep his apprehension in check.

'I just need more information... that's all. I want to put her in the frame for it or strike her out. You're the one in contact with Corkscrew, not me, so I need to speak to you about it.'

'Well, speak,' Jamie retorted shortly.

'No, not on the phone. I've got too many questions. If she's in Glasgow I'll come up. If she's the bomber we can finish it together.'

Finish it together? I don't think so.

'You're serious... You're coming here?' he asked doubtfully.

'Well, you can't come down here, not at this point in the game, and I do need to see you.'

Put like that it was plausible but still not quite right. 'When are you coming?'

'It'll be a day or so... I've got things to arrange here. How will I contact you? Where are you staying?'

He thought about that for a moment. Had the Brigadier really cut him adrift after his first meeting with Liam back in October... pulled off all the tails? 'I don't know, is the answer to both questions. I've been with my parents for a few days but I'm moving out. I don't want them involved when this goes down... If it goes wrong...' He didn't finish but Clara picked up anyway.

'Okay, I understand... In that case, phone me tomorrow. I'll know then when I'm coming up... we can fix something.'

'Yeah, right,' he said, unable to keep the antipathy out of his voice.

There was silence for a moment before Clara responded. 'I'm on your side, Jamie. I always have been, you know that. I just need to see you.'

'Okay, okay. I'm sorry. I'm tired, forget it. I'll call you tomorrow afternoon. That do?'

'Yes, that'll do. Take care.'

She hung up, leaving him staring at the phone. His gut was churning. Her farewell was clipped, and that was not like her; not like her at all. Something wasn't right... but what?

Chapter Fifty-four

Jamie eased the bike out onto Great Western Road and joined the light flow of traffic heading west. It was a dry, cold afternoon with bright sunshine glistening on the hoar frost that clung to the grass verges, trees and hedges. The pavements and roads were clear of ice now, a change from early morning when conditions had been treacherous.

Conor had left the Raeburn house around ten that morning, urging Jamie to phone him regularly. They had drunk Jamie's Laphroaig well into the night, ably assisted by his father. That had curtailed conversation on their plans for the immediate future but Conor got the impression that Raeburn Senior grasped more than he let on.

Conor's main concern was that Jamie would sully forth, without backup, to face the Irishmen on his own. In his mind he likened Jamie to a Scottish "Captain America", or Super-jock, ready to take on the forces of darkness, anywhere, any time... and crazy stunts like that could get him killed. He refused to leave until Jamie promised "not to do anything stupid" without him. Jamie had laughed; did that mean they could do stupid things together, he asked.

And now, here he was, breaking his promise... though only a tiny bit, he told himself. He wasn't being *that* stupid. He stuck to the speed limit. The last thing he needed now was to be stopped by an overzealous cop. The Walther tucked into his trousers at the small of his back would take some explaining.

As he passed the police station at the junction of Garscadden Road South and Great Western Road he opened the throttle on the Bonneville a little and accelerated past the slower traffic. Drumchapel appeared on his right, the rows of flats on Heathcot Avenue seeming to glow in the sunlight.

The landmarks flew past now but he still kept close to the speed limit. The Boulevard Hotel, the Kilbowie roundabout with Hardgate off to his right and Clydebank to his left. Next up on his right was Clydebank Crematorium, where he had supposedly been earlier in the day. He didn't let his conscience bother him. What his mother didn't know wouldn't hurt her.

He felt elated. The Bonneville was running as well as ever, its big 650cc engine straining to be given its head. Passing the slip road leading to the Erskine Bridge with Old Kilpatrick on his left, he twisted the throttle grip on the handlebars and pushed his speed up to 85mph. Bowling flew past. He could easily top the ton, he mused confidently, but he would keep that for another day. Content with the bike's performance, he throttled back and allowed his speed to drop to 70mph, falling further as he drove through Milton. The Dumbarton turn appeared on his left and he swung into the bend.

He was almost at his first objective, the demolition site at Victoria Road. The whisky bond and Dumbuck House Hotel were the final landmarks before the houses on the outskirts of the town appeared. Traffic was building but it was still moving. Jamie slowed to 30mph now, going with the flow along Glasgow Road, under the railway bridge and then turning into Victoria Street. Castle Street was next. The demolition site or, more accurately, demolition sites, were off to right and left.

The old roads were unmarked. Some buildings had already been brought down and mechanical diggers were filling lorries with rubble for transport off site. Men in hard hats moved about like ants, crawling over mounds of brick and mortar, directing the diggers. Further away, he could see rows of old tenement buildings. These were being stripped systematically of anything that was recyclable... wood, cable, lead and copper piping. He sat astride the bike at the side of the road, looking in through the security fencing, looking for the building that housed the weapons cache. It had to be part of the line of buildings being stripped, ready for the wrecking ball. But which. He couldn't get close enough... or could he?

There was a gap in the fence and a well-trodden path over the waste ground led towards the buildings beyond. No work was underway near the path and he assumed it was a short-cut used by the workers to get to the shops on the main road. He took out his cigarettes and lit up, considering his next move, when two labourers came across the waste ground towards the gap. His assumption about a short cut had been right.

He dismounted and strolled to the gap, waiting for them to squeeze through. Both men gave him a disinterested look as they negotiated the final few feet to the hole. Jamie didn't wait till they were through before asking: 'I was wonderin' if there was any work goin'?' he said as they closed on him.

'Don't know mate,' the closer man said. 'Ye'd need tae ask ower at the site office.' He turned as he straightened up, pointing back the way he had come. 'It's ower there,' he continued. 'They buildin's that are bein' stripped oot, wan o' them has the site office an' the bit the security men use. Ye cannae miss them. They're the wans wae the windaes boarded up. Aw the rest ur open tae the wind an' rain.'

The second man pushed through and both set off down towards the Glasgow Road. Jamie considered for a moment then squeezed through the hole in the fence. What was the worst that could happen? Nothing drastic. He followed the path, his boots crunching on the hard, frosty ground. Noise built up around him; engines, the clang of metal on metal, chain saws then the shouting and cursing of the men. Nobody stopped him. No one seemed interested.

He made it to the first tenement block. Here, where there had once been windows there were now just gaps all the way up from ground to top floor and the roof slates had been removed. Skips filled with the valuable slate stood nearby. The next block was a mirror image of the first. It wasn't until he reached the final block that things changed... and he still hadn't been challenged. Either nobody here knew what was stored in the place or, if they did, their security was shit. The final block wasn't too unlike the others, gaping holes for windows on the first, second and third floors, but the windows of the ground floor flats were boarded up. He looked up and noticed that the roof was still intact. This had to be the place.

He decided to push his luck. He turned towards the close entrance when a heavy set man in his fifties appeared in the opening, eyeing him suspiciously. 'Whit ur you efter?' he demanded, continuing to block the entrance.

'Ah'm lookin' fur the site office,' Jamie retorted in his best Glaswegian dialect. 'See if there's any work.'

The man stepped aside. 'First door oan the left... right up the hall tae the end. Ye'll find the gaffer in there. 'The first door's ma office. Security,' he added pompously.

"Office", Jamie thought, laughing inside. 'Right-oh, thanks,' he said, squeezing past the man's enormous belly. The smell of the man's body odour was almost overpowering, which was probably how he managed to incapacitate trespassers, Jamie mused... If he could catch them.

He strode to the door and entered, following the fat man's instructions to the letter. The door at the end of the hall was slightly ajar and he could hear voices coming from beyond. He pushed through and found a big man sitting behind a desk talking on the telephone. This wasn't like the security guard at all. He was big but it was mostly muscle and the donkey jacket he wore bulged in all the right places. He had a white hard hat on his head. The man looked up as Jamie entered, paused in his conversation and knitted his brow in a question, then nodded Jamie to wait.

'Someone's just come in. I'll phone back in five minutes but get those lorries organised or there'll be hell to pay.' He said no more but crashed the handset back onto its cradle. 'What can I do for you?' he asked.

'Ah'm lookin' for work,' Jamie went on, continuing the pretence. The man regarded him sceptically and Jamie knew what he was thinking. 'Ah've been abroad,' he said. 'Ah'm just back an' need tae find a job.'

'Have you got a trade?'

'Time served welder... worked a John Brown's, but the yards are nae use now. There's nothin' doin'.'

The man nodded knowingly. 'Aye, times are hard,' he said. 'We're nearly finished here,' he went on. 'Couple of months and we'll be gone but there's new work in Glasgow. The way they're going we'll be knocking the place down for the next twenty years,' he laughed, but he was serious. 'You look reliable. I can give you a name and an address. Write in. Say Bill Tolland, that's me, told you to write. You might just be lucky.'

Thanks,' Jamie responded quickly. 'Ah really appreciate it.'

The man wrote down the details on a scrap of paper and added his own name at the bottom before handing it over. 'You didn't give me your name,' he said, pen still poised.

'It's Michael, Michael Ferryman,' Jamie replied, smiling gratefully.

'Right Michael. I'll give them a call... tell them to expect something from you. Now, if you don't mind, I've got an arse to kick,' he said, lifting up the phone again.

Jamie grinned and left him to it.

Fatty was still at the door, smoking now. Jamie was grateful for that. It killed the sour smell of his sweat. He edged past him, holding his breath, and returned to his bike. That wasn't too difficult, he congratulated himself, and now he knew exactly where the guns were. Now, it was time to visit Alexandria.

He rode the bike back down onto Glasgow road and turned to the centre of town, following the signs. The Sheriff Court was there somewhere too. Just before the town centre he turned right onto the B830, rode under the railway bridge, passed the old power station at Hatfield Gardens that had once provided the power for Dumbarton's trams, and on up to the Stirling Road, the A813.

The familiar scenery of the night before flashed past and in minutes he was turning onto Bridge Street and crossing the River Leven. Alexandria was just ahead. Now all he had to do was find Margaret Drive.

He stopped on Main Street and dismounted, propping the bike up on its stand. He was in the main shopping area and people, mainly women, were bustling past. Raising the visor of his helmet, he accosted an older woman with heavy shopping, hoping she could direct him. She gave him a suspicious look but his smile won her over and she seemed glad to put her bags on the ground to catch her breath.

'Margaret Drive,' she repeated thoughtfully. 'Now, let me think. There's new houses up near the bypass... I think it's up there,' she said.

'How do I get there?' Jamie probed.

'Och, it's not far,' she assured him. 'Your best way is to turn round and head back down Main Street, past the fountain, and then take next on your right... that's Gilmour Street. If you go right to the end of Gilmour Street that should take you into Margaret Drive... I think.'

Jamie gave her another winning smile. 'If you want to jump on the back I'll run you home with your shopping,' he joked.

The lady laughed. 'If I was twenty years younger I would take you up on that,' she threw back. 'As it is, I don't think I could hold onto these bags and to you at the same time... so I'd have to dump the shopping. You've made an old woman's day,' she continued, letting out a theatrical sigh.

Jamie grinned and remounted the bike. He let her walk off a way before starting the engine, conscious of its throaty roar. When she disappeared into a nearby shop he turned the key and brought the beast to life. A number of people turned, startled, then carried on with their lives. He was just another man on a bike.

He checked the traffic and did a quick U-turn, following the woman's instructions. The fountain was unmissable, he had passed it on his way in, standing as it did at the junction of Bank Street and Main Street. Just over a hundred years old and built with Aberdeen granite and sandstone from

Bannockburn, it was topped by a bird, a heron. Water had once flowed from the fountain and from the bird's beak but that, like everything else these days, had gone. It wasn't a fountain any longer, just a pretty, ornamental pile of stone.

Jamie turned right into Gilmour Street and followed it to the end, a long straight of about 250 to 300 yards. Just as the old woman had said, it became Margaret Drive where it turned right to run parallel with the bypass. He pulled to the side of the kerb and scanned the length of the road ahead. It was a cul-de-sac. There were houses on his left, only four or five, the odd numbered side of the road. The houses on his right, fairly new semi-detached houses with small front gardens, stretched away from him. Number 44, he guessed, was somewhere towards the end, about 250 yards away.

It was quiet. With it being a dead end there was no through traffic and the bike would be noticed. He decided to ride to the end of the road, take a quick look at the house and the neighbouring properties, and then return. He could get away with it once, he reckoned; twice would be pushing it and three times would arouse suspicion.

He moved off, following the road slowly as if looking for a particular house number, his head turning to cast his eye over the buildings. On the odd numbered side, after the few houses there the ground was open with a tree screen bordering the road beyond, probably to deaden traffic noise, he assumed. 44 Margaret Drive was, he discovered, the last semi-detached house in the street and beyond that lay a wooded area. There were Venetian blinds on all the windows and they were angled such that the occupiers could look out but no prying eyes could see in.

The house next door had curtains, not blinds, and these were open. The tenants or owners of this house didn't seem to mind who looked in and the same could be said of the bulk of the other houses in the street. They had nothing to hide and anyway, he doubted that many people walked along here. He turned the bike in the tiny turning circle at the end and, careful not to let his eyes rest on number 44, made his way back down to Gilmour Street.

He was interested in the woodland at the end of the road and decided to check it out from another angle. He rode about fifty yards and turned left into Smollett Street. The houses here were older, red sandstone being prominent. He could see the trees above the roof line of the houses towards the end of the road on his left and what appeared to be open land straight ahead and off to the right. Interested, he rode the Bonneville to the end of the road, coming to a halt outside the last house.

There, he discovered, the road took a sharp 90 degree turn to the right and continued down towards the main road, running along the boundary of a public park. A gap in the fence and hedge edging led to a tarmacadam pathway that made its way across the grass to some small buildings in the distance. To the left of the path was a stretch of grass and beyond that, the trees. It was well-established woodland with a variety of trees, mainly deciduous, their leafless branches interlocking and stretching skywards like spidery fingers. In spring and summer, the foliage would form an umbrella of green over most of the ground below. Now, it stood bare and desolate.

He dismounted from the bike and strolled into the park. No one was about. The small buildings he had sat close to a children's play area, swings and roundabouts abandoned, the chains of the swings giving a melancholy squeak as they swung in the wind. He walked about ten yards, surveying the tree line, finally finding what he was looking for. Everyone loves a shortcut and the inhabitants of Margaret Drive were no different.

The path, turned to mud by the recent passage of feet, snaked out from the trees and made its way towards the gap in the fence. It could only lead to one place, he surmised, and that was Margaret Drive. He smiled to himself. That knowledge might come in handy at some point... If it were summer now and not the depths of winter, it certainly would.

Satisfied with his day's work, he returned to his bike, and prepared to head home. He kicked the machine into life and was about to move off when movement back at the treeline attracted his attention. Jamie waited, letting the engine idle, and watched as four figures emerged from the wood. They trudged, single file, over the muddy grass, their shoulders hunched against the cold. Liam Fitzpatrick was in the lead, followed by the Fionn Doherty. He couldn't remember the names of the others but they were the same men he had seen in the Clelland Bar in Gorbals back in October.

Intrigued, he switched off the bike's engine and waited. The four men were making for the gate leading to the street. Jamie dismounted and bent over the engine, apparently tinkering. The men exited the park and turned in the direction of the main road, following what Jamie discovered later was Park Street. They passed within a few yards of him but paid him no attention. They were too busy grumbling, complaining about something to Liam Fitzpatrick who was pointedly ignoring them.

Jamie remained beside his bike until the men had covered about 100 yards, passing the junction with another road. Before starting the engine again. The men were heading for what he took to be Main Street, about another 100 yards ahead. There was nowhere else they could be going. The park, Christie Park according to a large sign on the fence, stretched all along the road on the left and there were no buildings he could see on the right. Main Street was the only possible destination.

Jamie rode his bike slowly down Park Street, passed Middleton Street, and was level with the deserted greens of Vale of Leven Bowling Club when the four men turned right into Main Street and disappeared from his sight. He accelerated, anxious not to lose them, and reached the junction with Main Street just in time to see the men climbing into the back of an old white mini-bus.

He turned right into the main road and stopped. He was still about 50 yards away. The mini-bus was facing in the direction of Dumbarton but that didn't mean it would head off in that direction. Minutes later, a plume of diesel smoke blew from the tail pipe and the driver pulled away, crossed the road and headed east towards Bonhill or Renton. Jamie followed, keeping well behind. Traffic was light. That was a double edged sword. On the one hand, he could follow the bus without difficulty but, on the other, he would be visible to Liam and the others. Liam wasn't the problem; Doherty was, and, if he was as paranoid as Jamie suspected him to be, he might be looking for a tail. The time was just after four thirty and darkness was falling. Soon, he would have to use his lights and that was an added give away.

The mini-bus turned left into Bank Street so Renton was ruled out. They were heading for Bonhill or beyond. He dropped back, allowing a Volvo Estate Car to pass him and take up station between him and the bus. The little convoy proceeded onto Bridge Street and crossed over the River Leven, where the bus turned right. The Volvo turned left, leaving Jamie once again directly behind his quarry. He reduced his speed.

This road, the A813, ran all the way to the junction with the Stirling road, the A82, with only housing estates off to left and right but Jamie doubted the Irishmen were about to visit anyone living locally. If that were the case there would be no need for the mini-bus, he reasoned. Their destination had to be Dumbarton or, more likely, Glasgow. If his instinct was right they could be meeting with Orlagh Duggan and the other eight members of the team. He felt elated. Glasgow or Dumbarton? He would learn the answer to that in a few minutes when they reached the Stirling road. Turn left and they were heading for Glasgow, go straight on and it was Dumbarton.

The bus turned left. Jamie smiled to himself. Tailing it just got easier. There was traffic on the Glasgow road, a lot of traffic, and it all had its lights on.

Chapter Fifty-five

Orlagh Duggan, or Olivia Hammond as the hotel staff knew her, turned heads as she strolled casually through the foyer of the Stakis Grosvenor Hotel. Men eyed her salaciously, women enviously. She was oblivious to it all... she had seen it all before. She could probably have any man she wanted but none of this crowd came anywhere near tempting. And she had other things on her mind in any event.

She smiled warmly at the desk clerk as she approached reception and asked him to call he a cab. The clerk, who looked as though he had just reached puberty, blushed and stammered as he acknowledged her request. He was so overcome he forgot to ask where she was going but it didn't matter, she would have lied anyway. Still smiling, she walked across to a large leather sofa placed strategically to the side of the main exit and sat down, crossing her long shapely legs to the accompaniment of barely suppressed male libido.

The Grosvenor stood majestically at the corner of Great Western Road and Byres Road, overlooking Glasgow's Botanic Gardens and only a stone's throw from BBC Scotland's headquarters in Queen Margaret Drive. It was a good choice, she mused, as she surveyed the other guests. They were all, to a man... *and* woman, well dressed and well off. People's perception of terrorists is that they lurk in dark places, hiding in the poorer areas of cities and towns or living in the suburbs where they are the man or woman next door. No one expects them to book into the best hotels... and that suited Orlagh.

There was, however, one drawback to staying here. Meeting her co-conspirators in the hotel was out of the question. The men of the three ASUs, with the exception of one or two, would appear out of place in this bastion of middle class snobbery. Hence the need for a taxi.

She had made four calls from her room. The first had been to a number in Keady, just south of Armagh. To anyone listening, it was innocuous. She spoke to a woman, ostensibly her mother, and advised her of her safe arrival, though she didn't say where. The message would be relayed to her father. He would know.

The second, third and fourth calls were made to the three safe houses where the members of her assault teams were staying. One call was made to the house in Alexandria, one to a semi-detached house in Ashgill Road, Milton, on the north side of Glasgow, and the third to a multi-storey flat in Charles Street, Garngad, again to the north of the city. Again, the content of her calls was bland. It was a needless precaution but one born out of habit. It was needless because the Brits couldn't possibly know about these safe houses. They had never before been used and the occupants were, on the face of it, hard-working members of the local communities. That illusion wouldn't last, she smiled grimly.

The calls were made to set up meetings with her teams. Three separate calls and three separate meetings. It was time consuming, and it was a nuisance, but it was necessary. She wanted to ensure containment if any one unit was compromised. God forbid that happened, she reflected, oblivious to the irony of invoking God's aid, but if it did, they couldn't compromise the others.

Her taxi arrived a few minutes later, the driver poking his head into reception and calling out her name or, more accurately, the name Hammond. She rose from her seat on the sofa and made her way out behind the man, heads again turning as she passed. She smiled to herself. If she could bottle the hatred in the women's eyes she could sell it back in the "The Six Counties" for spraying on peelers and Brit soldiers. She'd make a fortune.

She settled into the back of the taxi and gave the address of the block of flats in Charles Street. If the cabbie wondered why a woman looking like her wanted to go to Charles Street, he didn't say. In fact, unlike most taxi drivers, he said nothing. Most of them have an opinion on something... actually, they have an opinion on *everything*, she mused, but this one was keeping them to himself which suited Orlagh right down to the ground.

The driver took her along Great Western Road and joined the new M8 motorway just beyond St George's Cross. She had been to Glasgow years before, when her mother had been alive, and this was new to her. There was nothing like this in Belfast and she took it all in. Ahead, she could see tall flats, twenty storeys she thought, counting them rapidly, and wondered if they were her destination. The driver came off the motorway at the Townhead interchange and before she knew it she was outside the block at number ?? Charles Street and the driver was twisting in his seat with his hand out. The fare was one pound and fifteen pence. She dug in her purse and gave him one pond thirty, telling him to keep the change.

She stepped out onto the pavement and looked up. The flat she was looking for was on the fifteenth floor. The flats reminded her of the Divis Road flats in Belfast but only in as much as they were high, everything else about them was different... no graffiti, no barbed wire, no wrecked and burnt out shells of cars... and the smell. It didn't smell the same.

The taxi drove off and she headed for the entrance, passing a group of women on their way out. They weren't like the women in the Grosvenor, not in the least, and it showed mostly in their eyes. If they were envious of her at all it was of her apparent wealth rather than her looks. They made some comments as they passed, comments she took to be insulting due to the use of the word "tart", but that was about the only word she could make out. They could have been speaking Swahili for all she knew.

There were two lifts, their metal doors firmly shut. She pressed the call button and waited. Above the lift doors a panel told the floor the lift was on. The lift currently on the tenth floor was still going up. The lift on the thirteenth floor started to descend. It stopped on the seventh floor and she could hear the doors grinding open and then closing before it moved again. It repeated that procedure on the fifth floor and then ground to a halt in front of her. She could hear voices and laughter from inside and then the door slid open to reveal a group of young men and two older men. No women. She stood aside to let them pass, fully aware of what was going through their heads. She smiled demurely and braved the wolf whistles and suggestions. She fancied the suggestions, they would make for an interesting night, but she didn't fancy any of the young men making them. They were still ogling her as she pressed the button for the fifteenth floor and the door closed.

The lift rose steadily, without stopping, all the way to the fifteenth floor. She alighted into a brightly lit hallway and four separate doors. She looked for the name Milliken on each door plate and found it at the third attempt. She knocked and waited. The door opened and a young woman appeared, a baby in her arms. She said nothing, just stepped aside. Orlagh was expected.

***

She left the flat just over half an hour later, her first unit briefed. It had gone well, better than she expected. There had been no rebellion. Not that they would have challenged her authority, they wouldn't dare, but the target might have spooked them. It didn't. She hoped her meetings with the second and third teams went as well.

Another taxi was waiting for her as she stepped out from the exit. Her next port of call was Milton. Not the house in Ashgill Road, she didn't want anyone seeing her going into or out of the house. This meeting was in a pub on Balmore Road and, for the first time, she felt nervous. She couldn't explain it.

She checked her watch. It was approaching five and it was already dark. She didn't know how long it would take to get to Milton but traffic was heavy now so it would be at least fifteen or twenty minutes, she guessed. She had told the men to be there at five when the pub opened and to wait for her in the lounge bar. She didn't want to arrive first.

The taxi followed Springburn Road, stopping at traffic lights and crawling at times. Eventually, the driver turned onto Keppochill Road and progress was faster then. At Saracen Street, the car turned right and joined more traffic, cars, lorries and buses, heading north towards Lambhill and Milton. They were crawling again, edging through traffic onto Balmore Road, then past Bilsland Drive and on towards Lambhill.

The pub was on the left, just before the canal. O'Malley's was an Irish pub, the name gave it away. As such, the presence of four Irishmen having a drink in the lounge wouldn't attract any undue attention. The taxi pulled up outside the brightly lit bar at twenty past five. Orlagh paid the driver and took a chance, asking him to return at six o'clock to take her to Partick. The driver grinned and nodded. He would be happy to do it... in fact, he would wait for her, and no charge. Orlagh smiled her thanks and left him there, reminding herself to leave the pub before the men of the ASU. The driver would remember her; she just didn't want him to remember her with *them*.

This meeting, like the first, went better than she had hoped. She knew these men well and they knew her. There were no problems on that score and the news about the target was received enthusiastically. They discussed the plan and their part in it. They didn't discuss the part the other units would play. Orlagh kept that to herself. The men drank slowly and little but they were happy to be out. Being cooped up in the house on Ashgill Road was getting on their nerves but she consoled them with the thought that they had just over two weeks to kill and then they would be heroes.

She left them at precisely six o'clock, telling them to enjoy a little more time of freedom before returning to the safe house. The taxi driver was snoozing lightly when she opened the door and climbed in, the smell of a recently eaten pie lingering in the air. The man rubbed his eyes and sat up, waiting for his next destination.

Orlagh grinned and settled back into her seat. 'Cavanagh's, Vine Street, Partick,' she said.

'Pub crawl is it?' the driver threw back, laughing himself.

'Yes, something like that,' she said, lighting a cigarette and closing her eyes. He took the hint.

***

Jamie followed the mini-bus into Glasgow, turning south at Anniesland Cross and following Crow Road. The vehicle could be heading for Hyndland or Partick, or even south of the river via the tunnel, but his gut told him its destination was Partick. Hyndland was too middle class for the boys in the bus, full of students and professional people... they would be too conspicuous.

His instinct was proved right again. The driver didn't head for the tunnel and, at the junction with Clarence Drive, stayed on Crow Road. Following now was less of a problem. The darkness helped, but none the less, he remained about 50 yards behind, allowing other vehicles to come between him and his quarry.

Finally, the driver turned off Dumbarton Road into Vine Street. Jamie rode straight on, turning as quickly as he could to return to the junction. The traffic was heavier now making the manoeuvre difficult and delaying him. He cursed again, anxious not to lose them. He needn't have worried. When he made it back to the junction he saw the bus stopped by the side of the road about 40 yards away, the four men clambering out onto the pavement.

He stayed out of sight and watched. There was some laughter, a brief conversation with the driver, and then the four men crossed the road, Liam leading, to enter a pub opposite. Jamie was now faced with a dilemma. He couldn't stay where he was on the main road, the police would move him, but Vine Street didn't afford much cover... and he needed to stay out of sight. The men were meeting someone, that much was obvious... they hadn't come all this way just for a pint, he mused, and if he wanted to see who it was he would have to take a risk.

Coming to a decision, Jamie swung the bike into Vine Street and drove down past the mini-bus. The driver was slumped in his seat, his head back and his eyes closed. That indicated the rendezvous was going to be relatively short. He did a U-turn and pulled to a halt at the kerb. He was now facing the mini-bus, about 20 yards away, on the opposite side of the road. He pulled back his left gauntlet and checked his watch. It read 6.19.

He considered his next move, contemplating the risk. He needed to see who was in the pub with the Irishmen and the only way he could do that was by going in. He might get away with sticking his head through the door, as though checking to see if someone he knew was there, but he would need to keep his helmet on. The only problem with that was that if the men and their contact weren't immediately in view, he couldn't hang about. But he had no alternative.

He eased the big bike back onto its stand and was just about to dismount when a black hackney cab entered the street and came to a halt behind the mini-bus. Something told him to wait and he settled back onto his saddle, watching carefully. He saw the interior light in the cab come on and a figure in the back, a woman he thought, leaning forward to talk to the cabbie. The driver was nodding and then the engine stopped. The cab's nearside door opened and the woman stepped out onto the pavement. She looked both ways, her eyes coming to rest for a moment on him, and then she crossed the road.

Jamie gave a low whistle. She was quite a looker... Tall, with long, dark hair - red maybe - it was hard to tell in the dark, and long, shapely legs that showed beneath her coat as it flapped open... and her breasts put Mae West to shame.

He looked back at the taxi and saw that the cabbie was taking a leaf out of the mini-bus driver's book. He was having a sleep. Coincidence? *Probably not, he mused,* and *if* not, then this might be the formidable Orlagh Duggan. He smiled grimly. On the other hand, it might just be a woman going to meet a friend, or her husband, for a quiet drink. The sleeping taxi driver said no to that but he had to be sure.

He swung off the bike and headed for the pub, looking at the name on the big signboard above the door as he did so. "Cavanagh's" it read, in bold gold letters on a dark green background. *That figures,* he thought with a smile. He stood by the door for a moment and then pushed it inwards and stepped inside, sweeping his eyes along the bar and then to both sides. He was disappointed at first. He couldn't see the four men *or* the woman but he couldn't wait. That would be suspicious. He was turning to leave again when, out of the corner of his eye, he saw a flash of red hair. When he turned back he saw the woman cross from behind the bar with Liam Fitzpatrick in tow. That was enough. He let go of the door, allowing it to swing shut just as the woman turned.

Jamie returned to the Bonneville and remounted. If she was suspicious at all someone would investigate, he was sure of that. He slipped his hand behind his back and felt the reassuring bulk of the Walther.

He waited. A minute passed, then two. No one came out from the pub. He waited another couple of minutes before allowing himself a brief smile. He knew what he had to do now.

Chapter Fifty-six

It was growing cold. Twenty minutes had passed since Jamie had poked his head into Cavanagh's and the mini-bus and taxi were still parked in Vine Street. He had driven the bike back out onto Dumbarton Road and parked in Merkland Street, making his way back to a small café that gave him a reasonably good view of the pub entrance.

He ordered a coffee and sat by the window, his helmet beside him on the table top. The place was empty. He imagined it might get busier as the night wore on but just now, at just after half past six, most people were home eating dinner. The café owner, a balding, middle aged man with an Italian accent, sat behind his counter reading and avoiding conversation, though his eyes flicked nervously in Jamie's direction from time to time. Jamie did his best to alleviate the man's stress by smiling at him from time to time but it seemed to have little effect... at least, it didn't make him appear any less apprehensive.

Jamie nursed his coffee and smoked a cigarette. A girl of about eighteen came in, flashed him a smile, and asked for a packet of Benson and Hedges and a packet of Wrigley's gum. If her skirt had been any shorter it would have been a boob tube, Jamie mused, grinning over at her. She had certainly brightened the place. She was still there when the pub door opened and the red headed woman stepped out. He finished his coffee in one gulp and picked up his helmet. The girl looked disappointed. He shrugged, smiled, and left her, running for his bike.

He was sitting astride the Triumph at the corner of Merkland Street, engine idling, when the taxi emerged from Vine Street and turned east towards Partick Cross. He waited, allowed a Corporation bus and two cars to pass before following, keeping a good distance behind.

The taxi kept up a steady speed and made the lights at the foot of Byres Road just as they changed from green to red. Jamie, caught behind a bus, saw the car turn into Byres Road, and cursed loudly. By the time the lights had changed to green again and he made it into Byres Road, the taxi was nowhere in sight. He rode steadily up towards Highburgh Road and University Avenue, slowing to look along both as he negotiated the junction but still there was no sign of the cab.

He passed Tennent's Bar on the corner of Highburgh Road and his thoughts flashed back to 1967. He hadn't been back in there since that fateful night when Jack Connelly had been stabbed... and probably never would. The lane drifted past on his right. Would he ever really be able to live with the events that happened there, he wondered. It was that "fate" thing again; at least, that was what he tried to tell himself, but it wasn't that... It was him. Everything bad that happened to the people he loved was down to him.

He felt a tear run down his cheek. He hadn't cried for a long time. Jack's funeral was probably the last time, but then it had been through grief and remorse; this was more through anger... anger at himself.

He had passed Hillhead Underground Station and the junction with Great George Street before he shook himself out of it. He had been riding on auto-pilot... and he had given up looking for the taxi with Orlagh Duggan on board, if it was Orlagh Duggan. He decided to head for home. The call to Clara could wait.

Byres Road was quite busy for a Wednesday evening. A week after New Year's day and the party spirit was still alive and well in Glasgow. The Christmas decorations, the flashing lights and glowing Santas were all gone but people were still stopping and shaking hands. That would go on for a couple of weeks yet. New Year was a bit like Christmas, it didn't last just one day.

The bars and restaurants were open and one or two shops still had their lights on. People drifted up and down the pavements, like two opposing tides, eddying constantly against one another. He rode on past Roxburgh Street, Cresswell Street, Loudon Terrace and the big sandstone building that housed the public library. He allowed his thoughts to wander again. It was a beautiful part of the city and yet some terrible things had happened here. He was still ruminating on that thought when his old friend fate played a hand again.

Ahead of him there was a squeal of brakes and the traffic backed up, red brake lights coming on in sequence. The traffic coming from Great Western Road had also stopped. An old man was being helped across the road by a group of people and drivers were coming from their cars. An accident of some sort. He was stopped just at the junction with Grosvenor Lane, the big bike's engine purring beneath him, when some thought made him turn to look into the lane. A black hackney was sitting in front of the hotel entrance and, as his eyes travelled from cab to the revolving hotel door, a saw a flash of red in the glass and then it was gone. It was her. He sensed it.

Quickly, he turned the bike and rode up the lane, passing the cab as it pulled away. He stopped outside and peered into the foyer through the glass. She was at reception, picking up her key, smiling at the receptionist... looking perfectly normal and, he had to admit, beautiful. And yet... she was neither, really..

He pulled away, back down to Byres Road, turned left and left again at the traffic lights taking him onto Great Western Road. He now had another part of the jigsaw in place. Maybe it was time to call Clara after all.

Chapter Fifty-seven

He stopped at Knightswood Cross and used the usual telephone box. Somebody had been using it for another purpose, it seemed, the wrinkled remains of a used condom lying ignominiously among the usual detritus of cigarette ends, matches and scrunched up fag packets. He couldn't imagine anything worse than a "knee trembler" in this place on a cold winter's night.

He lifted the handset, fed in coins and dialled. Clara answered.

'Kensington 2779,' she said.

'It's me,' Jamie responded without introduction. He heard her laugh.

'Of course it's you,' she retorted, still laughing. 'No one else phones me here.' Jamie didn't believe that for a minute but he let it go. 'I'm coming up to Glasgow next week,' she went on without further ado. 'I'll be there on Monday. Can we meet on Monday evening?'

'I suppose so,' he replied, sounding a little brusque even to his own ears. 'Where will you be staying?' he continued, trying hard to take the edge out of his voice.

'I haven't booked yet. Probably somewhere in the city centre; the Central Hotel or the Ivanhoe.'

'Can I make a suggestion?'

'Of course you can... what is it? She was intrigued.

'The Grosvenor Hotel... It's on Great Western Road, the West End... you'd like it there.'

She laughed again, suspiciously this time. 'Come on Jamie, you don't work for the Glasgow Tourist Board, if there is such a thing, so why the interest in this place?'

'There's someone staying there I think you should meet... Well, maybe not meet, more have a look at,' he qualified.

'And who would that be?'

'Orlagh Duggan.' There was silence for a moment before Clara responded to the news.

'Ah,' she said, and that was it. Nothing else.

'You don't sound enthusiastic.' There was another pregnant silence. He found it unnerving.

'It's just... well, she is the reason I have to see you.'

The pause in the middle was unsettling and the silence that followed was all down to Jamie this time. His nerves kicked into overdrive. The feeling that something was wrong was back, and how! 'What's the problem?' he probed, a little apprehensively, dreading the answer.

'Just some questions,' she responded easily. 'I'll tell you all about it on Monday... and I'll take up your suggestion about the Grosvenor. Do you want to meet me there for dinner on Monday evening?'

'For dinner?'

Clara laughed. 'Yes, dinner... don't worry, darling, you can trust me; I won't try to get you into bed again.'

That's not the problem, Jamie mused. I'm not sure I can trust myself.

'Yeah, okay... say seven in the lounge. We can have a drink first.'

'Perfect. Now, tell me how you know Orlagh Duggan is staying there.'

There was no need for silence now. 'I went down to Dumbarton today,' he started. 'I visited the arms cache... and there was no security I could see. The guns and other stuff must be well hidden.'

'You were taking a chance,' she threw in. 'What if you had been seen?'

'That was a risk I had to take... but I calculated it first. I didn't think it likely any of Corkscrew's ASU would hanging around.'

'Fair enough; what else?'

'I went on to their safe house after that. Nice, quiet area... out of the way. It's at the end of a cul-de-sac with a wood beyond and behind it. They can come and go through the wood without attracting attention... there's a well-used short cut...'

'And what was your calculation on that one? Did you think they wouldn't be hanging around there too?' she interrupted, caustically.

'Don't worry; I was careful. They did see me, right enough,' he went on and heard her gasp. 'But they didn't recognise me,' he laughed, cutting off her comment. 'I was wearing a crash helmet with the visor down.'

'You're incorrigible,' she said, recovering a little. If it was a complaint it didn't sound like one, Jamie thought. 'But that still doesn't explain how you know Duggan is staying in the Grosvenor Hotel,' she continued, back to business.

Jamie's laugh simply increased her apprehension. 'Corkscrew and his pals went for a run in a mini-bus... I followed them.'

'Good God, Jamie, are you out of your mind... If you're seen the game will be up.'

'Calm down, I wasn't seen. I'm not completely stupid... and I have a well-developed sense of self-preservation.

'Don't patronise me,' she retorted tetchily.

'I'm not patronising you, I'm just telling you like it is. Believe me, no one saw me. I followed Corkscrew and his boys to a pub. They met Duggan there and, when she left, I followed her.'

'How do you know it was her?'

'She fit the description Corkscrew gave me... And who else would they meet?'

'And you're sure you weren't seen?'

'Christ, Clara, how many times do I have to tell you?' he exploded.

There was another of those silences that occur when people don't know quite what to say next. It was Clara who found her tongue first. 'I'm sorry,' she said diffidently. 'I just can't help worrying about you... You know that.'

'Yes, I *do* know that... just try not to think about it,' Jamie replied. He thought about saying "don't think about *me*" but discarded the idea, it wasn't going to happen. He tried to steer the talk away from that particular subject but all of the other subjects were equally troublesome. He went for the Orlagh Duggan question; he had to face it sometime so why not now. 'While we're on the subject of the Duggan woman; what is it you want to ask me?' he asked.

Clara wasn't ready to play that game. When she posed her questions she wanted to be able to look him in the eye. She wanted the truth. He could lie to her but his eyes couldn't. 'I told you, it's just a few questions... nothing to get worked up about. We'll talk about it on Monday and maybe by then we'll know the target.'

'Yeah, alright,' Jamie replied, giving up the fight.

'Until then, be careful. No more taking risks... that's an order.'

'Yes, ma'am,' he replied, snorting a little laugh. 'I'll see you at the Grosvenor on Monday... seven o'clock.'

He hung up the phone quickly. He didn't know if she was going to say she loved him but if she was, he didn't want to hear it. His life was already too complicated... but talking to Clara had given him an idea.

Chapter Fifty-eight

'Still no word from your man,' Conor said after they had gone through the preliminaries. 'Have you been behaving?' Jamie's soft laugh suggested he hadn't.

'Of course I have... I promised, didn't I.'

'Why don't I believe you?'

Jamie's laugh grew louder. 'Because I'm me?' he suggested. 'Listen, Conor, I'm a big boy. I went down to Dumbarton and Alexandria for a look see, that's all... On the bike, helmet and all. I can't just sit on my arse and wait to see what happens; I need to be doing something.'

'Yeah, yeah, okay... It's just that I worry when you head off on one of your expeditions, that's all.'

'Aye, you and everyone else,' Jamie retorted, immediately biting his tongue. He hoped Conor didn't come back on that.

'Are you still looking for somewhere to stay?'

'No, I've sorted that. I'm moving out tomorrow... told my mother I'm heading back south.'

'That as quick. How the hell did you find somewhere?'

'It was easy, actually. It's a hotel... and I can kill two birds with one stone.'

'It isn't exactly a safe house. What if...'

Jamie didn't let him finish the question. 'I need to be contactable, Conor. A hotel has phones... a rented place doesn't, unless it's shared and that's no good.'

'Okay, that's one bird; what's the other?'

'What?' Jamie retorted, confused.

'Two birds with one stone, you said, so what's the other?'

'A place to stay *and* be contactable; that's two.'

'Bullshit! Come on, Jamie. I know you... there's something you're not telling me.'

Jamie laughed affectionately. 'You're not as dumb as you look, Conor,' he joked.

'I'll take that as a compliment. So, what is it?'

'You're not going to like it... and you'll do your big brother thing again...'

'It's a woman?' Conor butted in, incredulous.

Jamie continued laughing. 'Sort of...'

'Who? The good doctor, huh?'

'No, not Clara...'

'Then it has to be the Irish broad... right?'

'Almost,' Jamie replied. 'She's Irish, right enough, but not the Irish broad you're thinking of.'

'You're talking in riddles again. How many Irish broads are there?'

'Two that matter... The one you know about and one you don't.'

'You're still doing it,' Conor retorted, irritated, and Jamie's laugh didn't help.

'The one you don't know about is the one co-ordinating the attack over here and she's also the one I'm trying to set up for the bombing in Coventry.'

Conor was quiet for a moment as he assimilated that piece of news. 'She's going to be staying in this hotel?' he asked at length.

'She's already there.' Jamie expected an explosion from the big American but it didn't materialise.

Instead, he sounded resigned when he did eventually respond. 'Okay, give me the name of the hotel and a number.'

It's the Grosvenor on Great Western Road. I don't have a number, but I'll phone you with it, and my room number, tomorrow.'

'You want me to come join you?'

Jamie laughed again. 'You never give up, do you? No, you have to stay there until Corkscrew contacts you. After that, we'll see,' he said. That, he hoped, was consolation enough for him..

Chapter Fifty-nine

Friday 11 January 1974

Jamie moved into the Grosvenor Hotel at lunch time. There had been a tearful, not unexpected, parting from his mother but she had said she understood. She wouldn't understand if she knew the real reason for his leaving, he reflected ruefully as he rode off on the Bonneville.

The bike could be a problem, he decided. It turned heads, a bit like beautiful women turn heads, and once seen it stayed in the memory for a while. In his present situation, that wasn't particularly good. He made a phone call from the coin box at Knightswood Cross, the usual one, and then made for Possilpark.

His short, cryptic message to Father Frank Daly was enough to guarantee the bike a safe haven. The old Priest asked no questions, simply greeted him warmly, let him change out of his leather biker's gear into more conventional clothing, and bid him good luck. 'Stay in touch lad,' he said. It was more a plea than a suggestion.

Jamie smiled, one of those enigmatic smiles the old man had come to know so well, and nodded. 'Pray for me Frank,' he replied softly, words the old Priest found more disturbing than anything he had heard from him before.

A taxi picked him up at the Chapel House and whisked him off to the hotel. He had booked by telephone the night before and his room was ready. It was a double on the second floor with a big window facing out over Great Western Road to the Botanic Gardens beyond.

The Grosvenor was one of those hotels Jamie knew well from the outside but had never visited or stayed in. His frugal Protestant upbringing baulked at the expense. That, of course, was before he met Sir Charles Redmond. His Protestant upbringing also baulked at the idea of killing and he had managed to get over that. He could handle the extravagance now too... especially as the Brigadier was picking up the tab.

He laid out his clothes and arranged his things in the drawers and wardrobe, taking particular care with the Walther. It wouldn't do for one of the chamber maids to find that. He chose to put it in the cistern in the toilet, carefully sealed in a plastic bag. No matter how fastidious the maids were, he doubted they would clean inside the cistern but he left a tell-tale just in case.

Satisfied with his work, he phoned Kate. She already knew he was moving, she just didn't know where. The news that he was staying in a hotel came as a pleasant surprise to her; at least he would be at the end of a telephone line if she needed him, she said. It made her feel a little less anxious... but only a little. Had she known *why* he was staying at this hotel, the "little less" would have been a hell of a lot more. But she didn't know, and she didn't ask.

His first task was to explain to Kate what to do should his mother try to contact him. If Kate answered the call it should be straightforward but it would be bloody disaster otherwise. And there was a good chance of that. Kate's mother didn't hang about when the phone rang and if she got to the thing first the proverbial cat would be out of the proverbial bag. Unless, of course, she was in on the subterfuge, but that was a decision he left to Kate. Other than that, his plan was simple; if his mother called, Kate would say he was out and would chat away for a while before promising to have him call back, which he would do later, from the hotel. It could work, just as long as his mother didn't insist on talking to them both at once. He prayed they could carry it off. His mother's wrath could be fearsome, not to mention the disappointment she would feel.

He called Conor immediately afterwards, giving him his room number and impressing on him the need to phone as soon as Liam Fitzpatrick made contact... no matter what hour of day, or night. If Jamie was out, Conor was to leave a message.

His calls done, he dressed in a pair of Levis denims, a navy blue Byford Polo Shirt and his suit jacket. Dark brown leather shoes completed the outfit, smart but casual and expensive enough not to look out of place in the hotel.

He left the room and made his way via the stairs to the ground floor and the dining room. He had eaten little that morning, his nerves playing up. Not nerves as to what he was doing, nerves about hiding it from his mother. She had a knack of sussing out his deceptions. Having completed the operation successfully, he decided to reward himself with lunch and a drink, though too much of both were not a good idea. He had to stay sharp.

The hotel restaurant was still moderately busy though the diners were, he guessed, mostly professional people enjoying a working lunch and not guests. He cast an eye around the big room, feigning disinterest, while all the time searching for Orlagh Duggan. His last sighting of her - his *only* sighting, in fact - had been hurried, and at a distance. He wanted to see her up close. He always preferred to have a close look at recipients of "the good news" - he never called them victims - before a hit to let him gauge their physical and mental strength. It limited surprises.

But he couldn't see her anywhere. Her flame red hair was unmistakable and none of the women in the restaurant came close. There were honey blondes and women with auburn tresses but no one with red like Orlagh's. He felt disappointed. He really did want to see her and, if possible, get close.

He eased his disappointment with a sirloin steak, rare, with "fries" and what the menu called "Roast Winter Vegetables" – which, to Jamie, were simply chips with carrots, parsnips and suede cut into thick slices – accompanied by a pint of French lager. That cheered him up somewhat but not entirely. He was still troubled by Clara's insistence on coming to "talk to him" about said Orlagh Duggan. He consoled himself with the fact that he still had the weekend to prepare for it, whatever it was, but that was a double edged sword... It also gave him the weekend to worry. That brought him to Roisin. It would help to know how she was bearing up. The last he had heard, her health was improving but she was still in the hospital. He wondered if she was still there now. He should find out, he decided.

A commotion near the door caught his attention and he turned, curious. The sight that greeted him brought a cold smile to his face. Orlagh Duggan, for it could only be Orlagh Duggan with hair like that, had arrived for a late lunch. One of the waiters, his mind more on her than the job, had lost his footing and distributed a tray load of plates and cutlery across the restaurant floor. Fortunately, the plates were on their way to the dishwasher and not a table of diners, so the mess was limited. Jamie wondered if chaos like that followed her everywhere.

She swept in imperiously, neatly sidestepping the disaster area as her eyes swept the room without resting on anyone or anything. Jamie watched her for a moment, his eyes crinkling in amusement, then looked away. She probably wouldn't notice him but he wasn't taking the chance. Apart from anything else, he didn't want to seem interested. If she did look, his disinterest might just intrigue her enough to make her interested in him. If she approached him, fine. It wouldn't happen the other way around.

He waited until she had settled then, pointedly ignoring her, pushed his plate away and rose to his feet. He thought he felt her eyes on him but resisted the temptation to glance across. Two could play at her game.

He left the restaurant and headed for his room. The maids had been. The bed was made up and the place was pristine. He made for the bathroom and checked the cistern. It hadn't been moved. The tell-tale was still in place.

He thought about Orlagh Duggan as he looked out over the busy road to the Botanic Gardens beyond. What a waste, he mused. She was a beautiful woman. She could probably have anything she wanted in life... well, almost anything, but the thing she wanted most was the thing she couldn't get so, while she had the world at her feet, she had decided to kick it in the balls. She might be beautiful to look at but inside she was twisted and ugly. Like he said; what a waste. He shrugged the thought away.

He took his heavy coat from the wardrobe, checked the room and left. As he passed through reception he could just see Orlagh at her table in the dining room, her eyes fixed on her food, ignoring everything around her. He allowed himself another little smile. She thought she was invulnerable but she was in for a shock.

Outside, it was cold. A weak sun was doing its best to thaw the ice and frost but it was losing the battle. Grit had been spread on the pavements and he could hear his boots crunch on it. Orlagh wasn't likely to be going anywhere in a hurry, he decided, so he had time for something else. On impulse, he crossed over Byres Road and made for the bus stop on Great Western Road. In the distance he could see a number 11 bus. Its route would take it along Great Western Road to Anniesland and beyond before it turned left at Knightswood Cross for its destination at Garscadden. It would do nicely.

He stepped down from the bus at the stop before Gartnavel General and The Pond Hotel. He was about He stepped down onto the pavement and started walking as the bus pulled away, the stench of diesel filling his lungs. He gathered his thoughts and wondered how to play it with Roisin, if she was still there. Be open, he decided. There was no point in building up expectation when there were still things to resolve and his upcoming rendezvous with Clara was still nagging away at the back of his mind.

The place hadn't changed much. It hadn't changed at all, really. The only thing that was different now was the colour. In October, it had been all brown and yellow and red, now it was white with an over wash of grey. It had been depressing then and it was more depressing now.

He rang the bell and heard the footsteps approaching on the other side of the door. It was like a jail, he mused, which, in a way, it was. Only difference was that here, in the main, the "prisoners" were locked up to prevent them harming themselves and not others.

A nurse opened the door and stood aside to let him enter. You could get in easily enough, getting back out was the problem. It was a different nurse from the time before but she was straight out of the same mould. She had a kindly enough face but you wouldn't want to get on the wrong side of her. He explained who he was and asked if Roisin was still a patient. She was indeed, the nurse informed him, but not for much longer. That the good news. The bad news was that her husband Trevor was with her but he could go up anyway. Jamie gave a mental shrug. He had to face the man sometime and at least he would learn if Roisin had told him what she had done, and why.

He made his way up the stairs and followed the passage to Roisin's room. He could hear voices behind the door. They seemed happy. He hoped he wasn't going to pour cold water on that. He knocked the door gently and the talking stopped. Slowly, he pushed the door open and stuck his head in, a smile fixed on his face.

The talking stopped and two faces turned to him. The reactions of both were entirely different. Roisin's face went through a metamorphosis from curiosity to surprise and then elation. Trevor's face remained wary and questioning.

'Jamie!' Roisin exclaimed, rising to her feet and rushing to him. That didn't help with Trevor, Jamie noted. 'You've come back,' she went on happily.

Jamie held her close and let his eyes drift to her husband. Trevor was watching closely. His expression wasn't malevolent but it wasn't exactly friendly either. He might as well jump in with both feet, he decided. 'Have you told him?' he asked, trying to keep it casual.

Roisin pulled back. The smile was still in place and her head bobbed up and down. That was positive at least. Trevor was still trying to come to terms with it all, probably trying to slot him into what he had learned.

'I've told him everything,' Roisin said quietly, turning to her husband for confirmation.

Everything? I hope not, Jamie mused.

Trevor stood up and Jamie now had the opportunity to gauge him properly. He was big and he was broad, at least two inches taller than Jamie and a good few inches wider. His face was still like granite but a crack or two had appeared. Jamie wasn't sure if he was smiling or grimacing. The man held out his hand and Jamie took it, feeling the strength there. The guy could probably crack walnuts with hands like that. Roisin had chosen well, he decided. Pity Trevor hadn't been around when rat face Doherty visited a couple of years before. Things would probably have turned out differently, he suspected.

'Everything?' Jamie asked, repeating the word.

'Yes,' Roisin replied simply and Trevor was nodding.

'*Almost* everything,' the big Englishman qualified in a voice that was strangely soft. 'What I don't know is where you fit in.'

Jamie pushed the door closed behind him and moved deeper into the room. There was a spare chair near the window and he pulled it over before lowering himself into it with a sigh. Trevor waited, still on his feet. 'Sit down, both of you, please. You're making me uncomfortable.'

He waited as both returned to their seats. They looked cautiously at one another before Trevor took his wife's hand and turned to face him. Jamie gave him his full attention. There was no hostility in the man's eyes but he wanted answers.

'Why did you come to see Roisin in October? How did you know?'

Jamie looked him straight in the eyes. 'I came because her cousin Liam told me the story...'

'Aye, so she said, but there's more to it than that. I'm not stupid.'

Roisin looked up at Jamie and he could tell from her imploring look that she hadn't told Trevor everything... The personal everything, anyway. He smiled at both of them.

'No, you're not stupid, I know that, but there's a limit to what I can tell you... for your own good,' he added after a short pause.

'So what *can* you tell me?' Trevor sounded a little disappointed and Jamie could understand why. If Roisin had told him about Doherty and her brother then he would be out for revenge.

'Tell me what *you* know,' Jamie countered.

Footsteps sounded in the corridor outside and all three fell silent. The padding feet grew louder as they passed outside the door and then faded. Jamie raised an eyebrow, inviting Trevor to respond.

'I know what she did,' he said quietly, 'and I know why. I would have done the same.'

Jamie laughed coldly. 'So would I,' he announced.

Trevor stared back at him, waiting for more. 'Is that it?' Jamie asked.

'What else is there?' the big man retorted belligerently.

'The future,' Jamie said simply.

'Who knows what that holds?' Trevor threw back.

Jamie smiled again, as cold as before. 'I do,' he said. 'And that's why I'm here.'

'You didn't get that from Liam,' the Englishman replied, laughing softly. 'The past, yes, but not the future.

'No, the future is all me and it's not rosy, believe me. Putting it simply, Roisin's in a dangerous situation. Nobody has forgotten about that bomb. People are still looking for the bomber... and they're getting closer.'

'How do you know that?' the Englishman asked dubiously. Jamie's frosty smile should have given him an inkling but he pressed on. 'It's been more than three years. The trail will have gone cold.'

Jamie gave him a pitying look and shook his head. 'Three years or thirty years, they won't give up...'

'I know that,' Trevor interrupted, frustrated. 'But as time goes by it gets more difficult, surely.'

'No it doesn't. And before you ask how I know all this, if I wasn't here to help Roisin then the show would be over. I won't go into detail, but I've got a job to do that involves Liam Fitzpatrick... he's here in Scotland by the way. That job is to help him disappear but there's another part to it.' Jamie paused, staring at the couple hard for a moment. Roisin looked fearful, Trevor looked lost. 'That other part was to quiz Liam on the identity of the bomber, find out who she is... and then kill her.'

The impact of that was immediate. Trevor's face contorted in rage and he started to push himself up out of his chair but Jamie was ready. He rose first and pushed Trevor back, forcing him down into his chair again. 'Now you are being stupid, Trevor,' he spat. 'If I was going to do that I would have done it in October, last time I was here. Think about it. And if I was going to do it now would I announce the fact? Get real.'

The big Englishman sagged back and stared at the ceiling, his mind in turmoil. When Roisin told him her story he had thought things couldn't get worse. He had adjusted to it, convinced himself everything would be alright, and now his hopes had been shattered. The nightmare was real.

He dropped his gaze from the ceiling at last and fixed his eyes on Jamie. 'I'm sorry,' he said.

'No need. I wanted to be sure you got the message. Brutal, I know, but now you know exactly where you stand.'

He turned to Roisin. Tears were welling up behind her eyes and he could see the dark clouds gathering. The last thing he wanted was her to relapse. 'I said I was here to help,' he said reassuringly, ' and I will. I have been, in fact, though how successfully I don't know. I won't go into it but, if I've got it right, you'll be off the hook in a couple of weeks. If I haven't, then we need to think of an alternative and the only one I can think of is that you disappear.'

'I can't leave Trevor,' she said, reaching out for her husband's hand. The Englishman looked lost.

Jamie nodded. 'I didn't think you would,' he said, 'but unless he agrees to disappear with you, you might have to.'

The couple looked at one another despairingly and then at Jamie. 'How can we do that?' Trevor asked. 'I'd be a deserter and I'd be hunted down. We would be on the run for ever...'

'Aye, if you stayed as Trevor and Roisin Evans, you would, but if you were somebody else with new passports, American for example...' He let the suggestion hang in the air.

Trevor laughed bitterly. 'And how do you arrange that?' he fired back. 'Apart from anything else it takes money, a lot of money.'

Jamie smiled benignly. 'Normally, yes, it does, but it's easier if you know someone.'

'And you do?' Trevor's scepticism was still evident.

'As it happens, yes, I do. It will still be difficult but it can be done. I hope we don't have to go down that road but if all else fails, it's your way out. It all comes down to you.'

'What's your other plan?' Trevor came back.

Jamie smiled again. 'You don't really want to know,' he said quietly. 'But if it works, you won't need to worry about disappearing. You'll just have to trust me on that.'

Trevor nodded and looked back to Roisin. It had been a lot to take in, Jamie knew that, but his judgement of the Englishman made him think that disappearing wouldn't be off the table. He saw the imperceptible little nod pass between them.

It was Trevor who spoke next. He said, 'Okay, we trust you... and if it comes to it, we'll all disappear together.' He smiled and turned to Roisin, squeezing her hand.

Jamie stood up and headed for the door. He stopped as he pulled it open, turning back to them. 'Be ready to go in the next couple of weeks, just in case,' he said, adding the last bit in an attempt to allay their fears. He doubted it worked but they were lucky, they had each other.

He left them then. At the main door he chatted for a moment with the nurse who had admitted him. He wanted to know how much longer Roisin would be there. "A couple of weeks, not more" the nurse advised. Jamie smiled. It was a timescale that fitted perfectly.

He struck off down the driveway towards Great Western Road, his mind churning over the options and the possible problems, not least of which would be his meeting with Clara. What exactly did she know, he wondered. He kept walking, shunning the bus this time. The exercise and the solitude, the time to think, would do him good he decided.

Chapter Sixty

Back at the hotel later, Jamie learned that a call had come in for him while he was out. As the receptionist reached back for the note, his mind wondered who had called; Kate or Conor? It couldn't be anyone else. The girl smiled as she handed over the note and gave him his key. He returned her smile absent-mindedly, slipped the folded note into his jacket pocket, and made for the lifts.

His timing couldn't have been better. As the lift door opened he saw a flash of red mane and Orlagh Duggan stepped out. He couldn't ignore her this time so he offered her a polite smile and stepped past her into the lift. She smiled back but there was more to it than politeness in it. If he had been of a mind he could have struck up conversation there and then but he wasn't of a mind. He had her interest. He just didn't want her to know she had his. He turned in the lift and faced her, returning her gaze while trying to appear aloof. She smiled again. He had thrown down a challenge and her smile said she was up for it.

Orlagh's smile said a little more than that. She had something in mind and he should have seen it. She was thinking "light relief", something to take her mind off the tension building in her. Sex was good for destressing, she found... especially good sex, and she was also thinking he could give her that. As long as she didn't mix business with pleasure all would be well, and she had time on her hands. Apart from anything else, he wasn't like the other men in the hotel... not by a long way. He wouldn't fawn over her and follow her around like a love-sick puppy and that was important. For a man like him, she suspected, there would always be another Orlagh just around the corner. He was like her in a way. By the same token, she mused, it would take more than a demure little smile to have him panting, but she would get there. She always did. She let her eyes linger on him as the lift door closed, hoping he would pick up the vibe, but he had turned away. He really was going to be a challenge, she decided.

Jamie smiled wryly to himself as the lift started to ascend. Getting close to Miss Duggan might be easier than he had anticipated. The problem might be in keeping her at bay. He thought about her for a moment. She was attractive... no, she was more than attractive, the lustful eyes of every other man in the hotel told him that, and she was confident. Intelligent, confident and beautiful; quite a combination, he decided. She was more than a country girl from County Armagh. She fitted in here as if she belonged. That told him she had been around, and not just in Ireland. If what he knew of her was to be believed, she was ruthless as well as intelligent, confident and beautiful. Left unchecked, she would rise high in the Organisation and that made her dangerous. That might prove important when he was discussing her with Clara.

The lift jarred to a halt at his floor and he stepped out into the corridor. It was empty. He stopped at his door and waited a moment before inserting the key and entering. Habit. He never opened a hotel room door with someone else in the corridor.

Once inside, he removed his outer clothes, took the scrap of paper from his jacket and threw it carelessly onto the chair by the dressing table. The note was short and to the point. "Mr Whelan phoned. He asked that you call him as soon as possible". Si it had been Conor, not Kate. There was no number but Jamie didn't expect one. He knew where to get Conor. He sat down heavily on the edge of the bed and smiled wryly. He felt disappointed. It was understandable. He was missing Kate and his kids more than he was prepared to admit.

He picked up the phone and dialled. It rang only twice before Conor picked up. 'Jamie!' the American exclaimed. 'Where the hell have you been? I called the hotel two hours ago.'

'Out,' Jamie retorted bluntly. 'I had someone to see.'

'Your man made contact,' Conor went on,' deciding to let things lie. 'He didn't say much; he didn't have time.'

'What did he say?'

'He has the details. There's a hijack involved and a massive bomb. The bomb is coming in separately. He's writing it all down and he's going to leave it in a dead drop.'

'Great,' Jamie responded sardonically. 'Where exactly?'

'He says you know his address... I didn't tell him you'd paid a visit. He says the road behind the house runs along a park on one side and a bowling green on the other.' He paused, waiting for Jamie to acknowledge.

'Uh-huh,' Jamie said, obliging.

'The bowling green in bounded by a brick wall about six feet high, he says, and next to the gate, low down to the left, a couple of bricks are loose. You'll find his note behind them. He says he'll make the drop tonight... and not to leave it too long before picking up.'

'That it?'

'Yeah, that's it, but the guy sounds scared.'

Jamie laughed coldly. He said, 'I imagine he is, and if he isn't, he should be.'

'So where were you?' Conor probed.

'I went to see if Roisin, Liam's cousin, was still in hospital.'

'Yeah, I know who she is... and is she?'

'Yes, but she has made a good recovery. She'll be out in a couple of weeks.'

Conor paused a moment. 'Why did you need to know if she was still there?' he asked eventually.

From his tone Jamie knew it was more than simple curiosity. 'Because I might have a problem with my original plan,' he replied.

'Your scapegoat?'

'That's the one,' Jamie confirmed, a grim laugh behind it.

'And what might be the problem?'

'Clara Whitelaw. She's the one the Brigadier has charged with finding the bomber and I don't think she's taken my bait. She wants to meet me, "face to face" to talk about it. If she knows something I don't, then I'm going to need a plan B.'

'Are you telling me or asking me?'

'I'm asking you, Conor; you're the only one I can ask... the only one I can trust.'

'You're back to passports and new identities.'

'Yes, as a fall back.'

There was silence for a moment before Conor responded. 'It can be done but it'll take time. If I was back in the States it would be easier but I'm not,' he said, stating the obvious. 'It'll take more than a couple of weeks. I need to speak to people. Make a case.'

'Then I'll find a safe house if I have to,' Jamie acknowledged. 'Don't do anything just yet.'

'Okay, I'll wait for your word on it. If it comes to a safe house I might be able to help,' Conor went on.

'I don't think a spare room in a brothel fits the bill,' Jamie retorted, unable to stifle a laugh.

The American joined in. 'No, brothels are for you bro, not for women and kids. Still don't know why you didn't go for that suggestion.'

Jamie laughed louder. 'Probably because it would take my mind off things and I can't afford that. Here, I can keep an eye on Miss Orlagh Duggan, though I think she's using another name, and wait for Clara. She's arriving Monday.'

Jeeze, Jamie. You sure like to surround yourself with women,' his friend remarked flippantly. 'I don't know where you find the energy.'

Yes, but only one of them really matters, Jamie thought silently.

'So, where is this safe house?' he asked, changing the subject.

'Middle of nowhere,' Conor chipped back with another laugh. 'On the shores of Loch Goil. Mary's folks have a place there.'

'Sounds good,' Jamie acknowledged. 'Keep it on the back burner... I might need it myself if this all goes pear shaped.' He said it with a laugh but Conor knew he was deadly serious.

'So what now?' the American asked.

'Well now I revert to being a guest at this fine establishment. I keep myself to myself and wait and tonight I head down to Alexandria and do my postman act.'

'Want company?'

'No, I can manage it myself, but thanks for the offer. You stay there in case Liam calls again with a change of plan. Enjoy your holiday, if you can.'

'Never did like long vacations.'

'Well this one is coming to an end pretty soon so try,' Jamie retorted. 'I'll need you at your best.'

'Okay kid, you got it. Phone me if you need me. Chou,' he said, finishing the call.

As Jamie replaced the handset he realised that was the first time in a long time that Conor had called him kid. His big brother instincts must be kicking in.

Jamie wasted no time in making a second call. He thought about Conor's remark about him surrounding himself with women and his immediate thought in response - only one of them really matters - and he had been ignoring her. Well, not exactly ignoring her, pushing her to the back of the queue more like. It was time to make amends.

The phone rang for a while before Emily Edwards answered. The sound of her voice told him she was of a like mind. Her tone was frosty. He tried to ignore it. 'Is Kate around?' he asked when the formalities had been dealt with.

'Yes, she's here, worrying herself sick,' Emily threw at him, reinforcing his earlier thought. 'What are you up to?'

You don't want to know, Jamie mused. 'working,' he replied. 'Kate knows what I do.' He tried to keep the irritation out of his voice. There was a sigh of exasperation from the other end of the line, then a swishing noise and the sound of something hard clicking against the handset, and finally Kate was on the line.

'I'm fine Mum,' he heard her say and then she was his. 'Hi baby,' she said softly, 'sorry about that. She doesn't understand and I can't exactly tell her, can I?'

'It's okay. I understand how she feels... I feel the same. I'm sorry.' He paused a moment, then said, 'How are you all?'

'We're fine... missing you, but otherwise we're okay. What about you?'

'I'm missing you too. I lie awake at night thinking about you and the fact you're not there beside me eats away at me. I want to curl up with my arms around you and sleep the sleep of the innocent.'

'Sleep?' she teased. 'You had better get that idea out of your head right now. You won't have time for that, at least until I drop off.'

Jamie laughed. 'I hope your mother isn't listening.'

'I don't care if she is... I love you. Just come back to me in one piece.'

'I will, don't worry,' he said, knowing all the time that not worrying was a luxury she probably wouldn't achieve.

They spent the next ten minutes talking about the future though neither of them knew what it held. They had their hopes though and that was enough. When he finally ended the call Jamie was more determined than ever to change his life. He didn't know how and he didn't know if he would be allowed to but he was going to try. He lay back on his bed and studied the ceiling going over everything that had brought him to this place. It was a long list.

Chapter Sixty-one

Jamie left the hotel about six that evening, missing out on dinner. On the way out he caught sight of Orlagh Duggan descending the stairs. Their eyes met for a moment before he turned away and exited through the revolving door but in that instant he saw the naked intent in Orlagh's eyes. He was going to have to disappoint her but not too brutally. The brutality would come later and he could do it, he knew that, but for now he wanted to talk to her. She, on the other hand, wanted more. It was there in her eyes. He would have to lead her on, flirt and tease a little, but no more than that. More would be like bedding the devil, he decided, and he had enough demons to deal with as it was.

Outside it was cold and dark. The temperature, hardly above freezing for most of the day, was dropping like a stone. Frost was forming on stationery cars and the pavements. The sky was clear and the moon cast a pale glow on the city. He couldn't see the stars but they were there, shrouded in the light pollution thrown out by the street lights and shop fronts.

He flagged a passing taxi and gave his destination as St Gregory's in Possilpark. The driver set off up Queen Margaret Drive and Jamie settled back in the worn back seat. He knew his surroundings well. This was all part of his past. They crossed the River Kelvin through Kelvinside, then Maryhill and into Ruchill. Street names came back to him, names that sent shudders through him in his younger days – Shuna Street, Curzon Street and Brassey Street – when walking there alone was not advised. He smiled to himself. Even walking there in company wasn't advised unless it was in the company of somebody known to the gangs that ruled here. He would have no qualms now. He was a different man now... or was he, he wondered. Roaming through this place had been risky but he had done it with Jack by his side and usually a couple of local girls... and that too had been unwise. The local guys were territorial. They hadn't like outsiders shagging their women. He grinned to himself. *Probably still didn't.* The things he and Jack had done chasing "nookie". A deep sadness engulfed him then. Jack was gone and he too might be gone in a couple of weeks. He hoped not, but nothing in life is guaranteed, he reminded himself... except death, of course.

With that dark thought in his mind the taxi turned right from Bilsland Drive into Balmore Road then swung left then right into Saracen Street, and more memories. He stepped back in time. Jack's home passed on his right. He looked up and saw a light on in what was the kitchen window and another in the living room. He could picture Jack's father and mother sitting there, alone now, their children all married and gone... all except Jack. Jack was dead and it should have been him. He wondered how they coped with his loss... if they coped. He should visit them, he reflected guiltily, but not tonight. Tonight was for other things.

***

Father Daly looked up from the table as his housekeeper, Mrs Murphy ushered Jamie into the room. The older man's face lit up in a bright smile and Mrs Murphy laughed. 'I thought he would bring you out of your grumpy mood,' she said, her Irish origins still clear in her voice.

'Oh, be off with you woman,' the old Priest joked, ' and bring us a pot of tea.' He stood up and pulled Jamie to him like a father would greet a son. 'You're back earlier than I expected. Twice in one day is flattering,' Frank Daly teased. 'I've been thinking about you,' he continued, serious again.

'And praying too, I hope,' Jamie said as the door closed.

'Aye, that too, after you left this morning I was troubled.'

'I'm sorry Frank,' Jamie responded. 'I should think before I speak sometimes,' he went on.

'Well, you still *look* fit and healthy,' the old man said but he noticed the darkness behind Jamie's eyes. Those eyes were the gateway to Jamie's soul but few people got through the gate. He was one who did and, he suspected, Kate, his wife, was too, but they were in a very small minority. 'What brings you back so soon?'

'I need my bike and a place to change into my biker gear.'

'You're leaving already?'

Jamie laughed at his friend's confusion. 'No, not leaving, I just have somewhere to go tonight.'

'And you can't take a bus or a train?' Jamie drew him a sideways look. The Priest smiled sheepishly, the extent of his naivety dawning on him. 'No, I don't suppose you can,' he continued. 'And will you be coming back tonight?'

'I certainly hope so,' Jamie replied, smiling now. 'But I'll probably be late.'

'I'll wait up,' Frank said, 'and don't even think about objecting.'

Jamie nodded slowly and a grin appeared. 'I wouldn't dream of it,' he retorted. 'Would you like me to bring something back?'

Frank Daly laughed conspiratorially. 'No, I've got a stash, but don't let on to Mrs. Murphy know, she'll have me doing penance for weeks. We'll talk when you get back.'

'Aye, okay Frank,' Jamie conceded, 'we'll talk.' He knew he could unburden himself without fear of it coming back to haunt him, but what he had to say would probably haunt Frank Daly till the end of his days.

***

Twenty minutes later, now clad in his leathers, Jamie clambered onto the Triumph and kicked the starter. The engine roared into life and he felt the machine tremble beneath him like a wild horse straining to be free. He slipped it into gear and rode down towards Saracen Street. The road had been gritted but it was still treacherous and he took his time to Bilsland Drive.

Stopped at the lights, he planned his route. A plume of smoke rose from the exhaust as the hot fumes hit the cold air, wreathing him in a toxic cloud of white. He held his breath, waiting for the lights to change, then sped off left into Bilsland Drive. He had chosen his route to Alexandria. He would keep to main roads. There would be less chance of ice or worse, black ice, on those. He would follow Bilsland Drive to Maryhill Road and then take the latter out past the old barracks and Summerston towards Bearsden. At Canniesburn Toll, "the Switchback", he would swing left towards Anniesland and from there it was a straight road to Dumbarton.

He maintained a steady speed, not too fast and not too slow. He had plenty of time. The night was young. Soon, he was on the Switchback Road which would morph into Bearsden Road. He felt a twinge of regret as he passed his and Kate's old home but he kept his eyes on the road, reluctant to look. They had been happy there until his past caught up with him and fucked it up. He shrugged off the bitterness. It gained him nothing.

The rest of the road to Dumbarton was covered without incident. Traffic was light. Even though it was a Friday evening people were staying home. From Dumbarton to Alexandria was a little more hairy. The roads were untreated and dangerous. If things went wrong later and he had to get out in a hurry that might prove difficult. *Que sera, sera*, he murmured to himself beneath his helmet and visor.

It was just after eight o'clock when he entered the outskirts of Alexandria and crossed the metal bridge over the River Leven. As far as lifting Liam's note from the dead drop he had only one problem. No time had been specified by Liam as to when he would make the drop. That implied he wasn't in control of the timing. Reading between the lines, the happy little band would probably visit a local pub or one of them, maybe two, would visit an off-license for a "carry out".

Liam's note might even be in the drop already, he mused, as he rode down Bridge Street. It was after eight and the men were Irish, so no different from their Scottish brethren, particularly their West of Scotland brethren when it came to drink. In Glasgow speak, they liked a good "bevvy". That led him to think they would already be in the pub downing pints of Guinness or sitting back in the safe house in Margaret Drive slurping cans of beer and tumblers of whisky. He decided to risk it.

He turned off Bank Street into Main Street and followed the road as far as Park Street. He remembered it well from his earlier visit. He took the left turn into Park Street and rode slowly. From memory, the park was on the right and the bowling green on the left just before the road end. Another road ran off to the left there but he couldn't remember its name. What he could remember was the fact that it would provide him with an escape route.

About half way along Park Street he pulled to a halt and sat for a moment. His nerves were tingling. The old sixth sense. He switched off the engine and listened. The road was deserted but he could hear faint laughter from up ahead. He strained his eyes but could see nothing. Then, out of the gloom, he saw four figures emerge from the park. They crossed the road towards the bowling green. They were about a hundred yards ahead of him, their voices loud. Four men coming from the park, he mused. Who else could it be but Liam's ASU?

They were still coming towards him, their mood light. A bit of R&R and no one knew they were here... at least they thought no one knew they were here. So why should his presence look suspicious? It shouldn't but that was little comfort. These weren't ordinary men and they didn't think like ordinary men.

He flooded the carburettor of the bike and kicked the starter. The engine spluttered and died as he knew it would. The men were about eighty yards distant now. As he cast a glance at them he saw one detach himself and kneel down as though tying a shoelace. The others kept coming. Jamie dismounted from the bike and pretended to fiddle with the engine. If they saw him they would think he was having trouble... He hoped. When he looked back at them again, the fourth man was hurrying to catch up with the group. They were now about fifty yards from him. He remounted the Bonneville, turned the switch and kicked the starter. This time the engine caught, a great cloud of white smoke being expelled into the air. Jamie pulled down his visor and revved the engine, the roar catching the men's attention but not their interest. At ten yards, he dropped the big bike from its stand and pulled away into the middle of the road, passing the four men a few seconds later. None of them paid him any attention. He smiled behind his visor. It was them, and the man who had fallen behind to tie his lace was Liam. His smile became a grin and by the time he turned left at the end of the road he was laughing aloud.

He rode the Triumph to the end of that road, Smollett Street he discovered, and stopped again. As with Park Street, it was deserted. The houses that lined the street were a mix of semi-detached and terraced and a school took up a substantial part of it. Lights were on in most of the houses, faint behind drawn curtains, and the school was in darkness. After a few minutes he restarted the bike and retraced his route. Park Street was empty, the Irishmen long gone.

He pulled to a halt at the gates to the bowling green and raised the bike up onto its stand, the engine still idling. Quickly, he dismounted and made his way to the gate. Left hand side, lower bricks he remembered. He ran his fingers along the joints looking a gap in the pointing. He found it easily. As his fingers reached the loose bricks they moved imperceptibly. A smile played at his lips as he pulled the brick free and probed with his fingers into the void behind. The paper was there, rolled into cylindrical form. He grasped it between thumb and forefinger and pulled, teasing the tube from the hole, then quickly slipped it inside his leather jacket.

Rising to his feet he scanned the roadway down towards Main Street. Nothing moved. The only sound was the hum of traffic from the A82 beyond Margaret Drive and a fox barking in the nearby wood. He checked his watch. It was still early and the Irish contingent was unlikely to return until last orders. He decided to reconnoitre the wood behind the safe-house. Knowing the lie of the land might give him an edge later.

He returned to the bike, slipped it down off its stand and manhandled it back into Smollett Street, pushing it about 25 yards along the road before once again raising it up on its stand. Smollett Street, like Park Street, was deserted. The populace was staying home tonight and, given the falling temperature, who could blame them. He retraced his steps and entered the park. He remembered the sign at the gate from earlier; Christie Park, it said, with edicts about ball games and dogs. The path running through the park was illuminated for the first twenty or thirty feet by the light spilling from the street lights on Park Street but beyond that it disappeared into a dark gloom. The wood to the left, stretching back to Margaret Drive, was in complete darkness with only the light of the moon as it flitted in and out of the clouds giving any illumination at all.

He left the path and crossed the grass towards the trees, grateful now for the freezing temperature. Without that he would be walking through a quagmire. Ahead of him he could make out a path, the result of hundreds, if not thousands, of feet tramping through the wood over the years. He followed it into the trees, stepping over fallen branches and slipping on ice covered puddles. The undergrowth on both sides was thick, the trailing, leafless, branches of wild bramble forming an almost impenetrable barrier on his left while, on his right, a burn trickled turgidly over frozen stones and discarded beer cans and bottles.

A gap appeared on the right, just over the stream, leading deeper into the trees. He took note of it. It might make a good escape route or even a hiding place, if needed, and the wood here would make a good killing ground. He reached behind him and felt the comforting bulk of the Walther tucked into his waistband. 'Not tonight,' he murmured to himself. 'I still don't have it all.'

He turned back to the path. Further ahead he could make out the lights of the houses on Margaret Drive and the glow of the street lamps beyond. The sound of the traffic on the A82 was louder here. He edged forward until he reached the fence at the rear of number 44. The path carried on along the side of the property to the road but Jamie stopped, crouching down behind the fence and boundary shrubs. A light was on in the kitchen and he could see a woman working at the sink. She wasn't young. In her fifties, he estimated, grey hair tied back in a bun. She looked like a schoolteacher with her heavy black glasses. An ordinary woman. He wondered if she knew who she was harbouring, then shook his head at his naivety. Of course she knew. When the Irishmen were eliminated what would happen to her? And if she had a family, what would happen to them? Only time would tell.

He stayed a moment. The woman continued working, oblivious to his presence, oblivious to the danger she was in. It wouldn't be him who brought it down on her but he was fairly sure someone would. She would be a loose end, as would the people providing the safe houses for the other ASUs, and loose ends always had to be tidied up. Sir Charles Redmond would see to that.

He straightened and made his way carefully back along the path to the Christie Park and from there to Smollett Street and the Bonneville. He wanted to get away from here.

***

Frank Daly was sitting by the fire reading when Jamie entered the room. The old priest looked up from his book and smiled, the younger priest who had shown Jamie in quickly taking his leave. There was no sign of Mrs Murphy other than a plate of sandwiches and a flask of tea or coffee. Jamie hoped it was the latter. Coffee went better with whisky.

Father Daly wasted no time, reaching down and lifting a bottle of Glenmorangie from the side of his chair, like a magician producing a rabbit from a hat.

'You're back sooner than I thought,' he announced happily.

Jamie returned his smile. 'It turned out to be easier than I thought,' he replied, unfastening his jacket and settling down into his usual chair.

'Pour yourself a coffee and help yourself to sandwiches. Mrs Murphy will be disappointed if they're still there in the morning and I'll get the edge of her tongue.'

Jamie grinned and levered himself out of his chair. He poured a coffee and looked to Frank, holding the flask aloft. The old priest shook his head.

'I'll settle for this,' he said, raising the bottle. 'Pass me a tumbler, there's a good lad.'

Jamie obliged and then had a look at the sandwiches. The bread was soft and he spied slices of gammon and cheese peeking out from between the layers of bread. He was suddenly hungry. He filled a plate and returned to his chair with a mug of coffee in one hand and the plate of food in the other. Father Frank grinned appreciatively. Jamie tucked in and the older man sipped his whisky.

'So where were you?' Frank probed, pretending innocence.

Jamie raised an eyebrow and smiled. 'Alexandria,' he replied. One word, no more.

'That would be the one near Dumbarton,' the priest added mischievously.

'Uh-huh,' Jamie agreed. 'Egypt was a wee bit too far, even with the Bonneville.'

'And are you going to tell me what you were doing there?'

Jamie's eyebrows lifted again. 'You know I can't, Frank,' he said, stuffing a mouthful of gammon into his mouth.

'That didn't stop you before,' the priest persisted. 'Same rules,' he added. Jamie let out a soft sigh. 'It's good for the soul,' he went on.

'I thought we'd agreed I don't have one,' Jamie retorted.

Frank laughed. Their talk was following the usual pattern. 'No, you say that, I say the opposite, and I'm trying to save it.'

'Big job, Frank.'

'Maybe, but I like a challenge. So are you going to tell me?'

'You're trying to save my soul, I'm trying to save the world… or the West of Scotland to be more accurate.'

Frank Daly frowned. 'From what?'

'As far as I can make out, a major terrorist attack; a bomb… A big one.'

'In Alexandria?' The priest's bushy eyebrows arched dubiously.

Jamie shook his head. 'No, not there, but close by. I don't know where exactly, not yet, but it's going to happen soon.'

'And how do you know all this?'

'Come on Frank, you know what I do and who I work for.'

'I thought you were finished with that?'

'Aye, so did I,' Jamie replied, forcing a smile. 'And after this I will be,' he added. Frank Daly wasn't convinced. 'I've been doing a lot of thinking,' Jamie went on.

'You've done that before, lad, but as far as I can make out action doesn't follow your thoughts... Not on that score anyway.'

'True,' Jamie conceded, finishing the last of the sandwiches and gulping down his coffee. He returned the empty plate and cup to the table and returned with a tumbler, holding it out like Oliver Twist. Frank picked up the bottle and poured a large measure.

'I take it you're leaving the bike here,' he said, adding a little more of the malt to the glass.

Jamie laughed. 'Even if that hadn't been my intention I sure would be now,' he said with a laugh, holding up the glass and examining it theatrically. 'Walking might even be a problem.'

They sat in comfortable silence for a moment, enjoying the whisky. This was the norm. Not only were they comfortable with the silence, they were comfortable with each other's company too.

'So, this crusade of yours,' the priest resumed at last. 'How many will it be this time?' He didn't refer to the subject of the "how many", they both knew.

'Quite a few,' Jamie admitted grimly. 'But if they don't cross over a lot more will.'

'And can you do it? Are you on your own?'

'No, I'm not on my own. Your first question is harder to answer though. A lot depends on someone else... That's where I was tonight, picking something up from him.'

'And what can he tell you?'

Jamie shrugged. 'Everything, I hope. He's part of it and when he knows, I'll know. I came back into this to save him... that was the deal, but it grew arms and legs. Now I have someone else to save as well as stop this attack.'

'Who do you have to save these people from?' Frank probed.

Jamie shook his head sadly. 'The man has been passing information to my people for a while. He's a tout, an informer, and his life is on the line. If the bhoys find him out he won't have an easy death.'

'But why you? Surely you could have walked away?'

'No Frank, I couldn't,' Jamie said softly with a gentle shake of his head. 'He saved my life a year ago and now it's up to me to save his.'

Frank Daly nodded. He understood Jamie Raeburn better than most, probably even better than his own father and mother. He knew what Jamie did but he couldn't condemn him for it. He knew the burden Jamie carried. 'And the other person?' he asked.

'The other is a young woman. A mother. One of your flock, Frank. She's a victim, more sinned against than sinner.'

'I can guess who is after the man but who is after her... and why?'

Jamie's smile was icy cold when he replied. 'She planted a bomb in Coventry a couple of years back. A lot of people died. It's retribution.'

'And how do you know all this?' the priest went on, though he suspected he knew the answer. Jamie's grim look confirmed it even before he replied.

'It's my people who are after her. They haven't identified her yet but they think the man I'm bringing out knows. My job was to get her identity out of him and…' He paused, a dark shadow passing over his face. The priest waited. 'You know the rest,' Jamie murmured at last.

'And *does* this man know her?'

A bitter laugh greeted that question. 'Oh aye, he knows her… And so do I as it happens. She's his cousin.'

'But if she planted this bomb why aren't the authorities dealing with it?'

Jamie's laugh was still bitter. 'I think you'll find it's "the authorities" that *are* dealing with it. They're the ones who give me my orders,' he continued dolefully. 'Anyway, I'm trying to save her, not kill her.'

'Why?'

Jamie smiled again. He had been expecting that question. 'Well, like I said, she's more sinned against than sinner and she has already paid a high price for something she couldn't avoid.'

'The world is a dark place,' Frank Daly murmured softly. 'Bombs, murders... Evil is everywhere.'

'Am I included in that?' Jamie asked, a wry smile playing at the edge of his mouth.

'You're a special case,' the priest returned, matching his smile. 'You're not a murderer, you're an avenger and avengers usually dispense justice.'

'Oh aye?' Jamie retorted, sounding dubious. 'That sounds good, but I'm not convinced.'

'Have you heard of Samuel Johnson?'

Jamie knotted his brow, thinking. 'English writer or philosopher?' he asked.

'He was a writer,' the priest agreed, nodding. 'He wasn't a philosopher though, more a moralist. He's better known as Doctor Johnson... Anyway, he explained it well: "Revenge is an act of passion; vengeance of justice. Injuries are revenged, crimes are avenged", is what he said.

Jamie gave another cold laugh. 'And is that how your God will see it?' he questioned.

'I certainly hope so,' the old priest replied. 'I believe he's a fair God. That's my *raison d'etre*.'

'Well I hope you're right, Frank,' Jamie said with a smile. 'When my time comes I'd like to go to a place where I'll be with the people who love me and not the other place with the people I've sent over. I'd have a hard job avoiding them.'

Frank Daly laughed. He said, 'For a man who says he has no soul that's quite a statement.' He picked up the Glenmorangie and waved it in front of Jamie. 'Let's have another of these.'

Chapter Sixty-two

Jamie returned to the Grosvenor in the early hours of the morning. The resident's lounge was still open and he could hear voices and laughter. They were louder than he expected, the drink no doubt playing a part in that. That would include him, he mused wryly.

He stuck his head in through the door, swithering over whether to have a nightcap. Orlagh Duggan was at a table, surrounded by drooling men, four of them to be precise, all middle aged, over weight and infatuated. They were also quite drunk and it was showing, their hands drifting to parts of Orlagh they wouldn't have dared touch had they been sober. Orlagh was playing them, sitting there like the Queen of Sheba. She knew she could have any one of them if she wanted but there was a slightly bored look on her face. Clearly, she didn't want.

As he was turning away, the nightcap forgotten, he caught her watching him. He smiled over and she smiled back. Then she rolled her eyes. He got the message but he wasn't joining in the game, not tonight anyway. He had probably drunk as much as the four hopefuls at the table and that put him at a disadvantage... with a woman like Orlagh Duggan at least. He let his eyes linger on her a while, just enough to confirm interested, then headed for the lift. He had some reading to do and a phone call to make.

He was physically tired but his brain was ticking over, fully alert. He withdrew Liam's note from his pocket and threw his coat and jacket onto the chair. He stretched out on the bed and unfolded the note. It had been scribbled quickly, no sentences, just shorthand notes, but it was enough. He read it quickly. What was there in the note took him almost to the finishing line. Almost, but not quite. He read it again: *"3 x units, peelers – ambulance – fire. Staged accident, heavy truck. Road (A817) blocked 5+half miles from A82 junction – accident at x roads on sharp bend/blind hill - time 00.30. Only target lorry expected on road with escort. Take out escorts. Heavy lorry in accident loaded explosive. My Unit to hijack fire truck from Garelochhead – firemen part time volunteers. Emergency call at 23.30 on 24th – overpower and take truck. Get yer arse there ffs. "* The last acronym brought a smile to Jamie's face... "ffs" - for fuck sake. The final part helped too. *"Now regulars at pub in Main Street, 8.30 till 10.00 – unarmed"* it said.

Jamie smiled again. *Don't worry Liam, old son, I'll be there.*

So, three Active Service Units involved, just as expected. One of these would masquerade as police, one as ambulance crew and the third, Liam Fitzpatrick's unit, as firemen. With them at the scene it would give the staged accident a look of authenticity. The target was a lorry with an escort and it would be on the A817 about five and a half miles from the Loch Lomond Road junction. He smiled grimly. Warhead convoy? It didn't sound likely.

From what he knew the nukes were transported in a multi lorry convoy with heavy protection. Twelve men, even with an element of surprise, wouldn't get close. The boys guarding these trucks were hard as nails and they wouldn't take their fingers off their triggers. It couldn't be that, he reasoned, so what the hell could it be? But first things first; he would need to take a trip along the A817, and then he would have to work what else to do. Part of that was simple enough. All he had to do was pass on this intel to Clara and let her and Sir Charles deal with it. The old man would see to it. That would take care of the fake cops and ambulance crew but it still left Liam and his bhoys. They were his responsibility... And so were the poor unsuspecting firemen who turned up at Garelochhead, he reflected grimly.

He checked his watch. It was ten to one. He smiled grimly, jealousy rearing its ugly head. His call might interrupt a torrid moment or, then again, it might initiate one when he hung up... if Clara and her man were back to sharing the same bed, that was. Part of him hoped they weren't, but that was unfair. He had no right to be jealous. He had made his choice. And it was the right one. And yet, his hand hovered over the handset for a moment before he picked up. Likewise, his finger hesitated for a second in the zero of the dial before he rotated it. He allowed himself another grim smile then dialled the remainder of the number.

He heard the ring tone and pushed all other thoughts from his mind as he switched persona. He was Michael Ferryman now... At least, he was Michael Ferryman if Mark Whitelaw happened to answer. He doubted he would be anyone but Jamie to Clara, no matter what.

Clara answered on the fourth ring. 'Yes,' she said shortly. No introduction, no unnecessary chit-chat.

Jamie grimaced. He wondered absently if she had been expecting a call from someone else. He said, 'Sorry, did I disturb you?' It was impossible to keep the edge out of his voice.

'Jamie?' The frost had gone. She sounded warmer.

'Aye, it's me. Expecting someone else, were you?'

There was a moment's silence then she said, 'Yes, I was actually. I'm sorry.'

Jamie didn't ask who she was expecting to call. He could make a shrewd guess. So they weren't sharing the matrimonial bed. Ah well.

'I wasn't expecting you to call,' Clara went on. 'We're meeting on Monday.'

'I didn't think this should wait and the sooner the Brigadier knows the better...'

'What is it?' she demanded, interested now. Whatever had been bothering her was forgotten.

'Corkscrew made contact. The attack is set for 25 January right enough... at half past midnight. It's a hijack. They're setting up an accident on the road to stop the traffic and then stealing a lorry. The wagon they use for the fake accident will be filled with explosives...'

'Where?' she interrupted.

'On the A817.'

'That tells me a lot,' she retorted shortly.

Jamie gave a frosty laugh. 'The A817 links the main road round Loch Lomond to Garelochhead which, as its name suggests, is at the top of the Gare Loch.'

'Which is significant how?'

Another laugh greeted that question. 'Faslane... Ring any bells?'

'HM Naval Base Clyde,' she responded quickly.

'Which is on which stretch of water?'

'Oh shit!'

'Aye, "oh shit",' Jamie responded sardonically.

'So whatever it is has to do with the submarine base.'

'Good thinking Sherlock, but what? I've been racking my brain. The hijack is taking place well away from the base, according to Corkscrew. And, unless they intend driving both lorries through the gate at Faslane, I can't see what they hope to achieve. Blowing up a couple of lorries miles from anywhere is pointless so I'm missing something. It can't be a nuke convoy; those are too heavily escorted. Twelve men against the MOD Close Escort Group and the Stand Off Escort marines would be suicide. The IRA aren't into that.'

'Is that all he gave you?'

'Other than how his lot get their fire engine, yes.'

There was silence between them for a moment. Not exactly awkward but uncomfortable, Jamie thought. He suspected the spectre of the bomber was behind it. That was still unresolved between them.

'So what now?' he said at last, breaking the peace. 'Will you phone the old boy or will I?'

'I'll do it.'

'And we're still on for Monday?' He detected a moment's hesitation before Clara responded.

'No,' she said, apparently having decided. 'I'll be with you tomorrow. Phone me again in five minutes,' she continued, taking charge. She didn't say goodbye, just cut him off.

Jamie sat quietly on the edge of his bed and contemplated their meeting. He hoped it wasn't going to be confrontational. That, however, was down to Clara. He suspected that his attempt to put the blame for the Coventry bomb onto Orlagh Duggan was going to be swept aside. Clara knew something. He had a sudden craving for a cigarette. He had a packet of Embassy somewhere, he remembered, and rose to search. He found the packet in the bottom of his luggage bag and tore it open. His Zippo was in his jacket pocket. He was never without that.

He lit up and dragged heavily on the cigarette, hacking up a cough. It had been a while since his last smoke, a couple of weeks, and he felt light headed. Kate would be disappointed. She thought she had won that battle.

He took in another mouthful of smoke and inhaled. No cough this time. The five minutes was up. He lifted the handset and dialled again. There was no delay this time before Clara picked up.

'Yes,' she said, repeating her earlier chilly welcome. Jamie smiled. She was still anticipating a call from someone else.

'It's me,' he said, 'not the other guy.' He heard he give a nervous little laugh before she responded and, when she did, she ignored his jibe.

'Do you have transport?' she asked.

'Yes, I've got transport,' he confirmed. He didn't say it was the Triumph but he didn't know why she was asking.

'Good. In that case pick me up at Glasgow Airport tomorrow afternoon. I'll be on the Heathrow flight arriving at one fifteen.'

'Uh-huh,' Jamie acknowledged, wondering how she would feel about sitting pillion on the Bonneville. That would be fun. It wouldn't work, of course, she would have luggage and, Clara being Clara, it would probably be more than a carry-on bag. He smiled to himself. He was tempted to take the bike, just for the hell of it, but that would only get her back up and he needed to stay on her good side. 'Okay,' he went on. 'I'll be waiting at Arrivals. Still staying at the Grosvenor?'

'Yes, I'll phone them in the morning. Can we reschedule our dinner meeting for tonight?'

'Aye, why not,' he said lightly. 'I'm not doing anything else. Hope you're in a better mood though,' he threw in.

He heard her sigh then force a laugh. 'I will be,' she said. 'I'll be with you.'

'Aye, right,' he said, trying to keep the groan out of his voice. 'You better get your beauty sleep then. I'll see you at the airport.' He cut her off this time. Now he had another problem to occupy his mind. Where was he going to get a car for one o'clock?

Chapter Sixty-three

Traffic on the M8 heading west was heavy, most of it carrying football fans to Ibrox Park for the Rangers v Aberdeen game. It was one o'clock, kick off at three, and already the "Bears" were congregating. He could imagine the atmosphere building up. Rangers and Aberdeen supporters weren't the best of buddies and the insults would soon be flying... Aberdeen supporters' proclivity for sheep being foremost in their counterparts repertoire. A few years earlier he would have been there, adding his voice to the clamour. Now, he couldn't care less.

He negotiated his way past the standing traffic at the Govan slip road and accelerated, the road opening up before him. The car was pretty good even if a bit ostentatious, but Yanks like big and ostentatious, don't they he mused. Finding it had been easier than he anticipated. An early morning call to Conor had produced a number for a dealer in Glasgow's East-end. The guy specialised in American cars for the sailors based at Holy Loch and he didn't ask too many questions. Which was a bonus. Jamie phoned, arranged a visit, and drove out twenty minutes later in a bright red 1965 Ford Mustang two door hardtop with cream leather interior and ninety-four thousand two hundred and forty miles on the clock. It was left-hand drive but after many months in France that didn't present him with a problem. Its 4.3 litre V8 engine gave him all the horses he needed beneath the bonnet, or the hood as the Yanks called it, and the ninety plus thousand miles on the clock was nothing for an engine that size. The only downside was the car's petrol consumption and with the Arab oil embargo brought in after the 1973 Yom Kippur war still in place and the coal miners' and railway strikes adding to the problem, that would be costly. But what the hell, it wasn't his money he was using, he thought with a grin.

As he passed the Hillington/Renfrew exit he opened the throttle further and pushed the speed up to 80 mph and the big car was still straining at the reins, like the wild horse it was named after. The landscape flew past; the Rolls Royce factory to his left and the housing estates of Renfrew on his right, built on the site of the old Glasgow Airport.

He parked in the nearest car park to the terminal at one fifteen and walked casually towards the Domestic Arrivals Hall. Even if the Heathrow flight was on time it would take time for the passengers to disembark and he had plenty of time. He lit a cigarette, feeling a little ashamed of himself. His self-imposed ban had been breached the night before and now he was hooked again. One day, he told himself, I'll give up for good... *Aye, one day.*

The terminal was busy, but mostly with passengers departing rather than arriving. The big Flight Information Board told him that Clara's flight had arrived on schedule so he shouldn't have long to wait. He began to rehearse his approach. Roisin was uppermost in his mind. The attack would take care of itself. All he had to do was take out Liam's three mates, Sir Charles could take care of the rest. The only thing still gnawing away at him was the reason for the hijack. Why blow up a lorry, two lorries he reminded himself, in the middle of nowhere?

It was just after one thirty when passengers began to emerge through the Arrivals Gate. Clara wasn't among them but most had only carry-on bags and, if his conjecture about her was correct, she would have at least one suitcase. Just as well he had brought the car and not the bike, he mused, but what Clara would make of it he dreaded to think. His guess regarding her luggage was proved correct when she appeared through the gate a few minutes later pushing a metal trolley loaded with one large suitcase and a carry-on bag perched on top. An attaché case was tucked under her arm. How long was she here for, he wondered, grinning wryly.

She smiled brightly as she picked him out in the waiting crowd. That was a bonus, Jamie mused. Maybe their meeting wasn't going to be confrontational after all. She pushed the trolley manfully towards him and stopped just short, abandoning it and coming to him. The kiss on the cheek was unexpected but things were looking brighter by the minute.

'Have you been waiting long?' she asked, smile still in place.

'No, not long. How was the flight?'

'It was fine. A bit bumpy leaving London but it settled down.'

Jamie reached for the trolley. He said, 'I'll make the drive to the hotel as gentle as possible. I take it you want to go straight there?'

'Yes, please. I telephoned this morning and they changed my booking. Are you still okay for tonight?'

Jamie nodded, smiling. 'Uh-huh, we're still on.' As he pushed the trolley the weight of her case registered. 'How long are you thinking of staying?' he asked.

'That depends,' she replied quickly and left it at that.

Jamie smiled dutifully but he wasn't happy. Her answer told him nothing. She was smiling, certainly, but that told him nothing either. He would just have to wait.

She followed him to the car park, chattering on about the flight, the weather in London, the weather here... anything but the reason for her being here. When he stopped by the Mustang her eyes opened wide. 'Where on earth did you find this?' she questioned. 'It's not exactly inconspicuous, is it?'

'Hardly,' he agreed, 'but I rather like it. It's comfortable and it's fast.'

'But not practical,' she threw back at him. 'You can't possibly use it for surveillance.'

Jamie laughed. 'Aye, that would be a tad difficult but maybe, in a perverse sort of way, it will help.' Clara was shaking her head. She probably thought he was losing the plot. 'Think about it,' he went on. 'If people know this is mine they'll be keeping an eye on it and while they're doing that, I'll be watching them.'

'By "people" I take it you mean Orlagh Duggan?'

Jamie shrugged. 'Yes,' he agreed. 'I want her to lead me to the other ASUs... and whoever is bringing the lorry load of explosives.'

'You've got other transport?'

'Of course.'

'Then why didn't you bring that today?'

Jamie laughed again. 'I couldn't fit you and your luggage onto the pillion.'

'Pillion? It's a motor bike?'

'Not just any motor bike, it's a Triumph Bonneville, a real beast. When I pull on my leathers and helmet no one but no one will recognise me, not even you.'

'Don't bet on it,' she laughed in response. 'I think I could recognise you anywhere. Anyway, enough of this. Are you taking me to my hotel or what?'

Jamie bowed. 'Your carriage awaits, Madame,' he said with a grin as he opened the door for her. As she slipped her long legs into the car he lifted her case and bag from the trolley and stowed them in the car boot. Clara kept the briefcase close to her throughout.

He slid into his bucket seat beside her and started the engine. Its throaty roar turned a few heads and Clara grinned. 'That's another reason you can't use it for following people; they would hear you long before you came into sight.'

However, when he climbed up the on ramp to the M8 and put his foot down, the look on Clara's face changed. The big car reached 80mph in a matter of seconds and flew along the motorway, leaving lesser vehicles in its wake. She seemed to be enjoying the thrill of it, he thought, even though her hands gripped the edge of her seat with white knuckles. He followed the signs for the Clyde Tunnel and braked as he reached the minor road, slipping in behind a Triumph Stag. This was the nearest thing Britain had to the Mustang but Jamie had to admit, the American car had the edge both in looks and in power. He smiled as he caught the driver of the Stag give him an envious look in his rear view mirror.

They drove under the river in convoy, Jamie keeping the Mustang tucked in behind the other vehicle and then, as they emerged from the tunnel into daylight once more he pulled out to the right and accelerated, leaving the Triumph in his wake. He was 100 yards ahead by the time he reached the junction with Victoria Park Drive North and Victoria Park Gardens South. The lights changed to red as he flew through the junction. The Stag didn't make it.

He followed the road to Anniesland Cross and then east on Great Western Road. Gartnavel appeared on their right, evoking thoughts of Roisin, but he pushed them aside. Minutes later he was turning into Byres Road and then sharp right into Grosvenor Lane and the hotel entrance. Clara breathed a theatrical sigh of relief as the big car ground to a halt but he knew it was false. Her eyes told him she had found the ride exhilarating.

'If Madame wishes to register I will attend to her luggage,' he said grinning.

She punched him playfully on the arm and opened her door. He slipped out his side and watched as she strode into the foyer through the revolving door. She certainly was something special. Her hair blew out behind her and her long coat flapped wide. She was wearing denim trousers, expensive, and knee high leather boots and. Sexy was an inadequate description. And just like Orlagh Duggan some days earlier, she was turning heads. He let out a sigh and headed for the boot.

By the time Jamie had unloaded the car and ferried the cases into Reception Clara had attended to the formalities of registration. She turned with a smile on her face and waved her key. As she walked over to join him the receptionist gave him a smile. She had read it all wrong but he couldn't blame her. It wasn't so long since she would have had it 100% right. Clara hadn't seen the smile. For that he was grateful.

They took the lift to the second floor and Clara followed the signs to her room. It was along the corridor to the right of the lift. Jamie hoisted the case in one hand and threw the bag strap over his shoulder. Clara still held onto the attaché case. She had opened the door and entered by the time he arrived, her coat already on the bed when he shuffled into the room and dumped the case and bag. Beneath the coat she was wearing a beige coloured roll neck sweater, tight enough to display everything she had on offer. He wondered if that was intentional. It certainly had an effect on him but, then again, he was a man.

'Have you found somewhere to stay?' she asked casually. Maybe too casually. Jamie raised an eyebrow questioningly. 'It's just a thought, but this *is* a double room and we're not exactly strangers,' she continued, explaining.

Jamie smiled awkwardly. 'I have actually,' he replied. 'Moved in yesterday.'

Clara shrugged. 'It was just a thought,' she repeated. If she was disappointed, she hid it well.

'I'll leave you to get settled,' he said. 'Need to park the car.'

'And you'll be in the lounge at seven?'

Jamie smiled easily. 'Oh yes, I'll be there,' he said.

Chapter Sixty-four

They met at seven as arranged, Clara looking radiant in a figure hugging black dress, its neckline plunging to a deep V that displayed all her charms. Not her usual "work" clothes, Jamie noted with a smile.

Jamie was wearing a pair of navy Farrah slacks, a white button down Oxford shirt with plain navy tie, and a navy and grey check Harris Tweed jacket with black shoes. Not quite in Clara's class, but tidy enough.

She was sitting by the bar nursing a gin and tonic when he entered. She rose instantly to greet him, kissing him affectionately on the cheek to the disappointment of a number of other single men who were eyeing her with interest. They sat down together and Jamie ordered a Laphroaig. "You look beautiful,' he said. It was a simple enough statement. And it was the truth.

Clara smiled and his heart fluttered. That wasn't a good sign, he decided. Temptations like Clara were difficult to resist. 'What's happening?' he went on, avoiding direct reference to Orlagh Duggan.

She smiled again, but it was different this time. 'All hell has broken loose,' she said, sipping her gin.

'What caused that?'

'The disappearance of a number ofmen on the Watch List all at the same time induces panic and Five are leading the pack.'

Jamie smiled. That wasn't hard to believe. 'What about Sir Charles; has he said anything?' he queried.

Clara's smile was still in place. 'Not yet,' she said.

'If this bloody thing goes tits up Five will be looking for a scapegoat,' Jamie remarked. 'He had better watch his back.'

'He can take care of himself. He has already organised the troops. All he needs is word on where the ASUs are holed up. I'm more worried about you,' she continued, her grey eyes lingering on his.

Jamie laughed softly. 'Don't worry about me; I can take care of myself too.'

Clara arched her eyebrows doubtfully. 'Even when you're busy looking after someone else?'

What's that about, Jamie wondered.

'Any more thoughts on Corkscrew's note?' she carried on, not waiting for his answer.

'Yes, lots, but they don't make sense. Why blow up a couple of lorries in the middle of nowhere? The key is the lorry they intend hijacking. We need to know what it's carrying. Without that we're stumbling about in the dark. We can stop them, sure, but if we step in too early we'll miss some of them. Something tells me that includes our American friend.'

'You think?'

Jamie laughed again. 'Yeah, I think.'

'Well it might interest you to know that he's missing too. He's supposed to be on holiday but his itinerary is vague. No one knows where he is.'

Jamie's laugh continued. 'Well I think we know where we'll find him,' he said.

Clara smiled and sipped her drink then cast her eye around the lounge. 'It's nice here,' she commented, changing the subject. 'Comfortable. Are you staying nearby?' she went on.

Jamie gave her one of his enigmatic smiles. 'Yes, I am actually,' he replied.

'And are you going to tell me where?'

'Later, perhaps.'

Her eyebrows arched again and then she laughed. 'Alright, be like that. Let's have dinner.' She threw back her gin and stood up, waiting for him.

Jamie grinned and lifted his glass. 'I'll take this with me,' he said. 'Laphroaig isn't a dink for gulping down like that.' He stood and offered her his arm.

Clara laughed girlishly and slipped her arm through his. 'Always the gentleman,' she said, leaning her head on his shoulder a moment before Orlagh Duggan sashayed into the lounge. Her eyes took in the scene and her eyebrows rose in surprise. Unlike Clara, Orlagh couldn't hide her feelings.

***

Clara leaned across the coffee table and flicked ash off her cigarette into the heavy glass ashtray. They were back in the lounge. The meal had been excellent. They had avoided shop talk and were relaxed together, much as they had been back at the beginning. Orlagh had dined at a table not far from theirs and Jamie noticed her surreptitious glances. When Jamie and Clara left, she was still there, sharing her table with one of her suitors from the night before. He afforded her a glance and caught her questioning look. A smile was all he gave her in response. She didn't follow them into the lounge.

Clara blew out a cloud of smoke and leaned over the table towards him. Her smoky grey eyes were burning into him. Jamie tried to look away but it was impossible. It wasn't her big grey orbs that were holding him, it was orbs of a different nature and the chasm between them.

'Stop it, Clara,' he murmured, his frustration showing. 'We're past that. It's over, remember? We decided we were going to be friends.'

Clara laughed and straightened up, her teasing finished. 'I remember,' she said, still laughing. 'But it's hard to stick to it when I'm with you.'

Tell me about it, he groaned silently. She had a point. 'It's hard for me too,' he admitted. 'I already told you that, but we're not here to reminisce,' he continued.

Clara stopped laughing and became serious. 'No, we're not, I'm afraid,' she replied.

Jamie noticed a hardening behind her eyes and started to worry again. It wasn't like her. The hardness in her eyes transferred to her voice and that was new. To him at least. Sure, she had been serious before, but her tone was different now.

'So why *are* we here?' he asked, taking the bull by the horns.

'I want you to answer some questions,' she said simply, smiling again, but it lacked warmth.

Then ask, for fuck sake. Put me out of my misery, he mused, but said nothing. He returned the smile and hid the thought.

She lifted the cigarette to her mouth and sucked in a mouthful of smoke, blowing it back out through pouted lips. Jamie reached for his glass and took a swallow of wine. Clara followed suit. She was in no hurry to enlighten him, it seemed.

Jamie decided to play along. The suggestion they meet for a meal hadn't struck him as deceitful. It wasn't something they hadn't done in the past, after all... Their *old* past, that is. He hadn't suspected an ulterior motive but now he was beginning to think he was mistaken. Whatever it was, Clara seemed to be having difficulty deciding how to play him. It was to do with Orlagh Duggan, he knew that, she had said as much, but what?

He sat quietly as she took another drink of her wine, a tiny red dribble running from her lips down her chin and gathering there. She laughed, nervously he thought, and wiped it away. More silence. A minute, then two, and then he cracked.

'Jesus, Clara, get to the point, will you. What the hell is going on?'

'Orlagh Duggan and the Coventry bomber is what's going on,' she retorted shortly.

'Okay. How, exactly?' he threw back.

'You suggested that Orlagh Duggan was the Coventry bomber,' she said softly, a fire igniting behind her grey eyes. 'Why?'

Jamie stared back at her, a bit like a rabbit caught in the headlights of an oncoming car. *Run, or you're dead, he mused.* This was going to take the performance of his life.

He knitted his brow and gave a derisory snort. 'You invited me to dinner to ask me that?' he said with a laugh but even to him it sounded hollow. 'I suggested she *might* be but I also said it might be too obvious.' It came out convincingly, at least he thought so, but it didn't have much impact.

'Yes, you did,' she agreed, a little sadly. 'But you've been playing me along, haven't you? You fed me little tit-bits of information, *convincing* little titbits, that painted the picture you wanted me to see, while at the same time telling me they might not be true... But you knew I wouldn't listen to that bit because what you were giving me was plausible and it all stacked up. You've been leading me by the nose, Jamie, and I let you. What I want to know is why?'

She didn't sound angry, he noted, more sad and disappointed. He didn't respond. He couldn't. What could he say? She knew it all. Denying it would get him nowhere and bluster would only disappoint her more. His old friend Guilt was back on the scene.

'Is Corkscrew involved in the charade?' Clara went on. Once again, Jamie stayed silent. She shook her head sadly, almost on the verge of tears, he thought. 'Who planted the bomb Jamie? You know, don't you? Why are you protecting her?'

Three questions that he couldn't answer. He cringed as the roof caved in on him. He looked away, unable to face her. He could lie with the best but a few people could see through the deceit to the truth. Four people, to be precise, he reflected wryly, and three of them were women. His mother, his wife and Clara Whitelaw. He forced himself to think. If she had worked all that out it wouldn't be long before she worked out everything else. She was almost there already. All that was missing was the name. He had always known she would crack it, given time. He had always been racing against the clock and now time had run out. He looked towards the bar and caught a waiter's eye.

The man came over, order pad at the ready. 'I'll have a large malt, Laphroaig,' Jamie said. The waiter nodded. Jamie looked at Clara then. 'Do you want a brandy?' he asked. He saw she was about to refuse so carried on quickly. 'You might need one when you hear what I have to say,' he said, forcing a smile. She looked back at him bleakly and nodded. 'And a large Remy Martin for the lady,' he said, turning back to the waiter, who jotted it down and left them to it. Jamie smiled grimly. The guy had probably seen it all before... *Just another domestic.*

'It's that bad, is it?' Clara probed as the waiter moved out of earshot.

Jamie forced another smile. 'Well, it depends on how you look at it,' he said enigmatically. 'Let's just wait till we have our drinks.'

Clara shrugged and took another cigarette from her packet of Sobrani. She offered him the pack, knowing he would refuse. The black cigarettes with their gold tips were too effeminate for him. He shook his head just as she knew he would. Why did she feel so sad about this, she asked herself.

They sat in a stony silence until the waiter returned with their drinks. He placed the glasses on the table and slipped the bill between them, waiting for payment. Jamie brought his wad of notes from his trousers pocket and peeled off a five, watching, amused, as the young man's eyes opened wide. They opened even wider when Jamie waved away the change. The man had been watching them curiously throughout the evening, probably wondering what "Beauty" was doing dining with The Beast, Jamie mused. He had to admit they appeared mismatched, he mused as he slipped the bundle of banknotes back into his pocket. That would give the guy something else to think about and probably an answer to his pondering.

When the waiter was once more out of range, Clara wrung her hands nervously and repeated her earlier question. 'Who is she, Jamie?' she asked, keeping her voice steady. Jamie sighed softly. He looked defeated, she thought, but that didn't make her feel any better. He lifted his glass from the table and sipped the Laphroaig. 'Before we get to that, I want to tell you a story,' he started. 'It's a pretty grim tale... that's "grim" with one 'M', not Grimm with two. It's not a fairy tale. It is the whole unedited truth.' That was a little misleading, he reflected, as he intended leaving out a few important details, but all in all it was enough. He took another mouthful of his whisky and waited for a reaction. She gazed back at him and sipped her brandy. Alright, he thought; in for a penny, in for a pound. 'Once upon a time,' he started, and then gave her it all. Chapter and verse. All except Roisin's name, that is, and anything Clara could use to identify her.

***

'Why should I believe you?' Clara asked as he sat back, finished with the story.

'Because it's the truth.'

'Is it? You've been lying to me up till now... What has changed?'

'You know it all. There's no point in me trying to mislead you anymore and my Mum always told me to tell the truth.'

'It's a pity you didn't remember that earlier,' Clara said quietly, her eyes locked on his. The burning behind them was gone. Now they were sparkling and filled with questions.

'I'm sorry,' he said lamely. He left it at that. There were only so many times he could apologise without getting on her nerves.

'You still haven't told me why you're protecting her.'

'Because it's the right thing to do.'

'How well do you know her?'

Jamie raised his eyebrows. 'Well enough,' he said.

'We're you lovers?'

He shook his head slowly this time. 'Not in the way you would define it, no,' he responded slowly.

'And how would I define it?' she threw back at him, much more quickly.

'Like we were... In a relationship.'

'Were we?'

'Christ Clara, where are you going with this?'

'Were you in love with her?'

He looked at her, bewildered. 'No, I wasn't in love with her. I was with her for four nights and five days and two of those nights were on a ferry between Glasgow and Belfast. Yes, we made love... we were both in a dark place, for what it's worth. We needed comfort and that's what we got. Love had fuck all to do with it and it still hasn't.'

He was speaking quietly, controlling his anger well, she could see that, but his frustration was obvious. She felt tears gathering in her eyes, tried to fight them.

'I'm trying to do the right thing, that's all. The girl doesn't deserve what happened to her.'

Clara wiped away the tears. 'How do you know she's telling you the truth?' she asked, controlled again.

'I spoke to her. I watched her cry, just like you're doing now. I saw what it had done to her and what it has done to her family. It isn't bullshit, Clara.'

They fell quiet for a moment. It was taking a lot out of both of them. Clara reached for her cigarette which was burning away in the ashtray but it was almost finished. She stubbed it out and scrabbled for another. Jamie handed her his lighter and watched as she brought the flame to the tip of the cigarette with a shaking hand. Another barb twisted in my soul, he mused, then smiled to himself... the soul I don't have.

'What do you want me to do?' Clara asked at last, blowing out a cloud of smoke.

'I just want you to do what you think is right,' Jamie said, his voice low. He wasn't demanding, wasn't pleading. 'If you can't go along with my Orlagh Duggan ploy then all I ask is that you give me some time to put something else in place. 48 hours is enough. After that, I'll tell you who she is.'

'By which time she'll be someone else,' Clara said, laughing softly. Jamie said nothing.

'And if I agree to your ploy, what then?'

'Then I'll kill Orlagh Duggan and the little shite who threatened her and I'll go over to Ireland and I'll kill her brother, the one who was behind it in the first place. He's the one you want really, not her.'

Clara was staring at him, her grey eyes calculating. 'Who is her brother?' she asked.

Jamie snorted quietly. 'If I tell you that you'll work out who *she* is.'

'And if I go along with you?'

'Then I'll tell you the rest.' He saw her smile. He wasn't sure if she believed him or not. 'If you tell me you're okay with it then I *will* tell you... You won't betray me.'

'You think not?'

'You won't Clara. You won't because you know I'd walk over broken glass to help you.'

'Would you? Really?' Her tone was surprised, not dismissive.

Jamie didn't answer. She knew he would, she just hadn't thought it through.

'Where is she now?' she asked, then smiled. 'Generally speaking, that is. I don't need an address.'

'She's here in Glasgow. Nearby in fact.'

She didn't seem surprised. 'Can I meet her?'

'Why would you want to do that?' he threw back at her.

'You believed her after you spoke to her; I'd like the same opportunity.'

Jamie gave her a penetrating look, smiling all the time. 'If I say yes, what guarantee do I have you won't just call in the cavalry as soon as we leave her?'

'My promise not to. If I don't believe her then you can have the 48 hours you asked for... Then I'll call in the cavalry,' she said with a little laugh.

Jamie nodded slowly. 'And if you do believe her?'

'Then you'll have persuaded me that Orlagh Duggan was the bomber even though I know she wasn't, even though I know she couldn't have been.'

'How did you find out?' Jamie queried, diffidently.

'By chance. I was going through some intel from the time of the bombing back in 1970. I was trying to make sense of things, clutching at straws, I suppose.'

'And?'

'I came across a Garda report prepared by their Special Branch. There was a bit of a scandal in 1970 involving the Irish Directorate of Military

Intelligence, *Stiúrthóireacht na Faisnéise* to give it its Gaelic name, or G2 to you and me. Remember it?'

Jamie shook his head, his face blank. 'Don't remember it... never heard of it, to be honest.'

'It was a bit of a mess. A fiasco, really. An Irish Army intelligence officer, Captain James Kelly, was implicated in an unauthorised covert operation supposedly with the knowledge of Charles Haughey - he was Minister of Finance at the time - and Neil Blaney who was Minister of Agriculture. The Garda Special Branch uncovered it... it involved £50,000 of a secret Irish government humanitarian fund of £100,000 being diverted to import, illegally, and smuggle arms and ammunition to the Provos. The only loser was Captain Kelly – he was forced to resign. Haughey was sacked but he'll probably end up Taoiseach one day. There was a trial but it collapsed and all three men were found not guilty.'

'Surprise, surprise,' Jamie responded with a quiet laugh. 'But what has it got to do with Orlagh Duggan?'

'Ah well, Special Branch were looking into everyone who might be involved and one of those implicated, though it never came out in the scandal or the trial, was Orlagh Duggan, though she wasn't identified by name.'

'So how do you know it was her?'

'Photographs, Jamie... You know, those little pieces of shiny paper with people's pictures on them, taken with cameras... In this case by surveillance cameras. She hasn't changed much over the years... Looked just like she did tonight in the restaurant actually.'

Jamie laughed. 'So you spotted her,' he said.

'She's difficult to miss.'

'As a matter of interest, how was she involved?'

'She was suspected of killing a Garda Special Branch officer. Part of the surveillance team. They arrested her, kept her in for a while, but there was nothing to tie her to the murder so they had to let her go.'

'I heard about that... She did it, didn't she?'

'Oh yes, she did it. they just couldn't prove it.'

'And this just happened to be around the time of the Coventry bomb?'

Clara let out a soft laugh. 'Not *about* the time, Jamie. She was in custody over the weekend the bomb went off. Like I said, she wasn't the bomber.'

Jamie shrugged. 'She still deserves to get the good news though,' he said.

'Yes, she does. The only question in my mind is whether the lady you're protecting doesn't. If I believe her story, Orlagh is all yours.'

Jamie nodded. Clara's proposal seemed fair enough. It all came down to trust. 'Okay, deal,' he said. 'I'll take you to meet her early tomorrow, right after breakfast.'

Clara took another drink of her Remy Martin Brandy, not a sip this time, and puffed on her cigarette. Her glass was nearly empty.

Jamie caught the waiter's eye and the young man fairly rushed over, his last tip more than enough incentive. 'A Laphroaig 15 Year Old and another Remy Martin... singles this time, please,' he said. The waiter hurried away.

'What do you think we should do about the attack?' Clara asked, carefully checking the man was out of range.

Jamie shrugged. 'I would leave them to it, right up until the last moment...'

'Why? If we act now we could nip it in the bud,' Clara interjected.

'Yes, we could, but we wouldn't get them all. We still don't know where the other eight men are holed up and we don't know where the lorry carrying the explosives is. My gut tells me that bloody Yank reporter is involved but I might be wrong.'

'What about the weapons cache?'

'Leave it. Watch it, sure, but if we close it down they'll run for the hills. If worst comes to worst the ASUs can be taken out when they turn up there, but we have to let Corkscrew's lot through.'

'But if we do that won't the explosives man be warned and simply abort?'

Jamie smiled coldly. 'Not if we let the bhoys pick up their weapons before we take them out. Then we can get our lot to take their places and turn up to welcome the bastard. And I'll be there too with Corkscrew.'

'Only two of you?' She sounded suspicious.

Jamie grinned. 'We'll have some help.'

'I won't ask who.'

'No, better you don't.'

They fell silent again as the waiter returned and placed the drinks before them. Jamie slipped him three pounds and waved him away. The guy was having a profitable night.

'What does Charles think?' Jamie asked when it was safe to do so.

'He told me to ask you,' she replied with a wry smile. 'But I think he'll do what you suggest. He thinks a lot of you, you know.' It was Jamie's turn to smile wryly.

'He once told me he thought you had what it takes to make it right to the top,' she continued.

'Aye, Lady Estelle said something similar,' he said. 'Frankly, I doubt it. Wrong class, wrong school, wrong university and wrong background. I don't fit the profile of top dog and, to be honest, I don't want to.'

'Things like that don't matter anymore.'

Jamie looked askance. 'Of course they do, and they always will. I'm not the sort of guy Lord and Lady Snooty would invite round for drinks and canapes. And that's another reason why you and I would never have made it. You would have been shunned, cut off from your friends, gossiped about behind your back.'

Clara looked hurt. 'That's only an excuse,' she said.

'No Clara, it isn't. You would have ended up unhappy and so would I. You couldn't fit into my world and neither could I in yours.' He paused a moment, then said, 'Can I ask you a question?'

'Of course.'

'Do your mother and father know about us?'

Clara blushed. 'No,' she said.

'What do you think they would take it if they found out?'

'I don't know.'

'Now, *that's* an excuse and you're avoiding the answer. You're not naïve, Clara. You know exactly how they would take it.'

'They liked you when they met you at Hazelgrove.'

Jamie laughed at that. 'I thought so too,' he said. 'But at that time I was *Monsieur de Rochefort* as far as they knew, employed by the French Government. That little "*de*" in front of *Rochefort* gave them the wrong impression. In France, you stick *de* in front of your name and everyone takes you as a member of the aristocracy.' He saw her disbelieving look and said, 'Don't tell me you didn't know that... I'm sure your parents did, and I'm pretty sure too that their attitude to me would have been different if I'd been introduced as Michael, one of Sir Charles' jolly band of assassins.'

Clara was quiet at that. He knew what she was thinking - had she ever meant anything to him? Lady Redmond's little pep talk came back to him then. 'Listen Clara, what started as a bit of fun between us – your share of the 10%, remember – became something else entirely. I fell in love with you. I shouldn't have done because deep down I knew it wouldn't work... It couldn't work; partly for the reasons I've just given you but mostly because I never stopped loving Kate. I'm sorry.'

'So am I,' she said, a little sadly, but she was smiling too.

'So we're still friends?'

'Someone once said – I don't know who – that ex-lovers who stay friends after they split are either still in love or were never in love in the first place. What do you think?'

If ever there was a loaded question, that was it, Jamie mused. He took the easy way out. 'I think they're right,' he said. She could work it out. He had already told her.

They fell into silence for a while, sipping their drinks. Clara lit another cigarette. Her hand wasn't shaking any longer. Jamie gave up the fight and lit one of his dwindling supply of Embassy. It was Clara who spoke next. She said, 'Will you stay with me tonight? Jamie narrowed his eyes. 'I just want you to be there with me. Nothing more, I promise... other than maybe hold me.'

He nodded slowly. Just holding her would be difficult but... His heart was already on his sleeve. 'Okay,' he said softly.

Clara pushed herself up out of her chair and held out her hand. 'Let's go to bed,' she said.

'Your room or mine?'

Clara's eyes widened as that sunk in and then she laughed. 'You swine,' she retorted, punching him playfully on the arm. 'I wondered why the waiter looked confused. You've been in the lounge before and you paid him in cash this time rather than put it onto your bill. You really are sneaky, Jamie Raeburn. You're right, us being together wouldn't have worked.' But she was grinning so everything was okay.

'You're here to keep tabs on Ms Duggan, I take it?'

Jamie nodded slowly. 'Yes, of course I am,' he answered. 'She'll meet up with the three ASUs again before the 24th, she has to, and I'll be waiting. That'll give us their locations and when we have those the Brigadier can send in the cavalry. When you pass that on make sure you tell him to wait. We want them all, don't we?'

Clara nodded thoughtfully before continuing. 'If you intend following her I hope you don't intend using the Mustang,' she said, heading off in another direction.

'What do you take me for?' Jamie started to laugh then grew quiet. Maybe it was time to let her into his plan for Orlagh.

'Listen,' he started, 'You won't like this, but I'm going to try to get closer to Duggan, without breathing in the exhaust fumes of her taxi.' He had her attention now and he was right, she didn't like it.

'I hope you're not planning what I think you are?' she said earnestly.

'She's alone here...'

She cut him off immediately. 'Alone maybe, but vulnerable she most definitely is not. I forbid it.'

'You forbid it,' he laughed. 'I'm not a member of Ultra now Clara, I'm here as a volunteer, and I don't take orders.'

'That's not what I meant,' she blustered. 'I don't want you getting involved with her, that's all.'

It all suddenly became clear to him. 'Woah, hold on,' he said quickly. 'You've got the wrong idea. You think I'm going to seduce her... get her into bed and hope for pillow talk? Listen, I've got no intention of screwing her... Though I might have to give her the impression I want to,' he added. He was laughing now. Clara wrinkled her nose and Jamie grinned. She didn't like it when he spoke crudely. It was the class thing again.

Her response, however, wiped the grin off his face. She said, 'I'm not worried about that. It's more her screwing you that bothers me. She's dangerous... the Garda Special Branch officer isn't her only victim. Why do you even think it's necessary, for God's sake? Her ASUs will walk right into the trap.'

'True, but we will miss out on the explosives transporter... and I want him.'

'Why? What's so special about him... or her?'

Jamie shook his head slowly. 'I don't know for sure, it's instinct,' he replied, his voice no louder than a whisper. 'But I think it's the Yank, if he is a Yank, and I think it was him that set me up at Kiltyclogher. If that is the case I want the bastard and whoever gave him the information in the first place.'

Clara looked back at him anxiously. She had never heard him sound so venomous. He was taking it personally and that worried her too. But she wouldn't sway him, she knew that. Reluctantly, she nodded agreement. 'Okay,' she conceded. 'We'll do it your way.' There was no point in even trying to dissuade him. He would do it his way, no matter what. She stood and held out her hand. 'Your room I think,' she said, smiling. She wasn't happy about the plan and not purely for operational reasons, she had to admit. In a practical sense, it had merit, but if he went anywhere near the bitch she would cut off his balls, she promised herself.

Chapter Sixty-five

Sunday 13 January 1974

Sunday was living up to its name. The sun was out, but that was about all. The temperature was still hovering around 32 degrees Fahrenheit. Freezing, or Baltic as they say in Glasgow. Jamie blew into his hands to warm them and scraped frost from the windscreen of the Mustang. The engine purred loudly under the bonnet as it heated up but it was keeping its heat to itself as yet. He checked his watch. 09.20. Still early.

They had breakfasted at eight. As far as Jamie was concerned the night had been uneventful. Clara chattered on through the early part, mostly letting him know she was worried about his plan to get close to Orlagh Duggan.

She may have capitulated to his demand earlier in the evening but she was still concerned about it. Orlagh had seen them together in the restaurant so how was he going to explain that, she asked him at one point. His reply had irritated her, he could see it in her eyes. 'I'm not going to explain it at all,' he told her. 'She can think what she likes.'

'And what if she thinks I'm your wife... or your mistress?' Clara went on.

He remembered laughing at that. In hindsight, not the best response and his words hadn't helped. 'Well she'll be right, one way or the other,' he said.

They had slept in the same bed. It was what Clara wanted, but, happily from Jamie's point of view, intimacy didn't come into it. Strange then that he still felt guilty when he woke, he reflected sombrely. That was probably because Clara's legs were wrapped round his and his arms were around her, he told himself, and nothing at all to do with the fact he had wakened with an unrequited erection. *Aye, right!* At least Clara hadn't taken unfair advantage, he thought gratefully.

He caught movement from the side of his eye and turned to find Orlagh watching him from the hotel doorway, a wry smile on her pretty face. She was dressed for the weather; heavy coat and boots and a furry hat, faux Russian and black, sat on her head, her red mane tucked beneath it. If she was heading out to make contact with her soldiers he was going to miss out, he mused, then gave a mental shrug. His trip with Clara was more important. On the other hand, he thought, maybe she's a good Catholic girl heading for the nearest chapel to expunge her sins. The thought brought a cynical smile to his face. That, he mused, might take her all day and cost a fortune in candles.

He heard the hotel's revolving door turn and his smile changed to one of amusement when Clara emerged. The two women looked at each other, Clara a little dismissively and Orlagh more than a little speculatively. He suspected he knew what Clara was thinking. Orlagh's thoughts were more of a mystery.

Orlagh moved aside to let Clara pass and she did so without a second glance, making her way to Jamie and planting a kiss on his mouth. 'I wonder what the bitch will make of that?' she whispered with a laugh as she pulled away from him.

Orlagh was already walking away, a spring in her step. Jamie could imagine her smiling. 'Not much, it seems,' Jamie said, nodding her in the direction of Orlagh's disappearing back. 'Come on, let's go visit Roisin.'

Clara cocked an eyebrow. 'So it's Roisin, is it?' she said. 'Trust me now, do you?'

'You gave me your word, that's good enough for me, so yes, I trust you. Get in,' he went on, opening the passenger door.

They settled down on the leather seats, Clara giving an involuntary shiver. The car's heater was blowing warm air up the windscreen but the seats were still cold. That was the drawback with leather car seats, Jamie mused; they burned your arse in summer and froze it in winter.

'Where are we going?' Clara asked as he pulled out into Byres Road and turned left.

'Not far... We'll be there in a few minutes.'

He stopped at the traffic lights, the left indicator clicking rhythmically. He checked the rear view mirror and spied Orlagh Duggan walking away from him down Byres Road towards Partick. It looked like the second option, he surmised. If she was meeting with her men she would have taken a taxi. Walking meant she was going somewhere close and the only place he could think of was church.

Clara tried to read his thoughts. 'Wondering where she's going?' she asked, turning her head to glance back at Orlagh.

He smiled. 'Not any longer... She'll be back in the hotel by half past eleven.'

'Psychic are you?'

He laughed aloud. 'Nah, if I was psychic I'd have avoided all the shit that's come down on me in the last few years.'

'Does that include me?'

The lights changed and he pulled away, turning left again into Great Western Road. He glanced over at her and shook his head. 'I wouldn't have avoided you,' he said. 'You're not one of the bad shit I would have ducked. In fact, you were one of the highlights of the whole thing.' He saw her lift an eyebrow and gave her a little laugh. 'Okay, you were the *only* highlight.'

'You're forgiven,' she said, grinning now. 'So, if you're not psychic, how do you know when Duggan will be back?'

'I'm guessing, but it's an educated guess. It's Sunday morning and she's a catholic.'

'She's going to chapel? You're joking!' The look on his face told her he wasn't.

The lights at Hyndland Road were green and he sailed through. Clara looked out at the big mansions lining the road here and gave a low whistle. 'Impressive,' she said. 'These would cost a fortune in London.'

'They cost a fortune here too,' Jamie commented dryly as he flicked the indicator left and began to slow down.

Clara turned her attention back to the road ahead. They were approaching a junction, a minor road leading off to the left. Beyond that, a hotel. In her peripheral vision, also off to the left, she saw a large, multi-storey building; modern, utilitarian. Beyond that, on the crest of a hill, surrounded by trees, stood an older building. It consisted of two long blocks, with barred windows on two floors, standing on each side of a taller, central tower. It was of a kind, she mused darkly. Victorian, built out of the way, to house those who society didn't know how to deal with. With the passage of time its initial isolation from public view had been eroded and now it was surrounded by large villas and a modern hospital... But they still didn't know how to deal with the poor buggers who ended up in its wards, she reflected. Yes, things had improved, but there was still a long way to go. When they finally gave up on ECT, electroconvulsive therapy, realising it didn't really work, something else abhorrent would take its place.

'Is that where we're going?' she asked, her voice low. Jamie nodded and swung the Mustang left then right, following Shelley Road before turning off to the left on an unnamed road towards it.

A sign by the side of the road read "Gartnavel Royal Hospital". It didn't say what the hospital's speciality was. It didn't need to. Clara knew exactly what it was. She was beginning to feel sorry for the girl already.

'You didn't tell me she was here,' she said accusingly.

Jamie gave her a quick glance as he pulled in front of the central tower and manoeuvred into a parking space. 'No, I didn't,' he agreed, then explained. 'I thought if I threw it in it would sound too much like a sob story and turn you off.'

'Am I really so hard?'

'More cynical than hard,' he laughed. It didn't mollify her.

'How long has she been in here?'

'I don't know exactly. It wasn't immediately after the bombing. She had her girls to think of and they were still babies. I think as the twins became less demanding her thoughts turned to what she had done... been forced to do,' he added after a short pause. 'And then it all took over. She tried to kill herself and then she was sectioned.'

'Did her family know what had happened?'

Jamie laughed bitterly. 'It depends what you mean by "family". Her husband hadn't a clue. Put it down to post-natal depression. Her brother, on the other hand, knew only too well because he was behind it.'

'Her brother?' Clara queried, surprised. 'You missed that bit out of the story too.'

'Aye, well, there were a few thinks I left out. They didn't affect the story, only what you would take from it.'

'Are you ready to tell me it all now?'

'Not quite,' he replied grimly. 'But I will after you've spoken with Roisin.'

Clara nodded thoughtfully, then said, 'Okay, let's get on with that.'

Jamie opened his car door and cold air flooded the cabin. He hauled himself out, swinging his arms around himself to keep warm. Clara emerged from the car, all efficiency. She pulled her coat tightly around her and waited impatiently. Jamie took the hint. He locked the car, though why bother, he mused. There was no one around here to steal it... Unless, of course, one of the patients managed to escape, he thought with a wry smile.

They stood together at the big door, clouds of white rising into the air with their breathing. Jamie pressed the bell push and waited patiently. Clara surveyed the surroundings. Pleasant enough, she thought, if you discounted the purpose of the big grey, forbidding building. It was time places like this were brought into the modern age, she mused. It frightened her so what would it do to someone suffering from paranoia?

Footsteps echoed on the wooden floor behind the door, a face appeared at the window panel on the left side and quickly disappeared, and then the locks were withdrawn. The door opened silently and a familiar face greeted them. Familiar so far as Jamie was concerned at least. It was the nurse who had shown him to Roisin's room on his first visit. While Jamie recognised her there was simply a blank expression on the nurse's face, albeit pleasantly blank.

'My name's Raeburn,' Jamie said, introducing himself, 'and this is my wife.' He swung an arm in Clara's direction, avoiding looking at her 'We've come to visit Roisin Evans, if that's okay?' he asked, smiling at the woman.

Recognition dawned on the nurse's face. The smile grew warmer. 'Ah, it's you,' she said. 'I was trying to place you... the miracle worker,' she added with a soft laugh.

Jamie smiled and Clara gave him a questioning look that replaced the surprise at being introduced as his wife.

'Hardly,' he replied, a little self-consciously. 'All I did was talk to her; she did the rest herself.'

'Come in, it's cold out there,' the nurse went on, standing aside to let them enter. She seemed oblivious to his protestation. 'Maybe we should get you in here on a regular basis to "talk" to the patients,' she continued. 'God knows, it worked with Mrs Evans, so who knows what it would do for some of the other poor souls.'

Clara smiled. Jamie Raeburn as a counsellor painted a strange picture in her mind but he did have a softer side. She knew that.

'Roisin is still in the same room but you're just in time. She's going home today,' the nurse went on. 'Do you want me to take you up or can you find it yourself?'

Jamie hid his surprise and smiled. He was genuinely pleased at the news but it was a surprise none the less. 'It's alright, we'll manage,' Jamie assured her, and headed off towards the stairway with Clara in tow. The nurse returned to her station at the reception desk and noted their arrival. The woman looked nice, she mused as she wrote down Mr and Mrs Raeburn in the Visitors' Book.

'Your wife?' Clara said as they climbed the stairs to the first landing.

'I couldn't think what else to say.'

Clara smiled at him. 'It's a nice thought,' she said quietly.

They turned right at the top of the stair and followed the corridor. Clara wrinkled her nose. Familiar smells assailed her nostrils – disinfectant, the sour odour of ancient vomit, human smells... fear, even. She would still be working in a place like this, she thought, if Charles hadn't persuaded her to join Ultra and her life would be so different. Maybe she would be a consultant now, or married to another doctor. Maybe she would be a mother... But she was none of these. It saddened her a little.

They passed a nurse about mid-way along the corridor. The woman, young and pretty, smiled at them, though more at Jamie Clara noted. Muffled voices filtered through doorways, a scream split the air but was quickly stifled. Clara looked at Jamie. He didn't flinch at the sound where most people would. He really was quite special, she mused.

Finally, Jamie came to a halt in front of a door. Roisin's room, no doubt, Clara thought. He hesitated, seemingly undecided about something, then turned to her. 'How should I introduce you?' he asked, his voice a whisper.

Clara smiled teasingly. She said, 'What's wrong with "your wife"?

'Nah, that wouldn't work,' Jamie replied, playing the game. 'You're too refined. She knows Kate is a nurse.'

'I'm a doctor... well, psychologist, I can do "nurse".'

'We're wasting time.'

'Okay,' Clara laughed, conceding the point. 'Why don't you tell her I'm a friend who is a psychologist who's here to talk to her. Will she buy that?'

Jamie nodded slowly. 'Yes, I think so,' he said. He turned back to the door, his hand now on the door knob. 'Shall we?' he said.

'Yes, let's,' Clara agreed. Strangely, she felt a little nervous.

Jamie pushed open the door and led the way. He thought about ushering Clara through before him but worried about the effect of that on Roisin. Roisin was up and dressed. She was sitting by the window, her usual seat Jamie reflected, and a small suitcase lay on the bed. He remembered she could see down to Shelley Road and the Pond Hotel from her seat at the window. She would be watching for Trevor, he surmised. She turned towards the door as they entered, her face going through a range of emotions – curiosity, disbelief and pleasure, in that order, then consternation, apprehension and, finally fear when she spied Clara. She stood up but didn't come to him.

Jamie saw her anxiety unfolding and moved quickly to her, putting his arms around her and pulling her close. 'It's okay,' he whispered soothingly. 'She's a friend. She's here to help.'

Roisin backed away and looked nervously at Clara. She still wasn't convinced.

'This is Clara,' Jamie went on quickly. 'She's a psychologist. I told her about what happened to you. Talk to her Roisin. She might be able to help you.'

Clara stood back, waiting. Given the reason for her being here, Roisin's reaction was perfectly natural. A lot now depended on how much she trusted Jamie Raeburn.

'I'm going home today,' Roisin said softly, her eyes flitting between them.

'Yes, I know,' Jamie acknowledged, easing her back down onto her chair. 'Listen, I just want to help... So does Clara here. You won't stop thinking about what happened. I just don't want you back in here again, so please, talk to her.'

Roisin looked up at Clara and then back at Jamie. She nodded slowly and forced a nervous smile.

'I'll help you all I can, Roisin,' Clara said quietly, smiling openly. 'I'm not here to pass judgement,' she continued. 'Believe me.'

Jamie crouched down beside her and reached for her hands. 'Talk to her Roisin. Tell her in your own words what happened and how it affected you. That's all you have to do.'

Roisin nodded again, her eyes locked onto him. 'Okay,' she said, her voice no more than a whisper.

Clara took of her heavy coat and laid it on the bed beside the suitcase. She pulled one of the spare chairs over beside Roisin and settled down, looking up at Jamie. Back off, her eyes were saying, let me take it from here.

Jamie did just that. He let go of Roisin's hands and straightened up, moving back towards the door. He was in a bit of a quandary. Roisin was leaving which meant Trevor would be arriving soon to take her home. He didn't want Trevor to arrive before Clara finished and he could prevent that by waiting outside in his car for the Englishman's appearance. On the other hand, he was concerned that Roisin would react badly to him leaving. He decided to wait.

Clara started speaking softly, smiling encouragingly, teasing the story from Roisin. Roisin began slowly, defensively, but with Clara's gentle prompting the words began to flow. Jamie began to relax. It was all coming out from her openly and it had the ring of truth. He smiled inwardly. It had the ring of truth because it was the truth.

Bothe women were engrossed in the story now, Roisin the storyteller and Clara the listener. Jamie eased the door open and slipped out into the corridor. If either woman saw him leave they didn't show it. He waited outside the door for a moment listening to Clara's voice. There was no break. He smiled again and headed for the stairs.

The nurse on duty at the door looked up as he passed. He held up his cigarettes and mimicked taking a smoke. She smiled back at him and then returned to her work. Outside, it was colder if anything. The sun was behind a screen of light grey cloud now, a ball of white brightness. His breath was coming from his mouth in clouds of white that lingered a moment before being absorbed into the atmosphere around him. He lit a cigarette and drew heavily on it. He had been anxious bringing Clara here but his gut was telling him the gamble had paid off. That would make life easier but if it didn't happen, he would deal with it. He would still have his 48 hours and he still had Conor.

He finished his cigarette and lit another. He had been outside now for about ten minutes. Not long enough. On the bright side, there was still no sign of Trevor and even if he arrived now, Jamie was confident he could delay him for a few minutes. As it happened, he didn't need to. He finished his second cigarette and tossed the stub away just as Clara stepped out from the hospital and a sleek blue Mk1 Ford Capri with smoke grey tinted windows pulled to a halt beside the Mustang. Clara stopped on the steps, a sixth sense telling her that Trevor Evans had arrived.

The Englishman heaved himself from the Capri and looked searchingly at Jamie before turning his gaze to Clara. He tilted his head slightly to the side, questioning her presence, then fixed his eyes on Jamie once more.

'She's with me,' Jamie said. 'A friend.'

Trevor turned away and reached into the Capri, stretching over to the back seat, his back to them. Jamie turned quickly to Clara. She had a tiny smile on her face as she nodded almost imperceptibly to him before Trevor re-emerged from the Capri, a toddler in his arms. The baby girl appeared to be asleep, cosily wrapped in warm winter clothing. Trevor looked at them both again, still wary, then held out the child to Jamie. Jamie hesitated, taken off guard, while Clara laughed. 'It shouldn't be too difficult; you've got four of your own,' she said.

Jamie took the child and held her against his chest. Trevor said nothing, simply gave them both a lingering look then turned back to the car for his second daughter. When he returned to them this time the child was tucked against him, asleep like her sister. He looked as if he wanted to ask if everything was okay but was afraid of what he might hear. Instead, he introduced them to the twins. 'This one is Molly,' he said, nodding down at the child in his arms. 'She's named after Roisin's aunt,' he explained needlessly to Jamie. 'The one you're holding is Edith, that's my mother's name.'

'Lovely names,' Clara said, entering the conversation.

Trevor looked at her fleetingly before turning his attention back to Jamie. He still couldn't find the courage to ask.

Jamie watched the anxiety grow in the big man. It was, he imagined, like visiting the doctor after tests to find out if you had something terminal. You wanted to know but you couldn't ask. You were hoping for the best but suspecting the worst. Human nature. He put the man out of his misery, just as a good doctor would. 'Everything is alright, Trevor. Nothing is going to happen to Roisin... It's all taken care of.'

The Englishman was close to tears. He struggled to speak and his eyes moved from Jamie to Clara as if he knew that she had something to do with it. She was more than a friend, he suspected, though what he could only guess. It didn't matter. The smile and the nod she gave him were enough.

'Does Roisin know?' he asked at length.

Jamie turned to Clara. The ball was in her court, momentarily at least. She gave him a slight shake of the head. 'No, Trevor, she doesn't,' Jamie replied then. 'You can give her the good news, eh?'

'You're not coming back up?'

'No, we'll leave you to it... but give me a number I can contact you on,' Jamie said, almost as an afterthought.

Automatically, Trevor handed Molly to Clara who took her with a little trepidation, cradling her in her arms like some fragile ceramic doll. It was Jamie smiling now. 'You'll make a good mother someday,' he said, biting his tongue as the words came out.

She smiled sadly in response. *Yes, maybe, if I had the right man beside me to be the child's father; but I won't, will I*, she mused. She said nothing but her eyes conveyed her thoughts. Jamie's old friend guilt tapped him on the shoulder again as he turned away, unable to hold her look.

He was saved from further discomfiture by Trevor. The big man had found a scrap of paper and a pencil and had scribbled down a number. 'That's the number at home,' he said. He didn't ask why Jamie wanted the number. He hoped he knew.

Clara handed him Edith and turned to the door, pressing the bell. Moments later, the nurse appeared, smiling this time. The Englishman took Molly, still asleep, into his spare arm. He was like a giant in a fairy tale, Jamie thought with a smile, a big friendly giant. Maybe someone would write a book about him one day.

'Thanks,' Trevor said softly. He was speaking to both of them now. 'You've brought a nightmare to an end.' The nurse smiled her agreement though her perception of the nightmare was way wide of the mark. 'Keep in touch,' the Englishman went on. That was addressed solely to Jamie.

'Uh-huh, I will, don't worry.' The look in his eyes carried an added message and Trevor broke into a smile. The door closed then and he and Clara stood on the step, both of them drained. He turned to her and put his hands on her arms. 'Thank you,' was all he said.

Chapter Sixty-six

'You're a hero; according to Roisin Evans, that is,' Clara said with a laugh as Jamie swung the car out of the parking space and headed for Shelley Road. 'And I'm not the only one you would walk over hot coals for, it seems. Roisin was quite informative,' she continued teasingly, 'though I think she was holding some things back... things even Trevor doesn't know about. Tell me, is this a service you provide only for damsels in distress or are men included?'

Jamie's replied with a snort. 'I'm no hero. I just do what's right, or at least I try to.'

'Only women?' she pressed.

'No, not only women. One or two are men.'

'Only one or two?' she laughed.

'Aye, the ones who mean a lot to me. The ones I really care about... and that goes for the women too.'

Clara was quiet for a moment. She looked at him sadly, pensively, before going on. 'I didn't know about what happened to your first wife,' she said, her mood sombre now. 'The dossier I read hinted at something but it didn't spell it out.'

Jamie stared straight ahead. They were at the traffic lights at the Shelley Road, Great Western Road junction. A picture of Lucie had formed in his mind and he felt a tears well up behind his eyes. How long had it been? Six, nearly seven years, and it had passed so quickly. He realised he hadn't thought of her for a while and hearing Clara speak of her like this now was almost too much. His old friend Guilt was waving to him from the darkness of his mind. He forced a grim smile before speaking.

'Her name was Lucie, Lucie Kent before we married, and the reason she wasn't mentioned in the file on me was because the man who wrote it up tried to keep my identity a secret. Including Lucie's name in it would have made it easy for the reader to identify me... Not that the Brigadier had much difficulty on that score,' he added, bitterly.

'I'm sorry,' Clara said awkwardly. 'I didn't mean...'

He cut her off. 'It's alright, forget it... Not your fault.' His face was set in a cold smile. 'It was fate, that's all. If Lucie hadn't met Max Kelman when she did, if she hadn't been coming into a fortune, if Kelman hadn't found out about it, then maybe she'd still be alive and I wouldn't be here. That's a lot of "ifs" that didn't happen and because of them I ended up killing a lot of guys... And a lot more since. I didn't set out to do that.'

'I know... I knew it from the beginning, from the first time I met you. I had reservations about you. You're not like any of the others.'

Jamie laughed then, his bitterness still showing. 'No, apparently I'm better than the rest, according to Sir Charles. Not sure I'm proud of that. It's all to do with my being a civilian. The others are all ex-military and still act like it. Seems I blend in better... with my victims, that is.'

'They're not victims, Jamie,' she retorted harshly. 'If you think of them as victims you're doing yourself a disservice. Victims equate to innocence, these people are not innocent.'

They drove in silence for a while and were approaching the hotel before Jamie spoke again. 'So you believed her?' he posed. He saw Clara nod out of the side of his eye before she replied.

'Yes, I believed her,' she answered simply.

'And Orlagh? You'll pin it on her?'

Her head was shaking now. 'No, I won't. If I could find out she isn't the bomber so can Charles. I have a better idea.'

'Which is?' he said, turning to her briefly as he negotiated the junction at Byres Road.

'Corkscrew can't give us the bomber. She's dead. But he can give us the monster behind it... and he already has... and Roisin confirmed it.'

'Brendan Kelly?'

She smiled as she replied. 'That's our man,' she said.

'And Orlagh walks away?'

'I doubt it. If she's involved she will have to disappear like the rest.'

'And can you find someone to fill the shoes of the bomber... someone who will satisfy Sir Charles that is?'

'He'll be too busy rubbing his hands with glee at getting the brains behind it but yes, I can find someone.'

Jamie brought the Mustang to a halt just beyond the hotel entrance and turned to face her fully at last. He felt awkward. 'Thanks,' he said quietly. 'I didn't know how you would react.'

She forced a laugh. 'Liar,' she said, holding his eyes with hers. 'You knew exactly how I would react.' Her laugh grew louder. 'Charles told me I was the only one who could get you to work on Fitzpatrick for the name. He thought I could manipulate you but all the time I sensed that it was you who would end up manipulating me.'

'I'm sorry.'

'Don't be. I'm not. Roisin Kelly doesn't deserve to die for something she had no control over... But I'm not doing it for her, I'm doing it for you because...' She paused, unsure whether to say it, then shrugged. 'Because I still love you,' she said, dropping her eyes. 'It's my way of walking over red hot coals for you.'

She saw the battle going on behind his eyes. She knew he was sorry. She didn't have to hear it. He was about to speak when she held up her hand and stopped him. 'Don't say anything,' she said. 'Let me believe what I want to believe, Jamie; don't take it away from me.'

'I wasn't going to...'

'Then that's enough,' she said, cutting him off. 'I'm going back to London tomorrow. I'll do what I have to do, you do your part. Can you?'

'Yes,' he said easily.

'Including Orlagh Duggan?' He smiled. It was a cold, hard smile and she found it scary.

His tone when he spoke matched it. 'Yes, including Orlagh,' he said, hoping he assuaged her doubt.

He pushed open the car door and climbed out into the cold. He shivered. Clara was watching him, concern showing. He smiled. His shiver had nothing to do with what was facing him over the next few days; it was all to do with the temperature, but Clara probably didn't see it like that. 'What?' he said, grinning at her. 'It's bloody cold out here, that's all.' He doubted she was convinced but it didn't matter. The only person he had to convince was himself and he had already done that.

She extracted herself from the car and pulled her coat tight around her. Her look softened and a smile formed at her lips. 'Okay, if you say so,' she said. 'I'm not going to argue. We've only got until tomorrow and I don't want to spend it fighting with you. Let's just make the most of it. We'll have lunch and then you can show me the delights of Glasgow... and tonight... well, that's up to you.'

She was teasing him. He knew that, but there is an old Scottish expression; half kidding, whole earnest. It seemed to fit her like a glove.

Chapter Sixty-seven

Monday 14 January 1974

Clara left the hotel by taxi just before mid-day on route to London via Glasgow Airport. She was booked on the one-thirty shuttle and would be back in her office by four with any luck.

Jamie had shown her Glasgow and a bit more besides but he didn't succumb to the craving that threatened to tear him apart. He knew, deep inside, that he would regret it forever if he did.

He helped load her luggage into the taxi, hugged her and kissed her tenderly. It wasn't all for show. He was going to miss her.

As the taxi disappeared down Byres Road towards Partick Cross he turned back to the hotel. He would miss her, right enough, he mused, but not as much as he was missing Kate right now. It had been ten days; ten long, bloody days. He had lied to her. Told her it might take a week, a little longer maybe, but he knew it would be much longer. Unless he managed to get everything from Orlagh Duggan before the date of the attack it would be another ten days before he was finished and another one or two before he could be with her. He needed to talk to her. And lie to her again.

He went straight to his room and picked up the phone. His finger danced over the dial and seconds later the ringtone came to him. The marvel of telephony, he mused, talk into a chunk of plastic at one end and someone miles away, hundreds, thousands even, could hear you. Just as well they couldn't see you, he thought. If they could, it would make it much harder to lie. Somebody would come up with that idea one day.

It was Emily Edwards who answered, her tone far from warm. 'So you've called at last,' she said censoriously.

If she was trying to sound severe she was succeeding, Jamie thought. He stifled a sigh. She was right, of course. She was up there on the moral high ground and he was down here in the swamp. He decided to take her criticism on the chin. Fighting it would only make matters worse, even though it had only been three days since his last call. 'You're right,' he said. 'I should have phoned before this. I'm sorry. It's been difficult.'

Wrong thing to say, he reflected instantly. What could possibly make it difficult to phone... in Emily Edwards' world at least. He held his breath, waiting for her barbed retort but Kate's arrival on the scene saved him. He heard a flurry of chatter, mostly muffled, as Kate gently took over. He could picture his mother in law with her hand firmly clamped over the microphone. Then there was a moment's silence before Kate's voice came down the line.

'Hello baby,' she said breathlessly. 'Don't pay any attention to mother,' she continued, quietly. 'She thinks you should phone every day.'

'And you don't?' he responded, laughing softly.

'It would be nice if you could but I know it isn't easy. I just wish I was there with you.'

'So do I,' he murmured. 'I miss you. It won't be long now,' he said. First lie, depending of course on how you defined long. She would ask; he knew she would.

'How long? Days? A week?'

He hated being right. 'Not days, a week probably,' he replied. He would say the same when the week was up and then it might be true. 'Has anyone tried to contact me?' he went on quickly, diverting her.

'Your Mum phoned the day before yesterday... Don't worry, I answered the phone. I told her you were away for a couple of days and she chatted with me for a while. She sounded happy. I don't think she was suspicious but maybe you should call her.'

'Yeah, I'll do that,' he replied absently.

'Are you being a good boy?'

She was teasing him but still, what a question. He was being good but if he told her what had been happening and what he was about to do he doubted she would see it that way. 'Yes, I'm being good,' he told her. 'I'm too busy trying to figure out how to resolve this mess to find time to be bad.'

'Good,' was her simple reply.

They spent another ten minutes talking about the children and the future. That was always the scope of their conversations on the phone. When the call ended Kate still sounded happy or as happy as she could be in the circumstances. He, on the other hand, was not. Lying to her didn't come easy but the truth was harder still.

He lay back on his bed and stared at the ceiling. What now, he wondered. Could he wrap this thing up before the twenty-fifth? If he could get the locations of the safe houses from Orlagh Duggan maybe, but there was still the lorry load of explosives to deal. Did she know where that was being hidden and who was bringing it? He smiled wryly to himself. Maybe.

He leaned over and picked up the handset again, this time dialling Conor. An unknown female voice answered, a soft, West Highland accent not unlike Mary's, Conor's wife. It could only be Mary's mother, he surmised, she didn't have a sister; at least she never spoke of one. 'Hello,' he said pleasantly. 'It's Jamie, Conor's friend, is he around by any chance?'

The response was warm and immediate. He could almost see her smiling. 'I get to speak to you at last,' she said. 'He never stops speaking about you. I feel you're one of the family. Hold on, he's just coming,' she continued. 'Come down and visit us... we're in Dunoon, not the far side of the moon.' She accompanied that with a soft laugh. 'Here he is,' she finished.

'Jamie,' the big American greeted him, clearly happy to get the call. 'You need me, I hope?'

'Your experience and your brain for now, don't get too excited,' Jamie replied, laughing at Conor's obvious frustration. The American wanted to be involved.

'Okay, shoot,' Conor said, shelving his disappointment.

'I've sorted the problem around Roisin. Clara has agreed to take her out of the frame.'

Conor let out a low whistle. 'How did you manage that?'

'I took her to meet Roisin.'

The stunned silence from the Dunoon end of the line wasn't unexpected and it was a long moment before Conor spoke. 'Took a chance there, kid. That could have ended badly.'

'If I'd thought that I wouldn't have taken her. We talked it out. She knew Duggan wasn't the bomber and had worked it out that I knew who was. I told her Roisin's story on the basis she give me 48 hours to make Roisin disappear. It was after that she asked to meet her... same terms. Anyway, she was convinced. She'll cover for Roisin.'

'So you don't need a hidey-hole and passports. That's a relief. How is she going to do it? She needs to convince your boss.'

Jamie laughed. 'She's going to do what you suggested in the first place. She's going to find someone who's dead to lay the blame on.'

'Makes sense. And that's it?'

'Not quite... She wants the man behind it dead.'

'Brendan Kelly,' Conor stated tersely. 'And you get the job?'

'Quid pro quo. I was going to do it anyway,' Jamie replied dismissively.

'Is that what you want to pick my brain on?'

Jamie laughed again. 'No Conor, that's for the future and it'll be across the water. It's something closer to home.'

'Okay, I'm listening.'

'It's eleven days until the attack takes place and we still don't know where the other ASUs are. Glasgow, yeah, but it's a big place. If Duggan doesn't meet up with them again before the day we'll be relying on taking them out at the scene and that could get messy.'

'Yeah, it could, but you'll have your SAS with you and probably some of your Ultra guys. That sort of limits the possible damage.'

'Aye, but there are still risks. We don't know exactly what they're going to do. We've got a lorry being hijacked, another loaded with enough Sodium Chlorate to blow a hole through to bloody Australia, and not a fucking clue as to what it all means.'

'So what do you want?'

'I want to know where our friends can get the quantity of Sodium Chlorate they need without arousing suspicion. I know it has to be mixed with sugar... I did it myself when I was a kid and blew up plastic models in the garden, but is there anything else it can be mixed with... something that'll make it more effective?'

'That all?'

'No, I want to know how they detonate it. Can it be detonated by firing an RPG at it?'

'It shouldn't be too hard to find that out. Why not ask your people?'

Jamie laughed quietly. 'I don't have people, Conor. But since you ask, I don't want the Brigadier picking the guy up before I get to him.'

'Okay, I get that. You think this dude has something to do with what happened to you in Ireland?'

'That's perceptive of you Conor; ever think of becoming a spy?' Jamie retorted, laughing.

Conor ignored the teasing. 'I'll get back to you later today,' he said. 'Meantime, watch your back.'

'I will... Give my love to Mary and tell her mother I'll be down as soon as I can... and I'll bring Kate and the kids.'

'That'll keep her busy,' Conor retorted, laughing. 'Better give a week's notice so she can clean the house. Chou, kid.'

The call disconnected and Jamie settled back on the bed. He wanted the mole more than anything else now. If the Brigadier got to the man before him chances were he would never find out who it was and that would be disappointing. He had a score to settle.

He sat staring at the window. The sun was out. A miracle, some might say. Two days of sunshine in quick succession in Glasgow in January probably did fall into that category. A walk would do him good, he decided. Clear away the cobwebs. Glasgow Botanic Gardens were just across the road and the glasshouses would be open. He had never visited them before, a failure shared by most of the city's citizens he thought. Time to find out what he and they were missing. He pushed himself up off the bed and took his coat from the wardrobe. The sun might be shining but that was misleading. This was Scotland... and it was January.

Chapter Sixty-eight

He returned to the Grosvenor in a better frame of mind. It wouldn't last but he didn't know that. He had spent a couple of hours in the gardens, making his way from glasshouse to glasshouse, marvelling at the plants on display. He had never, in his wildest imaginings, thought that such exotic florae could exist in a city with an atmosphere heavy with pollutants and a climate that matched the frozen wastes of Siberia.

It was late in the afternoon and the sun was sinking rapidly, casting long shadows. Lights were coming on in the imposing buildings along Grosvenor Terrace and the hotel was lit up like a Christmas tree. This was where the rich had lived years ago. Some of them still did, he mused. It made him angry. The disparity between rich and poor was still there. He laughed quietly to himself as he recalled Clara's suggestion that class didn't matter these days. It didn't matter to the rich, maybe, but to the poor buggers scraping a living to survive it was there alright.

He shivered a little as he crossed Great Western Road. Soon it would be dark and the temperature, such as it had been, was already dropping. It would be another cold night and a heavy frost was promised. He would stay in the hotel tonight and see what developed with Orlagh Duggan. At least he could keep an eye on her in comfort. He checked his watch, an action that brought a cold smile to his face. Fionn Doherty still had his watch, the one Kate had given him, and in a few days he would take it back.

The hands told him it was just after four o'clock. If her flight had been on time Clara should be in London sitting at her desk. He wondered if she had briefed the Brigadier and if so what his reaction had been. He would find out soon enough.

He walked the short distance to Grosvenor Lane and turned right towards the hotel entrance. The Mustang was still where he had left it the night before, the windows heavy with ice and a covering of frost forming on the bodywork. He wouldn't be driving tonight so it didn't matter.

He wondered if Orlagh Duggan was still in the hotel. His trip to the Botanic Gardens had been impulsive, like most of his life, he mused wryly. If Orlagh had decided to meet her troops today he would have missed out on the opportunity to pinpoint the safe houses. He shrugged mentally. Fuck it. He had needed the time to think. Anyway, he doubted she would be in contact with the bhoys again so soon. It was only five days since her last rendezvous with them and there were still ten days to go till the big event. These boys knew what they were doing so she had no need to babysit them. But that raised another question. Why was she here so early? He could understand the men of the ASUs disappearing from across the water and lying low but she didn't need to be here. Unless... she was meeting the someone else! And that someone else had to be the man bringing in the explosives. He smiled grimly. He would get the bastard. That was a promise.

He was still thinking that through when he pushed through the revolving door into the heat of the hotel foyer. He looked around. It was quiet. Understandable. January wasn't the height of the tourist season in Glasgow. Come to think of it, there wasn't a tourist season in Glasgow.

The receptionist caught his eye and gestured him over. She was smiling and waving a slip of paper. He turned in her direction.

'There was a call for you while you were out, Mr Ferryman,' she said, holding out the slip of paper to him.

Conor must have been quick off the mark, he mused as he took the proffered note. 'When did the call come in?' he asked.

'About twenty minutes ago,' the girl advised. 'I took the call myself. The caller seemed quite agitated... she insisted we get the message to you the moment you returned.'

The hairs on the back of Jamie's neck stood on end. The word "she" the trigger. Only two women knew where he was, Kate and Clara, and a call from either of them in an agitated state didn't bode well. He thanked the girl, retrieved his key and made immediately for the stairs, the note still folded in his fingers.

He waited until he was in his room before opening the slip of folded paper. The words stared back at him and a wave of relief swept over him - *Dr Whitelaw phoned at 3.45, asked that you call back urgently, important development. No number left.*

His relief was in the fact that nothing had happened to Kate or one of his children. Nothing else really mattered, he realised as he reached for the phone. They came first, last and everywhere in between. Whatever was troubling Clara was secondary but judging by the speed of her call it must be serious. He gave a grim little smile. Just about everything to do with Ultra was serious. He dialled her office number and she answered immediately.

'Whitelaw,' she said, her usual greeting.

'It's me. I didn't expect a call, sorry.'

'Where the hell have you been?' she demanded irritably. Agitated she certainly was.

'Out,' he snapped back. 'Why don't you just calm down and tell me what it is that's got you so stressed. It's not like you.'

'I'm sorry. It's the hijack. We've just identified the target and it's worse than we imagined,' she said, the tension seeming to ease from her a little as she spoke.

'What is it?'

'A convoy carrying spent submarine reactor fuel leaves HMS Clyde, Faslane, at 23.30 on 24 January. It takes the waste to the rail yards at Glasgow and from there it is transported by train to Windscale for reprocessing.'

'They're hijacking a fucking bin lorry, is that what you're saying?' It was a bad joke and he knew it.

'You could say that,' she replied stiffy. 'But this stuff isn't going to a landfill site. If it was, it would be buried in concrete for the next couple of hundred years.'

'But it's waste; surely it can't be that bad... is it?'

'Maybe not as bad as a nuclear bomb going off or one of the missiles exploding on the base, but bad enough apparently. The waste contains a lot of nasty stuff.'

'How nasty?'

'Some of it is *very* bad, I'm told.'

'How do they transport it?'

'It's carried it in heavy, lead lined, steel containers, completely sealed. They load the containers onto trucks at Faslane and offload them at the railhead.'

'Well, that accounts for the RPG7s Corkscrew said they have,' Jamie mused aloud. 'Those things can crack open battle tanks so a couple of steel containers shouldn't stand in their way. What's the Brigadier saying?'

'Not much. It's out of his hands now. The Prime Minister has been kept in the loop all along but when this came out he insisted that the Heads of MI5 and SIS be briefed so if there's a mole in either it'll be out soon enough. The SAS is on the way to Scotland as we speak. If this attack is successful it'll be a major disaster.'

'How long have I got?'

'To do what, Jamie; find the locations of the safe houses or get Corkscrew out?'

'There's no "either or" there Clara. It's a package,' he fired back.

'24 hours, 48 at a push. The SAS will take out the arms cache in Dumbarton first and a protective ring is being thrown round the submarine base. That part is still being kept hush-hush. As far as the locals are concerned it's just an exercise. They have them all the time. Whatever happens, if the twelve men of the ASUs are still on the loose and we don't have the big bomb, the waste convoy won't leave the base.'

Jamie's head was reeling. He thought of family and friends and his next question was one he was reluctant to ask. But he needed to know. 'What's the contamination risk?' he said at last.

Clara let out an anxious laugh. 'That's the problem. No one knows exactly, or, if they do, they're not saying,' she admitted. 'Nothing like this has happened before. Nuclear power stations have plans in place to combat leaks and the convoys too have procedures in place, but these only deal with accidental leaks, not a major catastrophe and this really is a nightmare scenario. Once it's out there God knows what will happen.'

'What *are* the experts saying?'

'Nothing definite, other than it will be bad, very bad some say. Others say the damage will be more psychological than physical but they're in the minority. It all depends on "unknown factors" like the weather at the time, wind strength, how bad the breaches in the containers are and how much explosive there is to blow it all up. If it gets into the atmosphere and the wind gets it you're looking at exclusion zones of maybe anything between 10 and 25 miles.'

Jamie couldn't prevent his shocked intake of breath. 'Jesus, that will take in most of Glasgow.'

'Yes, and the US base at Holy Loch,' Clara added.

Jamie let out a bitter laugh. 'They're the last of my worries just now. They shouldn't be there; that was just another political sell out.'

'But they *are* there and this could have major political consequences.'

'So fuck the people of Dumbarton and Glasgow as long as our American allies are okay, is that it?' He thought of Conor and immediately regretted his outburst.

'Don't be stupid,' Clara retorted angrily. 'That's not what I said.'

Jamie stared blankly out of the window, forcefully calming himself, breathing deeply. Clara heard the rasping sound of it and waited. She understood what was going through his head. He had family and friends there. She would feel the same if this was happening in London. Eventually, she heard his breathing settle.

'Okay,' he said at last. 'What do you want me to do?'

'I'll let Charles tell you that,' she said calmly. 'He wants to speak to you. It's important, so hang on while I get him.'

Jamie hung on. He heard her chair scrape backwards on the wooden floor and then the opening of her door, the familiar scrape there too. There was muffled conversation, two voices only. It went on for a while and during that time Jamie felt his anger building. Then the sound of footsteps echoed on the parquet flooring again, two sets, one heavy one light, and then the Brigadier was on the line.

'Raeburn, Clara tells me you're in the same hotel as the Duggan woman so there's something I want you to do. Urgently.'

There were no preliminaries, no niceties, no "sorry about this old chap", the old boy was all business. 'Yes,' Jamie replied sharply.

'From what you say it seems you think Duggan knows the whereabouts of the three ASUs. Is that correct?'

'I don't *think* it, I know it,' Jamie retorted, still keeping his emotions in check. 'She met with them a few days ago.'

'Corkscrew told you this?'

Jamie responded with a cold laugh. 'I followed him and his mates from Alexandria. They met her in a pub in Glasgow and then I followed her back to her hotel. This hotel. Corkscrew confirmed later that she had met all three units.'

'And you took a room in the hotel, yes?'

'Yes, to keep an eye on her. I was hoping she might lead me to the other units eventually.'

'I'm afraid eventually isn't quick enough. Clara tells me you're planning to get close to the woman.'

'Yes, I had that in mind but it seems it has been overtaken by events.'

'Rather, old son,' Sir Charles replied. 'We don't have time for a gentle, probing approach now. We need to know where those ASUs are. If Duggan knows, get that information from her... by fair means or foul. Do I make myself clear?'

Jamie hesitated a moment before responding. 'Not really,' he said, his voice low and cold. 'You'll need to spell it out for me.' The implications of the words "fair means or foul" were not sitting well with him.

'Very well,' the Brigadier retorted sharply. 'What I am saying is wring it out of her. Threaten her, beat her, do whatever is necessary to get that information... and get the name of the contact carrying the explosives.'

'Just his name? Don't you want to know where to find him?' Jamie retorted insolently.

'Of course I bloody want that,' Sir Charles exploded. 'This isn't the time for your childish games, Raeburn. Lives are at stake.'

He had him there, Jamie mused. And yet, something in him still wanted to fight back. He had been drawn into the Brigadier's shadowy world against his will and now he was being dragged deeper down into the morass. 'So you want me to pull out her finger nails with pliers, is that it Brigadier?' he said softly.

'We don't have time for this. We have to nip this in the bud, clear up the mess before it gets any worse. If we manage that we can deny everything. Clara has told you what the naval trucks will be carrying. If word of this gets out there will be panic and serious consequences.'

Jamie laughed scornfully. 'Serious consequences for whom Brigadier? As far as I can see the only people likely to suffer serious consequences are you and the Prime Minister when the people up here realise they've been sitting on a fucking time bomb for years.'

'Don't be insolent Raeburn and watch your language,' the old man retorted.

'You want me to torture the information out of her; why don't you just say it instead of all this "whatever means necessary" crap? Or don't you like the idea any more than me? You fought against people who used those methods and now you're telling me to use them. That's hypocrisy, Brigadier.'

'It is *not* hypocrisy. There is no alternative. We need that information and we need it now. I don't have time to enter into a philosophical argument on the rights and wrongs of it; just do it. When you have the information call either myself or Clara immediately and we will take care of the rest.'

'And afterwards? What do I do with Duggan?'

'What you're paid to do. Kill her.'

'And Corkscrew?'

'He's your responsibility. Get him out. I take it you have something planned for that. If you need help with it, ask.'

'No, I don't need help. Corkscrew and I have it all arranged. Just keep the SAS or other Archangels away from his ASU. Those three men are mine. I've got a score to settle with one of them.'

'Don't turn this into a personal vendetta Raeburn. It is too important to get bogged down in some private little war.'

Jamie laughed dismissively. 'Don't worry Brigadier, my private little war is part of your public big one. I won't get bogged down.'

'Very well. I'll hand you back to Clara,' the old man said. 'Just one thing though Raeburn... You are still an Archangel until I say otherwise. Don't forget that.' He handed the phone to Clara before Jamie could respond.

Clara said nothing. She was there at the end of the line. He could hear her breathing. 'Well, that's me told,' he said, addressing her bitterly.

'I'm sorry.'

'Are you? Really? About him ordering me to torture Orlagh Duggan or the fact that I'm still an Archangel?'

'Both,' she replied quietly. He believed her.

'So what now? When I get the information to you... if I get it, that is, is that when my 12 hours starts?'

'The 12 hours is my estimate of when the SAS will go in to clean up the arms cache. If you locate the other ASUs you'll have another 12 hours at least, probably longer. They will need to recce the houses and plan their attack. They'll go in at night when people are in bed. They won't want witnesses. The terrorists have to disappear.'

'Aye, so I gather. Alright, I'll go now and mug up my manual on tearing out finger nails and the effective use of burning cigarette ends.'

'Don't, Jamie, please. Charles doesn't want this any more than you but there really is no other way. If there were he would tell you to use it.'

'Aye, but he's not the one doing it,' he replied harshly, then relented. It wasn't her fault. 'Okay, okay, I'm sorry, It's just... it's a slippery slope and when I step on it there might be no going back. What happens to an Archangel who goes AWOL?' he asked, laughing to make it sound like a joke. But it was no joke. He'd thought about it before and would have done it if the Brigadier hadn't agreed to his "early retirement". That didn't last long, he mused bitterly.

'I'll pretend I didn't hear that Jamie. Don't worry, I'll talk to him, but you have to do what he wants now... Not just for him. If this goes wrong and the Militia blow up this nuclear waste lots of people will suffer. You don't want that.'

Well, she had that right, he mused. He didn't want to talk about it anymore. He had had enough. 'I'll call you,' he said, ending the call before she had a chance to respond.

He settled back on his bed, staring at the ceiling. What was happening to him? Worse, what the fuck was he becoming? Could he live with himself afterwards? This mess wasn't his problem, he was just a cog in the bloody wheel, and yet here he was was being dragged in, like a swimmer caught in a whirlpool. This had to be the end. Suddenly he needed a drink... and then a chat with Frank Daly.

Chapter Sixty-nine

He decided to forego the drink. If talking to Frank didn't help, that would be plan B. The Mustang was where he had left it the day before. Ice was forming on the windows and frost gathering on the bodywork. Earlier in the day the sun had melted the ice and frost of the night before but it was an endless cycle. The cold nights produced the hoar frost and the warmer days melted it. He almost wished it would rain.

The drive to St. Gregory's didn't take long even in the heavier rush-hour traffic. He could drive the route with his eyes closed - straight up Queen Margret Drive to Maryhill Road, across into to Bilsland Drive, past Ruchill Hospital to Balmore Road, take a right at the traffic lights there and then follow his nose into Saracen Street. St Gregory's was at the end. It would take him no more than ten minutes. Not long enough to compose himself, and he really needed to. Explaining his predicament would be difficult enough without approaching it haphazardly. But then again, that wasn't new he reflected with a grim smile. Every time he visited Frank for "confession" it was the same. No matter how long he had to prepare, he was never composed.

It was just after five o'clock. Bad timing, he mused. Frank would be sitting down to dinner soon and an invite to eat with him was something he couldn't refuse, but he had no appetite. Not now. There was always the chance that the priest would be out visiting a parishioner but he hoped not. He really did need to unburden himself. It was strange, he thought. Usually, he apologised for laying his worries on his mentor but that was far from his mind this time. On earlier occasions he had already made up his mind to do something and his talks with the priest were only to salve his conscience. He had taken advantage of the older man on those occasions, he thought regretfully. But not this time. This time was different. This time he had doubts; he hadn't made up his mind and he didn't know if he could go through with it.

He parked the big car on the gravel in front of the Chapel House, the headlights sweeping across the building and illuminating it. The exhaust roared and he caught sight of a twitching curtain at the ground floor kitchen window. By the time he had hauled himself out of the car Mrs Murphy was at the door waiting for him, her expression, initially curious, changed instantly as she recognised his bulk coming towards her.

'Och, it's you,' she said, smiling. 'I should have known; you're the only one who would come up here in a behemoth like that,' she said, laughing then. 'Don't you be taking Father Francis out in that,' she giggled, 'or he'll be wanting one for himself.'

Jamie joined her laughter. *Behemoth*, he thought laughing, only Mrs Murphy could come away with that word, and *Father Francis...* that must be his

Sunday name. 'Aye, it's a bit more powerful than his old Morris,' Jamie replied, grinning. 'He could visit all his parishioners in jig time in it.'

'Come away in,' the older woman said. 'I think he's having a wee nap before dinner but he'll be pleased to see you. You brighten up his days, I think.'

That was surprising. If anything, Jamie thought his visits would depress the old boy. He always came with a problem or two. When he thought about it, priests were always hearing people's problems and absolving with their sins and his were a bit out of the ordinary. That was putting it mildly, he thought, smiling inwardly, but maybe that was how he brightened up Frank's day. He hoped that was the case.

He followed Mrs Murphy along the corridor to the sitting room. She knocked gently on the door and pushed it open. Frank Daly was snoozing in his usual chair beside the fire, with only a small table lamp illuminating the room. It was warm, warm enough to put anyone to sleep, Jamie thought. Frank stirred and opened his eyes, rubbing them gently and focussing on his visitor. It took him a moment and then his face lit up with a smile.

'I'll leave you to it,' Mrs Murphy said quietly as she ushered Jamie in and pulled the door closed behind her. Both men listened to her footsteps fading down the hall before speaking.

'Well, well, you're back again, and so soon,' Frank Daly said, laughing. 'This is becoming a habit, Jamie. You'll be turning up for Mass soon,' he joked.

'Don't hold your breath, Frank,' Jamie retorted, joining the laughter. 'I don't even go to my own church so there's little chance of me coming to yours.' It was said in a way that didn't give offence and Frank Daly simply smiled and nodded.

'But you believe, lad, that's what's important, and deep down inside, you're a good man.'

'I don't know about that,' Jamie said quietly, serious again. 'I'm not sure I do believe and your definition of good must be a bit different from mine.'

The Priest laughed again. 'Aye maybe, but it's mine that counts. So what brings you to me this time Jamie Raeburn?' he went on, pointing Jamie to the chair facing him.

Jamie settled into the chair. It squeaked under his weight and the air was expelled from the cushion like a sigh. He took his time, looking at Father Daly a while before starting. 'I'm in a bit of a quandary, Frank,' he said at last. 'I have to decide whether to do something... something most people think is abhorrent.'

The Priest smiled drolly at the irony of that statement. He doubted Jamie had picked up on it. 'Something abhorrent,' he repeated. 'Then it must be serious,' he laughed. 'Then again, most people think killing is abhorrent. What can it be that's worse than that?'

Jamie gave him a melancholy smile. He didn't bother explaining his moral justification for killing. They had rehearsed it often, he and Frank. The Priest knew his mind and accepted it... and still thought he was "good". He wondered if tonight would change his mind. 'I've been ordered to torture someone,' he said, his voice no louder than a whisper.

'Ah, I see,' the Priest responded, though in honesty he didn't see. 'And who is it you are to torture and, equally importantly, why?' he asked. He watched as Jamie wrung his hands nervously. That was unlike him, Frank Daly thought, his eyes never leaving Jamie's face.

'The why is probably more important than the who, Frank,' Jamie continued. 'Where I go there is usually a death...'

'Aye, that's usually the case, from what you've told me,' the Priest interrupted. 'What makes this time different?'

'You already know part of it, we spoke about it, remember? The planned IRA attack and the informer I have to bring out safely?'

'Yes, I remember. He's the man you said saved your life,' Frank Daly replied, a little sceptically, Jamie thought.

Jamie nodded. 'That's the one,' he said. 'It was all straightforward... or as straightforward as these things can be,' he continued, smiling ruefully. The Priest said nothing. Jamie hesitated. He was getting into dangerous waters, he realised, but he trusted the man facing him. 'The attack is due to take place in a couple of weeks, less in fact, on 25 January,' he carried on at last. 'There are three IRA units involved. That's twelve men, and there is a woman is in command. One of those units, the one with the informer in it, is in a safe house in Alexandria.'

'Not very safe if you know about it, is it?' Frank Daly mused aloud. Jamie simply smiled.

'We know now where the attack is going to take place. It's going to involve them hijacking a lorry, maybe two, and blowing them up.'

The old Priest broke in again. 'It seems you know a lot about it,' he said. 'Your informer has been working hard. The question is, knowing all that, why haven't you done what you came to do?'

Jamie smiled gloomily. It was the obvious question for someone who couldn't see the whole picture. 'There's a problem with that Frank. Trouble is, we don't know all we need to know. We only know where that one active service unit is; the whereabouts of the other two are still a mystery. We need to get them all. We do know where their weapons cache is and we could take them out there but it would be messy and it would be impossible to keep a lid on it.'

'Why would you want to keep a lid on it?'

Jamie smiled again. 'Politically, the whole thing has to be deniable. The terrorist have to disappear. All of them,' he added. 'The powers that be don't want the public to know anything about it. They think it will cause panic, and they're probably right.'

'Panic?' the Priest queried, clearly missing the point. 'Why should it cause panic if you've thwarted it?'

Jamie sighed and wrung his hands again. 'The attack is supposed to take place no more than five miles from Faslane Naval Base and, as the crow flies, probably only about twenty from the American base at Holy Loch. Some people in the area are already nervous about those two.'

The Priest digested that information then shook his head. 'I still don't understand. If you stop this attack surely the people will have their confidence restored... and it will deter others from trying it.'

Jamie gave him a cold little laugh. 'In normal circumstances that might be right, but these aren't normal circumstances.'

'Explain.'

'You know what's at Faslane, don't you?'

'Yes, of course, submarines carrying those appalling Polaris missiles.' As he said it an inkling of the truth began to dawn on him. 'You think it's to do with those?' he asked, alarmed now.

'It is to do with the submarines, not the missiles Frank. Do you know anything about nuclear powered subs?'

The old Priest shook his head. 'Physics was never one of my strong points,' he said.

'Nor mine,' Jamie conceded, 'but they are powered by a nuclear reactor. Unlike a diesel engine, it doesn't spew its waste out an exhaust. It collects it and every so often the nuclear waste produced by the reactor has to be removed and reprocessed.'

'For someone who isn't into physics you seem to know a lot.'

'Only what I've been told, Frank. Anyway, the waste is taken from the base to Glasgow and is then moved by rail to England where it is reprocessed. It's the waste trucks the terrorists are after. They want to blow up the waste and spread it as far as possible.'

The Priest was looking at him, wide eyed. 'How dangerous is it?'

Jamie smiled grimly. 'Dangerous enough from what I've been told. The experts aren't sure of the fallout,' he went on, oblivious to the pun. 'From what we know, the IRA are bringing a lorry load of explosives to do the job. They've also got RPG7s available...'

'Rocket propelled grenades,' Frank said, thinking aloud. His face was grey.

'Aye, they've got enough of those to start a small war. They need to be stopped Frank. That's why I'm here though I won't be alone.'

'And the person you've been told to torture knows where these men are?' Frank asked, putting two and two together and coming up with the right answer.

'I don't know that for sure, Frank, but I'm almost certain.'

Frank Daly shook his head forlornly. 'That's all you have?' he asked. Jamie nodded, his head down. 'It's a big step to take based on what you think, isn't it?' Frank continued quietly. 'Is that why you have doubts?'

'No, not really. I just don't like the idea of doing it. The person I'm talking about has to know the details; they're co-ordinating the whole thing so they must know.'

'You think,' the Priest said.

'Yeah, okay, you're right; I think... and that's not enough, but tell me Frank, is torture always wrong?'

The old Priest raised his eyebrows. 'Morally? Yes, definitely,' he said. 'But I can see situations the morality might take second place.'

Jamie looked at him searchingly, his eyes narrowing.

The Priest gave a small chuckle and went on. 'Sometimes the greater good trumps the moral argument,' he said. 'If there is a planned atrocity where a great many people might be killed, for example, innocent people, and it could be stopped by getting information from one of the perpetrators, then that might justify torturing that man. Balance the safety of the majority against the pain and suffering of that one man... The majority wouldn't see it as abhorrent then, I imagine. But, another but, I'm afraid, and it's an important one,' he continued with a bitter laugh. 'The justification for it is only in stopping the atrocity. The person brutalised has to have the information and the torturers have to be sure of that. If the person doesn't have the information and the people carrying out the torture suspect that might be the case or aren't convinced, then it is simply gratuitous violence. What I'm saying, Jamie, is that you need to be sure of your source. "I think" doesn't get you there, you have to be certain.' The Priest paused, his eyes searching Jamie's face. 'Is that what you wanted to hear?' he asked gently.

Jamie forced a smile. 'I don't know what I wanted to hear, Frank. Truth is, I'm scared.'

'Afraid of dying this time?'

Jamie laughed wryly. 'No, dying doesn't bother me; it comes to us all eventually.

'What else is there to be afraid of?' the Priest asked, leaning forward in his chair, closing in on him.

Jamie shook his head sadly before continuing. He looked steadily at Frank Daly, then said: 'For the last few years I've been justifying what I do by telling myself I'm doing the right thing. I kill evil people; it's me and the other Archangels against the Forces of Darkness,' he said, punctuating that bit with a hollow, self-deprecating laugh. 'What I'm afraid of is that I'm becoming one of them. Worse, maybe.'

'You're not evil, Jamie. Evil people have no conscience. The very fact that you're sitting here with me now proves that you do.'

'You always see the good in me, Frank.'

'That's because there is good in you.' The Priest sat back in his chair again. 'So what are you going to do?'

Jamie laughed coldly. 'I'm going to balance the greater good against the individual involved. If I'm sure they know what I need to know then I'll do what I have to do, I suppose, and try to live with it afterwards. Until I'm sure I'll do nothing.'

'Then you've just proved my point. You're not evil.'

'But you'll pray for me anyway?'

The Priest smiled. 'I always do, lad,' he said. 'Every day.'

Chapter Seventy

Jamie returned to the hotel in a better mood than when he left. That made two times today he had felt like that. This time, however, he hoped it would last a little longer. As far as he could see, every light was on in the Grosvenor, turning its façade into a beacon of sanctuary in the cold dark night. He had spent the time during the return journey reflecting on Frank Daly's words. Those were his beacon of sanctuary.

Orlagh Duggan was the key. There was no "if" about that. He had been naïve to think he could sweet-talk any worthwhile intelligence from her and now the plain truth was staring him in the face. The only way to get it was to force it from her. But still he baulked at the idea. Think of the greater good. That had to become his mantra, for now at least.

The heat in the hotel foyer hit him as he pushed through the revolving door. The uniformed commissionaire was inside tonight rather than in his usual spot on the step outside, a sure sign that the temperature was dropping. Unlike here, he mused. It was like standing in front of a blast furnace.

He checked at reception. There had been no calls so Conor hadn't got back to him. His advice was to stay available after six o'clock and it was now nearing seven. He hadn't eaten. Frank Daly had invited him to stay, as he knew he would, but he had politely declined. He didn't want to upset the formidable Mrs. Murphy. He still didn't feel hungry. It wasn't so much that; he just had no appetite. He had too much on his mind.

As he entered his room he locked the door and pulled the security chain across, securing it to the door jamb. He didn't normally bother, but then, he didn't normally sit in his room stripping and reassembling a Walther PPK, did he, he mused.

The gun was still in its protective wrapper inside the cistern. The tell-tale he had left in place, the tiny sliver of matchstick wood jammed between the cistern lid and the body, was still in place too, confirming that no one had been poking about. He hadn't expected that anyway. He was in an hotel. No one here knew him or what he did. He was just another guest... but over the last few years he had developed a sense of paranoia. That, he realised, came with the job. Everyone in this business, on all sides, was guilty of it, if guilty was the right word. It was a defence mechanism. It made you act as if someone was always out to get you which, in the field, was probably true.

He sat on the bed and unwrapped the weapon. It gleamed dully in the light from the bedside lamps. It was, he mused, a thing of beauty, sexy even, perfectly engineered to do a job that no one in their right mind could describe as beautiful. It was an instrument of death. Why, he wondered, did man produce such beautiful things - this Walther, pearl handled revolvers, ornate swords and jewelled daggers – all with the same purpose? No doubt a psychologist or psychiatrist could come up with an answer but it was too deep for him.

He let his fingers work expertly on it, taking it apart, almost lovingly, the way he and Kate would undress each other before making love, though stripping was part of the process too. He caressed the individual parts of it the way he caressed his wife's body. He loved his wife and it struck him, in a strange way, that he loved this Walther almost as much. Not in the same way, obviously, nothing could compare to his love for Kate, but he had a bond with the gun. If he looked after it, and cared for it, it would look after him.

He rebuilt it then, working the parts carefully to ensure their efficiency; the magazine catch in the grip frame behind the trigger, the safety catch on the slide and the pressures of the double action trigger. He smiled appreciatively. Old Carl Walther had designed one hell of a gun. He checked the magazines. Four of them, each loaded with 9mm short rounds, 28 rounds in total. More than enough to take out Doherty and the other two men, even without help. He would keep it close now. He would need it soon. He stood up and slipped the pistol beneath the waist line of his slacks at the small of his back just as the telephone rang.

He reached for it quickly, anticipating Conor on the other end of the line. He smiled as the American's voice came to him, the deep baritone he knew so well.

'Hey kid, sorry it took so long,' his friend started.

'Don't worry about it. I've had an eventful afternoon anyway.'

'Oh yeah?' the American replied.

It was a "tell me more" response but it could wait, Jamie decided. 'I'll tell you later. What have you discovered about the sodium chlorate?'

'Quite a lot. It's amazing what you can do with weed killer. You can mix it with a lot of other shit. It makes a low power explosive in most cases but if you pack enough of it into a large container and mix it in the right proportions with red phosphorus, 50/50 in that case it makes an impressive impact explosive. There's other ways. You can mix it with plain, good old fashioned sugar or aluminium powder. It burns hot. If it's the mix with red phosphorus it has to be hit to be detonated...'

'An RPG warhead would do the trick?'

'Yeah, and some. If it's packed into a large container and hit with an shell it'll be like the 4th of July.'

'Where do you get the stuff?'

'It's surprisingly easy kid. The sodium chlorate is in most proprietary weed killers. Red phosphorus is used to make matches. If they've got access to the pure stuff it'll improve the performance. If it's packed into a lorry container God knows what it'll do. How many tons is that? Christ, it'll probably flatten everything for miles around.'

'So we need to find it. It won't be easy tracing its supply chain... they probably used legitimate purchasing channels. The only way is through Duggan,' Jamie said, quieter now. 'That brings me to something else I need help with Conor... and this time I need you with me.'

'When?' the American demanded, a hint of excitement in his voice now.

Jamie hoped he didn't get too excited. 'As soon as possible,' he said. 'And bring the Browning.'

'It's that sort of help, is it?' Conor said, a little less enthusiastic now. He didn't expect an answer.

'When can you get here?'

'Tonight, if you need me as quickly as that. I can leave in half an hour, be there about eight-thirty, maybe nine, depending on the roads.'

'Wait until the morning. It's probably safer. I'll book you a room here.' He hesitated a moment before posing another question. 'That little cottage you mentioned, Mary's folks' place, is it still available?'

'Yeah, no problem kid. I'll bring the keys, but if you're thinking of staying a while we'll need fuel and food. It'll be cold... worse than a New York winter.'

'Don't worry about that. We won't be staying long. You did say it's isolated?' he queried.

'Sure is. Nearest cottage is about a quarter mile away.'

'And it's off the road?'

'Yes,' Conor replied, a little hesitantly this time. 'What you thinking of using it for?'

Jamie gave him an icy laugh. 'We'll be entertaining a guest,' was all he said.

Conor realised that was all he was going to get and left it at that. All the same, he had a bad feeling about it but his trust in Jamie overcame it. 'Okay,' he replied breezily. 'I'll see you at your hotel tomorrow morning about eleven.'

'Good... and thanks, Conor.'

'Nada kid. Ciao.'

Once again Jamie was listening to the purr of dial tone. He thought of phoning Kate but if he did she would worry. Two calls in quick succession would set alarm bells ringing. He checked the time. It was just after seven o'clock. The restaurant would still be open but he still had no appetite. He took the Walther from the waist band of his slacks and slipped it beneath his pillow. It formed a comforting lump. Five minutes later, still fully clothed, he was lost in a fitful sleep.

Chapter Seventy-one

Tuesday 15 January 1974

The morning found him still on top of the bed, his clothes wrinkled and creased. He rubbed a hand over his face, conscious of needing a shave. His mouth was dry. The curtains were open, just as he had left them, and it was still dark outside. He rubbed his eyes and checked his watch. It was just after six thirty and the hotel was still asleep. Soon, the kitchen staff would begin preparing breakfast and guests would stir.

He felt tired. No matter he had slept for ten hours, it hadn't been a restful sleep. He had dreamt bizarre dreams, the faces of Orlagh Duggan, Kate, Roisin and Clara Whitelaw filling most of them. Torture had been the underlying theme, the victim interchangeable.

He slipped his hand under the pillow and retrieved the Walther. He held it loosely in his hand, for reassurance as much as anything else, then laid it carefully on the bedside unit. He rose, slid out of bed and made for the shower, undressing as he went, his clothes leaving a trail behind him. The shower was over the bath, the taps fulfilling the double functions of filling the bath or forcing the water through the shower head thanks to a simple plunger. He ran the water into the bath, adjusted the temperature and pulled the plunger upwards. Instantly, a jet of cold water was emitted from the shower head before turning hot. He stepped in.

The shower revived him. He stood beneath the jet for many minutes, letting the water beat on his head and course down over his skin. He washed at a leisurely rate and, when finished, turned the dial of the shower to cold. The shock of the cold water made his shiver momentarily but it did him good.

He stepped from the bath and dried himself roughly with a large towel. His skin tingled. Naked, he walk from the bathroom and selected clothes from the wardrobe; clean underwear, a brown checked, long sleeved Ben Sherman button-down shirt, a pair of Wrangler jeans and black socks. His brown leather brogues lay beside the bed where he had discarded them. He dressed quickly, slid the gun into his waist band and selected his single breasted brown leather jacket from the wardrobe. It was long enough the hide the Walther.

The appetite he had lost the day before was now back with a vengeance. As he stepped from his room he could smell the appetising aromas of frying bacon, sausages and all the trimmings. He was early. The benefit of that was that he could eat alone without distraction, principally the distraction of Orlagh Duggan. He didn't want to see her now. Later tonight, or even tomorrow, would be soon enough.

He ate like he might not eat again. Cereal and orange juice was followed by eggs, bacon, square sausage, black pudding and everything else that was available in the buffet. Two cups of strong black coffee and two slices of well browned, almost burned toast, finished the job.

He left the hotel just after eight o'clock having booked a room for Conor. He left the Mustang. Hiring a van was on his list of things to do and with all his skills, driving two vehicles at once wasn't one of them. He caught a taxi in Byres Road, directing the driver to the East End of the city or, at least the east end of the city centre. He was heading for the Barras. The open air market and the stalls in the covered areas would be closed but he wasn't interested in those. His destination was Bill's Tool Store in Bain Street. It was open even when the market wasn't and it would supply him with everything he needed; oxygen and acetylene gas cylinders, tubing, a heating torch – a big one about two feet long - a mask and gauntlets. He could have used an Oxford Pot Welder for the task but he wanted to scare Orlagh. Oxy-acetylene would do a much better job of that, he reckoned. He would pay for the goods and pick them up later when he had acquired the van.

He had thought a lot about what he had to do and how he should do it. The thought of inflicting pain on Orlagh Duggan... not just pain, he reminded himself, but *excruciating* pain, turned his stomach. He smiled wryly as he reconciled that thought with his normal jobs for Ultra. Absurd irony.

The taxi dropped him in London Road. It was just before nine o'clock but the shop would be open. It was cold but milder than the day before. The sort of weather that brings Glaswegian men out in T-shirts. He knew this place well but it had been a long time since he had walked this street. He smiled as he remembered his father bringing him here the weekend before he had started his apprenticeship in John Brown's... the best tool and work clothes supplier in Glasgow his father said, and in Jamie's opinion, he was right.

The shop was open and already workmen were at the counters. He knew exactly what he was looking for and found them quickly. In the great scheme of things they weren't expensive. The lance was nearer three feet in length which suited him fine and he chose an expensive visor. He also threw in a pair of dungarees. The last thing he wanted was singe marks on his clothes. He paid and left the equipment behind the counter, promising to return later in the day to uplift it. No problem.

His next task was to find a suitable vehicle. Something utilitarian, ordinary, anonymous and cheap was what he was looking for. That ruled out the usual hire companies who liked to plaster their corporate info all over the sides and backs of their vehicles. The hirer was a mobile advertising board and anonymous these vehicles were not. This might be a problem, he thought disconsolately. He was still scratching his head trying to find a solution when a fly-posted announcement stuck to a lamppost caught his eye: *Massive De-Stockage - Commercial Vehicles: Vans, Lorries, Lifting Equipment. City Auctions – Tuesday 15 January at 10.00. Viewing Monday 14th 10.00 – 16.00 and Tuesday 15th from 09.00.*

It was worth a visit, he decided, especially as the auction site was no more than a short walk away. He set off briskly along Gallowgate, heading east, and after 100 yards turned left into Barrack Street. The auction site was another couple of hundred yards on his left behind a high stone wall that was crumbling dangerously in places. A crowd was already in evidence, filing into the area through a narrow gate. He mingled freely with them and surveyed what was on offer. The site had been split into areas containing different vehicles; small vans, large vans, lorries, heavy trucks, digging equipment and vehicles with hoists for working at heights. He made for the vans. Dealers were already there, picking over the carcasses like vultures. He lurked close to two older men who seemed to know what they were talking about as they checked out what was beneath the bonnets of a few vans. There was a proliferation of ex Post Office Telephone vans and Royal Mail vans as well as a number from the old Corporation. Commer vans, Morris vans and a few battered Fords. The Post Office vans were all painted in dull khaki, or mid-bronze green to give it its posh name, of the old Post Office. For safety reasons, the colour had changed in recent years to bright yellow. He wouldn't need one of those. These old vans had the Post Office logos covered over with white paint. Easy enough to remove, he thought. They were all supposed to be "runners", able to be driven away that day if paid for in cash, which was perfect. Quickly, with the aid of his two unsuspecting "experts", he picked three that suited him. Three Commer vans, utility work vehicles that, in the main, would have been well looked after in the Post Office garages and workshops. His two "advisors" seemed to think so too. He would get one of them, no matter how much he had to fork out.

He made his way to the auction office and registered. A bored looking girl in a tight white jumper and an even tighter skirt issued him with a card. His number was 1313. His lucky number twice, he mused with a smile. The auction was starting soon and the vans were first up. With luck, he would be out of here in an hour and a half with one of the vans... provided it started, he thought with a grin.

One hour and forty three minutes later, his bid of £150 won the second of the Commer vans. The two dealers he had followed around were keen on his first choice. He decided to let them win it. Only fair, he thought. And his good deed was repaid immediately; either that or his lucky numbers were in play. Whatever, the van he was after was running smoothly when the auctioneer's assistant drove it through to the bidding arena and it was still running smoothly when he drove it out into Barrack Street ten minutes later. It was £150 well spent and the Brigadier would never miss it.

He returned to Bain Street and found a space in front of the tool store. It didn't take long to load the gear. One thing about this whole mess, he knew how to use the equipment. It was just that he had never used it for anything like this before.

He was still thinking along those lines when he parked the van in Great George Street, a few hundred yards down Byres Road from the Grosvenor. Far enough... he hoped. He locked the van and walked down Great George Street without turning round. It would be there when he came for it again, he was sure of that. The sky was clouding over, promising rain. It was warmer, about 5 degrees, he thought. He was thinking the temperature in degrees

Celsius after his sojourn in France. It would be about forty Fahrenheit to the locals... positively tropical. The good thing about the rain and the rise in temperature was that the roads would be clear of ice tonight. Those lucky numbers were coming in handy.

Conor Whelan was in the lounge bar. He was sipping a coffee and making conversation with one of the barmaids, effusing Bostonian charm. He waved Jamie over, introducing him to the girl as "my big Scots buddie" but giving no name. He was shrewd enough to hold back on that. For a start, he didn't know what name Jamie had registered under. The American ordered him a coffee, an Americano he called it, black with a touch of milk added. Jamie added two sugars and they found a quiet table, allowing the girl to return to her work.

'Nice room you got me,' Conor said as they settled down. 'Near yours?'

Jamie gave him a smile. 'Same floor, three doors along,' he replied.

'And the lady?'

Jamie's smile disappeared, replaced with a grimace that said Orlagh Duggan was no lady. 'Third floor, room 314. She's booked in as Olivia Dunlop.'

'Yeah? You work fast kid. How'd you get all that?'

'You're the spy, Conor, how do you think? I hung about reception while she was there picking up her key. The receptionist called her Miss Dunlop and the sleazy guy with her called her Olivia. I can add.'

Conor laughed and sipped his Americano. 'So what's the plan and how do I help?' he asked after casting a wary eye around their surroundings. There was no one within hearing distance.

'You've brought the keys of the cottage?'

'Sure,' the American replied, patting his pocket. The jingle of metal confirmed it.

'I should have asked before but does it have an electricity supply?'

'Yeah, they managed to get rid of the oil lamps years ago. There's a generator out back in case the grid supply is cut off. Sometimes in winter that happens when the lines come down.'

'Good,' Jamie responded. Conor was looking at him expectantly, expecting more. An explanation even. 'What?' Jamie asked.

'You mentioned a guest. You taking the Irishman there?' Jamie's smile when he replied was scary, Conor thought.

'No, not the one you know about, another one... one of the other three; the one who was with Liam Fitzpatrick at Kiltyclogher.' Conor's eyes narrowed. 'He'll have company,' Jamie continued. 'I'm bringing the lady you spoke of earlier.'

Conor paled visibly. 'What exactly are you planning kid?' he asked. He didn't know if he would like the answer.

Jamie looked around the lounge bar. It was beginning to fill with lunch time guests. He finished his coffee and placed the cup back on the table. 'Let's go somewhere else for a real drink and I'll tell you,' he said, smiling coldly.

Conor left his coffee unfinished and followed Jamie out into reception. He saw an attractive female descending the stairs, red hair and well stacked he noticed, with legs all the way up. She was one classy broad, he thought. Strangely, Jamie ignored her and pushed out through the revolving door into Grosvenor Lane, Conor following, turning back for another look at the red headed beauty who was smiling at him... or was she, he wondered. Her eyes seemed to be more on the kid than on him.

'Who was the dame with the red hair?' he asked as he hurried after Jamie to Byres Road.

'Olivia Dunlop, aka Orlagh Duggan.'

'She's quite a looker,' Conor remarked. Then said: 'Got the impression she likes the look of you.'

'You think?'

'Hey kid, you know me, when it comes to women I've got built in sensors, a bit like your 6th sense. You ask, you'll get, kid.'

Jamie's smile was still there. 'Then I guess I'll ask,' he said, laughing quietly.

Chapter Seventy-two

They went to the Curlers Rest, a two storey white painted, old fashioned, pub that had been there for as long as Jamie could remember. It was a fixture in Byres Road, sitting just beyond the junction with Great George Street and next to Hillhead Underground Station. The place was crowded but they were just two more men in for a lunchtime drink. The conversations around them were the usual for a Glasgow pub; women, football, drink and the weather and not necessarily in that order. No one listened to anyone else's' conversation, they had heard it all before.

Jamie ordered two pints of McEwan's 80/- and they found a spot near the door shunned by most because of the draught each time a customer entered or left. That suited Jamie.

Conor listened with growing unease as Jamie filled him in on what was now known. The prospect of nuclear material being released into the atmosphere over Faslane filled him with a cold dread. He thought of his family and of other American families in Dunoon. Friends too. The spread of the contaminants could easily reach there and the consequences were unthinkable. By the time Jamie had finished on the background, he was almost at his wit's end.

'So what are we going to do?' he asked.

'We're going to stop it,' Jamie retorted blandly. 'The only thing we need is the locations of the safe houses and where the explosives are coming from. When we've got that information we'll wrap it all up.'

'We?' Conor probed. 'I hope others are involved.'

Jamie laughed. 'Don't fret, it's all in hand. The SAS are in Faslane already. They will take out the arms cache soon and the convoy with the waste won't leave the base unless this whole thing is wrapped up.'

'So back to my question; what are we going to do?'

Jamie sipped his beer. 'We're going to get that information,' he said.

'How?'

'From Orlagh Duggan. She's the lynchpin. She knows where the ASUs are hiding out and she has to be the one liaising with whoever is bringing in the explosives. We get it from her.'

'Yeah, just like that?' Conor remarked dubiously.

Jamie was smiling icily again. 'Yeah, just like that,' he said, mimicking his friend. 'We'll ask her nicely and she'll tell us. I might have to give her an incentive, but she *will* tell us.'

'And then?'

'Well, then you leave me and I do what I have to do,' Jamie replied, sighing softly.

'And this Irishman you spoke of; where does he come into things?'

'He's the incentive,' Jamie said, finishing his beer. 'Come on, finish your beer and I'll show you what I've got planned,' he continued, placing his empty tumbler on a small ledge beside the door and waiting. Conor was a little slower but then, he wasn't born and bred in Glasgow where downing pints of beer was an art form. If there was a world championship for drinking beer in the quickest time, Jamie mused, it would probably be held by a Glaswegian... in perpetuity.

They left the pub and walked to Great George Street. The van was parked up the hill and Jamie walked right to it, ignoring the driver's door and opening the back doors. Conor looked inside. The interior was dark, gloomy even, but he had no difficulty identifying the equipment. The meagre light glinted on the lance and the two gas cylinders and the lance. The gauntlets and visor lay beside the cylinders and the dungarees were neatly folded on the floor of the van.

'Thinking of doing a bit of welding?' the American asked, unsure what all this was for.

Jamie grinned. 'A bit of burning is a more accurate description of what I have in mind,' he said.

'Shit!' was all Conor could say in response. He could add two and two as well.

'How long will it take to drive to the cottage?' Jamie asked, not allowing him to dwell on it.

'It's just outside Lochgoilhead... take us about an hour and a half, I reckon.'

'Right, let's go get lunch and then we'll head over there. Did you borrow Mary's old man's car?'

Conor nodded. 'Yeah, I've got an aversion to your ferries, trains and buses. They're cold and dirty most of the time.'

Jamie smiled knowingly. He couldn't argue with that. 'Okay, you take it and I'll take the van. When we get there we'll unload my gear and then I'll follow you to Dunoon. You can return the old boy's car and we will head back here.'

'To the hotel?'

'Aye. We'll have dinner and then we'll set off again.'

'Where this time?'

Jamie hesitated. Too much information might freak Conor out but keeping him in the dark was no good either. 'We're heading back to the cottage but this time we're stopping off in Alexandria. That's when you'll need the Browning,' he said casually. Conor said nothing. 'We'll take out Fitzpatrick's ASU. I want one of them alive. The smallest of the group, looks a bit like a skinned rat. He's the one we're taking to the cottage.' Conor nodded slowly. He still had nothing to say though, Jamie noted.

'Aren't you wondering what's going to happen to the others,' he asked. Conor simply shrugged. 'Seeing a different side of me?' Jamie asked.

'No, not really, just a different view of the same side I think. I keep thinking I got you into this, kid. I'm sorry.'

'We've been down this road before Conor... I got myself into this, you had nothing to do with it. I am what I am.'

'Yeah, but...'

Jamie held up a hand stopping him. 'No buts Conor. Just accept it. You've helped me out plenty since and you're helping now. Come on, let's go eat,' he said, finishing the discussion.

Chapter Seventy-three

They left the Grosvenor shortly after two o'clock that afternoon. Lunch had been eaten in silence, both of them engrossed in thoughts of their own. There had been no sign of Orlagh. Jamie agonised over that. Maybe she had rendezvoused with her troops, he reasoned, and if that were the case he would have been able to avoid what was still to come. On the other hand, she could have eaten early or ordered room service... or maybe she was *being* serviced, he mused crudely. There were enough men here who would oblige. He shrugged these thoughts away. It was too late now to worry about it.

Jamie left a few minutes ahead of Conor, telling the American they would meet in the car park of Esquire House at Anniesland Cross. 'It's at the corner of Fifth Avenue,' he said, teasing a smile from the big American.

'If only,' he murmured.

The van started on the first turn and Jamie pulled away, down to the junction with Byres Road, and turned right. The fuel gauge was telling him he was running on fumes but the engine was running well. Like all diesels, it chattered away, a bit like an old Singer sewing machine. None the less, his first priority was to find a filling station. From memory, there was one near The Pond Hotel and another at Anniesland. With luck, he would make it and 1313 was still in play.

The clear blue sky of previous the previous days was gone, replaced by the slate grey that was more common at this time of year. Just above the roofs of the buildings it was a pale colour, darkening as it rose into the firmament until it was almost black. It was already raining. Tiny spots, like mist, formed on the windscreen. He waited until his vision was almost totally obscured before turning on the wipers, breathing a sigh of relief as they swung across the glass leaving circular streaks but at least he could see.

There was a filling station at the Pond and he swung off the road. He had seen nothing of Conor. He filled the tank. Fifteen gallons of diesel it took, the smell of it catching in his throat and clinging to his hands and clothes. He paid £5.25, bloody robbery he mused.

When he pulled into the car park at Esquire House Conor was waiting, a cigarette dangling from his lips. He gave Jamie a wave and started the engine of the Austin 1100 and pulled away. He took the lead, Jamie swinging in behind him onto Great Western Road.

Conor's estimate of the time it would take turned out to be accurate and they arrived at Lochgoilhead an hour and twenty minutes after leaving the filling station. The cottage was on the outskirts of the village and set in its own grounds, well off the road, a major bonus as far as Jamie was concerned. It was just as Conor had described it. The garden ground, if it could be called garden ground, extended to about half an acre, and was screened by a dense line of mountain ash trees along the perimeter. Even in winter, without foliage, they presented a decent barrier. He couldn't see the nearest house and the village itself was about a quarter of a mile away. It was looking better and better.

He stretched and yawned as Conor approached from the Austin. He had parked to the side of the cottage allowing Jamie to park the Commer near the front door.

'What do you think?' Conor asked.

'Perfect,' was Jamie's enthusiastic response.

The interior of the cottage was even more appealing. The front door lead into an open plan living room with kitchen off. There were two doors leading off, one serving the bedroom, the other the bathroom. The floors were of stone. Rugs were dotted around the living room and bedroom but the kitchen and bathroom floors were bare and cold. The walls were rough stone, pointed in white cement and the windows were the old casement type. At night, without a fire in the grate, it would be cold and judicious use of the lighting available would increase discomfort. Lighting the blowtorch in the dark might bring about the desired result without having to resort to unpleasantness. He hoped so.

Quickly, he and Conor unloaded the equipment and stored it in the bathroom. It was there - if things went to plan – that Fionn Doherty would meet his Maker and in doing so, hopefully, loosen Orlagh Duggan's tongue. Disposing of Doherty wouldn't cause him any grief. The man was an animal. Orlagh Duggan, on the other hand, might be a different matter.

Jamie wasted no time. He could not afford to; it was at a premium. As soon as the welding gear was safely stored away he rushed Conor into setting off again to finalise this part of the plan. They would stop in Dunoon where Conor would return the Austin and then catch the Western Ferries roll-on/roll-off ferry, either the MV Sound of Scarba or MV Sound of Shuna, from Hunters Quay to McInroy's Point just west of Gourock. With luck, they would be back at the Grosvenor in time for dinner. After that, the real fun would start.

Chapter Seventy-four

They arrived back in Glasgow just after five thirty and Jamie once again parked in Great George Street. The journey had tired them both but the thought of what lay ahead had the adrenalin pumping. When it was all over Jamie thought he would sleep for a week, preferably with Kate beside him.

After showering and changing in their rooms at the Grosvenor they met again in the hotel bar at six thirty. They ordered drinks, a pint of beer for both, and avoided any conversation about later. They had discussed it on the journey back from Dunoon and both knew what lay ahead. This was Jamie's act. Conor was there for show more than anything else but he was prepared to join in if he had to. He hoped he wouldn't have to. In all his years in the Navy and then in the CIA he had never killed a man. He wondered if he could and wondered how Jamie managed it.

From the beginning, when the kid had killed Max Kelman and the other members of the Kelman gang, Conor had marvelled at how he insulated himself from the consequences. He had known men who killed before he met Jamie Raeburn. Some killed for fun; they enjoyed it. Others killed because they had to but with each killing a little part of them died too. Jamie fell into the second category, at least in part. He killed because he had to, not because of some psychopathic urge, but he seemed to hold onto life at the same time. There couldn't be many like him, Conor mused.

The plan was simple enough. Jamie reasoned that the more complicated it was, the more likelihood there was of it going wrong. It had to be quick, clean and quiet... or as quiet as possible given that there would be gunfire. The silencer on his Walther had better be good!

They were finishing their meal when Orlagh Duggan entered the dining room with her usual poise. She was really quite special, Jamie mused wryly, and in any other circumstances he might admire her. She was almost breathtakingly beautiful and at the same time utterly evil, if what he had learned of her was true. He smiled to himself. It's strange, he thought, how in nature some of the most beautiful animals are the most dangerous... and the female of the species is more deadly than the male, as Rudyard Kipling so aptly put it. She smiled demurely in their direction and both men returned it, but Jamie knew this was no shy, retiring maiden. She was cold and calculating, and probably more dangerous than all the men of the three IRA Active Service Units put together. Her eyes lingered on them and Jamie gave her another, brighter smile now. Her face lit up.

If she had a weak spot - and he sincerely hoped she had – it would be in her belief that she could have any man she wanted. Just looking around the room she probably had good cause for believing that. The usual suspects were there, the overweight and balding with money preening themselves like peacocks, chests thrown out and straining against the already strained cotton, linen or silk of their expensive shirts. Her beauty was a blessing but it was also a curse. He had no doubt she had had many lovers, but he suspected that none had lived up to her expectations. She was always disappointed. He smiled quietly to himself. He was going to be no different... a major disappointment.

He felt Conor nudge him and nodded ever so slightly. She was coming over. His smile had won the day. He was on the hook and all she had to do was reel him in... She thought.

She stopped next to their table and they could smell her perfume. It was heady and certainly not cheap. What the chic urban terrorist of today was wearing. It made him wonder again why she was involved in the terror at all. Her father was worth a small fortune though much of it was probably derived from arms smuggling and other nefarious transactions. Maybe that was it, he mused, it was part of her life style. Being a terrorist was what kept her in the style she was used to. Maybe it was nothing at all to do with patriotism or nationalist fervour; maybe it was all down to personal betterment, greed and ambition.

'Leaving so soon?' she said as she surveyed the empty plates on the table. 'Every time I come in you seem to be leaving,' she went on. 'It's as if you're trying to avoid me.'

Jamie smiled up at her. 'Just bad timing,' he said easily. 'You're the last person I'd try to avoid,' he continued, massaging her ego a little, not that it needed massaging.

Her smile widened. 'We've both been here for days and we haven't had a conversation, let alone a drink. Do you think I'll eat you?' The last bit was said with a laugh, the kind of laugh that said that's exactly what she would do. Her deep, soft Irish accent was seductive and her Irish eyes were certainly smiling.

Jamie felt Conor's foot tap him under the table. 'It's his conscience,' the American said. 'Believe me, I know him. He's fighting an inner battle,' he went on with a smirk. Orlagh's brow knotted questioningly. 'He's married,' Conor explained.

Orlagh's eyes widened as if in surprise but Jamie knew it was all put on. She had seen him with Clara and had probably done the sums. She had already reached that conclusion, it was just her method of reaching it that was flawed. 'You're married?' she said, the inflection in her voice continuing the deception.

Jamie stared right back at her, a smile behind his look. 'Yes, I'm married. Is that a problem?' he asked, hoping her Catholic upbringing hadn't made adultery a taboo; it certainly hadn't stopped her killing but some people, most he reflected, only follow the Commandments they want to follow. She probably honoured her father and her late mother and maybe she didn't take the Lord's name in vain. He doubted she coveted her neighbour's ass but by the same token probably wanted him to covet hers. As for the rest... bearing false witness, making idols – she was her own idol – stealing, murder and adultery, they were all up for grabs.

'It's not a problem for me,' she said. 'You seem to be the one with the problem... are you?'

'I'm fighting it.'

'Well, if you win the battle I'll be here... but I'm only here for a few more days so don't waste time.' She fluttered her eyelashes and her smile was for him and him alone.

Conor's foot kicked him gently again. A little *I told you so* tap on the ankle. Ask and you're in, Conor had said, or words to that effect. He broadened his smile. 'How about tomorrow?' he said. 'You got anything planned?'

'What's wrong with tonight?'

Jamie shrugged apologetically. 'My Colonial friend, here, and I have got some business to attend to tonight,' he said, patting Conor on the arm. 'Otherwise I'd take you up on that.'

'Well later, maybe. I'm not a great sleeper,' she said coyly, conveying a message. 'If you make it back early, I'll be in the lounge bar... If not,' she added, smiling and holding out her room key fob for him to see. 'You'll find me there. Don't be shy.' And with that she swayed off to find a table, well aware that both men were watching her.

'Will you?' Conor whispered lewdly.

'Not if I don't have to,' Jamie replied smiling wryly. 'There are some things even I won't do.'

'Yeah, it would be a hell of a sacrifice,' Conor retorted, grinning.

Jamie simply shook his head. 'Come on, time to get the show on the road. If we get to Alexandria early we might get back here early.'

'And your lady friend will be in the bar, remember.'

'Maybe I'll stay out late,' Jamie laughed. 'Her eating me doesn't appeal.'

'Yeah, like I said, a hell of a sacrifice.'

Chapter Seventy-five

The evening traffic was light. It was raining lightly, a smir that settled on the windscreen and glistened on the road beneath the streetlights. There was no moon, heavy cloud cover having taken care of that. Apart from the rain, it was a perfect night for what they had to do.

They had taken the Commer. It was cold, the van's heater labouring to keep the windscreen from misting up let alone heat them, and Conor was shivering. Jamie had parked in Smollett Street, about 100 yards from the park entrance. The road and pavements glowed dully beneath the streetlamps as the light thrown down from them reflected off the gathering rainwater. It was depressing.

'Are we going to sit here and wait or go find them?' Conor asked, hoping Jamie would confirm the former. He was to be disappointed.

'We're going to wait for them down there in the park. They'll come out from the safe house in about twenty minutes,' Jamie stated confidently, looking down at his watch. The time was ten minutes past eight.

'You some sort of clairvoyant or do you know something I don't?'

'These boys are Irish so they like a drink,' Jamie said, laughing sarcastically. 'They go to the pub every night... at least, I *hope* they do. If they decide to stay home tonight we're on to plan B.'

'Which is?'

'Fuck knows,' Jamie laughed. 'Maybe I'll just have to go and knock the door.'

'Christ, you're joking, right?'

Jamie was still laughing. 'Aye, I'm joking. Maybe I should send you,' he teased and watched Conor's face pale. 'Relax,' he added quickly. 'That's a joke too. Don't worry, they'll be here. The pub beats the boredom of four walls and Coronation Street on the telly. They probably can't even swear with their landlady around. They've settled into a routine and that means heading for the pub every night. He checked his watch again. Only two minutes had passed thought it felt like hours. Nerves, he thought. I'm out of practise. He shrugged and opened the van door. 'Come on,' he said. 'Let's go and set up the meeting.'

'Jesus, Jamie, you make it sound like a social night,' Conor retorted as he stepped down from the van. He heard Jamie chuckle and shook his head in amazement. The kid seemed as cool as a cucumber.

They walked together to the park and Conor followed him through the gate. The grass was slippery. They picked their way carefully up the well-trodden path towards the trees. The frozen ground of the last few days had thawed and turned to mud that clung to their shoes but Jamie was striding ahead confidently. Conor guessed he had been here before... Had probably planned tonight's little escapade then, he thought.

They were well into the trees and near the burn when Jamie stopped. It was quiet. The only sounds were of the water in the burn eddying round stones and the hum of traffic on the nearby by-pass.

'They'll come down this way,' Jamie said confidently, confirming Conor's thought about earlier planning. 'I'll wait in the trees here. You head up the path a bit and then hide yourself. Stay hidden. When they pass you, come out behind them and follow but don't get too close and stay out of my line of fire,' he instructed. Conor looked uncertain, he thought. 'Okay?' he asked quietly. The American nodded but the look of doubt was still there. He would need to calm the big guy down. 'Don't worry,' he said encouragingly. 'You won't have to do anything unless any of them manage to turn and try to make a run for it. If that happens just stand your ground and let them get a good look at your Browning. That should be enough,' he said, finishing with a soft laugh. He patted Conor on the arm. 'You ready?' he asked. Conor nodded again, more determined this time. 'Okay, on you go,' Jamie said and moved off the path into the trees.

Conor moved off too and picked his way gingerly over the muddy path for about another ten yards before turning to look back. When he did, Jamie was nowhere to be seen. It was as if he had simply melted into the darkness. He gave a mental shrug and stepped off the path into the trees. The ground was more solid here. After about another five yards he found a tree with a trunk thick enough to conceal him from the anyone on the path but in the darkness that would have been difficult enough anyway. He was nervous and his palms were sweating. He pulled his collar tight round his neck, took the Browning from his coat pocket, and waited. He wasn't surprised to find his hands were shaking. He smiled nervously to himself and checked the safety on the gun. It was off and a bullet was in the chamber. He was all set. He knew what to do; he had been trained in the use of firearms. The only question in his mind now was, when the time came, could he?

He heard the Irishmen coming five minutes later. Well, he assumed it was the Irishmen. Who else would be crazy enough to be out on a night like this? That brought a smile to his face as he stood there shivering. Yeah, who else would be crazy enough? A quick glance at the luminous hands of his watch told him it was eighty twenty-eight... bang on time. They were talking easily amongst themselves, sauntering along the path without a care in the world. A boys' night out. Sink a few drinks and eye up the broads. It was hard to believe these bastards were going to set off a bomb that could kill thousands... Or maybe they didn't know, he mused. They would probably be the first to succumb, and with the knowledge of that on your mind you wouldn't be on your way for a drink sounding like you were off to the high school ball.

They passed his hiding place in single file, still laughing and joking though it sounded strained. Fitzpatrick could be any one of the four, he reflected. He had never met the man. Jamie had described the one he wanted alive, a thin, rat faced little runt, and the second in line had those characteristics. At a guess, if Fitzpartick was in command of the ASU he would be point man or the back marker.

Conor was stepping out from behind his tree when all conversation stopped. In the darkness he could just make out all four men on the path. As his eyes adjusted, a dark figure stepped out from the trees beyond them, blocking the path. What followed was like a scene from a Keystone Cops movie as the man at the front of the line stopped suddenly and each of the men behind stumbled into the man in front. It would have been comical if it hadn't been so serious. The confusion came to an end abruptly. There was a sound like a soft cough and the leading man, a big, broad shouldered man, suddenly tumbled backwards. Weasel face, second in line, was taken unawares and tried to grab the man to support him but the man's momentum and weight were too much for him and both fell awkwardly to the ground, weasel face trapped beneath the bigger man. The man third in line, a tall gangly individual, younger than all the others, looked around in panic, his eyes darting to Jamie, then the men on the ground and finally behind him. He could see a shadowy figure in front of him and the other two men on the ground.

The man was about to bolt, Conor judged, and prepared himself. His hand was shaking as he brought the Browning up into firing position but he controlled it. This was his moment of truth. He had never shot a man before. The soft cough saved him from the test. The young man's head was thrown back and he toppled backwards, collapsing like a sack of potatoes. Three down, he mused, which had to mean Fitzpatrick was the back man. As Conor was reaching that conclusion Liam Fitzpatrick raised his hands in the universal gesture of surrender. Good decision, the American reflected; after all he didn't know who was doing the shooting.

But weasel face wasn't down, Conor suddenly realised. The small man had worked free from the restricting bulk of his friend and was pushing himself up. Surrender was the last thing in this man's mind, it seemed. His face was contorted with rage as he launched himself at Jamie, pushing off like a sprinter from the blocks with his hands reaching forward like claws. Conor held his breath.

Jamie, however, was ready. As Doherty's momentum brought him within striking distance, Jamie stepped lightly to his right and brought the Walter down in a clubbing motion, tearing skin on the Irishman's temple and stopping him in his tracks. The man sank to the ground but he wasn't finished. Neither was Jamie. As Doherty started to rise, Jamie's boot caught him under the chin, snapping his head back and forcing him down again. He rolled over and managed to rise to his hands and knees when a hard kick to his solar plexus knocked the wind and the last of the fight from him. He sank forward into the mud again, only his eyes showed any sign of life.

It had all happened so quickly, Conor reflected. He had been spellbound. The kid is in a class of his own, he mused. As he watched, Jamie crouched down beside the man, took a handful of his hair and pulled his face round to him. He smiled briefly and then thrust the silencer of the Walther viciously into Doherty's mouth. The man yelled and cursed. 'Hello Fionn,' Jamie said. 'Fancy meeting you here.'

Fionn Doherty tried to focus through the pain. In the darkness all he could make out was the vague outline of Jamie's features. It was someone he knew, or should know. The man certainly knew him. He struggled against the hand gripping his hair and the muzzle of the gun in his mouth and felt fear for the first time. Eventually, the man removed the ugly tube of the silencer from his mouth. He sucked in a deep breath, the cold air sending pain shooting through him as it hit the nerve ends of a broken tooth. He grimaced and let out another curse. 'Who the feck are ye?' he mumbled through swollen lips.

Jamie almost admired his defiance... almost. 'You could say I'm a ghost,' he said. 'When dead people come back to exact vengeance on the living that's what they are, isn't it? Ghosts?' Doherty looked confused, lost even. The man still hadn't placed him, Jamie mused, smiling grimly.

Doherty's struggle was ended by Liam Fitzpatrick. Recognising Jamie's voice he lowered his hands and stepped forward, picking his way gingerly over the bodies of Finnegan and Macari to the two men. 'For feck sake Dermott,' he whispered, his voice shaking. 'We don't have time fer this. Just shoot the cunt.' He was shaking now, reaction setting in.

Conor stood back, his Browning still held loosely in his hand. Not surprisingly, he found that his hand was shaking again. He had to agree with Fitzpatrick, they didn't have time for this. Two men lay dead on the ground and another was immobilised. Someone could come through the wood at any time but Jamie seemed intent on dealing with weasel face here. He was about to speak when Doherty reacted.

'Feckin' Dermott,' he hissed as understanding dawned. He pushed himself up, straining against Jamie's restraining hand in his hair, his hands forming two claws ready to strike. He didn't make it. Jamie's right hand swung once again and the heel of the Walter impacted on Doherty's head near the first point of impact and the Irishman flopped forward, head first into the mud. This time he didn't get up.

'Shoot him,' Liam urged, his voice still shaking.

Jamie smiled grimly. 'Not yet Liam. I need him.'

Liam Fitzpatrick stared at him, lost for words. 'What the fuck for?' went through his mind but he didn't ask. He had seen enough to know that Dermott Lynch or whatever his fucking name was, wasn't a man to challenge in a situation like this. He had suspected it at Kiltyclogher, now he knew with certainty.

Jamie straightened up. He was back in control of himself, Conor mused as he looked on anxiously, but then again, he always had been, the big man reflected. 'What now? he asked, his voice no louder than a whisper.

Jamie's grim smile was back in place. He fished in his trousers' pocket and pulled out the keys for the van, tossing them over casually to the American. 'Go and get the van,' he instructed. 'Bring it down to the park gate and turn it then park next to the bowling green. The wall hides you from prying eyes. When you see Liam and me coming, get out and open the back doors.'

Conor nodded and took off, glad to be away from this place. He moved as quickly as he could, slipping precariously on the treacherous surface.

Jamie watched him disappear into the darkness then turned to Liam. 'Help me get these down to the van,' he said. 'We can't leave them here; no loose ends.'

'What about him?' Liam asked, nodding in the direction of Doherty.

Jamie's smile chilled him. 'I've got plans for him,' was all he said. He walked over to Macari and Finnegan, bent down and removed their belts, handing them up to a bemused Liam. 'Tie up Doherty's ankles and wrists with these,' he ordered. 'As tight as you like.'

As Liam moved away Jamie turned back to the bodies. Macari's face was a picture of surprise, his eyes wide open, staring at the sky. The tiny hole between them the only evidence he wasn't simply asleep. A pool of blood would be gathering beneath his head where the exit wound, a bigger hole, lay against the muddy earth. He turned his attention to Finnegan then. This was a boy, he thought, still in his teens by the look of him. What made them do it, young guys like him, he wondered. Patriotism? What exactly is that, he mused. Then he thought about his part in the boy's end. He looked at peace. His features were soft, his eyes open, like Macari's, but without the surprise in them. The bullet this time had entered just above the left eye. He shook his head sadly and, with two fingers, gently closed the eyes. The lad was wearing a scarf; a red tartan scarf wrapped loosely round his neck. Jamie unwrapped it, lifting the boy's head from the muddy ground with one hand as he slipped it off with the other. He put it in his pocket and lowered the head again. When he removed his hand, it was slick with blood. He sighed heavily and wiped it on the wet grass.

Liam Fitzpatrick was watching him. Jamie was an enigma to him. One minute a cold, calculating killer, next a gentle compassionate man. He couldn't come to grips with it. Just as Jamie had wondered what drove people like Pearce Finnegan, so Liam wondered what drove him. He didn't even contemplate patriotism. It was something else, something much more complex.

Jamie caught Liam's searching look and smiled. 'There's something else you have to do,' he said quietly, snapping the Irishman out of his reverie.

'What?' Liam asked uneasily.

'Go back to the house and tell your landlady, the lady with the grey hair and the glasses, that plans have changed. Pick up all your gear and theirs too. Leave nothing.'

'Mrs Porter, you know her?' Liam asked, surprised.

Jamie gave him a quiet laugh. 'No, but I've seen her. The night you left the message I came back here and checked the place out. Does she have any family?'

Liam nodded. 'A daughter, fourteen years old.'

'No husband?'

'She's a widow.'

It was Jamie's turn to nod, a reflective nod. 'Go and tell her it's all off. Conor and I will bring the van round to the front in twenty minutes. Be ready.'

'Why?'

'Because I'm not into killing misguided old ladies and their children. You tell her the plans have changed and you're all heading back home. You're going to disappear and so are they,' he went on, nodding in the direction of Finnegan and the other two. 'The attack isn't going to happen. Everyone involved is going to vanish off the face of the earth and no one will know anything about it. She'll hear nothing and just get on with her life. Do the job well.'

Jamie bent down then and took hold of Doherty's bound wrists. The man was still unconscious but he'd come round soon enough. 'You take Finnegan,' he said as he began dragging Doherty down the path to the tree line, the man's heels etching two ragged parallel lines in the mud. Liam followed suit, taking hold of Finnegan's wrists, one in each hand and working backwards, pulling the boy as gently as possible. Of them all, he thought sadly, Finnegan was the least deserving of death.

Jamie reached the tree line just as Conor drove into Park Street and started his three point turn. By the time he reached the main path through the park, the Commer was parked in front of the bowling green wall, its engine idling roughly. He scanned the roads. They were empty. Fate was still dealing him a fair hand. He continued along the gravel, dragging Doherty none too gently. Liam followed, his treatment of the dead Finnegan less brutal.

Conor was waiting nervously by the back doors of the van when they arrived. Unceremoniously, he gripped the belt that bound Doherty's ankles and, between them, he and Jamie tossed the Irishman into the back. The man landed in a heap but made no sound. Jamie smiled grimly. That wouldn't last, he thought. Conor repeated his work with Finnegan, gripping the boy's ankles, but sensed Liam's mood and gently they slid the boy's body onto the floor. The gesture was for Liam's benefit, not Finnegan's Jamie mused; the boy was long past feeling anything.

Only Macari remained to be brought down and Jamie decided to do that himself. He ran his eyes over Liam. The Irishman didn't look too bad, considering everything. His clothes were relatively unmarked. Only mud on his shoes, lower trouser legs and hands gave any sign of what had taken place. There was no blood spatter anywhere on him, that was the main thing. 'You'll do,' he said, patting Liam lightly on the arm.

Then he turned to Conor. 'That bastard in there will come round soon,' he said, referring to Doherty. He withdrew Finnegan's scarf from his pocket and handed it over. 'Gag him with this,' he went on. 'We don't want him screaming blue murder and upsetting the locals.'

Conor nodded and took the scarf. He was already climbing into the back of the van when Jamie lead Liam away back to the park, his arm resting on the Irishman's shoulder. As they approached the scene for the second time Jamie stopped and faced Liam again. He repeated his instructions. 'Remember, you tell her there's been a change of plan. If she asks how, tell her you were contacted in the pub.' Liam nodded repetitively as he listened. 'Your new orders are to head home and you're back to pick up all your gear. If she asks about the others, they'll be coming in a van... which they will,' he added, laughing mirthlessly. 'Make sure you pick up everything and make sure you're convincing. Alright?'

Liam nodded again. He looked anxious. Jamie smiled grimly. 'You'll be saving her life... her life and her daughter's,' he said quietly. Liam looked up and regarded him steadily. Jamie knew what he was thinking.; he was thinking the same thing. *Could I really kill them?* No, he decided, but someone else sure as hell would if it was thought she was a loose end. People in the shadowy world of espionage don't like loose ends. 'Just do it, Liam,' he said quietly. The Irishman dropped his eyes and nodded.

'Good,' Jamie responded, patting him on the arm again. 'I'll take Macari, here, down to the van. You wait here for five minutes then head back to the house. Five minutes should be enough for you to have made it to the pub and back, we don't want the old dear getting suspicious.' He checked his watch. 'It's quarter to nine now. Conor and I will bring the van round to the front of the house in twenty minutes, that should give you enough time. Don't get involved in any chat with her, get in, get your gear and get out. We'll be outside at five past nine. Make sure you are too,' he instructed. Liam shrugged and forced a smile.

Back in the van, Conor sat in the front passenger seat with the window open and looked uneasily towards the park. His nerves were tempered by what he had seen... the ruthless efficiency of what he had seen, more particularly. Jamie Raeburn was a natural leader. He issued instructions and others carried them out, including him, he mused, the guy who saw himself as the kid's "big brother" and protector. In truth, it was the other way round. It made him think again of a plan that had been forming in his head for a while now, a plan that involved them both. He smiled contemplatively. Could they get away with it, he wondered.

Minutes later, though to Conor it seemed like hours, he heard rather than saw Jamie emerging from the dark shadows of the trees onto the grass. As with Doherty, he was dragging the dead man by the wrists. When they reached the gravel path the sound of the man's heels on the stone came to him; a grating sound which, though virtually silent, seemed like a continuous roll of thunder to him. He was getting too old for this, he reflected, which took him back to his plan again.

Jamie was breathing hard when he arrived at the van. Macari was much bigger and heavier than Doherty and the effort had been taxing. Conor descended from the cab, opened the rear doors again and took hold of the man's ankles. With a practised swing they lifted Macari from the ground and slung him into the van where he landed heavily on top of Doherty. The smaller man suddenly came to life, struggling against his bonds and wriggling free while garbled noises came from behind the gag. Jamie grinned. 'Glad you're still with us, Fionn,' he said, withdrawing the Walther from his belt.

The Irishman's face reddened and more noises came from his gagged mouth. Nothing intelligible. Jamie was turning away, ready to close the van doors, when he suddenly stopped. 'Almost forgot,' he said. 'You've got something of mine.'

Doherty looked up at him, puzzled. Jamie leaned into the van and took hold of the man's wrists, pulling him violently towards him then concentrating on his left wrist. He found the catch of the watch bracelet and undid it as Doherty twisted and turned, finally slipping it from the man's wrist. Doherty sagged back onto the floor.

'This is my watch,' Jamie said. 'You took it from me at Kiltyclogher just before you pissed on me you slimy wee shite,' Jamie said calmly. He saw Doherty's brow knot as he tried to work it out. 'The "dead Brit" didn't die Fionn. He's still here, alive and kicking.' He slipped the watch onto his right wrist, straightened up and slammed the doors shut, leaving the man in darkness.

'Come on, Conor, let's get out of this rain,' he said, moving down the driver's side of the van while Conor went down the other. They hauled themselves inside and Jamie adjusted his seat. Conor's legs were much longer than his and the seat had been pushed right back to let the American drive. The heater was still blasting out lukewarm air and the windows were still misted with condensation but at least it was dry in here. Their wet clothes would add to the condensation problem but there was nothing they could do about that other than wipe the screen with a rag that sat beside them in the central console next to the gear stick. He checked his watch again. It was almost fifteen minutes since he had left Liam in the wood. Dragging Macari out had taken longer than he thought. It was time to go. He slipped the van into gear and drove back along Smollett Street.

Chapter Seventy-six

Liam emerged from the safe house in Margaret Drive at exactly eight minutes past nine. Jamie knew that because he had just checked the time on his watch, his "new" watch, the one retrieved from Doherty. The Irishman was struggling with four bags and the woman of the house was standing in the doorway, framed in the light from the hall. Conor looked at Jamie and shrugged. His message was clear; Liam would have to struggle on his own.

Jamie had parked carefully, making sure the rear and interior of the van couldn't be seen from the house. Neither could the occupants of the cab, though if she looked carefully, the woman would make out their shapes, not their features.

Conor sat nervously in the passenger seat. He was more or less the same build as the dead Irishman, Macari, but a close look at his face would give the game away. He saw the woman wave and waved back while doing his best to keep his face shielded from view. He held his breath and Jamie grinned. 'This isn't funny kid,' Conor griped.

Jamie laughed a little more. 'Relax,' he said. 'She would need 20/20 vision to see you properly, we're twenty yards away, it's pissing down and it's dark... and she wears glasses.'

Conor smiled but he wasn't convinced.

Liam headed for the back of the van. That took him out of Mrs Porter's line of sight. Jamie slipped out of the van on her blind side and joined him, quickly opening the doors. Liam threw the bags in, smiling.

'You'll need to join them,' Jamie said ruefully. 'There's no room up front.' That wiped the smile off the Irishman's face.

'With them?' he said, horrified. He wasn't talking about the bags.

'Aye, but don't worry. They won't bite. Now give the old dear a wave and let's get away from here,' Jamie told him and took him by the elbow, helping him in.

Liam mumbled something Jamie didn't catch, waved, and climbed in. Doherty was conscious, blood streaming from a gash at the side of his face where the Walther had caught him. His eyes were burning with uncontrolled fury and loathing.

Liam ignored him. He didn't care what Doherty thought. The wee bastard would be dead soon anyway. He wondered what Dermott had in store for him and smiled icily. He took some comfort from the fact it was unlikely to be pleasant. But still, if he had had his way, Fionn Doherty would already be on his way to hell, just like the other two. He settled himself against the bulkhead facing the man and drew his knees up to his chest, returning Doherty's malevolent stare. Two could play, he mused, and smiled unpleasantly.

He felt the van settle to the right as Jamie returned to his seat in the cab and then they were moving. It was dark in the back of the van now. All he could see was the bundled shapes of Macari and Finnegan lying in a tangled heap near the door and the vague form of Doherty across from him. He couldn't make out Fionn's features now but, by the same token, Fionn couldn't see his. He didn't give a shit. He knew the wee shite was looking at him thinking up ways of making him pay for what he had done. So what, he mused. It would never happen. Fionn Doherty was at hell's gate waiting for it to open and it would... soon. Very soon, he hoped.

His thoughts turned to Dermott then. He smiled to himself. Dermott wasn't his real name, he knew that. Roisin knew, but she had never told him. That didn't matter. Dermott, or whatever his name was, had come through for him. That was all that mattered. The events of the last half hour filled his mind then and he smiled to himself again. When the man, Dermott as it happened, had emerged from the trees, he had almost shit himself. One second he was strolling with the others through the wood to the pub and next second, Finnegan and Macari were dead and he thought he was next.

Fionn had surprised him, right enough. Self-preservation, he supposed. It put his own actions to shame, not that it did the wee bugger any good. The only surprise was that the man facing them had clubbed him down with his gun rather than shoot him there and then. It was then he had heard Dermott's voice and the warm glow of relief filled him. That must be what salvation feels like, he mused, and closed his eyes.

He didn't know how long the journey took and he had no idea where they were. The first part had been through the town, Alexandria to Balloch he imagined. Some meagre light had filtered through the filthy rear windows but after that there was nothing but darkness. The drumming noise from the tyres on the road surface was almost hypnotic, a subdued roar like a continuous drum roll, and he had dozed for a while. He awoke not long before they arrived at their destination. The van was labouring up a long incline and then he was thrown from side to side like a ragdoll as the it twisted and turned tortuously on the downward leg. Now, with the van stopped and the engine off, the silence was deafening.

He felt the van lurch as Jamie and Conor descended and then the rear doors were thrown open. It had stopped raining and a pale moon was flitting in and out of the clouds painting everything in a ghostly white light. The smell of wet grass filled his nostrils and he drew it in thankfully. Jamie, or Dermott as Liam knew him, stood there, an amused grin on his face. 'Sorry about that Liam, old son,' he said. 'But we've arrived now so you can get out.'

Liam pushed himself up awkwardly off the floor and eased himself forward in a crouch then jumped down onto the ground. His muscles screamed in protest after the cramped conditions of the journey but he felt good. He breathed in the cool fresh air. They were in the countryside, the smell of damp grass and wood smoke in the air told him that, but where, he had no idea.

He looked around as his eyes adjusted. They were in a clearing surrounded by trees. A stone cottage stood off to his left. All around was darkness, the sort of darkness you only get in the countryside away from the big towns and cities. It felt comforting. He had never been afraid of the dark. He turned around, a full 360 degrees. The darkness seemed to have swallowed them up though he thought he saw a light flickering in the distance, how far he couldn't tell. 'Where are we?' he asked at last, turning to face the man he now saw as his saviour.

'Paradise,' Jamie replied, a wry smile on his face as he hauled Doherty from the van by his ankles and let his body drop to the ground with a resounding thud. Doherty had the presence of mind to throw his head forward as he fell and took the full force of the fall on his shoulders and back rather than his head. He tried to scream through the gag but it came out like a gargled screech.

Jamie knelt down beside him and undid the belt around the man's ankles. Without waiting, he straightened up and hauled Doherty to his feet.

The Irishman struggled and stamped his feet as the blood in his legs started to circulate again. His ankles and calves throbbed with the pain of it.

Jamie smiled unpleasantly. He knew what Doherty was thinking but he wouldn't get the chance. 'Inside,' he hissed, pushing him towards the door with Liam following.

The inside of the house was warmer, but not much. A kettle was sitting on a gas stove, not quite boiling. Liam looked around. The house was basic but clean. The furniture was old but solid and the walls were bare stone. He wondered who lived here.

Conor knelt by the hearth doing his best to light a fire. Scrunched up newspaper filled the grate and a blue flame licked at it, spreading quickly. The American threw some kindling on top and stood up, watching proudly as the flames caught. Larger pieces of wood stood piled beside the grate and, when the kindling was glowing red, he placed two of these on top. The kettle was now boiling.

Doherty was lying face down on the stone floor where Jamie had thrown him. He had given up groaning; he knew it did no good. No one was listening.

As Conor made a brew, Jamie pulled an envelope from inside his jacket. It was crushed and appeared bulky. Without speaking, he held it out to Liam.

'What is it?' the Irishman asked.

'Your future, *Mr King*,' Jamie replied. 'There's a passport and some cash in there, the rest of your money is in a Swiss Bank Account. It's all written down. Your part is finished.'

'I don't think so,' Liam retorted cautiously. 'There's still Roisin.'

Jamie smiled and it was warmer now. 'You don't need to worry about Roisin. She's in the clear.'

Liam looked at him for a long moment, weighing up his words, struggling to believe. 'Seriously?' he said at last.

'Seriously,' Jamie confirmed.

Liam was close to tears. 'I'll not forget this,' he said, his voice shaking with emotion. 'I owe you.'

Conor Whelan, standing behind the two men with cups of steaming hot tea in both hands let out a chuckle. 'Yeah, me too,' he said. 'Jamie here has lots of favours to call in.'

Liam looked at the big American and took the cup before turning his eyes back to Jamie. 'So it's Jamie, is it? I knew Dermott wasn't your real name.'

'That's what gave me away this time,' Jamie said, laughing quietly as he thought back. 'When you asked Brigadier Redmond for my help from the man you "saved" at Kiltyclogher and called him Dermott, it didn't take him long to work things out. When he realised we knew each other before then he knew he could use it, and use it he did.'

'I'm sorry.'

Jamie laughed. 'Don't be. You said you owe me but I was only repaying a debt. You took a hell of a risk that night. If you hadn't shot me and faked my death I wouldn't be here tonight, my wife would be a widow and my kids left without a father. You don't owe me a thing. We're even.'

He sipped the burning tea handed him by Conor, smiling warmly at the big American as he did. 'And that goes for you too, Conor. You don't owe me anything.'

'That means diddly-squat to me kiddo. You saved my life. You can't wipe that out.'

Jamie shrugged, still smiling. 'You've repaid it more than once... I don't want you feeling you owe me anything; you don't.' He took another drink of the scalding tea and looked down at Doherty then. Subject closed.

Liam saw his pensive look and raised an eyebrow. 'What are we going to do with him?' he asked. 'Why did ye bring him with us? Ye should have killed the wee shite back in Alexandria.'

'Patience, Liam,' Jamie replied, the cold smile back on his face. 'Like I said, he's useful.'

'How's he feckin' useful? He's a psychotic wee killer who knows feck all. What possible use can he be? I don't get it,' he said, his frustration coming out again.

'You don't have to get it and you don't need to stay if you don't want to. If you don't have a strong stomach, maybe you should disappear for a while. I'm taking the van back to Glasgow. Conor is staying to keep an eye on Doherty. You can come with me.'

Liam looked at both men in turn. Neither man was giving anything away. It was confusing but from what he had learned of Dermott, or Jamie, he reminded himself, told him he wasn't keeping Fionn alive on a whim. He was curious. 'Nah, I'll stay with the big man,' he said. 'He makes a grand cup o' tea... an' I do have a strong stomach. I'm a feckin' plumber fer fuck sake,' he added, finishing with a laugh.

Jamie smiled again. It was becoming a habit, he mused. 'Okay, in that case you can help him dispose of Macari and Finnegan. You can dig one grave each,' he said, turning back to Doherty and crouching down. 'As for you Fionn... well, we'll see,' he whispered.

Fionn Doherty glared back at him. If looks could kill he would be dead, Jamie thought. Lying there, facing God knows what, the bastard was still planning ways of making him pay. He was evil personified, it was there in his eyes. They were dark, black, fathomless pools. Even when he smiled, which wasn't often, there was no feeling in it. Just an emptiness. He wasn't the sort of man you'd invite to dinner with your wife and kids; they'd have nightmares for weeks afterwards. He just lay there, bound and gagged and plotting.

He straightened up again and turned to Conor. 'Leave him where he is. If he needs to piss or crap, tough. You do not untie him. Leave him there. Got that?' Conor nodded.

'Conor's in charge, Liam. You do as he says, right?'

'Aye right, he's the man.'

'I'll be back late morning if everything goes to plan... Then the fun will begin.' He finished off his tea and threw the dregs onto the now glowing fire where they hissed and quickly evaporated. 'Right, let's get Macari and Finnegan out of the van. Have you picked a spot for them?'

Conor gave him a humourless smile. 'Sure have, kid. Nice spot overlooking the loch. Never seen anyone visit in all the times I've been here. They won't be disturbed.'

'Good,' Jamie nodded appreciatively. 'We wouldn't want anyone disturbing their sleep,' he chuckled coldly, his eyes back on Doherty. 'But what will we do with you, Fionn,' he said, as though thinking aloud. 'One hole or two... or maybe even three or four. Depends how long you take to die, I suppose,' he added. Fionn just stared back emptily, still plotting. Jamie simply shrugged. Left alone he'll start to think about it. For the moment, he has something to focus all his hate on, Jamie mused; me.

Chapter Seventy-seven

Glasgow was still awake when he arrived back. Just. It was nudging half past eleven when he parked the van in his usual place in Great George Street and sauntered down to Byres Road. A few couples walked by him, laughing, flirting. Students, he thought. The pubs were closed, the Salon picture house was closed and even the restaurants were closed. How long would it be, he wondered, before Glasgow caught up with the world? They could start with the pubs and everything else would follow.

He had left Conor and Liam with clear instructions. He had no doubt they would follow them. The rest was up to him.

As he pushed through the revolving doors into the hotel foyer he looked himself over. He had managed to get most of the mud off his trouser hems and his shoes but there were still traces. Other than that, he thought he looked okay. The resident's lounge was still open. There was music; Frank Sinatra was extolling the virtues of New York, the city that never sleeps. Somebody should do that for Glasgow, he mused with a smile... I Belong tae Glesga has limited appeal.

A woman's laugh broke into his thoughts. Orlagh. It couldn't be anyone else. She would be holding court with her usual subjects. The faces changed but the bald heads and the fat guts didn't. She played them. They bought her drink, flattered her – not that she wasn't worth the flattery – and vied for her attention, hoping they would get the chance to show how virile they were; or thought they were. He was pretty sure none of them had managed to get off the starting block.

It was time, but he would have to be careful; play it cool. He was conscious of the Walther tucked into his belt at the small of his back. That was another reason for not ending up one on one with her tonight. It wasn't the main reason, the main reason was about 300 miles away. He took a deep breath and stepped into the room. Only one person noticed him, everyone else was too busy noticing her. He gave her a smile and headed straight for the bar.

He hauled himself up onto a stool. The barman, the same one who had been on duty when he had been here with Clara, gave him a professional smile and waited for his order. 'Laphraoig,' Jamie said, returning the man's smile. As the barman turned away he called him back. 'I've had a shitty night,' he said, loud enough to be heard by Orlagh if she was listening. 'Make it a double, and have one yourself.'

The man's smile suddenly became genuine. 'Thanks,' he said. 'I've had a busy night myself,' he added, his eyes taking in the group surrounding Orlagh.

Jamie let his eyes drift to the mirror behind the bar. It gave him a perfect view of the table and the group. The table was littered with empty and part drunk glasses, pint jugs and spirit tumblers. They certainly had been making a night of it, it seemed. As his eyes moved from the table to Orlagh herself he noticed her looking back at him, a wry smile on her face. He nodded at her reflection and her smile widened.

The Laphraoig arrived. He added a drip of water from a jug on the bar and raised the glass to his lips. Orlagh was still watching him. He stopped mid-sip and raised the glass in a silent toast. She smiled again. None of her suitors seemed to notice she wasn't smiling at them but, judging by the number of empty glasses on the table, that wasn't surprising. He sipped at the whisky, letting the heavy, peat laced liquor swill around his mouth before swallowing. Five minutes, he guessed, before she let them down gently. They would all leave with her, he assumed. She was the sole reason they were all still here at this time of night so it was a safe guess. Say another five minutes before she was back... and then? He allowed himself a little smile. He'd need to be convincing.

He took another sip of the Laphraoig and kept his eyes on her in the mirror. She was back with the crowd, giving them her undivided attention, stroking their egos. She was good. He imagined that in any walk of life she would be successful. It was a pity she had chosen the route she was now on. Success in that field was always limited and the competition brutal. To coin a phrase; they didn't take prisoners... But neither did Orlagh. If what he had learned of her was true, she was an effective operator with an impressive list of victims. That made him shiver. The same could be said of him.

His estimate was bang on. The five minutes had flown past. He saw her rise from her chair, heard the collective disappointment and watched as glasses were speedily emptied as they all vied to be the one to escort her to the lift... and hopefully her room. Ironic, he thought. These guys all wanted to shag her and she wasn't interested; he didn't and she was.

She swept close to him as she left, almost close enough to touch. She had gone out of her way to do that, manoeuvring through tables and past chairs when the direct route was simpler. It was her way of telling him to stay put. Her scent filled his nostrils. It smelled expensive. Pearce Duggan's haulage business must be good, he mused, though he suspected he was skimming a little off the top in the gun running too. As a side-line, it was probably very lucrative. He was a top man so a blind eye would be turned to it as long as the guns and explosives kept flowing.

He turned as she passed, following her passage. Her behind swayed tantalisingly in the tight mini dress and it was easy to see what made normally sane men lose their minds. As temptations went, her bum was up there with the best and the legs were a match. He could easily imagine what was going through those men's minds. It was going through his.

When the bar was empty he called the young barman over. 'When do you finish?' he asked.

The lad smiled wanly. 'When you do,' he said.

'I'm going to keep you a bit longer then but I'll make it worth your while.' The young man nodded. 'The lady that just left; what was she drinking?' Jamie asked.

'Whiskey, Irish... She likes the Bushmills, the ten year old.'

'Figures,' Jamie said with a soft laugh. 'In that case, pour a double and leave it here with me.' He watched, amused, as the young man raised one eyebrow. The lad had seen the other hopefuls leave with their tails between their legs and probably thought he was wasting his money. Who knows, he mused, maybe he's right. 'And I'll have another Laphraoig, a single this time. Just add it to my glass,' he said, handing it over.

The barman moved down the bar and turned to the whiskies ranged behind him whilke Jamie thought about the next stage. He hoped his charm and a promise would be enough to get Orlagh to Lochgoilhead. If not, he had a problem. Tying her up and throwing her into the boot of the Mustang in broad daylight wasn't an option... But tonight, when no one was about, he might get away with it. One scream, however, was all it needed to scupper that plan.

The barman returned and placed the glasses beside him. He still seemed amused. 'Do you want these put on your room tab?' he asked.

Jamie shook his head and brought out a wad of notes. 'How much?'

'Two pounds and ten pence,' came the reply.

Jamie peeled off a five pound note and slipped it across the bar to him. 'Keep the change,' he said. 'I did say I'd make it worth your while.'

The lad grinned appreciatively and headed for the till then spent the next few minutes polishing glasses. He wondered how long it would be before this man gave up hope and headed for his room. And it would be his *own* room. The Irish woman was a tease, no more, no less. He had seen it all before. Or thought he had.

When Orlagh Duggan reappeared and hoisted herself up onto a stool next to Jamie the young man's eyes almost popped out of their sockets. Jamie suppressed a grin but not nearly enough. Orlagh caught it and her eyebrows knitted. 'Am I missing something?' she asked, Her voice was deep, like sweet black treacle, and eminently sensual.

'My friend behind the bar thought I was wasting my time waiting for you,' he said, pushing the glass of Bushmills towards her.

She laughed, deep and throaty. 'And did you tell him it's you that's been playing hard to get?' she asked, turning to the young barman and giving him an innocent smile. 'I'll bet he didn't, did he?' she went on. The young man laughed and shook his head. She turned back to Jamie. 'What kept you?' she probed. 'Apart from it being a shitty night?'

That confirmed she had heard his earlier remark to the barman, Jamie thought, smiling. 'Just too much to do and not enough time to do it. The old story,' he quipped.

'Where's your American friend? Was it all too much for him?'

Jamie kept the smile on his face. Was that an innocent query or was she interrogating him? *Don't get paranoid*, he chided himself. If she had any doubts she wouldn't be here. 'He got caught up in something,' he replied, trying to give the impression that the something he got caught up in had a beautiful smile and other memorable assets.

'Ah,' she said knowingly. 'I'm glad you didn't get caught up in the same something,' she said, her eyes locked onto his.

He was finding it difficult to keep up the pretence. Her eyes, a sparkling, translucent green, were having an almost hypnotic effect on him. Added to her smile it was hard to believe she was the evil harridan he knew her to be. He swivelled on his stool and felt the Walther press against his back. He eased back, releasing the pressure.

'So, what are we going to do now?' she asked, almost purring. 'The night's young.'

He smiled apologetically. 'My shitty night has had a knock on effect,' he said, sounding regretful. 'I have to get up early in the morning... site visit.'

'Site visit?' she repeated. She sounded disappointed. 'Is that the truth or are you letting me down gently? Still guilty?'

He laughed, pitching it just right. 'No, it's the truth, and I'm as disappointed as you are, believe me.'

'I don't believe you.'

He gazed into her eyes. 'I wouldn't be able to do you justice tonight,' he said. 'I'm tired... it's nothing to do with guilt. I'm no angel,' he added. He grinned as he said it. If she only knew, he mused.

Orlagh misinterpreted the grin. If he wasn't an angel she would bring out the devil in him, she thought. She didn't know how right she was but it wasn't the devil she would like. 'So how are you going to make it up to me?' she whispered. She left no doubt as to how she expected him to do that, letting her hand drop onto his thigh. She got the reaction she wanted. 'You're not exhausted then,' she laughed. 'And you're certainly alive.'

Jamie forced a smile, consoling himself with the thought that there wasn't a man alive who wouldn't react as he had done. It was a physical thing, a natural reaction. We're all just animals, he reminded himself.

She was talking again, her fingers still running up and down the inside of his thigh. 'I'm waiting,' she said, her voice dripping like honey. 'How are you going to make it up to me?'

'I'll find a way,' he assured her, laughing now. 'But I'll be away most of tomorrow, sorry.'

'So I have to amuse myself all day?' she retorted, pretending hurt. 'I'd set tomorrow aside,' she continued, pouting.

Suddenly his night just got better. That was his opening. It also confirmed she wasn't planning on meeting with her ASUs or anyone else for that matter. 'Yeah, well I'll be on my own too,' he said, baiting the hook and gazing longingly into her big green eyes.

She waited a moment. 'Your friend isn't going with you?' she asked coyly.

'I think he's going to be tied up all day,' Jamie replied, laughing.

'Lucky boy,' she said. 'Where are you going exactly?'

'A client is interested in a plot of land in Argyllshire... a nice little cottage and about ten acres,' Jamie responded, gilding the lily. 'Nice place. They're thinking of opening a holiday park. The scenery is supposed to be breathtaking.'

'Quiet, is it?'

'Supposed to be.'

'No nosy neighbours?'

'It's a holiday home in the middle of nowhere. Nearest neighbours are about half a mile away so nosy they're not,' he laughed.

'A holiday home? Are the owners there just now?' she asked.

She was nibbling. He might just land her if he played this right, he mused. 'It's the middle of winter,' he replied. 'So no, they're not there just now. I've got the key in my car.'

'Sounds romantic,' she said softly, her fingers becoming active again after a period of inaction.

'Yeah, I suppose it does,' he said... 'You could always come along for the ride,' he said, as if the idea had just entered his head. 'But you don't have to,' he added quickly... 'I mean, well, it'll be cold and, well maybe you'd rather stay here in the heat.'

'Alone? No, I like the idea of coming along for the ride,' she said, fluttering her eyelashes and playing the double entendre for everything. 'I know a few ways to keep warm,' she added, with just the right amount of lewdness.

Aye, I'm sure you do, Jamie mused. So do I.

'Are you serious? You want to come?'

'Oh yes,' she laughed. 'I want to come... Are you going to take me?'

She emphasised "come" and "take me" just enough, Jamie mused, laughing inside. She must have been watching too much "Up Pompeii" with Frankie Howerd. 'Well, if you're sure,' he said. 'I'd love the company.'

Orlagh picked up her Bushmills and drank some down. 'Oh, I'm sure,' she said.

Jamie looked at his watch. They had been sitting for about twenty minutes and he hadn't touched his drink. He yawned theatrically and picked up his tumbler, taking a mouthful of the Laphraoig. He looked at the glass for a moment then brought it to his lips and finished what remained. Sacrilege, but some sacrifices are necessary in life. He hoped he didn't have to make another one tomorrow. 'I'm leaving early, right after breakfast,' he said. 'You okay with that?'

'Yes, I'm okay with that,' she confirmed. 'Knock my door on the way down,' she said... 'Or you could just give me a gentle shake,' she suggested.

God loves a trier. Jamie smiled. 'We'll leave that till Thursday,' he replied.

Her eyes lit up lasciviously. 'Wow,' she responded huskily. 'A whole day and a whole night... though maybe after that I'll have to wake you,' she laughed, letting her hand wander again by way of demonstration.

'Aye, maybe you will,' he said.

***

They left shortly after that, Jamie leaving another two pound notes on the bar for the grateful barman. Orlagh clung to his arm as the lift ascended and stopped at the second floor. 'My room's on the third,' she said impishly.

'Yeah, I know, but mine is just along the corridor here.'

'Don't I even get a goodnight kiss?' She was blocking the lift door, preventing it from closing.

Jamie sighed inside but smiled none the less. She moved closer, her right hand snaking round his neck while the left slipped lower, onto his hip, dangerously close to the Walther, and eased him gently but firmly towards her. Her mouth was on his then, lips parted, her tongue probing. Caught in his own trap, he mused, as he responded, pulling her into the lift and pressing her against the wall. The lift door closed and he hoped it would move. Up or down, it didn't matter, as long as someone on another floor pressed the call button. Nobody obliged. The kiss seemed to last forever before he finally managed to disentangle himself. She had certainly set his pulse racing.

Orlagh smiled, gave him a final peck on the lips, and pressed the button to open the door for him. He smiled again and backed out. 'That was just a taster,' she said. 'Tomorrow's another day.'

The lift door closed as he stood there and he heard the hum of the motor as it started to climb again. He was getting in over his head. The girl was a man eater and he was on the menu. It would be easy to be her hors d'oeuvres, main and dessert, he mused. In normal circumstances that wouldn't be so bad but his circumstances weren't normal. He'd got in over his head once before and lost his way with Clara. That wasn't going to happen again.

His room was cold when he finally let himself in. That was a bonus. He was feeling pretty hot just then. He stripped, showered, dried himself and slipped between the sheets. He didn't set the alarm. He would be awake in plenty of time. He closed his eyes and thought of Kate. She was smiling at him, shaking her head, sending him a message. Orlagh Duggan was an attractive woman but her attractions were limited and definitely skin deep. Kate, on the other hand, was sublime. He fell asleep with a smile on his face.

Chapter Seventy-eight

Wednesday 16 January 1974

He was out of his room at seven thirty on the dot. Breakfast was 07.30 till 09.30 and he had warned Orlagh he was leaving early. He felt refreshed. The events of the night before had been consigned to memory. He wouldn't think about them again unless he had too.

He climbed the stairs to the third floor and took the corridor to room 314. Automatically, he ran a hand through his hair and checked his breath. The minty-ness of the toothpaste was still there, thank God. His mouth had been like a sand pit when he woke; too much Laphraoig too late at night.

He knocked gently and was surprised when the door opened almost immediately. A beaming smile greeted him. He ran his eyes over her, thanking God that she was dressed. She had chosen clothes well for the occasion. A black mini skirt clung to her hips and half of her thighs. Black boots, the long ones up over the knees, covered the bottom part of her legs with a tantalising gap between the hem of the skirt and the top of the boots giving him a glimpse of the assets she clearly had. On top she was wearing a burgundy coloured polo neck in a shaggy, woollen fabric. Angora came to mind for some obscure reason. She had done her hair, her eyes and her lipstick to produce a perfect picture of the siren she undoubtedly was. She was in the wrong business; had made the wrong choice. Sir Charles could have used her. She could probably prise secrets from any man. She was a modern day Mata Hari.

'Well?' she said. 'Will I do?'

She knew damned well she would do, Jamie mused, but probably liked to hear it anyway. 'Yes, you'll do,' he confirmed. It wasn't too difficult to sound convincing. 'But I hope you're wearing something on top,' he went on. 'It'll be bloody cold where we're going.' *For the first part anyway, he mused darkly.*

'Well, apart from you, I thought I'd take a coat,' she teased. 'Come in, I'll just get it,' she said, standing aside.

Jamie stepped into the room. He hid his reluctance well. The day was starting badly from the seduction point of view but perfectly in every other respect. On the seduction front, he suspected she wasn't going to hold back. But, on the bright side, it seemed that she suspected nothing. He had another worry. He was beginning to like her. If that feeling grew over the journey to Lochgoilhead could he stick to his plan, he fretted.

She stood in front of him now, a long suede Afghan coat with a fur collar draped over her shoulders. The usual "wet dog" smell associated with these coats was masked by her expensive perfume. He had to hand it to her. She was a walking fashion statement. Christ, he fumed, what a waste. 'Come on,' he said. 'I think I need to build up my energy.' That made her smile.

They breakfasted alone, first guests in the dining room that morning. The chat was just as Jamie anticipated, flirtatious and filled with suggestiveness. He could live with that. With luck, it would set the tone for the drive. For him though, maintaining the right balance was crucial. Too suggestive and he might have her wanting to pull off the road for a taster... and there were plenty of isolated spots on route for that.

Two of her suitors from the night before entered the dining room as they were leaving. She gave them a beaming smile and hung on to Jamie's arm. The guys gawped but her smile kept their hopes alive. She had the ability to make men think she wanted them, even when she was hanging on the arm of another man, Jamie noted. Talent like that shouldn't be squandered, he mused. The thought disturbed him. That sort of thinking wasn't a good idea, he reminded himself.

The cold air outside cut into them. It was a clear morning, the rain of the night before having cleared away. There was a light frost on the ground but the morning sun would soon burn it off. The road should be clear Jamie guided her towards the Mustang and opened the passenger door. She knew it was his car; she had been watching him and the Mustang for days now but she still squealed with delight as she sank into the leather seat.

Jamie walked round the car. Her eyes followed him. He could just see them through the lightly frosted windscreen. Suddenly, he had the feeling he might have bitten off more than he could chew. He opened his door and slipped into the car. Their breathing was filling the interior with steam that condensed on the windscreen and side windows. Body temperature was clearly higher than that outside. Orlagh leaned across towards him as he settled in and planted a kiss on his cheek. It suddenly got warmer. He started the engine and leaned back. Soon, the heater would clear the windows and they would be off. Orlagh smiled in anticipation of what she expected at their destination. She had no idea.

Chapter Seventy-nine

He was almost there. Too soon to congratulate himself that he hadn't been side-tracked on route but a feeling of relief was building in him; almost as much as the feeling that he might not be able to go through with his plan. But what then? What did he do with Orlagh Duggan?

The talk on the journey had surprised him. As they settled in, Orlagh seemed to relax and the conversation moved away from the flirting and innuendo of earlier. She began to talk of her past though she was careful that the past she talked of was the fictitious Olivia Hammond's past and not Orlagh Duggan's. She was spinning him a story but much of it, he suspected, was based on fact and Orlagh's real background. He knew a little of that but, to be fair, what he knew was coloured by her recent activities. What he was learning now painted a different picture of a young woman trapped in a past she wanted to escape from.

She was bright and intelligent. She was an only child, like him, but she had been born and raised in rural Ireland. Her mother was her heroine. She had died when "Olivia" was at University and that had a profound effect on "Olivia's" life. Her father ran the family business and leaned heavily on her mother. With her mother gone her father had gone off the rails and "Olivia" had stepped in. But she wasn't her mother. She didn't have the control over her father that her mother had been able to exert. Now, she was her father's advisor and advice, she pointed out, could be ignored.

Jamie found himself liking her despite the blood on her hands. That, he mused, was exactly what he hadn't wanted to happen. Liking someone and then threatening to do what he had in mind didn't sit well.

She had finished her own life story by the time they reached Luss on the banks of Loch Lomond. Only once on the journey had she hesitated and that, tellingly, had been when they passed the junction with the A817. Jamie had been waiting for a reaction. He got it. She seemed to drift away from him for a while, her mind on other things - which it clearly was – and was lost in her thoughts. He didn't intrude. Who knew what she was thinking and probing could do more damage than good.

After Luss, she was back in control of herself. She began to ask questions of him. It was time for his falsehoods, all well-rehearsed. Again, much of what he told her was based on his real background which reinforced his belief that she had given him much of hers. He was an only son, born and brought up in Glasgow. He had been a welder, had married, lost his first wife and married again. He spoke of Kate and his children but kept it brief. Orlagh knew he was married, he couldn't avoid it, but people contemplating adultery tended not to discuss their spouses with their intended paramour. He told her he too had gone to university, studied languages and had worked as an interpreter for a while. He had lived in France. He was now working with a company that found property for international clients and that's what he was doing today.

Most of the story was true and, because of that, easy to respond to. If questioned, his answers were automatic; not stilted or vague. He suspected Orlagh worked on the same principle. The best lies contain about 90% truth.

They stopped at the top of the Rest and be Thankful. The morning sun was out and they stood together looking back down the mountainside in the direction of Arrochar and the torpedo testing range on Loch Long. There was a chill in the air but the sun was warm on their faces. They stood side by side, Orlagh's arm interlinked with his as they watched the shadows cast by drifting clouds move irresistibly across the landscape until finally absorbed into the deep gloom on the western slopes of the mountains. The sight was breathtaking. Jamie had seen it before but it always filled him with awe. Orlagh seemed transported. Looking at her, her face full of innocent wonder, he found it hard to believe she was who she was.

They finished the last part of the journey in relative silence. Only relative silence. Talk had reverted to flirting and innuendo mode. Orlagh probably felt comfortable with that, Jamie thought. He, on the other hand, didn't.

The cottage looked deserted. He had insisted on that. No fire, no smoke from the chimney, no smell of burning wood. Conor and Liam would have heard the Mustang; everyone within half a mile would have heard it, he mused.

'It's beautiful,' Orlagh said, surprising him. 'I can see why someone would want to buy it; it's so peaceful.'

Not for long, Jamie reflected grimly. Soon, Doherty's screams would shatter the tranquillity. After that, hers? He hoped not; he really did. But it didn't matter. The chances of anyone hearing were minimal. A dark memory suddenly intruded... Lucie with Kelman in Carr Wood the night he raped her. "Scream all you like" he told her, "nobody can hear you". If he did this he was no better than Kelman.

Orlagh was out of the car now, drawing in the cold fresh air. She was smiling at him. That didn't help. He had never been close to any of his targets, not personally anyway. His kills had always been at close quarters, sure, but he hadn't known any of his targets. This time it was different. His resolve was evaporating. He had to steel himself.

He climbed out of the Mustang and forced a smile. She's the key, he reminded himself. *She has all the information needed to clean up this whole mess in that beautiful head of hers and I'm the only one who can get it from her. The time for self-recrimination is later.* He took the house key from his jacket pocket and handed it to her. 'I'll let you do the honours,' he said.

Orlagh smiled coyly and turned to the door. It was a big, old fashioned lock and a big old fashioned key, about three inches long with a ring at one end encircling a heart. She looked at it a moment, smiled, showed him the heart and then, very carefully, inserted it into the lock. She turned it, expecting resistance, but it rotated smoothly, its teeth engaging with the grooves in the lock. It might have been old fashioned but it was well oiled. There was a loud click as the lock disengaged. She turned to him, smiling archly, then pushed it open.

She didn't see him at first in the dim interior but his struggles caught her attention. Doherty was sitting in the centre of the room, naked, though she couldn't see that just yet. For now, he was just a vague form set in the darkness. His arms were twisted behind his back and his were legs bound to the legs of his chair. The furniture and rugs had been moved exactly as he had asked and the curtains pulled closed. It was cold, freezing cold and Jamie saw Orlagh shiver. Was it the temperature or the atmosphere that he had created that induced her trembling, he wondered. He hoped it was the latter. He wanted her terrified from the start and the place did look just as it was supposed to; terrifying. Conor and Liam had done well.

It took her a moment to react. She hesitated, saw the struggling shape of Doherty, heard the incoherent gurgling from behind the gag, and then turned back, her brow knitting worriedly. She saw the smile on Jamie's face but it wasn't the pleasant, heart melting smile she had witnessed the night before and in the car on the way here. It was a cold, detached smile. And then she saw the Walther.

'I'm sorry Orlagh,' he said, sounding like he really meant it.

The use of her name registered immediately. She drew her brow together. She knew she was in trouble. 'What's going on here?' she asked, surprising herself by keeping her voice steady. 'Why have you brought me here? And who's Orlagh? You're frightening me Michael,' she went on, her voice rising. She threw a look back over her shoulder at the struggling form in the centre of the room and gave a little shudder.

Jamie eased her backwards into the room, the Walther pointing directly at her midriff. She couldn't see his face clearly now, his features in darkness with the sunlight behind him. She saw his free arm rise to his left, heard a soft click, and the room was filled with light.

'It's over Orlagh,' Jamie said softly. 'We know all about the attack...'

'What attack?' she blustered. 'This is madness. I don't know what you're talking about. My name is Olivia. You've got me mixed up with someone else.'

Jamie's smile was still in place. He saw her tense, ready to spring at him, then regain control. She seemed to sag and then began to sob. It was a masterful performance. 'I'm not this Orlagh person, whoever she is,' she said. 'I don't know about any attack and you're scaring me. Please, you have to believe me.'

The chairs and table had been moved against the walls. Jamie indicated one of the easy chairs and pointed her to it. 'Sit down,' he instructed. He didn't shout but his voice carried all the authority it needed. She sat down and only then looked at the man tied to the chair in the middle of the room. He lay slumped forward in the chair now, his face and upper body badly bruised but no more than that. She recognised him immediately and her shoulders sagged imperceptibly. 'You know Fionn, of course,' Jamie said. 'Though I doubt you've ever had the pleasure of seeing him like this.' Orlagh was staring up at him, refusing to look at Doherty. 'Fionn's been helpful; very helpful,' he went on. 'The rest of the unit are dead... Macari, Finnegan and Fitzpatrick,' he added, throwing in the names. He was conscious of Doherty struggling more at the mention of Liam's name, fighting against his bonds and his gag. He took a step towards the hapless man and brought the Walther down in a vicious, curving swing against the Irishman's head. The struggling stopped and Doherty's head lolled forward.

'Who are you?' Orlagh pleaded, her voice quivering.

'Well, my name's not Michael, just as yours isn't Olivia,' he replied easily. 'Let's just say we're on opposing sides.'

'MI5,' she retorted, contempt creeping into her voice.

'No, not them and not SIS either, or SAS come to that. I'm a sort of special trouble-shooter and that's why we're here. I want some information from you... and we can do it the hard way, or the easy way; it's up to you.' He kept his voice steady, conversational even. He could threaten without raising his voice. 'Fionn told us most of it... the hi-jack, the arms cache in Dumbarton... the SAS will have taken that out by now, by the way... and then there's the lorry load of explosives,' he added after a heartbeat.

'If you know all that you don't need me. There's nothing more I can tell you,' she said contemptuously. 'And even if there was, I wouldn't.'

Jamie gave a hollow little laugh. 'I sort of guessed that, Orlagh. But there are things you know; things I want you to tell me. I don't really want to hurt you.'

She spat at him, spittle catching him on the cheek. He wiped it away. She waited for the retaliation but there was none. He simply looked at her, pityingly. She laughed, a brittle little laugh. 'You expect me to believe that?' she said. 'You'll wait a long time before I'll tell you anything, you devious Brit bastard,' she hissed.

The initial shock had worn off and now she was ready for whatever he threw at her, he guessed. He would have to take control again.

'I think it's time I gave you a little demonstration of what's in store,' he said softly, his eyes watching her unblinkingly. 'Fionn, here, hasn't exactly volunteered to help but he doesn't really have a choice.' He waved the Walther in Doherty's direction. 'I've seen some of Fionn's handiwork first hand,' he went on. 'He's quite a dab hand when it comes to inflicting pain but I think what I have in mind takes things to a new level.'

Orlagh snorted derisively. 'If you think torturing him will get me to tell you anything, you're mistaken. He means nothing to me. Do what you like to him.' Jamie's laugh in response got to her. She was trying to rile him, get under his skin, divert him from his plan, but he seemed inured to it all. It was her who was getting annoyed and, if she was honest, a little worried. She expected to die. That came with the territory. Torture was something she hadn't expected and her blustered defiance was waning.

'Conor,' Jamie called out, taking her off guard. 'I need you to keep an eye on our guest while I get Doherty ready.'

Conor appeared in a door off to her left. He wasn't smiling. If anything, he looked a little sick, she thought.

'Ah, the American,' she said softly. 'I should have known.' Both men ignored her.

'Keep your Browning trained on her. If she moves, knee-cap her... and don't be misled, she's dangerous,' Jamie said quietly. Conor nodded.

Orlagh watched as the American withdrew the big automatic from his jacket pocket and held it loosely in his right hand. The muzzle was pointing at the ground but she was under no illusion that he would use it. Her attention moved to Jamie who had moved behind Doherty. Without warning, he hooked his arm around the man's neck and pulled, tipping him backwards. Doherty struggled against his bonds but it was pointless, she could see that. Slowly at first, Jamie began to drag the chair towards the door the American had emerged from, leaving a trail of faeces and urine on the stone floor. Doherty's head thrashed aimlessly from side to side. It was pointless. She could see the fear in his eyes and then he was gone, dragged out of sight to face whatever was behind that door. She heard something metallic being dragged across the stone floor and then there was silence. The tension in her was building. She heard someone speaking, the voice low and indistinct, and then sobbing and whimpering.

She could feel her heart racing in her rib-cage. And then the whimpering became a long, drawn out, muffled moan. That sent a shiver down her spine. She had always despised Fionn Doherty. The man was a psychopath, inhuman even, but hearing him moan like that filled her with terror. She remembered her father telling her that Fionn was useful to The Cause because he didn't know what fear was. Clearly, he had that wrong. She heard the voice again, Jamie's, clearer now, booming out from the room. He said: 'Bring her in.' That terrified her even more.

Conor Whelan stood back and waved the Browning, pointing her towards the door. She rose slowly. The American, unlike the Brit, looked nervous. She deemed it sensible not to move quickly. A 9mm bullet through the knee might be the result. She pulled her Afghan coat tightly around her and shuffled towards the door. A feeling of dread filled her. She had already guessed that was the sole purpose of this "demonstration", but she couldn't fight it.

She stopped in the doorway, the American two paces behind her. Fionn Doherty was still strapped to his chair. He had stopped whimpering but his eyes were wide, a wild look in them. A pool of urine lay on the floor beneath him and the stench of shit filled her nostrils. She raised a hand to her mouth and gagged. It was then she spotted Jamie. He was behind Fionn and he had changed into a boiler suit. His hands were hidden by two heavy leather gauntlets and in one he held what looked like helmet of sorts. In the other, he was holding a rod. He was smiling but, strangely, he seemed sad.

'Can you remember anything we talked about on the way here?' he asked, almost gently.

She could remember all of it. She had liked him then. She had been thinking about the sex that was promised. The bastard had played her. She nodded slowly.

'I told you I was a welder once,' he said. 'In fact, I did a job for your lot back in 1967 in Belfast. Opened a safe for them. Cut through the steel with an oxy-acetylene cutter. Do you know how hot a cutter like that gets?' he asked.

Orlagh shook her head. Her feeling of dread was growing, threatening to engulf her.

'6000 degrees Fahrenheit,' he said, casually, as if discussing it with an apprentice. 'As hot as Hell. It can cut through steel in minutes. Can you imagine what it would do to flesh and bone?'

She stared at him wide eyed and open mouthed. The horror invoked by the thought left her speechless. She understood now why Fionn had wet himself and was sitting in his own shit. She felt her stomach churn.

Jamie wasn't smiling now. He was deadly serious. She turned her eyes away from his look. She watched him lift his hand, the one with the helmet, and place the helmet on his head. It reminded her of a deep sea diver's helmet, dull black and heavy with an oblong glass panel in front to see through. She watched, transfixed now, as he turned to two containers standing against the wall and turned knobs on the top of each. A sickly sweet smell assaulted her olfactory nerve as the acetylene began to flow. The oxygen mixed as Jamie opened the second valve. The shock came seconds later as he flicked his Zippo and the flame at the end of the lance ignited, a bright white light burning into her irises. She felt the heat even from where she stood by the door and could only imagine what it felt like to Fionn Doherty.

As she watched, Jamie moved round Doherty and brought the lance down towards the man's right foreleg. She heard a scream and realised it came from her. 'Stop, just stop,' she yelled, trying to make him hear over the hissing of the burning gases. She couldn't see anything now, the intensity of the flame had blinded her.

Jamie turned off the gas and the room turned dark again. He smiled behind the mask. It had been easier than he thought. It seemed she had a soft side after all. If she saw his smile she would see his relief. He didn't want her to see it; not yet. He still had to get her to talk. This was only the first hurdle and he might have to go over it all again. He looked down at Doherty. The man was slumped forward in his chair, blubbering, a large blister forming on his right shin where the heat of the torch had seared his skin. There was a faint smell of burned flesh, but it could have been worse.

He placed the lance against the wall and pulled off his helmet, his hair wet with sweat. He had forgotten how hot it was working with equipment like this. Orlagh stood still where she was, her eyes following his every move. He smiled coldly and walked towards her.

She flinched as he took her by the arm and pulled away but his grip was tight. Tight, but not painfully so, she realised with surprise. She had expected force, violence even, but he gently manoeuvred her back through the door and into the big room. She realised now this was the main living room of the cottage and started to pick out the furniture in the gloom. Everything had been pushed back against the walls, chairs, tables, rugs, everything, to create the big open space she had first seen. Her eyes were adjusting to the gloom when there was a swishing sound and sunlight filled the area. She screwed her eyes tightly shut against the glare.

By the wall, the American had finished opening one set of curtains and was starting on a second. She took in her surroundings again. The curtains were in a heavy jacquard material, a deep burgundy colour. Perfect for keeping out the light and for shutting out the winter nights. The furniture was old but solid. As she watched, her arm still held by Jamie, the American began moving the furniture back into place. Moments later, she was standing by the easy chair she had been in earlier, though now it was positioned next to the big, open fireplace. The grip on her arm was still there, firm but surprisingly gentle. She took in the kindling in the grate, the newspaper twists, the framed photographs on the mantle; an older couple, a beautiful young woman with children, on her own and with a man, the American. She looked over at him. His face had changed. Before he had looked apprehensive. Now, his expression was softer but there was resolve in his eyes.

Neither of the men said anything. The younger one was clearly in charge and this whole thing had been stage managed to create fear in her. It had certainly achieved that. The silence now was another part of it. All she could hear was the incoherent gurgling of Fionn Doherty in the other room. What was going to happen to her, she wondered. She was going to die, that was a given, she assumed, but how she died was the question that filled her head now. The sight of the glowing torch in the younger man's hand, the heat of it, the sight of Fionn Doherty writhing helplessly as the white hot tip of the flame seared his skin made her shudder.

The grip on her arm relaxed. The American was lighting a fire in the grate and she watched as blue flames licked around the wood. Even flames like that could burn skin. She couldn't bear to think what the white heat of the torch would do. As she trembled she felt the grip on her arm released. She heard her captor speak.

'Sit down Orlagh,' the voice said. It was said like a friendly invitation rather than a command, the sort of thing you would say to a visitor. She looked at him. The smile was back on his face, warmer than before. He was handsome. Tall, strong and handsome, she mused, and consoled herself with the thought that she probably wasn't the only one who had been ensnared by that smile. She smiled back at him wanly. He held her future in his hands. Future, she thought, if I have one.

Jamie pulled up a seat and sat down facing her. Close but not too close. The Walther was now in his boiler suit pocket, out of sight but readily available. He smiled at her again, keeping malice out of it. He had shown her what to expect if she didn't co-operate and the message had got through. He sincerely hoped it had. He didn't want to have to do it again, this time for real.

'I want you to talk to me Orlagh,' he said softly. 'I need you to tell me where your other two ASUs are hiding out and I need you to tell me the arrangements for meeting up with the explosives.' He kept the smile in place.

'Who are you?' she asked.

'It doesn't matter who I am,' he replied quietly. 'It wouldn't make any sense to you if I told you anyway. I'm a ghost,' he added with a soft laugh.

'You'll kill me anyway... what do I gain by telling you anything?' It wasn't said defiantly, Jamie noted, more with sad acceptance of the inevitable.

'I'm going to kill Doherty,' he said. 'You? I don't know,' he added thoughtfully.

She laughed for the first time since she had left the car. 'I don't think so,' she said disdainfully. 'You've lied and manipulated me all the way through this.'

He nodded slowly. 'Aye, I have, but that was necessary. Killing you isn't necessary unless you make it so,' he replied.

She looked into his eyes, trying to read what was behind them. She wasn't the first to do that either, she imagined. There was sadness in them, she thought. Was that a sign that he was lying to her again or was it something else. 'If you're going to kill Fionn, you have to kill me. I'm a loose end.'

He nodded again. 'Yes, you are,' he admitted. 'But there are lots of ways of tying up loose ends; killing you is only one of them.'

'Then you could apply the same logic to Fionn,' she retorted.

Jamie laughed. The ice was back in it and the look in his eyes had changed. 'Nah,' he said. 'Fionn Doherty and I have history. I promised someone I would kill him and I'm going to keep my promise.'

She watched him as he leaned back in his chair, his eyes softening again. The fire had warmed the room now and she was feeling the heat beneath her Afghan coat. Tiny beads of sweat were forming on her brow. She opened the coat, revealing her long shapely thighs and the formidable curve of her breasts beneath the tight sweater. She didn't do it in any hope of distracting him. She knew that wouldn't work. She just needed to cool down.

'Take it off if you're too warm,' he said, smiling and trying to ignore the obvious attractions. 'I'm a little hot myself,' he added. He was a master of understatement. He got up from his chair and began to strip off the boiler suit, taking the pistol from his pocket and placing it on the mantle well out of Orlagh's reach. He didn't think she would be foolish enough to try for it but why take the risk. He stepped out of the black overalls and retrieved the Walther, tucking it into his belt at the small of his back, its usual resting place. Finished, he sat down and waited.

Orlagh hesitated a moment then pushed herself up out of the easy chair and followed his example, peeling off the heavy, ornate coat and laying it over the back of her chair. She stood facing him, like a model posing for a magazine photoshoot, then sat back down. Jamie caught Conor's eye and suppressed a grin. He could read his friend's mind but now wasn't the time or the place.

Orlagh sat down again, crossed her legs and placed her hands in her lap. She looked at him tentatively then dropped her eyes. 'What do you want from me?' she asked.

'I want the safe houses where your ASUs are and I want the man bringing in the explosives... If I'm right, that'll be the Yank newspaper reporter.'

Her head came up sharply. 'He told you about him too,' she said, sounding surprised. She was referring to Fionn, of course.

Jamie didn't disabuse her. He simply nodded.

'You could wait and get them all together,' she suggested.

He nodded again. 'Aye, we could, but that would be a bloody mess. It's better if we take them down when they least expect it. And I want the Yank before anyone else gets to him.' He saw her brow knitting together as she tried to work that one out. She couldn't. He helped her out.

'About a year ago I was sent to a nice little place called Kiltyclogher. Not exactly a tourist hotspot but it was popular when I was there. A few people came down from Belfast to welcome me and we had a big party at a guy called Malone's house. I was hoping to have a private chat with Mr Malone but, unfortunately, Fionn got there before me.' He paused for a moment. She was taking it all in, her eyes told him that, but they told him something else as well; she knew what he was describing.

He went on with the story. 'When I got there the party was over and the other guys were outside. I couldn't see them, but I knew they were there. Anyway, poor Mr Malone was past talking. Fionn had obviously passed the time enjoying a cigarette or two and in the absence of an ashtray had stubbed them out on him... I didn't bother counting the number of burns.' He gave a short laugh. 'Cigarettes aren't quite as effective as an oxy-acetylene torch,' he continued, 'so they didn't get what they were after... So they waited for me, thinking I might be able to help them out.

'That's when I became acquainted with Fionn Doherty and Liam Fitzpatrick,' he carried on, his voice take on a harder edge. 'I was stupid. I knew they were waiting for me that night but I went in just the same. I should have walked away.'

'How did you know?' she asked, interrupting his flow.

He laughed again. 'I just knew. I've got this sixth sense that tells me when I'm in the shit. It was screaming at me that night.'

'Then why didn't you just leave it, like you said?'

'Good question. I don't know... Maybe I thought the mission was bigger than me.'

'And was it?' His face took on a strange look before he replied. A sardonic smile, she thought.

'I think you already know the answer to that Orlagh,' he said softly.

She dipped her head to avoid eye contact and tried to put that to the side, but she sensed he could read her mind. Why deny it, she thought. 'They said you were dead,' she said, lifting her head and looking him in the eye again.

'Aye, I imagine they did,' he said, almost as though thinking aloud. 'To be fair, I'm sure they believed it,' he continued, leaning forward in his chair, closer to her, and lifting the hair on the left side of his head. He turned his head slightly to the right.

The ugly, ragged scar left by Liam's bullet stared back at her, a deep, white fissure. Orlagh gave an involuntary gasp and saw him smile.

'Not very pretty, is it?' he said, letting his hair fall back into place. 'I hope I never go bald; I'll scare my kids with that... a bit like Frankenstein's monster. But that wasn't all. I took a 9mm bullet through the top of my thigh. That scar's impressive too. Pity you didn't get a chance to see it,' he went on, grinning now. 'In fact, that was worse than the head wound. I nearly bled to death from that one.'

There was silence between them for a moment before Orlagh spoke again. 'They were only doing what they thought right,' she said defensively.

'Oh aye, we can agree on that point,' Jamie replied, the grim smile back on his face. 'But stealing watches from corpses and pissing on them is taking things beyond that.' He paused for a moment, eyeing her speculatively. What he read from her expression told him she agreed with his last sentiment.

Conor was watching closely. He was becoming alarmed by Jamie's casual approach to the Irish woman now. He drew Jamie a warning look but got only an imperceptible shake of the head in response.

'I've killed a lot of people Orlagh. That's not a boast, just a statement of fact. It's not something I'm proud of, but when I've killed, I've done it quickly and cleanly and I didn't stop to steal their jewellery or piss on them. Like you said, they were only doing what they thought right, fighting for their cause... Like you are now. I respect that... but Fionn Doherty, well...' He left that hanging there. But his message was clear. You I respect, Fionn Doherty deserves none.

Silence fell between them again. Conor, lounging near the window, watched and waited. The sun was beating in through the glass now and dust mites danced in the air as the room grew warmer. He was still reeling from Jamie's sudden disclosure. It was as if he had decided to treat Orlagh Duggan like an equal which, on reflection, perhaps she was. They were both soldiers fighting in the same war. Still, it was a risky ploy... gentle persuasion was unlikely to work. This broad, from all accounts, was hard-line terrorist. People like that tended to have a blinkered view. It was their way or no way.

He recalled his Vietnam days. They tried that there too; winning "hearts and minds" it was called. It didn't work in 'Nam, he doubted it would work now.

'Were you going to take part in the attack?' Jamie asked, breaking the silence, and changing direction. Orlagh averted her eyes but nodded. 'What did you hope to achieve?'

'We were going to hold the British Government to ransom... force them to negotiate unification.'

Jamie laughed softly and shook his head. 'And killing hundreds, maybe thousands, of innocent people was going to achieve that how exactly.' He saw her brow knit curiously. 'That's what would happen when a massive bomb scattered nuclear waste into the atmosphere. You and your boys would be the first to die but the fallout would spread over a big area. People would die; lots of people, men, women, kids and all of them painfully.' She laughed. It sounded a little hysterical, he thought.

'That wasn't the plan,' she said. 'The only people who would die would be the men escorting the convoy. They're soldiers. That's the risk they take; just like us.'

Jamie stared at her pensively. Either she was bluffing or she really believed that. If she believed it, what was the alternative plan... or had she and her father been conned? 'You were going to hi-jack a lorry load of nuclear reactor waste and blow it up. That was the plan, Orlagh.'

'You're wrong,' she retorted defiantly. 'We would gain nothing from that. We would be pariahs.'

Jamie smiled grimly. That assessment was spot on. 'So what *was* the plan?' he asked

Conor held his breath. If there was an alternative strategy would Orlagh divulge it? More to the point, could they do anything about it?

A moment passed in silence. Both men kept their eyes on Orlagh. Finally, she gave a sigh. 'I don't suppose it matters now,' she said quietly. 'It's not going to happen. The plan was to stop the waste convoy, attach our trailer with the bomb to one of the tractor units and then run it back to the base with one of the escort vehicles. If necessary, we would take out the guardhouse, and run the truck as far as possible into the base... right against the weapons store. And then we would demand that negotiations start.'

Jamie laughed aloud. 'You're crazy; you're *all* fuckin' crazy. You'd never get past the guards. That's not just any naval base, it's the British Navy's Nuclear Submarine Base. The security around that place is impenetrable. Who sold you that croc of shit?'

Orlagh stared back at him defiantly but doubt was beginning to gnaw at her. She was going over things in her head; things she had accepted without question at the time. She had never trusted the American but her father thought he was the messiah. It wouldn't have mattered of she had raised doubts, her father would have gone with this anyway. The prize was too great. Suddenly, she knew they had been duped. It all began to make sense. They were all supposed to die. Kevin *bloody* Sparke had set them up... And he would walk away.

Chapter Eighty

'Kevin Sparke,' she said softly, her voice clear. 'His name is Kevin Sparke... He's an American journalist; he's also been supplying us with guns and explosives for a while now.' She was looking Jamie straight in the eye. 'He passed us information too. It was him who told us a Brit was coming for Gerry Malone.' Her admission took Conor by surprise, less so Jamie.

'And the explosives? I take it he doesn't want to be in for the kill,' Jamie said sardonically, his voice matching hers. It was a bad choice of words but Orlagh didn't seem to notice. 'So what's the arrangement?'

She didn't hesitate. 'There's a farm south of Glasgow, Torhead farm, it's isolated, out on the moor between Glasgow and Stranraer. We were to pick up the lorry there.' Jamie smiled calmly. Conor, conversely, bit his lip. 'It never really stood up,' Orlagh continued. 'He's an American. What did he expect to gain from this?'

'Yeah, I was wondering the same thing,' Conor mused aloud, getting involved for the first time. 'Either way you play it, you and your people become outcasts. If it's the bomb blowing up the nuclear waste the contamination would spread as far as Holy Loch and beyond; if it's the threat of blowing up the Polaris arsenal at Faslane the public reaction here and the political fallout would achieve the same result. The USS Canopus would have to up-anchor and sail off down the Clyde within days. That's very un-American whatever way you look at it.'

Jamie refused to be side-tracked. 'When is the hand-over?' he demanded.

Orlagh smiled bleakly. 'He'll be at the farm on Saturday; the nineteenth. The plan is to call me from there...'

'Call you where?' Jamie interrupted.

'At the hotel. We meet, he gives me the keys of the truck and the instructions for arming the bomb and then he leaves me to it.' She didn't mention the fact that Sparke hoped they would be doing more than just meeting.

'But you won't be there,' Jamie mused aloud.

'No, I won't,' she said, smiling. She wouldn't have to fight Sparke off and that was a bonus. Probably the only good thing to come out of this mess.

'So what will he do?'

'He'll leave the truck at the farm and disappear, I suppose. If he doesn't get to speak to me he'll assume I've been compromised.'

Jamie laughed coldly. 'That's one way of putting it,' he said. He paused, holding her eyes. 'I'll need the exact location of this farm,' he continued. 'I need to scout it out before he arrives... How many men at the farm?'

Orlagh shook her head slowly before replying. It was one thing giving up Sparke; he had set them up. It was something else playing Judas to the volunteers at the farm. 'Three; the farmer and his two sons. His wife is there too. What will happen to them?' she asked.

'Are they armed?'

'No.'

'What do they know about the operation?'

'Nothing. All they've been told is to expect a lorry that has to be hidden for a few days.'

'They don't know what's in the trailer?'

'No, and they're not stupid enough to look inside.'

Jamie smiled at her reassuringly. 'In that case, nothing will happen to them... unless they get in the way. What they don't know won't hurt them... But if you're lying to me Orlagh...' He left her to work it out.

'I'm not lying,' she protested.

He nodded slowly, accepting her word on it. That left only the addresses of the safe houses but that, he knew, would be a harder nut to crack. Still, there was no point in putting it off. 'I need the safe houses,' he said.

She shook her head. 'I can't,' she said plaintively. 'I can't betray them.'

Jamie gazed down at her. He had expected that response but his expression gave nothing away. He was about to respond when Fionn Doherty regained consciousness. The noise made all three in the room turn. Orlagh gave a visible shudder. Jamie remained expressionless. Conor pushed himself away from the wall near the window, ready to quieten Doherty again but Jamie stopped him with a quick shake of the head. Conor leaned back against the wall. The noise from the bathroom continued, louder now. A mix of grunts, moans and gasps for air.

'Loyalty is a great thing, Orlagh,' Jamie said. 'But misplaced loyalty is a waste. Would you have felt the same for Fionn there?' he asked, nodding in the direction the bathroom. She didn't respond. 'He didn't take too long to give you up,' Jamie continued quietly, his voice barely audible over the din. 'You know your boys better than I do,' he went on. 'How many of them are as loyal as Fionn, do you think?' He paused to let her think about that. 'When you get right down to it, how many of them would lay their lives on the line for you? One, two... all of them? Or none of them.'

He turned away from her. Fionn Doherty's clothes lay in an untidy bundle near the bathroom door. He stooped down and scooped them up then stepped into the room, out of Orlagh's sight. He threw the bundle into the lap of the struggling man who stopped his noise and glared up at him, an animal frenzy in his eyes.

Jamie bent low, close to the man. 'I'm going to untie you Fionn and you're going to get dressed,' he said softly. 'If you try to take off the gag I'll hurt you much more than you've been hurt up to now. Understand? Just nod,' he said casually.

Doherty nodded resentfully. Jamie undid the binding on the man's writs and stood back, the Walther back in his right hand. A wounded animal is often more dangerous, he mused, and Doherty was a wounded animal. 'Now, untie your legs and get dressed,' he commanded.

The Irishman bent forward and undid the ropes binding his ankles to the chair legs. The stench of faeces was almost unbearable but Jamie ignored it. Stiffly, Doherty pushed himself up, his anger simmering. Slowly, he began to dress, his hate filled eyes never leaving Jamie. The vest and underpants covered the mess on his lower body but did nothing to kill the smell. He pulled on his trousers and then his shirt, his movements slow and deliberate. Jamie stayed well back. The only weapon of note in the room available to Doherty was the chair but he would never make it. He saw Doherty think about it then come to the same conclusion. He smiled. 'Good choice Fionn,' he said softly. The Irishman drew him a hateful look. 'Put on your shoes,' Jamie went on. 'We're going for a walk.' Doherty knelt down and slipped on his shoes, loosely tying the laces. Jamie picked up the man's jacket and threw it to him. 'Don't want you getting cold,' he said wryly.

Doherty slipped on the donkey jacket and pulled it tightly round him. Jamie waved the pistol towards the door. 'Out,' he said... 'And remember, not a sound.'

Orlagh looked up as they emerged from the Bathroom, Doherty in the lead. She could see his face better now. The bruises were livid and his jaw was swollen. Blood seeped from below the gag that was bound tightly across his mouth. His eyes darted around the room. There wasn't fear in them, just unbridled loathing and hatred and she shuddered at the thought that some of that loathing and hatred was aimed at her. She looked away from him.

Jamie looked enquiringly at Conor. The American read his mind. 'Down towards the loch,' he said. 'About a quarter mile. There's a copse about fifty yards from the shore. It's inaccessible other than through the garden out there. No one ever visits. The locals say it's haunted.' He grinned coldly. 'Maybe after today it will be,' he added.

Jamie nodded slowly. 'Okay. Look after our guest,' he said. 'I won't be long.'

Orlagh watched as he ushered Fionn Doherty out the door into the sunlight. She had the feeling it was the last time the sun would shine on Fionn. She looked down into her lap and thought about her predicament. She was a woman in a man's world. Fionn Doherty resented her. How many of the others felt the same? All of them probably, she thought. Her life was hanging by a thread and it was in the hands of the man who had just left... and she had a decision to make.

Chapter Eighty-one

Jamie was back in twenty minutes. The first thing Orlagh noticed was that Fionn Doherty wasn't with him; the second was his mud covered boots. She had spent the twenty minutes arguing with herself. She wasn't winning any arguments.

'Nice spot,' Jamie said, addressing Conor. 'And far enough away from the house not to be a problem.'

'Yeah, I thought so too,' Conor replied, laughing awkwardly.

Jamie turned to Orlagh. 'You want to go see it?' he asked softly.

She looked away from him and felt tears building up behind her eyes. Was this it, she wondered. This man was an mystery. Part of him seemed caring and gentle, another part, a bigger part it seemed now, was cold and ruthless. She had seen both sides of him. Her big problem was in deciding whether she could trust the warm, caring and gentle side. She was about to find out, she realised.

She decided to answer his question first. She kept her eyes down in her lap. 'No, I don't want to see it. I don't want to go anywhere near it,' she said. She waited for his response. She waited a long time. When she looked up he was watching her, smiling. 'What will happen to me?' she murmured.

He was still smiling. 'I don't know,' he said. 'It isn't up to me.' He shrugged. 'But, if you want my opinion, I think you've got a better chance of seeing your next birthday if you give me the safe houses.'

Orlagh looked away again. Eight men. Was it worth it? Was *she* worth it? He was still watching her... examining her more like. It was as if he was reading her mind. He was, she soon discovered.

'I know what you're thinking,' he said softly, almost gently. She looked up at him again and realised he was reading her like a book.

'Let's go for a walk,' he continued, taking her heavy Afghan coat from the chair and handing it to her. She backed away, her eyes wide, the fear surfacing. He laughed softly. 'It's alright,' he said. 'I'll bring you back in one piece... Promise.' She watched him take his automatic pistol from his pocket and offer it to Conor. 'Does that make you feel any better?' he asked.

'What if I run?' she demanded, plucking up the courage from somewhere.

He shrugged nonchalantly. 'Where would you run to? And why would you? I just want to talk, and when I'm done, I'll leave you to your decision.'

She took her coat from him and eased her arms into it before pulling it tightly shut and fastening all the buttons. He said nothing, simply turned to the door and held it open. She felt the cold hit her again and shivered. He was watching but gave no indication he had noticed. Instead, he walked past her out into the cold air and waited for her to follow.

She stepped out from the house and breathed in the cold, fresh air. She knew it was her imagination playing tricks on her but she still had the smell of burning flesh in her nostrils from earlier. He was ahead of her, walking slowly down the drive to the roadway beyond, his back turned to her. She looked around. The loch was about four or five hundred yards away just as the American had said. There was a house off to the left, further away, and someone was at home. Smoke rose from the chimney before being whipped away by a strengthening wind. She thought about running but he was right... Where could she run to? The distant house? And what would she say when she got there? She laughed to herself. Anything she said would just make matters worse.

Jamie was still walking. He was giving her all the time in the world. He reached the gate leading to the main road and stopped, throwing a glance back over his shoulder. She was watching him. He smiled and waited. He knew she would come and she did. As she started walking, so did he, turning left onto the main road and heading towards the village and the lochside. He was still ahead of her.

Orlagh quickened her pace, making a conscious effort to catch up. Something told her being out here with him was important but the whole situation was crazy. Bizarre, even, she thought. One minute he was threatening her with unspeakable violence and now, here he was, calm as you like, strolling ahead of her down to the village as though none of that had happened. He wasn't going to kill her; she was sure of that. She couldn't say where her certainty came from but it was there. The threat of torture too had been just that... a threat. It had been theatrical and, God knows, it had frightened her. But that was what it was supposed to do.

She was with him when they entered the village. It was really just a scattering of small cottages with the odd two-storey house, smoke drifting up from chimneys into the cold, still air. She could smell the burning wood, feel the cold nip the skin on her face and see the sun shimmering on the still waters of the loch ahead. She suddenly felt alive and, more than anything now, she wanted to stay alive. She saw him looking at her, a smile playing enigmatically at the corners of his mouth. She had reached her decision and he had won; and he knew he had.

He led her through the village. They met no one. It was as if the population had been spirited away, she mused, and maybe they had. He was capable of anything, it seemed.

'Where are you taking me?' she asked. If she had asked that earlier, she would have been apprehensive. Not now. A feeling of calm had settled on her.

'Down to the loch,' he replied easily. 'It's quiet and we can talk. Fresh start,' he added.

She nodded and followed. He was taking her away from the torture house, away from where he had brutalised Fionn Doherty, away from the horror. Now it was up to her.

They reached the lochside. Like the village, it was deserted. The sun danced on the tiny ripples on the water, reflecting up into their eyes with an intensity that blinded. Jamie found a rocky outcrop and chose two large boulders, wiping the dampness left by the frost off with his hands. He sat on the rougher of the two, waving her in the direction of the other, a big, round flat-topped stone. She eased herself down onto it, bending her knees and pulling her Afghan coat tightly closed.

He rummaged in his pockets and brought out a battered packet of cigarettes and a scuffed lighter. She hadn't smoked in a long time but now seemed the right moment to start again. He offered the pack across and she nodded. She took one of the cigarettes and placed the filter tip between her lips, waiting patiently as he flipped the top of the lighter and flicked the small abrasive dial against the flint. The spark ignited the petrol soaked wick and the flame rose high. She pulled hard on the cigarette, drawing in the nicotine laced smoke, and gave a cough. She saw him smile, lift the flame to his own cigarette and light it.

They sat for a moment in silence and looked out over the loch to the shore beyond. Trees were everywhere. Tall evergreen conifers interspaced with the bare branches of deciduous giants. Soon, buds would begin to appear on those naked branches and leaves would spring from them. New life.

Jamie broke the quiet. 'I brought you here to tell you some things,' he started. 'My plan was to show you that sometimes we're not masters of our own destinies... sometimes we have to do things we'd rather not do.' He let out a short snorted laugh. 'I certainly have,' he went on. He paused, his eyes now fixed on her. 'I'm not going to kill you Orlagh,' he said softly. 'My orders were to get the information about the safe houses from you and the plan for delivery of the explosives... "by whatever means necessary". The performance back there was a charade. 'I wasn't going to torture you.'

'I know,' she replied, smiling for the first time. 'But it's not up to you, is it?' He smiled back, sadly she thought. If he was surprised by her statement he didn't show it.

'No, it isn't up to me; it's up to you,' he said. He paused again and she sensed hesitation. He drew heavily on his cigarette, inhaled and then blew the smoke back out through his nose, two long streams of white that drifted away in the air. 'I did something once,' he said softly and Orlagh sensed a confession. It didn't quite amount to that but it painted a picture. 'I thought I'd got away with it but the past has a habit of catching up when you least expect it. You probably feel a bit like that just now,' he went on. 'I was given a choice... do things for a certain organisation or face a life behind bars, away from my wife and my family. I probably wouldn't have seen daylight again,' he continued, a wry smile now in place on his face.

'What did you do?' she asked, automatically.

'I killed a few men. The fact that I had good reason to kill them is irrelevant. Even if you kill bad guys you go to jail...' he paused again and laughed now. 'Unless, of course, you're working for the right people. The man who gave me the choice is one of those "right people" and my gut tells me he'd be prepared to make you the same offer.' He left that sitting there.

They sat quietly again, looking around them, gazing at the beauty that surrounded them, like a couple of lost tourists. Jamie finished his cigarette and flicked the stub into the water that lapped the stone shore a few feet away.

'What would I have to do?' Orlagh asked tentatively.

'Sell your soul,' he replied. He wasn't laughing. 'You're a beautiful, intelligent woman, Orlagh. It would be a shame to throw it all away on a lost cause. I'm not talking about the dream of a united Ireland,' he added quickly. 'I'm talking about this failed attack. That's the lost cause. It isn't going to happen, and the men you're trying to protect are already dead; they just don't know it. If you tell me where they're holed up, they'll die there. If you don't, they'll be killed when they go to pick up their weapons and uniforms in Dumbarton or when they try to mount the attack. Either way, they're finished. You won't be giving them away. Someone else has already done that. So why sacrifice yourself?'

Orlagh looked away. She was wrestling with her conscience again. His words made sense but they didn't make it right. But then, did anything make things right? And he was right; she would be sacrificing herself for nothing. She reached her decision almost without thinking. '13 Ashgill Road, in Milton, Glasgow. It's a semi-detached house. Four of the men are there,' she murmured quietly. 'The others are in a flat in Garngad, but...' She hesitated, remembering clearly the young girl who had opened the door, her baby clutched tightly in her arms.

'But what?' Jamie probed gently.

'There's a girl and a baby in that flat. She lives there with her husband. Her man doesn't know anything about the plan and neither does she. They were asked to put up four men for a few weeks. They agreed... what else could they do?'

Jamie nodded slowly. 'If I promise you they won't be harmed will you take my word for it?'

She looked at him searchingly, her eyes staring into his. She nodded, mimicking his gesture. 'Yes,' she said quietly.

'Then I promise you, nothing will happen to them,' he said simply.

It was enough. 'The flat is at 22 Charles Street. That's in Garngad. It's on the 15th floor and the name on the door is Milliken.' She looked at him pleadingly before going on. 'If anything happens to the family...'

He stopped her with his hand raised in front of her. 'If they know nothing they won't be harmed. I give you my word.' He was staring at her as if willing her to read between the lines. 'But if it turns out they *do* know the plan...' He didn't finish. He didn't need to. Orlagh knew exactly what was coming.

'They don't,' she said, closing the subject.

Jamie heaved himself up off his rocky seat and stretched. 'In that case they've got nothing to worry about and neither do you. Come on,' he said, offering her his hand to help her up. 'I've got a call to make and you might as well hear it.'

They stood together in the red telephone box in the centre of the village. Unlike the phone boxes in Glasgow and other big cities, it was clean, fresh and in perfect working order. For most of the people of Lochgoilhead it was probably their only link with the outside world so they looked after it. In other respects, it was just like the phone boxes in Glasgow; small and claustrophobic. One person filled it comfortably; two were generally uncomfortable, unless they were only there for a quickie, Jamie reflected, amused. But that wasn't going to happen with Orlagh.

He leaned an elbow on the main box and fed coins into the slot while Orlagh pressed her back against the side windows. They made an odd sight, he imagined. He dialled the numbers quickly, forcing the dial back with his finger each time instead of allowing it to return normally. The usual clicks came back down the line followed by the ring tone and then Clara's voice.

'Whitelaw,' she said abruptly.

'It's me,' Jamie responded. 'I've got the information we've been waiting for. Is the Old Man around?' His clipped response and the tone of his voice told Clara he wasn't alone.

'Yes, he's here,' she confirmed. 'Where are you?'

'Lochgoilhead,' he answered shortly. 'I need to get an assurance from him before he sends in the troops,' he added.

'Okay, hang on; I'll get him.'

He heard her footsteps on the parquet floor as usual, the noise of her door opening, muted conversation and then footsteps returning. The door closed then.

'Hello Michael,' Sir Charles greeted him. 'Congratulations. Did you get it all?'

Jamie ignored the praise. It meant nothing. 'Yes, all of it, but there's a proviso.'

'And the girl? What have you done with her?' the Brigadier carried on, ignoring the "proviso".

'I haven't done anything with her, Brigadier. She's here with me now, actually. What would you like me to do with her?' he asked, his eyes never leaving Orlagh. He saw her stiffen. Saw the fear resurface. Pity that, he thought, but it was necessary. He knew how to play Sir Charles, she didn't.

There was a longish pause while the Brigadier thought it out. Orlagh's trepidation mounted. Jamie relaxed a little.

'I take it she has been co-operative,' Sir Charles came back at last.

'Very. That's why she's still here.' He was stating the obvious.

'So, what do you suggest we do with her?'

Jamie laughed softly. 'You're reneging on your responsibility, Brigadier. You take the decisions, not me.'

It was the Brigadier's turn to laugh. It sounded dry. 'Yes, and you ignore them Michael,' he said quietly.

'Well, you know me.'

'Yes, I do, only too well. But back to my question... what do you suggest I do with her?'

Jamie smiled again, easing Orlagh's tension a little. He had noticed the subtle change from "we" to "I". That wouldn't have registered with Orlagh but as far as Jamie was concerned, it was a step in the right direction. 'I think she could be useful to you,' he replied. 'The way I was useful; the way Corkscrew was useful.'

'Don't speak in the past tense, Michael. You're still useful. You've redeemed yourself. I take it the proviso you mentioned earlier has to do with Miss Duggan,' Sir Charles went on, making no comment in response to Jamie's suggestion.

'Yes, and no. It doesn't relate to her personally. She asked me for an assurance in relation to one of the safe houses. I gave it.'

'Did you indeed! And now you're passing it on to me, are you?'

'That's right,' Jamie replied shortly.

'So, what is this assurance?'

'One of the safe houses is a family home... a man, woman and baby live in it. They haven't got a clue as to why the men are there. They were made an offer they couldn't refuse, so to speak. They're not to be harmed.'

'And if I refuse?'

Jamie laughed frostily. 'Then I won't give you the address.'

Orlagh's eyes opened wide in surprise. He kept dumbfounding her and he'd just done it again.

'You're insufferable, Michael; insufferable and insubordinate,' Sir Charles retorted, sounding just a little irritated.

'Aye, you've said that before, but you still use me. Now, tell me, do we have your assurance?'

'And if they know about the plan after all?'

'I've already gone into that. Miss Duggan knows the consequences but she's adamant they don't know a thing.'

'Alright. You have my assurance,' he said finally. 'Now, give me the addresses and the information on the explosives delivery.'

Before Jamie could reply, Orlagh grabbed his arm and pulled the phone from his ear. 'Do you trust him?' she demanded anxiously.

Jamie smiled and shook the phone free from her grip. 'Yes, I trust him,' he answered. 'I might not always like him, but I trust him,' he went on, knowing Sir Charles was listening to every word. 'He has never gone back on his word to me... and he won't now. Okay?' Orlagh nodded.

'Okay Brigadier; here we go,' Jamie started, and then went on to give chapter and verse. When he finished there was a moment's quiet before the Brigadier responded. His words didn't come as a surprise to Jamie but Orlagh's anxiety went through the ceiling.

'I'll arrange matters surrounding the safe houses,' he said. 'I'll leave you to deal with Mr Sparke, if that is his name. If the information Miss Duggan has given you is correct, you've got three days to prepare. I take it you're still in touch with your American friend?' he went on.

'Uh-huh,' Jamie responded, without going into detail.

'In that case, perhaps it would be a good idea to involve him in this. Sparke, after all, is supposed to be a countryman of his. I'll speak to his superior in Washington. As for Miss Duggan, I think she and I should have a little chat. Stay in Lochgoilhead for the moment. I'll have a helicopter pick her up. After that, you'd better get moving. I'll head up to Glasgow and we'll meet on Friday. The Central Hotel, two thirty. Bring Mr Whelan with you. Clear?'

'Clear.'

'Good, I'll see you on Friday... and well done,' Sir Charles added before cutting the line.

'Aye, right,' Jamie murmured, smiling sourly.

Orlagh was still anxious. It was printed on her face. 'Where is he taking me?' she asked.

'London, I imagine,' Jamie replied. 'And you can start thinking about your future,' he went on. 'You've still got one. He wouldn't be sending a chopper for you if you didn't.'

'Would you have shot me if he told you to?' she asked. Jamie didn't reply. He looked at her a moment and smiled. It was one of his enigmatic smiles, she mused, so maybe the answer was yes and maybe it was no. She would just have to hope it was the latter.

They left the phone box and walked back to the cottage, still looking like tourists, Orlagh thought. That would soon change.

An hour and a half after returning to the cottage the whop, whop, whop of a helicopter's rotating blades disturbed the calm. People emerged from their houses, curious. Sitting in the passenger seat of the Mustang she saw their inquisitive looks. They were all still there when the Westland Whirlwind helicopter lifted off the ground and swung away over the steely grey water of the loch. She didn't look like a tourist now, she mused, smiling nervously.

Her thoughts returned to Jamie. She still didn't understand him. She hoped one day she might get the chance.

Chapter Eighty-two

Friday 18 January (Morning) Liverpool.

Kevin Sparke smiled easily as he stepped off the gangplank of the overnight Dublin to Liverpool ferry. He was relaxed. Everything was coming together perfectly and in a few days he would be home, feted as a hero. Until then, he was on holiday. That, at least, is what he had told anyone who asked, though few did. He had few friends, only acquaintances. Still, he had dropped out of circulation a week earlier. Announced to his landlady he was taking a holiday in England; a touring holiday, he said. He had always wanted to visit Wales, he told her; The Welsh mountains. Then there would be The Lake District and the Yorkshire Dales and he would finish the grand tour in London. He would be back at the end of January, he told her, and paid for another month in advance for his room. He had smiled as she thanked him. Told her that if anyone was looking for him he would be "out of touch" but if she took a name and contact he would get in touch as soon as he returned. She assured him she would do that, grateful for the advance payment, and wished him a good holiday. He was such a nice young man. Always polite, never any trouble and always punctual with his rent. She never thought to question why anyone would take a touring holiday round some of Britain's most exposed landscapes in the middle of winter.

He had left his digs that day and had booked into a little hotel in Bray. While there, he stayed in his room most of the time, emerging only to eat, and he avoided contact with people. He paid for five night and left the hotel on the afternoon of the seventeenth. A taxi took him to the ferry port in Dublin. He boarded the ferry, went immediately to his cabin and stayed there for the whole of the voyage, leaving as the ferry docked. To all intents and purposes, he had disappeared. He had every right to feel relaxed.

When Sparke emerged from the port building, a car was waiting for him. The driver, a big man in an ill-fitting suit, sat hunched behind the steering wheel. His eyes, constantly on the move, scanned the crowd leaving the terminal and the traffic coming and going. The man knew his role and he was good at it. He didn't know his passenger but had been given a description of the man. He also had a recognition code and his passenger had details of the car. There would be no mistakes. There *couldn't* be any. The man was important. His orders had come from the top and they were specific; get the man safely to a haulage firm in Warrington, leave him there and then forget he had ever met him. And he intended to do just that.

Sparke spotted the car immediately. It was exactly as described; a dark blue Austin 1800, registration G97 FBO. He eased his way through the crowd towards the car, avoiding eye contact and attracting no attention. He wanted no one to remember him. He reached the car, opened the rear door and slipped inside.

The driver, watching his approach in the car's mirrors, turned to him immediately. The first thing he saw was the arrogant smile on Sparke's face. He decided instantly that he didn't like this man, but liking him wasn't part of the task. Deliver and forget, he reminded himself. 'It is cold, isn't it?' he said, delivering the first part of the recognition code. His accent wasn't local. In fact, anyone hearing him would have been hard placed to link it to anywhere.

'I imagine it's colder in Moscow,' Kevin replied, completing the code.

The arrogance was in the man's voice as well as his eyes, the driver noted. He nodded acknowledgement, turned in his seat and switched on the ignition. The engine fired immediately. Without another word he checked his mirrors, signalled his intention to leave his parking spot and pulled out onto the exit road. No one followed.

The drive was completed in silence. It was early afternoon when the 1800 pulled off the main Warrington Road into an industrial area and stopped outside a haulage yard. and darkness had fallen by the time the driver pulled up outside the haulage yard. An articulated lorry stood off to one side of the yard, in the shadows. The yard was encircled by a high wire fence topped by barbed wire and was lit by powerful arc lights. Two large stone buildings took up a big part of the area and a smaller block housed what appeared to be offices. Lorries were being loaded, the doors of the two big buildings wide open, light spilling out, open and fork lift trucks shuttled back and forth.

Kevin Sparke sat in the back of the car, watching the activity. The driver remained silent, as he had done throughout the journey, and watched his rear view mirror. They sat like that for more than half an hour until the activity on site ceased and the lights extinguished. Three lorries drove out of the yard past them and disappeared into the distance, their red tail lights fading. The storage units' doors were closed and most of the lights in the office block went out, one after another, until only two windows remained lit.

Sparke opened the car door without a word, picked up his bag, and slipped out, closing the door quietly behind him. He strode off, through the unlocked side gate, and made his way to the office, turning only once as he reached the door.

His driver sighed heavily with relief, switched on the car's ignition, and drove away. His task was completed and he was well out of it. His passenger was someone else's problem now. As the big Austin faded from view Sparke pushed open the door and stepped inside. He was in a utilitarian brick build block with a central passage and small offices off to each side. There was a small reception desk and telephone switchboard and a sign announced "Welcome to Brogan Animal Feed and Fertiliser Ltd". He smiled coldly and gave a small cough to announce his arrival.

A door at the end of the passage opened and a large, balding man with a drinker's face and matching belly, appeared in the passage. 'You'll be Mr Sparke, I take it,' he said, taking in his visitor.

Kevin nodded and began his walk up the passage. The big man retreated back into his office and was settled behind his desk when Kevin appeared in the doorway. He looked around, trying to hide the feeling of distaste he felt. The office, like the man, was a mess. Papers were strewn about; invoices, orders, shipping notes. How anyone made sense of them he could only guess.

'Mr Brogan, I presume,' he said, sounding just a little pompous.

'No, actually my name is O'Hara, Mr Brogan left us a while back,' the big man retorted with a frosty smile.

'And where is he now?' Kevin asked, he didn't like loose ends and Brogan, he suspected, might be one of those.

The man laughed. It wasn't a warming sound. 'I imagine he's sharing tales with Lucifer,' he said. 'When I said he left us a while back I meant he's dead. His daughter inherited the business and I married her... so here we are. Don't worry yourself, everything is in order. Mr Duggan's request was expected.'

Kevin came into the office and sank into a spare chair, dropping his bag on the floor beside him. 'The papers?' he asked.

'They're in the cab,' the big man replied and slid open a desk drawer. When his hand reappeared there was a Makarov PM pistol nestling in it. He placed it on the desk and pushed it across to Sparke. 'One Makarov pistol, as requested,' he said, slipping his hand back into the drawer and reappearing with two metal clips. 'And two spare magazines,' he went on. 'Twenty-four rounds should be enough, I take it?'

'I certainly hope so,' Kevin said, grinning. 'Your boys will be doing most of the work. They have everything they need?'

'Yes, everything was delivered about two weeks ago. It's safe and can be picked up when needed.'

'Good. In that case I will change out of these clothes into something more appropriate and leave you in peace.'

The big man hauled himself up out of his chair and pointed to the room opposite. 'You can change in there,' he said curtly. He had decided he didn't like this man one bit. He was too full of himself, and the sooner he was gone, the better. There was still the problem of the lorry, of course, but he would report that as stolen in the morning. By that time, this man and his cargo would be in Scotland and the number of the truck and trailer changed. What Sparke did with it then was his business.

Kevin rose and picked up his bag. They didn't shake hands. The feeling of distrust was mutual. He entered the other room and pulled the door closed behind him. He was in another office, secretary he guessed. There was a hint of scent in the air, a tidy desk, typewriter and photographs on the top of a grey metal filing cabinet. Mr O'Hara featured in a few of these, his arm around a younger woman in some. Kevin smiled to himself. He wondered if Mrs O'Hara knew.

When he returned, he had changed into jeans, working boots, a heavy cotton shirt, checked pattern, and a donkey jacket. Now he looked exactly as he wanted to look... like the driver of a heavy goods vehicle. O'Hara looked him up and down. If he had a comment to make, he kept it to himself. Kevin favoured him with a smile but only his lips demonstrated it; his eyes were cold.

O'Hara returned his gaze equally coldly but said nothing. He could have wished him good luck but he had his own view on what this man was up to. He knew what had been loaded onto the trailer; he had supervised it, after all, and a load like that could only have one purpose. He wanted nothing more to do with it and, more, he didn't want it coming back to bite him. He watched dispassionately as Kevin Sparke crossed the yard and circled the lorry, inspecting it.

Sparke climbed up into the cab and the engine coughed into life. With a flick of a switch all the vehicle's lights illuminated and then he climbed back out to repeat his inspection, checking every light. O'Hara smiled grimly but there was grudging respect in it. The man took no chances.

Five minutes later, satisfied, Sparke clambered back into the cab and engaged first gear. The heavy lorry lurched forward as he came to grips with the unfamiliarity of the clutch. He eased the vehicle towards the big double gates, lining it up with the road beyond, and accelerated, disappearing into the darkness in a cloud of exhaust smoke. He settled back into his seat, lit a cigarette, and considered the journey ahead. He would stop at Gretna, just over the border with Scotland, and sleep there. He would drive on to Glasgow tomorrow, having changed the registration plates, and there he would meet Orlagh Duggan. He grinned at the thought of wiping the smug smile off her pretty face..

Chapter Eighty-three

Same day, South of Glasgow

A cold wind blew in over the Fenwick Moor from the west. There was sleet in it. If the temperature dropped another degree or two it would turn to snow. Jamie huddled down in his parka and surveyed the farm about three hundred yards away with powerful binoculars. Lights were on in the windows and smoke whipped away from the chimney. He was downwind and could smell it. Peat, great for burning to keep warm; better, in his opinion, for flavouring whisky.

Beside him, Conor Whelan lay prone in the wet heather. They had been there for an hour, having hiked across the moor from the B764, the Eaglesham Moor Road. The trek had taken them the best part of an hour and a half, laden as they were with heavy Bergen rucksacks containing all they would need. The ground underfoot had hindered them too. It was marshy and treacherous and progress had been slow, punctuated by occasional falls and regular cursing. The Commer sat in the layby at the foot of Ballageich, a hill on the north side of the moor topped by a stone cairn. From there, on a good day, you could see for miles in any direction; but not tonight. Not even the lights of Glasgow to the north, East Kilbride to the east or Kilmarnock to the south would be visible tonight.

About twenty miles south of them a squadron of SAS troopers was enjoying the comforts of the RNAS base at Prestwick Airport, HMS Gannet. A Westland WS-61 Sea King helicopter stood on the hard standing with its engine idling and its rotors turning lazily. If worst came to worst, it could have the troops here in minutes; the back-up force, just in case anything went wrong. Sir Charles, put in charge of the clean-up and cover up operation by the Prime Minister, had made it abundantly clear that had better not happen. Conor had received a similar warning from a voice at the other end of a call from Washington.

With the immediate threat of a nuclear disaster removed, the politicians on both sides of the Atlantic were now back in their comfort zones; what Conor described as "ass covering mode". Jamie smiled grimly. The political consequences of this plot ever leaking were now considered even more toxic than the fucking bomb itself, he mused.

'Nothing?' Conor enquired, his voice no louder than a whisper. Jamie shook his head. 'Did you believe Duggan?' Conor continued. 'You think the folks down there aren't in the loop?'

Jamie shrugged but the heavy parka he wore hid the gesture from Conor. 'I don't know,' he admitted. 'But if she was lying her lifespan will be considerably shortened. Sir Charles doesn't forgive and forget.'

'Yeah, but if she *was* lying our lifespans might be shortened too, kid... considerably,' Conor responded sourly, voicing his real concern.

Jamie laughed quietly. 'Don't worry, I've got your back... and there are only three of them.'

'*If* she was telling the truth,' Conor threw back, unconvinced.

The radio squawked, a quick burst of static. Jamie checked his watch. It was eleven o'clock. The Brigadier insisted on hourly updates, even if they had nothing to report. Jamie grinned as Conor switched the set to transmit, cursing under his breath, and sent a squawk in reply. There was nothing to report. They were in position and watching.

'What do you think?'

Jamie scanned the farmhouse and outbuildings again. Lights had gone out on the ground floor and one window on the upper floor was now illuminated. Bedtime, he surmised. This was a working farm. The family would go to bed early and be up at the crack of dawn... before that at this time of year. 'I think it's nearly time I went down for a look,' he said. 'It'll be midnight in an hour. I'll give it thirty minutes then make my way down. That should give me enough time to check the place out and get back before the next squawk.'

'What about the dogs?' Conor asked, voicing concern. They had heard the barking when they arrived. At least two, probably three, but Jamie had shrugged off concern. This was a sheep farm, he had argued, and they would be sheep dogs, not guard dogs.

He was equally unconcerned now. 'They'll be inside,' he said. 'Shepherds look after their dogs,' he added. Conor hoped he was right.

'I'm getting too old for this,' Conor griped as he lit the small stove and started to boil water. They had built screens of heather round their position so there was little risk of detection. Certainly not from the farmhouse and only crazy people would be out on the moor at this time of night and in this weather. That description sort of summed them up perfectly, he thought... a couple of crazies.

He boiled the water and made the brew, passing one tin mug to Jamie and wrapping his frozen fingers round another. 'I've been thinking about retiring,' he said casually as Jamie raised the can to his lips.

'You'll be lucky,' Jamie laughed, before sipping the scalding tea. 'I tried it; the old bugger wouldn't let me.' The "old bugger" he was referring to was Sir Charles Redmond. He had no doubt Conor had an "old bugger" manipulating him too. They were both just marionettes controlled by puppet masters.

'I've been giving it some thought,' Conor went on. 'Thought we might work together on a little venture.'

Jamie lowered his mug and looked at his friend curiously. 'A little venture?' he queried, laughing quietly. 'Isn't that what we're on just now?'

'Exactly... we've got skills, kid. We complement each other; I'm the brains, you're the muscle,' he joked. 'Think about it,' he continued, warming to it. 'There are people out there who will pay big money to learn from us.'

'What? How to analyse intelligence and kill people?' Jamie scoffed.

Conor wasn't put off. 'Not exactly. I was thinking more along the lines of survival training. It's confidence building. Company executives would lap it up.'

'Aye, and what about your lot and mine?' Jamie countered, still sceptical.

'I've been thinking about that as well,' Conor responded. 'We could offer a service to them. We can't get out... can't just walk away, but we can be consultants. You've got skills old Sir Charles doesn't want to lose and I like to think I've got skills too, so we offer to pass those on... and be available for them to call on us in an emergency.'

'I was beginning to like the sound of it until you spoiled it there,' Jamie came back with a laugh. But it had him thinking. It might work. Might.

He looked down at his watch. Time was passing quickly. Down at the farmhouse all the lights had been extinguished, all except a small light above the main door. That probably stayed on all night. It was deathly quiet. There were no trees and the wind blew past silently, rustling nothing. Off in the distance, a sheep bleated mournfully. The place really was desolate and yet, in the sunshine, it would have a certain wild beauty, he imagined.

'It's nice to dream, Conor,' he said, after a moment, but he sounded a little less dubious than before.

'Sometimes they come true, kid,' the big American said, smiling and patting him on the shoulder. 'Don't write it off.'

'Tell me more later. For now, keep an eye on things here. I'll be back before midnight.' With that, Jamie rose to a crouch and drifted off into the darkness.

He made good progress. The land nearer the house was better drained than the section of moor they had crossed on the way in. He found a trail through the heather and gorse, beaten down by years of use by man and beast, maybe even centuries of use, he thought.

He circled around the farm. It was bigger than he had imagined. The farmhouse itself was substantial, built from stone, with two floors and a slate roof. It had probably been in the family for generations, which begged the question; what were they doing supporting the IRA?

Behind the farmhouse there were sheep pens and an enormous barn. He had made out the top of its roof behind the house from his hide in the heather but that had been misleading. It was bigger than he had guessed. Big enough to park an articulated lorry and still leave space for whatever else was inside. He decided on a closer inspection. Slower now, crouching a low as possible, he left the cover of the heather and edged towards the sheep pens. The ground was soft and muddy here, churned up by the tiny cleft feet of sheep. The animals were probably brought in during the worst of the weather, the ewes at least, to protect them. Especially if they were carrying lambs. He skipped round the pens. His boots left imprints in the mud but he noticed other footprints, removing all concern.

He reached the barn and edged along the wall, his back pressed fast against the wooden slats. The door was unlocked but heavy. It was a big, double door with one side held tight by an enormous slip bolt that fitted into a hole on the concrete base. The other door moved freely. He held his breath and eased it open. It was warm inside and as his eyes adjusted to the darkness he discovered why. At least sixty sheep were herded together in a large pen. The smell of wet wool and dung greeted him as he stepped deeper inside. The sheep jostled about nervously but remained quiet. He scanned the cavernous space. An old tractor sat against one wall and some drums, like oil drums, were stacked nearby. The main floor was of concrete and looked as if it had been recently cleared. A ladder led to a loft and he could make out bales of hay.

He had seen enough. He eased back out into the yard and closed the door. He debated whether to take a closer look at the house but decided against. The dogs were an unknown quantity. If they caught his scent or heard his movements they could bring the whole house down on him.

He followed the same route in reverse on his way back. As he passed the front of the house again he noted a Land Rover parked in the shadow between the house and the barn. It wasn't new, the registration plate told him that much, but if it was in daily use it would be serviceable. As such, it was a means of escape for their quarry. He would need to remember that.

He was back with Conor at five minutes to midnight, grinning as the American jumped with surprise. 'Who did you expect? The ghost of Fionn Doherty?' he laughed, as he settled down beside his friend. Conor's response was a short expletive. 'When they come through this time tell them we've done a reconnaissance. The barn has been cleared though it's full of sheep to one side. It looks like the lorry is expected. There's an old tractor in the barn and a Land Rover parked outside the house... registration PVA 335. Other than that, there's nothing. You good with all that?' Conor nodded. 'Good. In that case I'm having a snooze. Wake me in two hours.'

So saying, he rolled onto his side, pulled his parka hood over his head and settled down. He was asleep before the radio squawked at midnight.

Chapter Eighty-four

Saturday 19 January 1974, Gretna Green

Kevin Sparke woke early. It was just after six o'clock. He had slept in the cab of the truck and his body was stiff and sore. The drive from Warrington the night before had taken longer than estimated, the cause being a multiple crash in fog on the motorway fifteen miles south of Carlisle. A journey that should have taken two and a half hours ended up taking four and a half. It did not shake his optimism. Even now, after spending the night contorted in a sleeping bag, his spirits were high.

He was in a lorry park surrounded by trucks of all shapes and sizes, rigid and articulated. If O'Hara had reported the lorry stolen and the police were looking out for it, they would have a hard job finding it here. He had changed the plates.

There was a toilet block with showers and a small, ramshackle transport café. He decided to shower then eat. The café was open twenty-four hours, which was good, but the quality of the food would be dubious. These places invariably sold fried meals dripping in fat and judging by the smell this one was no different. He would settle for a coffee and a sandwich.

He followed his plan, avoided contact with other drivers, and pulled out of the lorry park at seven and headed for the A74. According to a sign, he was 85 miles from Glasgow. Without stops, he would be at the town of Hamilton at around eight-forty-five. He had memorised his route. He would leave the A74 just beyond Hamilton and take the road to East Kilbride, what the British called a "New Town". Beyond East Kilbride, in the direction of a place called Busby, he would turn left onto the Eaglesham Road and then the road was straight through to the road leading to the farm. With luck, he would be there at around nine thirty. He smiled to himself again. He had thought a lot about Orlagh Duggan during the night and he was thinking about her again now. He would enjoy putting his thoughts into practise.

The lorry handled well. The tank was full of diesel when he left Warrington and still had enough in it to complete its mission. After that, it wouldn't be going anywhere else.

He drove steadily past the towns dotted along the A74 and ticked them off his mental list. These were his waypoints: Kirkpatrick-Fleming, then a place with the bizarre name, Ecclefechan, then Lockerbie, Elvanfoot, Crawford, Lesmahagow – another strange name – to Larkhall, and finally Hamilton. The road was monotonous. Endless hills rising on both sides dotted with tiny white spots; sheep. It might look pleasant to some people but he wasn't into landscapes.

Just after nine o'clock he reached a large roundabout on the outskirts of East Kilbride.

The sign said "Whirlies", another bizarre name, but it was a bizarre roundabout. He was making good time. He hoped his team was ready.

***

Jamie and Conor alternated two-hour shifts, one watching the house while the other slept. At least, Jamie slept, Conor tossed and turned most of the time during his down time and complained through all of it. First light was at around seven twenty that morning. Strangely, it seemed to Jamie, the house was still quiet.

Activity commenced ten minutes later. Lights came on in the house, smoke drifted up from the chimney and was blown away by the strengthening breeze. Two young men emerged and made their way to the barn. Strangely, there was little or no conversation between them. They acted like strangers. Both were big men, one a little bigger and a little older, and there was no family resemblance, Jamie mused.

He continued to watch through the binoculars as Conor prepared "breakfast" from their ration packs - Ration, Complete GS 24 hour, the packs said. Cordon bleu it was not but if soldiers survived on it, so could they. There was porridge, a bacon burger, biscuits and a chocolate drink. Conor lit the stove and boiled water. They had brought with them a petrol cooker - "Cooker, Petrol No2" – in preference to the tiny folding Hexamine cookers issued with the ration pack. It was easier to light, having a built in windshield, and did not give off toxic fumes like the Hexamine tablets.

They ate in silence and watched the farm. The sheep were brought out from the barn and secured in the pens. Animal feed was poured into the troughs and loud bleating filled the air as the hungry beasts began to eat. It all seemed normal, Jamie thought, but "seemed" was the word that stuck in his mind. Something wasn't right.

It wasn't until almost eight when that "something" became apparent. Two more men left the farm house. That brought the total to four when, according to Orlagh, there should only be two plus the father and mother. A cold shiver ran down his spine. The odds had just worsened.

The radio came to life. 'Control to Ringwraiths, come in, over,' the voice of the operator came through. It was a new voice. A new operator. The shift had changed.

Jamie grimaced and Conor grinned. The Brigadier's insistence on these identifiers amused them but the old boy was deadly serious. 'Ringwraith 1 receiving, go ahead, over,' Jamie replied.

The voice of Sir Charles himself came on then. He sounded tinny and remote. 'The MGB GT is registered to an address in London,' he reported. 'Special Branch have it on their files. It's home to a Hungarian émigré but Special Branch think he's something else. He has a wide range of friends... Quite a cosmopolitan group, in fact, including some Members of Parliament, over.'

Jamie switched to back to transmit. 'The farm has been reinforced,' he reported blandly. 'At least two extra men... Fit looking; military background

I'd guess. That fits with the car being a two seater. I hope there's not more of them,' he added.

'No sign of our American friend yet?' the Brigadier came back.

'Negative.'

'Okay, continue surveillance. We'll check with your new Irish girlfriend re the additional troops. Over.'

'Affirmative. Ringwraith 1 over and out,' Jamie responded tightly, bridling at the Brigadier's "new girlfriend" reference, before switching off.

Conor had listened in to the exchange and raised an enquiring eyebrow. 'I wonder if the Hungarian has Irish friends,' he said.

Jamie gave him a snort. 'The old boy said his friends were "cosmopolitan" so you never know,' he said. 'Though I doubt it.'

'You could always take them out with the rifle.'

'True, but if I do that Sparke will run and I can't take him down. He has to be breathing when we hand him over.' He picked up the binoculars and scanned the moor. He focussed then on the farm and worked his way back along the farm road to the main road about half a mile away. The farm road was little more than a track running in what was almost a straight line from the Eaglesham Moor Road to the farm, disappearing from time to time when the track dipped below the level of the heather bordering it. They had surveyed it quickly on their way in. Although it was little more than a track it was well maintained with only a few biggish potholes. The MGB wouldn't be slowed too much by it, he thought, although the mud would help. There was a wood about 1200 yards away to the west, off on their right. Beyond that the main A77 ran south from Glasgow through Fenwick to Kilmarnock, Prestwick and Ayr. It was far enough away to cause him no concern.

Down at the farmhouse the four men were talking outside the barn. He focussed the binoculars on them, studying their faces. Two of them looked like brothers; same build, same hair colour, same facial likeness. The other two men were slightly older. Late twenties or early thirties, he guessed. Their expressions were harder and they were obviously used to giving orders and having them followed. NCOs in some man's army, he surmised, it was in their body language. Something else was showing in the body language too; the younger men didn't like being ordered around, but it didn't look like they had much alternative.

'What are you thinking?' Conor probed.

'The two young guys are the brothers, the farm boys. They're the ones we were told about. The older guys are professionals. I don't think they were expected and I don't think the farm boys like them being here. When push comes to shove, I think we can forget the farmers. It's the other two we need to worry about.' He stopped for a moment, thinking things out. 'The farm was to be used to hide the truck until it was needed. That's straightforward enough; drive it into the barn and close the doors... So why are the other two here? And what is the paint for?'

'Back up for Sparke,' Conor suggested. 'Or maybe they're the painters, their job is to change the appearance of the lorry.'

'I don't think he needs back-up. From what Orlagh gave us, he was bringing the truck, setting up a meet with her to hand over the keys and instructions, and then heading for home... wherever that is,' he added thoughtfully. You don't need back-up for that. The guy's no shrinking violet. Maybe you're right; maybe they're here to change the lorry into something else... But what?' he finished pensively.

'So what do we do?' Conor asked, nervous again.

'We wait.'

***

Sparke drove into Eaglesham village at twenty minutes past nine. He was the third vehicle in a convoy of three heavy lorries polluting the place with diesel fumes. Ahead of him was a set of traffic lights and beyond that a hill that seemed to climb up forever. The road was narrow and the odd car or two were parked at the kerb. Negotiating the hill with this load in the face of oncoming traffic would have to be done in low gear. The smell of diesel would hang in the air for a long time, he thought, amused. How the people here put up with it was beyond him. From what he had seen up until now it was a busy road. A quick look in his mirrors picked out another two lorries and a stream of cars closing up behind, and it was still early. He grinned. Capitalist democracy was no better than Communism dictatorship in that respect. In Russia, the peasants had no control over their lives. It was no different here, it seemed.

The traffic lights turned red and he came to a halt behind the lorry in front. The first lorry had caught the lights and was now labouring up the hill. A malignant cloud of black smoke followed its progress. He sat with the engine idling and saw a police station off to his right. Nothing to worry about there. The policemen in a place like this probably had nothing to do all day long and sat on their fat arses drinking tea. Very British. He didn't know, of course, that Brigadier Sir Charles Redmond had commandeered the place.

The lights changed and the truck in front, an articulated lorry like his, moved away. He slid the gear stick into first and let out the clutch. The truck eased forward slowly then gained speed just before the incline. The lorry in front was already labouring and his was following suit. They were at the head of a larger convoy now, a mix of lorries, cars, vans and a bus climbing slowly - endlessly it seemed - up the hill.

Finally, after what seemed an age he pulled out of the village but the climb continued. Car drivers, frustrated by the slow progress, edged their vehicles out in the hope of overtaking only to pull in again as an oncoming vehicle flashed its lights and its horn blared. He smiled to himself and refused to let the frustration get to him. He had only a mile or two to cover now and this was, after all, the greatest day of his life. He tucked himself into the slipstream of the truck in front and relaxed.

***

It was Conor who picked out the truck as it turned off the Moor Road onto the farm track. He nudged Jamie. 'We've got company,' he said. 'Articulated truck with a big trailer at ten o'clock.'

473

Jamie twisted slightly backwards and to his right, bringing the powerful binoculars to bear on the vehicle. He saw the driver hunched over the steering wheel then ran his eyes along the trailer. It was big, about thirty feet long; a giant container on wheels, four on either side towards the rear. But it was the name on the side that held his eye - Brogan Animal Feed Ltd - in big, bold lettering. 'That's our boy,' he said calmly, though there was never any doubt.

'Sheeeit,' Conor murmured, sounding a little awed. 'If that thing is full of what we think it is it'll blow a hole through to China.'

Jamie nodded thoughtfully. 'Yeah, makes you wonder, doesn't it?' he posed.

Conor looked over at him, his brow puckering. It hadn't made him wonder; tremble, sure, wonder... No.

Jamie treated him to a frosty smile. 'You don't need all that shit to blow up a waste container,' he said, voicing his thoughts. 'They've got RPGs, remember? Once the waste is out it'll spread in the wind. The bomb will help, sure; lift it up into the atmosphere... But you wouldn't need that lot down there to do that.'

'So?' Conor prompted, but he had already worked out the answer and it made the nightmare a thousand times worse.

'So what Orlagh Duggan told us is probably true. The plan is to penetrate Faslane.'

Conor laughed. 'That's crazy,' he said. 'Holding the British Government to ransom will never work. You Brits are devious bastards. If they think that will work they're pissing in the wind.'

'I don't think nuclear blackmail forms part of the plan,' Jamie said quietly. 'At least, not the IRAs plan,' he added. 'And I think I know why the two new guys are here... They brought the final piece of the jigsaw with them.'

'Christ... If you're saying what I think you're saying then it isn't just nuclear waste that would be released into the atmosphere.'

Jamie smiled grimly. 'No,' he agreed, gravely. 'It would be then real thing.'

They were quiet for a moment as the gravity of what they were thinking sank in. Meanwhile, the lorry continued its progress down then track towards the farm. It was moving slower now. On a summer's day it would be travelling faster, followed by a cloud of dust. Not today though. The winter snow and rain had coated the track with a film of slippery mud that slowed momentum. A small mercy but maybe an important one, Jamie mused. He took up the binoculars again, turning them back to the farm. What he saw now was a hive of activity. The barn doors were opened wide and the old tractor had been moved out. A large space had been cleared to the front. There was still no sign of an older man or woman and from what he could see the two younger men weren't willing participants. They appeared to be afraid of the older men, Jamie thought. It was in their movements. Thy sprang into action when spoken to, throwing nervous looks at the other men, and did nothing when left to their own devices. He remembered the blood on the barn floor and guessed what had happened to Mum and Dad. That's what happens when you get mixed up in things you shouldn't, he thought, then laughed aloud. He was one to talk. Conor turned to him, surprised by the sound. Jamie just carried on laughing and shook his head.

Conor didn't know what to think. A laugh was the last thing he expected. He hoped Jamie wasn't losing it, but something told him he needn't worry.

'Radio in,' Jamie ordered. 'Tell them what we think,' he continued. Sharing the credit with Conor hadn't occurred to him, no less than sharing the blame if he were wrong. They were in this together. He smiled then. Maybe that's the way it's supposed to be.

As Conor made contact with the Brigadier, Jamie picked up the rifle. The L42A1, the main sniper rifle of the British Army, is a 7.62mm bolt-action rifle with a muzzle velocity of 2,750 feet per second, faster than the speed of sound. It has an effective range of 800 yards and is fitted with a ten round detachable magazine. The hide was approximately 400 yards from the farm. Even if he wasn't a marksman, which he was, he couldn't miss at this range and his target would be dead before the sound of the shot reached him. All good, except he couldn't kill the American and the sight of bodies dropping dead around him would probably set him running. With the best will in the world, they couldn't race the MGB. He could try to blow out the tyres if the guy did make a break for it, but that carried the risk of the bugger killing himself when the car totalled. He ran his hand lovingly down the stock of the rifle. 'Not today old girl,' he murmured silently.

Conor was tapping him on the arm, holding out the radio microphone with one hand and the headset with the other. 'Sir Charles wants a word,' he said, pulling a face.

Jamie laid the rifle on the heather beside him, covering it carefully, before taking the proffered instruments. He held one earphone to his left ear with his left hand and keyed the transmit on the microphone with his right. 'Ringwraith 1 receiving, over,' he said automatically, early training coming back.

The Brigadier didn't bother with formalities. He cut straight to the chase. 'How sure are you about this?' he asked.

Jamie switched to transmit. 'Pretty sure. Why have two extra bodies here if all he's doing is hiding the truck? And the boys who have arrived are professionals; it's in everything they do. I think the older couple, the father and mother, are dead,' he finished.

'Explain,' Sir Charles threw back immediately.

'I found blood on the barn floor last night. Might be animal but I doubt it. There's been no sign of the couple and the boys look nervous.'

There was silence for a moment with just the static hiss of the radio filling the void. Jamie looked at Conor who was digesting the news about the blood. He shrugged an apology. The radio came to life again.

'If you're right, I want the device. Get it. Over.'

'And the American?' Jamie responded.

'I want him too. Something tells me he's not what he seems.'

Jamie cursed softly under his breath before replying. 'That might make things difficult. We're 400 yards from the farm. Covering that distance without being seen will be a bloody miracle. If I can use the rifle I can take them all out and get you the device. Over.'

'I want the man... So do you, remember that. I don't care how difficult it is, just do it. I can't send in the Regiment. That'll blow it completely.'

'Sod off,' Jamie murmured before switching to transmit. 'Okay. You're the boss. Ours not to question why and all that shit,' he added bitterly.

'Just do it Ringwraith 1. Over and out.' The Brigadier was gone and only a steady hum remained.

Jamie turned to Conor and gave him another shrug. 'Your little joint venture idea is beginning to look appealing,' he said, smiling bitterly.

'This just keeps getting better and better,' the big American replied sarcastically.

'Yeah, well it's us or the end of the world as we know it Jim,' Jamie threw back, misquoting Dr McCoy of the Starship Enterprise. 'Know any good prayers?'

***

Kevin Sparke wrestled the big steering wheel of the truck on the last fifty yards to the farm, fighting to keep the heavy vehicle on the road. The mud beneath the wheels was making it slide constantly and his correcting manoeuvres were throwing it in from side to side. The weight of the cargo kept pushing him forward as he applied the brakes. Sweat beaded on his brow. Finally, with the speed dropping, he regained control and brought the giant truck to a halt in a loud hiss of air brakes.

He wiped the sweat from brow with the back of one gloved hand and applied the handbrake, letting the vehicle idle. He saw the four men. No fifth man and no woman, he noted with a grim smile. He stretched, eased his neck muscles and opened the cab door. One of the older men came towards the truck, the other remained with the farmhands, a Makarov automatic pistol tucked into his belt. That would be enough to discourage the boys, he thought. He swung his legs out of the cab and jumped down onto the wet ground, sliding momentarily before regaining his balance.

He looked at the man approaching. There was a Makarov tucked into his belt too, he noted. He wondered which of them had disposed of the farmer and his wife. This one, he thought; he had the look of a killer.

'Where are the man and woman?' he asked.

'In the barn, sir,' the man reported. 'It was unfortunate. The man had a shotgun which he thought he could threaten us with.'

'No matter,' Sparke replied, changing to Russian. 'It was coming to them all in the end anyway. When the truck is ready we will dispose of these two as well. Is everything ready?'

The man stood rigidly to attention. 'All as directed, Major,' he confirmed, giving Sparke, or Igor Volkov as he now was, his KGB rank.

The two farm boys looked on, bemused. They looked at one another, their fear growing. Igor smiled. Simple bastards, he mused. Still, dying will probably be better than living the rest of their lives in this shit hole. 'Okay,' he said, addressing his compatriot. 'Let's get the truck changed and then you can install and arm the device. I've got a rendezvous with the woman whose deluded men will deliver the bomb. How long should the operation take?'

'Four hours, no more Major,' the man advised.

'Good. That is perfect. I will take the sports car... You know what you have to do when I leave?'

'Yes major. We tidy up here and remain in place until the truck is taken by the Irish people. Then we return to London in the Land Rover.'

Volkov smiled a wolf like smile. 'Excellent Starshina Fedorov. You and Sergeant Stepanov will be rewarded for your efforts. Now, let us get this thing finished,' he said. 'I will use the house to change. Where have you left my things?'

'Your suitcase is in the main bedroom on the upper floor Major. The facilities in the farmhouse are basic but adequate. If you give me the keys of the truck I will start work.'

Volkov handed over the keys and stood for a moment, surveying the surrounding countryside and watching as his subordinate climbed into the high cab of the truck and familiarised himself with the equipment. What a forsaken place, he thought as his eyes roamed the bleak countryside. But it has nothing on Siberia, he mused. When it comes to bleak, we Russians rule the world. His face broke into a rare smile.

Chapter Eighty-five

Jamie watched everything unfolding below him, his Bausch and Lomb binoculars focussed on the new arrival and the man with him. What he saw convinced him his theory was dead-on. The new man, Sparke, was in charge and the man addressing him did everything but salute. He passed the glasses to Conor.

'Take a look,' he said. 'These boys are military; no doubt about it.'

Conor put the binoculars to his eyes, adjusting the setting, and scanned the scene. There was no doubt about it. The whole thing was being handled with military precision. Those ol' boys down there were soldiers alright but they weren't American soldiers. That made things better... and worse. Better in that he wasn't dealing with a rogue countryman, worse in that these guys would be ready for anything. Maybe it was time to call in the cavalry. He suggested the same to Jamie.

'Shouldn't we call in some help?' he asked, though his brain told him what the response would be. It was an exercise in futility even asking.

'You heard the man,' Jamie replied quietly. 'We are the fuckin' cavalry this time.' He took back the binoculars and swung the glasses out to the west towards the Clyde Estuary and then back over the farm towards the east. The hills around them blocked off the towns and villages and all he was seeing was heather and gorse... and cloud. Lots of cloud. It was moving in quickly from the west. Was it his imagination, he wondered, or was it getting warmer? He looked down at his watch. It was now almost ten o'clock. Time to report in. And it wasn't his imagination... it was getting warmer.

He decided to pre-empt the Brigadier's call. He handed the binoculars back to Conor, picked up the transmitter microphone and switched on. The lights glowed. 'Ringwraith 1 to base, come in, over,' he said, holding one earphone to his left ear. Nothing. He repeated the call. 'Ringwraith 1 to base, come in, over.'

This time the operator responded. The same girl. He could picture her in the warmth of the police station, sitting hunched over the radio set and trying to relieve her boredom by reading or dreaming. No doubt the local plods would be wondering what the hell was going on. They didn't get much excitement. If the girl was good looking it would probably make their day. 'Base to Ringwraith 1, receiving, over.'

'Target has arrived. Sparke seems to be in charge. Lorry has been moved into the barn and Sparke has headed for the house. Visibility good. Chances of approaching farm unseen are slim, over.'

It was the Brigadier who came on now. 'Understood. It's imperative you prevent Sparke from leaving. Capture and hold if possible. Acknowledge, over.'

'Yeah, I get that, Brigadier,' Jamie responded irritably. 'But heading down there now isn't likely to achieve that. I'd probably end up dead and our man would bolt. Suggestions? Over.'

There was a hint of hesitation before Sir Charles responded. 'Point taken,' he continued at last. 'Maintain surveillance and advise if target is preparing to leave. Over.'

Jamie smiled grimly. His message had got through. Committing suicide wasn't in the job description. 'Acknowledged,' he replied quickly. 'Over and out.'

He switched the radio to stand-by and turned to Conor. 'Time for another brew, my good man,' he said with a laugh. 'Fuck knows what happens now but if he orders us down there I'll be tempted to mutiny.' He stopped for a heartbeat, his eyes fixed on Conor. 'If it comes to it I'll go in alone. You stay here.'

'Like fuck I will, kid.' Conor protested. 'We're in this together.'

Jamie held up a hand and stopped him. He was expecting Conor's objection. 'You need to stay here and watch,' he said. 'If I get topped someone has to stop the bugger. That's your job. You report that I'm down and then you leave it to the Brigadier. He'll send in SAS. You stay put here.'

'No way. I can't let you.'

'I'm not asking you to let me Conor. I'm being selfish. If anything happens to me, I want you to look after Kate and the kids. If you come with me and we both go down that'll leave two families without Dads... So you have to stay. Now make the fuckin' tea,' he finished, turning away and bringing the binoculars back to his eyes.

Maybe it was time to pray, he thought, though whether it would do any good was debateable. But a miracle would be handy.

***

The radio remained silent and time passed with mind numbing monotony. It was mid-day. The men came and went from the barn and Sparke had reappeared, now dressed in fashionable western clothes. He disappeared into the barn and re-emerged with the man he had spoken with earlier. The man was wearing overalls and had a breathing mask round his neck, hanging loosely by straps. They talked again and walked together to the trailer Jamie had seen on his reconnaissance the night before. He watched as the junior man undid the ties holding the canvas cover and eased up a flap. Sparke looked inside and Jamie could see a satisfied smile appear on his face. Clearly, whatever was in the trailer was important. And it didn't take "Brain of Britain" to guess what it was.

Jamie rolled over on his side. 'The warhead is in the trailer,' he announced. 'It's almost time, I think.'

He turned back onto his stomach and looked west. The cloud that had been coming in was building and a fog was forming. Visibility was down but it was still greater than a mile. He thought about it, trying to remember how fog formed. 'You're the navy man,' he said without turning to Conor. 'How does fog form?'

Conor answered right away. He had been watching the weather and had been thinking the same thing. 'This time of year it can come after a spell of really cold weather when there has been snow or ice on the ground. When warmer wet air moves in over the cold ground it creates fog. The technical term is Advection fog. It can get pretty dense at times... and we might just get lucky,' he added, smiling as his eyes drifted westward.

'Have you been praying?' Jamie asked, laughing softly.

'No, not me kid, but I sure hope somebody has.'

Jamie smiled. It hadn't been him either and it wouldn't be the Brigadier. That left only one suspect. 'Good old Frank,' he murmured.

'Frank? The old priest?' Conor queried.

'The very same.'

'What does he know about all this?' Conor responded, a little concerned.

'Fuck all,' Jamie retorted with a laugh. 'But he prays for me every day, or so he says. He's trying to save my soul, but I've told him he's probably wasting his time. It's too big a job. Anyway, if anyone's been praying it's him and let's face it, he's got a closer relationship with the Big Man upstairs than either of us. Maybe the miracle we need is on its way.'

They both turned and looked west. Landmarks that had been visible minutes earlier were now hidden by a bank of mist. Visibility was still about half a mile though, technically fog, but not nearly thick enough for Jamie to risk approaching the farm. Not yet, but it would be soon. Very soon.

Chapter Eighty-six

The mist began to swirl around the farm, gradually enveloping it. And the men working in the barn were blissfully ignorant of its encroachment. In fairness, it meant nothing to them. They weren't leaving the place for a few days in any event.

Sparke, or Volkov, on the other hand, was livid. He had returned to the farmhouse just after noon, eaten a meal of bread and cheese, and fallen asleep. The drive up from England had taken a lot out of him. Lack of sleep during the night added to his fatigue and even the excitement of what he was now part of failed to keep him awake. He woke at two o'clock, refreshed. His mood was momentarily lifted. He was ready for the Irish bitch now, he mused happily as he stretched and pulled back the curtains. That was when his mood changed.

He ran downstairs from the bedroom he had commandeered on the first floor and out into the yard. He was shouting at the top of his voice, gesticulating wildly as the fog crept in relentlessly.

'Fools,' he screamed as the men, startled by the noise, rushed from the barn. 'I told you I was meeting with the Irish woman this afternoon. Why did you not waken me?'

'I'm sorry Major,' the Starshina, or Sergeant Major, apologised quickly, tucking his Tokarev TT-33 automatic pistol back into his belt. 'We were busy in the barn and did not realise.'

The other men, Sergeant Stepanov and the two farmhands, watched nervously as Volkov fumed, fighting to keep his anger under control. He looked away, up the hill towards where Jamie and Conor lay hidden. The mist had now settled on the hilltops and visibility was down to about 150 yards. He cursed violently. If he didn't leave here now he would not be meeting with Orlagh Duggan today. But the mist was thicker on the hilltops and he had no way of knowing whether the fog extended beyond that to Glasgow.

He kicked irritably at some loose gravel with the toe of his boot and turned back to face the Starshina. 'Okay Fedorov, what's done is done,' he said, dismissing the matter, though his tone belied it. 'Is the device armed?'

Fedorov bowed his head. 'Not yet Major. We have finished the alterations to the truck and trailer and have created the space in the centre of the load to site it as ordered,' he reported. 'I was awaiting your instructions for the timer before finishing. I was not given the co-ordinates.'

Volkov cursed inwardly. That was his fault, but he would not admit it; not to these fools anyway. Not to anyone, for that matter. He put it down to the fatigue. 'Very well,' he said. 'The device is to be set to explode at 02.00 hours in the morning of 25th January, just less than six days. But first, let me see what you have achieved.'

Without another word he strode past Fedorov and headed for the barn. The Starshina followed in his wake, rolling his eyes at his comrade Stepanov who trailed dutifully behind while keeping a watchful eye on the farm boys.

The sight that greeted Volkov when he entered the cavernous barn cheered him a little. He was still smarting at being cheated out of an afternoon of sex with Orlagh Duggan but that could wait, he told himself. This was bigger than personal gratification. Much bigger.

The lorry had been transformed. The tractor unit stood apart from the trailer. It had been resprayed a dark olive green and British military markings adorned the front wings. He nodded, satisfied. 'You have done well, Starshina,' he said, before turning his attention to the enormous trailer.

The original canvas covering had been removed and now lay bundled in the far corner of the barn. New material had been stretched over the metal frame, starting at the front end of the trailer and sheet metal had been inserted beneath it. About half the trailer had been converted. The material covering was the same colour as the drab olive green of the cab but was devoid of lettering. Beside the trailer, some of the sacks from the load had been stacked in a neat pile. It was about 20 cubic meters of explosive, he estimated, about one quarter of the trailer's volume. The sacks had been removed to create a space for the device and when that was armed they would be replaced. Finally, the remaining metal plates would be installed and the drab green material stretched over them. When that was done, the trailer would be a ticking bomb. Literally.

Volkov's enthusiasm was returning. He had all but forgotten his missed opportunity to make Orlagh Duggan pay for her constant put-downs. He clapped his hands enthusiastically. 'I take it all back, Fedorov. You and Stepanov have done a magnificent job.' He said nothing about the farm boys who had executed most of the hard labour. 'It is time, I think, to install the device. We will link the trailer to the motor unit and then load the device. When the device is in place we will arm it and replace the sacks. When the cover is pulled over it will look exactly as I wished; indistinguishable from the real thing.'

The Sergeant Major nodded and shouted an instruction to his subordinate who immediately prodded the two boys into action at the point of his pistol. They trotted from the barn into the fog and were almost immediately lost to sight from inside. Volkov cursed again. The fog could ruin everything depending on how long it lasted.

He stood at the barn door. About 20 yards away he could just make out the vague shapes of Sergeant Stepanov and the two men labouring around the farm trailer. The old tractor coughed into life, the black smoke belching from its exhaust adding to the fug around them. The air was filled with cursing and grunting as the men strained to connect the trailer to the tractor's tow bar and then it began to move. He turned away as the tractor approached the barn, unable to hide his delight. Soon, the device would be in place and his destiny would be assured. And then he would be out of here. This fog could not last forever.

***

On the hillside, Jamie and Conor watched as the fog drifted in. It was relentless. Visibility dropped rapidly. Soon the farm was enveloped in the thick mist and visibility was down to fifty yards and dropping. In the deathly silence they could hear indistinct voices floating up to them. There had been a commotion earlier. Angry shouting. But again, they had been unable to make out what was being said.

'I think it's time I made my move,' Jamie said, smiling grimly at his friend.

Conor shook his head slowly. 'Uh-uh,' he replied. 'It's time we made our move. The fog changes everything. If I stay here, I won't have a clue what's going on down there. If you get taken down, I won't know. I have to come with you.'

After a moment's indecision, Jamie gave a reluctant nod. It made sense but Conor had never been involved in anything like this before. Apart from being forced into a period of unwelcomed field work back in 1967 and 1968, he had spent all of his career behind a desk. Knowing what to do and actually doing it are two different things. Entirely different things, Jamie reflected grimly.

'Are you sure you can handle it?' he asked quietly.

'Yeah, I can handle it,' Conor stated adamantly. 'I know what's at stake.'

'Okay, we'll go in together. Stay close to me but not too close. Two targets rather than one, right?'

Conor nodded. He was nervous but that was a good thing, he supposed. Jamie, on the other hand, looked as cold as ice. It was becoming more and more apparent that Jamie was what he would call a real pro. He had watched him over the previous weeks. He had seen him strip and rebuild weapons as if it were second nature. He had witnessed the clinical killings of the two Irishmen in the wood at Alexandria and had watched him set up the "torture chamber" at the cottage in Lochgoilhead. He shuddered at that particular memory, remembering Fionn Doherty's screams and the look on Orlagh Duggan's face. He thanked God he hadn't had to witness the oxy-acetylene torch in real action. What he had seen was enough. And now, here he was, taking command like a field commander should. He was a natural.

Jamie was speaking again, delivering more instructions. 'You take the rifle,' he said. 'It might come in useful but I don't want it to slow me down. We'll take only our pistols and knives, everything else we leave here. The farm track is over to our right. We'll make for that and follow it in. There are boulders strewn along the verge. We'll scatter a few of those buggers on the roadway just in case our American friend tries to make a run for it though I doubt he will in this fog. But nature being nature, it might change at any second and give him an opportunity. A few big rocks should stop him enough for us to catch him. Better report in,' he finished and reached for the radio transmitter.

The lights glowed in the fog as he switched on. The time now was exactly two sixteen. He flicked the transmit switch. 'Ringwraith 1 to Control, Come in. Over,' he said, his voice steady. He repeated the call again before the female voice acknowledged.

'Control to Ringwraith 1, receiving, over.'

'I'm moving on target, over.' Jamie was brief and to the point.

The Brigadier's voice came on line. 'Control to Ringwraiths, good luck. Report when completed, over.'

'Affirmative,' Jamie replied curtly then broke the transmission.

Conor looked at him questioningly. 'How long do you think he'll wait before he sends in the heavy brigade?' he asked.

'Fuck knows, but I hope we're still around and breathing when they get here,' Jamie retorted grimly. 'Ready?' he queried. Conor nodded once and they moved off together, heading due west towards the farm road. 'You know,' Jamie went on, smiling sheepishly. 'Maybe it's a good thing you're with me. Last time I did something like this on my own, I nearly didn't come back.' That was the last thing Conor Whelan needed to hear.

Chapter Eighty-seven

They reached the farm track in ten minutes. That was a little slower than Jamie had wanted. Their progress had been hindered by thick banks of fog that settled on the moor, cutting visibility to zero at times. They stumbled and fell over hidden heather roots, cursing under their breath. It was hard going. Their clothes were soaked through. Fine beads of moisture clung to them and coated their thick woollen hats. Strangely, for the first time in his life, Conor Whelan felt truly alive. It really was true, he mused. The nearer to death you come, the more you really live. He suspected Jamie shared that emotion.

Reaching the track improved things. They found large rocks to block the roadway easily enough. These were abundant on both sides, scraped aside and left in the ditches when the road was formed years before. They had been discarded then as useless. They weren't useless now.

Within minutes they had manhandled a number of heavy boulders onto the track to form a barrier across the road. It would stop a car, Jamie mused, but the truck might be more of a problem. If it had built up sufficient speed and momentum it might just manage to crash through. He smiled grimly. It was unlikely. The weather would see to that. Then he remembered his chat with Conor earlier... "nature being nature, it could change at any second" he had said, and that was worth remembering.

Satisfied with their makeshift roadblock, they began their approach to the farm. Jamie hugged one side of the track while Conor took up a position a little behind him on the side. Jamie shut the American from his mind. He was a big boy, he could take care of himself, he argued, but a tiny element of doubt remained.

They were close to the farm buildings now. They couldn't see anything but the sounds of men working carried in the stillness. Grunts and curses drifted to them. It was as if the sounds were magnified by the moisture suspended in the air around them. They were close now. Suddenly, the stuttering roar of the tractor engine coming to life halted them in their tracks. Jamie waved a cautionary signal to Conor and melted into the verge at the side of the road. Conor followed suit on his side.

The noise settled to a constant hum. Metal clunked on metal. The tappets in the tractor's engine, worn by age, rattled incessantly like accompanying timpani. The vehicle was moving, the change in pitch and direction of the sound told them that, and it was moving away from them rather than towards them.

Jamie emerged from the gloom on Conor's right and gave him the signal to move forward. Talking was impossible now. Any sound would be amplified and would be carried to the men in the barn. Those men, oblivious to the approaching danger, had no such qualms. There was a lot of talk. The tractor had stopped and in the absence of its engine noise the voices were clear. It was almost as if they were standing next to the group and in this fog that might just be possible, Jamie mused. He stopped and listened.

A man was speaking. The voice was distinct. He could make out every word... and it wasn't English, not even the bastardised version Americans use. His instinct had been right. He turned to Conor, about six feet away and barely visible. He motioned him over. The big American crouched low and came to him, kneeling by his side on the mud lined track. 'Hear that?' Jamie whispered, his voice almost inaudible.

Conor nodded, his expression a mixture of surprise and relief, the relief coming from the realisation that Sparke wasn't an American. 'They're Ruskies; Sparke's a fucking Ivan,' he hissed softly, his face breaking into a grin. 'That sure as hell makes my life easier.'

'You think so? These boys will be good; they wouldn't be here if they're not. All we've got up our sleeve is the element of surprise; when we lose that things will get hairy. And we still want Sparke alive. That makes it harder, not easier. But at least we know what he looks like now.'

'What about the farm boys?' Conor whispered.

Jamie shrugged. 'If they get in the way, shoot them,' he said coldly. 'Come on. Let's finish this.'

They eased forward again. The track ended and they were in the farmyard. The voices were closer now, off to their right. They passed the sheep pens like two ghostly shepherds, the sheep watching them cautiously. The farmhouse appeared in the gloom and then the bulk of the barn. There was light filtering through the fog, a square patch of light grey set in the darker surrounding mist. The sounds were coming from the light.

Suddenly, another engine started up. It was a bigger, more powerful engine than that of the farm tractor, the roar deafening. Lights pierced the fog, beams reaching out only to be diffused and pushed back by the swirling mist. There was a crunch as gears engaged and then the light beams receded as the vehicle moved deeper into the barn. There was a loud metal clunk, a moment of revving engine, and then silence descended again.

Inch by inch, Jamie and Conor approached the source of the noise. Both men had their guns ready, pointing towards the sound. Jamie's heart beat fast; Conor's raced.

Suddenly, they were at the barn door. They stepped out of the fog and into the light, light swirls of mist following them and clinging to them like ghostly fingers. They were in the barn, light from arc lamps illuminating the scene in front of them. Automatically, Jamie moved to his right and Conor moved left, keeping distance between them, and then they stopped, awed by the sight.

The truck tractor unit, once a light blue, was now drab green. The military markings were clearly visible on the front bumper and wings. The trailer, deeper in the barn, was partially covered in fabric of a similar colour. It had been transformed completely.

Conor couldn't contain himself. 'Holy shit,' he murmured. 'They really mean to do it.'

Jamie nodded and cast his eyes over the little group around the trailer. The two farm lads were there, lifting and laying sacks from a pile beside the trailer and placing them on the flat bed. Sparke was beside them, watching progress, a smile on his face. From what Jamie could see, sacks were stacked eight or nine high, higher than the men working with them. The two Russians were nowhere in sight but the sacks being loaded onto the trailer were quickly disappearing. That meant the Russians, the men presenting the greatest danger, were behind the wall of sacks, protected.

The old Massey Ferguson tractor was parked just beyond Sparke with its trailer facing back towards the door. The drop gate was down and the bed of the trailer was empty. Jamie felt his heart drop. That could only mean one thing; the nuclear device was already on board the artic lorry trailer. He prayed to God it wasn't armed.

He measured the distance between himself and the group of men. Fifteen yards, he estimated; forty-five feet, give or take. He and Conor were both still just inside the door, their backs to the barn walls and guns raised, frozen into immobility. They couldn't stay there, Jamie assessed instantly. Yet any movement now might attract attention, even if they stepped back outside. They were between the proverbial rock and the hard place. If the two Russians had been in view, it would have been easy. He could take them both out at this range before they knew what was happening. Forty-five feet was okay. But they weren't in view; they were hidden behind the sacks and as soon as he was spotted, they would come into play.

Gesticulating gently, he motioned Conor to move further away to increase the distance between them. The closer they were the easier they were to kill. Conor saw the slow movements of Jamie's hand and eased, little by little, to his left. The men around the trailer were still engrossed in their work but the farm boys were clearly nervous. Jamie guessed what was in their minds. When the loading work was finished, so were they, he reckoned.

It was one of the brothers, the older one, who saw them first. He was probably looking for an escape route and probably imagined he had found salvation. His eyes moved over them and then, as their presence registered, he turned back in surprise. He said nothing but the obvious double take and, perhaps, a soft gasp of surprise was all it needed.

Sparke, or Volkov, turned to follow the direction of the man's gaze and finally came to rest on Jamie. What he saw was a man dressed in military clothing, fog swirling lightly around him and a weapon in his hand. If he was shocked, he hid it well. Without hesitation, he shouted a warning and threw himself to the ground, crawling for the cover of the tractor.

Then all hell broke loose. The two farm lads made a break for it, running for the barn door. On reflection, Jamie mused, they had no alternative, but deliverance was a forlorn hope. They were a loose end... for both sides. Jamie was already moving, throwing himself to his right. Conor, reacting instinctively, hit the ground to the left. As Jamie made contact with the ground he rolled over, levered himself up on his elbows and raised the Walther, traversing towards the trailer, looking for a target. A face appeared above the sacks, eyes narrowed, expression set. Jamie swung his aim towards it but the farm boys, running in panic now, careered across his path and blocked his aim.

A shot rang out, and then another, the noise amplified in the enclosed space. The older boy, leading the charge, pitched forward, a gaping hole appearing in his neck where the bullet had exited. The lad's heart was still racing, pumping blood through his arteries. Most of it sprayed out from his torn aorta, covering Jamie in a fine red mist.

More shots filled the cavernous building. Jamie's ears rang. He wiped the first man's blood from his face and cleared his vision just in time to see the second farm boy hit the concrete, face down, two bullets through his skull. His body bounced once, like a rag doll dropped from height, then came to rest, his head across his brother's thighs.

Jamie twisted and fired off two quick shots but the face above the sacks was gone. He looked anxiously to his left. Conor was prone on the ground, elbows crooked, his Browning aimed at the trailer. He scanned the rest of the barn then, his eyes carefully searching beneath the body of the enormous trailer. If the Russians came for them, that was the route they would take, he reckoned. The other man, Sparke, was behind the Massey Fergusson tractor, crouched behind one of the large rear wheels. He could make out a sliver of the man's jacket sleeve, nothing else. He didn't even know if Sparke was armed but common sense said he was. So, three against two. The Russians on the trailer weren't moving, but that wouldn't last. They weren't stupid. He and Conor controlled their means of escape... unless there was a side door he hadn't seen on his visit during the night. Either way, the Ivans would have to come for them.

And it would be sooner rather than later, he mused grimly. It wouldn't take these boys long to work out the odds. He and Conor were alone, for the moment, but for how long? That question would be running through the Russians' minds. And they would err on the side of caution and move quickly. They might think they had a chance of getting out. They might think that Jamie and Conor had simply stumbled upon them. He smiled sourly. He didn't think they'd be that stupid.

But he and Conor couldn't stay where they were either. They were exposed. The element of surprise was gone. Now it was kill or be killed and he knew that the Russians would be thinking the same. He turned to Conor and waved backwards towards the barn door a few feet behind them. Conor nodded and immediately began to slither backwards, crabbing towards the fog filled gap. Jamie waited a moment, his Walther moving between targets, the trailer to the left and the tractor to the right.

He turned momentarily to check on Conor's progress. The American was clear, now just a vague shape in the fog. He took a deep breath and began to follow his friend, pushing himself backwards on his belly. That was when the Russians made their move.

There was a sudden explosion of sound in the confines of the barn as all three men opened fire simultaneously. Bullets buzzed past him, some hitting the concrete floor of the barn and throwing up particles of concrete before ricocheting away. Bits of concrete stung his face and blinded him. He closed his eyes and could feel the tiny fragments of grit behind his eyelids, tearing at his pupils. Everything was happening so quickly. Those first shots were to keep him and Conor pinned down, he knew that, but that was about to change. They would show themselves and start to pick their shots and here, spread-eagled on the floor, blinded, he was defenceless. He thanked God Conor was clear.

Blindly, he pointed his Walther towards the sound of the Russian guns and fired. Conor, realising his predicament, opened up behind him. A series of shots from the heavy calibre Browning High Power whined over him and embedded themselves in the sacks. Small cascades of powder and granules trickled from the holes in the sacking and collected on the floor beneath.

Volkov, hidden behind the tractor, now joined the battle. Crawling on his belly, he moved himself around the big tyre. He was hidden in shadow beneath the tractor body. He could see Jamie clearly and a malicious grin formed on his lips. Gently, he eased himself up on his elbows and took aim, bringing the sight of his Makarov PM to bear on Jamie's exposed skull. His firing position wasn't perfect but it was good enough. Gently, his finger applied pressure to the trigger.

Conor, peering into the barn from his position by the door, caught a slight movement by the tractor. He knew Sparke, or Volkov, was there somewhere but he was hidden in the gloom. The man was dangerous, that went without saying. The simple thing to do would be find him and kill him but he was learning quickly that in Jamie's particular line of work the simple thing was rarely achievable. Sparke was to be taken alive. Still, he should keep the bastard's head down at least. He shifted aim from the trailer to the tractor. He did a quick count. He had fired off seven shots which, by his reckoning, left six still in the magazine. More than enough. He raised the sight a fraction and aimed at the wide wall of the tractor tyre. The gun kicked in his hand as he fired three shots in quick succession. All three hit their target, the 9mm bullets ripping into the thick rubber. The tyre, under enormous pressure, ripped apart on impact.

Volkov was about to fire when Conor's three bullets hit the tyre. The sound of escaping air and the loud bang that followed along with the sudden drop of the vehicle onto the tyre rim startled him. He moved as he fired. Two shots. The first screamed over Jamie's head. The second, more by luck than intention, scored a line across his back, tearing through his parka and his clothing and searing his skin before embedding itself in the barn wall.

Jamie felt the bullet burn across his right shoulder blade. Another scar to add to his collection. His sight was returning slowly but his eyes still stung. Blurred shapes appeared before him, melting into background then reappearing. He could feel tears run down his cheeks. He guessed Conor would be panicking by now and waved a reassuring hand. It was time to get out of here, if he could. From the direction of the shot that had wounded him he realised that Sparke was now in the game.

Volkov was engrossed in his own problem now, the tractor settling low on one side and effectively trapping him. He could still move but doing so would, he thought, bring more fire down on him. He lay still, watching. The man on the ground was moving again, slowly but surely making for the relative safety of the fog. If the man managed that, then he and his men would be trapped in the barn... And then it would only be a matter of time before reinforcements arrived. He couldn't let that happen.

'Fedorov! Stepanov! The man on the ground is still alive. Kill him! Don't let him reach the safety of the fog,' he screamed.

Jamie translated the man's words and gritted his teeth. Sparke was quick on the uptake but then, that was only to be expected. He began to slither backwards with a bit more urgency. Conor wouldn't understand a word the Russian had said but, with luck, his tone of voice would give him a clue. Without covering fire, Jamie would be dead in seconds. Conor's Browning banging away gave a moment of comfort, but only a moment. Three shots in quick succession and then silence. Jamie grimaced. He knew the reason for that and if he could work it out, so too could the Russians. How long would it take Conor to change magazines, he wondered. Two seconds? Three... five? He closed his eyes and prayed.

The Russians on the trailer didn't hesitate. They had worked it out. They rose as one and peppered the area around Jamie, but their shots were hurried. They faced the same dilemma; how long would it take Conor to change the magazine and re-join the fight?

Bullets cracked into the concrete around Jamie, then whined off harmlessly. One, closer than the others, impacted a few inches in front of his face throwing slivers of concrete and grit up into his face. A chunk of concrete slashed his cheek just below his right eye. He felt the warm blood run freely down his cheek. Too close for comfort, he mused... much too close. He kept moving, his Walther held out in front of him. He tried to remember how many shots he had fired. Two initially and then three from his position here, or was it four? Five shots at best, six at worst. The Walther magazine held seven 7.65mm bullets and that left him dangerously short. He fumbled in his parka pocket with his left hand and found one of his spare magazines. He clutched it tightly and brought it out. One shot, maybe two, eject and replace. Two seconds, no more.

Conor returned to the game. Three shots whistled over and the Russians sank behind the heavy sacks once again. Jamie looked up painfully, his eyes still smarting. Sparke was still behind the tractor and wasn't going anywhere in a hurry. The other two were hunkered down on the trailer. He didn't take time to think, simply pushed himself up onto his feet and ran. Conor loosed off another salvo, five shots, evenly spaced. Jamie threw himself headlong towards the barn door. He almost made it.

Sparke had seen him push up off the ground. The Russian too was on the ground, lying beneath the tractor's main body. As Jamie rose, he presented the man with a better target. Sparke raised his Makarov. Lying prone as he was, aiming was difficult, but his target was only about six or seven meters away. He fired then lowered his aim and fired again just as Jamie launched himself towards the barn door.

The first bullet flew high and wide. The second ripped through his left calf. If he had been on his feet it would have brought him down, but he was already flying headlong through the air, his momentum carrying him to safety. Before the Russian could fire again the fog had enveloped him.

Jamie hit the ground heavily and rolled towards Conor who was still firing, his target now Sparke who was trying to wriggle further back into the deep shadows. Conor stopped firing and looked down anxiously. Jamie had propped his back against the barn wall and was examining his leg. A dark stain spread across the material of his trousers around two neat holes about four inches apart. The bullet had punched straight through the muscle but missed the bone. He gritted his teeth and forced a grin. 'More holes than a fuckin' pin cushion,' he joked, easing Conor's tension. 'Went clean through,' he went on. 'I'll be fine in a minute. Keep an eye on those buggers. They can't stay in there and they know it.'

He removed his emergency medical pack. It was the first time he had ever bothered to carry one on a mission but Conor had insisted. Thank you Conor, he thought as he slit his trouser leg above his boot and peeled back the blood soaked material. The holes were neat but blood was pumping out from both. He unwrapped a field dressing and began to wind it around his leg. Pain was kicking in. He pulled the heavy bandage tightly round the wound, slit the end and tore two strips to allow him to tie it tightly. Conor could have done it quicker but Conor had his hands full.

Sparke, or Volkov, was rallying his troops. He was shouting what sounded like instructions, Conor thought. He looked towards Jamie with a shrug. Jamie gave him another painful smile. 'He's telling them they have to get out of there,' he said. 'He thinks we'll have reinforcements arriving,' he continued and then his face grew dark. 'He's just told them to arm the fucking bomb,' he hissed.

Conor was trying to work out how Jamie knew all that when Jamie spoke again and everything became clear. 'Yesli vy vooruzhite bombu, vy nikogda ne vernetes' v Mat'-Rossiya. Ty umresh' zdes,' he shouted. Conor wasn't alone in being stunned into silence. Jamie forced another grin. 'I told them that if they arm the bomb they'll never get back to Mother Russia; they'll die here,' he explained.

'You speak Russian?' Conor whispered, astonished.

'Aye... I did a degree in French and Russian. Did I not tell you?'

Conor shook his head in amazement. 'No, you didn't. What else have you kept from me?'

Jamie laughed. 'I told you before, you're the spy. I'm just the blunt instrument and right now we're dealing with three very desperate men.'

Volkov was shouting instructions again. He had overcome his shock. So, one of these men spoke Russian. No matter. It changed nothing. 'Starshina

Fedorov, I order you to arm the device. Set it to the time I gave you earlier,' he instructed.

'Twenty-fifth January Starshina,' Jamie shouted, startling Volkov more than the others. He heard the Russian curse loudly. 'We know it all, Sparke, or whatever your real name is... when, where and what. Your time is running out. If you arm the device now you are finished. We will simply disarm it or move it to some place where the fallout will be limited.' He paused and laughed evilly. 'We might even chain you to the thing and let you fry when it goes off. You would have six days to regret your impulse before you simply evaporate,' he added chillingly.

'Ignore him Fedorov. Arm the device.'

'But Major...'

'No buts, Fedorov. Do it,' Volkov screamed.

Jamie's cruel laugh filled the barn. 'He's playing with your life Fedorov. Arm it and you and your comrade are dead. Throw down your weapons and stand up. You can walk away. We will not stop you.' Conor looked at him as though he had lost his mind. Jamie gave him a smile and shrugged. 'They're foot soldiers, nothing more. How far do you think they'll get before they're picked up?' he whispered. 'We want Sparke. They're not important. If they leave now, he's alone. How long do you reckon before he throws in the towel?'

Conor returned his shrug. He wasn't convinced, but it wasn't his call. If it went wrong, Jamie would carry the can, not him. 'You're the boss, kid,' he said softly.

There was a deathly silence in the barn. Outside, the fog was thinning but it wasn't lifting. Visibility was now up to about twenty yards. Jamie watched the trailer while Conor kept his eyes on Sparke.

Maybe it was time to give the two Russians a carrot. They already knew what the stick was. 'The fog is thinning out, Fedorov,' he called out. 'You can still get out before the SAS get here. Take the sports car. There are large rocks blocking your route about 50 meters along the way. Once you clear a path through you are clear.'

'Sparke's getting agitated,' Conor whispered, just loud enough for Jamie to hear. 'His boys must be thinking about it.'

Jamie grinned, raised a finger to his lips and waited.

On the trailer Fedorov and Stepanov were weighing up their options. There weren't many. Neither man looked at Volkov. They both knew what that would lead to. And they didn't like the situation they found themselves in. Death was staring them in the face. The question was, could they trust the British man?

'What do you think?' Stepanov, the junior man asked quietly, keeping his voice low so as not to allow the Major to hear.

Starshina Fedorov shrugged. He had been in tight situations before but none that he didn't think he could get out of. This was new territory. They were trapped in here with the Major, a zealot, who would sacrifice them in the blink of an eye. If they remained here for much longer any chance of escape would be gone, and he didn't fancy being here when the British SAS turned up. Things were bad enough now. When they arrived, the game was up. They could always do what the Major suggested, arm the device and then fight their way out, but somehow he didn't think they would make it. The first thing the British would do was disable the vehicles. And even if they did manage to overpower their opponents and get out of here, they would probably meet the reinforcements coming in. No matter how he looked at it, all he could see were negatives. 'I think we're fucked,' he replied eventually.

'Me too,' the younger man agreed. 'But can we trust them?'

Fedorov smiled wryly. 'Who? The British or the Major?' he asked.

Stepanov looked at him glumly. He had been thinking about the Major, worrying more than thinking, and Fedorov's words made sense. How would the Major react if he and Fedorov surrendered? Badly, he suspected. But what else could they do? If the Britisher was to be believed more soldiers would be arriving soon. They had no reason to doubt that. In fact, it was the obvious conclusion. It was stupid to think that these two men had blundered in here without anyone knowing where they were. Added to that, they seemed to know everything about the Major's plan. The sensible thing to do was lay down their guns and give themselves up. He hoped Fedorov saw it that way too.

Fedorov had already made up his mind. He gave his friend a slight smile and another shrug. He had his back pressed against the sacks of the sodium chlorate mixtures lining the side of the trailer. He patted a space beside him and gave a shake of his head indicating that Stepanov should join him. The younger Russian crawled across, keeping low, and sat down. They were both now hidden from Volkov's sight. Fedorov smiled again.

'It is time,' he said. 'When I give the word push back against the sacking. When the sacks fall, jump. But first, remove the magazine from your weapon and throw both towards the door. The British have a sense of honour; they won't shoot unarmed men.'

Stepanov wasn't convinced. And there was the other problem. 'What about Major Volkov?' he murmured.

'Fuck him!' Fedorov threw back at him. 'He wants us to commit suicide so that he can be a hero. Are you with me?'

Stepanov nodded slowly. A slim chance of survival was better than no chance at all. He flicked the magazine release on his Tokarev and let the magazine drop into his hand. Fedorov did the same. Then, as one, they threw their pistols over their shoulders in the general direction of the barn door and followed up with their magazines.

They remained silent. Shouting anything would simply forewarn the Major of their intentions and Fedorov didn't want that. He hoped that the sight of the two big Tokarev TT-33 landing on the floor of the barn in front of them would be enough of a message for the British. He smiled again.

'Now Alexi,' he said, using his companion's given name. 'Push and pray, both at the same time.'

Digging their feet hard on the ridged base of the trailer, they pushed backwards. At first, nothing happened. All of their efforts seemed to be absorbed by the sacks behind them. Straining hard, sweat beading on their brows, they pushed again. The sacks moved. They pushed again. A little more movement. Fedorov pushed himself up, raising his back higher against the line of sacks. Stepanov followed his example. They pushed backwards, co-ordinating their efforts and slowly but surely the heavy bags at the top of the pile began to wobble. They thrust back harder. The wobbling sacks began to sway, gently at first, then violently until, suddenly, the top four rows succumbed and fell outwards onto the concrete floor.

At the door, Jamie and Conor saw the two Tokarev pistols sail through the air and crash to the floor with two dull thuds. The magazines followed in quick succession. Jamie raised an eyebrow and smiled at Conor. The swaying sacks drew their attention then. 'They're coming out,' he whispered. 'Watch them closely. If it looks like a con, don't wait, aim and fire.' Conor nodded.

Beneath the tractor, Volkov was unaware of what was taking place until the guns hit the floor. Even then, he was unsure. He heard the thuds as metal hit concrete but couldn't see what had caused the noise. He was agitated. Fedorov had not responded to the order to arm the weapon. That did not, of course, mean that he wasn't obeying the command but something made Volkov doubt it. He moved uncomfortably, wriggling further back beneath the tractor, trying to find a spot from where he could see into the gap between the rows of sacks. It was difficult. The chassis of the tractor was rubbing against his shoulders, chaffing his skin. He forced himself through, gritting his teeth. He edged clear just as the sacks toppled and crashed to the ground. The top layer fell further out from the trailer and two burst on impact with the ground. A cloud of sodium chlorate rose into the air. His brain was still working out what had happened when Fedorov and Stepanov leapt from the trailer, hurdling the lower layers of sacks.

He saw the two men through the cloud of chemical dust. They crashed to the concrete floor a few feet in front of him, rolled and came up fast with their arms and hands thrown up in the air. He cursed in disbelief. They were deserting their post. They were abandoning him. He didn't think twice. Determinedly, he held his Makarov out in front of him in a classic two handed grip, raised the barrel and fired. Bullets spat from the gun barrel.

Stepanov went down first. He had only just started to run when the first 9mm bullet from Volkov's Makarov hit him low down on his back, tore through his kidney, ripped apart his intestines, punctured his left lung and exited through a large hole between the eighth and ninth ribs on his left side. The second bullet followed a similar trajectory but exited through the middle of his chest after smashing his sternum. He was dead before his body hit the floor.

Fedorov made it a little further. He had been marginally ahead when they jumped and made it to his feet first. He was running full tilt for the barn door when he heard the shots that killed his friend. He didn't hear the shots that killed him. Volkov was clinical. He ignored the dust settling around him, focussed on the running figure and fired. Two more shots, rapid fire. The first hit Fedorov on the left shoulder, spinning him to his right. The second, the killing shot, entered his skull between his right eye and his ear. It tore through his brain and exited through the left side in a spray of blood and brain tissue at a little less than its initial velocity of 1,030 feet per second. His momentum carried him a few paces further before he crashed down in a pool of sheep slurry.

Jamie was moving before Stepanov's body came to rest. Sparke wasn't about to give up, so much was clear. He had to move the lorry. Crouching low, he scurried across the concrete floor, skirting the sheep pens and slipping precariously in the slurry on the floor. The lorry was ahead of him. To his right he could barely make out Sparke through the dust particles floating in the air. The man was still beneath the tractor, a yellowish-white powder covered both him and the ground around him. Sparke saw him and raised his weapon.

The dust was drifting, cloud like, towards the barn door as though being sucked out into the fog. Jamie saw Sparke's movement and fired off a quick shot before throwing himself towards the safety of the lorry's bulk. A shot from Sparke's Makarov whistled harmlessly past and thudded into the barn wall. Jamie made his way to the cab door, opened it and hauled himself up into the vehicle. He was hoping the keys had been left in the ignition after it had been reversed into position to link up with the trailer. Keeping his head low, he searched for them beneath the steering column. They were there. He sighed with relief.

Slowly, he eased himself up onto the driver's seat. He didn't know if he was presenting a target to Sparke or if the height of the cab blocked him from the Russian's view. It didn't matter. He had to take the chance. Pressing his foot on the clutch, he turned the key in the ignition. The engine, still warm, started immediately. He gripped the gear change and pushed forward, hoping he had made the right choice of gear. Stalling the engine was the last thing he needed now. Gently, he let out the clutch and felt it bite just as the window to his left shattered and shards of glass showered him. He felt the nip of cuts to his cheek but ignored them. They were the least of his worries. Another bullet from Sparke's Makarov hit the roof of the cab to his left and ricocheted off past his head and out through the window to his right, taking the glass with it.

Slowly, the heavy truck eased forward. The headlights pointed out the door only to be reflected back by the fog beyond. He could see Conor crouched low, his back to the wall, his Browning High Power aimed towards where he imagined Sparke to be. Flashes erupted from the barrel but the roar of the truck's engine blotted out the sound of the shots. He saw Conor lurch to the side then fall. Sparke had spotted him.

Jamie's heart sank at the thought of the American shot and wounded, or worse. And then the lorry was entering the gap that was the doorway, forming a physical barrier between Conor and the Russian. Jamie drove on and the fog swirled around him. The vehicle was travelling slowly, just under 5mph. He carried on, trying desperately to remember the layout of the yard ahead. He checked his mirrors, watching the far end of trailer. He could barely make it out but it was still emerging from the light inside. Suddenly, it was clear. He drove forward another ten to fifteen yards and pressed hard on the brakes. The compressed air hissed and the heavy lorry lurched to a stop. He pulled the gearshift into neutral, switched off the ignition, ignored the hand brake and threw open the cab door. He was down and running back towards the barn in seconds.

An eerie silence had descended on the place. Cautiously, he edged around the door and searched for Conor. His friend was still on the ground but he had moved from where he had fallen. He was in shadow near the sheep pens. Then he searched for Sparke. The man had emerged from beneath the tractor and was sitting still, his back propped against the punctured tyre of the vehicle. He was covered in dust and was coughing harshly. As Jamie watched, the man clutched his stomach and vomited. A stream of putrid bile flew from his gaping mouth. His breathing was laboured.

Around him, piles of sacking and powder lay in great mounds. As part of their preparation for this Jamie and Conor had read up on the detrimental effects of sodium chlorate. He remembered clearly now – a toxic dose of more than half an ounce would lead to severe gastro-enteric pain, vomiting and diarrhoea. There could also be breathing difficulties, including lung failure, and damage to kidneys and liver. Sparke was way over half an ounce exposure. 15 grams was about the lethal dose for an adult and by the look of him, the man was way over that limit too. And all that was without the effects of the red phosphorus. Taking him alive now had just ceased being a possibility.

Jamie's main concern now was Conor. Ignoring the Russian, he ran to his friend. The American smiled bleakly and a wave of relief swept over him. Blood saturated Conor's parka but he was still alive and still conscious. Quickly, he bent down, eased his arm under the big American's body, and then, straining under his weight, pulled him towards the door. It took a while but eventually he managed to pull Conor clear.

Once outside he laid the American down and returned to the barn. Sparke was still propped against the tyre, his head down, chin tucked into his chest. His chest was expanding and contracting rapidly, his breathing quick and harsh. The dust had settled on everything. Tentatively, Jamie took a step into the barn, his footprints leaving a dark pattern on the dust covered concrete. He moved slowly lest he disturb the powder again.

Sparke raised his head and smiled bitterly. His gun was still in his right hand but he had no strength to raise it. Jamie aimed his Walther at the man then lowered it. There was no need to waste a bullet. The man only had minutes to live. He made his way over and crouched down beside him. What drove men to this, he wondered. Human evolution hasn't taken us far from the jungle, he mused; we are still little better than animals. Sparke was trying to speak. Jamie craned forward, listening.

'Who are you?' the Russian croaked. Jamie smiled gently, something Volkov found incongruous.

'I'm an archangel,' Jamie said softly. 'I've come to send you to the other side.'

The Russian coughed up more bile. It trickled from his lips and dripped onto his shirt front. He knitted his brow incomprehensively then shrugged it away with an almost imperceptible shake of his head. 'Sigareta, pozhaluysta, a cigarette please,' he mumbled, switching between Russian and English.

Jamie brought out his packet of Embassy. He knew it wasn't his best ever idea but what the hell. The packet was battered and crushed but the few cigarettes inside had survived. He handed the packet to the Russian. Sparke dropped the Makarov from his fingers and took the packet. He struggled to open the flip top and Jamie took pity on him. He retrieved the packet, withdrew a cigarette and slipped it between the Sparke's lips. 'Spasibo,' the man said, a painful smile softening his drawn features.

Jamie pulled a box of Bryant & May matches from his pocket. He had considered lighting the cigarette with his Zippo but the sodium chlorate all around them changed his mind. He placed the box in Sparke's left hand and then, without saying another word, he rose and walked quickly away, back out into the fog. He knew what was coming. Thank God the bomb was out, he mused grimly. He didn't know for sure but he suspected that the extreme heat generated by an explosion of sodium chlorate and red phosphorus might be enough to trigger the nuclear device. It was better not to put it to the test. He didn't look back.

He reached Conor and helped him to his feet. He said nothing but the American sensed the urgency. With Conor leaning heavily against him, they made it to the lorry. Straining hard, he helped his friend into the cab. Time was running out. Bundling Conor inside, he shut the door and ran to the driver's door. He climbed the step and hauled himself into the cab, reaching immediately for the ignition. He turned the key, heard the engine roar into life, selected first gear, and drove off. Fog swirled around the truck blocking out everything. He threw caution to the wind, pushed down on the accelerator and hoped for the best. He was driving from memory, nothing else.

Back in the barn Sparke, or Volkov, fumbled with the matchbox. His sight was failing. He coughed and tasted bile in his throat. Matches fell to the floor beside him and he felt about blindly for them. As his fingers found them and locked onto one, he thought about what the man had said. An archangel, he thought with a wry smile. Perhaps there is a God after all. He heard the lorry engine and stared up at the barn roof, half expecting the man to be staring back down at him, but his sight was gone. Finally, he returned to the task of lighting the cigarette. With the match in his right hand and the box in his left, he aligned the two and dragged the match head down the abrasive strip.

The flame of the match flared before him, a bright light in the darkness that was settling around him. He brought it to the tip of the cigarette and dragged deeply on the smoke. He held onto the match until the flame burned his fingers and then, with a manic grin, threw it away.

The match landed in the midst of a pile of powder that had formed when the sacks had fallen from the trailer. It guttered for a moment and then flared as the sodium chlorate ignited. As the flame intensified the sodium chlorate decomposed. Oxygen was released and the fire intensified. Soon, the area around the Russian was burning fiercely. Volkov paid it no heed. He was already dead. The heat was intense. Almost immediately, the flames reached the undamaged sacks on the barn floor.

Outside, Jamie was driving on autopilot. The lorry accelerated, slowly at first, and then its momentum built up. He checked the mirrors. Behind him, he saw a bright yellow glow light up the fog. It was like a supernova, glowing more and more as the intensity of the firs grew. He was still gazing in the rear view mirrors when the truck struck the line of boulders strewn across the track. He lost control as the steering wheel was wrenched from his hands. The lorry slewed left and began to jack-knife Suddenly, there was a noise like an underground train passing through a station and the air was sucked from the cab. The lorry cab was shaken by the force of the explosion and was thrown up into the air like a toy before crashing back down to earth. Its wheels buckled beneath it. Miraculously, the trailer stayed on the ground, the weight of its cargo acting as ballast against the effects of the blast.

A split second later debris rained down from the heavens. Giant chunks of masonry, wooden beams, brick and concrete crashed onto the roof of the cab and the fabric covering the trailer. The cab was crushed by the weight of falling stone and the fabric of the trailer sagged under the strain.

Just before he lost consciousness Jamie saw the glow from the explosion illuminate the sky. It seemed to burn intensely for a moment and then fade. He turned to Conor. His friend's eyes were closed and he had a peaceful look on his face. He could have been asleep but there was no sign of life, no rise and fall of the chest, no sound of breathing. He felt his eyes fill up. This couldn't be the end. He fought back against the force crushing the life from him. His sight blurred and blackness settled around him. He was slipping away. His last thought was of his wife. She was smiling, holding out her hands to him, willing him to come to her. He reached out and then she was gone, leaving him alone in the darkness.

Postscript

The name on the shingle read "W & R SURVIVAL TRAINING LIMITED". It summed up the business accurately. The owners were survivors. The business premises, sitting deep in woodland off the Inverary to Dalmalley road, were newly constructed on a chunk of land acquired from Argyll Estates. A grateful government had seen to that. It had also ploughed a sizeable sum into the development. They were, of course, getting something in return.

Jamie Raeburn and Conor Whelan, the W and R of the business, stood outside the main building. It was a long wooden construction that contained eight single bedrooms, a communal sitting room, a modern kitchen and dining room, four shower rooms and two toilets and two lecture rooms. All of that was on the ground floor, available to all. Beneath the building sat a gymnasium and a shooting range. These were off limits to most people.

Things had changed in the eight months since the events at Torhead Farm. The British and U.S. Governments decided that the fewer people who knew about it the better. A cover up was quickly orchestrated with Brigadier Sir Charles Redmond the conductor. He was also the man who persuaded the British Government to back Conor and Jamie's survival training company, though that too was something few people knew. The money for the development filtered through numerous channels and shell companies and it would take an army of accountants a lifetime to trace its origin. The British and American Governments wanted it to stay that way. In return, Jamie and Conor agreed to provide specialist training to certain individuals chosen by certain Government Departments. That too had to remain secret. In addition, they would have access to Jamie and Conor in exceptional circumstances. That, Jamie had reluctantly agreed, was a small price to pay. They had already paid a bigger price.

***

Eight Months Earlier

It was early evening when the fog finally lifted from Fenwick Moor. A Westland WS-61 Sea King helicopter hovered above what had once been Torhead Farm. Nothing of the place remained. Dead sheep littered the ground on the periphery of the explosion and what had once been a substantial farmhouse and farm buildings was now reduced to a smouldering pile of rubble spread around an enormous crater.

About 120 yards from the epicentre of the explosion, the soldiers found what was left of a British Army lorry. That was unexpected. They radioed in the discovery and were advised to approach with caution. They were also reminded that two friendly operatives had been observing the farm at the time of the explosion and it was imperative they be found. That, thought their commander, was highly unlikely.

The troops dismounted from the chopper and fanned out. Given the devastation they didn't expect much opposition but they were professionals. They approached the scene slowly. They found no living thing. The Russians and the two farm hands had simply disappeared in the conflagration. The exploding sodium chlorate and red phosphorus mixture had spread out from the barn, searing the heather and throwing the debris almost 200 yards. On the outer radius they found the remains of sheep, mostly burned alive. The smell was noxious.

The lorry sat within that radius but it had been luckier than the sheep. The cover had been partially blown off the trailer and sacks littered the ground. Some had burst open but, by some miracle, there had been no secondary fire or explosion. If the truck had been closer to the main blast it too would probably have disappeared, the SAS commander thought grimly.

When his men found the nuclear device on the trailer, he shuddered at the thought of what might have been. The gleaming metallic cylinder sat askew on the trailer floor surrounded by debris. Large pieces of stone and concrete lay around it but, by some miracle, the device was still intact. The whole area was littered with the lorry's other cargo. Some of the sacks had burst open, spewing out their red and yellow contents; others were intact, piled on top of another on the ground. The soldiers quickly identified the sodium chlorate and red phosphorus. Wisely, they left the device where it was in the midst of the sacks. There were others, more expert than they, who would deal with it.

After that, they turned their attention to the cab. The metal was twisted and torn and large chunks of masonry that had fallen from the sky had crushed the roof. It was as if a giant had smashed his hand down on it. Large pieces of wood, roof trusses and beams probably, peppered the ground, some sticking up into the air like enormous javelins. One of these pieces had pierced through the centre of the cab's roof and had splintered on impact. A trooper, climbing up onto the lorry's twisted access step, tried to view the inside. In the deep gloom he saw what he thought was a human arm. He called urgently for light and was passed a powerful lamp. Everything came into focus and he could make out two bodies, trapped by the twisted metal and wood and bleeding heavily.

He reached for a blood soaked arm and searched for a pulse, astonished when he found one. He called it in to the others and immediately four other troopers climbed onto the twisted wreckage and began pulling at the debris with their bare hands. Freeing these men was now the priority. Who they were, friend or foe, was irrelevant. All that mattered was getting them out.

It took two hours to free them and only with the help of specialised equipment quickly brought in. An elderly man had arrived with technicians from the United Kingdom Atomic Weapons Research Establishment (UKAWRE) at Aldermaston and an army of Spooks. The old guy was clearly in charge and everything took on greater urgency. Brigadier Sir Charles Redmond had that effect on people.

Jamie and Conor were removed from the wreckage and were immediately transferred to a waiting Sea King helicopter. Seconds later, the machine's Rolls Royce engines roared and it rose smoothly up off the ground, hovered a moment, then spun slowly on its axis and headed north west towards Glasgow's Southern General Hospital. Brigadier Redmond remained at Torhead Farm. The cover up was already under way.

The explosion had been heard for miles around. It shook and broke windows in nearby Kilmarnock and the surrounding towns and villages. Windows on high flats in East Kilbride were rattled too. A cover story was needed and Brigadier Redmond was the man to provide it. He was good at that.

A story was put out that the cause had been poorly stored propane gas cylinders at the farm. It was said that there had been twenty cylinders involved. The media warned people of the dangers of keeping such gas cylinders. The explosion was headline news for a day or so until it was replaced by another disaster and was quickly forgotten. The cover up had been a success.

The nuclear device was made safe and was carefully removed from the trailer by anonymous men in protective clothing. It was wrapped in heavy black sheeting, sealed into a large wooden box, and transported to Aldermaston. It provided a mine of useful data for the scientists. Few people knew how close they had come to Armageddon. If Major Volkov had survived and made it back to Mother Russia he would have spent the remainder of his days breaking rocks in the stony tundra of Siberia. Dying at Torhead Farm was an better option.

Jamie and Conor spent two weeks in virtual isolation in hospital. Their wounds were treated and, towards the end of their stay, they were debriefed, their brains picked clean of every tiny detail of the operation. Before their discharge they put their plan to the Brigadier. He said he would think about it. He did.

There were still one or two issues for Conor and Jamie to deal with along the way. Conor's issues revolved around what had occurred at Torhead Farm. Jamie's were of a more practical form and involved "tidying up" of loose ends, as Sir Charles put it.

In May, three months after the Torburn Farm firefight, Jamie and Conor travelled to London for a "business meeting" with Sir Charles. While Conor conducted business, Jamie carried on to Dublin. He was away for five days. It was no coincidence that during those five days the unexplained and accidental deaths of Pearce Duggan and Brendan Kelly occurred.

The men had met in a pub in Armagh and had been driving back to Duggan's farm when they were involved in a fatal road accident. Their car apparently left the road at speed and ploughed into an ancient oak. There were no witnesses... none that came forward anyway. The oak had survived; Pearce Duggan and Brendan Kelly did not.

Both men had been drinking and seatbelts were not worn. Seatbelts didn't go with their macho image. They were hard men. The RUC investigated but did not dig too deeply. They found skid marks on the roadway. One set only. There was nothing to suggest any another vehicle had been involved. They surmised that the most likely cause had been an animal, probably a deer, straying onto the road. Duggan, the driver, taken by surprise, had swerved to avoid the beast and lost control. It was enough. Both men were known IRA men and senior IRA men at that. They were no loss. Case closed.

Duggan and Kelly were given the usual IRA send off. Many hundreds turned up for their funerals and a squad of masked volunteers fired the obligatory salute. The British authorities watched from afar and let them get on with it. The funerals took place on Jamie's fifth day in Ireland, three days after the accident. He stood alone, watching the proceedings from a distance, emotionless. Another debt paid.

Also watching from a distance was a young woman. She was tall and beautiful with cropped short blonde hair. She too was alone. She had a scarf pulled tightly over her head and her face was partially obscured by dark glasses. She saw Jamie Raeburn at the back of the crowd. His presence didn't come as a surprise. She smiled wanly as a solitary tear rolled down her cheek. He was one man she would never forget.

Back in Scotland, the Evans family got on with their lives. It took a while for Roisin to recover fully but she progressed little by little, putting the past behind her. News of her brother's death didn't come as a shock. Actually, it brought her a sense of release.

William King, plumber, arrived in Western Australia in February 1974. He had a little money and soon found employment. He was, the locals decided, an easy-going individual who smiled a lot and enjoyed life to the full. He would go far, they all agreed. He was bonzer. Liam Fitzpatrick had simply disappeared. His departure from this earth along with that of Doherty, Macari and Finnegan and eight other volunteers was put down to death in action. They were all volunteers. They knew what to expect if things went wrong and it was generally assumed that things had, indeed, gone wrong.

No one really knew what had happened to them. Only Pearce Duggan and Brendan Kelly knew what the men had been involved in; and Orlagh, of course. No one spoke about Orlagh. They would be remembered. They were heroes, martyrs. But in the end, most people just wanted to get on with their lives.

Liam Fitzpatrick's mother, Roisin's auntie Molly, consoled herself that Roisin was safe and well and she still had her other children around her. She didn't believe Liam was dead. She was his mother; she would know... and she didn't.

In London, Clara Whitelaw tendered her resignation to Sir Charles. Needless to say, the old boy refused to accept it. She was important to the continued existence of Ultra, he assured her, and he didn't have long left. He said it jokingly but the old saying - half joking, whole earnest - thought of by Jamie in the lead up to the firefight at the farm could apply.

For Kate Raeburn and Mary Whelan life returned to normality. Their husbands were free at last from the dangers of their clandestine lives... or so they thought. The two families became, in effect, one large family. With the closeness between Jamie and Conor that had always been the likely outcome.

Frank Daly, Father Frank, was a frequent visitor to the Raeburn house outside Inverary. He drove there in his old Morris Countryman and occasionally spent a night or two with the family, especially when Jamie opened a bottle of malt. He was still trying to convert Jamie. He didn't expect to succeed but he enjoyed the challenge. And he still prayed for him. Jamie had a special place in the old man's heart. Frank Daly said nothing but he sensed that Jamie Raeburn wasn't entirely free of his past... He doubted he would ever be. And there was still the matter of who had betrayed him.

Lightning Source UK Ltd.
Milton Keynes UK
UKHW021304270822
407818UK00004B/77